VAMPIRE WARS

THE VON CARSTEIN TRILOGY

THE VON CARSTEINS are the most infamous vampires to stalk the Warhammer Old World. Their very names – Vlad, Konrad and Mannfred – conjure up images of doom, death and destruction. This omnibus edition collects all three of Steven Savile's Von Carstein novels, into one gore-drenched volume.

Inheritance – The rise to power of the dark and sinister Vlad von Carstein at first goes unnoticed, however, once he has established his rule in Sylvania, a plague of evil is set loose on the Empire. Can anyone save the land of the living from this bloodthirsty family of vampires?

Dominion – A new evil threatens the Empire when the insane Konrad von Carstein comes to power. Savage and bloodthirsty, he and his vampire servants embark on a reign of terror and conquest.

Retribution – The way lies clear for return of the greatest and most dangerous Vampire Count of all – Mannfred von Carstein. Divided by conflict, the rulers of the Empire must put aside their differences and unite to battle this threat from the new lord of Sylvania, or the land of men will be lost forever...

More Warhammer omnibuses from the Black Library

GOTREK & FELIX: THE FIRST OMNIBUS
by William King

(Contains the novels
Trollslayer, *Skavenslayer* and *Daemonslayer*)

GOTREK & FELIX: THE SECOND OMNIBUS
by William King

(Contains the novels
Dragonslayer, *Beastslayer* and *Vampireslayer*)

THE VAMPIRE GENEVIEVE
by Jack Yeovil

(Contains the novels
Drachenfels, *Genevieve Undead*, *Beasts in Velvet* and *Silver Nails*)

BLACKHEARTS: THE OMNIBUS
by Nathan Long

(Contains the novels
Valnir's Blood, *Broken Lance* and *Tainted Blood*)

THE AMBASSADOR CHRONICLES
by Graham McNeill

(Contains the novels
The Ambassador and *Ursun's Teeth*)

A WARHAMMER ANTHOLOGY

VAMPIRE WARS

THE VON CARSTEIN TRILOGY

Steven Savile

For Lindsey Priestley, editor and friend. This book could not have happened without you. In other words, it is all your fault.

A Black Library Publication

This omnibus edition published in Great Britain in 2008 by
BL Publishing,
Games Workshop Ltd.,
Willow Road, Nottingham,
NG7 2WS, UK.

10 9 8 7 6 5 4

Cover illustration by Wayne England; design by Darius Hinks.
Map by Nuala Kinrade.

A CIP record for this book is available from the British Library.

ISBN 13: 978 1 84416 539 1
ISBN 10: 1 84416 539 6

Distributed in the US by Simon & Schuster
1230 Avenue of the Americas, New York, NY 10020, US.

THIS IS A DARK age, a bloody age, an age of daemons and of sorcery. It is an age of battle and death, and of the world's ending. Amidst all of the fire, flame and fury it is a time, too, of mighty heroes, of bold deeds and great courage.

AT THE HEART of the Old World sprawls the Empire, the largest and most powerful of the human realms. Known for its engineers, sorcerers, traders and soldiers, it is a land of great mountains, mighty rivers, dark forests and vast cities. It is a land riven by uncertainty, as three pretenders all vye for control of the Imperial throne.

BUT THESE ARE far from civilised times. Across the length and breadth of the Old World, from the knightly palaces of Bretonnia to ice-bound Kislev in the far north, come rumblings of war. In the towering World's Edge Mountains, the orc tribes are gathering for another assault. Bandits and renegades harry the wild southern lands of the Border Princes. There are rumours of rat-things, the skaven, emerging from the sewers and swamps across the land. And from the northern wildernesses there is the ever-present threat of Chaos, of daemons and beastmen corrupted by the foul powers of the Dark Gods.
As the time of battle draws ever near,
the Empire needs heroes
like never before.

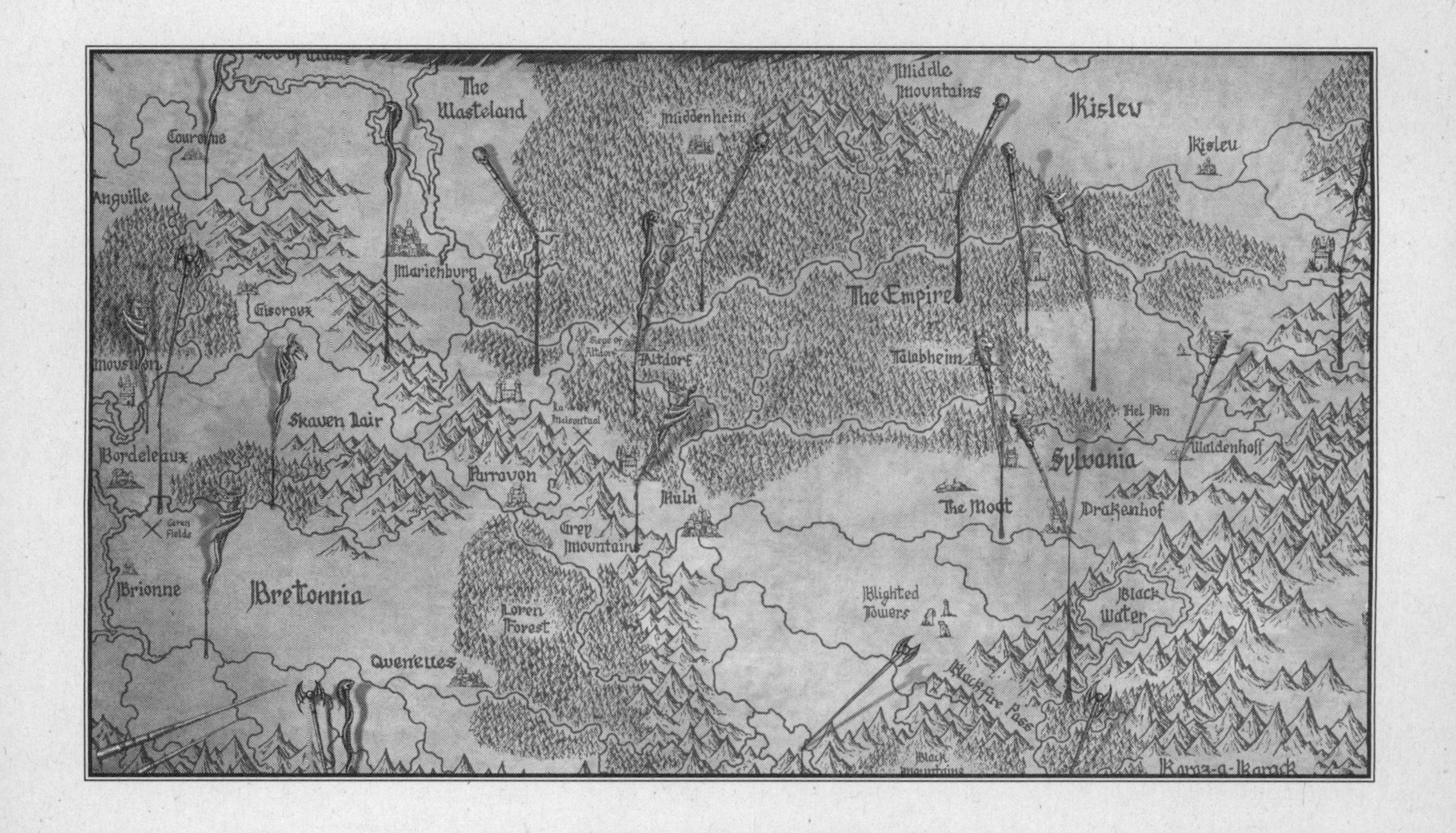

The Wasteland
Middle Mountains
Kislev
Middenheim
Couronne
Anguille
Marienburg
Kislev
Gisoreux
The Empire
Altdorf
Talabheim
Skaven Lair
Hel Fen
Bordeleaux
Parravon
Sylvania
Waldenhof
The Moot
Drakenhof
Grey Mountains
Nuln
Brionne
Bretonnia
Blighted Towers
Black Water
Loren Forest
Quenelles
Blackfire Pass

CONTENTS

AUTHOR'S INTRODUCTION

FORGET DRAGONS, HERE be spoilers. Read on at your peril, or read the book and then come back and read the introduction. Gone? Okay, we'll just sit here and talk behind your back until you come back. Back? Fantastic, okay, so here's the thing – fantasy always struck me as being the stories of heroes pitted against impossible odds, and those heroes were always more interesting to me as a reader when they were normal men and women confronting the daemons, devils and demi-gods. What is fun about reading the tales of the greatest swordsman in the West with his magical blade and his lightning reflexes, unbeatable in combat, ad nauseum? You know the drill, you've read the books, seen the movies, bought the t-shirts and all that malarky, right? I know I have.

Growing up I always had odd heroes. Other people talked in reverent tones of Trevor Francis and Peter Barnes, Stevie Highway and Kevin Keegan (okay that dates me), where as I was always more awed by Peter Cushing and Christopher Lee. Look at the evidence, as presented in those old Hammer House of Horror productions: every Friday night on Channel 4 or BBC2 the borders between the living and the dead would be blurred for just a few hours. Cushing would find himself in Dracula's Castle with dawn approaching, the evil Count (because, let's face it, to a thirteen-year-old Christopher Lee pretty much epitomised evil back then) at one end of the huge dining table, Cushing's Van Helsing at the other, with only candlesticks and untouched food between them and nary a weapon in sight. Yet Cushing would leap onto the table, grabbing the silver candlesticks to make a crucifix and run along the table, driving the Count back with nothing but faith, and hurl himself at the thick velvet drapes to let the day in... how could a football player ever be considered a hero after that? Week after week, be it in the tales of Victor Frankenstein or the Werewolf or the Mummy, these old studio productions shaped a young viewer planting the seeds of this dark love into his heart.

Fast forward far more years than I'm willing to admit and we arrive at a flurry of emails (and what kind of dark magic would those have been back in the day of Christopher Lee's Dracula?) and an opportunity knocked – would I be interested in a series of fantasy vampire novels? I am going to share the secret of my success now, so pay attention, it's the secret handshake that has been passed on to me from generations of writers gone before, a four word mantra: *I can do that.*

I knew when I set out that I wanted to maintain the sense of humour established by Kim Newman in his Vampire Genevieve books, so buried hundreds of little tips of the literary and televisual hat within the manuscripts. That was the easy part – though it was no less amazing when one reader, Barry Green, compiled a list of about fifty of them and mailed it to me for confirmation. I didn't mention at the time that he had missed about one hundred and fifty more, I thought I would save that now to drive the poor fellow mad scouring the pages again and again.

But then, of course, came the hard part, taking hundreds of years' worth of history and making a coherent driving narrative out of the existing Games Workshop material which was a challenge all of its own. The aim was not to humanise the vampires, which meant trying to stay out of their point-of-view for large parts of the trilogy, which in turn meant finding a sympathetic way in, someone to root for as the evils mounted and the Old World teetered on the brink of unlife.

I had Vlad von Carstein, my Lee-esque vampire who oozed seductive charm and gothic broodiness, that part was easy – but where was my Cushing? My hero? The greatest swordsman in the west? I think not, remember, dull, dull, dull. An anti-hero then? Flawed characters are always more interesting, so instead I wrote the first scenes with Jon Skellan and Stefan Fischer, but even as I set the first words down I knew that they could never be my heroes – as mortal men their lives are like dust motes in the schemes of the eternal dead. But then who could be the hero? Who could provide a sympathetic point of view for *centuries*? In the original outline for the first book Skellan never made it out of the castle on Geheimnisnacht. He scored his pyrrhic victory and had no reason left to live. Besides, he was far too damaged to be a real hero, he was your good man who fell into darkness. That gave me the arc I needed – a hero's fall, and eventual redemption. Only, of course, the deeper Skellan fell, the more irredeemable he became. It was unrelentingly bleak. Indeed, more than once I have had folks comment on the fact that each time they thought they had worked out who the hero was going to be I killed them. I guess being a hero in the Old World was a dangerous business.

Skellan always interested me, primarily because he was utterly loathsome, even as a human being. When he turned, there was more darkness in him than in many of his kindred bloodsuckers, a reflection of the darkness that was in him as a man.

Of course that makes for plenty of angst and readers wanting to slit their wrists around page 250, so there had to be a counterpoint, some kind of hope. Because that is what fantasy is all about really, going right back to that opening comment about heroes, and the best heroes being ordinary men and women – the thing that sets them apart is that they never lose hope.

So when Vlad hurled the corpse of the White Wolf of Middenheim from the spire in what was no more and no less a fit of pique, I knew I had my counterpoint, my hope, a man so entrenched in all that is good the darkness of his new nature couldn't hope to completely undo the man he had been. Jerek Kruger stepped comfortably into the shoes of my hero, the perfect foil for Skellan's nihilistic urges.

From that moment on the series was always about these two. Both normal men tormented by the world around them, changed. They were not the mythic counts, the greatest swordsmen, the most powerful mages, they were two normal men driven and separated by the most common thing: love. I always knew one would fall and one would be redeemed. Love drove Skellan to madness and held Kruger back from its brink.

But that is how it has to be in the epic stories, isn't it? Hopes are lost and clung to, plans fall into tatters, swords are raised against devils and men, it is Van Helsing with his silver candlesticks all over again, faith surmounting the insurmountable, and the price of victory needs must be huge – in this case a man's immortal soul.

Steven Savile
August 30th, 2007

DEATH'S COLD KISS

THE OLD PRIEST fled the castle.

Lightning seared the darkness, turning night momentarily into day. The skeletal limbs of the trees around him cast sinister shadows across the path that twisted and writhed in the lightning. Thunder rolled over the hills, deep and booming. The rain came down, drowning out lesser sounds.

The primeval force of the storm resonated in Victor Guttman's bones.

'I am an old man,' he moaned, clutching at his chest in dread certainty that the pain he felt was his heart about to burst. 'I am frail. Weak. I don't have the strength in me for this fight.' And it was true, every word of it. But who else was there to fight?

No one.

His skin still crawled with the revulsion he had felt at the creature's presence. Sickness clawed at his throat. His blood repulsed by the taint of the creature that had entered Baron Otto's chamber and claimed young Isabella. He sank to his knees, beaten down by the sheer ferocity of the storm. The wind mocked him, howling around his body, tearing at his robes. He could easily die on the road and be washed away by the storm, lost somewhere to rot in the forest and feed the wolves.

No.

The temple. He had to get back to the temple.

He pushed himself back up and lurched a few more paces down the pathway, stumbling and tripping over his own feet in his need to get away from the damned place.

There were monsters. Real monsters. He had grown numb to fear. A life of seclusion in the temple, of births and naming days, marriages and funeral rites, such mundane things, they somehow combined to turn the monsters into lesser evils and eventually into nothing more than stories. He had forgotten that the stories were real.

Guttman lurched to a stop, needing the support of a nearby tree to stay standing. He cast a frightened look back over his shoulder at the dark shadow of Drakenhof Castle, finding the one window that blazed with light, and seeing in it the silhouette of the new count.

Vlad von Carstein.

He knew what kind of twisted abomination the man was. He knew with cold dark certainty that he had just witnessed the handover of the barony to a daemon. The sick twisted maliciousness of Otto van Drak would pale in comparison with the tyrannies of the night von Carstein promised.

The old priest fought down the urge to purge his guts. Still he retched and wiped the bile away from his mouth with the back of his hand. The taint of the creature had weakened him. Its sickness was insidious. It clawed away at his stomach; it tore at his throat and pulled at his mind. His vision swam in and out of focus. He needed to distance himself from the fiend.

His mind raced. He struggled to remember everything he knew about vampires and their ilk but it was precious little outside superstition and rumour.

The oppression of the pathway worsened as it wound its way back down toward the town. The sanctuary of rooftops and the welcoming lights looked a long, long way away to the old man. The driving rain masked other sounds. Still, Guttman grew steadily surer that he was not alone in the storm. Someone – or something – was following him. He caught occasional glimpses of movement out of the corner of his eye but by the time he turned, the shadow had fused with deeper shadows or the shape he was sure was a pale white face had mutated into the claws of dead branches and the flit of a bat's wing.

He caught himself looking more frequently back over his shoulder as he tried to catch a glimpse of whoever was following him.

'Show yourself!' the old priest called out defiantly but his words were snatched away by the storm. The cold hand of fear clasped his heart as it tripped and skipped erratically.

A chorus of wolves answered him.

And laughter.

For a moment Guttman didn't trust his ears. But he didn't need to. It was a man's laughter. He felt it in his gut, in his bones and in his blood, the same revulsion that had caused him to black out at the feet of von Carstein when the man first entered van Drak's bedchamber.

One of the count's tainted brood had followed him out of the castle. It was stupid and naïve to think that von Carstein would be alone. The monster would have minions to do his bidding, lackeys who still clung to their humanity and servants who had long since given it up. It made sense. How could a creature of the damned hope to pass itself off among the living without an entourage of twisted souls to do its bidding?

'I said show yourself, creature!' Guttman challenged the darkness. The rain ran down his face like tears. He wasn't afraid anymore. He was calm. Resigned. The creature was playing with him.

'Why?' A voice said, close enough for him to feel the man's breath in his ear. 'So your petty god can smite me down with some righteous thunderbolt from his shiny silver hammer? I think not.'

Brother Guttman reeled away from the voice, twisting round to face his tormentor but the man wasn't there.

'You're painfully slow, old man,' the voice said, behind him again somehow. 'Killing you promises to be no sport at all.' Guttman felt cold dead fingers brush against his throat, feeling out the pulse in his neck. He lurched away from their touch so violently he ended up sprawling in the mud, the rain beating down around his face as he twisted and slithered trying to get a look at his tormentor.

The man stood over him, nothing more than a shape in the darkness.

'I could kill you now but I've never taken a priest. Do you think you would make a good vampire, old man? You have a whole flock of dumb sheep to feed on who will come willingly to you in the night, eager to be fed on if your holy kiss will bring them closer to their precious Sigmar.' The man knelt beside him, the left side of his face lit finally by the slither of moonlight. To Guttman it was the face of ultimate cruelty personified but in truth it was both beautiful and coldly serene. 'What a delicious thought. A priest of the cloth becoming a priest of the blood. Think of the possibilities. You would be unique, old man.'

'I would rather die.'

'Well, of course. That goes without saying. Now, come on, on your feet.'

'And make your job easier?'

'Oh, just stand up before I run out of patience and stick a sword in your gut, brother. You don't have to be standing to die, you know. It isn't a prerequisite. Swords are just as effective on people lying in the mud, believe me.' He held out a hand for the priest to take but the old man refused, levering himself up and stubbornly struggling to get his feet beneath himself.

'Who are you?'

'Does it matter? Really? What's in a name? Truly? Turned meat, cat's urine and mouldy bread by any other names would still smell repugnant, wouldn't they? They would still stink of decay, rot, so why this obsession with naming things? There is no magic in a name.'

'What a sad world you live in,' Guttman said after a moment. 'Where the first things that come to mind are riddled with corruption. Give me a world of roses and beauty and I will die happily. To live as you do, that is no life at all.'

'Do not be so hasty to dismiss it, priest. They have an old saying in my hometown: Die reinste Freude ist die Schadenfreude,' the man said in perfect unaccented Reikspiel. 'The purest joy is the joy we feel when others feel pain. Now I believe it is the only genuine joy we feel. The rest is transitory, fleeting. Soon the darkness will be all you have left, and the light and your precious roses and everything else you think of as beautiful will be nothing more than memories. The knowledge of this gives me some slight happiness I must confess. When you've been reduced to nothing, then let us see how much of the so-called beautiful you choose to remember. My name is Posner. Herman Posner. Say it. Let it be the last thing you say as a living creature. Say it.'

'Herman Posner,' Brother Victor Guttman said, tasting the name in his mouth. The words were no more evil than any others he had said. There was nothing unique about them. They were not tainted with vile plague or ruined by undeath. They were just words, nothing more.

'A rose or rot, priest? You decide,' Posner said. His hand snaked out grabbing the old man by the collar and hauling him up until his toes barely touched the floor. Guttman struggled and fought, kicking out as Posner drew him in close enough for the priest to taste the redolent musk of the grave on his breath. The creature's touch was repulsive.

It didn't matter how much he kicked and twisted against Posner's grip; it was like iron.

He felt the teeth – fangs – plunge into his neck, biting deep, hard. The old man's body tensed, every fibre of his being repulsed by the intimacy of the kill. He lashed out, twisted, flopped and finally sagged as he felt the life being drained out of him.

And then the pain ended and Posner was screaming and clutching his own chest.

Guttman had no idea what had caused the vampire to relinquish his hold. He didn't care. His legs buckled and collapsed beneath him but he didn't pass out. He lay in the mud, barely able to move. He was sure his tripping heart would simply cease beating at any moment and deny the vampire its kill. There was a delicious irony to the thought, the beast gorging itself on dead blood, only realising its mistake when it was too late.

Posner lifted his hand. The skin beneath was burned raw with the mark of Sigmar's hammer.

For a moment the old priest thought it was a miracle – that he was saved. Then the cold hard reality of the 'miracle' revealed itself. The silver hammer he wore on a chain around his neck had come loose from his clothing and as the vampire leaned in the silver had burned its mark on the beast. Silver. At least that part of the stories was true. The metal was anathema to the lords of the undead. He clasped the talisman as though it might somehow save him. It was a feeble gesture. Posner leaned over him and grasped the silver chain, ignoring the hiss and sizzle of his own flesh as he yanked the holy symbol from around Guttman's throat, and tossed it aside.

The stench of burned meat was nauseatingly sweet.

'Now let's see how you fare without your pretty little trinket, shall we?'

Before Guttman could scramble away Posner had him by the throat again, fingernails like iron talons as they sank mercilessly into his flesh. The pain was blinding. The priest's vision swam in and out of focus as the world tilted away and was finally consumed in an agony of black. The last sensation he felt as the pain overwhelmed him was the vampire's kiss, intimate and deadly, where his fluttering pulse was strongest. Guttman's eyes flared open and for a fleeting moment the world around him was intense, every colour more vibrant, more radiant, every scent more pungent, more aromatic, than they had been through his whole life of living with them. He was dying, drained of life and blood, and this intensity was his mind's way of clinging on to the memories of life, one final all-consuming overload of the senses. Victor Guttman let it wash over him. He felt his will to live fade with his thoughts as he succumbed to Posner. He stopped struggling, the fight drained out of him.

Posner yanked his head back better to expose the vein and sucked and slurped hungrily at the wound until he was sated. Grinning, he tilted the old man's head and dribbled blood into his gaping mouth. Guttman coughed and retched, a ribbon of blood dribbling out of the corner of his mouth. His entire body spasmed, rebelling against the bloody kiss and then he was falling as Posner let go.

The vampire walked away, leaving the old man to die.

To die, Guttman realised sickly, and become one of their kind. An abomination. No. No. It cannot happen. I will not kill to live. I will not!

But he knew he would.

In the end, when the blood thirst was on him and his humanity was nothing but a nagging ghost he would feed.

Guttman clawed at the mud, dragging himself forward a few precious inches before his strength gave out. His erratic breathing blew bubbles in the muddy puddle beside his face. His hand twitched. He felt himself slipping in and out of consciousness. Every breath could easily have been his last. He had no idea how long he lay in the mud blowing bloody bubbles. Time lost all meaning. The sun didn't rise. The rain didn't cease, not fully. He tried to move but every ounce of his being cried out in pain. He was alone. No passing carters would save him. He had a choice – although it was no choice at all: die here, now, and wake as a daemon, or fight it, grasp on to the last gasp of humanity and hope against hope that something in the temple could stave off the transformation and buy him precious time. Death was inevitable, he had always known that, accepted it. He would meet Morr, every man, woman and child would eventually; it was the way of the world. He promised himself he would do it with dignity. He would die, and stay dead. Judge me not on how I lived but how I die... who had said that? It made a grim kind of sense.

On the hillside around him the cries of the wolves intensified. It was a mocking lament. He knew what they were, those wolves. He knew how the beasts could shift form at will. He dreaded the moment their cries made sense to him, for then his doom would be complete.

He dragged himself another foot, and then another, almost blacking out from the sheer exertion. His face held barely inches above a muddy puddle, he stared at his own reflection in the water, trying to memorise everything he saw. He knew the image would fade, knew he would forget himself, but it was important to try to hold on to who he was. Another foot, and then another. The old priest clawed his way down the long and winding road. He felt the steel breeze on his face as he craned his neck desperately trying to see how far away the city lights were.

Too far, they taunted him. Too far.

He would never make it.

And because of that he was damned.

Desperately, Victor Guttman pushed himself up, stumbled two unsteady steps and plunged face first into the mud again. He lay there, spent, cursing himself for a fool for coming to the castle alone. The chirurgeon was long gone, probably safely at home in his bed already, tucked up beside his shrew of a wife while she snored. Or he's lying dead in a ditch somewhere. He was just as alone when he left the castle. Just as vulnerable. And probably just as dead. Guttman thought bitterly.

Again he stumbled forward a few paces before collapsing. Five more the next time. He cried out in anger and frustration, willing someone to hear him and come to his aid. It was pointless, of course. The only people abroad at this ungodly hour were up to no good and would hardly come to investigate cries on the dark road for fear of their own safety. Thieves, robbers, bandits, lotharios, debauchers, drunks, gamblers and vampires, children of the night one and all. And not a Sigmar fearing soul amongst them. He was alone.

Truly alone.

MEYRINK AND MESSNER were passionately arguing an obscure point of theosophy, the older man being driven to the point of distraction by the younger's sheer belligerence. He was impossible to argue with. There was no reasoning, only absolutes. The arguments were black and white. There was no room for the grey spaces of interpretation in between. Normally there was nothing Meyrink enjoyed more than a good argument but the youth of today seemed to have abandoned the art of reason in favour of passion. Everything was about passion. Meyrink laid aside the scrimshaw he had been carving and rolled his neck, stretching. The carving was therapeutic but his eyes weren't what they had been even a few years ago and the close detail gave him a headache from straining. He felt every one of his years. Brother Guttman would return soon. Perhaps he could make young Messner see reason.

'Perhaps, perhaps, perhaps,' Meyrink muttered bleakly. He didn't hold out a lot of hope.

'Ah, is that the sound of quiet desperation I hear leaking into your voice, brother?'

'Not so quiet, methinks,' Meyrink said with a lopsided grin. He liked the boy, and was sure with the rough edges rounded off his personality Messner would make a good priest. He had the faith and was a remarkably centred young man.

'Indeed. I was being politic. Come, let's warm our bones beside the fire while we wait for Brother Guttman's return.'

'Why not.'

''Tis a vile night out,' Messner remarked, making himself cosy beside the high-banked log fire that spat and crackled in the hearth. He poured them both cups of mulled wine.

'For once I'll not argue with you lad,' Meyrink said wryly.

The night stretched on, Meyrink too tired to debate. He looked often at the dark window and the streaks of rain that lashed against it. Messner was right: it was a vile night. Not the kind of night for an old man to be abroad.

They supped at their cups, neither allowing the other to see how much the old priest's lateness worried them until a hammering on the temple door had them both out of their seats and almost running through the central aisle of the temple to answer it. Meyrink instinctively made the sign of the hammer as Messner threw back the heavy bolts on the door and raised the bar. It had been many years since they had left the temple open through the night. It was a curse of the times. He didn't like it but was sage enough to understand the necessity.

Messner opened the door on the raging storm.

The wind and rain ripped at the porch, pulling the heavy door out of the young priest's hands.

For a heartbeat Meyrink mistook the shadows on the threshold for some lurking horror, distorted and deformed as they were by the storm, but then the wine merchant Hollenfeuer's boy, Henrik, lumbered in out of the driving rain and dark, a bundle of rags cradled in his arms. It took

Meyrink a moment to realise that the rags weren't rags at all, but sodden robes clinging wetly to slack skin and bones, and that Henrik had brought Brother Guttman home. The old priest's skin had the same blue pallor as death. His eyes rolled back in his head and his head lolled back against the boy's arm, his jaw hanging loose.

'Found 'im on the roadside a couple of miles back. Carried 'im 'ere.' Henrik grunted beneath the strain. He held the old man in his straining arms like a sack of coals. 'No idea how long 'e'd been there. 'E's still breathing but 'e's not in a good way, mind. Looks like 'e's been attacked by wolves or summink. 'E's got some frightenin' wounds where 'e's been bitten round the throat.'

'Put him down, put him down,' Meyrink flapped. 'Not here, no, no, not here. In his room. In his room. Take him to his room. What happened? Who did this to him?'

'I don't know,' Henrik said, tracking the storm into the temple. Behind him, Messner wrestled with the door. Meyrink moved in close, feeling for the old priest's pulse. It was there, faint for sure, but his heart was still beating and his blood was still pumping.

They carried the broken body of Victor Guttman up the winding stairs to his bare cell and laid him on the wooden pallet he called a bed, drawing the blanket up over his chest to his chin. The old man shivered. Meyrink took this as a good sign – there was still life enough in him to care about the cold.

He sent Henrik on his way, urging him to summon Gustav Mellin, the count's chirurgeon. He pressed a silver coin into his palm. 'Be convincing, lad.' The wine merchant's boy nodded and disappeared into the storm.

Meyrink went back to the old priest's cell where Messner was holding a silent prayer vigil. He cradled Guttman's fragile hand in his, whispering over and over entreaties to Sigmar, begging that His divine hand spare the old man from Morr. It was odd how the young man could be so adamant in the face of theory and yet so devout in the face of fact. His blind faith was as inspiring now as it had been annoying a few hours ago. Meyrink hovered on the threshold, looking at the young man kneeling at the bedside, head bowed in prayer. Guttman was clinging to life – a few words, even to the great and the good, wouldn't save him. It was down to the old man's will and the chirurgeon's skill, if he arrived in time. When it came down to it that was their prime difference: Meyrink was a realist, Messner an idealist still waiting for the brutality of the world to beat it out of him.

Meyrink coughed politely, letting Messner know he was no longer alone.

'How is he?'

'Not good. These wounds...'

'The bites? If that is what they are.'

'Oh that is what they are, without doubt. Whatever fed on him though, it wasn't wolves.'

'How can you be sure?' Meyrink asked, moving into the cell.

'Look for yourself. The first set of puncture wounds are precise and close together, suggesting a small mouth, certainly not a wolf. And there are nowhere enough teeth or tearing to match the savagery of wolves. If I didn't know better I'd say the bite was human.'

'But you know better?'

Messner shook his head.

'Then let us content ourselves with the fact that the world is a sick place and that our dear brother was set upon by one of the flock. It makes no difference to the treatment. We must staunch the blood loss and seal the wounds best we can, keeping them clean to keep out the festering. Other than that, perhaps you are right to pray. I can think of nothing else we can do for our brother.'

They did what they could, a mixture of prayer, medicine and waiting. Mellin, the chirurgeon arrived at dawn, inspected the wounds clinically, tutting between clenched teeth as he sutured the torn flesh. His prognosis was not good:

'He's lost a lot of blood. Too much for a man to lose and still live.'

'Surely you can do something?'

'I'm doing it. Cleaning up the wounds. If he deteriorates, my leeches will be good for the rot, but other than that, he's in the hands of your god.'

Guttman didn't wake for three straight days. Mostly he lay still, the shallow rise and fall of his chest all that distinguished him from the dead, though he did toss and turn occasionally, mumbling some incoherent half words while in the grip of fever dreams. The sweats were worst at night. In the darkest hours of the night the old priest's breathing was at its weakest, hitching and sometimes stopping for long seconds as though Guttman's body simply forgot how to breathe. Messner only left his bedside for a few moments at a time for daily ablutions. He ate his meals sitting against the bed frame and slept on a cot in the small cell, leaving Meyrink to oversee the day-to-day running of the temple and lead the congregation in prayers for Brother Guttman's swift recovery.

The fever ran its course and on the fourth day Victor Guttman opened his eyes.

It was no gentle waking: he sat bolt upright, his eyes flew open and one word escaped his parched mouth: 'Vampire!' He sank back into the pillow, gasping for breath.

The suddenness of it shocked Meyrink. He thought for a moment that he had misheard, that the dry rasp had been some last desperate plea to the gods for salvation before the old priest shuffled off the mortal coil, but it wasn't. He had heard correctly. Guttman had cried vampire.

Meyrink stared at the sutured wounds in the old man's throat, his mind racing. Could they truly be the mark of the vampire? The thought was ludicrous. It hadn't even crossed his mind. Vampires? But if they were... did that mean Victor Guttman is one of them now? Tainted? He was a priest of Sigmar surely he couldn't succumb to the blood kiss...

Meyrink took the old man's hand and felt none of the revulsion he was sure he should if Guttman had been born again into unlife.

'It's not too late, my friend,' he said, kneeling at Guttman's bedside. 'It's not too late.'

'Kill... me... please,' the old man begged, his eyes rheumy with pain. The chirurgeon had left nothing to dull the pain and Meyrink was loathe to let the man loose with his leeches. 'Before I... succumb... to it.'

'Hush, my friend. Save your strength.'

'I will not... kill. I will... not.'

REINHARDT MESSNER TURNED the brittle pages of the dusty old tome. He was tired, his enthusiasm for the search long since gone and the ink on the paper was a degree less intelligible than a spider's scrawl. The words had long since begun to blend into one. Beside him Meyrink grunted and shifted in his chair. It had been three days since Brother Guttman's return to the land of the living. During that time he had faded in and out of consciousness. He refused food, claiming he had no appetite. He drank little water, claiming he had no thirst. This disturbed the young priest. No hunger, no thirst, it was unnatural. It added a certain amount of credence to the old man's story of vampires but Messner refused to believe there was any real truth to it. Still, he studied the old tomes looking for some kind of geas that might be used to seal Guttman in the temple. It was useless. There was nothing.

The few references to the vampiric curse he had found revolved around fishwives' gossip and stupid superstitions about garlic and white roses. The only thing of any use was a single line about silver being anathema to the beasts. Other than that there was nothing of substance. One had ideas of how to keep a vampire out of a building, not keep it trapped within one – though for a while he hoped the solution might be one and the same.

'This is out of our province,' he admitted grudgingly, closing the book in a billow of dust. 'Short of sealing Brother Guttman in a silver lined vault, which is both impractical and impossible given the cost of the metal, I have found nothing. I hate to say it, but this is useless. We are wasting our time.'

'No, it has to be in here somewhere,' Meyrink objected, for once their roles of donkey in the argument reversed. Meyrink was being the stubborn ass refusing to see the impossibility of their situation. If

Guttman had been infected – and that was how he thought of it, a disease – then the best thing they could do for the old man was drive a stake through his heart, scoop out his brains and bury him upside down in consecrated ground.

If…

'You know it isn't, brother. This is a wild goose chase.'

'What would you have us do? Slay our brother?'

That was a question he wasn't prepared to answer. 'Nothing good comes of death,' he said instead, hoping Meyrink would take it as his final word.

'Yet we cannot stand guard over him night and day, it is impossible. There must be a way.'

A thought occurred to him then: 'Perhaps magic runes…?' They could place runes on the doors and windows to act as locks barring Guttman's ingress and egress, thus confining the vampire to the crypts.

Meyrink spat. 'Would you consort with the servants of Chaos?'

He was right, of course. The practice of magic was outlawed – it would be next to impossible to find anyone to craft such magic, and even if they could, for how long would the magic remain stable? To rely on such a warding was to court disaster, for certain, but Messner knew there was hope in the idea. Could such a series of runes be created to turn the old temple into a sanctuary for Guttman?

'The count would have access…' and then he realised what he was saying. The count.

Von Carstein.

The vampire count.

He made the sign of Sigmar's hammer.

There would be no going to the castle for help.

THE DOORS AND window frames of the temple had been inlaid with fine silver wire; bent into the shape of the runes the mage had sworn would keep the undead at bay. Meyrink had had no choice but to employ the man, despite his deep-seated distrust of magicians.

Meyrink studied the silver swirls.

There was nothing, as far as he could tell, remotely magical about the symbols that had cost the temple an Emperor's ransom. The man had assured the priests that the combination of the curious shapes and the precious metal would turn the confines of the temple into a prison for any of the tainted blood. He had sworn an oath, for all the good it did them now.

Like the windows and doors, the entrance to the crypt itself was protected by a serious of intricate metal swirls that had be laid in after Victor Guttman had been led below. Together, the mage had promised, these twists of metal would form an impenetrable barrier for the dead, keeping those without a soul from crossing. Again, Meyrink had no choice but to believe the man, despite the evidence of his own eyes.

Meyrink descended the thirteen steps into the bowels of the temple.

The crypt was dank, lit by seven guttering candles that threw sepulchral shadows over the tombs, the air fetid. Guttman had refused the comforts of a bed and slept curled up on a blanket in a dirty corner, ankles and wrists chained to the wall like some common thief.

It hurt Meyrink to see him like this: living in the dark, hidden away from the world he so loved, shackled.

This was no life at all.

'Morning, brother,' he called, lightly, struggling to keep the grief out of his voice.

'Is it?' answered the old man, looking up. The flickering candlelight did nothing to hide the anguish in his eyes or the slack skin of his face. 'Time has lost all meaning underground. I see nothing of light and day or dark and night, only candles that burn out and are replenished as though by magic when I finally give in to sleep. I had the dream again last night...'

Meyrink nodded. He knew. Two more girls – they were no more than children in truth – had succumbed to the sleeping sickness and died during the night. Two more. They were calling it a plague, though for a plague it was a selective killer, draining the very life out of Drakenhof's young women while the men lived on, seemingly immune, desperate as those they loved fell victim. It was always the same: first they paled, as the sickness took hold then they slipped into a sleep from which they never woke. The transition was shockingly quick. In a matter of three nights vibrant healthy young women aged as much as three decades to look at and succumbed to an eternal sleep. Meyrink knew better: it wasn't a plague, it was a curse.

'Did I...? Did I...?'

He nodded again.

'Two young girls, brother. Sisters. They were to have been fifteen this naming day.'

Guttman let out a strangled sob. He held up his hands, rattling the chains in anger and frustration. 'I saw it... I...' But there was nothing he could say. 'Have you come to kill me?'

'I can't, brother. Not while there is hope.'

'There is no hope. Can't you see that? I am a killer now. There is no peace for me. No rest. And while I live you damn the young women of our flock. Kill me, brother. If not for my own sake, then do it for theirs.' Tears streaked down his grubby face.

'Not while you can still grieve for them, brother. Not while you still have compassion. When you are truly a beast, when the damned sickness owns you, only then. Before that day do not ask for what I cannot do.'

'HE HAS TO die!' Messner raged, slamming his clenched fist on the heavy oak of the refectory table. The clay goblets he and Meyrink had been drinking from jumped almost an inch, Meyrink's teetering precariously before it toppled, spilling thick bloody red wine into the oak grain between them.

'Who's the monster here? The old man in the dungeon or the young one baying for his blood?' Meyrink pushed himself to his feet and leaned in menacingly. It was rapidly becoming an old argument but that didn't prevent it from being a passionate one.

'Forty-two girls dead, man! Forty-two! What about the sanctity of life? What is the meaning of life, brother, if you are willing to throw it away so cheaply?'

'We don't know,' Meyrink rasped, his knuckles white on the tabletop. 'We just don't know that it is him. We have no evidence that he gets out. He's chained up in there. There are wards and sigils and glyphs and all sorts of paraphernalia aimed at keeping him locked up down there, helpless... harmless.'

'And yet every morning he feeds you stories of his dreams, talks of the young ones he has seen suffering at the hands of the monstrous beasts. He regales you in glorious detail, brother. The creature is taunting you and you are too stupid to realise it.'

'No. Not too stupid. It is compassion. The old man raised you as he would his own son, from when the temple took you in fifteen years ago. He cared for you. He loved you. He did the same for me in my time. We owe him–'

'We owe him nothing anymore. He isn't Victor Guttman! He's a daemon. Can't you get that into your thick skull, man? He barely touches the food we take down for him for a reason, you know. It doesn't sustain him. Blood does. Blood, Brother. *Blood*.'

'Would you do it? Would you turn murderer and kill the man who might as well have been your own father, everything he did for you? Would you? Take the knife now, go down into the crypt and do it, cut his heart out. Do it, damn you! If you have so little doubt, do it...'

'No.'

'Well I am not about to.'

'I know men who could,' Messner said softly, wriggling around the impasse with a suggestion neither man really wished to consider. Bringing in outsiders. Part of it was fear – what would happen if people realised the priesthood of Sigmar had been infected with the tainted blood of vampires? Another part was self-preservation. The streets had been rife with rumours for days. Two witch hunters were in Drakenhof, though from what little Messner had managed to learn they were not church sanctioned Sigmarite witch hunters, and were barely in the employ of the Elector Count of Middenheim. Their charge had been issued nearly a decade ago, now their hunt was personal. They had come to town a week ago, looking for a man by the name of Sebastian Aigner, who, if the gossips were to be believed, they had been hunting for seven years. He was the last of a bunch of renegade killers who had slaughtered the men's families, burning them alive. Metzger and Ziegler, the witch hunters, had found the others and extracted their blood debt. They had come to Drakenhof looking to lay their daemons to rest, and perhaps, Messner thought, they could purge the temple of its daemon in the process. 'They could tell us for sure. This is what they do.'

Meyrink looked sceptical.

'Forty-two young women, forty-two. Think about it.'

'That is all I have been doing, for weeks. Do you think I don't lie awake at night, imagining him out there, feasting? Do you think I don't sneak down into the crypt at all hours, hoping to catch him gone, so that I know beyond a shadow of doubt that he is the killer my heart tells me he isn't? Always I find him there, chained to the walls, barely conscious, looking like death itself, and it breaks my heart that he is suffering because of me!'

'Forty-two,' Reinhardt Messner said again, shaking his head as though the number itself answered every objection Brother Meyrink voiced. And perhaps it did at that.

'Talk to them if you must, but I want no part of it,' Meyrink said, finally, turning and stalking out of the room.

Alone, Messner righted the spilled goblet and began mopping up the mess. It was, it seemed, his destiny to clean up after Meyrink.

MESSNER GREETED THE younger of the two with a tired smile and held out a hand to be shaken.

Metzger ignored it and didn't return the smile. There was something distinctly cold about the man, but given his line of work it was perhaps unsurprising. The older man, Eberl Ziegler, nodded and followed Metzger into the temple. He, at least, had the decency to bow low before the statue of Sigmar Heldenhammer and make the sign of the hammer whereas the other just walked down the aisle, toeing at the seats and tutting at the silver runes worked into the window frames. His footsteps echoed coldly.

Messner watched the man, fascinated by his confidence as he examined every nook and cranny of the old temple. Metzger moved with authority. He lifted a thin glass wedge from the front table, beside the incense burner, and tilted it so that it caught and refracted the light into a rainbow on the wall.

'So tell me,' Metzger said, angling the light up the wall. 'How does this fit with your philosophy? I am curious. The taking of a human life... it seems... alien to my understanding of your faith. Enlighten me.'

Behind Messner, Meyrink coughed.

'Sacrifice for the good of mankind, Herr Metzger. Sacrifice.'

'Murder, you mean,' Metzger said bluntly. 'Dressing the act up in fancy words doesn't change it. You want me to go down into the basement and slay a daemon. I can do this. It is what I do. Unlike you I see no nobility in the act. For me it is a case of survival, plain and simple. The creatures would destroy me and mine, so I destroy theirs. So tell me again, why would you have me drive a stake into the heart of an old man?'

'He isn't an old man anymore. Victor Guttman is long gone. The thing down there is a shell, capable of ruthless cunning and vile acts of degradation and slaughter. It is a beast. Forty-two young women of this parish have suffered at the beast's hands, witch hunter. Forty-two. I would have you root out the canker by killing the beast so that I do not find the words forty-three coming to my lips.'

'Good. Then we understand each other.'

'So we kill to stop more killing?' Brother Meyrink said, unable to hold his silence. 'That makes as much sense as going to war to end a war.'

'We love to hate,' the witch hunter said matter-of-factly. 'We love to defeat and destroy. We love to conquer. We love to kill. That is why we love war so much we revere a killer and make him a god. In violence we find ourselves. Through pain and anger and conflict we find a path that leads us to, well, to what we don't know but we are determined to walk the path. It has forever been so.'

'Sigmar help us all,' Meyrink said softly.

'Indeed, and any other gods who feel benevolent enough to shine their light on us. In the meantime, I tend to help myself. I find it is better than waiting for miracles that will never happen.'

'How do you intend to do it?' Meyrink asked.

Messner paled at the question. Details were not something he wanted.

The witch hunter drew a long bladed knife from his boot. 'Silver-tipped,' he said, drawing blood from the pad of his thumb as he picked himself on the knife's sharpness. 'Surest way to do it. Cut his heart out of his chest, then burn the corpse so there's nothing left.'

Messner shuddered at the thought. It was barbaric. 'Whatever it takes,' he said, unable to look the witch hunter in the eye.

'Stay here, priest. I wouldn't want to offend your delicate sensibilities. Ziegler, come on, we've got work to do.'

THEY DESCENDED IN darkness, listening to the chittering of rats and the moans of the old man, faint like the lament of ghosts long since moved on. His cries were pitiful.

The candles had died but tapers lay beside fresh ones. Metzger lit two. They were enough. Death was a dark business. Too much light sanitised it. His feet scuffed at the silver wrought into the floor on the threshold. It was nothing more than mumbo-jumbo. There was no magic in the design. Some charlatan had taken the temple for all it was worth. It was amazing what price people would pay for peace of mind.

The fretful light revealed little of the dark's secrets.

Carefully Metzger moved through the crypt, Ziegler two steps behind him, sword drawn in readiness for ambush. Metzger had no such fear. The only things alive down in the crypt were either too small or too weak to cause any serious harm. There was no sense of evil to the place. No taint. He raised the candle, allowing the soft light to shed more layers of pure black in favour of gentler shadows.

The old priest was huddled in the corner, naked and emaciated, his bones showing stark against the flaked skin. He barely had the strength to lift his head but defiance blazed in his eyes when he did so. Suppurating sores rimmed his mouth. There were dark scars where he had been bitten. Metzger had no doubt about the origin of the wound. It was the cold kiss of death: a vampire's bite. The old man had been fed on, of that there was no doubt. But that didn't mean that he had been sired into the life of a bloodsucking fiend.

Again, there was no residual evil that he could discern, only a frightened old man.

He trod on a plate of food that lay untouched at Guttman's feet, the plate cracked and mouldy cheese smeared beneath his boot. A nearby jug of water was nearly empty.

'Have you come to kill me?' The old man said. It sounded almost like a plea to Metzger's ears. The poor pathetic wretch had obviously tortured himself to the point of madness with the dreams of blood feasts. It was natural, having been fed upon to dream of feeding in the most feverish moments of the night when the kindred vampires were abroad. But dreams were not deeds. A true vampire would feel no remorse. There would be no tortured soul beginning for slaughter. There would be only defiance, arrogance, contempt, as the love of hatred boiled away all other emotions.

'Yes.'

The fear seemed to leech out of Guttman, the puzzle of bones collapsing in on themselves as his body slouched against the cold crypt wall.

'Thank you.'

'It will hurt, and there will be no remains for loved ones to come cry over, you understand? It can be no other way. The curse is in you, whether you killed these women or not.'

'I killed them,' Guttman said forcefully.

'I doubt it,' Gundram Metzger said, drawing the silver dagger from his boot. 'Does this scare you, priest? Does it make your skin itch and crawl?'

Guttman stared at the blade as it shone in the candlelight. He nodded.

'Make your peace with Sigmar,' Eberl Ziegler said from behind Metzger. He turned his back on the murder.

A litany of prayers for forgiveness and for the safe passage of his soul tripped over Victor Guttman's lips, not stopping even for a moment as Metzger rammed the silver knife home, between third and forth rib, into the old man's heart. His eyes flared open, the truth suddenly blazing in his mind. His screams were pitiful as he succumbed to death's embrace. He bled, pure dark blood that seeped out of the gaping wound in his chest and pooled on the floor around him.

Metzger stayed with the old priest as he died, a pitiful old man in chains.

He hung there, limbs slack, body slumped awkwardly, head lolling down over his cadaverous ribs, where the knife protruded from his chest cavity.

'It's over,' Ziegler said, laying a hand on his friend's shoulder. 'Come, let's leave this place. Bringing death to a temple leaves me cold.'

'In a moment my friend. Go to the priests, tell them the deed is done, and fetch the paraffin oil from the cart. This place needs cleansing of the stench.'

'But–'

'No buts, old friend. The place must be purged. The priests can find more walls to praise their god. But not here. Now leave me for a moment with the dead, would you? I need to pay my respects to a brave old fool.'

He sat alone for an unknowable time, the candle burning low in his hand, unmoving, waiting, alone with the dead priest.

The pungent reek of paraffin drifted down from above. It was a sickening, stifling smell. Disembodied voices argued, Ziegler's the loudest as he continued to douse the temple in oil. The place would burn.

Victor Guttman's eyes flared open in the dying light and his hand flew to the silver blade still embedded in his heart. He screamed as he yanked it out and sent the knife skittering across the crypt floor. The flesh around the wound was seared black.

'I tasted his blood,' Victor Guttman rasped, his head jerking up as he strained against his chains, all trace of the man gone. 'I want more!'

Guttman twisted and jerked, tugging at the chains that bound him, but there was no escape.

'No,' Metzger said softly. 'I told you I was here to kill you, consider this my promise delivered.' With that he stood, collected his silver knife and slipped it into the boot sheath, the gesture itself a mocking bow to the beast chained to the cold stone wall.

He walked slowly up the stairs, the creature raging in the darkness he left behind.

Ziegler was waiting at the crypt's entrance, his face grim. He held a bottle in his hand, a rag stuffed into its mouth. He passed it to Metzger who lit the end with the last of his candle's dwindling flame.

Together they stood at the huge wooden door, the cocktail of lamp oil and fire burning in Metzger's hand. He tossed it deep into the body of the temple where the glass shattered off the statue of Sigmar. Flames licked at the stonework, tongues of blue heat lashing out to consume the wooden seats. Metzger and Ziegler backed out from the intense heat as the conflagration took hold and consumed the temple.

He turned to the younger priest, Messner, who had begged his help.

'The beast is dead.'

'But...'

'There are no buts, the beast's evil cannot survive the fire. It is done. Deliver payment to Herr Hollenfeuer's wine cellar.'

'How can we pay? We have nothing left. You've destroyed everything we ever had!'

Metzger shook his head sadly. 'No, young sir, you did that. I am merely the tool you chose for its destruction. Do not blame the sword for the soldier's death, blame the man wielding it.'

HIGH ABOVE THE blaze, three men stood watching the towering inferno with perverse delight.

Vlad von Carstein, the vampire count of Sylvania, watched the flames intently. Beside him, Herman Posner turned to his man, Sebastian Aigner: 'Go out and feed. Make sure the fools down there know that they killed an innocent man. I want the knowledge to tear them apart.'

Aigner nodded. 'It will be as you wish.'

'Poor, stupid, cattle,' Posner said, a slow smile spreading across his face. 'This place promises a lot of sport, my lord.'

Von Carstein said nothing, content to watch the Sigmarite temple turn to ashes and smoke.

INHERITANCE

PROLOGUE
Death and the Maiden

DRAKENHOF CASTLE
Late winter, 1797

THE OLD MAN was dying an ugly death and for all their skill and faith there was nothing either the chirugeon or the priest could do to prevent it. Nevertheless they busied themselves by plumping the sweat-stained pillows that propped the old man up, and fussing like fishwives with candle stubs and curtains to keep the shadows and the draughts at bay, and still the bedchamber was bitterly cold. Where there ought to have been a roaring fire the stacked logs and kindling remained unlit. The two men lit smoke to ward off the ill humours and offered prayers to benevolent Sigmar. None of it made a blind bit of difference. Otto van Drak was dying. They knew it, and worse, he knew it. That was why they were with him; they had come to stand the death watch.

His bottom lip hung slackly and a ribbon of spittle drooled down his chin. Otto wiped at it with the back of a liver-spotted hand. Old age had ravaged the count with shocking speed. Otto had aged thirty years in as many days. All of the strength and vitality that had driven the man had fled in a few short weeks leaving behind a husk of humanity. His bones stood out against the sallow skin. There was no dignity in death for the Count of Sylvania.

Death, he finally understood, was the great leveller. It had no respect for ancestry or nobility of blood, and his death was determined to be as degrading as it could be. A week ago he had lost control of the muscles in his face and his tongue had bloated so much so he could barely lisp an intelligible sentence. Most of the words he managed sounded like nothing more than drunken gibberish.

For a man like Otto van Drak that was perhaps the most humiliating aspect of dying. Not for him the clean death of the battlefield, the bloodlust, the frenzy, the sheer glory of going out fighting. No, death, with its macabre sense of humour, had other humiliations lined up for him. His daughter had to bath him and help him go to the toilet while he sweated and shivered and barely managed to curse the gods who had reduced him to this.

He knew what was happening. His body was giving up the ghost one organ at a time. It was only the sheer force of his will that kept him breathing. He wasn't ready to die. Otto was contrary like that; he wanted to make them wait. It was one final act of stubbornness.

Using a cold compress his daughter Isabella leaned over the bed and towelled the sweat from his fevered brow.

'Hush, father,' she soothed, seeing that he was trying to say something. The frustration ate at his face, sheer loathing burned in his eyes. He was staring at his brother, Leopold, who slouched in a once plush crimson velvet chair. He looked thoroughly bored by the whole charade. They might have been brothers but there was no fraternal bond between them. Her mother had always claimed that the eyes were gateways to the soul. Isabella found them mesmerising. They contained such intensity of emotion and feeling. Nothing could be hidden by them. Eyes were so expressive. Looking into her father's now she could see the depth of his suffering. The old man was tormented by this degrading death but it would be over soon.

'Not long now,' the chirurgeon said to the priest, echoing her thoughts. He bent double over his case of saws and scalpels, rummaging around until he found a jar of fat-bodied leeches.

'Perhaps there is small mercy in that,' the priest said as the chirurgeon uncapped the jar and dipped his hand in. He stirred his hand through the leeches and lifted one out, placing it on the vein in Otto's neck so that it might feed.

'Leeches?' Isabella van Drak asked, her voice tinged with obvious distaste. 'Is that really necessary?'

'Bleeding is good for the heart,' the chirurgeon assured her. 'Reduces the strain if it has less to pump, which means it can keep on beating longer. Believe me, madam, my beauties will keep your father alive much, much longer if we let them do their work.' The young woman looked sceptical but she didn't stop the chirurgeon from placing six more of the bloodsuckers on her father's body.

'All... talking about me... like I am... gone... Not... dead... yet...' Otto van Drak rasped. As though to prove the point he broke into a violent coughing fit before the last word was clear of his lips. He slapped ineffectually at the leeches feeding off him.

'Be still, father.' Isabella wiped away the mucus he coughed up.

'Damned... giving up... without... a fight.' Otto struggled to form the words. The frustration was too much for him.

Leopold pushed himself up from the chair and paced across the floor. He whispered something in the chirurgeon's ear and the other man nodded. Leopold stalked over to the window and braced his hands on the windowsill, feeling the wainscoting with his fingers. Listening to the old man's laboured breathing he dug his nails into the soft wood.

A jagged streak of lightning lit the room, throwing gnarled shadows across the inhabitants. Thunder rumbled a heartbeat later, the vibrations running through the thick walls of Castle Drakenhof. Leopold could barely keep the smug smile from his face. Rain lashed at the glass, breaking and running like tears through his reflection. He chuckled mirthlessly. Crying was the very last thing he felt like doing. 'You'll be damned anyway, you old goat. I'm sure the only reason you aren't dead already is that you are terrified they're all waiting for you on the other side. That's right isn't it, brother of mine? All of those wretched souls you put to death so cheerfully. You can hear them, can't you, Otto? You can hear them calling to you. You know they are waiting for you. Can you imagine what they are going to do to you when they finally get the chance at retribution? Oh my... what a delicious thought *that* is.'

Otto's eyes blazed with impotent rage.

'Come now, Otto. Show some dignity in your final hours. As Count of Sylvania I promise you I will do all I can to dishonour your memory.'

'Get... out!'

'What? And miss your final breath, brother mine? Oh no, not for all the spices in Araby. You, dear Otto, have always been an incorrigible liar and a cheat. Dishonesty is one of your few redeeming features, perhaps your only one. So, let me put it this way: I wouldn't be surprised if this was all one grand charade. Well, I won't be a laughing stock at your expense, brother. No, no, I'll wring the life out of you with my bare hands if I have to, but I won't leave this room until I've made sure you are well and truly dead. It's nothing personal, you understand, but I am walking out of here Count of Sylvania, and you, well the only way you are leaving here is in a box. If the roles were reversed I'm sure you'd do the same.'

'Damn you...'

'Oh yes, quite possibly. But I'll cross that bridge when I come to it, which looks like it will be a good while after you've already gone trip-trapping over it, eh? Now be a good chap and die.'

'Vile...'

'Again, quite possibly, but I can't help wondering what father would think if he could see you. I mean, no disrespect, but you are a mess, Otto. Dying obviously doesn't become you. It hasn't changed you much, either, for that matter. So much for learning the error of your ways. You are still too cheap to light a damned fire in your bedroom so we have to freeze while we wait for you to pop off.'

'Damn you... your children... damn all... rot... in pits... of hell. Never let you... be... count.' Otto clawed at the bed sheets, the skin around his knuckles bone-white. '*Never!*'

Lightning crashed once more, the bluish light illuminating the sickening fury in Otto van Drak's face. Twin forks struck somewhere along the mountain path between the castle and the town of Drakenhof itself. Fat rain broke and ran down the glass of the leaded window as another jag of lightning split the storm-black darkness. The wind howled. The wooden shutters rattled against the outer wall.

'I don't see that you have much say in the matter, all things considered,' Leopold said. 'That sham of a marriage you so conveniently engineered for Isabella with the Klinsmann runt, well it was laughable, wasn't it. I can't say I was surprised when the boy threw himself from the roof of the Almoners Hall. Still, all's well that ends well, eh, brother?'

Sitting down on the edge of the old man's bed, Isabella dabbed away the blood-flecked saliva that spattered his chin and turned her attention to her uncle. She had known him all of her life. At one time she had worshipped the ground he walked on but with age came the understanding that the man was a worm. 'And I suppose I have no say in the matter.'

Leopold studied his niece for an uncomfortable moment as she brushed the long dark hair back from her face. She was beautiful in her own way, pale-skinned and fine-boned. The combination crafted a glamour of delicacy around the girl though in truth she owned the foul van Drak temper and could be as devious as a weasel when the mood took her.

'None, I'm afraid, my dear. Would that it was otherwise, but I am not the law-maker. By accident of birth you came out... female. With no sons your father's line ends, and mine, as eldest surviving male begins. With your betrothed coming to such an... untimely end... well, that is just the way it is. You can't tamper with tradition, after all it becomes traditional for a reason. Though,' Leopold mused thoughtfully as though the idea had just occurred to him. He turned to look at the priest. 'Tell me, how does the benevolent Sigmar look upon the union of close family, say uncles and nieces, Brother Guttman? Being the kind of man I am, I might be convinced to make the sacrifice to set my dear brother's mind at rest. Wouldn't want to see the only good thing he ever managed to create forced into whoring on the street, would we?'

'It is frowned upon,' the aged priest said, not bothering to look at Leopold when he answered him. The priest made the sign of Sigmar's hammer in the air above Otto's head.

'Ah, well. Can't say I didn't try, my dear.' Leopold said with a lascivious wink.

'You would do well to mind your tongue, *uncle*.' Isabella said, coldly. 'This is still my home, and you are alone in it, whereas there are plenty of servants and men-at-arms here who remain loyal to my father, and in turn, to me.'

'A woman scorned and all that, eh? Well of course, dear. Threaten and bluster away. You know I love you like my own flesh and blood and would never see you suffer.'

'You would turn your back so you didn't have to watch,' Isabella finished for him.

'Damn, you've got spirit, girl, I'll give you that. A true van Drak. Heart and soul.'

'Hate... this. I don't... want... to die.' The leeches at his throat and temples pulsed as they fed on Otto van Drak. In the few minutes since the chirurgeon had placed them they had bloated up to almost a third again their size and still they sucked greedily at the dying count's blood.

'Pity you have no choice in the matter, old man. First you die, and then you will go to Morr and I am sure the Lord of the Underworld will delight in flensing your soul one layer at a time. After the kind of life you've led I can't imagine any amount of grovelling and snivelling by our friend the priest here will help you avoid what's coming to you.' Leopold said. 'Tell me, Brother Guttman, what says your god on this matter?' Leopold asked the stoop-shouldered priest of Sigmar. The man looked decidedly uncomfortable at being addressed directly.

'Only a repentant soul can be shrived of the taint of darkness,' the priest answered. Isabella helped the aged holy man kneel at Otto's bedside.

'And there you have it, brother, out of the mouthpiece of blessed Sigmar himself. You're damned.'

'Are you ready to unburden your soul of its sins before you meet Morr?' Victor Guttman asked Otto, ignoring Leopold's gloating.

'Get... away... from me... priest.' Otto spat a loose wad of phlegm into the priest's face. It clung to the cheekbone just below the old man's eye before slipping down into the grey shadow of his stubble. The frail priest wiped it away with a shaking hand. 'I have nothing ... nothing... to repent. Save your breath... and mine.' Otto trailed off into a fit of raving, spitting out half-formed words and curses in a senseless torrent.

'Father, please,' Isabella said softly but it was no good, the old man wasn't about to be convinced to cleanse his soul.

'Oh, this is wonderful stuff, Otto. Quite wonderful,' Leopold gloated. 'Do you think I have time to summon the priests of Shallya and Ulric so you can alienate their gods, too? Any others you would particularly like to offend?' Another jag of lightning split the darkness. If anything the storm was worsening. The shutters clattered against the stonework outside, splinters of wood tearing free. The wind howled through the eaves, moaning in high pitched chorus from the snarling mouths of the weather-beaten gargoyles that guarded the four corners of the high tower. 'Every bitter word that froths from your mouth is rubbish, of course, Otto, but such marvellous rubbish. Give it up. All this breathing must be awfully tiresome. I know I am growing tired of it.'

The laughter died in his throat.

Three successive shafts of lightning turned the black night for a heartbeat into bright day. The storm lashed the countryside. The trees bent and bowed in the gale. Skeletal branches strained to the point of breaking. Thunder grumbled around the hilltops, the heavy sounds folding in on themselves until they boomed like orc war drums.

A shiver chased down the ladder of Leopold's spine one bone at a time. Behind him the priest pressed Otto to confess his sins.

'It's pointless,' Leopold said, turning to smile at the earnest priest. The old man's hands trembled and every trace of colour had drained from his face. 'If he starts at the beginning he won't make it out of his teens before Morr takes him. Our Otto has been a very bad boy.'

'Morr... take... you...' Otto cursed weakly as a fit of coughing gripped him. He hacked up blood. Brother Guttman took the towel from Isabella and made to wipe up the red-flecked saliva but Otto jerked his head away with surprising strength. 'Get... away from me... priest... won't have you... touch me.' Otto slumped back exhausted onto his pillows.

As though the sheer force of Otto's loathing had undone him, the priest staggered back a step, his hand fluttering up weakly toward Isabella to prevent himself from falling as his knees buckled, then swayed and collapsed. The side of his head and shoulder cracked off the rim of the bedside table with the sick sound of wet meat being tenderised.

Mellin, van Drak's chirurgeon, moved quickly to the fallen priest. 'Alive,' he said, feeling the faint pulse at Brother Guttman's throat. 'Though barely.'

Lightning rent the fabric of the bruise-purple sky, the incessant drumming of the fat rain stopped suddenly.

The frail priest contorted in a series of violent convulsions, almost as though his body were somehow earthing the raw electricity of the storm. And then he lay deathly still.

In the deafening silence that followed there was a single sharp knock and the door opened.

A terrified man-servant stood in the doorway, head down, humble. A hauntingly handsome man pushed past the servant, not waiting for his formal introduction. The stranger was easily a head taller than Leopold, if not more, and had to stoop slightly to enter the bed-chamber. In his hand he held a silver-topped cane. The handle had been fashioned into the likeness of a dire wolf, teeth bared in a feral snarl. The shoulders of his cloak were a darker black where they were soaked through with rain and water dripped from the brim of his hat.

'The noble Vlad von Carstein, my l-lord,' the servant stuttered. With a wave of the hand, the newcomer dismissed the servant who scurried off gratefully.

The sound of rain rushed back to drown the silence in the very heart of the storm.

The newcomer approached the bed. His boots left wet prints on the cold wooden boards. Leopold stared at them, trying to fathom where the man had come from. 'Out of the storm,' he mumbled, shaking his head.

'I bid thee humble greeting, Count van Drak,' the man's accent was peculiarly thick; obviously foreign. Kislevite perhaps, or further east, Leopold thought, trying to place it. 'And you, fair lady,' he said, turning to Isabella, 'are quite enchanting. A pale rose set between these withered thorns.'

Her face lit up with that simple compliment. She broke into a lop-sided smile and curtseyed, never taking her eyes from the man's. And such eyes he had. They were animalistic in their intensity, filled with nameless hungers. She felt herself being devoured by his gaze and surrendered willingly to the sensation. The man had *power* and he was not averse to exploiting it. A slow predatory smile spread across his face. Isabella felt herself being drawn to the newcomer. It was a subtle but irresistible sensation. She took a step toward him.

'Stop staring, woman, it is quite unbecoming.' Leopold snapped. 'And you, sir.' He turned his attention to the stranger. 'Thank you for coming, but as I am sure you can see, you are intruding on a somewhat personal moment. My brother is failing fast and, as you only die once, we would like to share his last few minutes, just the family, I am sure you understand. If you care to wait until... ah... afterwards, I would be pleased to see you in one of the reception rooms to discuss whatever business you have with the count?' He gestured toward the door, but instead of leaving the newcomer removed his white gloves, teasing them off one finger at a time, and took Isabella's hand. He raised it to his lips and let the kiss linger there, ignoring Leopold's blustering, the convulsing priest and the chirurgeon as they were clearly of no interest to him.

'I am Vlad eldest of the von Carstein family–' the newcomer said to the dying count, ignoring Leopold's posturing.

'I don't know the family,' Leopold interrupted somewhat peevishly.

'And neither would I expect you to,' the stranger countered smoothly. He regarded Leopold as though he were nothing more interesting than an insect trapped in a jar of honey, the sole fascination being in watching it drown in the sticky sweetness. 'But I can trace my lineage to a time before van Hal, to the founding of the Empire and beyond, which is more than can be said of many of today's nobility, yes? True nobility is a legacy of the blood, not something earned as the spoils of war, wouldn't you agree?' Vlad unclasped the hasp on his travel cloak and draped it over the back of the crimson chair. He set the wolf's head cane down to rest beside it, laying his white gloves over the snarling silver fangs, the wet hat on top of the gloves. His raven black hair was bound in a single braid that reached midway down the length of his back. There was an arrogance about the man that Leopold found disquieting. He moved with the grace of a natural predator stalking tender prey but equally there was no denying the fellow possessed a certain magnetism.

'Indeed,' Leopold agreed. 'And what, pray tell, brings you to us on such a foul night? Does my brother owe you thirty silvers, or perhaps he had your betrothed executed on one of his foolish whims? Let me assure you, as the new count, I will endeavour to make good on whatever debt you feel the family owes you. It is the very least I can do.'

'My business is with the count, not his lackey.'

'I don't see what–'

'There is no need for you to see anything, sir. I was merely in the vicinity, travelling to the wedding of a close friend, and I thought it right and proper to pledge fealty to the *current* Count van Drak, to offer my services in any way he might see fit.'

In the bed Otto chuckled mirthlessly. The chuckle gave way to another violent fit of coughing.

'Marry...' Otto's eyes blazed with vindictive glee. 'Yes,' the dying count hissed maliciously. 'Yes... yes.'

'Preposterous! I will not stand for this nonsense!' Leopold spluttered, a flush of colour rising in his cheeks so the broken blood vessels showed through angrily. 'In a few hours *I* will be count and I will have you drawn and quartered and your head on a spike before sunrise, do you hear me, fool?'

Otto managed something halfway between a cough and a laugh.

On the floor, the priest of Sigmar was gripped by a second, more violent, series of spasms. The chirurgeon struggled to hold him fast and prevent the old man from biting off or swallowing his tongue in the depths of the fit.

'Like... hell... will... see you *ruined* first!' Otto spat, an echo of his true self in his final defiance.

'Sir,' Vlad said, kneeling at the bedside. 'If that would be your will, I came to be of service, an answer to your prayer, and as such I would gladly accept the hand of your daughter Isabella as my wife, and would that you were alive to see us married.'

'No!' Leopold grabbed at Vlad's shoulder.

The priest's heels drummed on the floor punctuating Leopold's outburst.

'Excuse me,' Vlad said softly, and then rose and turned in one fluid motion, his hand snaking out with dizzying speed to close around Leopold van Drak's throat.

'You are annoying me, little man,' Vlad rasped, lifting Leopold up onto the tips of his toes, so that they were eye to eye. He held him there, Leopold kicking out weakly and flapping at Vlad's hand as the fingers tightened mercilessly around his throat, choking the very life out of him. Leopold struggled to draw even a single breath. He batted and clawed at Vlad's hand but the man's grip was relentless.

And then, almost casually, Vlad tossed him aside.

Leopold slumped to the floor, retching and gasping for breath.

'Now, we do appear to have a priest, could you rouse him?' Vlad von Carstein told the chirurgeon. 'Then we can get on with the ceremony. I would hazard that Count van Drak does not have long left, and it would be a shame to rob him of the joy of seeing his beloved daughter wed, would it not?'

Mellin nodded but didn't move. He was staring at Leopold as he struggled to rise.

'Now,' Vlad said. It was barely above a whisper but it was as though the word itself possessed power. The chirurgeon fumbled for his bag and knocked it over, sending its contents skittering across the floor. On hands and knees he picked through the mess until he found a small astringent salve. Shaking, he smeared the ointment on Brother Guttman's upper lip. The Sigmarite priest shuddered and came to, spluttering and slapping at his mouth. Seeing Vlad for the first time, the aged priest recoiled, reflexively making the sign of Sigmar's hammer in the air between them.

'We have need of your services, priest,' Vlad said, his voice like silk as his words wrapped around the priest, caressing the man into doing his bidding. 'The count would have his daughter wed before he passes.'

'You cannot do this to me! I won't allow this to happen! This is my birthright! Sylvania, this castle... it is all mine!' Leopold blustered. He needed the support of the wall to help him stand.

'On the contrary, good sir. The count can do anything – *anything* – that he so wishes. He is a law unto himself. If he bade me reach into your chest and rip out your heart with my bare hands and feed it to his dogs, well,' he held his hands out, palms up, then turned them over as though inspecting them. 'It might prove difficult, but if the count willed it, believe me, it would be done.'

He turned to Isabella. 'And what of you, my lady? It is customary for the bride to say "yes" at some point during the proceedings.'

'When my father dies *he*,' Isabella levelled a finger at the cringing Leopold, 'inherits his estate, the castle, the title, everything that by rights should be mine. All my life I've lived in the shadow of the van Drak men. I've had no life. I've played the dutiful daughter. I've been possessed – and now, my father is dying and I hunger for freedom. I hunger for it so desperately I can almost taste it, and in you, perhaps finally, I can realise it. So give me what I want, and I will give myself to you, body and soul.'

'And what would that be?'

She turned to look at her father in his death bed, and saw the malicious delight in his face. She smiled: 'Everything. But first, a token... A morning gift, I believe they call it. From the groom to the bride as proof of his love.'

'This is ridiculous!' Leopold shouted, his voice cracking with the strain of it.

'Anything,' Vlad said, ignoring him. 'If it is in my power to give, you shall have it.'

She smiled then, and it was as though she sloughed off the years of subjugation with that simple expression of pleasure. She drew him to her and whispered something in his ear as he kissed her delicately on the cheek.

'As you wish,' Vlad said.

He turned to face an apoplectic Leopold.

'I am a fair man, Leopold van Drak. I would not see you suffer unduly so I have a proposition for you. I will give you time to ponder it. Five minutes ought to suffice. Think about it, while the priest gets ready for the ceremony, and my wife to be makes sure her father is comfortable, and then, and only then, after five full minutes have passed, if you can look me in the eye and tell me that you truly wish me to stand aside, well then, I will have to accede to your will.'

'Are you serious?' Leopold asked somewhat incredulously. He hadn't expected the stranger to back down so easily.

'Always. What is a man if there is no honour to be found in his word? You have my word. Now, do you accept?'

Leopold met Vlad's coldly glowing eyes. The startling intensity of the hatred he saw blazing there had him involuntarily backing up a step. He felt the wall and the ridge of the windowsill dig into the base of his back.

'I do,' he said, knowing it was a trap even as he allowed himself to be shepherded into it.

'Good,' Vlad von Carstein said flatly. In four quick strides he was across the room. With one hand he picked Leopold up by the scruff of the neck, the other he rammed into the man's chest, splintering the bone as his fingers closed around the already dead man's heart. In a moment of shocking savagery he wrenched it free and hurled the corpse through the window. There were no screams.

The dead man's heart in his hand, Vlad leaned out through the window. Lightning crashed in the distance. The eye of the storm had passed over Drakenhof and was moving away. In the lightning's afterglow he saw the outline of Leopold's body spread out on a flat rooftop three storeys below, arms and legs akimbo in a whorish sprawl.

Isabella joined him at the broken window, linking her fingers with his, slick with her uncle's blood. But for the blood the gesture might have been mistaken for an intimate one. Instead it hinted at the darkness inside her: by taking his hand she was claiming him and the life he offered every bit as much as he was claiming her and the power her heritage represented.

The power.

'Your gift,' he said, offering the heart to her.

'Throw it away, now that it has stopped beating I have no use for it,' she said, drawing him away from the window.

Somewhere in the night a wolf howled. It was a haunting lament made more so by the wind and the rain.

'It sounds so... lonely.'

'It is missing its mate. Wolves are one of the few creatures that mate for life. It will know no other love. It is the creature's curse to be alone.'

Isabella shivered, drawing Vlad closer to her. 'Let's have no more talk of loneliness.' Rising onto tiptoes she kissed the man who promised to give her *everything* her heart desired.

CHAPTER ONE
A Fisher of Devils

A SYLVANIAN BORDER TOWN
Early spring, 2009

THE LAND WAS devoid of life. No insects chirped, no frogs croaked, there was no bird song, not even the whisper of the breeze stirring leaves in the trees. The silence was unnatural. The malignancy, Jon Skellan realised, infected everything. It was ingrained in the very earth of the land itself. Its sickness ate away at everything; decay only an inch beneath the surface. The trees, still bare despite the turning of the season into what ought to have been the first flush of spring, were rotten to the core. Scanning the skeletal branches overhead Skellan saw that the only nest was empty, and judging by the way the twigs had been unravelled by the weather, had been empty for a long time. It was a spiritual canker. The land – this land – was soaked in blood, cruelty and despair.

Skellan shuddered.

Beside him, Stefan Fischer made the sign of Sigmar's hammer.

The two of them were chasing ghosts but what better place to come looking for them than the barren lands of Sylvania?

'Verhungern Wood. Starvation Wood, or Hunger Wood. I'm not sure about the precise interpretation of the dialect into Reikspiel. Still, the name seems disturbingly appropriate, doesn't it?'

'Aye, it does,' Fischer agreed, looking at the rows of dead and dying trees. It was difficult to believe that less than two days walk behind them spring in all of her beauty was unfolding in the daffodils and crocuses along the banks of the River Stir. 'Forests are meant to be living things, full of living things.' And by saying it out loud, Fischer voiced what had been bothering Skellan for the last hour. There was a total lack of life around them. 'Not like this blasted, barren place. It's unnatural.'

Skellan uncorked the flask he carried at his hip and took a deep swig of water. He wiped his mouth with the back of his hand and sighed. They were a long way from home – and in more ways than simply distance. This place was unlike anywhere he had ever been before. He had heard tales of Sylvania, but like most he assumed they were exaggerated with fishwives' gossip and the usual tall tales of self-proclaimed adventurers. The reality was harsher than he had imagined. The land had suffered under centuries of abuse and misrule, which of course made their arrival here inevitable. It was their calling; to root out evil, to cleanse the world of the black arts and the villainous scum who dabbled in them.

The pair had been called many things; the simplest, though least accurate, being witch hunters. Jon Skellan found it interesting that the agony of grief could earn a man such an epithet. He hadn't made a conscious choice to become the man he was today. Life had shaped him, bent him, buckled him, but it had not broken him. Now, seven years to the month, if not the week, since the riders had come burning and looting to his home, here he was, chasing ghosts, or rather looking to finally lay them to rest.

'All roads lead to hell,' he said, bitterly.

'Well, this one brought us to Sylvania,' Fischer said.

'Same place, my friend, same godforsaken place.'

The ruining of one lifestyle and the birth of their new one had been shockingly quick. Skellan and Fischer had married sisters and become widowers within a quarter of an hour of each other. The highs and the lows of their lives were bound together. Fate can be cruel like that. Skellan looked at his brother-in-law. No one would ever mistake them for family. At thirty-six, Fischer was nine years older than Skellan, a good six inches taller and a stone heavier where the muscles had started to slide into fat, but the two men shared a single disturbing similarity: their eyes. Their eyes said they had seen a future filled with happiness, and it had been snatched away from them. The loss had aged them far beyond their years. Their souls were old, hardened. They had experienced the worst that life could throw at them, and they had survived. Now it was about vengeance.

A beetle the size of a mouse skittered across the ground less than a foot in front of his feet. It was the first living thing they had encountered in hours and it was hardly encouraging.

'Have you ever wondered what it might have been like if...' He didn't need to clarify the 'if'. They both knew what he was talking about.

'Every day,' Fischer said, not looking at him. 'It's like walking out of the storyteller's circle halfway through his tale... you don't know how it is supposed to end and you keep obsessing over it. What would life have been like if Leyna and Lizbet hadn't been murdered? Where would we be now? Not here, that's for sure.'

'No... not here.' Skellan agreed. 'No use getting maudlin.' He straightened as he said it, drawing himself upright as though shrugging off the heavy burden of sadness thinking about Lizbet always brought with it. It was, of course, an act. He could no more shrug off his grief than he could forget what caused it in the first place. It was simply a case of managing it. Skellan had long since come to terms with his wife's death. He accepted it. It had happened. He didn't forgive it, and he didn't forget.

There had been seven riders that day. It had taken time, almost seven years to be exact, but six of them were in the ground now, having paid the ultimate price for their sins. Skellan and Fischer had seen to that, and in doing so they showed the men no quarter. Like their victims, like Leyna and Lizbet and the other souls they sent to Morr in their frenzy, they burned. It wasn't pretty but then death never is. They caught up with the first of the murderers almost three months later, in a tavern drunk to the point where he could barely stand. Skellan had dragged him outside, dunked him in the horse's watering trough until the murderer came up coughing and spluttering and sober enough to know he was in trouble. The knee is a very delicate hinge protected by a bone cap. Skellan shattered one of the man's kneecaps with a brutal kick through the joint, and dragged him screaming into the room he lodged in. 'You've got a chance,' Skellan had said. 'Not a very good chance, but more of one than you gave my wife.' It wasn't true. Unable to stand, let alone walk, the man didn't have a chance against the flames and the smoke – and even if by some miracle he had dragged himself clear of the fire, Skellan and Fischer were waiting outside to see he joined the ranks of Morr's dead.

There was no satisfaction in it. No sense of a wrong having been righted or justice having been done.

It was all about vengeance and one by one the murderers burned.

At first it had been like a sickness inside him, and it had only grown worse until it became an all-consuming need to make the murderers pay for what they had done. But even their deaths didn't take the pain away, so for a while he made them die harder.

By the time they caught up with the fourth murderer, a snivelling wretch of a man, Skellan had devised his torture jacket. The coat had extra long sleeves and buckles so that they could be fastened in such a way that the wearer was trapped, helpless. The coat itself was doused in lamp oil. It was a brutal way to die, but Skellan justified it to himself by saying he was doing it for Lizbet and for all the others the murderer had tortured and burned alive. Lying to himself was a skill he had perfected over the seven-year hunt. He knew full well what he was doing. He was extracting vengeance for the dead.

It was guilt, he knew, that drove him. Guilt for the fact that he had failed them in life. Guilt for the fact that he hadn't been there to save them from the savagery of their murderers, and his guilt was an ugly thing because once it had wormed its way into his head it refused to give up its hold. It ate away at his mind. It convinced him that there was something he could have done. That it was his fault that Lizbet and Leyna and all of the others were dead.

So he carried with him his own personal daemons and didn't argue when he heard people cry: 'The witch hunter is coming!'

They walked on a while in silence, both men locked in thoughts of the past, neither one needing to say a word.

After a while the wind picked up, and carried with it a smell they were painfully familiar with.

Burning flesh.

AT FIRST SKELLAN thought it was his mind playing tricks on him, bringing back old ghosts to torment him, but beside him Fischer stopped and sniffed suspiciously at the air as though trying to locate the source of the smell and he realised the burning wasn't in his mind, it was here, now. There would be no burning without fire, and no fire without smoke. He scanned the trees looking for any hint of smoke, but it was impossible to see more than a few feet either way. The entire forest could have been on fire and without the press of heat from the conflagration he would never have known. The wind itself offered no clues. They had walked into a slight declivity that cut like a shallow U through the landscape. It meant that the wind was funnelled down through channel before folding back on itself. The tang of smoke and the sickly sweet stench of burned meat could have come from almost any direction. But it couldn't have come from far away. The smell would have dissipated over any great distance.

Skellan turned in a slow circle.

There was no hint of smoke or fire to the right, or where the valley spread out before them, and the withered line of trees masked any hint of smoke to the left but the fact that there were trees to hide the fire where everywhere else was barren told Skellan all he needed to know.

'This way,' he said, and started to run into the trees.

Fischer set off after him but found it difficult to keep up with the younger man.

Branches clawed at his clothes and scratched at his face as he pushed his way through them. Brittle twigs snapped underfoot. The smell of burning grew stronger the deeper into the wood they went.

And still there were no sounds or signs of life apart from Fischer's laboured breathing and bullish footsteps.

As he pushed on, Skellan realised that the press of the trees began to thin noticeably. He stumbled into the clearing without realising that was what he had found. It was a village, of sorts, in the wood. He pulled up short. There was a scattering of low houses made of wattle and daub, and a fire pit in what would be the small settlement's meeting place. Early spring mist clung to the air. The fire was ablaze, dead wood banked high. A body had been laid out on top of the wood, wrapped in some kind of cloth that had all but burned away. A handful of mourners gathered around the pyre, their faces limned with soot and tears as they turned to look at the intruders. An old man with close-cropped white hair appeared to be officiating over the ceremony.

Skellan held up his hands in a sign of peace and backed up a step, not wanting to intrude further on their grief.

'Peculiar ritual,' Fischer muttered as he finally caught up. 'Burning the dead instead of burying them.'

'But not unheard of,' Skellan agreed. 'More common during times of strife, certainly. Soldiers will honour their dead on such a funeral pyre. But this, I fear, is done for a very different reason.'

'Plague?'

'That would be my guess, though by rights an outbreak in a village this small would wipe the place out virtually overnight and burning the first victims won't matter a damn. How many live here? One hundred? Less? It isn't even a village, it's a handful of houses. If it is the plague, I pity them because they're doomed. I doubt very much whether this place will be here when we come back through these woods in a few months time. We *should* leave them in peace, but we're not going to. Let's give them some privacy to complete the ritual then I want to talk to some people. The burning of the dead has my curiosity piqued.'

'Aye, it is an odd thing, but then we are in an odd place. Who knows what these people think is normal?'

They waited just beyond the skirt of the tree line until the fire burned itself out. Despite their retreat out of sight the mourners were uncomfortably aware of their presence and cast occasional glances their way, trying to see them through the shadows. Skellan sat with his back against a tree. He whittled at a small piece of deadfall with his knife, shaping it into the petals of a crude flower. Beside him Fischer closed his eyes and fell into a light sleep. It always amazed the witch hunter how his friend seemed capable of sleeping at any time, in any place imaginable. It was a useful skill. He himself could never empty his mind enough to sleep. He worried about the smallest details. Obsessed about them.

Even this close to the small settlement the woods were disturbingly quiet. It was unnatural. He had no doubt about that. But what had caused the animals to abandon this place? That was the question that nagged away at the back of his mind. He knew full well that animals were sensitive to all kinds of danger; it was that survival instinct that kept them alive. Something had caused them to leave this part of Verhungern Wood.

Jon Skellan looked up at the sound of cautious footsteps approaching. Stefan Fischer's eyes snapped open and his hand moved reflexively toward the knife on his belt. It was the old man who had been leading the funeral; only up close Skellan saw that it wasn't a man at all. Her heavily lined features and close-cropped white hair had rendered the woman sexless over distance but close up there was no mistaking her femininity. There was a deep sadness in her eyes. She knew full well the fate awaiting her settlement. Death hung like a sword over her head. A heady mix of perfumes and scents clung to her clothing. She was trying to hold the sickness back with pungent smelling poultices and essences of plant extracts. It was useless of course. The plague would not be fooled or deterred by pretty smells.

'It isn't safe for you here,' she said without preamble. Her voice was thickly accented, as though she were grating stones in her throat while she spoke.

Skellan nodded and pushed himself to his feet. He held out his hand in greeting. The old woman refused to take it. She looked at him as though he were insane to even contemplate touching her. Perhaps he was, but death held no fears for Jon Skellan. It hadn't for a long time. If plague took him then so be it. He would not hide himself away from it.

'I'll be the judge of that,' he said. 'Plague?'

The old woman's eyes narrowed as she looked at him. She transferred her gaze to Fischer, and rather like a mother berating an errant child scolded. 'And you can forget about your knife, young man. It isn't that kind of death that haunts these trees.'

'I guessed as much,' Skellan said. 'From the pyre. It brought back memories...'

'I can't imagine what kind of memories a funeral pyre would bring back... oh,' she said. 'I am sorry.'

Skellan nodded again. 'Thank you. We are looking for a man. He goes by the name of Aigner. Sebastian Aigner. We know he crossed over the border into Sylvania two moons back, and that he is claiming to be hunting a cult, but the man is not what he seems.'

'I wish I could help you,' the old woman said ruefully, 'but we tend to keep ourselves to ourselves here.'

'I understand.' Skellan bowed his head, as though beaten, the weight of the world dragging it down, and then he looked up as though something had just occurred to him. 'The plague? When did it first show up here? The first death?'

The old woman was surprised by the bluntness of the question.

'A month back, perhaps a little more.'

'I see. And yet no strangers passed through?'

She looked him squarely in the eye, knowing full well the implication of what he was suggesting. 'We keep ourselves to ourselves,' she repeated.

'You know, for some strange reason I am not inclined to believe you.' He looked to Fischer for confirmation.

'Something doesn't smell right,' the older man agreed. 'I'd be willing to wager our boy is tucked away in there somewhere.'

'No, he's moved on,' Skellan said, watching the old woman's face for any flicker of betrayal. It was difficult to lie well, and simple folk were more often than not appalling when it came to hiding the truth. It was in the eyes. It was always in the eyes. 'But he was here.'

She blinked once and licked at her lower lip. It was all he needed to know. She was lying.

'Did he bring the sickness with him?'

The old woman said nothing.

'Why would you protect the man who had, by accident or design, condemned your entire village to death? That is what I don't understand. Is it some sort of misguided loyalty?'

'Fear,' Fischer said.

'Fear,' Skellan said. 'That would mean you expect him to return...'

Her eyes darted left and right, as though she expected the man to actually be close enough to overhear them.

'That's it, isn't it? He threatened to come back.'

'We keep to ourselves,' the old woman repeated but her eyes said: *Yes he threatened to come back. He threatened to come back and kill us all if we told anyone about him. He damned us, either he kills us or the sickness he brought with him does... there is no justice in our world anymore.*

'He has a month on us. The distance is closing. I wonder if he looks over his shoulder nervously, expecting the worst? He can run for his life. It doesn't matter. It isn't his life anymore. It is mine. One day he will wake up and I will be standing over him, waiting to collect my due. He knows that. It eats away at him the way it ate away at his friends, only now he is the last. He knows that, too. I can almost smell his fear on the wind. Now, the question is where would he go from here? What are the obvious places?'

'Do you really think Aigner would be that stupid, Jon?' Fischer asked. He was talking for the sake of it. He was looking over the old woman's shoulder. The mourners were clearing away the ashes, gathering them into some kind of clay urn.

'Absolutely. Remember he is running for his life. That has a way of driving you forward without really thinking clearly. He sees limited choices. Always going forward, looking for shelter in the crush of people that civilisation offers. So,' he smiled at the old woman. 'Where can we go from here? Are there any settlements nearby big enough for us to lose ourselves in?'

'Like I said, we keep to ourselves,' the old woman sniffed, 'so we don't have much call for visiting other towns, but there are places of course, back on the main track. You have Reuth Losa four days' walk from here. It is a market town. With spring people will be gathering now. Beyond that you've got Leicheberg. It is the closest we have to a city.'

'Thank you,' Skellan said. He knew the lie of the land. The old woman had given them directions without having to betray her people. Sebastian Aigner had left here a month ago, heading for Leicheberg. It was a city, with all of the inherent distractions of a city: taverns, whores, gambling tables and the simplest things of life itself, food and a warm bed. Even running for his life it would slow him down. The press of people would give the illusion of safety.

Over her shoulder they were digging a small hole in the dirt for the urn.

'Might I?' Skellan asked, holding up the wooden flower he had carved while waiting for the funeral to end.

'It would be better if I did,' the old woman said.

'Perhaps, but it would be more personal if I laid it on her grave.'

She nodded.

Skellan took her nod as tacit agreement and walked across the small clearing. A few of the other villagers looked up as he approached. He felt their eyes on him but he didn't alter his stride. It took him a full minute to approach the freshly dug grave.

'How old was she?' he asked, kneeling beside the churned soil. He didn't look at anyone as he placed the delicate wooden flower on the dark soil.

'Fourteen,' someone said.

'My daughter's age,' Skellan said. 'I am truly sorry for your loss. May your god watch over her.'

He made the sign of the hammer as he rose to leave.

'I hope you kill the bastards that did this to my little girl.' The man's voice was full of bitterness. Skellan knew the emotion only too well. It was all that was left when the world collapsed around you.

He turned to face the speaker. When he spoke his voice was cold and hard. 'I certainly intend to.'

Without another word he walked back to where Fischer and the old woman waited.

'That was a kind thing you did, thank you.'

'The loss of anyone so young is a tragedy we can ill afford to bear. It was only a token, and it cost me nothing.'

'Truly, but few would have taken the time to pay their respects to a stranger. It is the way of the world, I fear. We forget the suffering of others all too easily, especially those left behind.'

Skellan turned to Fischer. 'Come, my friend. We should leave these good people to their grieving.'

Fischer nodded, and then cocked his head as though listening to some out of place sound in the silence of the forest. 'Tell me,' he said, after a moment. 'Has it always been this quiet here?'

'Quiet? Heavens, no,' the old woman said, shaking her head. 'And at night it is far from quiet. There's no denying that a lot of the creatures left with the coming of the wolves. They don't bother us and we don't bother them. They hunt at night, during the day they sleep.' She leaned in close, her voice dropping conspiratorially. 'Be careful though, when you are walking at night. Keep to the paths. Don't leave the paths. Never leave the paths. Verhungern isn't a safe place at night.'

With that final warning she left them on the edge of the trees. They watched her shuffle towards the mourners at the graveside. Fischer turned to Skellan. 'What on earth was that all about?'

'I'm not sure, but I am not in a hurry to find out, either.'

They kept well within the cover of the trees as they worked their way around the settlement until they came upon the narrow cotter's path that led through the trees back towards the main road and would eventually arrive at the market town of Reuth Losa. They had no more than a few hours of walking before nightfall and he had no intention of sleeping in the forest. It was a godforsaken place. The old woman's warning echoed in his mind. Keep to the paths. Skellan had his suspicions about what she meant. He was well aware of the horrors that walked abroad come nightfall.

They walked on awhile in silence, leaving the trees of Verhungern Wood behind. The road ran parallel to the forest for miles. The oppressive feeling that had been weighing the two men down since they entered the forest lifted almost as soon as they returned to the road. Neither man commented on it. Fischer dismissed it as nothing more than his nerves and imagination combining to play tricks on him. Skellan wasn't quite so quick to dismiss the feeling.

In the distance a dark smudge of mountains came into view but quickly lost its definition to the falling night.

THEY MADE CAMP by the roadside, not far enough away from the menace of the dark trees for comfort. Normally they would have eaten fresh meat, caught and killed less than an hour before they ate it, but there was no game to be hunted so they had to make do with the dry bread they had carried with them for three days since crossing the River Stir, and a hunk of pungent cheese. It barely touched their hunger.

Sitting at the makeshift fire, Skellan scanned the brooding darkness of the trees. It was disturbing how the shadows seemed to shift as he stared at them, as though something inside them moved.

'Not the most hospitable place we've ever visited, is it?' Fischer said. He chewed on a mouthful of hard bread and washed it down with a mouthful of water from his hip flask.

'No. What would make a man run into this blasted land? How could anyone choose to live here?'

'The key word is *live*, Jon. Aigner is hoping we'll lose him in this hellhole. And I can't say that I blame him. I mean, only a fool would willingly march into the wastes of Sylvania with nothing but mouldy cheese and stale bread to keep him alive.'

In the distance, a wolf howled. It was the first sound of life they had heard in hours. It wasn't a comforting one. It was answered moments later by another, then a third.

Skellan stared at the blackness beyond the trees, suddenly sure that he could see yellow eyes staring back at him. He shivered.

'They sound as hungry as I feel,' Fischer moaned, holding up what remained of his meal.

'Well, let's just hope they don't decide you're fat enough for the main course.'

'Hope is the last thing to die, you know that,' Fischer said, suddenly serious for a moment.

'Yes, always the innocents go first, like that girl back there.'

'Do you think he killed her? I mean, it doesn't seem like his style,' Fischer said, worrying at a string of cheese that had somehow gotten stuck in his teeth. The older man poked at it with his finger, digging it out.

'Who knows what depths the man is capable of stooping to. When you consort with the dead who knows what sicknesses you carry inside you? Aigner is the worst kind of monster; he wears a human face and yet he revels in depravity. He is sick to the core, yet he looks just like you or me. See him in a crowd and no one would be able to tell, but that sickness eats away at his humanity. An evil. He courts death. Is it any wonder he is drawn to the blackest arts? No, we will find our man, in Leicheberg or somewhere close, wherever the sickness of mankind is at its worst. That is where he will be. And then he will burn.'

A chorus of wolves howls filled the night, the baying cries echoing all around them.

'It isn't going to be easy to sleep tonight,' Skellan muttered, looking once again at the shadows cloaking the fringe of Verhungern Wood.

'I'm sure I'll manage,' Fischer said with a grin, and he wasn't lying. Within five minutes of his head hitting the bedroll he was snoring as though he didn't have a care in the world.

Skellan gave up trying to sleep after an hour, and instead concentrated on listening to the sounds of nocturnal life stirring in the forest. He could hear the wolves, padding back and forth just beyond the tree line. He thought again of the old woman's warning to stay on the path. He had no intention of moving away from the dubious safety the path offered. It seemed, at least, that the trees acted as some kind of natural barrier that the wolves dared not cross.

It hadn't been his imagination. Sickly yellow eyes really were watching them from the forest. A wolf, a giant of a wolf, came close enough to be seen through the silver moonlight. The creature was easily twice the size of a big dog with a long snout and jowls that Skellan imagined curled back in a snarl, saliva flecking the animal's yellowed teeth. The wolf remained there, stock still and staring back directly at him, long enough for Skellan to feel his heartbeat triple as it thudded against his chest and his breathing become shallow with the onset of fear, but it didn't leave the shelter of the trees. Skellan didn't move. He didn't dare to. A single sudden movement could cause the animal to launch an attack and he was in no doubt as to who would come out on top in a fight between man and this particular beast. Beside him Fischer slept like a babe, oblivious to the wolf.

As quickly as it came, the wolf was gone. It ghosted away silently into the darkness. Skellan let out a breath he didn't know he had been holding. The tension drained from his body with surprising speed.

He heard more wolf howls as the night wore into morning but they were always distant and getting further away each time. He ached. His back ached, the base of his spine the focal point for the irregular jabs of pain that helped keep him awake all night. The inside of his arms burned from being always ready to reach quickly for his knife. The bones in his legs transmogrified to lead and weighed down through the tired muscle encasing them. With exhausted sleep there for the taking the sun rose redly on the horizon.

Daybreak.

Fischer stirred.

Skellan kicked him with the flat of his foot. 'Sleep well?'

The older man sat up. He knuckled the sleep from his eyes. Then, remembering, shuddered. He exhaled, hard. The breath sounded like a hiss of steam. 'No. No not at all.'

'Looked like you did all right to me,' Skellan said, unable to keep the bitterness of exhaustion out of his words.

'I dreamed... I dreamed that I was one of them, one of the wolves prowling the forest. I dreamed that I found you in the darkness, that all I wanted to do was feed on your flesh... I had to fight every instinct in my body just to stay still, to wait back behind the line of the trees because some part of me, the human part of the wolf, remembered you were my friend. I swear it felt like I stared at you for hours.' He stretched and cracked the joints in his shoulders, first the right shoulder, then the left. 'Morr's teeth, it was so real. I swear I could taste your fear on the air with my tongue... and part of me thought it was the most delicious thing I had ever tasted. I was inside the head of the thing but it was inside me too.'

'If it makes you feel any better you didn't move so much as a muscle all night, and yes, I was awake all night.'

'Doesn't matter. I'll be happy when we are away from here.' Fischer said with absolute conviction.

'I won't argue with you there.' Skellan rose stiffly. He hunched over, stretching out the muscles in his back. He grunted. He moved through a series of stretches, using the exercise to focus his mind. Fischer's dream disturbed him, not because he thought his friend had some latent psychic talent that stirred conveniently for him to enter the beast's mind, but because, perhaps the wolf, or whatever it really was, had found a way into his friend while he slept. That possibility made putting as much distance between themselves and Verhungern Wood their main priority.

They walked for the best part of the day, the wolves' howls receding into the distance, before exhaustion overcame them, forcing them to bed down beside a brackish river. Signs of life returned to the countryside. It was a gradual thing, a blackbird watching with beady eyes from a roadside hedge, a squirrel spiralling up a withered tree trunk, black-bodied eels in the river, but mile by mile and creature by creature the world around them was reborn, making the earlier absence of wildlife all the more disturbing.

The following evening the bony hand of Reuth Losa's infamous tower poked above the horizon. Even from a distance the tower was impressive in its nightmarish construction. Five bone-white fingers accusing the sky, their moonlit shadow reaching far out across the swampland beneath the imposing tower. Skellan hadn't seen anything like it before and he considered himself a man of the world. It was unique. It could have been a dead man's hand reaching through the mountainside.

A rancid stench emanated from the swampland. Marsh gas. The land itself bubbled and popped with the earth's gases. For all that, they ate well that night, in the shadow of Reuth Losa. Fischer trapped a brace of marsh hares, which he expertly skinned and filleted and boiled up in a tasty stew with thick roots and vegetables, and for the first time in two nights Skellan slept dreamlessly.

The market town itself, swallowed in the shadow of the great tower, was not what Skellan had been expecting. When the pair finally arrived at dusk on the fourth day, the streets were deserted. With grim resolve the two men walked down the empty streets. Skellan's fist clenched and unclenched unconsciously as he moved deeper into the eerie quiet. The houses were single storey wooden dwellings, simple in their construction but sturdy enough to withstand a battering from the elements. Windows were shuttered or boarded up.

'I don't like this place one little bit, my friend,' Fischer said, pulling at one of the nailed-down boards barring a ground floor window. 'It's not natural. I mean, where is everyone? What could have happened to them?'

'Plague,' Skellan said, looking at the sign painted over one of the doorways across the street. 'My guess is they ran to the next town, taking the sickness with them. Still, he's been here,' Skellan said. 'We're getting closer. I can feel it in my gut. We're close enough to spit on him.' He walked across the street and pushed open the first door he came to. The mouldering stench of rotten food met him on the threshold. He poked his head inside the small house. Light spilled through cracks in the shutters. The table was still set with an untouched meal of sour pork. Flies crawled across the rotten meat. Piles of white maggots writhed with a sick pulsing life where there should have been potatoes. The place had been abandoned in a hurry, that much was obvious. He backed out of the room.

Fischer faced him from an open doorway across the street.

'Ghost house!' he called over. 'It's as though they disappeared off the face of the earth.'

'Same here!' Skellan called back.

It was the same story in every house they explored.

On the street corner they heard the distant strains of melancholy music: the sound of a violinist's lament. They followed the elegiac melody, faint though it was, through the winding ribbon of streets and boarded up houses, tracing it to its source, the old Sigmarite temple on the corner of Hoffenstrasse. The façade was charred black from fire and stripped of its finery but it was still an imposing place, even if it was only a shell. The wooden steps groaned under their weight. The door had been broken back on its hinges where it had been battered down.

'Something happened here,' Fischer said, giving voice to the obvious truth. Temples didn't burn down of their own accord, and streets didn't lie deserted by chance. The Sylvanian motto might well be to leave the questions to the dead but Skellan wasn't some superstitious bumpkin afraid of the dark and forever jumping at his own shadow. Strange things were afoot and their very peculiarity only served to pique his curiosity. Inevitably the riddles would play out one way or another when they confronted the musician, and in doing so, no doubt, would lead back somehow to Sebastian Aigner.

They moved slowly, carefully, aware that they were walking into the heart of the unknown.

The music swelled, bursting with the musician's sorrow.

The damage to the outside of the temple was nothing compared to the systematic destruction of the inside. All signs of the religion had been scoured from the building. It had been gutted, pews stripped and broken up for firewood, in turn used to purge the life from the place. The stained glass windows were ruined, shattered into countless shards of coloured glass that lay melted and fused into ingots across the dirt floor. The lead had been stripped from the roof and sunlight dappled through like a scattering of gold coins. The altar had been cracked in two and the life-size statue of Sigmar lay on its side where the Man-God's legs had been shattered. The effigy's right hand had been broken off. Gahl-maraz, the Skull Splitter, Sigmar's great warhammer, lay in the dirt, the Man-God's cold stone fingers still curled around its shaft.

Sitting at the feet of the fallen idol an old man in a simple muslin robe played the violin. He hadn't heard them approach, so lost was he in the sadness of his own music.

Skellan's feet crunched on debris as he picked his way forward to the musician. The music spiralled in intensity then tailed away in a simple farewell. The old man laid the instrument on his lap and closed his eyes. Skellan coughed and the old man nearly jumped out of his skin. He looked terrified by the sudden intrusion into the solitude of his world.

'Sorry,' Skellan said. 'We didn't mean to startle you. We just arrived in town... we were expecting more... people.'

'Dead or gone,' the old man said. His voice was brittle with disuse, his accent thick and difficult to understand. Pure Reikspiel, it seemed, did not survive this far from the capital. The thick dialect would take some getting used to. 'Those that didn't succumb to the sickness fled to Leicheberg in hopes of outrunning it.'

Fischer picked up a piece of the fallen statue. 'What happened here?'

'They blamed Sigmar for not protecting their daughters from the wasting sickness. At first they came and prayed, but when their children continued to sicken and die, they turned on us. They were out of control. They came in the night with torches and firebrands and battered down the doors. They were chanting "Wiederauferstanden" over and over as they set fire to the temple.'

'The risen dead...' Skellan muttered, recognising the word and its cult connotations. 'Strange things are afoot, my friend. Strange things indeed.'

'Describe the symptoms of this sickness, brother,' Fischer prompted, sitting himself beside the old man. He had his suspicions already but he wanted them confirmed.

The old priest sniffed and wiped at his face. He was crying, Fischer realised. It must have been hard for the old man to force himself to remember. He was their shepherd after all, and his flock had scattered because he couldn't protect them.

'The Klein girl was the first to fall, a pretty little thing she was. Her father came to the temple to beg us for help because she was getting weaker and weaker, just wasting away. There was nothing we could do. We tried everything but she just continued to sicken. It all happened so shockingly fast. It was all over in a matter of a few nights. And then there was Herr Medick's eldest daughter, Helga. It was the same, no matter what we tried, night by night she literally faded away before our eyes.'

Fischer thought of the girl whose funeral they had stumbled across. A wasting sickness, the old woman had said. He didn't believe in coincidences.

'I'm sorry,' Skellan said. 'It must have been difficult. Nothing you did helped?'

'Nothing,' the old priest said. 'The girls died. There was nothing I could do. I prayed to benevolent Sigmar for guidance but at the last he turned his back on me and my children withered away and died.' There was an understandable bitterness in the old man's voice. He had given his life to helping others, and when they needed him the most he had proved helpless.

'How many?' Fischer asked, knowing that two or three deaths could still fall into the realm of chance.

The old man looked at him, eyes brimming over with guilt and tears. 'Sixteen,' he said. 'Sixteen before they finally fled from the wasting sickness. They were all girls. No more than children. I let them down. Sigmar let them down. The children of Reuth Losa are gone now; there is no hope for my town. I failed it.'

Fischer looked at Skellan.

Sixteen was well outside the realm of chance.

'You did all you could, there was nothing else you could do, you said so yourself.'

'It wasn't enough!' the old man lamented. He hurled the violin away from him. It hit the head of the Man-God and snapped its neck. Sobbing, the priest crawled across the debris to the ruined instrument.

'Come on,' Skellan said.

'Where are we going?'

'You heard the man, the survivors fled to Leicheberg. That means the cultists and Aigner. If we find one, no doubt we will find the other.'

They left the old man on his knees, cradling the broken instrument to his chest like a dying child.

CHAPTER TWO
Afraid of Sunlight

LEICHEBERG, SYLVANIA
Early spring, 2009

THE OLD LADY had been right: Leicheberg was to all intents and purposes a city, even by Empire standards, though its inhabitants hardly seemed like city-dwellers. Their faces were pinched and weathered by hunger, their eyes sunken with the familiarity of disappointment, their frames bowed with the burden of living from day to day. They lacked that spark, that vital flame that danced mischievously in the eyes of folks back home.

Back home.

They had no home.

They had forfeited it when they began the hunt for their wives' killers.

There was no beauty in their world now, so perhaps that was the reason the people they encountered looked so listless, so drawn, worn, beaten and broken? Perhaps it was a reflection of their own spirit they saw in these strangers' eyes?

The two strangers could walk the streets without attracting stares. Food queues lined up at the market stalls, thin-faced shoppers bickering over the last few morsels of not-quite-rotten vegetables. Puddles muddied the streets where the spring rain had nowhere to drain away.

The place smelled of close-packed unwashed bodies, cabbage and urine. No one gave Skellan or Fischer a second glance.

The pair had been in Leicheberg for a week. They had rented a small room in a seedy tavern off the central square called The Traitor's Head. The name more than suited the establishment. It was a den filled with iniquities galore making it the perfect place to gather rumours. People's lips loosened when they drank. They talked out of turn. Spilled secrets. Skellan was not above listening to the drunken ramblings of braggarts and the pillow talk of prostitutes.

They had spent the first two days in the city in search of refugees from Reuth Losa, specifically those who had lost daughters to the mysterious wasting sickness that the old priest of Sigmar had described. Those few they found told the same sad story, how the sickness had come from nowhere, their daughters rising in the morning light-headed and woozy after a restless night, only to weaken over successive nights as the sweats and fevers gripped them, until they finally fell into a deep sleep from which they couldn't be woken. The parents spoke of candlelight vigils, useless prayers, fussing physicians and the same bitter swansong of death. There was precious little to be gleaned from delving into their sorrow. That much was obvious. While no one had anything to say directly about Sebastian Aigner, they had plenty to say about the Wiederauferstanden.

The Risen Dead was indeed a cult. Few would talk about them in any great detail for fear of retribution from unseen hands. It seemed the cult had infiltrated various levels of Sylvanian society, from the beggars and thieves at the bottom to the ranks of the nobility at the top. It was indeed tied to the worship of the undead. From what Skellan and Fischer could glean, the followers worshipped those abominations for being more than human. They *aspired* to be like these monsters.

The very thought of it left Jon Skellan cold; how could anyone in their right minds dream of being such an unholy parasite?

'You said it yourself, Jon, it's a sickness,' Fischer said.

They were walking through the market square looking for a trader the locals called Geisterjäger, the Ghost Hunter. His real name was Konstantin Gosta and he specialised in selling locks and chains he made himself from his small stall in the market place. He had a reputation for complicated mechanisms, the kind of thing you would use if you wanted to keep something precious safe from thieving hands. The Ghost Hunter was the best. He could design anything you wanted from tiny mechanisms to massively complicated combination locks that worked on convoluted mechanical techniques of cogs and tumblers having to fall into an exact predefined sequence.

'I just can't believe that people would willingly do that to themselves,' Skellan said, shaking his head.

'You mean you don't want to believe. We've both seen enough of it to know it's true.'

'Blood sacrifices to try and raise the dead.' He ran his hand through his hair and looked around the crowded square. 'The stupidity of it.' He spied the Ghost Hunter deep in conversation with a woman. She left without buying any of his wares. Rather than approach the locksmith immediately they stayed back inside the anonymity of the crowd and watched him. He was polite, said hello to passers by, but very few stopped to examine his wares and those that did, didn't part with any of their hard-earned coins. Judging by the few minutes they saw it was difficult to imagine the locksmith earning enough to make ends meet. The obvious answer of course was that he didn't, not legitimately. His knowledge of locks could be used not only to manufacture them, but also to open them. By day a locksmith, under cover of darkness the Ghost Hunter was a thief. There were few better in this day and age.

'A word, Gosta?' Skellan said, moving up beside the smaller man.

Without turning to see who was talking to him, the Ghost Hunter muttered, 'Take scruples, I've got no use for them. Better off getting rid of the word from my vocabulary.' He scratched at the palm of his right hand compulsively. The man was wound tightly, permanently fidgeting, shifting from foot to foot, scratching different parts of his body in a cycle from scalp, to cheek, to scalp and down to the fillets of his left arm, his side, the side of his face, just beneath the left ear, and back to the top of his head.

'Funny, Gosta, but not the word I had in mind.'

'No?'

'No.' Skellan leaned in close, making sure the Ghost Hunter appreciated the seriousness of his enquiry. 'I want to talk about Wiederauferstanden.'

'That's a mouthful,' he said, not meeting Skellan's eyes as he spoke.

'It is, so let's say the Risen Dead, if you prefer?'

'I do,' the smaller man said, shifting from foot to foot uncomfortably. 'Look, I don't know much. It isn't my thing, messing with the dead. I'm an honest criminal. What do you want to know? Maybe I can help, maybe I can't.'

'I want a way in,' Skellan said, not bothering to sugar-coat his most basic need.

'Not happening,' the Ghost Hunter said, shaking his head as though to emphasise the point. 'Not a prayer.'

'Are you trying to tell me that you can't name the right names? Put me in touch with the right person? I don't believe that for a second, Gosta.'

'Oh, I can name them all right, I can even tell you where they like to play their little games, that still won't get you inside the organisation though. They're the kind of group that comes looking for you; you don't go looking for them, if you know what I mean, stranger. They play their cards mighty close to their chests. And asking too many questions is likely to get you a cosy spot in a hessian sack at the bottom of the River Stir. You will, of course, have been chopped up into little pieces to make sure you fit in that cosy sack. That the kind of help you are looking for? I'm not going to help you kill yourself, least not without a good reason.'

'We can take care of ourselves. Give us an address then, I'm specifically looking for a piece of scum named Aigner, Sebastian Aigner. I don't know if he is part of this Risen Dead cult but from what I know of him, and the little I know about them, I wouldn't be surprised.'

'It's your death warrant, mister. Just as long as you understand that. I don't want no widow holding me responsible for your stupidity.'

'Just give me the address.'

The Ghost Hunter shifted uncomfortably. His eyes darted around furtively making sure no one who mattered was close enough to overhear what he was about to say.

'I ain't heard of your Aigner fella, but if he's mixed up with the Risen Dead, you'll probably find him down near the end of Schreckenstrasse, there's an old tower that used to be part of the Sigmarite temple. The temple's long gone, but the tower's still there. The Risen Dead use it because it still has access to the old catacombs. If you value your life you won't go anywhere near the place, mind.'

'Thank you,' Skellan said.

'Your funeral, big guy.' The locksmith turned away, eager to distance himself from Skellan and Fischer.

'I guess that means we're going for a walk,' Fischer said with a wry grin.

'Now's as good a time as any,' Skellan agreed.

They picked a path through the market-goers. The place smelled of urine and cabbage where it should have been filled with the heady smells of roasting pork, boiling bratwurst and sauerkraut. Famine took its toll in less obvious ways too. A woman sat on the stoop of a dilapidated building plucking feathers from a stringy-looking game bird. Her daughter sat beside her holding two more birds by the ankles. The two birds flapped and twisted in the girl's grip as though aware of what fate had in store for them. These three birds garnered the woman envious looks from those without the coin to buy even a few tough legs or sinewy wings. Two doors up a barber with a cut-throat razor trimmed and shaped an elderly man's beard. A wood carver was making some sort of pull-along toy on wheels while beside him his partner fashioned more practical things, the shafts for arrows, spoons, bowls and a miscellany of odds and ends that could be sold for cash including love tokens and trinkets.

'Do you trust him?' Fischer asked, stepping around a shoeless urchin playing in the mud. The child tugged at his trouser-leg, begging for coins.

'As much as I would trust anyone in this rat-infested hole. So not much, no. That doesn't mean his information isn't good though, just that his primary interest is survival at whatever cost. If selling us out pays well, you can bet that is exactly what Gosta will do.'

'So we could be walking into a trap?'

Skellan nodded. 'Absolutely.'

'Now there's a comforting thought.' Instinctively, Fischer reached down to feel for the familiar reassurance of the sword belted to his hip. Cold steel had a way of calming even the jitteriest of nerves. Right in front of him a woman with a young child cradled in her arms backed up a step and looked frightened enough to bolt. She was staring at his hand poised just above the sword's hilt. 'It's all right, it's all right,' he said, holding up his hands to show they were empty and that he had no intention of cutting her down where she stood. It didn't matter; the woman was already disappearing into the crowd.

He had sensed the same kind of nervousness in many of the citizens during their short stay in Leicheberg, as though they were used to the summary dispensation of brutal justice. Indeed the reputation of Sylvanian justice was one of the terrible swift sword, quick to anger, and unforgiving in its delivery. Fairness was not a word associated with Sylvanian society. For centuries the people had lived under the grip of the tyrannical van Draks, and they were familiar with the madness of their masters. Things had changed with the coming of the new line of counts, the von Carsteins, but next to the depravities of the last van Drak just about anyone would have looked like blessed Sigmar himself.

SCHRECKENSTRASSE WAS A long claustrophobic alleyway of close-packed houses that crowded into the street itself as the upper storeys leaned in close enough for the neighbours to touch fingertips if they reached through their open windows. Just as the Ghost Hunter had promised, the remains of the old Sigmarite temple were at the very far end of the street, on the furthest outskirts of the city. There was a tower, four storeys high, and some rubble. The tower stood alone, distanced from the rest of the buildings by the gap where the main chapel of the temple itself had once stood.

Skellan drew his sword.

Beside him Fischer did the same.

He looked at his friend and nodded. They matched each other step for step as they moved across the rubble. Skellan could sense eyes on him and knew they were being watched. It stood to reason that if the cult were using the tower for some nefarious purpose they would set lookouts – probably in the tower itself, and in one of the abandoned houses along Schreckenstrasse, an upper window with a good view of the door of the tower. He didn't look around or hesitate, even for a heartbeat. Three quick steps took Skellan up the short flight of stairs to the door. Rocking on his heels, he span and delivered a well-placed kick parallel to the rusty old lock mechanism that sent the door bursting open on buckled hinges. A hiss of noises and smells came rushing out from the darkness within.

Skellan stepped through the doorway. Fischer followed him.

Fischer was not overly fond of the dark or cramped spaces. What waited beyond the door tested the older man to the full.

The air was stale, thick with sweat and fear and the metallic tang of blood.

Precious little daylight spilled into the room, barely enough for Fischer to see much beyond his outstretched fingers with any clarity as he fumbled forward into the darkness, his eyes adjusting to the gloom, but he could hear slobbering sounds, and gasping, other noises too, whimpering, heavy things scrabbling about. None of the sounds were comforting. His hand gripped tighter around the hilt of his sword. He had no idea what secrets the treacherous heart of the darkness held, but knew he was about to find out. The sound of his own pulse was loud in his ears. He clenched his teeth and shuffled another step forward. A few chinks of light wriggled in through cracks in the boarded-up windows. They offered few clues as to the nature of the Risen Dead's business with the old tower. Someone groaned in the darkness. The noise raised the hackles along Fischer's neck. The sound was one of desperation; whoever had made it was suffering.

'I don't like this,' he whispered. His foot stubbed against something then. He toed it tentatively. It yielded. He kicked at it a little more forcefully. The voice groaned again. Fischer knew then what he was kicking: a body. 'Give me some light, damn it,' he cursed. He couldn't tell if the person was dying, drunk or drugged. He stepped over the body.

Skellan felt his way around the wall until he found what he was looking for, a torch. There was oil beneath the sconce. He dipped the dry reeds in the foul smelling liquid and then lit it with a spark of tinder. The air was moist but it didn't stop the reeds from catching and burning with a blue flame. He held the torch aloft. The flame cast a sickly light across the room. Fischer straddled a woman's body that had been bound and gagged. Dark patches showed through her clothing. Blood. There were rakes and hoes and buckets, hammers, saws and other tools from the tower's previous life scattered about the place. A staircase spiralled up into darkness, and down into deeper darkness. Skellan followed it down into a storeroom. Fischer followed a few steps behind him. Wooden shelves and barrels lined the small storage room but Skellan found what he was looking for:

In the centre of the floor was a three-foot by three-foot moss-covered trapdoor with a large iron ring in the middle.

He passed the torch to Fischer and gripped the iron ring with both hands. The trapdoor creaked on its rusty hinges as he pulled. The musty air of the grave escaped from the hole. Somewhere in the darkness beyond the torch, the moans and sighs swelled with excitement.

'I really don't like this,' Fischer repeated.

'It's the entrance to the old catacombs,' Skellan said.

'I know what it is, I still don't like it.'

'Aigner's down there.'

'You don't know that.'

'I can feel it. He's down there.' Skellan took the first step, crouching to descend into the darkness.

Fischer stood frozen.

Skellan took the torch from him.

With plaintive sigh Fischer followed him into the hole.

The stairs led them down deep beneath the ground. Fischer counted more than fifty steps. The tunnel was carved out of the earth itself and braced by aging timbers. They had to stoop; the ceiling was so low it was impossible to stand up straight. The sword offered little comfort against the press of the featureless darkness. At the bottom of the staircase the tunnel forked in three directions, each one leading off into a deeper darkness.

Skellan pressed a finger to his lips to emphasise the need for silence. He could hear something, in the distance. It took Fischer a moment to work out what it was: the low resonant rumble of voices chanting.

They moved cautiously down the centre tunnel, heading straight for the heart of the catacombs.

A horrendous cry cut through the tunnels. It was human. Female. Whoever was responsible for that scream, Fischer knew, was suffering. 'Come on,' he rasped at Skellan's back, driving the fear from his mind. The woman was alive and she needed them, that thought was enough to force the older man into action. They staggered forward. Suddenly the tunnel opened out into a chamber. There were corpses and bones everywhere, stacked one on top of another. Bodies wrapped in dirty bandages were piled into holes in the earth. Bare bones jumbled haphazardly; femurs, fibulas, tibias, scapulas and skulls made a sea of bones from the dead of Leicheberg. Some were broken, their ends ragged, others were sheathed in mould. Had these people ever been given a proper burial, Fischer wondered?

On the far side of the space an arch led into a second, bigger, chamber. Torches had been lit in the second room. In their light Fischer saw deformed shadows dancing on the earthen wall. They came together in one writhing mass.

In front of him, Skellan grunted, and stepped through the arch.

Gritting his teeth, Stefan Fischer followed him.

The sight that greeted them when they stepped through the arch was like something lifted straight out of their worst nightmares.

The woman who had screamed lay in the centre of the floor. There was a row of cages behind her but Fischer only had eyes for the woman. She had been slit from throat to belly, and though still barely alive, six cadaverous wild-eyed creatures clawed over her, sucking greedily at her still-warm blood as it leaked out of her. Her blood streamed down their chins and smeared across their cheeks. Ghouls, Fischer realised sickly, watching the creatures as they sucked at their fingers and lapped at the gaping rent in her torso. It was impossible to believe that these monstrosities had ever been human; they had more in common with daemons drawn from the pit than with decent everyday people.

The woman was dead but shock and denial kept her heart pumping weakly for a few more minutes, prolonging her suffering.

Something inside Fischer broke. He felt it happen. A small part of his sanity splintered away and left him forever.

Fury swelled to fill the emptiness inside.

He charged forward, swinging his sword in a frenzy of slashing. It was a blur of steel in the flickering torchlight. The first ghoul looked up as Fischer's blade sliced through its neck; the thing's head lolled back exposing a second, ear-to-ear grin that had been opened by the sword. Blood bubbled in the gaping maw. The second saw the tip of Fischer's sword plunge deep into its own eye, burying itself in the ghoul's brain, before it slumped forward over the woman's eviscerated corpse. The ghoul's body was wracked by a series of shockingly violent spasms as the life leaked out of it. Fischer kicked the corpse aside, yanking his sword free of the ghoul's head and delivering a huge sweeping arc of a blow that cleaved clean through the neck of a third ghoul. Blood gouted out of the severed wound. The ghoul's still-grinning head bounced on the floor and rolled away. The sheer ferocity of Fischer's attack was monumental. The weight of the blow unbalanced the older man and sent him staggering forward, barely able to control his own momentum. He lurched two more steps, plunging his bloody blade into the gut of the fourth ghoul even as the monstrosity launched itself at the witch hunter. He twisted his wrist, opening the wound wide. The ghoul's guts spilled out of the ragged wound in its stomach. The fiend's clawed hands closed around the blade, pulling Fischer closer by drawing his blade deeper into its gut. It breathed in his face, grin wide as it leaned in to bite off part of Fischer's face. Its teeth had been sharpened into fangs. Its breath reeked of the sour fetid stench of the grave. Fischer recoiled instinctively, his movement jerking the ghoul off balance. It fell at his feet, dead, its guts spilling out across the floor.

Fischer was breathing hard.

Skellan said something behind him but he wasn't listening.

Two of the fiends remained.

He stared at them.

Judged them.

The last vestiges of humanity had gone from their eyes. One gazed listlessly into the air, intoxicated from the dead woman's blood. It had no idea that what remained of its life could be measured in a few heartbeats. The other matched his gaze with one of its own, filled with cold animalistic cunning. It was calculating the threat Fischer posed, whether it needed to fight, flee or feed. It was hard to believe the creatures had ever been human. They had descended so far from basic humanity that they wallowed in the realm of the monstrous.

They *were* monsters.

Fischer launched a second brutal attack. He held nothing back. He threw himself at the remaining ghouls. He slashed and cut and stabbed in a wild frenzy, hacking into the helpless creatures. He cut at their arms as they tried to protect themselves. There was no control, no finesse to his fighting. His sole purpose was to kill. Screaming, he span on his heel, bringing the sword round in a wide arc with the full spinning weight of his body behind the downward slice of the blade as it cleaved into the ghoul's neck and buried itself deep in the beast's chest. He couldn't pull his sword free.

Skellan dispatched the final ghoul with clinical precision. He stepped up behind the creature, yanked its head back and cut its throat. In the space between two heartbeats the deed was done. He rolled its corpse over with his foot. There were no marks or symbols carved into its flesh. Nothing to identify it as one of the Risen Dead, but the thing's ghoulish nature was in no doubt.

'How could anyone fall so far?' he asked, shaking his head.

Beside the dead girl Fischer fell to his knees. The sword slipped through his fingers and clattered to the floor. He gasped for breath almost choking between huge heaving sobs. Tears streamed down his cheeks. She hadn't just been opened up; the ghouls had feasted on most of her internal organs.

'You couldn't have saved her,' Skellan said gently, resting a comforting hand on his friend's shoulder. 'She was dead before we even entered the room.'

'Always... too late...' Fischer spat bitterly. He was trembling as the adrenaline fled from his body.

'Not always,' Skellan said, finally seeing the row of cages and the emaciated shadows huddled in their darkest corners. The cultists obviously intended to serve these poor souls to the ghouls for food. 'Not always.'

He stepped carefully around the corpses and opened the first of the cages. There were two women in there, barely older than children really, their faces smeared with dirt and caked with dried blood. They looked absolutely terrified. Skellan tried to calm them but they shook their heads wildly from side to side and pressed themselves further into the corner, out of Skellan's reach. They stank of urine and stale sweat.

There were six more women in the other cages.

Still weeping silently, Fischer helped Skellan release them.

Sigmar alone knew how long the poor wretches had been trapped in the catacombs waiting to be fed to the ghouls. The confinement had done nothing for their minds. They mumbled and talked to themselves and stared straight through their rescuers as they tried to shepherd them back upstairs.

They refused to go outside into the street. They started screaming hysterically and beating at their faces with their hands and scuttled back into the darkest part of the tower, pressing themselves desperately against the wall as though trying to disappear into it.

It took Skellan a moment to understand. 'They've been down there so long... they are afraid of the sunlight.'

CHAPTER THREE
A Knife in the Dark

LEICHEBERG, SYLVANIA
Spring, 2009

SEBASTIAN AIGNER WAS a phantom.

A ghost.

He wasn't real – or at least that was how it was beginning to feel to Jon Skellan after three weeks in Leicheberg. They were close, he knew, close enough for Aigner to feel them breathing down the back of his neck, but the closer they got to Aigner the more elusive the man became. They were always a step or two behind him.

Gathering any kind of reliable information had proven to be a nightmare. Every avenue turned out to be a blind one.

If the usual slew of information traffickers knew anything, they weren't talking. Greasing the bureaucratic palms wasn't helping either. The magistrates had nothing to say.

Aigner might just as well not exist.

The few hints and whispers Skellan and Fischer did manage to scare up quickly faded into nothing. The man had friends and those friends were influential enough to help him disappear. That in itself worried Skellan. Gossip spread. It was in people's nature to talk. Rumours developed a life of their own. The blanket of ignorance surrounding Sebastian Aigner was unnatural.

A lesser man might have given up the ghost and let Aigner simply vanish into thin air, but not Jon Skellan. Aigner was his obsession. The all-consuming need for revenge drove him. Aigner had led the band of looters who had murdered his wife, and for that there could be no forgiveness. Without forgiveness it was impossible to forget. Thoughts of Sebastian Aigner ate away at Jon Skellan night and day.

For three weeks they had been spreading the word, making it known that they would pay good currency for information about Aigner or the Risen Dead. They made no effort to hide their whereabouts. They wanted people to know where to find them when their tongues loosened by need or greed.

Fischer took a healthy swig of ale and slammed the empty tankard down on the beer-soaked table. He let out a rumbling belch and backhanded the froth from his mouth.

'I needed that!' Fischer made a big show of enjoying his drink.

'I'm sure you did,' Skellan said.

The Traitor's Head was full with its usual mismatched clientele. Skellan didn't drink. At the beginning of the night he ordered a goblet of mulled wine then nursed the same drink until it was kicking-out time. He sipped at it occasionally, but Fischer was far from certain the alcohol ever touched his lips.

An open fire crackled in the hearth, the sap still trapped in the wood snapping and popping under the heat. A vagabond fresh from the road warmed his grubby hands by the fire.

The serving girl bustled between tables, platters of roasted fowl and stringy vegetables balanced precariously in her hands. Her blonde hair was plaited in a neat tail that coiled down to her ample breasts. The smile on her face was strained. She put two plates in front of Skellan and Fischer.

'Amos wants to see you,' she said, leaning in as she took Skellan's money from him. Amos was the owner of the Traitor's Head. It could of course mean anything, but Skellan chose to read it as a sign their luck was changing.

'Thank you, my dear.'

'Don't thank me, I'll be glad when you are gone. You boys are bad for business,' the girl said bluntly. 'Skulking in shadows and making people uncomfortable with all of your questions. Sooner we're rid of you the better.'

Business in the tavern was slow. Between them they could have counted the number of drinkers on their hands and had a few fingers to spare. They were the only diners. The lack of trade was painfully obvious, as was the reason for it. The occasional furtive glance of the drinkers at the bar toward the witch hunters made sure of that. It wasn't uncommon for folk to fear them. In smaller hamlets where superstition ruled over common sense their arrival often led to unnecessary deaths, girls stoned or burnt for witchcraft as the accusations flew. Cities like Leicheberg were different, but not so much different. Very few places welcomed witch hunters.

The tavern door banged open, and a giant of a man came in out of the night. He kicked the dirt off his boots and dusted the road out of his hair. He had a lute strung across his back. He looked round the taproom, nodded to a fellow at the far end of the bar, and walked briskly over to shake hands with Amos who was already drawing him an ale from the cask. The stranger's familiarity with the patrons and the tavern keeper put Skellan at ease.

'Deitmar!' Amos bellowed, the folds of fat around his three chins wobbling with excitement. 'As I live and breathe!'

The troubadour bowed theatrically, making a grand sweeping gesture out of removing his travelling cloak. He draped it over a barstool. 'Amos Keller, you are a sight for sore eyes! A beer, make it cold, and where is that delightful daughter of yours? Aimee? Aimee, come out here and give your uncle Deitmar a hug, lass!' He swept the serving girl up in a huge bear hug and span her round so that her toes barely touched the floor. Putting her down again he planted a kiss on her forehead. 'Damn, it is good to see you again, girl.'

Skellan watched the reunion with a hint of jealousy.

'It's been too long,' she said, and it was obvious that she meant it.

Again Skellan felt a pang of envy at the easy acceptance the troubadour got; he was welcomed with open arms. It was a long time since anyone had welcomed either Skellan or Fischer so warmly.

'Seven years,' he said aloud, not realising he had spoken.

'What?' Fischer pressed, leaning in.

'I was just thinking out loud,' he said. 'It is seven years since anyone welcomed us home like that.'

'Makes you think about what you're missing, doesn't it? Seeing people happy.'

'Aye, it does. Makes you realise what was stolen from you.'

'That's another way of putting it.'

'It's the truth, no matter how you dress it up,' Skellan said. He hadn't taken his eyes off the newcomer. 'It was us that died that day, you know. Not just the girls. Aigner killed us. He took our lives away as surely as if he had stuck a sword in our guts. We aren't the men we would have been.'

'No, we aren't,' Fischer agreed. 'But that might not be such a bad thing, Jon. In the last seven years we have changed a lot of people's lives, and I honestly believe most of those changes have been for the better. That wouldn't have happened without... without...'

'I know,' Skellan said. 'That wouldn't have happened without Lizbet and Leyna dying. I know that but that doesn't make it feel any better.'

The troubadour sank into a threadbare velvet seat by the fire. He put his feet up on the small three-legged wooden footstool and began tuning his instrument, running his fingers through a series of off-key scales. He tightened the strings until he was happy with the music he made. Some of the drinkers turned to face the fire. A travelling singer was a rare treat in these parts.

'Now who in their right mind would travel to this godforsaken piece of the underworld?' Skellan wondered. The troubadour was well dressed for a traveller but not lavishly so; his clothes weren't heavily patched and the colours were still vibrant. He obviously didn't lack for coin which made even less sense. For a musician of any kind of skill there was money aplenty to be made in Talabheim, Middenheim, Altdorf, Nuln, Averheim and the Moot, and the other towns and cities of the Empire. The man could obviously play – the way his fingers moved through the warming up exercises proved he could more than ably carry a tune. 'Someone with no choice in the matter,' he answered his own question with the only solution that made any sense: the man was gathering information for someone. It was the perfect disguise for a spy.

Skellan thought through the possibilities: the troubadour was an agent, either of the Empire, perhaps the Ottilia or the Grand Theogonist, the two were always trying to gain the advantage over each other; or on the other side of the conflict there was the enigmatic Vlad von Carstein, the Count of Sylvania. The man was a mystery but few spoke against him because the atrocities of Otto van Drak's reign of blood and fear were still fresh in their minds. The man could, of course, be playing both sides. It was not impossible.

Skellan smiled to himself. Deitmar the wandering troubadour was someone worth talking to in this city of madmen and crooks.

The musician began to play, a rousing shanty to get the blood flowing. The drinkers banged their wooden tankards on the bar and stamped their feet appreciatively.

Skellan slipped away from his table, caught Amos Keller's eye, and gestured for him to follow somewhere quieter. The big man moved down the bar. He left the tankard he was towelling out on the counter and ducked through the door that led to the snug, a quiet part of the bar where men with money could pay for solitude.

'Your girl said you wanted me?' Skellan said, stepping into the room behind Amos. He had no idea what to expect from the encounter but for some reason he wasn't expecting good news. The troubadour's music picked up pace. The riot of sound swelled as the drinkers got into the spirit of things, banging their fists and stamping their feet ever more enthusiastically. No doubt Fischer was hammering his clenched fist on the tabletop and singing along at the top of his lungs.

'I ain't gonna beat around the bush. You and your friend are bad news. Real bad news. I put up with you because I feel sorry for you, but this morning things went past feeling sorry.'

'What do you mean?'

'Fella came in here, told me I had two choices, number one was turf you out on your ear, the other was empty the place tonight, and leave the door open so some of his boys could come in and take care of you. You've made yourself some enemies, lad, and they want you out of their hair.'

'Did you recognise the man?'

'Aye, I did, but I ain't about to tell you who it was, I don't want to end up in the river in the morning, if you get my meaning.'

'So, you're asking us to leave I take it?'

'Got no choice, but I can tell you this much for nothing. The fella you are hunting, Aigner, he ain't been in Leicheberg for weeks.'

Skellan grabbed the barkeeper by the throat and pulled him close enough to taste the sour smell of his breath on his tongue. 'Are you sure?'

'Certain. He disappeared a few days before you boys arrived. He paid good money to keep folks quiet. He didn't want you following him.'

'And you knew all along?' Skellan's voice dropped to barely above a whisper. His eyes blazed with righteous fury. 'He bought your silence? How much was it worth, Amos? What value do *you* place on my wife's life? Tell me! How much was she worth to you?' He was shaking. The troubadour's music was loud enough to drown out his shouting in the taproom.

'Ten silver,' he said. 'And the promise of ten more where they came from for each week I kept you here. That's what the fella was here for, he came to pay Aigner's debt.'

After seven years of hunting the man, to be so close only to be lied to, cheated out of his revenge. It was too much. Skellan erupted: 'Give me one good reason not to kill you, right here, right now. One reason, Amos. Give me one reason.'

Beads of perspiration dribbled down the corpulent barkeeper's face. His fat lips trembled. His huge arms, like ham-hocks, had turned to jelly.

'One reason,' Skellan repeated. 'Why I shouldn't snap you in half right now?'

'Aimee.' Amos barely managed to say his daughter's name.

Skellan let him go. That was the difference between the hunter and his prey. Skellan was still a human being. He still cared about family and love and people, even if he was alone in the world.

He closed his eyes. 'Are they coming tonight?'

'Yes... an hour after lights out. I'm sorry. I didn't want this. I was frightened. They... They're going to kill you.'

'Well, they are going to try.' Skellan opened his eyes again. The red mist of fury had fallen away. He was thinking now, planning how best to stay alive to see dawn.

'Aren't you going to run?'

Skellan shook his head. 'No point, they attack here when I am expecting it, or they ambush me on the road when I am not. This way the odds are stacked slightly back in my favour. This is what I want you to do, act normally. You haven't spoken to me tonight. All right? Come lights out get Aimee and go sleep in the stables. I can't promise it will be safe but it has to be safer than your rooms.'

'What are you going to do?'

'The less you know, the better,' Skellan said, rather more harshly than he had intended. He softened. 'It is safer for you and Aimee that way.'

'I don't want any killing, not under my roof. That's why I warned you, to give you a chance to run before they arrived.'

'And I appreciate it, Amos. I do. But it is too late for that. Now we are playing last man standing and I intend to win.'

The barkeeper wiped the sweat from his brow with the same towel that he had been using to dry the pitcher with before. 'You're every bit as crazy as Aigner said you were...' For the first time there was a genuine cold-to-the-marrow fear in Amos Keller's voice as the stories of Jon Skellan's relentless hunt came back to him: the slaughter of Aigner's friends, the ritualised burning, the cold-blooded nature of the assassin. 'I shouldn't have said anything. I should have let you rot here trying to pry your answers from closed mouths until the Wiederauferstanden were ready to send your soul to Morr and gotten fat off the proceeds... But oh no, not stupid old Amos Keller... had to go and feel sympathy for the murdering lunatic in his lounge and try to warn him. Stupid, stupid fool, Amos, you should have just kept your nose out of it and let folks get on with killing each other.'

'Are you quite done?' Skellan asked, obviously amused by the barkeeper's rambling admonition of himself. 'People are going to be getting thirsty. Go do what you do. If you see one of my so-called assassins I want you to warn me. It will go badly for you if you don't. Do you understand? I want you to send me a drink over. I won't be ordering another one tonight, so any drink arriving at my table is a sign that a would-be murderer has entered the bar.'

Amos nodded reluctantly.

'Now, I am going back through to sit with my friend and listen to the music. I suggest you put a smile on your face. It shouldn't be so hard to do. Think about it this way, in the morning we'll be gone one way or another.'

Skellan pressed a silver coin into the barkeeper's fleshy hand. 'In advance, for that drink.' It was enough to pay for twenty drinks, with change. Amos took the money without a word. He pocketed it and left.

Skellan followed him through to the taproom a few minutes later.

The final few strains of a bawdy tale of a frisky tavern wench and a lusty sailor petered out to a round of enthusiastic applause. He slid into his seat. Fischer looked at him quizzically but he didn't answer. The next song was a ballad. The troubadour introduced it as 'The Lay of Fair Isabella'. It was quite unlike anything he had sung so far. His fingers played lovingly over the lute's strings, conjuring something of beauty from them.

Skellan closed his eyes and simply appreciated the music.

It was a love song of sorts.

A tragedy.

The troubadour's voice ached as he sang of the fair lady Isabella's sickness, her porcelain skin waxen as she faded in the arms of her love, beseeching him to save her even as she withered away to where death was the only answer.

The words washed over him and began to lose meaning, simply folding into each other. Deitmar's voice was mesmeric. He held the bar-room of drinkers rapt with his velvet tones. They hung on his every word as he played them like an expert puppeteer.

The nature of the music shifted, lowering an octave conspiratorially. Skellan opened his eyes. It was another trick of course, the troubadour manipulating them into thinking he was imparting some dark secret, but it worked, Skellan sat forward and listened intently as Deitmar whispered, barely above a breath, no rhyme or reason to his words:

'When in the long dark night of the risen dead
Callous Morr crept unto fair Isabella's bed
The lament lingered bitter on his lips
Even as he stooped low to kiss
Her broken soul
That one so fair should fall so foul
To waste away before her time
Fragile flesh and brittle bone
The treacherous remains
While love lay dying.'

And then, with a flourish, the music and the dying lady returned to vibrant life, resurrected by Deitmar's beautiful song. Two images caught Skellan's attention. Surely it was no coincidence that the troubadour mentioned the Risen Dead and the wasting sickness in the same breath.

'We need to talk to him before the night's out,' he said, leaning over to talk in hushed tones to Fischer. The other man nodded; obviously he had caught the oblique reference as well. 'And before the trouble starts.'

That caused Stefan Fischer to raise an eyebrow.

'Seems we've been played for fools, I'll explain it later.'

Fischer nodded.

The troubadour played nine more songs before taking a break to soothe his voice with a goblet of Amos's mulled wine. Skellan and Fischer moved to sit beside him at the fireside.

'If you've no objections?' Skellan said, sitting himself.

'Not at all, sometimes it is just as nice to share a drink with a stranger as it is to share one with a friend.'

'Indeed,' Skellan agreed. It was a refreshing to hear a man with a decent command of Riekspiel. Surrounded by the thick Sylvanian accents he had begun to forget what it sounded like. 'I must say I was quite taken with one of your songs. I assume you wrote it. I haven't heard it before… "The Lay of Fair Isabella" I believe you called it?'

'Ah, yes, though I fear my voice pales next to the beauty of fair Isabella herself.'

'Truly?'

'Truly, my new friend. Isabella von Carstein, the lady of Drakenhof. Fairer beauty and fouler heart you have never seen. To see fair Isabella is to lose one's soul. But what a way to die.'

'She sounds… interesting,' Skellan said with a wry grin. 'Not that I would ever trust a minstrel's romantic soul for a reliable account. You wandering spirits have a habit of falling in love daily, a new great beauty in every new town.'

Deitmar laughed easily.

'You know us so well. But believe me, in this case, what I say, that isn't even the half of it. She owns beauty enough to stop your heart dead should she so desire, and more often than not, she does. The woman is the most powerful in all of Sylvania and she is ruthless with it. Morr's teeth, even death itself can't take the woman. She has power over it, it would seem.'

'Indeed,' Skellan leaned in, listening intently. 'How so?'

'It's no secret, she was dying. She fell victim to the wasting sickness that is scouring the country. She fought it tooth and nail. Nothing the chirurgeons and the faith healers could do made the damnedest bit of difference. It was killing her. Just like all of the other girls across the land. The sickness was no respecter of her beauty or her power. To Morr, she was just another soul. Word was the priests even came to shrive her of her sins at the last. And you know what? The next afternoon, she rose from her deathbed, and she was radiant. More so than ever before. She was alive. The fever and the sickness had broken. It was a miracle.'

'Truly. I've seen the effects of this sickness. It isn't pleasant. Like you say, I have yet to encounter a survivor.'

'Isabella von Carstein,' Deitmar said with passion. 'Death holds no dominion over her.'

'Tell me,' Skellan said, as though the thought had just occurred to him. 'The night of the risen dead? You mentioned it in your song.' Mimicking Deitmar's trick with the song, Skellan leaned in and dropped his voice to a conspiratorial whisper. 'Would it have anything to do with the Wiederauferstanden?'

'The Cult of the Risen Dead?' If the troubadour was surprised by the question he masked it well. 'Only the obvious, that the cult believe there will be a night when the dead shall rise, when the barrier between this world and the next will fall. They call it the Night of the Risen Dead. Isabella von Carstein lives and breathes where all others afflicted with the wasting sickness rot in the dead earth. She is a beacon to their kind. They see an unholy miracle. She died at the hands of the priests and the chirurgeons, all their skills and faith couldn't save her, and yet she rose again. Death itself could not hold her. She is everything they dream of, everything they adore. The Cult of the Risen Dead worships the woman. To them Isabella von Carstein is reborn. She is death risen. She is immortal.'

'She is their leader?'

'Define leader, my friend. The misguided fools worship her heart, body and whatever is left of their blackened souls.' Deitmar said earnestly. 'Does that make her their leader? Perhaps, but then is Sigmar your leader?'

'I don't follow any so-called divinity. Give me ale, give me women with enough soft pink flesh to wrestle with, give me a sword, things I can see and touch with my own two hands, those are worth believing in. Thank you, my friend. Now, at least, I have a place to begin my search. Drakenhof.'

'It is three weeks' inhospitable travel. The roads are poor; the old counts were never ones to invest in things that didn't immediately reap rewards, and well, let's just say the countryside is at best unforgiving. I don't envy you the journey... but for one more look at fair Isabella it might just be worth it.' Deitmar winked at Skellan, a lascivious smile spreading up to his eyes. There was mischief written all over his face. 'If you know what I mean.'

'We are ever driven thus, are we not? Puppets to the whims of our hearts.'

'Exactly. And what shadow plays the heart does perform! Well, I should set about earning my keep before Amos decides better of it and turfs me out on my arse. It has been my pleasure, neighbour. May you find what you are looking for in Drakenhof.'

The troubadour played on deep into the night.

More customers came as the night wore on, but business was far from brisk.

After an hour or so Skellan leaned over to Fischer and said: 'I'm turning in for the night. I'll see you upstairs when you've finished up. We need to talk.'

Fischer nodded, took a deep swallow of his drink and pushed back his chair. He followed Skellan up to the plain room they rented above the taproom. It was a simple chamber with two beds, a chair, and a full-length mirror. There was a threadbare rug over the rough timbers of the hardwood floor. Sinking back onto his bed, Skellan explained the situation: that Aigner was gone, drawn to Drakenhof if this Countess Isabella really was the evil Deitmar claimed, and assassins of the Risen Dead intended to make sure they never caught up with him. Fischer listened. He moved the chair so that it faced the door.

'So they are coming tonight?'

'In a couple of hours, yes.'

'I assume we are going to surprise them.'

'Naturally.'

'All right, if you were them what would you do?' Fischer was already thinking through what he would do in the assassins' place. Sleep was their natural enemy. The longer the night wore on the less chance the witch hunters had of making it through to dawn. It stood to reason then that the assassins would come during the dead of night.

'I'd send three men, there are two of us but two on two there is always the chance that even with the element of surprise against us, we could somehow survive. Aigner knows us. He will have transferred his paranoia on to the rest of the cult. The third assassin adds a level of security.'

SKELLAN WAS RIGHT.

When they came, there were three of them. They moved quietly down the corridor, pausing at the door to listen. The door handle turned slowly. It was a simple ruse, but in the dark it would be effective. The pillows had been bolstered to look like the rough outline of sleeping men beneath the bedcovers. The trickery wouldn't hold up to close inspection but that didn't matter. There would be no time for it. The door opened, groaning slightly on dry hinges. The silhouette of a man filled the doorway.

He stepped into the room.

Another shape moved in behind him.

He was less than an arm's length from where Skellan stood, cloaked in the shadows behind the open door.

In the chair, Fischer waited, willing the third assassin into the small room. The man stayed back. Fischer's finger itched on the trigger guard of the small hand-held crossbow he held levelled at the dark outline of the first man as he approached the bed. Moonlight glinted silver on the assassin's blade.

Skellan coughed, clearing his throat.

Fischer pulled the trigger. The bolt flew true, slamming into the gut of the assassin as he plunged his dagger into the bundle of bed linen. The man grunted in pain and staggered back, sagging against the wall. He slumped to the floor clutching the bolt in his gut.

Skellan moved quickly, stepping out of the shadows to press the point of his dagger up against the second assassin's throat.

'Do it,' the man rasped.

'With pleasure,' Skellan whispered in his ear as he rammed the knife home. The assassin folded in his arms, the life draining out of him. Skellan cast him aside. 'Come on my beauty,' he goaded, seeing the third assassin frozen in the doorway.

Before the man could flee, Fischer put a second crossbow bolt high in the man's thigh. He went down screaming in agony. Skellan dragged him into the room and slammed the door shut.

It was all over in less than a minute.

'Who sent you?' he hissed, grabbing hold of the shaft of the crossbow bolt and jerking it violently. The man shrieked in pain. 'Talk!'

'Go to hell!'

'Not nice,' Skellan whispered, pushing the bolt deeper into the man's thigh. 'You can die here, like your friends, or you can limp away. It is up to you. Now, who sent you?'

The colour had drained from the assassin's face. Sweat pooled in the creases of his neck. His eyes were wide with pain.

'I can make it worse, believe me. Now I am asking you again, who sent you?'

'Aigner,' the assassin said through clenched teeth.

'Better. Now where is the son of a bitch?'

The assassin shook his head violently.

'And we were doing so well,' Skellan said quite matter-of-factly as he yanked the crossbow bolt clean out of the assassin's leg. The man's screams were pitiful. 'I'll ask you again, last time. Where is Aigner?'

'The temple... Drakenhof.'

'Good.' Jon Skellan smiled mirthlessly. 'You should thank me.'

'Why?' the man cursed, clutching at the wound in his leg.

'Because I am going to give you the chance to see if you really can rise again. You shouldn't have come here tonight. You shouldn't have tried to kill me. That made things personal.'

'I am not afraid of death,' the assassin whispered, wrenching his shirt apart to expose his bare chest. 'Kill me. Do it!'

Mystical sigils had been scrawled across the man's flesh. The ink had seeped deep beneath the skin and into the muscle beneath.

'Do you truly believe they can bring you back? A few lines of ink?' Skellan pressed the tip of the knife into the man's chest, enough pressure behind it to draw a bead of blood.

'You know nothing, fool. Nothing!'

The assassin threw himself forward onto the knife. The blade buried hilt deep in his chest. The man shuddered once, a gasp escaping his lips, and collapsed into Skellan's arms.

He kept his promise to Amos. They were long gone come sunrise.

CHAPTER FOUR
Gathering Darkness

DRAKENHOF CASTLE, SYLVANIA
Late summer, 2009

VLAD VON CARSTEIN fascinated Alten Ganz.

The two of them watched ravens bickering over scraps in the courtyard below. Their dance was filled with savage beauty. The count watched the ravens, mesmerised by their wings and beaks as they fought over the crumbs put out by the cook.

'Fascinating, aren't they?' the count observed. 'So like us, and yet so different. This is basic nature, Ganz. This dance of wings and feathers is nothing more than the survival of the most desperate. It is a fight, every day. Feeding comes down to snatching the bread from the mouth of another bird. It is that or starvation. There is no sharing in their world. The bird willing to blind its brother for the sake of a piece of bread will feed like a king. The one that isn't, the one that won't fight for its life, will starve.'

At times there was an intense darkness to the way the Sylvanian count saw the world. He obsessed over the play of life and death. The dance of mortality, he called it. 'It is all about movement, Ganz. They dance toward the end of the song.'

'And life is the song,' the cadaverous young man finished, sensing where his master's thoughts were going.

'Ah, no, life is merely a prelude to the greatest of all songs.' Down below, the hungriest raven took flight, sleek black wings beating, its prize gripped firmly in its beak. The others were left to fight amongst themselves over the last few morsels. 'Death is the full rapturous movement. Never forget that, Ganz. Life is but fleeting, death is eternal.'

There were times when the count's predilection for darkness verged on the nihilistic. Like today, Ganz had found the man standing lonely vigil on the battlements of Drakenhof Castle. His quest for solitude was not uncommon. At sundown he would often come to the highest point of the castle and survey his domain as it unfurled beneath him. The wind pulled at his cloak, whipping it around his legs as he turned away from the squabbling birds.

'Have the cook put out double the amount of scraps tomorrow. I like the birds. They should have a home at Drakenhof.'

'As you wish, my lord.'

On some days the darkness seemed to radiate from Vlad von Carstein's heart and pulse outwards, consuming not only the man but many of those closest to him. The man was a complex composite of contradictions. Where on the one hand he was ruthless in dealing with those that stood against him, he had it in him to make sure the birds did not go hungry. It was a tenderness he didn't convey to his fellow man.

In that the Count of Sylvania was an enigma, even to his chancellor.

It wasn't arrogance. It wasn't even a symptom of power. It was a genuine indifference to his fellow man.

He walked slowly along the narrow battlements, pausing every few steps to look at some peculiarity he saw in the landscape below. Ganz mirrored his pace step for step as the count moved away from the courtyard to brace himself against a parapet towering over a razor of jagged rocks far, far below. He stayed a hesitant step behind von Carstein. The count was talking, in part to himself, in part to the wind, and of course, to Ganz. He listened to the count's musing. He never knew what he might hear next: a fragment of long forgotten poetry; an element of philosophy; history so wrapped up in story that it sounded like a cherished memory; or on a day like today, a death sentence.

'Rothermeyer is a thorn in my side, Ganz. He has a greatly inflated opinion of his importance in this life and the next. I want him taken care of. Make him the same offer you made Sturm and Drang. Be persuasive. He has two choices, I do not particularly care which of the two he takes. After Heinz Rothermeyer, pay a visit to Pieter Kaplin. Kaplin is doing his best to make a mockery of my generosity, Ganz. He is playing me for a simpleton, and that cannot be allowed to happen. There will be no choices for Pieter. You will make an example of him. Others will quickly tow the line. If not, they can always be replaced. Just make certain they are in no doubt as to what will happen to them if they continue to defy me.'

'My lord,' Ganz nodded, shuffling back a step. The drop from the battlements was a long one to the rocks below and while von Carstein obviously enjoyed flirting with death, Ganz much preferred the safety of solid ground. His balance was not as unerringly good as the count's. The man ghosted around the battlements with the preternatural grace and precision of one of those black-winged birds he was so fond of. 'It will be as you wish. Pieter Kaplin will rue the day he incurred your wrath.'

'You make me sound like an animal, Ganz. Remember, there is beauty in all things. Is the wolf driven by wrath when it stalks its tender prey? Were those birds down in the courtyard driven by blood fury?' He shook his head to reinforce the point he was making. 'No, they kill through necessity, through nature, they are killers through need. The gods made them and placed that basic need within their spirit. They need to kill. So they make a beautiful dance of the savagery, they don't seek to tame the wild beast within them. In that they are so unlike humans. Humans seek to subvert nature, to tame the savage beast that lurks within their soul. They build monuments and temples to gods who knew the darkness of their own souls and used it to their advantage. They revere Sigmar and his mighty warhammer, conveniently forgetting that that very warhammer was a tool of death. They wall themselves in. Build houses of sticks and stones and call themselves civilised. Humans are weak, they fear what might happen if their bestial nature is unleashed. They forget that there is beauty in *all* things – even the darkness – when they should be embracing it.' Von Carstein lapsed into silence, lost in thoughts of death and beauty.

This was another aspect of the count's personality: his mood could swing abruptly from merely thoughtful to this deeply melancholic brooding as he lost himself inside his own labyrinthine thoughts. It afforded him an air of introspection. The man was quite obviously brilliant, blessed with an intellect verging on sheer genius, he was well read and versed in every subject he cared to talk about and quick enough of wit to read people as well as he read those books.

Alten Ganz had never encountered anyone even remotely like Vlad von Carstein.

'Have Herman Posner accompany you, along with a few of his most trusted men. I have a feeling Posner is the perfect mixture of violence and cunning to tip Rothermeyer over the edge. Tell me, Ganz, do you believe Heinz will bend his knee and accept my rule? I tire of all this petty squabbling.'

'He would be a fool not to,' Ganz said, without really answering the question.

'That is not what I asked though, is it?' von Carstein said. He toyed with his signet ring as he spoke, turning it so that it was back-to-front on his ring finger, then completing the turn again. It was the closest thing the count had to a nervous tic. He toyed with the signet ring when he was deep in thought or puzzling through a problem. It was a habit Ganz had seen demonstrated on many an occasion.

'No, my lord.'

'So tell me, Ganz, honestly. Do you believe Heinz Rothermeyer will finally bend his knee to me?'

'No, my lord. Rothermeyer is a proud man. He will fight you to the last.'

Vlad von Carstein nodded thoughtfully, his gaze off somewhere in the middle distance where the night consumed the town of Drakenhof far below their vantage point.

'I agree,' he said at last. 'So, you know what you will have to do.'

'Yes, my lord.'

'Then go, time is fleeting, I would have these thorns picked from my flesh before they bleed me further.'

GANZ LEFT VON Carstein alone on the battlements. There was no telling how long the count would remain out there, the man craved solitude. Few in Drakenhof Castle dared approach their lord and he seldom sought out the company of others, save his wife Isabella and Ganz.

Isabella von Carstein was her husband's equal in every way. She was beautiful and cruel, a dangerous combination. Unlike Vlad she was predictable in her cruelty, though. Ganz had long since found her measure. She craved power in all shapes and forms. It was a simplistic desire compared to the confusing nature of her husband, but in that she proved the perfect balance, the perfect foil, the perfect mate. When the count had thought he had lost her to the wasting sickness he had been desolate. At first he had railed at the chirurgeons and the physicians, urging them to find the miracle that would cure his wife, and then when medicine failed he sought a higher salvation. He stood lonely vigil on the highest stones of the castle wall, night after night, as though proximity to the gods in the sky might somehow convince them to save his beloved Isabella. It was only on the final evening, when her carers feared her spirit had passed too far into Morr's kingdom to ever find its way out, that Vlad banished everyone from her chamber and sat the loneliest of vigils, the death watch for his own wife.

But she didn't die.

The count emerged the next day exhausted, physically drained to the point of collapse, and sent the gawkers on their way. My wife will live, was all he said. A simple four-word announcement. His wife did live. He was right. That night, looking better than she had in months, Isabella von Carstein emerged from her bedchamber to show the world that truly, she would live. By the grace of the gods she had conquered the wasting sickness that had so ravaged Sylvania.

The narrow stone stairwell led to a gallery still high above the main house of the castle. The walls of the gallery were lined with portraits of von Carstein by some of the nation's most beloved artists, each one seeking to capture on canvas some of the count's most hypnotic qualities. It was the eyes they focussed on. Some might have considered the obsession with his own image vanity, but the more he grew to know the count, the less Ganz believed he was a vain man. No, it was just another dichotomy within the man. There were no mirrors in the castle, none of the usual trappings of narcissism that went with self-obsession. The paintings were obvious things of beauty and the count was an admirer of all such creations. He spoke often about great beauty being a gift from the gods themselves, a blessing, so he chose to surround himself with the pictures just as he surrounded himself with fine porcelain and marble statuettes, adorned himself with delicately crafted jewellery and furnished his home with plush velvets and brocades.

It was about collecting things of beauty.

Hoarding them.

Oddly, there were no portraits of his wife in the gallery.

Ganz walked briskly through the long room, pushing aside the thick red velvet drape at the far end and descending a second tightly spiralled stair into the servants' quarters. Unlike the refinements elsewhere, there was an edge of decay about these rooms. The tapestries on the walls were worn a little threadbare in places. The colour was spotted and uneven after years of sunlight had leached them of their vibrancy. They showed scenes of the Great Hunt, some nameless, faceless van Drak count leading yapping dogs and men on a chase after wild boar. Given the mad van Draks' well deserved reputations as barbarous fiends, Ganz suspected the invisible prey ran on two legs rather than four. The stained glass window at the far end of the hallway scattered a hypnotic array of yellows, greens and reds across the carpet.

Ganz stalked down the hallway. Halfway along, two servants' staircases led to different levels of the castle, the longest one descending directly into the kitchens, the shorter one leading to another gallery, this one overlooking the main hall.

Ganz took the short staircase two and three steps at a time.

He was out of breath by the time he reached the bottom.

The gallery was designed to show off the grandeur of the main hall and the count's obsidian throne. This was Ganz's favourite place in the whole castle. From here he could observe the comings and goings of the count's court unseen. Life played itself out in the room below, the scheming of the petty barons, the pleas for clemency, the terrible swift sword of the count's justice, the everyday life of Sylvania, it all happened down there.

From here Ganz watched, studied, and learned. He was not so different from Isabella von Carstein, he too craved the power his close association with the count conferred, but he wasn't so ignorant as to believe himself irreplaceable. Far from it, he harboured no illusions as regards his own beauty: he was not something the count would willingly choose to have about his person. He had to *make* himself irreplaceable. That meant gathering knowledge, knowing each and every man in the count's court, knowing their weaknesses and how to exploit them.

The count was right; life in his court really was very much like the ravens they had watched squabbling over scraps of food. Survival came down to being willing to sacrifice others in order to ensure your continued existence.

Alten Ganz was a survivor.

It was in his nature.

The main hall was abuzz with activity. Some lesser noble from the outer reaches of the county had taken it upon himself to make a pilgrimage to Drakenhof to petition Vlad von Carstein for aid in feeding his own people. The count had laughed in his face dismissively and told him to get on his knees and beg. When the noble did as he was told von Carstein laughed even harder and suggested that he might as well kiss the dirt at his feet for all the respect he had for a man who would beg at the feet of another. Instead of aid, von Carstein disenfranchised the noble, allowing him to leave Drakenhof with the shirt on his back and nothing more, no shoes, no trousers, no cloak to guard against the elements, and promised to send one of his most trusted family members to the man's home to rule in his stead. 'A man should be able to care for his own, not prostrate himself at the feet of strangers and beg for mercy. It is a lesson you would all do well to learn.' That was the count's judgement and the ramifications of it were still playing out in the main hall hours later.

GANZ FOUND HERMAN Posner in the drill hall, running a number of the count's soldiers through a series of punishing exercises. Posner was taller than Ganz by a good six inches, and had a much heavier build, all of it due to his well-defined musculature. While the others looked on, Posner duelled a younger soldier. Posner used two short slightly curved swords while his opponent opted for a longer blade and a small shield. Posner's swords wove a dance of death between the two men, keeping his opponent at bay with dizzying ease. The blades shimmered in the torchlight. Such was Posner's skill that the two blades appeared to blur into one, so quick was the movement.

As Ganz stepped onto the duelling floor Posner's left-hand blade snaked out to nick the young soldier's cheek, drawing a line of blood with the shallowest of cuts. He bowed to his opponent and turned to Ganz who was applauding slowly as he walked across the floor.

'Very impressive,' Ganz said.

'If it isn't von Carstein's esteemed chancellor. To what do we owe the pleasure, Herr Ganz?' Posner said, his sepulchral tones echoing loudly in the vast emptiness of the drill hall.

'Work. We are going to visit Baron Heinz Rothermeyer. The count would have him brought to heel.'

'Hear that, men?' Posner said to the men who had been watching his duel with the young soldier. A feral grin spread slowly across his face. 'The count wants us to instil just the right amount of terror in the baron's heart to convince him mend his ways, eh?'

'Something like that,' Ganz agreed.

Posner sheathed his twin blades in the scabbards slung low on his back.

'When do we leave?'

'Sunrise,' Ganz said.

'Too soon. We have to make preparations for the journey. Sundown. We can travel under cover of darkness.'

'So be it, sundown tomorrow. Be ready.' Ganz turned on his heel and left. The echo of steel on steel rang in his ears before he was halfway across the duelling floor.

'Better!' he heard Posner encourage one of his men. The count had selected Posner for a reason, and for all that Ganz disliked the man, he was the first to admit that Posner was among the best at what he did.

And what he did was kill people.

CHAPTER FIVE
Something Wicked This Way Comes

ACROSS SYLVANIA
Early autumn, 2009

FIVE BLACK BROUGHAM coaches rolled through the night.

Horses' hooves drummed like thunder on the hard-packed dirt of the makeshift road.

Clutching the reins tightly in their fists the five coachmen driving the broughams hunched low over the footboard irons, their occasional whip cracks spurring their teams of horses on to greater speeds. The coachmen wore heavy road-stained travel cloaks and had hoods pulled high over their heads and scarves wrapped around their faces.

The brougham coaches bore the crest of von Carstein on their doors.

The further north they travelled the worse the condition of the roads became. Three of the five coaches had had to be re-wheeled after rocks in the road had broken the existing wheel's felloe. One coach had needed its elliptical spring replaced and the other had developed cracks in its axle and had broken a lynchpin. None of the carriages had escaped unscathed.

The coaches afforded the travellers some small luxury, with Herman Posner and his men sharing four of the broughams, leaving Ganz alone in the fifth. Even so, tempers among the passengers had long since worn thin, and several frayed to breaking point. It was inevitable, Ganz realised. His travelling companions were killers. They craved space and solitude, perhaps to contemplate or come to terms with the murders they were prepared to commit in the name of their master, or perhaps simply to clear their minds of the tedium of the endless road.

After a month cooped up in the carriages it was inevitable that a few fights would break out, but whenever they did Posner was quick to stamp them out. The man ruled his soldiers with an iron fist and backed his threats up with the steel of his twin blades. Few pushed the arguments once Posner interjected himself into them. It was part fear, part respect, Ganz realised, appreciating the man's leadership skills. He was very much like the count in that regard, commanding the love and the fear of his servants.

They travelled by night and slept in the velvet darkness of the brougham coaches by day. It was a peculiar arrangement and Ganz found himself missing the touch of the sun on his face but he was growing used to it.

At sundown every day Posner put his men through a rigorous series of exercises aimed at minimising the effects of the journey on their bodies and keeping their minds sharp. Much of the exercises looked, to Ganz, like an elaborate form of dance, with Posner focussing on the footwork of his seven warriors as he drove them through a punishing series of blocks, strikes, parries and cuts.

Posner practised what he preached. He matched his men exercise for exercise and then pushed himself further still, focussing on his body dynamics and balance. The man was the consummate athlete. He manipulated his own body with preternatural grace. Without doubt, the man was a deadly adversary.

The eight of them together would be more than a match for local militia.

Rothermeyer's barony, Eschen, was one of the smaller outlying territories along the north-west border of the province, between the Forest of Shadows and the fork in the River Stir, a mere four days' travel from Waldenhof, Pieter Kaplin's home. The coaches might easily have been travelling through the Lands of the Dead for all the life the land offered. Given the season, the trees ought to have been a thousand shades of copper and tin. Instead, they were thick with lichen and mould, while others were lightning split, stumps of rotten trunks and dead wood. On the roadside dilapidated buildings crumbled to rock dust and rubble, and barren fields lay where there should have been a bountiful harvest waiting to be reaped. The sickness had spread to the very soil itself, poisoning the province.

Ganz rode alone in the last carriage. With plush red velvet banquettes and padded backrests the interior was luxurious, the drapes were thick enough to block out the sun, even at the height of the day, and the banquettes were more than comfortable enough for sleeping on.

He had thought through what he was going to say to Rothermeyer a thousand times, couching it in terms as disparate as a friendly warning and a pat on the back to outright threat and physical violence, playing through all of the wayward baron's possible responses in his mind. It was like an elaborate game of chess, trying to see through to the endgame with the best possible strategy. Soon enough it would move out of the realm of the imagination and become all too real. And it would come to blows, as he had told the count. Rothermeyer was no fool, and being on the very fringe of the count's territory it was little surprise the man felt invulnerable.

Vlad von Carstein's reach may have been long, but Rothermeyer must have been gambling on the fact that it was almost impossible to exert any real control on his barony over such great distance. The miles were his greatest protection from the count. They could also, just as easily, prove to be his death warrant as they had proved to be for Pieter Kaplin.

No doubt Rothermeyer knew they were coming. The five black broughams bearing von Carstein's crest had raised more than a few eyebrows as they cut through the night, and their practice this evening had been witnessed by a handful of farmers and their curious families from Eschen's outlying farmsteads. The strangers would most certainly be the topic of conversation for miles around and it was only to be expected that the lesser baronies they had swept through along the way would send word of their passing. It was part of the culture of fear that enveloped Sylvania. The black coaches could only mean ill news for someone further up the road. The word would spread by messenger birds: von Carstein's men were coming.

Those barons yet to fall in line with the count's rule would hear of the black coaches coming their way and would know fear.

Ganz admired the simplicity of the count's manoeuvre. Instead of travelling like any anonymous wanderer trudging the roads of the province by foot or horseback, the sumptuous brougham coaches not only afforded comfort, they made it plain exactly who was travelling in them. The knowledge that the count's men were abroad would be more than enough to stir the ever-present fear and self-loathing of the Sylvanian people.

The coachman rapped on the ceiling of Ganz's carriage, three sharp knocks.

The chancellor rolled up the velvet curtain, drew down the glass window and leaned out through the opening.

'What is it, man?' Ganz shouted over the noise of the wheels and the horses' hooves.

'Just crossed the River Stir, sir, and that's Eschen in the distance. We'll be there by dawn.'

Ganz strained to see through the gradually lifting darkness but it was impossible to make out more than a smudge of deeper darkness along the line where the land met the night sky. Sunrise was little more than an hour away. Eschen would be a hive of activity already, bakers preparing the day's bread, grooms readying the horses, stable boys mucking out the stalls, servants slaving away to make their work of the day appear effortless. How the coachman could possibly know that that inky smudge on the horizon was Eschen baffled him but Ganz was gradually coming to suspect that there was more to this peculiar entourage than met the eye.

In the month they had spent on the road the coachmen had barely said a word to each other, though they occasionally spoke to him in low inflectionless voices, and they did not fraternise with Posner's men. The five drivers were vaguely disquieting. It was something about them, a peculiar quality they all shared. Five deeply introspective men, almost identical in build, focussed so utterly on the road as though their very lives depended upon mastering it, permanently wrapped up against the elements despite the fact that it was late summer, drifting into autumn, and the nights were pleasantly balmy. Little more than the arch of their brow and the shadowed recesses of their eyes were exposed, and still they were capable of seeing for miles in the dark with greater clarity than Ganz could during the day.

Slowly, as the first blush of the sun began to rise and the distance to the town narrowed, the outline of Eschen came into focus.

It was a daunting silhouette, far grander in scale than Ganz had expected this close to the edge of the province. Not as vast as Drakenhof, Eschen still verged somewhere on the border between being called a town and a city. Spires rose into the reddening sky, and the rooftops of two and three-storey buildings crowded in on each other. Ganz's knuckles whitened as his grip on the sill of the carriage door tightened. Eschen Keep rose on a mile long crag-and-tail mount behind the houses, a brooding sentinel watching over the streets and houses below. Most surprising of all though, the thing that Ganz had most definitely not expected, were the high walls. Eschen was a fortified town.

It made sense, given the proximity of the Kislev border. Fortifications would act as a deterrent to prospective raiders.

As they drew closer Alten Ganz's suspicions began to crystallise.

The walls were new and had nothing to do with keeping raiding parties at bay.

Rothermeyer's rebellion was more serious than von Carstein suspected. The man was making preparations for civil war. Walling his city was a declaration of intent. Ganz could only wonder how many more of the border barons were with him in this. It would be a foolish man who stood alone against the might of Vlad von Carstein, and from the little Ganz knew about Heinz Rothermeyer the man was a lot of things, stubborn, honourable, curmudgeonly, but he was not a fool.

The coaches thundered on towards the gates of the walled town.

Ganz forced himself to reassess the situation. When they embarked it was to warn an errant baron from stepping out of line, not put down a burgeoning rebellion. Suddenly he felt like a fly crawling into the spider's sticky web.

Two soldiers standing square in the middle of the road blocked their entry through the Eschen Gate. More soldiers in the livery of Rothermeyer lined the battlements above them. Ganz studied the men. They ranged in age, two were very young, and another was well into his fifth decade. They were nervous. It was in their body language. They were tense. Expecting trouble. With good reason, considering the fact that their baron had obviously been plotting his coup for some considerable time. The next few minutes were going to be interesting.

'Hold!' one of the guards blocking the road demanded.

The front coach slowed to a complete stop, the horses' flaring nostrils mere inches from the guard's impassive face. The man didn't so much as flinch. His companion stepped around the front of the horses and walked up to the door of the front carriage.

Ganz reached through the open window for the door handle and opened the door. He climbed out of the coach cautiously, stiff from the long hours of travel.

'We seek an audience with the baron,' Ganz said, walking up to the soldier. 'I trust you will see to it that word gets up to the keep so we are properly welcomed, as befits our status as emissaries of the count himself.' Ganz craned his neck to look up at the soldiers on the battlements, meeting their gaze one by one and letting them know that he was taking care to remember their faces.

'Baron Rothermeyer does not recognise the claim of your master, sir. If I allow you to enter Eschen it is as a common traveller. Have you coin to pay for your food and board? We won't allow vagrancy, baron's rules.'

Ganz looked at the soldier, and shook his head very slowly from side to side. A slow smile reached his lips.

'Listen carefully,' Ganz said. 'I am going to pretend you haven't opened your mouth just yet. First impressions are so very important.

Now, let me tell you who I am. My name is Ganz, Alten Ganz, and I am chancellor of the Count of Sylvania's court. That would make me one of the most powerful men in the land, wouldn't you agree? Now, I am going to let you into a secret, and then we can begin again. The last person who used a similar tone when addressing me currently resides within the cold dirt of one of the many cemeteries in Drakenhof city. So, should we try again? We seek an audience with the baron.'

'Like I said, *chancellor*, the baron does not recognise the legitimacy of your master's rule. You are welcome to visit our city as a traveller. There is not, I am afraid, very much to see, but you must understand that any audience will be on the baron's terms, if indeed he should choose to grant one. I am also to inform you that there is, unfortunately, no room for your entourage in the keep itself, though there is a single chamber that has been made up for you and your man. Might I recommend the Pretender's Arms for your companions, it is a fair-sized tavern about half-way up Lavender Hill.' He pointed over his shoulder in the direction of the crag-and-tail rock formation leading up to the keep.

'This is preposterous,' Ganz said, shaking his head in disgust. 'Does the baron not realise the implications of such an affront to the count? Never mind, don't answer that. Of course he does. For every action there is a reaction, it is predictable. Rothermeyer knows full well that von Carstein will look to extract punishment for this stubborn display of resistance, and yet he goes ahead with it. Very well, soldier, open the gates.'

The second soldier stood aside. Together the two men raised the huge wooden brace barring the gate, and pushed the doors open to allow the black brougham coaches to pass.

The leading coachman cracked his whip above the horses' heads and the carriage lumbered forward. Likewise, the others followed in tight procession through the gate and into the cramped streets of Eschen. The steel-wrapped wheels clattered on the cobblestones and the horses' hooves clip-clopped loudly in the relative quiet of the early morning. The streets were tight and wound narrowly in a series of twists and turns like the meander of a great river. The spectre of Eschen Keep was ever-present, looming over the procession as it moved slowly up the incline of Lavender Hill toward the keep itself.

The Pretender's Arms was indeed almost half way up the long tail of the hill. Two stable boys and a dour faced groom waited for them by the coach house gates. The boys looked as though they had just been dragged rather violently out of bed and hauled down to the courtyard. The soldier from the gate must have sent a runner on to warn them that they were coming. No doubt he had some sort of reciprocal arrangement with the tavern. Ganz's coach pulled level with

Posner's as it peeled away toward the tavern's courtyard. He saw Posner's impassive face staring out through a chink in the curtained window. The man looked anything but happy at the baron's affront. Ganz gestured for him to pull down his window so that they could talk.

'I will have word sent down to you when I am settled. Get some sleep, tonight we will sort out this idiocy of Rothermeyer's.'

'Indeed we will,' Posner said coldly.

The manner with which he said it sent a shiver the length of Ganz's spine. Herman Posner was not inclined to offer forgiveness; it was not a part of the warrior's personality. He would answer the slight in his own way, Ganz had no doubt about that. Posner pulled up his window again and let the curtain fall so that he could no longer be seen.

'To the keep!' Ganz shouted up to his own coachman, and sank back into the velvet banquette to wait out the final few minutes of the ride. He closed his eyes.

When he opened them again the coach was slowing down at the gates of Eschen Keep. Again, two soldiers blocked the coach's path. A third soldier came around the side of the coach and knocked on the door. Ganz drew the black curtain aside.

'Yes?' he said, any hint of civility gone from his tone.

'The baron bids you welcome to Eschen, Herr Ganz. The chamberlain will take you to your room, and a girl has been assigned to see to your... ah... needs during your stay at the keep. Your coachman is to return to the tavern where the rest of your companions are staying. The baron trusts that this will meet with your approval.'

Ganz sighed. 'No, of course it doesn't meet with my approval, soldier. But I will show good grace and accept the decision. For now.'

The soldier banged on the side of the carriage and the brougham rumbled forward beneath the barbican. Eschen Keep was a formidable bastion, immune to assault from three of its four sides thanks to the jagged rocks of the crag it was built on. Though the mile-long tail of rock formed a gradual incline, the keep itself was several hundred feet above the town below. The wind was strong in the narrow bailey, the curtain wall doing little to prevent a battering from the elements. The coach rolled to a stop and Ganz opened the door and clambered out. The air tasted fresh. It stung his cheeks as he turned to survey his surroundings.

Eschen Keep was undoubtedly built for war. Unlike many of the baronies of Sylvania whose keeps and castles were ostentatious displays of wealth to separate themselves from the commoners, Eschen with its wall walks, murder holes and narrow arrow slits was made to hold off a full frontal attack. It wasn't a home, it was designed for protection during the strife of war. No doubt within the keep itself measures had been taken to survive a prolonged siege as well. Despite himself, Ganz could not help but admire Rothermeyer's audacity. The man had almost certainly bled his coffers dry in this last stubborn defiance of von Carstein's rule.

It was a pity that the gesture was futile.

A raven flew overhead, cawing raucously. Ganz couldn't help but think back to that evening on the battlements with the count and wonder if it was a sign. An acceptance of superstition came naturally to most Sylvanians.

The chamberlain and the girl waited on the steps of the keep. The man could have been Ganz's doppelganger; it was like looking at himself only thirty years older, the same cadaverous features, sunken cheekbones and hollowed-out eyes, and a willow-thin frame that was all awkward angles. The man's white hair was brushed back over his scalp and instead of a fringe he wore a harsh widow's peak. The girl on the other hand was, as the count would have said, a thing of beauty. She had an olive tint to her complexion and almond-shaped eyes. Her oval face was heartbreakingly pretty, high cheekbones and lush full kissable lips. But Ganz's eyes were drawn back to hers. At first they appeared to be green in the dawn's early light but the closer he looked the more certain he was that they were in fact a kaleidoscope of colours and it was the colour of her shawl and the sun that made them look green.

The man bowed stiffly as Ganz approached, the girl curtseyed. She moved as pleasingly as she looked.

'Greetings,' the chamberlain said, holding out his hand to take Ganz's travel cloak. Ganz unclipped the hasp and with a flourish draped it over the man's outstretched arm. 'Follow me, please.'

'Lead the way,' Ganz said, moving into step beside the girl.

His first impression of Eschen Keep was that he had had the right of it when he assumed Rothermeyer had emptied his treasury making the place as defensible as possible. The place was spartan. There were no wall hangings or tapestries or other decorations aimed solely at being easy on the eye. Everything about the keep was functional, the corridors narrow and the ceilings low to make swinging a sword difficult, tight spiral stairways, the corkscrew of stairs favouring the right-handed defenders fighting a retreat. Ganz followed the chamberlain to a small room on the second floor.

'Klara will draw you a bath so that you might wash the road from your skin, and I will have your luggage brought up to the room. Rest. You will be summoned when the baron is ready to greet you. If there is anything you need, Klara will see to it. I trust your stay will be a pleasant one, Herr Ganz. If there is nothing else I will leave you to Klara?'

'Thank you. That will be all,' Ganz said.

'As you wish.' The white haired man bowed again, as stiffly as before, and left the two of them alone.

'I will see to your bath.' The serving girl's voice was husky and thickly accented. Where some might have seen it as a flaw, for Ganz it only added to her curious appeal.

'Please,' he said, moving to the window. The view from the window was surprisingly similar to the view from his window in Drakenhof Castle, but then, he reasoned, how different could an endless cluster of rooftops, towers and spires look? The room itself was smaller though, and like the corridors leading to it, it was bare of ornament or decoration. There was a large metal tub in the corner of the room, and a cauldron of water bubbling in the hearth. Four large porcelain jugs filled with cold water were lined up beside the tub, a fifth jug stood empty. Klara took this jug to the cauldron and filled it with steaming hot water, which she poured into the metal bath. The water hissed against the cold steel.

'If you would like to undress, I can prepare the bath and bathe you?'

'Ah... no. It's all right, I can manage by myself. Just fill the tub up, leave some lye so that I can scrub the dirt out of my skin, and I will be more than happy.'

'I am to care to your every need, herr. I would not wish to disappoint my baron.'

'Disappoint is a word for lovers, not servants, girl. You displease your master or you give him pleasure. It would please me greatly if you drew a nice hot bath and then left me in peace to savour it, understood?'

'Yes, herr,' Klara said, lowering her eyes. She drew a second jug of steaming hot water from the cauldron and emptied it into the bath.

It took her a few minutes to fill the tub and cool the water sufficiently for Ganz to submerse his whole body. She left him alone to undress.

The bath was good. Being on the road, forced to live like an animal for the last month, made soaking in the hot water all the more luxurious. Ganz closed his eyes and tried to enjoy the feel of the water on his skin. He remained that way, head back, eyes closed, simply savouring the sensation of being clean, until the water was barely tepid. He soaped himself, rinsed the lather of acerbic lye off with icy cold water from the final jug, and clambered out of the bath and towelled himself dry. He wrapped the wet towel around his waist and stood by the window once again, this time paying special attention to the layout of this side of the keep and the streets below. He locked certain landmarks in his mind, using them to orientate himself. Knowledge of what could become hostile surroundings was invaluable.

He turned away from the window at the sound of a knock on the bedroom door.

'Come in,' Ganz said, expecting Klara to have returned from whatever errand she had fetched herself off on. It wasn't the almond-eyed servant girl who opened the door.

An elderly man, frail-boned, with snow-white hair fastened in a topknot, corsair style, leaned on a silver-tipped cane in the doorway. His hands were liver-spotted, the skin hanging loosely on the brittle bones beneath. The old man was frail but he wasn't weak. There was a difference. Ganz knew who his visitor was immediately.

'Baron,' he said by way of greeting. 'You have me at a disadvantage.'

'As was my intention, Herr Ganz. A naked opponent has, ah, less chance of hiding things, so to speak.'

The old man's eyes were bright and hinted at a sharp mind at work in his old body, which was so rarely the case with the aged. The old baron came into the room and closed the door behind him. He lowered himself gingerly down onto a hard wooden chair. 'Now, let's get something straight, shall we? I don't care for your master and I have no intention of kowtowing to his every whim. I am the lord of my dominion. These are my people here. I care for them. Your master in his cold empty castle hundreds of miles away is nothing to me.'

'Ah, now, you see, Baron Rothermeyer – may I call you Heinz?' without waiting for the baron's consent, Ganz went on: 'You see, Heinz, you have put me in a difficult position here because I *do* care for my master and he sent me to you to give you a chance. Every mile of this godforsaken journey I have fervently hoped there would be a wise man waiting at the end of the road, not a fool. Stubbornness will only get you killed, Heinz. Surely you can see that.'

The old man stiffened slightly in his chair. 'Do not presume to threaten me in my own home, young man. You are alone here. Your erstwhile assassins are in a tavern half a mile away. I am surrounded by people who love me and would willingly die doing my bidding. You on the other hand, well, no one would so much as hear you scream.' Rothermeyer coughed, hard, dredging up a lungful of phlegm. It rattled in his throat before he swallowed it back. 'Am I making myself clear?'

'Abundantly,' Ganz said, adjusting the towel. His semi-nakedness made him feel far more vulnerable than he would have leaning over a tabletop in some diplomatic chamber in the heart of the keep. 'But perhaps I am not making *myself* quite so clear, Heinz. I live for my count and likewise I would willingly die for him. I am sure that if you so chose you could have your men make me scream. The prospect does not frighten me even half so much as disappointing my count.

That, I believe is a mark of my devotion to him. He is a righteous man, a powerful man. He is good for this nation of ours. But Heinz, I have to tell you that your stubbornness has ceased to be amusing to von Carstein. I was told to offer you a choice. It is the same choice the count has offered other errant barons, and it is a simple enough one: bend the knee to him during the festivities of Geheimnisnacht or face his wrath. If you swear subservience, your petty rebellions will be forgotten, that is his promise. He is a man of his word, Heinz.'

'It won't happen,' the old man said flatly.

'That is a shame. Might I urge you to think it over? What is it they say? Decisions made in haste are most often repented at leisure.' The cold had begun to draw goose pimples out of Ganz's bare skin but he made no move to cover himself.

'The decision was made a long time ago, son.'

'And you set about preparing to defend yourself from its ramifications? Is that what the wall is all about?'

'Something like that, yes.'

'And now judgement has come to your door. I pity you, Heinz. Honestly, I do. If you kill me, another will come, and another after him, and they will keep coming until Eschen has been purged from the face of the world. He won't spare you because of your age. He won't humour a senile old fool. Have you no sense of what you are doing to those people you claim to love? You are signing their death warrants. Is it worth it? The death of everyone who loves and respects you? I can't believe it is. I can't. But trust me, this petty show of defiance guarantees that it is only a matter of time. So, because of you, I pity them, too. The count is not by nature a merciful man.'

Rothermeyer stood awkwardly, his weight on the cane. 'You speak very prettily for a thug, son. What are you, von Carstein's pet scholar?'

'I don't want anyone to suffer unduly.'

'But what constitutes unduly in your eyes?'

'People dying needlessly, which is exactly what will happen,' Ganz said with a surprising amount of passion in his voice.

'Better to die free than enslaved to a monster like Vlad von Carstein. Haven't you realised that yet?' Rothermeyer walked slowly over to the door, and then paused with his hand on the handle, as though something had just occurred to him. 'I don't see that we have anything else to talk about. Erich, my chamberlain will see you are fed, and returned to your men by sundown. I expect you out of Eschen by nightfall. And, in time, expect you to return with your armies to crush what you see as my petty rebellion. If death by a thousand cuts awaits me, so be it. I will meet Ulric in the Underworld with my head held high that I lived as a man and died as one.' The old man invoked the name of the warrior god. 'As you so rightly said, I am an old man.

Death does not frighten me the way it used to.' Heinz Rothermeyer closed the door behind him as he left.

'Why waste a thousand cuts, you old fool, when one will do?' Ganz muttered at the wooden door.

The meeting hadn't proceeded the way he had hoped it would but it had gone very much the way he had expected it to.

Ganz unwrapped the damp towel and dressed in clean clothes from his travelling chest.

Klara didn't return.

He lay on the bed and closed his eyes, content to doze for a few hours before rejoining Posner at the Pretender's Arms.

Food was brought to the room an hour before noon: a plate of fresh fruit, pumpernickel bread, aromatic cheeses and thick slices of various cold meats. It was a platter fit for nobility. Ganz ate ravenously. He hadn't realised it had been so long since his last real meal. The melange of flavours on his tongue was mouth-wateringly delicious. He ate until he was sated then he checked the sun through the window. It was a few hours past the meridian.

'Time to end the dance,' he said to himself. He looked around the room for some kind of bell-pull to summon the chamberlain but there was nothing of the sort that he could find. He opened the door. The passageway was empty. He walked back the way the chamberlain had led him a few hours earlier. Ganz found a servant boy walking hurriedly up the main staircase.

'Boy!' he called. The youngster stopped in his tracks and turned to look back quizzically. 'See my bags are brought from my room and have my coachman ready my carriage.' The boy nodded and skipped back down the stairs. Saying nothing, he hustled down the passageway Ganz had just left. Ganz made his way out to the courtyard. A few servants were busy with whatever chores their daily life forced on them. He crossed the courtyard to the stables. His black brougham was parked outside. The moribund coachman sat on the flatbed, reins wrapped tightly in his fist as though he had been expecting Ganz's imminent return. With a shiver, Ganz realised the man had in all probability never left his seat since dropping him off earlier.

'We are going to meet up with the others at the tavern down the hill, a boy is tending to my luggage.' He opened the door and clambered into the velvet cool darkness of the carriage.

HE WAS SEETHING by the time he found Posner, asleep in his own carriage in the courtyard of the Pretender's Arms twenty minutes later. Posner and his men hadn't bothered with renting out a dormitory. Instead they chose to sleep in their broughams just as they had done every day for the last month. No doubt Posner had decided that whatever the outcome of

Ganz's treating with the old baron, Rothermeyer would be dead come morning and they would be back on the road, so there was no point in making themselves comfortable. Giving the circumstances of his return from the keep he couldn't fault Posner's logic.

The soldier was laid out in a state of what looked like peaceful repose when Ganz opened the door to his coach and clambered in. Posner lay on his back, arms folded across his chest, heels together, on the velvet banquette. He was amazed the man could sleep like that. The carriage smelled stale – damp earth and mildew. It was a graveyard reek.

'He wasn't prepared to give so much as an inch,' Ganz said, sitting himself down on the bench opposite Posner's makeshift bed.

'You didn't seriously expect him to, did you?' Posner said, without opening his eyes.

'No,' Ganz conceded grudgingly.

'Then why the long face? You gave him his chance; he chose his own fate. It is more than many people get to do, remember that, chancellor. The consequence of his choice might be a visit from my men but it was still his choice. In his place I like to think I would have the courage to make the same choice. It is uncommon for an old man to have the courage to die gloriously. They prefer to slip into their dotage and dwell on things that once were and might have been but for one twist of fate, one bad decision, one love lost, one mistake made. Now, however, it is out of his hands. Come nightfall death will walk in his house. I fully expect that he has left the door open for us.'

'Just make it quick and clean,' Ganz said, a bad taste lingering in his mouth from the whole business. 'He is an old man.'

'It won't be either,' Posner said. 'Now leave me in peace, I must clear my mind for the killing to come.'

Ganz waited out the hours to nightfall in his own carriage. The minutes and hours dragged by, giving his guilt time to fester. The plain-speaking old man had gotten under his skin. He was fully aware of the consequences of his stupid rebellion and yet he refused to simply bow to the rule of von Carstein, which would have been enough to save his life. Instead he chose to stand up against the storm of the count's wrath even though it meant his own death. He didn't know if it was bravery or stupidity but whatever it was, it made Ganz respect the old man as much as he pitied him.

SOMEWHERE DURING THE long wait he fell asleep. He awoke to the frenzied sound of wolves baying in the distance. He opened the carriage door and staggered out into the night. A sickle moon hung in the clear sky. He had no idea how long he had been asleep or what time it was. The four other carriages were empty. For once, the coachmen were nowhere in sight. Their absence disturbed Ganz more than it ought to have, but the more he thought about it the more he realised that he had never seen the strange men leave the coaches.

The wolves howled again, a lupine chorus that echoed around the hilltop. He had no idea how many of the beasts there were out there but it was certainly a hunting pack and judging by the rabid baying they had scented their prey.

The sound caused the fine hairs at the nape of Ganz's neck to rise like hackles, prickling with the black premonition of fear. He knew, unreasonably, what they were hunting, long before the first wolf came loping back into the courtyard of the Pretender's Arms, the baron's blood still fresh on its muzzle. More of the great beasts came padding back into the forecourt, jowls slick with the blood of Heinz Rothermeyer and those unfortunates who loved the old man enough to die with him.

A huge wolf, almost twice the size of the others, came bounding into the courtyard. Ganz backed up against the side of one of the brougham coaches, feeling the door handle dig into his spine. The great wolf veered towards him, head thrown back as though driven crazy by the smell of his fear. Less than a foot from Ganz it raised up onto its hind legs and slammed its fore paws into the carriage door either side of Ganz's face. Its foul breath stung his eyes. He squirmed but there was no way he could wriggle out beneath the creature's claws before its jaws closed on his neck and ripped his throat out if it so desired. The wolf's feral eyes regarded him as though he was nothing more than a slab of meat.

Posner's words came back to him, ghosts in his mind: *It is uncommon for an old man to have the courage to die gloriously.*

There was nothing glorious about it, he realised. Death was dirty. He felt the warm trickle of urine dribbling down the inside of his leg.

The wolf's huge gaping maw appeared to stretch as the beast arched its back and let out an almost human howl. It was as though the wolf had raked its claws over his soul. Ganz felt his knees begin to buckle and the world around him began to shift and lose its shape and definition as it swam out of focus.

He fell amongst a curious mix of howls and laughter from all around the courtyard. He blacked out. He had no idea how long for. Seconds. Minutes. It was impossible to say.

When he looked up he saw Herman Posner standing over him, smears of fresh blood around his mouth and across his cheek. Of the wolf there was no sign.

'The baron is dead,' Posner said, scratching behind his ear. 'As are most of his household. It is time we left town, chancellor.'

There was something about Posner's eyes as he stared down at him that stirred up Ganz's most primal fears.

He realised what it was.

They were feral.

CHAPTER SIX

The Night of the Dancing Dead

DRAKENHOF
Early winter, 2010

IT HAD BEEN a hard year for Jon Skellan.

Failure weighed heavily on him.

The agony of dead ends and false hopes were etched now in every crease and wrinkle of the witch hunter's face. His eyes betrayed the depth of his suffering.

Jon Skellan was a haunted man.

His ghosts were not kindly spirits come to shape his future, they were bitter revenants that came tearing up from his past with hate enough to turn any heart black. Wearing the guises of loved ones they taunted him with his failure. They threw it in his face, branding him useless, their accusations dripped with the venom of self-loathing because that, after all, was exactly what these ghosts he carried with him were: projections of his own self-loathing, his own bitterness, his own hate. It was Skellan who couldn't bear to look at himself in the mirror anymore.

He knew that and yet still he let them get to him.

He obsessed on one unassailable fact: Sebastian Aigner was still out there. Still alive.

The murderer's continued existence taunted Skellan day and night.

It was as though the pair were locked in some perverse game of cat-and-mouse that was being played on the streets of Drakenhof. Several times since their arrival in the city Skellan and Fischer had come within a whisker of confronting Aigner, Aigner having moved on mere minutes before their arrival. They were close enough they could smell the man's rank body odour in the musty air of the taverns and gambling dens, only for them be left scratching their heads with the murderer having seemingly vanished into thin air by the time they made it back out onto the street.

A long time ago Skellan had reached the only reasonable conclusion he could: that some very powerful people were shielding his wife's murderer.

It wasn't a pleasant thought. It made him doubt who he could trust, made him spurn help where it was offered and made him turn on those who offered friendship.

So he stayed, and he waited, forcing himself to find patience where there was only the desperate need for resolution and restitution. He listened to the stories surfacing almost daily. First it was tales of the wasting sickness ravaging the Sylvanian aristocracy, and the tragic accidents that befell those who sought to oppose the rule of Vlad von Carstein, and then it was the anti-Sigmarite outbreaks that saw more and more of the old temples defiled.

More and more of the whisperers offered their own copper coin's worth of wisdom along with the rumours. Every third or fourth gossip fastened on the Cult of the Risen Dead and how they were not so slowly removing all traces of Sigmar from the Sylvanian countryside. Some could not hide their glee at the return to the older faiths; others remained more sceptical, sensing that there was more to this religious purge than simply some resurgence of the old ways and pointed to the name chosen by the cult, the Risen Dead. It played on centuries of fear, something the peasantry were all too familiar with.

Perhaps the most telling gossip revolved around the miraculous recovery of the count's wife Isabella and the fact that, unsurprisingly, she was a changed woman after the sickness, forever wan and pale. The gossips spoke about how she never left the chambers she shared with her husband, save by night.

Even now, almost a year on, Skellan remembered well the clandestine meeting he and Fischer had had with Viktor Schliemann, one of the two physicians who had attended the countess during her prolonged illness. The man had been terrified, always casting glances back over his shoulder as though afraid of who might overhear their conversation. The most memorable thing about the meeting though was the fact that Schliemann was adamant that Isabella von Carstein's heart had stopped. That she was in fact dead when he left the room.

This was immediately before the count had called the physicians fakes and dismissed them from his service.

Schliemann had been brutally murdered the morning after that meeting with Skellan.

Skellan had no fondness for coincidences. It was obvious that Schliemann had paid the highest price for his loose tongue.

Someone had wanted him silenced, which only went to convince Skellan that he had been telling the truth, that Isabella von Carstein had died and been resuscitated. It was no wonder that she had become so important to the followers of the Risen Dead. She was one of them. She had crossed over to the other side, she had breathed the foetid air of Morr's underworld, and yet she was back, walking amongst them once more, pale-faced and afraid of sunlight. She was a creature of the night, a human owl.

The old temples destroyed, the dead risen, the nobles falling victim to the same peculiar wasting sickness that meant that the castles across the land had become home to sallow-skinned nocturnal folk, these rumours all pointed to the same fundamental truth: that there was something rotten in the province of Sylvania.

Skellan made the sign of the hammer reflexively, and gazed up at the spectre of the count's gothic castle perched like some bird of prey on the mountainside, all sharp edges and jagged black towers with their blind windows staring back down at him. The castle was like nothing he had ever seen teetering there on the sheer face of the rock. The bird of prey analogy was a good one, Skellan thought wryly, though it could easily have been some misshapen gargoyle perched up there instead.

With money running low they had had a small stroke of good fortune and taken to lodging with Klaus Hollenfuer, a wine merchant in one of the less run-down parts of the city. Hollenfuer was a good man, sympathetic to their quest for justice. He could have charged them an arm and a leg for the spacious room above his wine cellar but instead of taking money he had them work off the rent, running the occasional delivery, but more often than not simply guarding his stock.

Hollenfuer didn't need them, he had a small legion of guards on his payroll and there were plenty of boys in the city who could have run his errands. They both knew that Hollenfuer kept them around because he felt sorry for them. The merchant had lost his own wife and daughter to bandits on the road to Vanhaldenschlosse a few years earlier. Part of him, he confessed one drunken evening over half-empty glasses, envied Skellan and Fischer for their relentless pursuit of Aigner and his murderous band of brothers and wished he had the guts to do the same to Boris Earbiter and his filthy horde of bandit scum.

The three of them were in the attic rooms above the wine cellar on Kaufmannstrasse. Skellan, his back to the other men, stared intently out of the small round window.

A low-lying fog had begun to settle in, it masked the city streets with a real peasouper thickness that made it difficult for him to see more than a few feet when he looked down at the streets below. Looking upwards though, toward the castle, the air was still bright and clear. The fog, however, was rising. In a few hours it would shroud the castle as completely as it already did the city streets.

He couldn't have wished for better weather for what he had in mind.

It was the perfect cloak for the subterfuge he was hoping to employ.

A steady procession of coaches and carts carrying the rich and the beautiful had been making their way up the curving road toward the black castle's lowered drawbridge all day. From a distance the gateway looked like a huge gaping maw waiting to swallow them. Totentanz, quite literally the Dance of Death, or at least a masquerade in honour of the departed, marked the eve of Geheimnisnacht. Vlad von Carstein had seen to it that absolutely anyone who was anyone would be under his roof to see in Geheimnisnacht.

Many of the coaches' passengers had travelled from the furthest reaches of the province to pay tribute to the count and his beloved Isabella, and in the process witness the unveiling of the artist Gemaetin Gist's portrait of the countess. That Gist, an old man deep into his final years, had undoubtedly created one final masterpiece was cause for jubilation. Gist hadn't accepted a commission in over a decade and many thought the old man would never hold a brush again until he was creating art for Morr in the halls of the dead. It was no small marvel that the count had somehow coaxed the man into doing one final portrait.

But then, the count was persuasive.

Drakenhof had been alive with talk of Totentanz for weeks. Seamstresses and tailors worked their fingers to the bone hurrying to create gowns to rival the beauty of their wearers. The vintners and dairy farmers crated and casked up the finest of their wares, delivering them up to the castle, the bakers and butchers prepared fresh meat and delicacies to make the mouth water. It seemed as though everyone had a part to play in the masked ball apart from Skellan and Fischer.

'Are you absolutely sure you can't be talked out of this?' Fischer asked, knowing that his friend had well and truly made his mind up and there was nothing he could do about it. He didn't like it, and he had being making his unhappiness plain ever since Skellan had shared his plan but the only thing to do now was to go along with it – ride the wave and see where it took them.

'Certain,' Skellan said, scratching his nose. It was something he did when he was nervous and didn't know what to do with his hands. 'He's up there, my friend. I know it. You know it. Can't you feel it? I can. It's in the air itself, so thick you can almost touch it. It's alive... It feels as though there is some kind of charge... A frisson. If I close my eyes I can feel it seep into my skin and cause my heart to hammer. It makes my blood sing in my veins. And I know what it means: he's close. So close. Here's my promise: it ends tonight, after eight long years. One of us will meet with Morr face to face.'

'Can you promise me it won't be you?'

'No,' Skellan said honestly. 'But believe me, if I go, I will do my damnedest to take the murdering whoreson with me.'

'Good luck to you, lad,' Hollenfuer said coming up behind him to rest a hand on his shoulder. 'It's a brave thing you are doing tonight, walking into the beast's lair. May your god guide your sword.'

'Thank you, Klaus. All right, let's go over this again, shall we?' Skellan turned away from the window. 'The final delivery is in little more than an hour, thirteen casks of various wines, two will be marked as Bretonnian. Those are the ones Fischer and I will be hiding in. Your man is waiting at the other end to uncork us, so to speak. A third cask, marked with the seal of Hochland, will contain our swords, and twin hand-held double shot crossbows along with eight bolts in two small belted sheaths. The weapons will be wrapped in oiled skins and floating in the actual wine.'

'We've been over this a thousand times, my friend,' the merchant said placatingly. 'Henrik is already up at the castle unloading an earlier shipment, your weapons are wrapped and ready to hide in the barrel. The last cart is loaded. All that remains is for you to go downstairs and for me to seal you in an empty cask of Bretonnian white. The journey to the castle will take an hour, perhaps a little more. Worry about what you will do once you are inside the castle. Let me worry about getting you in there.'

'I'm still not entirely happy about this,' Fischer said. 'I've got a bad feeling. It just keeps niggling away at the back of my mind and it won't go away.'

'That's your "old woman" instinct,' Skellan said, with an exaggerated wink at Hollenfuer. 'You know it *is* rather overdeveloped. When this is all over you'll make a wonderful harridan or shrew, my friend.'

The merchant didn't laugh. In part because he shared Fischer's misgivings but he wasn't about to voice his concerns. 'So, what say we get to work, lads?'

'Aye, the day isn't getting any younger,' Skellan said.

The three men went down four flights of stairs to the cellar where the dray was already loaded, the two carthorses harnessed and ready to roll. The barrels on the flatbed were various sizes and showed different signs of age and wear, a few of them were a dark wet brown and branded with the maker's mark while the others were made of pale dry wood. The two Bretonnian casks were barely big enough for them to squeeze into. Hollenfuer had reasoned that the smaller casks would be less suspicious than the larger beer barrels, though if an over-enthusiastic guard decided to help unload the cart he would be in for a hefty surprise.

Skellan climbed into one of the barrels, drawing his knees up tight to his chin and lowering his head. Hollenfuer pressed the lid down then hammered the seal into place. He had drilled two small air holes just beneath the second metal band cinching the barrel's girth somewhere near where the stowaways' face ought to be, but they were so small they would let precious little air into the suffocating confines of the barrel. They were big enough to keep him alive though.

It was dark and claustrophobically uncomfortable.

An hour in there was going to be nothing short of hellish.

After a few minutes he heard the banging of Fischer's cask being secured, and then the third lid being nailed shut on their weapons. One weapon didn't make it into the third cask. Skellan wore it on a leather thong around his neck, the glass phial cold against his skin as he cradled it close to his chest. It had cost him almost all of the money he had left but if it helped Aigner burn it would be worth every last coin of it.

And then they were moving. The slow gentle sway of the cart quickly became nauseating. Skellan tried to clear his mind of all thoughts but they kept coming back to the same thing – the face of the man he intended to kill.

Sebastian Aigner.

The cask muffled the sounds of the world. It was impossible to tell where they were along the road. He caught occasional snatches of Hollenfuer whistling. The man couldn't carry a tune to save his life.

Every few minutes, the sweat pooling in the hollows of his collar and the base of his spine and behind his knees, Skellan twisted around to suck in a few precious mouthfuls of fresh air. The inside of the cask was choked with the bouquet of rancid wine. Several times he had to fight back the urge to gag. Before long he found himself getting dizzy on the intoxicating fumes.

The cart jounced and juddered on the roughshod road, bouncing Skellan around in the dark. Numbness, like a thousand stabbing pins and needles, seeped into his arms and legs as his blood stopped circulating properly.

And then, after what felt like an eternity, he felt the cart begin to slow and eventually come to a standstill.

He could barely make out the strains of muffled conversation. He used his imagination to piece it together: the guard questioning the wine merchant, demanding his bill of lading, then satisfied, telling him where to leave the delivery using an unseen passage so as to avoid being seen by the steady stream of guests.

Someone banged three times in rapid succession on the lid of Skellan's barrel.

His heart stopped.

He didn't dare breathe or move.

Everything hung in the balance. It could all be over in the matter of a few seconds. Years in pursuit of justice come to nothing. He closed his eyes, waiting for the inevitable shaft of sunlight as the guard cracked open the lid of his hiding place – but it didn't come.

The cart rumbled forward again.

A shaky sigh leaked between his lips. They were inside the castle walls. They were rapidly approaching the critical moment, transferring the barrels from the cart into the count's cellars. If anything were going to go wrong it would be in the next few minutes. Skellan sent a silent prayer to Sigmar.

The barrel bumped sharply as the cartwheel rattled over a jagged stone and for a moment all sensation of movement ceased – then suddenly the barrels were being manhandled off the cart and rolled down planks into the cellar. Skellan caught himself on the brink of crying out. The shock of the violent disruption to his surroundings was both nauseating and agonizing as his body slammed into the barrel's inner wall and squashed his face up against the lid. As suddenly as it began, the turbulent spinning stopped and the seal was being broken on the lid of his wooden prison.

As the lid came off Skellan arched his back and pushed upwards, desperate to get out of the claustrophobic barrel. Like a diver surfacing after too long beneath the surface, he gasped, gulping down the musty cellar air greedily. He retched, almost choking on the air.

Hollenfuer's cellar boy Henrik hunched over the second Bretonnian white cask. He wore a look of steady concentration on his face as he worked the tip of the metal crowbar between the seal and the wood and levered it loose. From inside Fischer pushed up with both hands, forcing his way out of the barrel.

Skellan's legs buckled as he tried to stand. He caught himself on the supporting strut of a peculiar wooden contraption that was halfway between a harness and a winch. He stood there for a long moment, shaking. Henrik helped Fischer stand. In the small rectangle of failing light at the top of the gangplanks leading up out of the cellar Hollenfuer nodded once, and banged the storm covers closed. Moments later they heard the distinct crack of a whip and the creaks and groans of the cart making a slow circle before returning back to the wine cellar on Kaufmannstrasse.

Skellan looked around the cellar. The cold stones were impregnated with years of damp and limned with creeping black mould. Henrik handed them their weapons. Skellan sheathed his sword and clipped the hand-held crossbow onto his belt. The extra bolts he slipped into a boot sheath. Beside him Fischer did likewise. With his sword at his side his sense of vulnerability subsided. He clapped his friend on the back.

The ceiling was low enough to force Fischer to stoop. The bigger man moved awkwardly toward the door leading up to the kitchens.

'No retreat, no surrender,' Skellan said, taking a deep breath and following him.

They paused at the door. Sounds of frantic activity filtered down to them. The hordes of kitchen staff were no doubt working madly to get everything perfect for the count's feast.

'If we don't make it out of this,' Fischer whispered, fear glistening in his dark eyes, 'what kind of existence would you choose in your next life?'

'The same life I had once before in this one: an unknown farmer living in an out of the way corner of the Empire, a good wife, happy. I would give anything to go back to that time. To be the man I was, not the man I became.'

Fischer nodded his understanding.

'I would like to go back to that day,' he admitted. 'Though I think I would choose to die with them second time around, rather than live like this.'

This time it was Skellan who nodded.

'Enough talking, my friend. Death awaits.'

So saying, he hefted a small cask of port wine onto his shoulder and pushed open the door and walked confidently up the narrow servant's stairway. Fischer followed, two steps behind him. Skellan ignored the looks of the kitchen staff and walked straight up to the man who looked as though he was in charge.

'Where'd you want it, squire?' he said, tapping the cask with his fingers.

The cook turned up his nose and waved him away. 'Over there, with the others by the door. Then go get yourself cleaned up. You're filthy, man. The count will have your hide if he sees you like that.'

Skellan grunted and turned away. There were several small barrels and one larger one stacked against the furthest wall. He put the cask down beside the others, and walked straight out of the kitchen door. The passageway divided into three, one fork going left, another right, while the third continued straight on. Without knowing which way to go, he opted to go straight on for sake of expediency. It would be easier to find his way back if it proved to be the wrong choice.

They moved quickly through the belly of the castle in search of a stairway leading up. It wasn't difficult to find one.

Noise drew them toward the great hall. The passageways increased in richness, going from cold stone to tapestry-lined walls with various depictions of hunting and reclined beauties, each passage opening into a wider one until it finally opened into the great hall itself, the buzz turned into a roar of noise.

The great hall was alive with a swarm of people flitting from place to place, the buzz of conversation constant. All of the guests wore peculiar skull masks, making it appear as though they themselves had risen fresh from the grave. As Skellan and Fischer entered the hall two young serving girls swooped down seemingly out of nowhere and pressed masks into their hands. Skellan took his gratefully and quickly covered his face.

'How in Sigmar's name are we going to find him if he's wearing a bloody mask?' Fischer cursed behind him.

The hall was already stiflingly hot, the air thick with humidity. Given the amount of people already present it was hardly surprising. Skellan noticed more than a few ladies fanning themselves almost constantly as they turned and turned about to survey the gathering. The place was a riot of clashing colours. Beside the count's obsidian throne a row of violinists and cellists conjured a symphony of music, the third concerto of Adolphus, the blind Sigmarite monk, each note resonating with a pure unblemished simplicity that bordered on the divine. Skellan stopped in the middle of the press of people and let the music wash over him like a crashing wave. It was beautiful; there really was no other word to describe it.

On the opposite side of the obsidian throne a large dais hand been constructed and on it stood Gemaetin Gist's portrait of Isabella von Carstein, hidden beneath a plain scarlet curtain.

There was a fluid grace to the way the guests moved across the floor as though they were all part of some huge orchestrated dance, but where it aimed at sophistication there was something decidedly more tribal and ritualistic about the whole performance.

Skellan scanned the dizzying array of facemasks hoping to catch a glimpse of the people lurking behind the bone. Cold certainty settled in his gut: Aigner was among them. He knew it. One of those masks hid the man who murdered his wife.

Skellan pushed deeper into the crowd.

Fischer struggled to match his momentum.

The music surged. Bodies swarmed and pressed on all sides.

Skellan stared at mask after mask, a hideous dance of death being played out before his eyes. It was hopeless. To be so close, within touching distance at least once, almost certainly, and not being able to recognise his quarry. He clenched his fists. More than anything at that moment he wanted to lash out with frustration.

The tempo of the music shifted into something more melancholy. Skellan stood in the centre of the great hall, looking left and right. And then, he looked up, at the gallery overlooking the floor. A cadaverous young man braced himself on the mahogany balustrade, studying the dancers as though he were watching a swarm of flies crawling over the carcass of some long dead animal. His distaste was obvious. Behind him were five men, two of whom bore a striking resemblance to the count himself. Some sort of family, Skellan reasoned. The other three were muscle, ready to interject if things on the dance floor got out of hand thanks to a rowdy drinker or an angry borderland baron making a scene.

Skellan scanned the second gallery behind him. Again it was lined with attentive spectators, well dressed but obviously guards. One wore twin blades in a curious double sheath on his back. While the blades were interesting it was the shaven head of the man beside the sword-bearer that stopped Skellan dead in his tracks.

The years had not been kind to Sebastian Aigner.

Far from it. In the eight years since he had ridden into Skellan's village with his murderous brethren the man had aged twenty. He looked different, not just older. It was something about the way he held himself. He looked like a man resigned to his fate. That was it. Skellan had seen the look before in those he had condemned to a fiery death. The mark of damnation hung over Aigner's head.

It was all Jon Skellan could do not to unclip the hand-held crossbow at his side and bury a metal-tipped bolt in the man's throat there and then. He imagined himself doing it, raising the small crossbow slowly, squeezing down on the trigger mechanism and watching the deadly bolt punch into Aigner's throat, the momentary look of shock, bewilderment, before the blood pulsed out of the wound, through his desperate fingers as he clutched at his throat trying to keep it back. An icy satisfaction settled like a smooth sided stone in Skellan's gut. It ended here, tonight.

'I see him,' he said just loudly enough for his words to carry to Fischer.

Fischer turned and quickly scanned the gallery. He almost didn't recognise the man. His shaved head and the heavy criss-crossing of scars on his scalp made Aigner look very different.

'It's him,' Fischer agreed.

He looked around the great hall for a stairway that led up to the gallery but there were nothing obvious. Several of the stone columns around the room were covered by thick velvet drapes, and magnificent tapestries hung from two of the four walls. Any one of them could have hidden a door or a staircase.

Skellan pushed toward the edge of the great hall, his head swimming with thoughts of vengeance. Bodies closed around him, cutting him off from Fischer. He kept pushing forward, squeezing through gaps that weren't really there. The time signature of the music shifted again, into a heady cantante, the violins replacing the voice of the singer as the music spiralled into its triumphant crescendo.

In the second of awed silence that followed, a collective gasp escaped the lips of the milling dancers. The count, Vlad von Carstein and his beautiful wife Isabella stepped through the oaken doors behind the obsidian throne. The man moved with predatory grace, the woman like his shadow. The pair were so perfectly in time with each other. The count raised his wife's hand high, and bowed low to a ripple of applause.

There was something about the man that set Skellan's skin crawling. It wasn't anything obvious. There was no mark of Chaos hanging over him. It was subtle but it was there. A faint nagging something. In part it could have been down to the arrogance with which the man carried himself, but that was not it, at least not all of it. He might not have been able to divine the cause, but the effect was plain to see, the partygoers viewed the count with awe. Death masks slipped down to reveal wide-eyed adoration. Vlad von Carstein owned these people body and soul. He had a mesmerist's draw on them.

Skellan knew that von Carstein was no different from a great puppet master: every one of the people in the great hall would dance to his whim. The woman on the other hand, was easy to read. There was a raw sexuality about her and she knew it. A measured look here, a slight smile there, a teasing touch, the tip of her tongue lingering just slightly too long on her fulsome lips, a toss of the head to accentuate the swanlike grace of her neck and the cascade of her dark hair as it spilled down her back. She played with them almost as well as her husband did, but where he carried a faint air of melancholy with him she radiated the self-assurance of power. Real power.

The crowd parted to let them pass.

Skellan used the distraction of von Carstein's arrival to slip away unnoticed. He glanced back over his shoulder. Toadying guests all hungry to get close to the count and his lady fenced Fischer in. Skellan had no choice. He couldn't go back for him and he couldn't risk waiting. The choices of a warrior were simple: in a difficult situation, press on, when surrounded, look for weaknesses in your enemy's strategy that can be exploited, when confronted with death, fight. He had no choice. Skellan left Fischer staring helplessly as his back as he disappeared through the crowd.

Behind him, Fischer tried to barge his way through the bodies but the sheer weight of people pushed him back.

'Friends,' von Carstein said, his voice cutting through the falling hubbub. 'Be welcome in my home, for today we celebrate the most fragile of things and the most finite, life, and revel in the infinite, death. We come together as faceless constructs, bare bones that make us indistinguishable from one and other, in that we are equal.' There were a few murmurs of ascent. 'Equal in life and in death. Tonight we throw our inhibitions to the wind and give ourselves over to the music of these fine players. We are blessed with wonderful food and wine brought in from the very finest corners of the province. So, I urge you to surrender to the spirit of Totentanz. It is, after all, the dance of the dead, and who are we mere mortals to withstand such august company? Raise a glass to the restless dead, my friends! To the ghosts, the shades, the ghouls, the wraiths, the wights, the banshees, the liches, the mummies, the nightmares, the weres, the shadows, the zombies, the spectres, the phantasms, and of course,' he slowed down, letting his voice sink to the merest whisper. The count didn't need to shout. His voice carried to each and every guest, raising goose pimples of anticipation along their flesh, 'the vampires.'

A burst of applause greeted von Carstein's toast. Cries of: 'To the dead!' echoed around the room.

Skellan reached the first of four red velvet curtains bearing the crest of Sylvania. One of them, he hoped, would reveal a short flight of stairs leading up to the gallery. He paused to look up at Aigner. The man appeared almost bored by the proceedings. Aigner leaned on the mahogany balustrade clenching and unclenching his fists. Beside him more of von Carstein's cronies were chuckling.

Skellan pushed aside the curtain. As he had suspected, the red cloth hid a passageway. This one led off deeper into the castle but there was no sign of a staircase leading up to the gallery so he let the curtain fall closed again. The second curtain hid a barred door. The third opened on to another passage that disappeared into the darkness of Drakenhof's lower levels. He slipped behind the final curtain and into a tight embrasure that turned into an even tighter staircase.

The music started up again behind him.

SKELLAN CLIMBED THE stairs. Countless thoughts chased through his head like blind runners stumbling across each other. He couldn't think straight. It didn't matter. He didn't need to. His hands trembled with anticipation as he pulled the leather thong over his head. The glass phial was all that he needed.

He was glad Fischer had become trapped within the surging crowd. He hadn't been entirely truthful. He knew the risks coming here. He was going to kill Aigner in front of hundreds of people. He didn't expect to walk out of Drakenhof. It didn't matter. All that mattered was that Lizbet was finally avenged, that the circle of violence closed here, tonight.

Death had long since ceased to frighten him – after all, what was there to be afraid of? Lizbet would be waiting for him in the Kingdom of Morr. They would be together again. In that, von Carstein had been right when he said death was cause for celebration.

He paused before he stepped out onto the gallery. The violins rose in shrieking chorus, masking the sound of his footsteps.

There were four men on the gallery with Aigner.

Skellan didn't care, he only had eyes for Aigner. The others were insignificant. His fist closed around the glass phial. One of the others, the shortest of the four, turned and saw him. A look of distaste spread across the man's face.

'Downstairs, you ain't allowed up here.'

'I go where I please,' Skellan said.

Aigner turned at the sound of his voice.

For a moment Skellan fancied he saw a glimmer of recognition in the murderer's eyes, but more likely, he saw it because he wanted it to be there. A cunning smile spread across the shaven-headed man's skeletal face.

'You do, do you?' Aigner said. His voice was every bit as hateful as Skellan remembered. 'Well, not today. Back downstairs before I decide to teach you a lesson you won't quickly forget.'

'I don't forget anything.' Skellan moved forward two more steps until Aigner was just beyond arms reach. 'Not my wife, not my daughter, not my friends.' He touched his temple. 'They're all in here. Like the murdering scum you brought to my village. They're in here. Burning.'

'Ahhh,' Sebastian Aigner said, realisation dawning. 'So *you're* the witch hunter, are you? I was expecting someone... taller.'

'Is this going to be a problem, Sebastian?' The swordsman with the twin curved blades asked. He instinctively moved to put himself between Aigner and Skellan.

'No,' Aigner said, shaking his head. 'No problem at all, Posner. Our friend here was just dying.'

Aigner's slow smile flashed in to a dangerous grin. His lips curled back on sharp teeth.

'You first,' Skellan said, taking one step forward and slamming his fist up into Aigner's face. The glass phial shattered spilling its contents into Aigner's eyes and down his cheeks.

Aigner's hands flew up to his face, slapping and clawing at the acid as it seared into his skin. Pink froth sizzled between his fingers. Blood ran down the backs of his hands. Skellan didn't move. Aigner staggered forward a lumbering step. His mouth moved but the incessant violins drowned out his screams; violent music to match Aigner's violent contortions as the acid ran into his mouth and down his throat, eating away at his flesh as it did so. He lifted his hands away from his face. Half of his right cheek was gone, dissolved in a mess of blood and bone. A rash of pustulent blisters seethed across his cheeks, chin and neck, popping, sizzling and spitting as the acid continued to melt into what was left of his face. Rage burned in his one good eye. The other was gone, black and blind where the acid had burned through it.

Skellan moved quickly. He reached for the hand-held crossbow at his waist, unclipped it and levelled it squarely at Aigner's chest.

'You killed my wife... Death isn't good enough for you.'

He squeezed the trigger mechanism twice in quick succession. Two feathered shafts slammed into Aigner's chest, punching him back off his feet. He sprawled across the gallery's floor, blood and gore leaking from the wounds. Writhing on the deck, Aigner gripped one of the bolts in his bloody fist and yanked it free. His face contorted with pain.

Standing beside him, Herman Posner drew one of his twin blades and tossed it to Skellan. 'Finish him off. This isn't pretty.'

'It shouldn't be pretty,' Skellan said flatly. He stepped over Aigner's body and raised the borrowed sword. None of the others moved. It was as though a spell held them transfixed. 'And it shouldn't be fast.' He plunged the blade into Aigner's gut, wrenching it left and then right to open the wound wider, then pulled it out.

'That won't do it,' Posner said. 'Take his head off.'

Skellan hesitated.

'Do it.'

Suddenly, Aigner reared up, his face contorted in a mask of rage. The skin had dissolved around his cheeks and lower jaw, baring razor-sharp fangs. His claws raked blindly toward Skellan's face.

Skellan stepped sideways and back a step, bringing the sword around in a savage arc. The wickedly curved blade cut clean through the murderer's neck and spine, sending his decapitated head bouncing and spinning across the floor. There was precious little blood, considering the wound. A trickle rather than a fountain. One of the count's men stopped it with his foot. Aigner's dead eyes stared accusingly at Skellan. For a heartbeat Aigner's body continued to rise before it slumped to the floor, dead.

The waspish violin music swarmed around them as the musicians played on, oblivious to the killing that had taken place mere feet from them.

Skellan stood over the corpse of the man who had ruined his life. This final vengeance did not taste sweet. There was no satisfaction in the slaying. He looked down at the ruined face, still hissing and sizzling as the acid burned away more and more of the fatty tissue. Given time the acid would strip the head of all its soft tissue and dissolve the brain so all that remained would be the clean white bone plates of the dead man's skull.

'That was personal, was it?' Posner asked.

'Yes.'

'And it is over now? Finished?'

'Yes.'

'Good. That is good. My man did wrong by you and you claimed your justice, I can respect that... but it leaves me with a problem.'

'How so?'

'You killed my man, I can't let you walk away from here without recompense.'

'I understand.'

'And yet you aren't grovelling pitifully for your life. I can respect that as well.'

'I am not afraid to die. I came here tonight expecting to. It doesn't matter to me if I walk away from here. I have done what I set out to do. From now there is no purpose to my life. The sooner I die, the sooner I am reunited with my wife.'

'Ahhh, so that is your story? I understand. But if I were you I wouldn't look forward to any tear-filled reunions in the halls of the dead just yet. What is your name?'

'Jon Skellan.'

'Well, Jon Skellan, you killed my man. As I said, this causes me a problem.'

'And I said kill me,' Skellan said.

'In time. But you see, killing you doesn't *hurt* you. You've said it yourself, you want to die. You are finished here. You have avenged your loved ones. So killing you doesn't give *me* my justice.'

Skellan saw Fischer lurking in the door behind Posner's shoulder. He had come up a different way to the gallery. His hand rested on the handle grip of his own short crossbow. Skellan shook his head. This wasn't what he wanted. This was about his life, not his friend's. He turned, as though to look over the balcony at the guests of the count's masquerade.

Posner followed the direction of his gaze.

'Oh, their time will come. But you, Jon Skellan, what to do with you? My instinct, I must admit is to kill you, but as we've established, I can't do that, and besides killing you doesn't solve the fact that I am a man short.'

'Just do what you want to do and have done with it.' Skellan said. Posner's curved sabre slipped through his fingers and clattered to the floor. 'I'm finished here.'

The music down below lapsed into momentary silence.

'No, you're not,' Herman Posner said thoughtfully. 'It's just beginning.' His grin revealed predatory fangs. In the lull between arrangements, with the others laughing, Posner's face shifted, his smile disappearing as his features stretched. His cheekbones lifted and the bones beneath his face formed and reformed as though liquid. His jaw elongated and the line of his ears sharpened as the animal beneath his skin rose to the surface.

The transformation complete, Posner's roar was purely animalistic.

He flew at Skellan, slapping aside his ineffectual defence, grabbed a fistful of hair and yanked his head back, exposing his neck. For a full five heartbeats Posner held him like that, locked in a parody of a lover's embrace, before he sank his teeth into the soft, ripe flesh and drank greedily.

Skellan's limbs flapped, for the first few seconds, fiercely as he fought for his life, and then more and more weakly as his will to live faded into oblivion. He felt himself slipping away, his sense of self fragmenting into innumerable shards, parts of his life, forgotten memories of childhood, of Lizbet, of happiness, sadness, anger, and all he could think was: *so this is death...*

Then he felt the warm sticky wetness in his mouth as it filled with blood. His own blood and Posner's blood mingling.

Sated, Posner threw his head back and howled before hurling Skellan's limp body over the balustrade and into the middle of the revels below.

It took a second and then the shrieks and the screams began.

From the doorway Fischer loosed two crossbow bolts; one fired high and wide into the ceiling of the great hall, the other embedded itself in the neck of one of Posner's men. He didn't fall. Reaching up the man wrenched the bolt free of the wound in his neck even as a tiny dribble of blood oozed from the gaping wound. The man snarled and dropped into a crouch, his face undergoing the same hideous transformation Posner's had moments before.

Fischer turned and ran for his life.

Down below, Vlad von Carstein's voice cut through the pandemonium. 'Ah, first blood has been drawn. Yes. Yes. Reveal yourselves. Let out the beast within! The festivities can truly begin! Drink! Drink the wine of humanity!'

From both galleries above the great hall von Carstein's vampires leapt over the balcony and fell upon the revellers.

What followed was nothing short of slaughter.

CHAPTER SEVEN

Kingdom of the Risen Dead

CASTLE DRAKENHOF
Early winter, 2010

GANZ HAD ALWAYS known the truth.

But knowing and believing were two very different beasts.

They were animals.

No. They were worse than animals.

When the music stopped there was only the sound of the screams.

The fiends leapt from the galleries and fell upon the terrified revellers in a frenzy of feeding. Their teeth and claws ripped and rent at the pretty dresses and the pale flesh tearing their prey apart piece by bloody piece.

Alten Ganz looked away.

On the gallery opposite him Herman Posner watched the slaughter with disinterest, as though he had seen it all before, which, Ganz realised with a shudder, he probably had. The man's face had metamorphosed into that of a beast: the beast within. Posner wasn't a man any more than the count was, or Isabella or any of the others. The night travelling, the thick velvet curtains to keep out the day, his preternatural grace, it all made sense. Ganz thought of all the evenings he had stood on the battlements listening to von Carstein lament the transient nature of life, his obsession with beauty, even the portrait gallery, the countless paintings of the count. It all made sense.

Posner saw him staring and, teeth bared, flashed him a dangerous grin.

Ganz looked away again.

People were dying all around him. There was nowhere he could look without seeing some act of brutality. Death, this death offered by von Carstein's vampires, was not pretty. It was bloody and wretched. There would be nothing left to bury but bones.

The count was in the centre of it, detached from the bloodlust of his kin. Unlike the others, his face had not undergone a grotesque transformation. The countess, though, had given herself to the feeding frenzy. Her gown was soaked in the gore of countless partygoers' lives and still she threw herself into the slaughter. The carnage was incredible.

In a matter of minutes they were all dead.

Only then did Posner join his monstrous kin on the killing floor. He walked through the bodies without thought for who or what they had been.

'Was it everything you dreamt it would be?' Posner said, his voice echoing weirdly in the suddenly silent hall.

'And more,' Isabella answered. She was on her knees, her face smeared with the blood of the newly dead aristocracy. She jumped up and rushed over to the dais where her portrait had been knocked to the floor in the fighting. She knelt over it, staring at the face she hadn't seen for so long. 'Do you think I'm pretty?'

'It does not do you justice, countess,' Posner said.

'You think?' A flush of happiness brought a smile to her bloody lips.

'Gist is a master, but even a master cannot hope to render such flawless beauty with a clumsy brush.'

'Gist is dead,' Isabella said, lost suddenly in the memory of it. 'I ate him.'

'Is, was, it matters not, countess. The choice of words is nothing more than semantics. The proof of his labours is there in your hands, a timeless reminder of your beauty. If you forget yourself you need only gaze upon it as it hangs on the wall to be reminded. And for us beauty never fades.'

'Yes.' Isabella mused. 'Yes. I should like that. I am beautiful, aren't I?'

'Yes, countess.'

'And it will always be this way?'

'Yes, countess. For eternity.'

'Thank you, Herman.'

Posner turned to see the count reaching out to his wife. There wasn't a single fleck of blood on him. 'Come,' he said. She rose and picked a path through the corpses like a butterfly flitting from flower to flower. Posner followed her and von Carstein to the battlements. Alten Ganz knew where the count was going – there was only one place he would go – so he raced up to the rooftops via the servants stairs, panting and gasping as he pushed himself to keep on running up the different staircases. He was already there when von Carstein arrived. The battlements were thronged with ravens nesting along the crenellations and in the eaves and crevices of the gothic architecture. Feathers ruffled and wings beat as the count burst out onto the roof with Posner and Isabella trailing in his wake.

'Geheimnisnacht,' von Carstein said, no hint of breathlessness in his voice. 'A night like no other. Do you have it, Ganz?' He held out a hand expectantly.

Ganz reached inside the folds of his cloak and drew out a single sheet of parchment. His hand trembled as he handed it over to his master. He had looked at the parchment and though he couldn't read most of the arcane scrawl he recognised it for what it was: an incantation.

'My thanks. This single piece of paper will change the world as we know it.' His words snatched away by the rising wind, von Carstein savoured the thought. 'No more will we walk in fear, no more will we hide in shadows. This is our time. Now. With this single piece of paper we change the world.'

Isabella wrapped herself around her husband's side, her hair streaming in the wind, naked hunger in her eyes.

Posner stared out over the battlements at the city below, shrouded in fog and darkness.

Ganz didn't move. He stared at the brittle parchment in his master's hand. Only it wasn't parchment or paper or even vellum, he knew, it was flesh and blood, or rather skin and blood. The incantation written in blood on a sheet of cured human skin. The letters were the faded rust of blood and the texture of the parchment was unmistakable.

'Read it, my love,' Isabella whispered.

'Do you know what this is?' Vlad asked. Without waiting for an answer, he continued. 'One page from the nine Books of Nagash. Hand-written by Nagash himself, the blood on this page was shaped with his own hand. This is but a fraction of his wisdom, a hint at the wonders that held the key to his immortality. These words unlock the Kingdom of the Dead. This one page is precious beyond money. This one page... the power in it... The words give life, revification of the flesh... They offer a way back for all those who have gone – imagine – with this there can be no death. Not as we know it. Not as a meaningful thing, the end of a life lived to the full. With this the dead will rise to stand at my side. If I will it they will fight at my side as I march across the Empire of mortal men. Death shall have no dominion. With these words I shall command the flesh. I shall return life where I see fit. Fight me, face my wrath, I shall kill my enemies and then raise them to fight *for* me as I conquer the world. With these few words I shall raise the dead from their earthly prisons. I shall speak and in speaking become a dark and hungry god. I, Vlad von Carstein, first of the Vampire Counts of Sylvania, shall have dominion over the realms of life and death. As I say, so it shall be.'

'Read it,' Isabella pressed. She nuzzled in close to Vlad, her tongue trailing luxuriantly across his cheek, kissing and nibbling up to his ear. She breathed heavily into his ear before the trail of hot wet kisses led to the Vampire Count's neck, her teeth closing to bite in a sensuous re-enactment of her own siring.

'No,' Ganz said. He held out his hand as though asking for the parchment back.

'You would that it stays the way it is? The way it has always been? With my kind forced to hide from daylight, vilified by the stupid masses? Hunted by fools with stakes and garlic cloves like wild animals fit for nothing but slaying?'

'No,' Ganz repeated. He was visibly trembling. Still he held his hand out as though he truly expected the Vampire Count to surrender the incantation without unleashing its curse on the world.

'Are you afraid, Ganz? Are you afraid of a world full of the risen dead? Are you afraid that they will see you as I see you? As meat?'

Ganz looked at them all one at a time, studying them and seeing them for what they were for the first time in his life. They were nature's predators. They hunted to survive. The slaughter downstairs was evidence of that. What was he to them? He knew the answer. The truth. He always had.

Prey.

They weren't equals. They weren't even comparable. They had eternity where he was a mote caught in the eye of time. One blink and he was gone.

'Kill me,' he said, looking the Vampire Count in the eye. 'Make me like you.'

'No,' von Carstein said, breaking eye contact.

'Why? Aren't I good enough? Haven't I proved my loyalty?'

'You are nothing more than meat,' Posner said, not bothering to hide his distaste of Ganz's humanity.

'Quiet, Herman. Of course you are loyal, and valued. It is precisely because of that that I cannot – no I will not – turn you. I need a man to walk in the world of day, to be my voice. I trust you Ganz. Do you understand? You are more valuable to me as you are.'

'As meat.'

'As meat,' the count agreed.

'When this is over?'

'It will never be over. Not truly.'

'And if I throw myself off the battlements?'

'You will serve me in death, a mindless automaton. Would you wish that upon yourself?' von Carstein asked in all seriousness. 'Would you choose an undeath as a shambling zombie?'

'No,' Ganz admitted.

'Then be happy with what you are, and serve me with all of your heart. Or I might let Herman eat it.'

'I'll be the last of my kind... the last living man in the Kingdom of the Dead.' The thought of it was more than he could bear. Ganz sank to his knees, and lowered his head until his forehead touched the cold stone of the castle's rooftop. 'Kill me,' he pleaded, but von Carstein ignored him.

The Vampire Count stood upon the highest point of the castle, the mountain's teeth rising into the moonlight behind him like ghostly fangs.

'Hear me!' he called out into the darkness. 'Obey me!'

And he began to recite the incantation. Even as the first words left his mouth the heavens above split with a mighty crack and the first fat drops of rain began to fall. The ravens exploded from their nests, cawing frantically as they circled, a seething mass of black wings. From nothing rose a storm so violent it ripped and tore at the roof slates of Drakenhof and sent the loose ones spinning into the night to shatter on impact as they fell from the sky. Posner stood implacably in the midst of the driving rain. Beside him Isabella's expression was one of delicious expectancy. Vlad's obsessive chant was caught and ripped away into the night by the rising wind, the impact of his words carried to the farthest corners of Sylvania. Driven, he plunged on, calling out to the vilest forces in the universe, demanding they bend to his will.

Ganz raised his head to stare at the man he revered. The winds howling around the battlements rose to gale force. Sheets of rain pounded the mountainside. Amid the eye of the storm the Vampire Count threw back his head and bellowed another command from Nagash's damned book. The words meant nothing to Ganz. The wind tore at von Carstein's clothes and hair, buffeting and battering him. He read on, caught up in the sheer power of the incantation, his words tripping over themselves in their eagerness to be free of his mouth. Thunder crashed. A spear of brilliant white lightning split the night.

The transformation of Vlad von Carstein was highlighted in another jag of lightning; in the space of a few gut-wrenching syllables his face elongated and hardened into the bestial mask of the vampire, the contours of his brow sharpened, a feral snarl curling his lips, baring long canine incisors. The Vampire Count threw his head back against the wind, demanding the dead rise and do his bidding.

'Come to me! Rise! Walk again my children! Rise! Rise! Rise!'

And across the land the dead heard his call and stirred.

Bodies so long underground the flesh had been stripped by maggots and worms clawed and scratched at the confines of their coffins, chipping and splintering their skeletal fingers as they tore through first the cloth shroud and then the coffin lid. In their mass graves, newly dead plague victims sighed and shuddered as the agony of life returned to their revived corpses, the sickness that had stolen their lives, eaten away at their flesh and stilled their heart not enough to deny the call of the Vampire Count. In secluded corners of the province, forgotten by all but the murderers who left them there, the dirt of the unconsecrated graves hidden in forests and fields and roadside ditches rippled and churned as their restless residents gave themselves to a slow painful rebirth.

And below them, in the great hall of Drakenhof Castle, the revellers stirred and sighed and found life once more in their bodies, their souls denied eternal rest, the demands of von Carstein's magic bringing them back as nothing more than mindless zombies; all that was, save for one.

Jon Skellan.

He tasted the blood of the vampire on his tongue where it mingled with his own, and felt the aching need to feed, the burning hunger that accompanied his damnation and the madness of knowing, of understanding, suddenly what Posner had done to him. Skellan knew what he had become and finally understood the tragedy of it: how his last greatest peace had been stolen from him. There would be no reunion with Lizbet in this life or the next.

Skellan's tortured screams rent the night in two.

CHAPTER EIGHT

Into the Barren Lands

SYLVANIA
Winter, 2010

STEFAN FISCHER RAN for his life.

He staggered and stumbled and forced himself to run on. Hunger ate away at him. Some days he was lucky and feasted on the meat of a giant rat or long nosed tapir, other days he subsisted on roots from plants, there were no fruits or berries. On the worst days he went hungry.

After three weeks of running the snows came. At first gentle, they didn't settle but as the climate continued to drop the snow stopped melting as it fell. Winter arrived.

It would be the death of him if he didn't find warmth and shelter soon. A few roots and bugs weren't going to be enough to keep him alive. And that was what it all came down to: staying alive.

He stumbled on, into the boggy marshland west of Dark Moor, the spectre of Vanhaldenschlosse black in the distance like the ghostly claws of a revenant shade. Insects and mosquitoes swarmed all over him day and night, biting and sucking at his blood. For every one he slapped away or killed, ten more swarmed in to take its place feeding on his fresh meat. The only respite he got from the bloodsucking insects was at night, if he managed to gather the fixings to make a fire. The smoke drove them away.

By cover of night he stole a coracle from a small settlement on the outskirts of the marsh and for the last three days had been poling the small boat slowly through the reeds and rushes. He had eaten nothing for two days. Hunger left him dizzy and delirious. In the delirium he remembered snatches of Geheimnisnacht, the masquerade, the beautiful people in their bone masks, and the slaughter that followed. There was a nightmarish quality to it but that was no surprise, every minute of every day since Geheimnisnacht had been part of one long unending nightmare.

His only thought now was that he had to escape Sylvania. He had to make it back to the Empire so that he might warn people of von Carstein's true nature.

Not that he expected anyone to believe him.

The dead rising from their graves, the count and his cohorts gathering an army of the damned to their side. Who in their right mind would believe him? It was hard enough for him to believe and he had lived through it. It was still fresh in his mind – and it always would be. The images of death and destruction had seared themselves into his mind's eye.

FISCHER STUMBLED DOWN *the narrow stairs, his heart hammering in his chest. Skellan was dead. That... that... thing had thrown his corpse over the gallery rail. The Totentanz was a trap and Skellan's death acted as the spring that sent the jaws slamming down. He staggered out of the stairwell. A woman still clutching her bone mask stumbled into his arms. Her throat had been torn out. The blood and the gore spilled from the open wound, down the front of her dress. She died in his arms, her lifeblood oozing out all over him. The great hall was in chaos. People screaming, running, dying. The vampires descended in a feeding frenzy. Flight was impossible. Everyone who ran for one of the exits from the great hall was chased down and slaughtered by one of von Carstein's vampires. He was going to die here, in this foreign place, unmourned, food for one of the damned. He staggered forward. The woman's dead weight dragged her from his hands. People were dying all around him. There was nowhere to run. Nowhere to hide.*

Something slammed into his back, propelling him off his feet. Fischer sprawled forward, arms outstretched to break his fall, and landed in a bloody pool of spilled viscera. The blood was still warm on his hands and face. The screams were unbearable. He slipped and slithered through the gore, pulling a dead man across his body and lay there under the gutted corpse, staring blankly up toward the ceiling and praying fervently that the vampires would miss him. It was almost impossible not to gag on the wretched stench of death. He wanted desperately to breathe but couldn't, not more than a sip of corrupt air at a time. It was all he could do not to cry out in revulsion. Tatters of flesh were stripped and thrown around the death room. Blood sprayed over everything. The feeding frenzy went on unabated, the vampires playing with the last few revellers, spinning them from vampire to vampire, cutting them and pushing them away until they tired of the game and bit their victims' throats out and drained every last ounce of blood before they discarded their corpses like rag dolls.

The vampires moved through the room, pulling trinkets and jewellery from the corpses and arguing over the spoils after von Carstein disappeared upstairs. He was lucky – they weren't looking for survivors, they were sated from the feeding and interested in gold and jewels. He had neither on him so he was left alone. The silence was unerring but it did not last long. Long minutes later it was replaced by cracks of thunder and the sound of rain lashing at the windows as a storm raged outside.

Still Fischer didn't move, even as around him the nightmarish scene of slaughter became a macabre resurrection, one after another the gutted, slashed, and gored partygoers rose awkwardly, answering some unheard call. In the midst of it all he saw Skellan rise, his hands going to the wound on his neck where Herman Posner had bitten him. Mimicking the dead, Fischer pushed himself jerkily to his feet. He wanted desperately to go to his friend – for a moment he though that it really was Jon Skellan there, that somehow he had survived the slaughter, where the others shambled about the great hall like mindless zombies Skellan appeared to be thinking, remembering what had happened. Then he screamed and his scream was far from human. It was the last trace of humanity fleeing from his vampiric form. Silent tears slid down Fischer's cheeks as he said a final goodbye to his friend. With the milling corpses bumping into each other as they struggled to retain control of their awkward limbs Fischer slipped behind one of the velvet curtains, moving slowly, like one of the lost souls he had just abandoned. No one followed him as he snuck into the kitchens and then down again into the cellars. And then he was out into the fresh air, the rain soaking him and washing the blood from his face as he staggered about in the darkness looking for a way out.

He stole a black stallion from the count's stables and rode it into the ground. The horse died beneath him. He cut the dead animal open, filleting a few cuts of meat from it, which he stuffed into his pockets, and then he ran.

THE RESURRECTIONS WERE not contained to the revellers either. In the six weeks he had been running Fischer had come across pockets of shambling undead, recently raised from gardens of Morr and mausoleums across the countryside, the dirt of the graves still clinging to their rotten flesh, all moving unerringly in the direction of Drakenhof Castle.

They were answering von Carstein's call.

The Vampire Count was drawing the dead to him, summoning them from the grave to his side. More and more bodies, almost as though he were raising an army… a monstrous undead regiment. But why? And it came to him then. Von Carstein could only have a single purpose for raising an undead army: to wage war on the Empire.

Fischer pushed the pole deep into the saturated ground, propelling the coracle deeper into the marsh.

He had to survive.

He had to warn people what monsters were coming their way.

Without his warning town after town would succumb to the same bloody slaughter that he had lived through on Geheimnisnacht.

He wouldn't – couldn't – allow that to happen.

He had to survive.

CHAPTER NINE
Succubus Dreams

SYLVANIA
Winter, 2010

The insects were gone and the air was fresh for the first time in more than a week.

Fischer was weak with hunger. The last thing he had eaten was a water rat that he had caught by dragging the net he had found beneath the wooden seat of the coracle through the marsh water. He had been hoping to find some kind of fish but for a starving man meat was meat. He ate it with relish only to throw most of it up less than an hour later.

He lay on his back in the small boat, looking up at the sky. Ravens circled above his head, drifting silently on high thermals. The winter sun was bright in the clear blue sky. Not for the first time he regretted not having returned to his room above Hollenfuer's wine cellars. As the winter deepened the risk of hypothermia heightened. The cold was his greatest enemy now. He had pushed himself to the point of exhaustion knowing instinctively that sleep could be as deadly as a knife in the gut. Not that sleep was something he welcomed now; every dream, no matter how fleeting, took him back to Geheimnisnacht and the slaughter in the great hall, the faces of the dead as they came back from whatever hell their souls had been consigned to, the bone masks scattered across the floor, slick with the blood of their wearers, and the vampires.

It was a constant struggle though, not giving in to the lure of exhaustion.

A smudge of black smoke on the horizon gave him a surge of fresh hope. Fire.

He pushed himself to his knees and grasped the wooden pole, sinking it deep into the muddy bottom of the marsh waters, his gaze focussed on the smoke in the distance, a litany of mumbled prayers tripping off his lips. Smoke promised habitation, a settlement of some sort, a place to get real food, warm clothing, and a real bed for a night.

Turgid brown water lapped against the side of the coracle as he propelled it toward the column of smoke.

As he neared he began to make out more shapes and details. It was a settlement, the thatched roofs glittered yellow in the sun. The realisation that he would be sleeping under a dry roof, out of the elements, for the first time in almost two months was almost too much for him to bear. He drew the pole out of the water, and hand over hand, plunged it back into the murky water, punting the small boat closer to the settlement. He began fantasising about roast meat and vegetables, a cooking fire with a grill spit and a haunch of wild boar turning over the flames, dripping fat that sizzled on the coals beneath it. Such was the intensity of the imagined sight Fischer began to salivate at the very thought of it.

He moored the coracle up against a small wooden jetty and clambered out. There were fifteen houses in total and they were all built on stilts so that they rested above the water level. Gangplanks and rope bridges joined the buildings, and each had its own small jetty where coracles and canoes were moored. Fischer had no idea why anyone would choose to live in the marsh, but at that moment he was not about to start complaining. The smoke was coming from one of the central houses, which was slightly larger than the others. The rope bridge swayed beneath Fischer as he traversed from one building to another. He lost his footing twice but didn't fall. His vision swam as dizziness threatened to overwhelm him.

He opened the door and stumbled into the welcoming warmth of a small communal hut. There were tables and chairs and a fire crackling in the hearth. There were three men in the room, who looked up, surprised by his sudden arrival. He knew what he must have looked like, collapsing through the door, his face and neck swollen with bites and stings and smeared with blood from his constant scratching at them, his hair tangled and foul with stagnant rain and sweat and his clothes utterly filthy with ground-in muck and gore, hanging off him as though he were a bag of bones, so much weight had he lost since fleeing Drakenhof.

Fischer staggered forward then stumbled and fell to his knees. He reached out a hand to grab on to something for support then fell forward. He blacked out. He had no idea how long for but when he came to he was lying on a makeshift pallet by the fire and there was a ring of concerned faces looking over him.

'Give the poor fellow some air, woman.'

'Hush your chatter, Tomas Franz, he's waking up.'

'Where?' Fischer's voice cracked. He hadn't spoken for so long it was difficult to form the words. 'Where am I?'

'Right 'ere. Middle of nowhere.'

'Take no notice of Georg. Welcome to our little village, stranger. You are, in Sumpfdorf. Vanhaldenschlosse is two days walk north-east of here, once you are out of the marsh. From there, it's maybe five days on to Eschen, ten due north to Waldenhof. A better question might be what brought you to us?'

He didn't have an answer – at least not one he cared to share. 'Trying to get... home.'

'Magda, fetch the poor man some broth. Jens, run to my house and get Olof to give you our extra blankets.' The woman commanded. She turned to Fischer, her voice immediately softening. 'What's your name, love?'

'Stefan Fischer.'

'Well Stefan, welcome to our home. You look like you need a place to rest your head. We ain't rich and we ain't proud but we don't mind helpin' folk in need. So rest up. We'll talk when you've had some of Magda's broth.' She smiled at him, and for a moment at least, the nightmares of the last few months faded away into the background. He was safe.

The boy, Jens, returned with a thick warm blanket that smelled of the woman's home: of smoke from the fireplace, of her skin, of food cooked and spiced and long since eaten. He accepted it gratefully. A shy young slip of a girl approached his bedside with a wooden bowl filled almost to the brim with steaming soup. He tried to take it from her but his hands were shaking so badly she ended up spoon-feeding Fischer while he slurped and swallowed greedily. The broth smelled delicious and tasted better. He burnt his mouth in his haste to swallow mouthful after greedy mouthful. There were vegetables in it, and some kind of stringy meat.

When he was done, the woman came and sat by his bedside and shooed the others away.

'So, Stefan Fischer, tell me your story. Nobody ends up in Sumpfdorf intentionally. Are you running away from someone or to someone? It is always one or the other.'

Fischer closed his eyes. She obviously thought he was some kind of criminal on the run from an angry magistrate. He didn't know where to start. Part of him desperately wanted to tell her the truth, all of it, just to unburden his soul, but a larger part insisted that this little haven would be safe from the insanities of the Vampire Count, that they didn't need to know about the slaughter and the gathering undead army. The horrors of the world would surely pass them by. He closed his eyes as he began to smudge the truth.

'I came to Sylvania with my friend. We were looking for a man. Now I am going home and... and my friend is dead. All I want to do is go home but I think... I think I can't... because I don't think it is there anymore... He was my home as much as any place was. We'd been together forever and now we aren't. So now I just want to get out of this godforsaken province.'

'A sad story, but then I expected nothing less. You are welcome here, Stefan Fischer. We don't have much, but what we do have is yours to share. Stay as long as you need. The world will be waiting for you when you leave. It doesn't go away, however much we might like it to.'

'Thank you. I don't even know your name.'

'Janelle.'

'Thank you, Janelle.'

'You are most welcome, Stefan.'

'Fischer. Call me Fischer. My friends do.'

'Fischer. Sleep, rest. If you need anything call Magda or my son, Jens. When you are recovered, if you still want to get out of Sylvania, I will have Jens escort you out of the marsh and put you on the road. Carry on to Warten Downs and eventually you'll come to Essen Ford, where you can cross the Stir back into Talabecland.'

THEY WERE KIND to him.

He stayed with Janelle and the good people of Sumpfdorf for five days, gathering his strength, eating well for the first time since leaving Hollenfuer's home, and sleeping. Sleep was a blessing. Only on one night did he dream of Skellan. It was a strange dream, tinged with nightmarish qualities but it wasn't frightening, only sad. In his dream Skellan's lost soul found him in the marsh and begged him for directions to Morr's Kingdom. The most haunting aspect of the dream was Skellan's sadness as he begged his friend. After years of searching for that final closure his soul was out there, cast aside, to wander in limbo for eternity while his soulless shell lived on, infected by von Carstein's evil. When the shade moved on its way Fischer was left with an uncomfortable sense of having failed his friend. Come morning he wished he had the courage to hunt down the vampire his friend had become, to release his friend from his torment, but daylight didn't bring with it false courage. The sun rising redly over the marsh only succeeded in convincing him that the whole world was going to hell and he was just one man, and alone there was nothing he could do to stop it.

True to Janelle's word Jens escorted him out of the marsh and onto the Warten Downs road. The parting was bittersweet. In Sumpfdorf he had found something he hadn't had for a long time, contentment. His spirit was at rest.

'You are welcome to come back to us, Fischer, when you have finished running. I want you to understand that. There will always be a place for you here.'

'Thank you, Janelle. I will come back one day, I promise.'

'You should not make promises you cannot keep. Say instead I will come back, if I can. Let there be no lies between us.'

Fischer smiled. 'I will come back if I can, Janelle. I think I found somewhere I could one day call home and that is something I never thought to have again.'

'You are a good man, Fischer. You will do what you have to and then you will come back to us. We will be waiting.'

Make no promises you can't keep, Fischer thought, remembering the farewell.

He was alone again, shadows on the road behind him, shadows on the road ahead of him. They had given him a fur-lined skin coat, and cleaned the filth out of his clothes. He had a pack with enough food for two weeks on the road and fresh air on his face. He felt almost human again.

Still, the road ahead promised to be a long soul-sapping journey.

'One foot in front of the other,' he said and started to walk.

THE DREAM OF Skellan haunted him, even under the full glare of the winter sun. He couldn't help but feel that he was running out on his friend when, perhaps more so than ever before, he needed him. That feeling of desertion stayed with him for the long days ahead. At the end of his third day on the road a garish gypsy caravan slowed as it was in the process of overtaking him. The travellers were in good spirits, singing songs in a language Fischer didn't understand. There were three of them up front on the flatboard seat of the painted wagon, a man, well-groomed with his fair hair wetted down and slicked back off his forehead. He was perhaps a little older than Fischer. On either side of him sat two women, one, fair like the man, who was obviously his daughter, while the other was dark and bore almost no familial resemblance. She was dangerously beautiful with pale skin and emerald green eyes. It was difficult not to stare.

'Evening, neighbour,' the man called down as the wagon drew level with Fischer.

'Evening.'

'You're on the road late, where you headed?'

'Home.'

'Indeed, and where would that would be?'

'Talabecland.'

'You are a long way from home, neighbour. Want a ride? There's room up here for one more. We don't bite.'

The dark-haired young woman leaned forward, her hair falling in front of her face. She brushed it aside slowly, her smile the first thing to appear from behind the cascade of raven black hair. 'Unless you ask us to,' she said mischievously.

'Saskia!' The man shook his head as though to say, 'What can you do?'

'If it's no trouble,' Fischer said, reaching a hand up. The man grasped it and hauled him up to the flatboard seat. The women slid along to make room for him.

They travelled well into the night.

The conversation was full of places the unlikely trio had travelled, from Kislev to Bretonnia and Tilea, far to the south of the Border Princes. They were entertainers, jongleurs. Their act was filled with music, juggling and acrobatics. During the night the man, Kennet, recited *Das Leid Ungebeten* in its eerie entirety. The Ballad of the Uninvited was the perfect ghost story for a dark night and Kennet's performance was spellbinding. His voice ached as he spoke, carried away by the keen lament of the restless dead. Ina, Kennet's other daughter, was quiet most of the time, content to listen to her father and play second fiddle to her sister. They drank cider and bitter wine, joking and telling stories. Fischer found it hard to imagine good people like these surviving in Vlad von Carstein's Kingdom of the Dead. During the ride he found his eyes wandering back to Saskia. There was something utterly compelling about her pale skin and emerald green eyes. Even though she was less than half his age Fischer found his thoughts wandering to places they hadn't visited for a long time. Desire was an emotion he had thought long since lost to him. Unlike Janelle who had made him feel safe, warm, content to be alive, Saskia set his blood on fire. Had he been a younger man it would have been easy to surrender, as it was, Fischer was not about to make a fool of himself so he contented himself with stolen glances and carnal imaginings.

That night Fischer slept fitfully, his dreams fragmented and troubled. The most disturbing snatches of them threatened to wake him. They revolved around Saskia, her dark hair falling across his face, her fingernails dragging down his chest as she nuzzled into his neck, her teeth nibbling, teasing, her breathy promise, 'Unless you ask us to' hot in his ear as her teeth sank into his neck.

He awoke in a feverish sweat, his clothes in disarray. Instead of feeling refreshed from a good long sleep he was exhausted. He felt as though he could sleep for another eight hours comfortably. He was alone inside the caravan. The caravan itself moved to the gentle sway of the road. He touched the curve of his neck, half expecting to feel a stab of pain from bite wounds. It was unblemished.

'Stupid old man, Fischer. Dreams are just dreams.'

He stretched and rearranged his clothing, making himself decent before he opened the back door. He climbed out and used the ladder on the side of the door to climb up onto the roof and join Kennet and the ladies in the driving seat. The sun, he noticed, was already setting.

'Why didn't you wake me?' he scratched his head as he sank down beside Saskia.

'We thought you needed your sleep.'

'Seems you were right. I haven't slept well lately. A lot on my mind.'

'I know. You talk in your sleep.'

'No.'

'Oh yes. You must have been having some pretty colourful nightmares. At one point you were screaming and clawing at the blankets. Were you being buried alive?'

He had vague memories of the nightmare, but all of the fragments of his dreams were disjointed. After Saskia fed off him he found himself back in Drakenhof's great hall, facing his friend over the corpses of the fallen, Skellan urging him to join him in von Carstein's vampiric horde, and then the bodies on the floor had begun to seethe and writhe as the undead slowly began to rise.

Fischer shook off the memory.

He broke his fast on a chunk of hard bread and cheese and watched the evening world go by.

As with the day before, Kennet told stories to help the time pass, and the girls sang songs. One in particular stood out. The troubadour, Deitmar Köln, had sung it in the Traitor's Head back in Leicheberg: 'The Lay of Fair Isabella'. Saskia's voice held Fischer mesmerised as it wove though the tragic story of the Vampire Count's bride, though in their telling Isabella was more than a victim, she was the instigator of her own sickness, hungry for the power of eternity. The retelling was revolting given what he knew – what he had seen with his own eyes: the countess covered in blood asking for reassurance that she was pretty, even as the monsters fed on the dead and dying. He wondered what death had done to her mind. Was she the same scheming power-hungry woman she had been in life? Or had death unhinged her mind and turned her into something far more dangerous?

'Stop,' he said. He was physically shaking. 'Stop. I don't want to hear this.'

But Kennet just laughed and the girls sang on.

Several hours down the road they came to a fork, one turning point leading away toward Hel Fenn, the other into Grim Wood. Kennet steered the caravan into the forest. Fischer lay back on the flat roof of the caravan, listening to another of Kennet's sagas. The leaves of the trees twined and intertwined overhead forming a perfect canopy. He couldn't see so much as a sliver of moonlight through them. Sleep soon claimed him.

Again, his dreams were troubled with hallucinogenic splinters of memory fused with the conjurations of his imagination, and again, woven in and out of those splinters of memory were fragments of dream that verged on the erotic: Saskia's lips touching his cheek, his neck, finding the hollow where his pulse was so close to the surface, and feeding off him. He struggled to pull himself out of the dreams but the more he struggled the more Saskia drank and the weaker he grew.

HE HAD NO sense of time when he awoke. The leaves of Grim Wood kept out the sunlight as well as they fended off the moonlight.

The jongleurs sat together upfront, singing a haunting refrain from the 'Trauerspiel von Vanhal', the tragedy of the great witch hunter himself. It was a melancholy song, and though Fischer knew it well he had not heard it sung since he was a young man. It was one of those pieces that had fallen out of fashion as he had grown older. It was surprising that these travelling entertainers knew it, and so many of the older ballads. There couldn't have been a huge call for this kind of material in the taverns and taprooms of the Empire.

Fischer felt utterly drained. He reached into his pack and ended up eating three days' worth of his food without entirely satisfying his hunger. He felt light-headed. The movement of the wagon made him feel vaguely sick.

His dreams on the third night were the worst of all.

In one jagged splinter of memory-cum-imagination he dreamed he was a man who dreamed he was a wolf who dreamed he was damned for all eternity to be locked in the flesh of a man. He dreamed of Saskia too. Her gentle touch and the sheer sensuality of her lips as she kissed his skin caused his pulse to trip and skip erratically. The smell of her as she leaned in, the sensation of her teeth sinking into his neck and sucking the very lifeblood out of him was intoxicating. And through it all, the laughter of Jon Skellan rang in his ears, taunting him as he surrendered to the blackness of oblivion.

He came awake with a start.

Sweat streamed down his forehead and chest. Again his clothes were in disarray, the buttons open. Red bite marks and abrasions covered his chest. Instinctively he touched his neck where Saskia had fed on him in the dream. He felt the sharp rise of a swelling just above the hollow between his neck and collarbone and within it the serrated edge of bite marks.

Panic flared in his mind. He scrabbled around looking for his sword, his knife, anything to defend himself with. They were gone. His pack was there, with its dwindling supply of food. He looked around the inside of the gypsy caravan but couldn't see anything that could be used as a makeshift weapon. He was groggy and struggling to think straight. The rational part of his mind insisted it had all been a dream, that in fact he was still dreaming, but the cold hard truth pressed against his fingers when he touched his neck.

He was trapped in a wagon travelling with at least one vampire through dense woodland thick enough to turn day into night, and he was defenceless.

He tried to listen to see if he could hear anything but through the wooden walls and over the trundling wheels it was impossible. His every instinct screamed: flee!

Fischer grabbed his pack and slung it on his back. He crept over the mattress and the tangle of sheets to the door, cringing at every creak and shift the wooden floorboards made beneath his weight. He braced himself inside the small doorway with his hand on the doorknob.

He closed his eyes and counted silently to ten, gathering his courage and mastering his breathing. The next few minutes were going to be vital, he knew. Whether he lived or died at the hands of these bloodsucking fiends depended on what happened next. He twisted the doorknob and eased the door open inch by cautious inch until it was wide open. The caravan was juddering as its wheels bounced over ruts and stones in the so-called road. The branches dragged down low in places, almost scraping the roof of the wagon. Fischer crouched down and watched the road, trying to judge a rhythm so that he could best time his jump.

'One... two... three!'

He sprang from the open doorway, hitting the dirt road hard, and rolled.

'Hey!' Kennet cried.

Fischer struggled to get his feet under him and hared off into the undergrowth, hoping the trees would give him cover enough to run for his life. He scrambled forward, slipped and had to use his hands to keep him on his feet as he barrelled forward deeper into the trees. Branches and leaves slapped in his face. Brambles tore at his arms as he pushed through them. Behind him Fischer heard the cries of pursuit as they crashed through the forest after him.

'I can *smell* you, Fischer! You can't hide. There is nowhere to go and your fear *stinks*! So go on, run!' Kennet's voice taunted loudly, goading him into running faster. 'Run 'til your heart bursts! Your blood will be good and hot. Soon enough we will all feed!'

Please no, Fischer prayed, pumping his arms and legs harder. It was almost impossible to run properly in the forest. His lungs burned. Fire flared through his thighs and calves. He slipped on a mulch of dead leaves and tripped over a piece of deadfall lying across his path. He barely succeeded in keeping his feet as he ducked beneath a huge overhanging branch. Pushing a swath of leaves out of his face he careened into a rotten tree trunk, pushed himself off it. Gasping for breath, Fischer continued his frantic flight. All the while the taunts of Kennet grew closer, harrying him. He stumbled and staggered on even when his legs wanted to buckle and collapse.

He heard them all round him, playing with him as they shepherded him toward wherever it was they had decided to kill him: Kennet behind him, Saskia to his left, Ina to his right. They called out to him, pushed him in different directions until his legs collapsed under him.

Sobbing, Fischer looked up as Kennet approached, his face twisted into the mask of the monster he actually was. Saskia no longer looked like some heavenly creature; her face was hard, daemonic and Ina's grin was feral as she moved to stand beside her bestial kin.

'Mine,' Saskia said, crouching down beside Fischer. She reached out and tenderly stroked his cheek. 'He always was.'

Fischer spat in her face.

'I'd rather die!'

'Oh you will, believe me, you will.' Her fingers sought out his pulse as it fluttered through his neck. She drew in a slow breath through her nose, savouring the feel of his life beneath her fingertips. 'Blood... such sweet music it makes.'

'Do it,' Ina urged.

'Come on then,' Fischer said stubbornly. 'Finish me, you freak! Do it!'

Saskia pricked his cheek with a fingernail, drawing a ribbon of rich red blood. She leaned in and laved the blood up with her tongue, playing with the blood across her lips.

Fischer went cold. He didn't move. He didn't panic. He didn't close his eyes.

He met her gaze and rasped: 'Do it, damn you!'

He felt her teeth close on the soft flesh of his throat and in that last second as he waited for death heard a sound, like a sharp intake of breath. Fischer winced as the first prickling of teeth sank into his throat but it wasn't matched with the agony of the vampire's feeding. Instead Saskia's head jerked back, her eyes flaring open. The blooded silver tip of an arrow protruded through the front of her throat, the fletching of the shaft tangled in her beautiful hair. He touched his throat. It was wet with a trickle of blood from where the arrow had scratched him. A second arrow thudded into her back, its tip piercing through her breast. Saskia's mouth worked in a silent scream. She slumped into Fischer's terrified arms. He held her, not knowing what else to do.

More arrows rained into the clearing, taking Kennet high in the chest, spinning him around and dumping him, dead, on his back. Ina took three arrows in the chest, and one in the face.

Six men stepped into the clearing. Quickly and efficiently they decapitated the vampiric jongleurs and began to dig two separate shallow graves, one for the three heads, the other for the bodies.

'It's your lucky day,' one of the men, a flaxen-haired youth, said, slinging his bow over his shoulder and helping Fischer to rise.

He felt an unwelcome hollowness inside at Saskia's death. It was as though he had lost something. A part of himself. It felt wrong in so many ways. She had been inhuman. A monster. She had been feeding off him for days, bleeding the life out of him. And yet, there was an ache where she had once been. He shook his head, trying to dislodge the unpleasant feeling. She was dead. He was alive. That was it. End of the story.

'Let me have a look at that,' the archer said. Fischer titled his head to expose the shallow wound. The archer prodded and probed the gash. 'Sit.' Fischer did as he was told. The man drew out a small sewing kit, and a hip flask. 'Drink a good swallow, it'll take the sting out. We need to stitch this up otherwise it'll never heal properly.'

Fischer uncorked the bottle and took a hearty swig. The liquor burned as it slid down his throat.

The archer talked while he doctored the wound.

'You're a lucky man, my friend. Another minute and we'd have been chopping your head off and burying you with the other fiends. Makes you believe in Sigmar, doesn't it?'

'I don't tend to believe in much of anything anymore.'

'Don't talk, it pulls at the stitching. I'll try and answer your questions without you having to ask them. My name is Ralf Baumann. I serve in the Ottilia of House Untermensch's grand army, beneath Hans Schliffen. For the last month we have been experiencing an uprising of sorts, undead, all along the Talabheim borderlands and the Ottilia herself ordered us into the field to police the situation.'

'It is worse than you fear, by far. Undeath is an epidemic in Sylvania.' Fischer said, ignoring the archer's instructions. 'The dead are rising to the call of Vlad von Carstein. The man is a monster. Man. Gah! He is no man. His humanity is long gone. The Vampire Count is a monster. He has slaughtered thousands only to bring them back as mindless zombies. I saw it with my own eyes on Geheimnisnacht. It was butchery. Anyone who has stood against him, he has seen them cut down and replaced by one of his own kind, a bloodsucking fiend. And once dead they get no rest. Oh no, he is raising an army of the dead to do his bloody work!'

Baumann remained impassive as he finished stitching the gash but the second he tied off the final stitch he exploded into action, running across the clearing to where his fellow soldiers were burying the dead and animatedly explaining what he had just heard. An army of the dead being raised by a Vampire Count was more, by far, than this small battalion of soldiers were equipped to handle.

Being caught in this no-man's land between the two factions, living and dead, would mean their death, no one harboured any illusions about that. And as they were all coming to understand, death at the hands of von Carstein was not the clean death a soldier deserved. It was the vile unending 'undeath' of a zombie resurrected to swell the ranks of the Vampire Count's immortal army.

They had to return to the main body of the Ottilia's army.

Schliffen had to know what they were facing.

And for that to happen they had to survive.

CHAPTER TEN
The Storm Before

ESSEN FORD, SYLVANIA
Winter, 2010

THE MORE HE got to know him, the more Ralf Baumann reminded Fischer of Jon Skellan.

It was the little things at first, gestures, throwaway comments, the way he talked of life and his philosophy of living, of his daughters back home in Talabheim, and of the wife he had lost to sickness two summers gone. They suggested the two men were not so dissimilar, yet the true mark of their brotherhood came in the form of their damnation. Neither Baumann nor Skellan were fully at peace with the world around them. They had lost their place in it. It was the most basic thing a human being had, the knowledge of his own place in the world, that sense of purpose that came with knowing who you were, but because these men lived on while those they loved rotted in the dirt, the serenity that came with innocence was lost to them.

Haunted by old ghosts who loved them too much to leave them alone, both men were victims of the survivor's curse.

It weighed as heavily on Baumann as it had on Skellan.

Given the choice of grief or action, Baumann, like Skellan had before him, chose to fight back and gave himself to it body and soul. It was in how they dealt with all the things they had in common that made the two men different. The fact that Baumann was not given to the same brooding introspection and fits of violent temper that plagued Skellan, but rather was quick of wit and passionate in his camaraderie made him a good companion for the long journey. The more he thought about it, the more Fischer came to think that the two were twin aspects of the same soul, darkness and light.

He found himself liking Baumann, a lot, and felt as though he had known the man far longer than he actually had.

It had snowed for seven consecutive days without letting up.

Every day the seven of them pushed on, matching the weather with their own stubborn determination, through valleys and along ridgelines of precarious rock, across frozen streams and snow-laden glades. It was tough going but on the evening of the eighth day they met up with outriders from Schliffen's force. They were camped outside of Essen, close to the fording point of the River Stir, waiting for the main body of the Ottilia's army to cross over from the Talabecland side of the water.

A pile of bones replaced the campfire.

'We're taking no risks,' Frank Bernholz, one of the outriders, explained. 'Twice now we've had to fend off these creatures. The fire attracts them. They aren't smart enough to stay away from Mouse's mace so he ends up grinding them down one at a time while we do our damnedest to keep the rest of the buggers at bay.'

Mouse, the smallest of the crew, grinned and patted the hefty studded mace by his side. 'Big pile of walking bones ain't no match for Bessie here.'

'I can well imagine,' Fischer said.

'When are you expecting the general, Frank?' Baumann asked, settling down on a stone beside the outrider. He cracked a piece of hard travel bread and started to chew on it.

'Yesterday. I sent Marius out to see what was holding him up. I don't like being marooned out here like some kind of sitting duck. Not my idea of a fun way to pass the time. I like it clean and honest. I like to know what I am fighting and to be able to look my enemy in the eye, knowing that he has as much to lose as I do when it comes to the crunch. Can't do it with these... these... *things*. We've lost three scouts in the last week, Ralf. Three good men.'

'It's a dirty business, for sure.'

'And it's only getting dirtier.'

'You do know what's coming, don't you?'

'I've got my suspicions, yeah. Not looking forward to facing whatever it is they decide to throw at us. It's not like fighting men. Men you know, you know the fear pulsing through their veins, you know the exhilaration, the weakness, you know when doubt sets in and more importantly you know when they are broken. A pile of walking bones doesn't think for itself and those walking corpses... They just keep coming and coming and coming. What have they got to lose? They're already dead. They don't know fear or doubt. They just keep on coming, wave after wave of them, and eventually even a good man will break. Maybe not on the first day or the second or even the third but the time will come when exhaustion wears him down, when doubt gnaws away at the back of his mind, when he makes a mistake and then what happens? He dies. Only it doesn't end there... Oh no, his corpse swells the ranks of the enemy and minutes after his death he is fighting against his friends. It's ugly.'

'Ain't that the truth.'

'They're out there now. You'll hear them when the sun finally goes down. Wolves howling at the moon and this eerie keening moan that seems to float all around the camp. We're in the jaws of a trap here and Schliffen knows it. We're his bait. That's why he's late.'

'That's a pretty cynical way of looking at the situation, my friend.'

'Is it? Take a look around, this is the ideal battleground, or as close as you're likely to get around here. You're not exactly wide open to surprises. This way Schliffen is picking the battleground. He knows the fight is coming. Like any good soldier he wants to make the best of what he's got. The water at our back means we're only vulnerable from three sides, and we're between two major branches of the Stir so von Carstein can only bring his army over piecemeal, buying us time to dig in. We've been fortifying for a week. There's some nasty surprises out there beneath the snow, for what good they will do us.'

'Every little bit helps. So, honest opinion: when's this all going to go down?'

'Reckon you boys got here in the nick of time. The natives are restless. They're gathering all around us, have been for the last few nights. They fall into some sort of daze during the day, but like I said, come sunset you can hear them and there are lots of them. The noise has been getting louder every night, as more of them gather. It's creepy as hell, let me tell you. I heard them feeding last night. It isn't a sound I particularly want to hear again. It's like pigs at the trough, but, well, they aren't pigs are they. They're just like you or me. Or they were. Once. Anyway, sundown tomorrow would be my guess, unless they are waiting for something special.'

'I assume Schliffen will be thinking the same way.'

'I've long since stopped trying to second-guess the general but I certainly hope so. Morr's balls, I've got no desire to end up shuffling around with strips of rotten flesh hanging off me. That isn't a way I want to go.'

Baumann patted the outrider on the back and rejoined his own men, filling them in on the situation. He painted a bleak picture.

'So we've become the bait in the trap?'

'That's about the sum of it.'

'Nice,' Fischer said ironically.

The men ate in silence, watching the sun dwindle and finally disappear beneath the horizon.

A cold wind blew through the camp. Baumann busied himself by sharpening his sword on a whetstone. The regular *scheeeel scheeeel scheeeel* of his stropping motion rang out into the darkness. It was met by the ululating cries of the undead as they crowded in around the camp. Fischer caught glimpses of them in the darkness, bone-white flashes picked out by the moon, darker shapes shambling inside the shadows. In the most basic of ways they reminded him of wild animals playing with their food. They weren't trying to hide. They wanted to be seen. Being seen inspired fear in the minds and hearts of the soldiers.

By nature men who dealt in death were a superstitious lot. They believed they would hear an owl call their name the night before their own deaths and insisted on having their sword in their hand as they died as though the blade itself would prove to Morr's attendants that they were warriors, and always when they went into battle they would carry two silver coins to pay their passage into Morr's halls should they fall. Burdened with these superstitions it was hardly surprising that the men saw the shuffling corpses as a promise of the fate that awaited them on the battlefield. Today those putrefied zombies were their enemy, but tomorrow they would be their sword brothers.

More and more as the night lengthened they heard the low keening echo around them. The enemy were moving and they were blind to it. Bernholz had them prepare firebrands to fight off any of the creatures who stumbled too close to the camp but he wouldn't allow his men to light them for fear that the fire would attract the zombies, wraiths and wights like moths.

Fischer thought the man was an idiot. Those things out there weren't human and they weren't moths attracted by curiosity to the bright light. They were either oblivious to it or they were afraid of it. Dead or alive, they still burned. So as he saw it fire was their one and only friend. He didn't speak out against the Bernholz though.

The listless apathy of resignation had settled about the small camp. The conversations were muted, the men slipping into their own thoughts as they prepared for the inevitable battle. They knew that Hans Schliffen was sacrificing them in order to draw von Carstein's undead out onto the battlefield of his own choosing. They accepted it. It was what they did. They were soldiers. They sacrificed themselves for the greater good. It was a simple maxim: soldiers died for what they believed in. Every one of the men in the camp that night knew it and accepted it.

They were even coming to accept the fact that their general had condemned them almost certainly to an afterlife of living death in order to give the rest of his men the best chance of survival. There were always casualties during any engagement. Tough decisions had to be made. People would die: friends, brothers, fathers, no one was immune to the bite of a sword or the punch of an arrow. While they honed the edge of their weapons they did their damnedest to empty their minds. None of them wanted to dwell on the day ahead. They might accept what Schliffen was doing to them but they didn't have to like it. They were soldiers. They followed orders; even ones they knew would get them killed. There was no point in arguing with the strategy. Schliffen had made his mind up, and in his mind baiting the trap was their best hope of defeating von Carstein's horde.

All they could do was wait.

Fischer pressed his back against one of the cold stones the outriders had ringed around the empty fire pit and closed his eyes. He was asleep in moments, this time dreamlessly. The younger men lay awake most of the night, unable to sleep. The calls of the dead plagued them and their own black thoughts tormented them. They envied veterans like Fischer their ability to sleep with the sword of Morr hanging over their heads.

Before dawn the snow gave way to rain: a few spots at first and then more persistent. An hour after sunrise the sky was still dark with steel grey clouds, bulbous thunderheads, and the rain sheeted down turning the snow into slush and the soaking the ground beneath. By noon, Schliffen's precious battlefield was mired. Fischer picked his way toward the centre but walking was almost impossible as every step sank into the sludge almost as far as his knees.

He scared a single raven up from the muddy field and sent it cawing off into the torrential rain.

Fighting in this was going to be a nightmare.

Their one hope had disappeared with the mud – their mobility. Now they were going to be slopping about in the mire, flailing around for balance and moving like zombies themselves. A bitter part of him wondered if von Carstein wasn't somehow behind the foul turn of the weather. The man was a daemon after all, why shouldn't he have mastery over the elements?

The mud soaked up his calf and over his knee as he struggled another step forward. He turned to look behind him. There was no sign of the body of the Ottilia's army. There were, however, plenty of signs to suggest the encroaching presence of the Vampire Count's.

Thousands of them. Tens of thousands. Sprawled out all across the killing ground between him and the line of the second tributary that formed Essen Ford.

Bodies.

Fischer stood, rooted to the spot, as his feet sank deeper into the sludge.

From what he could see the dead had simply collapsed where they stood and lay in a sprawl of limbs. He wanted to believe that whatever hold von Carstein had over them had failed, that they were safe. But he didn't believe it, not for a second. They were puppets, their strings had been laid aside but von Carstein could easily pick them up again and make them dance to whatever whim he saw fit to satisfy. Even with Schliffen's rearguard they were doomed. No quarter would be asked or given. The Vampire Count would bring the full wrath of his army down on their heads come sunset and all of the strategies and all of the gamesmanship in the Old World wouldn't save them.

He slumped forward onto his knees.

The thought of running crossed his mind but he dismissed it before the idea was even half formed. After all this running there was nowhere left to run to. He had done what he had set out to do. He had spread the word. Vlad von Carstein's secret was out in the world now. The people who needed to know it knew.

And yet tears streamed down his cheeks.

The tears surprised him. He wasn't afraid. He had always known this day would come.

Tonight he would stand beside Baumann and Bernholz and the others and he would be proud to do just that. War made heroes out of normal people. Here, on the fields of Essen Ford, heroes would be born.

And heroes would die.

CHAPTER ELEVEN

The Swords of Scorn

ESSEN FORD, SYLVANIA
Winter, 2010

THE SOUNDS OF the battlefield were all wrong.

There were screams as soldiers fell and fierce battle-cries answered by the stampede as swords clattered off shields, the cacophony intended to instil fear in an enemy that knew no fear. Despite the screaming, the drumming and the stamping feet there was no ringing clash of steel on steel.

The fight was no ordinary fight.

Swords slashed through the torrential rain, cutting at the dead arms as they clawed and scratched and pulled at the soldiers. The dead stumbled forward and the living lurched backwards desperate to evade their outstretched arms and suffocating embrace. The ground beneath their feet was treacherous. It was virtually impossible to fight. They were reduced to trying to stay alive. They staggered and lurched as they struggled to fend off the dead, their movements mimicking von Carstein's monstrous regiment as they struggled to keep their balance.

No matter how desperately the Ottilia's soldiers fought, the dead kept on coming, surging relentlessly forward without fear or concern for their own safety.

Fischer fought for his life beside Baumann, the flaxen-haired archer proving himself as deadly with a sword as he had shown he was with a bow. There was no smile on his face now though, only grim determination to stay alive as the dead threw themselves at them. Twice already during the fighting Baumann's blade had deflected a blow aimed at sweeping Fischer's head clean off his shoulders.

Fischer ducked under a wild blow, jamming his sword up into the gut of a woman. Half of her face had been eaten away by maggots. He wrenched the sword left and right violently slicing deep into her spinal cord. Her torso buckled, folding over itself. Fischer dragged his sword free. Unable to support itself her body collapsed at their feet but still she clawed at them, tugging at their feet. Her clawed hands hooked around Baumann's ankle and almost succeeded in toppling him before Fischer's sword cleaved through her wrist. He kicked her severed hand away as another zombie trampled over her writhing corpse. There was no time for thanks.

The pair fought on, lungs and arms burning with exhaustion. The sheer weight of numbers was overwhelming. The dead climbed over each other to get at them.

All across Essen Ford it was the same.

The dead were a tidal wave, an undeniable force beyond the limits of nature sweeping everything away in their path. Von Carstein's army was relentless and lethal. They had no need of weapons. They threw themselves bodily at the terrified soldiers, dragging them down into the sinking mud and once they had them down the dead swarmed over them, clawing, biting and rending at their flesh until they had stripped the fallen soldier of his humanity.

It was barbaric.

It wasn't a battle, it was butchery.

Ghouls, once men like Fischer and Baumann before they sank so far as to become cannibalistic eaters of the dead, picked over the corpses as the combatants trampled them into the mud. The vile creatures stripped away fillets of fresh meat and gorged themselves on it. Friends, foes, the ghouls were indiscriminate in their feeding.

Fischer parried a raking claw aimed at putting his eyes out and rammed the point of his sword into a woman's throat. Her blood-matted hair fell across her face. Where she should have had eyes were empty sockets stitched up with mortician's thread. She threw herself forward onto the sword, trying to snare him in her deadly embrace. Fischer couldn't drag his sword free. Her bloody locks fell in his face as she threw all of her weight at him. Fischer felt himself buckling under her.

Screaming, Fischer heaved himself upright and sent her spinning away across the muddy field, his sword still stuck in her throat. She bucked and thrashed trying to wrench Fischer's sword out. He cursed and hurled himself forward, landing on top of the blind woman. He punched at her face, slamming his fist into it again and again until it felt like he was pounding a slab of raw meat. Still she clawed at the sword. Fischer pushed himself to his feet as another two undead grabbed at him. He slammed an elbow into the face of the first hard enough to rupture its nose and spray blood into its eyes. He grabbed the hilt of his sword before the second dead man could stop him.

Baumann cut the dead man down before Fischer could turn to meet the challenge.

More came to fill the gap left by the fallen dead.

There was no end to it.

Around them good men died only to rise again and turn on them.

IT HAD BEEN like that for six hours. Even before the first blow had been struck whispers spread through the ranks, the Vampire Count had offered the outriders clemency should they abandon the Ottilia and serve him. None did. Schliffen had arrived on the field of battle an hour before von Carstein unleashed the full might of his horde. It didn't matter. More than half of the outriders had fallen and been absorbed into the ranks of the undead before Schliffen and the body of the Ottilia's army arrived. Their horses were useless in the muck and mire. They couldn't run and the mud only served to bog them down and topple them giving the ghouls more meat to gorge themselves on. There was no questioning their bravery though, even when von Carstein himself entered the fray, his nightmare steed snorting licks of fire from its flaring nostrils as the Vampire Count's wailing blade cleaved through terrified ranks of human defenders. The shrieking of the sword as it cut through the air was mortifying. The soldiers who weren't cut down fled and dragged more down in their panicked wake as they tried to escape the hungry blade. Von Carstein himself mocked them, laughing manically as he cut and hewed through the living and almost negligently raised them in his wake, bringing them into his legion of the damned.

Fischer stared in awe at the nightmare.

It was an awesome beast, blacker even than true black and easily five hands higher than the biggest horse Fischer had ever seen. Everything about the mount and its rider radiated pure unmitigated evil. The creature reeked of it. Von Carstein's mane of black hair was matted with the rain. He twisted in the saddle, standing on black iron stirrups and learning forward. His sword wailed its hideous threnody as it sheared through the neck of a terrified Imperial soldier. The man's head fell beneath the nightmare's hooves and was sucked into the mud.

More vampires came behind the count, led by a giant of a man who had no need of a nightmarish steed to inspire terror, his twin curved blades were more than enough. The vampire's face was splashed with blood, none of it his own. He licked his lips and savoured the taste of his defeated foes. The treacherous battlefield didn't appear to hinder him as he ghosted through the living and the dead, his twin blades blurring into a single steel blue arc. His vampires and wolves trailed in his deadly wake.

Some of the risen dead recovered weapons from the fallen, skeletons with swords and pikes and spears came at them.

In a flicker of movement in the corner of his eye Fischer saw Bernholz was in trouble. A revenant shade had risen up behind him, ethereal claws coming down to rake through body and soul. The shock of the cold would be enough to throw Bernholz's focus, giving the three putrefied corpses crowding around him the chance they needed to bring him down. He couldn't shout. The warning would go unheard over the sounds of carnage and feeding. He had to do something.

Without thinking about what he was doing Fischer grabbed a handful of mud-clogged hair on a decapitated head and heaved it up into the air so it arced through the air and came down hard on the shoulder of one of the zombies crowding in on Bernholz and landed at its feet in a splash of snow and sludge. Bernholz backed up a step. It saved his life. The revenant shade's claws sheared through his back and out of his chest causing the soldier to scream in shock and pain but his backwards step had given him space enough to regain his composure as the zombies lurched forward. The outrider gutted one and decapitated another. Even then there was no letup for him as dire wolves snapped at his legs and dregs clawed their way through the mud seeking to bring him down.

Something slammed into Fischer's back and sent him sprawling forward and his sword spinning out of his hand. He tasted the mud and the blood of the fight as his face ploughed into the sodden ground. His sword had fallen tantalizingly out of reach of his fingers. He scrabbled toward it but before his hand could snatch it a heavy foot came down on his back, pinning him in the mud.

'Well, well, well, look who we have here.'

Despite its mocking tone he knew the voice.

Fischer squirmed beneath the crushing weight of the foot. He craned his neck to see the twisted features of his best friend sneering down at him: Jon Skellan. Only it wasn't Skellan. It was the soulless, heartless, dead thing wearing Skellan's bloodless corpse. It might have his memories and share his skin but it wasn't his friend. It was an animal.

Skellan kicked Fischer. 'Up, my friend. Time to die like a man.' Blood clung to Skellan's teeth where he had fed. His eyes were searing pits of anger.

'You're not my friend, not anymore.'

'Have it your own way. Up. I've got no patience for cowards and you stink of fear, Fischer. You absolutely reek of it. Now get up.'

Skellan kicked him forward as he struggled to rise so he kissed the blood-soaked dirt. Fischer put his hands under him again and started to stand only for Skellan to kick him off-balance again. He lay there in the mud, utterly drained. He lacked the will to move. Around him the sounds of the battle muted and lost their clarity as his senses narrowed their focus to the space between him and Skellan, shutting out all of the screaming and the dying, the driving rain, the keening of the undead and von Carstein's hideous wailing sword.

'So this is how it ends then?' Fischer said looking up at Skellan.

The vampire sheathed his sword and offered his hand.

'It doesn't have to. Take my hand. Join us. We can always use a good man. The Blood Kiss will set you free, believe me. I am a different man. Before it was all petty vengeance. My life was consumed with it. Posner freed me of the shackles of mortality. Now the strength of death flows through my veins in place of blood. The weakness is gone. There is no pity, no compassion, and no stinking mercy. I am vampire. I am immortal, what need have I to fear anything? It is a gift. The greatest gift.'

'No. You don't believe that. It is a curse and you know it. It is an abomination, even nature refuses you a reflection now so repugnant are you to the world. And you forget in your new arrogance, Skellan, you can die. You can die very well. Like Aigner. Remember him? Remember the man who murdered Lizbet? Remember the monster he was? That is what you are. How does it feel? You didn't slay the beast, you *became* the beast.'

'He was weak.'

'He was strong enough to destroy everything you loved.'

'And what is love if not weakness?' Skellan sneered, baring razor-sharp fangs. His features contorted, burning with bestial anger. 'I am not the man I was. I am more than that. I am immortal. I will be here when you are dust. I will see the rise and fall of empires. I am immortal.'

Suddenly, oddly, Fischer realised that the rain running down his face could well be the last thing he ever felt. He tilted his face up to meet it, savouring it for a moment before answering Skellan.

'So you keep saying, but you forget there are countless ways you can die a final death, and when you do you will be condemned to eternal torture in the realm of the dead, so cling to your unlife, Jon Skellan, live in fear of that final terrible judgement.' He reached into his shirt and pulled out the silver pendant Leyna had given him on their wedding night: the hammer of Sigmar.

Skellan recoiled, a look of utter revulsion on his bestial features. 'You and your miserable Man-God!' he spat. 'Stay as meat, you ignorant fool! You are nothing more or less than cattle to us.' He swept his arm out in a grand gesture, encompassing the whole field. 'You are part of our herd, Fischer. You are bred for one specific purpose: so that we might feed on you.'

Fischer's fist closed around the silver trinket.

'Then feed, *friend*. You wouldn't be the first to. Hell, you wouldn't even be the prettiest. Drink! Here's my throat, I am offering it to you. Drink damn you! Drink!'

'What are you waiting for?' Herman Posner asked curiously. He had come up behind the pair without either of them noticing. The man moved like a ghost across the battlefield. The fighting had all but died out in several parts of the field. A gibbous moon hung in the air behind Posner's head. Without turning, Posner rammed one of his twin blades into Bernholz's chest as the outrider came up behind him, sword raised ready to deliver a huge killing blow. It was coldly done. Posner didn't even acknowledge the dying man as Bernholz's eyes flared wide and blood bubbled out of his mouth as it sagged open in shock. The sword slipped from his fingers and fell into a puddle of mud and blood. The man was dead before he hit the dirt.

'Well? He's meat. Feed, lad. Don't let good food go to waste. Didn't your mother teach you anything?'

Before Skellan could respond the cries went up across Essen Ford: the Ottilia's forces were routed, the battle was won and there were still hours to go before the sun rose redly on the killing ground and the dead sank back into whatever hell held them once more. It was over.

Posner's crew moved amongst the living and the dead, spreading the word: the Vampire Count wanted the survivors.

All of them.

Skellan hauled Fischer to his feet and pushed him forward, driving him hard toward the pavilions the dead were erecting for their master away from the worst of the carnage. He staggered and stumbled through the mud. He wasn't alone. The survivors – of whom there were precious few – were being herded like cattle toward von Carstein's pavilion. He saw Schliffen, beaten and battered, his head down as he shuffled toward the tents, and Baumann, cut and bleeding but head raised defiantly as two of Posner's vampires jabbed him forward with the bloody tips of their swords. The vampires were beaten bloody; one's face was badly disfigured where Baumann had put his eye out and shattered its nose, and the other had lost half of its jaw where Baumann had almost cleaved its head in two.

Fischer saw countless bodies hunched over the fallen. He knew what they were: ghouls picking over the corpses, feeding. Normally he would have expected the survivors to gather the dead for burial, but not this time. The dead of Essen Ford would swell the ranks of the Vampire Count's monstrous army.

They had lost more than just their lives.

They had lost their deaths.

CHAPTER TWELVE
Spilling Tainted Blood

ESSEN FORD, SYLVANIA
Winter, 2010

Von Carstein walked down the line of prisoners.

He moved slowly, taking the time to examine each of the men facing him. Ganz walked two paces behind him. Buoyed up with the bloodlust of victory he felt like one of *them*. He felt immortal. Eternal. He felt the thrill of victory course through his veins. He felt the vitality of life pulsing through his body. He was alive. For the first time in years he felt it. He experienced it all as one huge sensory overload: the rain on his face, the tang of blood and dirt as he breathed, the sudden richness and clarity of the colours that made up the world around him, the infinite shades of greens and browns, even the coppery taste of his own blood in his mouth, all of it came together in one exaltation of life. And that was when he realised that he had more in common with the cattle von Carstein had lined up for inspection than he did with the Vampire Count and his hellish minions. He was human. Humanity was weakness.

Ganz looked at the row of faces, the resistance beaten out of them, the resignation to their fate written harshly in their dulled eyes.

They were meat.

Meat for the beast.

'You,' von Carstein said. 'These are your men, yes?'

The man nodded.

'I will give you a choice, a simple one. Think carefully before you decide. I am not in the habit of letting people change their minds. You spurned my offer of clemency so your life is forfeit. That is not in doubt. Your choice is this, serve me in life, or serve me in death. It matters not to me. Either way, I own you.'

Hans Schliffen stiffened physically. 'You cannot be serious.'

One of Posner's vampires moved up behind the general, hissing in his ear as he gripped his arms and pinned them behind his back. 'The count is always serious.'

'Indeed. Ganz, pick a soldier, any soldier, and cut his throat. Show the good general here just how serious I am.'

Ganz walked the line, relishing the looks of pure terror in the soldiers' eyes as he paused in front of them, each one silently begging him not to choose them, to move on and take one of their friends instead. He stopped in front of Baumann because unlike the others there was no fear in his gaze, only defiance as he stared Ganz down. A slow smiled spread across Ganz's face. He stepped forward and, with one swift twist of the wrist, grabbed a handful of the man's hair and yanked his head back. He brought his other hand up and rammed the dagger he had concealed in it deep into the archer's throat. Baumann gagged, blood burbling through his fingers as he clutched at the wound. It was a surprisingly slow death. No one dared move, least of all Ganz. He stared with sick fascination as the man he had just stabbed died.

Von Carstein held out his hand, palm up and made a slow lifting gesture. Baumann's body twitched and jerked in response as the newly-dead muscles answered to his will. Less than a minute later Baumann was standing back in his place in the line, his head lolling back slackly on his slashed throat, the life burned out from his eyes.

'In life or in death, general? I am quite serious.'

'You... I can't...'

'Allow me to help you some more, general. You see I own you all. How I dispose of you is my prerogative. You should have thought about that before you crossed me. You, you, and you,' von Carstein said, selecting three of Posner's vampires, including Skellan. 'Choose one of the cattle and feed.'

The three vampires came forward, looking over the line of prisoners. Few had the strength left in them to even look at them as they walked the length of the line, slowly, adding an edge of menace to the execution by drawing out the selection of their victims.

Skellan stopped behind Fischer and leaned in to whisper in his ear: 'You should have joined me, my *friend*, but it is too late now.'

'Couldn't even face me, could you?' Fischer said. They were the last words he ever spoke. Skellan sank his fangs into Fischer's neck and fed greedily, sucking the very lifeblood out of him. Fischer's body stiffened, spasmed violently and then slumped as the life left it. Skellan continued to drain every precious ounce of blood from him, swallowing the thick warm liquid hungrily.

Along the line the two other vampires fed, then threw the empty corpses to the floor.

Von Carstein raised the three dead men with an almost negligent flick of the wrist. Their bodies jerked and spasmed as the Vampire Count manipulated them back into their places in the line. Their movements were a grim parody of life.

'Now, general. Pick one of your men.'

Schliffen shook his head. 'No. I won't. This is... You are a monster. This is barbaric.'

'Do not try my patience, general. Pick a man. If you don't, I will.'

Schliffen shook his head crazily, not willing to sacrifice any of his surviving soldiers.

'Why do you insist in making everything so difficult, general?' von Carstein sighed. 'Very well, I will choose for you. You, come here.' The Vampire Count singled out a young man, no more than nineteen or twenty years of age. The young man shuffled forward. He sniffed. Snot and tears streamed down his cheeks.

'It is your lucky day, soldier. I am not going to kill you but I am going to kill each and every one of your friends here. I want you to run back to the Empire and tell everyone that Vlad von Carstein is coming. Make them understand that I am hungry for blood and that I am tired with living in the darkness and shadows. I want you to tell them what kind of monster I am. How I executed the survivors of your army. I want you to tell them how I fed my pet vampires with your friends and how when everyone was dead and the ghouls had sated themselves I raised each and every one to serve me in death. Do you understand me?'

The petrified young soldier nodded.

'Then go before I change my mind.'

The young man stumbled away, staggered and started to run. Von Carstein laughed at him as he slipped and fell, pushed himself up and managed four more steps before he fell again. He turned to Posner.

'Kill them all.'

'With pleasure, my lord,' Posner said. 'You heard him men, feeding time!'

The vampires descended on the line of prisoners in a feeding frenzy.

In the chaos Hans Schliffen broke free his guard's grip and dragged the wailing sword from the sheath at von Carstein's side. The blade screamed a warning even as Schliffen brought it around in a brutal arc. It was all over in a single heartbeat. Posner saw the blow coming and tried to push the count out of the way but von Carstein stiffened and snarled at his warrior. That snarl froze on his dead face as Schliffen's blow clove von Carstein's head clean from his shoulders.

The Vampire Count's tainted blood sprayed out of the gaping stump.

As one the risen dead fell where they stood.

Posner reacted first, dragging his twin curved blades free of their sheaths and hurling himself at Schliffen. The general aimed another wild swing at Posner but the vampire danced beneath it and rose, snarling, both blades coming together to shear through Schliffen's arms only inches above the wrists. Screaming in agony Schliffen stared as the stumps of his arms pumped out his lifeblood.

'Bind him and burn him,' Posner rasped. 'I want the man to suffer.'

Two of Posner's vampires dragged the screaming general through the mud to where a third was lighting a brazier. When the flames leapt to angry life they forced Schliffen's bloody arms into them. The stink of burned flesh and the general's shrieks filled the air. The vampires ignored Schliffen's screams and held his arms in the fire until the stumps were dry and caked with charcoal, the wounds cauterised.

Posner came over to where Schliffen lay curled up on the floor cradling the blackened stumps protectively to his chest.

'You'll wish you were already dead, soldier. The count might have offered you a mercifully quick death. I won't.' There was no sign that Schliffen heard him. Posner turned to the three vampires standing around the brazier listening to the general's juices spit and crackle in the roaring fire. 'Four horses, bind the man to them arm and foot... and then lash the damned animals until he's been ripped limb from limb. Do it slowly. I want him to know. I want him to feel it as he is pulled apart. It is the least I can do for the count.'

He turned his back on the whimpering general. He walked back toward the white pavilions where the rest of his vampires were done feeding on the prisoners. Their thirst for blood slaked the vampires threw the corpses to the ghouls to finish.

He smiled to himself. He would take von Carstein's signet ring and use it as a sign of power, to validate the transition between one ruler and the next. And then there was the crazy bitch von Carstein had saddled himself with, Isabella. He would take her too. He would make her scream his name: Herman Posner, Count of the Vampires!

The land would hear her screams and quake at his coming.

Posner had expected to see that sycophant Ganz weeping over von Carstein's body, tearing at his hair and wailing, but Ganz was gone.

More worryingly, there was no sign of von Carstein's corpse.

CHAPTER THIRTEEN
King of Dust

ESSEN FORD, SYLVANIA
Winter, 2010

Ganz fled from the battlefield, carrying the dead count's body and severed head in his arms as he stumbled toward the safety of the trees.

His grief was absolute.

He staggered forward, talking over and over mindlessly, saying the same things.

'It will be all right. It will be all right. It will be all right.'

No matter how many times he repeated the promise a distant part of him knew that things could never be all right again. Von Carstein was dead. His count was dead.

He cradled the lifeless body in his arms.

It seemed inconceivable that a wreck of a man like Schliffen could slay the Vampire Count in his moment of triumph. It wasn't right. Von Carstein was man of vision. He saw beauty in all things. In all...

That wasn't true. That was his grief speaking – it was all he could hear. The world around him was dead. A wasteland. The Vampire Count had proved his ruthlessness and in doing so turned Alten Ganz into a cold-blooded killer. He couldn't think for the incessant yammering of his guilt inside his head. On and on and on. Snatches of conversation came back to him, and in every one at least one voice was always the count's. Tears streamed down his face. Tears of grief and guilt. He had seen Schliffen wrestle free of his guard's grip and lunge for the count's sword but he hadn't done anything. He had simply stood there and stared like a rabbit caught in the hunter's sight, waiting for the killing blow to thud home. If he had done something... if he had at least tried... the count might still have been alive.

He had no idea what he was doing.

Ganz plunged blindly into the forest, stumbling into tree trunks and tripping over trailing roots. Thirty paces in, where the undergrowth thickened into an impenetrable tangle, he fell to his knees and laid the dead Vampire Count on the blanket of mildewed leaves and rotten twigs. He knelt there sobbing until the grief dried itself out and there were no more tears left to fall.

He arranged the count's clothes, making him look presentable. The count was always so careful with his appearance. He held the dead man's head in his hands. Brushed the long black hair back so that it didn't fall across the eyes, and laid it reverentially in place. Ganz couldn't bear the look of shocked betrayal in the count's dead eyes. He reached out and closed them. Von Carstein's skin was cold. Far too cold for someone who had died such a short while ago, he knew.

'But he didn't just die... He's been dead as long as I have known him.'

Ganz folded the count's arms across his chest.

The von Carstein signet ring was caked in blood.

It could have belonged to anyone; enough blood had been shed that night, von Carstein in the thick of the fighting. But it didn't belong to just anyone, Ganz knew. It was the count's blood.

The thought of taking the ring, keeping it for himself, entered his mind.

'Robbing the dead's not right,' he muttered.

Ganz gathered leaves and branches to cover the count's body. The ground was too hard for him to dig even the shallowest of graves with his bare hands so instead he made a cairn, piling dead leaves, branches and stones over von Carstein's body to protect it from hungry animals.

He stood over the cairn. He didn't know what he was supposed to do. So he did nothing.

'Goodbye.'

He walked slowly back toward the white pavilions.

Posner was struggling to subdue Isabella. She was in a rage the like of which Ganz had never seen before. She frenziedly tore at her own hair, at her clothes, and at anyone unfortunate enough to be within arm's reach. Three of Posner's vampires lay in the pool of tainted blood at her feet. Her claws had shred their faces and her fangs had ripped their throats out.

Ganz couldn't begin to imagine how she felt, her love, her eternal love, cut down in a single blow. Surely the loss would unhinge her already fragile mind.

CHAPTER FOURTEEN
Of Swords and Ashes

ESSEN FORD, SYLVANIA
Winter, 2010

Posner's rise was bloody and brutal.

He cut down any and all that stood against him.

Loyalty amongst the lords of the undead was not a natural thing; the shadows had grown dark in their hearts. They were kindred but that didn't mean they would even so much as shed a tear for a fallen brother. Few would miss von Carstein and all, without exception, would relish the opportunity to rise in his place. That lack of basic loyalty to the old count and his widow meant that few around the camp grieved. While Isabella sobbed her heart out and railed against the heavens at the unjustness of it all, each in their own way were wondering and planting hooks that might lead to alliances and in turn power. They hungered for it.

There is no vampiric society, no aristocracy or blue-blooded royalty amongst the undead. Vampires crave power, and through strength and cunning they take it. Frailty is punished by death: final, true death. There is no natural succession amongst those left behind. No birthright. No passing of the torch from generation to generation. Power is taken with strength.

Herman Posner understood that.

He walked through the subdued camp, seeing the alliances taking shape around him. Seeing potential pockets of rebellion rising up. Before they could bear fruit he crushed them. Those who refused his right to rule the dead were given one chance, a choice, much as Vlad himself had done only hours before with the cattle.

Where von Carstein had said 'Serve me in life or serve me in death,' Posner offered a slight variation to his brothers: serve me in life or serve me with your death.

His men culled the ranks of the vampires that night, shedding the weak and those most loyal to the old guard. The killing left behind a core he could, in some small way, trust.

It was not a luxury he would rely on.

Treachery, Posner knew, lay close to every vampire's stilled heart.

Still, he savoured his moment of victory.

He would find Isabella and make her an offer she would be a fool to refuse, cementing his place as the new count.

With the worst of the storm gone, and the rain drizzled out, the night was brightening. Storm clouds had blotted out the stars but they returned as a restless wind chased the clouds away. The wind rustled and mumbled through the encampment. A ruddy glow came from the embers of the campfire the vampires had built to burn the various parts of Schliffen's corpse. The dying light cast a reddish glow over the faces of the vampires who still stood around the fire ring, watching the murderer burn to ash and smoke. They had not spoken or moved as long as the fire had been burning.

Posner left them to their vigil.

He drew back the flap on the main pavilion and ducked inside.

The pavilion was opulent with gothic splendour. The count, as ever, had surrounded himself with things of great beauty, rugs from Amhabal and Sudrat in distant Araby, scents in the oil burners from Shuang Hsi in far-off Cathay, decorative clamshells from Sartosa, bone candelabra hand-carved in Ind, and much more. Von Carstein had been a collector. He had gathered souvenirs as others gathered memories. Posner picked up a jewelled egg von Carstein had stolen from the palace in Praag.

It was surprising the things von Carstein had chosen to keep near him during the march on the Empire. The egg was priceless, like so much of von Carstein's art. It had a name... Azovu? Posner marvelled at it. The egg was carved from a solid piece of heliotrope jasper, and decorated with yellow and white gold scrolls set with brilliant diamonds and chased red gold flowers. There was a tiny drop ruby clasp that opened to reveal a miniature replica, in gold and diamond, of Arianka's glass tomb. There was a perverse irony in the design. He assumed it was Walpurgis's work. The man was twisted enough inside that he would have made a truly great vampire.

He put the egg back on the wooden dresser where he had found it. In this tent alone there were treasures enough for him to live like an Emperor for years.

He had no use for von Carstein's trinkets.

Only his power.

The count had possessed a page from one of the nine great books of Nagash. If he had one page there would be more, surely. Posner could only imagine the possibilities those books would open up if a single page could raise the dead into an unstoppable army.

That was the kind of power that Posner craved.

Real power.

Not petty little treaties and pacts that relied on backstabbers to remain trustworthy.

Von Carstein's wailing sword lay on the table in the centre of the pavilion. The man's blood was still on it, dried into a caked layer like rust on the dark blade. Posner picked it up and examined it in his hands. The sword let out a gentle keening moan.

Posner smiled, hefted the sword and tested it with a few quick swings. The balance was exquisite, quite unlike anything he had ever wielded. It was as though the blade itself possessed a will of its own; its preternatural balance and timing no more than its own selfish lust for blood and slaughter. After four dizzyingly fast passes, high and low parries and thrusts, the wailing blade was crying out for blood and Posner found it almost impossible to lay the blade aside. It was inside his skull crying out to be fed. He dropped the sword and backed away from it in disgust.

The thing was alive.

A vampiric sword for a Vampire Count; it was a bloody partnership forged in the pits of Morr's underworld for sure.

'What do you want?'

He hadn't even seen Isabella huddled in the corner, clutching one of her dead husband's shirts to her heaving breast.

'You,' Posner said without a trace of irony or passion.

'I can smell him on it,' Isabella said, lost for a moment in the sensory deception of the shirt. 'He's still here. He hasn't gone. He hasn't left me.'

She was a wretched mess huddled on the floor, pressed up against the edge of von Carstein's elaborately carved coffin. Her eyes were rimmed red and the veins showed bluely through her pale skin. She looked like death.

Posner knelt down beside her and reached out tenderly to brush her hair back where it had fallen into her eyes. 'He's gone. I can't believe it either but he's gone. Now it is time for you to stand up and be strong, Isabella. Beautiful Isabella. There isn't a creature out there tonight who wouldn't see you dead, do you understand that? You are the last link to the past, to Vlad. They would bury you beneath a Sigmarite temple if they could.'

She shook her head violently, reacting to his tone if not his actual words. He looked deep into her eyes but she showed no sign of understanding what he was saying. She had receded somewhere deep inside herself. He didn't know how to reach her. All he could do was talk.

'I can help you,' he said, trying to put as much conviction into his voice as he could. 'Walk out of here with me. Stand by my side. Join with me and none can stand against us. I can protect you from them, sweet beautiful Isabella. I can keep you safe. I can be your count.'

'No,' she said, wriggling around beneath his hand. 'No. No. He wouldn't leave me. No. He's coming back. He *loves* me!'

Posner did his best to stifle his exasperation. He stood and hauled her up to her feet.

'Come out with me. Let them see us together. You don't have to say anything. Just stand there and be beautiful, Isabella. Can you do that? Can you do that for me?'

'No,' she said again.

Posner slipped his arm through hers. 'Lean on me.'

'No.' It was as though it was the only thing she could say. An endless stream of denials. No. No. No. No. No.

Gently, he guided her out of the tent.

They were all looking at him, he knew, the darkness couldn't hide their curiosity. They were looking at him to make a mistake. He didn't make mistakes. He was Herman Posner.

'It ends here, now. I claim this woman as my bride by right of strength. Any who would dare to challenge that right, speak now or forever hold your silence.'

'I challenge you,' said a voice Posner had thought never to hear again.

CHAPTER FIFTEEN
From Dust Returned

ESSEN FORD, SYLVANIA
Winter, 2010

HE WAS LOOKING at a ghost.

It wasn't possible.

Death for a vampire was final, there was no return from the torments of eternity. It was the end.

Your soul was shredded. There was no rest. No resurrection. No return. You were an empty vessel. There was nothing that *could* come back.

And yet…

Vlad von Carstein stepped through the crowd. His mane of black hair was blown back in the wind, exposing the line of dried and flaking blood that marred his neck.

But it couldn't be von Carstein. Posner's mind ran wild, impossible thoughts tumbling over each other in their clamour to be heard. One thought though was louder than all of the others: von Carstein was dead.

Posner had seen it with his own two eyes. Schliffen had taken the Vampire Count's head clean off his shoulders with that damnable wailing blade. It was impossible. He couldn't be alive. It had to be Ganz. The weasel had to be behind this charade somehow. Posner couldn't see the man.

This had to be some kind of trick. It had to be.

'I would be grateful if you would unhand my wife,' von Carstein said casually. Posner felt the coldness of his stare.

'You aren't him. He's dead.'

'Aren't we all?'

Some of the vampires chuckled at the count's gallows humour. Posner didn't raise so much as a smile. It felt as though his hastily-constructed world was coming down around his shoulders.

And then he did smile, and it was full of cunning; a predator's smile.

'You've got nothing here. Your sycophants are gone. Even the weasel Ganz has abandoned you. My vampires are all around you. Mine. They are loyal to me.'

'Loyal?' the Vampire Count said mockingly. 'What do any of us know of loyalty, Herman? You especially. I would have thought you knew better.'

Posner pushed the woman away from him. 'You want her? She's yours. You have,' he glanced up at the sky, 'until the cloud has passed completely across the face of the moon to run for your life. Otherwise I will strike you down where you stand. You already died once. Killing you again shouldn't be so difficult if one of the cattle can manage it. Go on, run.'

'No.' It was Isabella, stumbling through the mud toward von Carstein. 'No. No.' She repeated. She ran into him, hammering her clenched fists on his chest and shrieking hysterically: 'Nonononononono!'

Von Carstein didn't flinch.

'I *liked* you, Herman,' he said, his voice laced with disappointment. 'But we all make mistakes.'

The Vampire Count snarled, releasing the beast within. The bones in his face cracked and elongated, his jaw distending to reveal lethal fangs. He pushed Isabella aside and dropped into a fighting crouch.

'Fight me.'

Posner reached back and with a hiss drew his twin blades. The moonlight glittered off the silver. He circled warily, eying the count. 'You intend to fight me with your bare hands, Vlad?' His grin was maniacal. The twin blades danced in his hands, weaving a hypnotic pattern of death between the two combatants.

And then he heard it: the keening wail of von Carstein's damned sword.

He couldn't turn. He daren't take his eyes off the Vampire Count as he slowly circled, looking for a weakness in Posner's defence.

He saw the cadaverous figure of Ganz out of the corner of his eye. He had the wailing sword in his hands.

Posner launched a lightning-fast assault. He threw himself forward, his swords whickering through the air either side of von Carstein's head but the count, with ungodly timing, rolled away from both lethal cuts without seeming to actually move. Posner dropped and swept out a leg, looking to topple his opponent, while matching it with the left-handed blade, slicing it in perfect time with the leg sweep. The manoeuvre would have eviscerated a lesser man. Von Carstein leapt backwards in a tightly controlled somersault and landed easily. He held out his hand for Ganz to give him his sword while Posner regained his balance.

'Herman, Herman, Herman.' Von Carstein hefted the wailing blade, switching it from right hand to left and back again. He moved up onto his toes then rocked back onto his heels. 'You're a man of few words.'

Posner's answer was silence.

Deep within himself Posner heard a sound. It repeated itself over and over. A *howl*. It was animalistic. Its grip on his soul was absolute. His face shifted as the beast within, the vampiric side of his nature, was unleashed.

'Death is too noble for a piece of filth like you.'

Posner sprang forward and lunged in a single fluid motion. It was so incredibly fast it was virtually impossible to see his blade as it flicked out in search of von Carstein's heart. Steel rang on steel as the count turned his blade away with an almost negligent flick of the wrist. In response, von Carstein's sword slipped inside his guard and twisted up toward his throat. Posner's parry was a blur. His left-handed blade caught the count's wailing sword and locked it there for a split second, giving his right-hand blade the fraction of a heartbeat it needed to lance inside von Carstein's defences and drive the tip toward his stomach.

Von Carstein caught the blade in the palm of his right hand. Posner stared at the blood as it leaked between the Vampire Count's fingers and across his signet ring.

The distraction was all von Carstein needed.

He stepped in, his left hand deftly disengaging his blade from Posner's and unleashing a high swing that buried the edge of the wailing sword deep in Posner's neck. At the last moment he pulled the ferocity from the blow, deliberately preventing it from cleaving through the man's neck.

Posner staggered sideways, his eyes wide with the shock of agony as his tainted blood gouted from the gaping wound. His left hand spasmed and his fingers lost their grip on the curved blade. It slipped through his fingers and fell. It landed tip first in the mud and stuck, quivering. His hand went to his neck as though trying to staunch the flow of blood. He tried to speak but all that came out was a strangled gurgle.

He saw the weasel Ganz standing beside Isabella.

It was all so close.

He could almost touch it.

He raised his right hand and hurled the sword end over end, like a dagger. The remnants of a smile twitched across his lips as he saw the heavy blade slam into the centre of Alten Ganz's chest, shattering the bone and piercing his heart.

Ganz staggered back. Posner saw him try to right himself before he toppled. It was a reflex action. He was already dead.

'Never did... like... you,' Posner managed. He broke off into a bloody gurgle of coughing. He raised his eyes to meet von Carstein's condemning gaze. 'Finish it then.'

'No,' Isabella von Carstein said, lucid for the first time in hours. 'Let me.' She held out her hand for her husband's blade.

The Vampire Count gave her the sword willingly.

Posner lowered his head, waiting for the final killing blow to fall.

And then he was dead.

CHAPTER SIXTEEN
The White Wolf

SCHWARTHAFEN, SYLVANIA
Dead of winter, 2049

DEATH WAS A constant companion.

It had been a long and bitter war. At times the Empire emerged triumphant and other times the forces of darkness swept over the living mercilessly. Death was never far away. They lived hand to mouth. They dared not look to the future. Still, in the darkness, a flicker of hope refused to be extinguished. They had lived with this evil, many of them, their entire lives. A few, the oldest of the men, could remember a time before the threat of the Vampire Count, von Carstein, of Sylvania. It had become something of a myth amongst the soldiers.

They had all lost someone to the conflict: brothers, fathers, friends, sisters, wives, mothers, daughters and lovers. Death was no respecter of sex. It didn't limit itself to the battlefields and the trenches. It spilled over into the streets of their home towns. Food was scarce even with the women planting and reaping the harvest. The bakers, the butchers and the grocers made best use of what little they had, eking out the precious ingredients like misers in the hope of fending off famine.

The war was harshest on the children and the elderly; those who knew no better and those who still remembered the life before, when fresh fruit and meat and dairy produce had not been luxuries money couldn't buy.

Sickness was prevalent. Disease flourished in the wretched conditions with scurvy claiming victims daily when food stores ran dry. Cholera and dysentery did the work of von Carstein's army, killing thousands.

The people of the Empire lived with it. They had no choice. Death was all around them, wearing many guises.

Forty years of fighting.

Forty years of dying.

Forty years of losing loved ones.

Forty years trying to cling on to the hope that one day, one day, they would be free of the blight that was Vlad von Carstein, Vampire Count of Sylvania.

Forty years.

Jerek Kruger shuddered at the thought. The undying count had been an ever-present bogeyman throughout the White Wolf's life. The dark was coming. The grand master could not remember a time in his life when he hadn't considered darkness the hour of the enemy. He wasn't a superstitious man; he had yet to meet a foe his two-handed warhammer couldn't vanquish. Even the dead could die, a fact that came as no great surprise to the warrior. Those things were animated, like puppets, they weren't *living*, and they didn't *breathe*. Cut the strings and they fell down.

He scratched at his wild beard. The cold sting of the wind numbed his face. It wormed its way beneath the heavy pelts he wore over his red lacquered armour. The waiting was the worst. He had lost a lot of good men over the years and seen them come back to haunt him in a way that most leaders could never imagine – on the battlefield, shambling forward, clutching the weapons that had failed them in life, their spirits crushed, their souls gone, he prayed, to a better place. Ulric protected them; that is what the men believed as they threw themselves willingly into the slaughter.

Jerek Kruger planted the carved head of his huge two-handed warhammer into the snow between his feet. The rune of Ulric sank more than halfway into the pure white. He knew full well what awaited him and his men over the coming hours. It had passed beyond glory. They were fighting for survival. It was a desperate fight and only grew more so as every casualty added one more to the Vampire Count's horde. If they fell here, if the Knights of the White Wolf failed on the fields of Schwarthafen, the gateway would be open all the way into Altdorf itself, the very heart of the Empire.

'We will not fail,' the grand master said, his voice like flint. Beside him his second-in-command, Roth Mehlinger, grunted his agreement.

'We cannot.'

This was his test, Kruger knew. This was the moment that would give meaning to their lives. These coming days the Knights of the White Wolf would face their greatest foe since their inauguration in the wake of the Chaos Wars. This was the moment they had been born for.

And yet the seed of doubt was there in each man's mind. Their foe was immortal. He had been struck down time and again only to rise with vengeance and unholy fury. No sword, no axe, no hammer could banish the fiend. Kruger couldn't allow himself to think that way. Thinking about von Carstein as eternal sealed his own fate and the fates of all of the men who looked to him for leadership. Von Carstein was a vampire. The beast possessed unholy strength, cunning, gall, but was a beast nonetheless. Johann van Hal, the witch hunter, had first named the evil, and naming is the first stage in slaying it. For all its power the beast suffered from the Hunger, the thirst for fresh, warm blood. They *had* to feed to survive. That was their weakness. For all their cold and cunning they were still driven by the most primal of all instincts, survival.

And to survive they had to feed.

Which meant they could not hide.

The sunlight was deceptive. It offered the illusion of safety. The white pavilions of the Vampire Count were visible across the battlefield. The dead were there, lying where they had fallen, waiting for night to rise again. Most sickening of all, though, were the humans who had flocked to von Carstein's banner. The fools allowed themselves to be fed on, night after night, and guarded the undead by day. These were men and women, innocent, stupid. They saw some tragic romance in the vampire's plight. They flocked to the undead lord, no doubt desperate to be given the Blood Kiss and join the ranks of his true followers. Jerek Kruger couldn't bring himself to think about their stupidity. These were the people he was fighting to *save*.

Sadness smouldered in his soul.

They could not see; they were children lost in a wilderness of mirrors where the hunters cast no reflection.

It was his duty to protect them, to save them from the darkness within themselves and guide them out of the maze of lies and deceits they had lost themselves inside.

He had sworn an oath to the Elector of Middenheim. He was a knight protector. They all were. Each and every wild-haired red-armoured warrior on the field of Schwarthafen. They were not there for glory. They were not there because some ancient principle of honour had been slighted. They were there to protect those that could not protect themselves. They were the last chance.

The last hope.

And they were a long way from home.

Middenheim with its lofty viaducts and deep catacombs was an impregnable fortress on a sheer-sided pinnacle of rock rising out of dense forestland. That was a fortress built to withstand almost any assault. Drawing up the wooden bridges effectively cut the city off from the outside world. But they weren't in Middenheim; they were in the Ulric-forsaken wastelands of Sylvania and they were lining up to face the greatest evil known to man. It was a fool's fight.

Kruger knew it. Mehlinger knew it.

And every other man out there that evening knew it.

Still they stood there implacably, ready for the fight of their lives.

The mood in the camp was sombre. Some men busied themselves tending to their mounts, rechecking the barding and the braces, the stirrups and the girth, while others oiled their platemail or knelt in prayer and supplication, offering devotion to the warrior god.

'Walk with me,' Kruger told Mehlinger.

Together they moved down the line, offering words of encouragement to the younger knights, sharing fond reminiscences with the older ones. Jerek Kruger was, among many things, a leader of men. They looked to him for guidance in this dark time. He made a promise to himself that he would not let them down. He knew them all by name and face, he knew their families, their stories. He was their father, for many of the men the bond was stronger than it was to their own flesh and blood. He took an interest in their lives, in them as people.

Mehlinger moved silently beside him. Kruger knew the men called him the Grand Master's Shadow. There were worse epithets for a knight. He was taciturn and dour, preferring his own company or the company of Aster, his horse. People were a burden, they thought and did strange things, acted in peculiar ways, and more often than not let you down. Mehlinger needed things he could trust around him, and in the Knights of the White Wolf he had a brotherhood he *could* trust but trusting still came hard to the man, Kruger knew. They all had their weaknesses but it was their strengths, when combined, which set them apart. Alone they were weak, together they were giants.

That was what made them what they were. They thought and acted as one. United.

That was what made the Knights of the White Wolf the most feared and revered fighting force in the Empire.

Nothing could stand against them. Nothing.

Until now.

He stood alone at the head of the army, gazing out into the lowering dark at the white pavilions of the Vampire Count. They were a thorn in his soul, drawing blood every time he moved within their shadows. The von Carstein banner snapped in the wind, the sigil impossible to make out from this distance. Kruger knew it well. It was a vile loathsome icon.

'When this is over, Mehlinger, I'll burn that damned banner and dedicate whatever years I have left to purging this blighted province of its taint.' He said it forcefully enough to be heard by a few of the men who were using oil and rags to tend to their warhammers.

'And we'll be right there with you!' one of the knights, a flame-haired bull of a man, Lukien Karr, roared.

Kruger nodded. 'Damn right you will be.'

He turned his back on the pavilions and looked up at the sun, already setting behind the hills and the treeline of Ghoul Wood. He slammed a gauntleted hand off his breastplate, saluting the men as he passed them on the way back to his command point.

'Ready the men. We ride when the sun dips beneath the horizon. I want every second rider equipped with burning brands, for the first pass their warhammers will be their secondary weapon. Understood? I want–' he very nearly said chaos but that wasn't right, he didn't want to invite chaos into the battle. He raised his voice so it carried down the line, a rallying call. 'Von Carstein's army is a shambles. These creatures burn, so we burn them. We purge their ungodly taint from the world. We hammer them into the ground and we sear them off the face of the earth. These things aren't human. They aren't our friends, our loved ones. They are diabolical shells, shades sent to taunt us, to draw out our grief and unman us. Well, no more. We will purge this wretched land of their daemonic taint with oil and fire if we must, but purge it we will. We ride tonight for more than valour, we ride for everything that is *right*. We ride for every innocent child of the Empire so that they might live in a world worthy of them! We ride for the survival of all mankind!'

Up and down the line the battle-hardened Knights of the White Wolf responded to Kruger's impassioned speech vigorously, hammering their breastplates with gauntleted fists over and over until the beating became deafening, and then, when the hammering was at its loudest, howling like the very beasts they took their name from.

Kruger slammed his gauntleted fist once against his breastplate and lifted it in salute to his men.

'We fight!' Mehlinger cried. 'Mount up! Night falls!'

'The White Wolves ride!' the chant went up. 'The White Wolves ride!'

Roused, they were an awesome sight.

Nothing could stand against them, Kruger promised himself. Nothing.

He turned away from his men. Mehlinger was right, where he had assumed they had a final hour, they had barely minutes as the sun dipped behind the treelined hills. Already shapes were emerging from the white pavilions: von Carstein's vampires.

On the ground the dead stirred.

CHAPTER SEVENTEEN

Riders on the Storm

SCHWARTHAFEN, SYLVANIA
Dead of winter, 2049

AT FULL GLORIOUS charge the Knights of the White Wolf were an awesome sight.

The thundering hooves of the warhorses sent shivers coursing through the earth itself. The cacophonous tattoo of their charge rent the night.

Rank upon rank of majestic chargers came at the rows of undead with flaming brands and warhammers swinging.

'For all of humankind!' Mehlinger bellowed, his words snatched away by the wind.

Kruger drove his spurs hard into his horse's flanks, urging her to open up into full gallop. The waiting was over: the helplessness of it, the doubt gnawing away at a man's courage, the uncertainty. Fighting was better. The old Wolf lived for the thrill of it. There was nothing in the world even remotely like the vitality of it: man and beast as one. The charred earth crunched under his horse's hooves. Grimly, Kruger wiped the sweat from his eyes with the fur cuff of his gauntlet.

Mehlinger blew his warhorn, trumpeting the command to full gallop.

The discipline of the line was precise; when the grand master gave his horse her head the rest of the line followed, matching their momentum beat for beat.

Kruger's smile was grim.

There was no evil in the world that could not be thwarted by men brave enough to stand up against it.

There was no fear here today. This was what they lived for.

His warhammer sang in the air as he whipped it round above his head.

The cry of carrion birds overhead matched it hungrily; the birds had some sixth sense, flocking to the killing ground long before the first blood was spilled.

The air reeked of sulphur, sharp and repugnant.

No waning of the light marked the arrival of night. Moments before the charge a bloom of blue light above the white pavilions chased up into the heavens, like lightning in reverse as it gathered into a luminous sphere. The ball of lightning shifted colour almost continuously as it climbed until it met the clouds with a clash of steel and a belly-deep rumble of thunder that rent the sky. Immediately the rain came down, hard. The fat drops bounced five and six inches off the battlefield, turning it quickly to sludge beneath the horses' hooves.

Kruger had heard stories of the Vampire Count resorting to sorcery to turn the tide of his battles. Von Carstein could conjure hordes of ravaging daemons for all he cared. They would die just the same. Kruger was nothing if not a practical man. He knew what the blossoming blue radiance was but, unnatural or not, rain was rain and his men were more than capable of riding through a storm. The redolent sulphur, the ball lightning, the sudden fury of the storm itself, all of it might be unnerving, Kruger thought maliciously, but they were incomparable to the sight of the White Wolves bearing down on you.

The white-hot fire of battle filled his senses, coruscating through his entire body.

This was what being alive was, at its very grandest.

Here, now.

And then the battle was joined in a horrifying destruction of flesh, blood and bone as the Knights of the White Wolf hit the ranks of the dead head-on, warhammers crashing into thick skulls and mashing through dead arms as they clawed out. Firebrands flew high into the air, arcing, some burning out in the torrential rain, others descending on the mass of undead with lethal fire, igniting on the desiccated skin of the zombies.

The dead met the charge kicking and screaming as they were trampled beneath the horses' hooves.

Already the ghouls had a feast of corpses to gorge themselves on. Bodies sprawled in pools of congealing blood. Some had lost arms, legs were crushed, heads stoved in. The ghouls treated them all the same: as meat.

Kruger's warhammer smashed into skulls and shoulders, cutting a swathe through the dead. This was his day. This is what he had been born to do. *He* was the immortal on the field, not von Carstein. The blood fury sang through his veins. He bellowed a fearsome battle-cry and threw himself into the fray. He booted a shambling zombie in the face so hard that the creature's jaw caved in, and lifted another, a child with dead eyes, off its feet with the staggering force of his hammer blow. The boy slumped with his arm hanging loosely at his side, forced himself to his feet only for Kruger's hammer to stove in his skull. The air around Jerek Kruger ripped and crackled with violence. He savoured it, channelling it inside, feeling it course through his veins and turning it into his own strength. That was his magic. He was a fighter.

He sought out von Carstein across the field of slaughter and found him.

'Face me!' the grand master roared, challenging the Vampire Count. His taunt carried across the fighting and was met by a sneer from the pale lips of von Carstein. Kruger stood in the saddle and roared his challenge again: 'Face me!'

Mehlinger's warhorn sounded three times in short succession, drawing the second rank of knights in a sweeping arc across the battlefield and sending the third rank in their wake to pick off the pieces while the front rank broke the back of the undead's force. The dead scattered aimlessly, lost for direction as the Vampire Count rose to meet Jerek Kruger's challenge, his sword wailing and shrieking like a daemon possessed as he wheeled his mount around and spurred the nightmare beast into a rash charge.

Kruger's heart slowed, his pulse, the noise of the battle, everything around him slowed as though trapped in molasses. He saw von Carstein riding at him, saw the carrion birds circling overhead hungrily, saw the dead falling beneath his horse's hooves, but it all happened so slowly. His heartbeat thundered in his ears. His battle-cry stretched out into one long deafening howl.

And then the world snapped violently back into place.

Kruger's warhammer sang as it whistled through the air. The white pavilions were battered by the wind and rain but still that damnable banner snapped and flapped tauntingly against the black sky.

The Vampire Count's horde was in disarray. The Knights of the White Wolf hammered them down, crushing them ruthlessly.

Kruger only had eyes for one foe: the Vampire Count.

Von Carstein's tainted blade cried out for blood as the Vampire Count flung himself forward. Ripples of moonlight shimmered on the cursed blade as it scythed through the air, aimed high at Kruger's neck.

The grand master took the blow on the shaft of his huge warhammer, the jarring impact shuddering through him. He slammed a fist into von Carstein's face. There was nothing pretty about the move. It was pure brutality. It was a bone-crunching blow that had the vampire reeling in his saddle.

Kruger pressed his slim advantage, bringing the butt of the warhammer's shaft to bear. He jabbed the end of it into von Carstein's face as he struggled to shift his balance. The vampire was quicker. He rolled under the blow, taking it on his shoulder, his sword snaking out and slicing uselessly off Kruger's breastplate. The speed of the counter was dizzying. No sooner had the wailing blade clattered off Kruger's mail than von Carstein brought it to bear again and again in two lightning fast nicks, either side of the grand master's face, drawing blood on both cheeks. The wounds dripped into Kruger's unkempt beard. They were marks of humiliation, nothing more, nothing less.

Kruger roared, his entire musculature driven by controlled fury. He brought his warhammer down in a crushing arc. The blow was clumsy. It missed von Carstein and cracked sickeningly into the head of the Vampire Count's nightmarish steed. The animal shied, bucking and twisting, as its hind legs buckled and spilled von Carstein from the saddle. The undead count leapt clear, landing lightly, a look of intense displeasure on his face. He brought the wailing blade to the centre, taking it in a two-handed grip, then waited, implacable, deadly.

Kruger wheeled his mount around and charged for von Carstein, his mind filled with the image of the count's head bursting like an overripe watermelon beneath his hammer blow.

Again von Carstein was too quick. He dived and rolled beneath Kruger's lethal hammer and between his mount's deadly hooves, coming out on the other side in a tight crouch, horse blood dripping from his sword where he had gutted the animal on the way through. The horse managed five more steps before it realised it was dead and collapsed. Kruger barely managed to roll free before the dead weight of the beast pinned him in the mud.

Von Carstein was on him in an instant, followed by a pack of howling ghouls who threw themselves on the dead horse, biting and tearing with their teeth and bare hands. Gouts of blood pumped from the animal's gaping stomach, soaking the vile creatures as they fed.

'You're a parasite. Your time here is done, vampire,' Kruger said, his grimace hard as he weighed the warhammer in his huge hands.

'And you're wasting your precious breath trying to goad me, savage. Time to die.' The vampire unleashed a lethal reverse cut, feinting first high to Kruger's left then pulling the blow a fraction before the White Wolf's block and dropping his right shoulder, rolling the cut so it actually came from underneath, shearing up for his throat. Kruger barely got out of the way in time to save his life as the wailing blade sliced away the lobe and more than half of his ear in a bloody mess. The pain was blinding.

He staggered back a step and countered with a punishing right cross, his meaty fist snapping the vampire's head back. One fang snapped under the impact, spraying blood. Kruger sprang forward raining blows on either side of von Carstein's head, slamming his club-like fist into the vampire's ear and his nose but the Vampire Count was strong, impossibly strong. After the initial shock of the blow von Carstein unleashed the beast within, sacrificing all pretence at humanity, and roared on the offensive, his bloody blade slashing and arcing between them.

They circled each other warily, each judging the other for signs of weakness, looking for the kill. Death was very close and Kruger did not care. He had never been more alive.

Von Carstein feinted left and lunged, the tip of the wailing blade slicing at Kruger's stomach. The knight slammed the cut away and launched himself two-footed at the vampire, his booted feet crashing into the Count's face. Von Carstein staggered back. Kruger rolled to his feet as the vampire reared up, sword slashing wildly in the air between them. The knight threw himself forward, blocking blow after blow with the shaft of his warhammer and answering each with a devastating counter aimed at the Count's head until the rune of Ulric slammed into the side of von Carstein's face, hurling him from his feet. He lay there in the pool of horse's blood, ghouls all around him feasting, as Jerek Kruger, chest heaving, stood over him.

'Today I conquer death, destroyer of worlds. Go back to the hell that spawned you, fiend.'

With that Kruger beat the life out of the Vampire Count, pounding his bones to a bloody pulp with his mighty warhammer. The carrion birds cackled and cawed, circling vindictively overhead.

Mehlinger's horn trumpeted. The Vampire Count had fallen and the remnants of his army were routed.

The tide of the battle had turned. Kruger sank to his knees, utterly spent. Dawn was still hours away. It didn't matter. They were victorious. The night was won.

CHAPTER EIGHTEEN
A Wolf to the Slaughter

MIDDENHEIM
Spring, 2050

BUT ONE NIGHT does not a war win when the enemy refuses to die. The sad truth is that victory on one field can easily turn to defeat on another.

Where the open fields of Schwarthafen suited the glorious chargers of the Knights of the White Wolf, the cramped serpentine streets of Middenheim imprisoned them. It was impossible to ride their horses and unseated they lost not only their mobility but their cohesion as well.

Without their powerful mounts the knights were nothing more than glorified infantry with unwieldy weapons unused to fighting at close quarters.

They were vulnerable to von Carstein's undead.

The city's isolation on the huge plateau, the Fauschlag, only served to hinder them all the more because their enemy was neither mortal nor flesh and bone. In his heart Kruger knew there was no way to fend off von Carstein this time. What use was iron and steel against the ghosts conjured by the Vampire Count?

Von Carstein held back his zombies and skeletons, crowding them on the viaducts into the city itself and in a vast ring around the base of the plateau.

Instead he unleashed the revenant shades, the wraiths and the wights and the ghasts and the ghouls, ethereal undead that ghosted through wood and stone as though it didn't exist. Middenheim was every inch the great fortress city that Ulric foresaw but in a matter of hours von Carstein turned it into a necropolis.

Middenheim, City of the Dead.

Lukien Karr was the first casualty. Brave, foolish Lukien. Bellowing the battle-cry of the White Wolves, the knight stepped into the path of a ghastly shade and met it steel for insubstantial talons. The wraith entered Karr, sank into his skin and chilled his heart and turned his blood to ice, then ripped itself free of the dead man, ectoplasmic ribbons of ichor fanning out behind the wraith as it screeched off up the narrow street toward the plague monument. It was over in a heartbeat. Karr fell to the cobbles, a look of abject terror frosted onto his face.

More died the same way, the spirits shrieking and laughing as they tore through the flesh of the knights, making a mockery of their life as the helpless warriors hurled their hammers and struggled vainly to fight off an enemy as insubstantial as thin air.

The cry went up for priests, the desperate hope that faith and holy water would stand firm where iron and steel had proved useless.

Jerek Kruger stood in the centre of it all, watching his men die and helpless to do anything about it. He burned with impotent rage.

The ghosts of von Carstein tore through the streets, they drifted, they flew, they emerged from solid stone walls, they came from everywhere and there was nothing Kruger could do but swing his warhammer and wonder why the revenant shades claimed the lives of those around him but left him alive. They swarmed through the Pit with its warren of decrepit shacks and tumbledown buildings. They swept through the makeshift hovels as easily as they did Middenpalaz, the graf's palatial home. They poured through the squares, moonlight shining through their transparent forms, and down the streets, an endless sea of incorporeal souls spilling out of the shadows and the spaces between. In the Graf's Repose succulents and hardy perennials choked and withered as the cold flush of death lapped over them in foetid waves. Von Carstein's dead army threatened all life.

The priests came shuffling into the streets, cowed by the terrifying might of the wraiths and the ghasts as they snuffed the life out of the knights trying vainly to protect them as they stumbled over lines of exorcism and banishment rituals. They joined together from all denominations: Ulric, Sigmar, Shallya, Myrmidia, Verena and Morr, bringing their bells and holy books into the streets, spraying blessed water at the shades and shadows, though fear had them cowering and tripping over the lines of the rituals, allowing the mellifluous wraiths to slide into their flesh and chill their blood to ice, culling the one defence the city of Middenheim actually had from the Vampire Count's wrath.

The high priest of Sigmar suffered the worst. As the old man raised his eyes to the Middenheim Spire he saw the implacable figure of Vlad von Carstein squatting amid the buttresses and the gargoyles. It was impossible for him to make out the sardonic mockery in the pale count's expression but still the old priest was overwhelmed by the sudden repulsive touch of the vampire's base evil. The priest knew that von Carstein only resembled a human, that his nature was in fact something far older, and far more malignant in origin. His tainted blood was ancient and far crueller than any living being's.

He revelled in savagery, in death, in sadistic slaughter and sacrifice. He excelled at it. He was the Lord of Death and he hungered for mortal flesh, mortal blood. The priest felt the taint of his hunger, felt himself succumbing to it, being overwhelmed by the bloodlust of the beast perched up amongst the gargoyles, mocking their heroics.

The cobblestones around the Sigmarite's feet frosted with rime, touched by the unholy cold of the hungry dead, ribbons of frost crystallising and crusting over the stone walls of his temple, solidifying into ice. The priest's breath fogged in the air in front of his face as he struggled to give voice to the words of banishment, merging with the spectral forms, his own breath giving shape and definition to the dead. And then they were inside him, not one wraith, but a whole ungodly host, devouring his eternal soul even as they congested his lungs and blocked his throat with ice so that he could not breath or talk, choking him slowly and painfully to death even as the Vampire Count's mocking laughter rang through the streets. As the cold wormed its way into the silver hammer around his neck, the holy relic cracked and split in two. The shards fell to the cobbles and shattered like glass. The priest clutched at his throat, clawing at his own tongue, trying to pull it out so that he might swallow one last desperate mouthful of air before he died.

Kruger watched helplessly, feeling wretched, responsible and helpless at the same time. The fact that the wraiths came shrieking into his face and then pulled away to claim another soul tormented the grand master. He bellowed his rage and chased the bodiless entities into the open square beneath the Middenheim Spire, slipping and stumbling on the frosted cobbles as the shadows writhed and good men died.

'It's me you want!' Kruger yelled, his cry whipped away by the icy wind. He had killed von Carstein once, but death held no dominion over the count. He had heard the stories of Bluthof where five lances had skewered von Carstein to the ground before the Count of

Ostland had buried his Runefang deep in the beast's heart. Three days later von Carstein returned to order the crucifixion of prisoners outside the town gates. At Bogenhafen Bridge a cannon ball had decapitated the Vampire Count. An hour later the cannon crew were dead and Bogenhafen was overrun, Vlad von Carstein at the head of the conquering army.

The beast refused to die.

Von Carstein's mocking laughter haunted Kruger until he finally saw the monster crouched between the leering gargoyles of the spire hundreds of feet above. Kruger didn't hesitate. He charged into the vault of the cathedral, the massive wooden doors banging closed behind him, the echoes folding in on themselves as they reverberated through the massive dome above his head. Stained glass images of Ulric and the White Wolves let in a wondrous array of hues, reds and golds and greens dappling the stone floor like a scattering of coins.

Kruger ran down the aisle. The leather grip of his warhammer was soaked with the cold sweat of fear; its reminder spurred him on. He crashed through the door at the rear of the temple and started up the spiral stairs two and three at a time. There were two hundred and seventy-six in total, curling up almost two hundred feet to the bell tower. The grand master's lungs were burning before he was halfway up, his legs on fire, but guilt drove him on viciously. Kruger gasped for breath as he slammed the door to the bell tower open.

Von Carstein was there, ringing a death knell with the hilt of his damnable sword on the huge brass bell, the sonorous clang resonating through the very fabric of the tower.

Kruger sucked in a deep breath, battling to regulate his breathing. He wasn't a young man anymore. He felt every one of the stairs he had just climbed.

'I wondered how many you were prepared to sacrifice before you remembered you were a man and came to face me,' von Carstein said, amicably. He sheathed his sword.

'All of this was to get me?' Kruger said, images of the slaughter flashing through his mind. He shook his head, trying to dislodge them. He focussed on the undead count's sardonic smile, his cold eyes that delved deep inside, stripping away secrets and fears as though they were layers of clothing draped over a soul. He gave his hatred for the monster facing him time to fester.

'So it seems, does it not?'

'I killed you once before, von Carstein. Who's to say I won't do it again?'

'Well,' the Vampire Count said, appearing to give the question serious thought, 'me. You interest me, something most humans fail to do. You have... qualities that it is easy to admire. I could use a man like you.'

'Over my dead body,' Kruger spat.

'That was the general idea, yes.'

The Vampire Count moved away from the prayer bell. He came toward Kruger, his smile widening with each step closer. He moved like a spider, cautious, with predatory cunning.

'If you kill me, this ends. You have your revenge. Let my men live.'

'Too late for that, I am afraid. My pets are hungry. I promised them some succulent morsels to eat and nothing tastes better than fattened wolf meat, believe me.'

'You disgust me. You aren't human.'

'Don't you ever feel it, Wolf? The thirst for blood? Oh, I can see it in your eyes. You do. You do. You feel it now. You feel it on the battlefield when you ride for your precious honour. You hide behind your fatuous code of chivalry but we aren't so different. You choose to justify your violence and thirst for blood behind mysticism, claiming devotion to your pathetic warrior god so you can make it holy. At least I am honest about it. I allow myself to delight in the hedonistic rush of killing. I revel in the naked savagery of death. It is in you already, Wolf. The beast is in your soul. You keep it caged but it comes out every time you hold that hammer of yours. Believe me, you would make a good vampire. You already have the taste for blood.'

'I am nothing like you.'

'No, of course, you are the honourable and decent savage whereas I am just the savage.'

'Shut up!' Kruger hissed, lashing out with his warhammer.

Von Carstein didn't move. He didn't even breathe.

Kruger lunged forward two steps, the old wooden timber beams of the floor groaning under his weight. He swung again, wildly.

Von Carstein exploded into brutal, astonishing, action. He sprang at the White Wolf, his black cloak billowing out behind him. His economy of movement was both lethal and hypnotic; there was a brutal precision to his kicks and punches as they came, hard and fast. It was all Kruger could do to ward off the first few. In the space between heartbeats he was driven to his knees by a rain of punishment so shockingly violent it was irresistible. He threw up his warhammer desperately but it made no difference. An open-handed strike to the throat had Kruger choking as he swallowed his tongue. Vlad stepped back, watching curiously as the grand master choked slowly to death.

'No,' he said, shaking his head. 'You don't get away from me that easily, Wolf.'

He reached down and grabbed the pelt around Jerek Kruger's shoulders and hauled him effortlessly to his feet. The grand master's eyes flickered convulsively as he hovered on the edge of death. Von

Carstein waited until his enemy was a second from death and sank his teeth into Kruger's throat. He drank hungrily, savouring the hot sweet coppery taste of the White Wolf's blood as it trickled down his throat. He pulled back before he completely drained the grizzled old warrior, grabbed a handful of hair and yanked his mouth open. Slowly, savouring the final delicious irony of the moment, the Vampire Count sank his teeth into his own wrist, drawing blood. He held the wound over Kruger's mouth, letting it drip down his throat.

Kruger's body shuddered, every ounce of the man's being revolting against the tainted blood as it pooled in his mouth... and then he swallowed and his eyes flared open as he gagged and gasped a first desperate breath in minutes.

He lurched away from the Vampire Count's Blood Kiss, reeling as his legs betrayed him. Clutching at a low beam, Kruger staggered toward the moonlight as it poured in through an open arch.

He turned to look back at von Carstein.

'It ends here.'

He turned back to the arch. He felt the kiss of the fresh air on his face, savoured it, one final proof that he was alive, and threw himself from the height of the great spire.

CHAPTER NINETEEN
Alone in the Dark

MIDDENHEIM
Spring, 2050

He awoke in claustrophobic darkness. He couldn't move. His arms were crossed over his chest. He could move his legs sideways about six inches. No more.

The darkness pressed down on him. He tried to move his arms, sliding them down his chest, working them around to his side. It felt worse. He was trapped. He couldn't think.

Then, in hallucinatory flashes it came back to him. The wights, the wraiths, the rime of frost across the city – his city – as the ghosts of the conquered ravaged it and up above, the mocking laughter of von Carstein as his friends – no, men, he didn't have friends, his men – died, and then he was falling. The space in between was blank. Each fresh revelation stripped away another little piece of his humanity. He felt no grief, only curious detachment as his life came back to him fragment by bloody fragment, his identity establishing itself there in the dark.

He had been Jerek Kruger. That was before. He didn't know who he was now. Or what.

Only that he was something else – something altogether alien to the man he had been, though he possessed all of Kruger's memories and longings and no doubt wore the dead man's skin and bones.

Jerek Kruger was dead. He knew that with cold certainty.

Von Carstein's taunts came back to him: *It is in you already, Wolf. The beast is in your soul. You keep it caged but it comes out every time you hold that hammer of yours. Believe me, you would make a good vampire. You already have the taste for blood.*

The fall...

He tasted something sour in his mouth. It took him a moment to realise what it was: dried blood.

You already have the taste for blood. He knew then what had happened to him, what the taste of rust in his mouth signified. He writhed about in the tight confines of the coffin, kicking and gagging at the same time. His feet drummed dully on the wooden lid of the coffin, the weight of the earth dampening the sound to a dull thud. He was underground. They had buried him. Panic flared in his mind. He wasn't just trapped he was buried beneath tons of dirt. The sudden understanding was suffocating. The thing that had been Kruger shrieked its terror, bucking and writhing against the tight confines of the coffin.

He worked his hands around until they were either side of his face.

The darkness was all consuming.

Through the haze of fear one single need emerged: hunger. He needed to feed.

The thought simultaneously revolted and excited him. He could taste the blood in his mouth and it tasted good. He wanted more. He needed more. Fresh blood.

He had to find a way out of this prison. He had to feed.

Von Carstein had turned him into a monster... or had he always been a monster? Had the vampire been right? Had the beast always been shackled within his soul just waiting to be set free?

He knew who he was. It came to him with shocking clarity. He was a vampire, like von Carstein who had fathered him.

He was von Carstein, as much as any son was part of its father: by blood.

Jerek von Carstein. He tasted the name in his mind. Jerek von Carstein.

They would pay for doing this to him. All of them.

Anger blazed inside him. White-hot fury. He had fought monsters all his life and in doing so had become the worst sort. He roared in pain and frustration, and pushed at the wooden lid with his feet and his knees and the flats of his hands. The thin wood cracked and began to splinter beneath the strain. A trickle of dirt spilled into the coffin, hitting him on the chest. He roared again and pushed with all of his might but the lid didn't give another inch. The hard-packed earth kept it lodged in place.

He was trapped. Buried alive... Only he would be alive forever.

Forever trapped in the suffocating darkness, unable to move, unable to do anything but think. It would drive him to madness.

But it would save lives up there... The thought came to him unbidden. As long as he was a prisoner in his earthly tomb they were safe up there: his men, their families, the people he had fought to protect against the beast that was von Carstein.

But their safety would be his undoing. He wasn't strong enough. He knew that already.

The taste of blood was metallic on his tongue, taunting him.

He didn't just need to feed, he *wanted* to. Von Carstein had turned him into a monster.

He beat his knuckles raw and bloody against the splintered wood in frustration. Clawed at the splinters, tore his nails scrabbling at the wooden lid trying to tear through it. Jags of wood cut into his fingers, shredding the flesh and paring it down to the bone in places.

And then the dirt came. Like rain.

The lid gave way, a huge crack opening down the centre, and the mud and the worms and the stones spilled into the coffin, trapping Jerek von Carstein completely. He opened his mouth to scream and the dirt poured into it, filling him.

He lashed out wildly but could barely move. *Choking,* he thought desperately as he swallowed mouthfuls of dirt. *Can't breathe... Can't...*

But there was no pain in his lungs. No light-headed dizziness. No desperate retching for breath. He didn't need it. He was dead already. The thought ripped away one of the final shreds of his sanity.

He raged against the suffocating press of the soil and the jagged splinters of the coffin lid, tearing at the dirt, clawing upwards, dragging himself through the hard-packed earth until, finally, his face broke the surface.

He was born again.

Born into death in a brutal parody of the way he had been born into life, the earth yielding him up, his mother in this undead life.

He opened his eyes to see his father looking down at him.

Jerek coughed up a lungful of worms and black dirt.

'Why?' he managed to ask. 'Why did you do this?'

'Because you owed me a death. Because I lost a good man but in you I found a better one. Because I saw into your soul. Because you were already a wolf. All of these reasons and none of them. Because I *wanted* to. You will work it out, in time. Now come, let's feed. There is a world of flesh and blood out here. Satisfy your hunger, Wolf.'

Vlad gripped Jerek's wrist and hauled him free of the grave.

CHAPTER TWENTY
Dusk Chorus

ALTDORF
Winter, 2051

Jon Skellan had all but forgotten what it was like to be human.

It had been so long since he last felt anything.

That was what he missed most, the simple sensation of feeling the air in his lungs as he drew a deep breath, of smelling the fresh cut grass and the bread rising in the baker's oven, the kiss of sunlight on his face.

Sunlight.

He had taken it for granted all his life. The sun rose, the sun set. It was as simple as that. He was sixty-nine years old, though he hadn't aged a day in decades. Skellan hadn't felt the sun on his face in forty-one years.

Forty-one years.

He couldn't remember what it felt like.

The only thing he did feel now was hunger. It was a dark desperate sensation that gnawed away inside him constantly, demanding to be fed and with an appetite that could never truly be sated. He wasn't the man he had once been; the base lust for revenge that had driven him for so long had faded with the death of Aigner and his siring. The traces of humanity had faded gradually over the years, being subsumed by the fundamental vampiric urge: the need to feed. He had come to enjoy the hunt and the kill. A predatory smile spread across his face. He could taste it, thick in the air:

Blood.

The coming days promised slaughter; a rare feast of blood, old, young, innocent and soured by bitter experience. The city of Altdorf offered a smorgasbord of death fit for the entire vampiric aristocracy of Sylvania. Von Carstein's malignant kin swelled the undead army for the final glorious assault on the heart of the Empire itself.

Altdorf. The Imperial capital stood on a series of islands amongst the broad mud flats at the confluence of the Reik and Talabec rivers.

The city's defences were pitifully inadequate. In desperation the fools had dug ditches and planted stakes as though they expected the vampires to rush forward and throw themselves blindly on the sharpened wooden spikes. More old wives' tales had driven the citizens of the capital to redirect the flow of the Reik itself so it formed a moat of running water. Inside the city walls the riverbeds had run dry and the defenders had taken to using them as expedient footpaths. It was quite ingenious how they had managed it but then, the city was renowned for its learning.

The effort was unnecessary, of course. Superstition turned them all into fools. They prayed blindly to their impotent gods for salvation and turned to legends, needing them to be true. They bent the Reik because they needed to believe doing so gave them immunity from the vampires; that the count and his kin couldn't cross a river of fast-flowing water.

Holed up in their damp cellars, hidden behind planks and boards that blinded their windows, the Altdorfers deliberately forgot about the zombies, the ghouls, the ghasts, and other revenant shades at von Carstein's disposal. They had little hope. Mothers cradled their babies in their arms, shivering, backs pressed against the cold stone walls, listening for the sound of the vampires coming, trying to summon the courage to kill their own flesh and blood rather than give them over to the monsters to feed off. Desperate sobs haunted the darkest places of the city. This was their doom.

Skellan thrived on it.

War had accelerated the process of decay; what could fail and powder and flake and rust and collapse, did. Nature had already begun the long process of ridding the land of the pestilential hand of man. The first stage was rendering the once-grand buildings to dust returned. Vines and creepers crawled up the sides of the great surrounding walls, undermining the strength of their foundations as they rooted in between the cracks where the stones mated, working them wider and making them weaker.

What nature started they would finish.

Mankind would suffer in its final hours.

Skellan looked up at the sky. Dawn was less than an hour away. He could sense the complacency creeping into the defenders as they manned the battlements. The archers knew that they were safe, for a few hours at least; von Carstein would not launch an attack so close to sunrise.

Safety was an illusion.

He turned to look behind him. Along the mud flats tens of thousands of mindless automata were crowded, piles of bones and rotten flesh gathered in an endless wave of violence waiting to crash against the defenders, and at the lumbering siege engines rolling slowly forward to the front line. Von Carstein's army appeared endless, stretching as far as the eye could see. He could only imagine the effect it had on the morale of the men facing it, waiting, grimly relieved that at least they had another day of living allotted to them, thinking that they would get to return home to their wives and children one last time before the nightmare was turned loose.

How wrong they were.

The sky remained black as the heart of night, no sign of dawn's first blush of light.

Skellan turned to the grizzled old wolf of a man beside him, as Jerek von Carstein in turn shifted to look at the first of the massive siege engines of fused body and bone lumbering into position. Skellan didn't entirely trust the count's pet even if Vlad himself seemed to think the White Wolf had been entirely tamed. There was something about him that rankled, though it was impossible for Skellan to put his finger on what it was. Of course duplicity and deceit were hardly strange bedfellows for any member of the vampiric aristocracy; they were all a bunch of murderous liars, cheats and thieves, Skellan included. Trust was not something to be blindly given.

The first of the huge siege engines lumbered into place, hundreds of von Carstein's zombies hauling on ropes to drag it forward. The vampires patrolled the lines, whipping the creatures to greater and greater efforts. The infernal machine was like some freshly rendered vision of hell, a confusion of arms and legs and screaming contorted faces fused together in an impossible jumble that towered over the battlefield. Carrion crows circled overhead, drawn by the stench of death that clung to the monstrous trebuchets and catapults.

Mouths moved, still screaming. The constructs were alive, or at least alive in death, animated by dark magic. Their screams echoed the caws of the carrion birds.

Eight machines were locked in place, in range of the high city walls, another eight waiting in reserve.

The sun showed no sign of rising. There would be no dawn to save them.

He wondered when the defenders would realise that in their final hours night had become eternal.

Skellan walked a slow path through the dead to von Carstein's white pavilion, where the count sat, the wailing blade in his lap, toying with the signet ring on his left hand, rolling it slowly around his long thin finger. Von Carstein looked up, his already pale features emaciated now with the strain of war. It was obvious he needed to feed. Skellan drew one of the count's aides aside and instructed him to bring fresh blood that he might share with von Carstein before they delivered the ultimatum. The swarthy manservant scurried off.

'Can you taste it?' von Carstein said without looking up from his sword. The blade moaned slightly beneath his fingertips.

'The fear? Oh yes, delicious isn't it. They are waiting for their precious sun but it isn't coming.'

'Everyone is afraid of the dark, Skellan. It is a primal fear. It goes back to when we lived in caves and used fire to keep the monsters of the night at bay. We could sit here for a month, in perpetual dark and then walk into Altdorf unmolested because fear will have done the fighting for us. I can feel it already, undermining them. They huddle in the dark places praying death will pass them by.'

'They know nothing,' Skellan said.

The manservant returned with a young girl. Her feet and face were covered in grime and she was trembling uncontrollably.

'Ask her,' von Carstein said. 'Ask her what is more frightening, being here with us now, or being locked in the dark waiting to be dragged before us. Well girl, which is it?'

'Yes,' Skellan said, moving in close to stand just behind her, his hand touching the softness of her cheek as silent tears fell. His accent shifted into a much purer Reikspiel, and he began talking to the girl in her own tongue. 'Which is it? The wait or the kill? Which frightens you more?'

The girl shook her head.

Skellan tangled his fist in her hair and yanked her head back. 'I asked you a question, I expect an answer.'

'W...w... waiting,' she stammered.

'That wasn't so difficult was it,' Skellan said, almost tenderly. 'Now, let's get you cleaned up shall we? Can't have you covered in mud like this. Manners cost us nothing.' He gestured for the lurking servant to bring a wet cloth and gently cleaned the grime from the girl's face, lingering over her tears. Done, he turned her around. 'Better, and now you only stink of fear, not mud,' he said approvingly, and sank his teeth into her neck. Even as she screamed and fought against him, until the strength left her limbs and her arms hung slackly at her side. Her eyes rolled up into her head. Skellan broke away, gasping as he swallowed the last mouthful of warm blood and tossed her over to von Carstein to finish off.

'Feed,' Skellan said. 'You need your strength.'

The count drained the last of the girl's blood and threw the corpse to a ghoul who dragged it outside so that it could strip the flesh from the bones and feast out of sight of its master.

Von Carstein stood, sheathing the hungry sword and fastening his cloak about his shoulders. He looked at Skellan and nodded. 'It is time.'

With that, he walked out into the eternal night, Skellan two paces behind him.

The Vampire Count moved through the ranks of the dead, eyes fixed on the city walls.

Skellan studied his master as he led the way. For all that he had come to admire von Carstein's ruthlessness in the pursuit of his vision of a Kingdom of the Dead the man was deeply flawed. He was not the perfect monster. He could be insufferable with his brooding and his philosophising. It was melancholic and introspective and had no place in the armour of a great leader. It was too human; too close to weakness and those other damnable human traits. It was a game to Skellan, and whether the cattle played by the rules or broke them the results were the same, he fed off them. He didn't care about them. They were just meat. Von Carstein's attachment to them left him with a cold feeling in his gut. And the woman, Isabella, she was nothing short of insane. Her instability however made her interesting. She understood, in some basic way, the game.

Skellan had heard tales of her habits, bathing in vats of virgin blood to preserve her good looks, drinking thirty and forty maidens in a single night in a glut of ecstasy, painting the walls of the palace with the blood of her victims after an orgy of killing and an hour later complain that she was lonely in the draughty old castle. That she was alone.

Von Carstein stood on a stone butte amid the mud flats and called out: 'Who speaks for your city?'

His voice carried easily, his accent thickening even as it amplified. It sounded brutal in Skellan's ears, lacking any refinement or culture. But that was the way of the new world: the monsters ruled.

There was a bustle of activity on the battlements, the guards obviously unsure how to respond to the situation. Von Carstein waited patiently, as though he had all the time in the world. Skellan knew well enough what they were trying to do. Soon enough they would learn that stalling for time was going to get them nowhere. The sun wasn't going to save them this time.

After a few minutes, a man wearing a simple white shift with the hammer of Sigmar emblazoned on it appeared. He looked surprisingly tranquil given the massive army of undead spilled out across the mud flats as far as the eye could see. Beside him stood an effeminate dark-haired fop who, even from a distance, looked mortally afraid. Skellan smiled to himself. The old man was a priest but he carried himself like a warrior, the simpering fool by his side, more likely than not, Ludwig von Holzkrug, pretender to the Imperial throne. Skellan ignored him and stared at the priest. He knew who he was. The man had aged in the years since they had last met but he was still recognisable as Wilhelm von Ostwald. The last time Skellan had seen him the man was a fanatical witch hunter. It seemed that the fanatic had found religion. It was a shame it wouldn't save his immortal soul.

'I, Wilhelm III, Grand Theogonist of Sigmar, speak for the people of Altdorf,' the old priest called down coolly.

'I, Vlad von Carstein, come in faith to make you an offer I urge you to consider and answer for the best of your people.'

'Speak then.'

'The sun will not rise today, the long night has begun. This is my offer to you, serve me in life, or serve me in death. The choice is yours. There will be no mercy if you chose to stand against me.'

The fop looked visibly shaken, imagining no doubt the unlife of servitude, a mindless zombie at von Carstein's beck and call. The priest on the other hand was unmoved.

'That is no offer, vampire. That is a death sentence. I will not sell my people into slavery.'

'So be it,' von Carstein said flatly.

He signalled for the siege engines to fire the first volley of flaming skulls into the heart of the Empire.

CHAPTER TWENTY-ONE
Curiosity Killed the Thief

ALTDORF
Winter, 2051

ONE FINAL JOB, the thief promised himself, and then it's time to get out.

It was all about portable wealth. Felix Mann was a rich man by anyone's measure. He had assets: he had invested wisely in property in the Empire's capital, a society house close to the Imperial palace and the Sigmar monument in Heldenplatz, on the border of the affluent Obereik and the Palast districts. The property was worth an Emperor's ransom but it couldn't exactly be packed up on a cart and shipped out to Tilea or Estalia. He could see the great bronze statue of the Empire's patron deity from the window of his bedroom. He wondered what the Man-God would think about the fate that was befalling his city.

'All good things come to an end,' he said to himself.

Talking to himself was a bad habit that he had developed recently.

There was a ship waiting in Reiksport that would spirit Felix out of the doomed city before it succumbed to the inevitable and fell. It was all down to timing, circumstance and taking that final opportunity. Felix wasn't a greedy man. He had no need of exceptional wealth; for all the majesty of his house and its finery, the trappings of the rich held no interest for him. Theft was a game where he pitted himself against the wits of his victims, the wealth he walked away with nothing more than a way of keeping score.

The thousands of undead feet shuffling across the mud flats sent vibrations running deep through the heart of the old city, tiny tremors of revulsion where nature shied away from the unnatural touch of the dead. Flaming skulls shrieked intermittently over the high walls, smashing and burning where they landed, spilling vitriolic fire throughout the timber-framed houses, and terror through the citizens. The skulls brought the horrors of the war home to them. Those skulls belonged to people who had stood against the Vampire Count. Tomorrow or the next day it might be *their* skulls shattering against the walls of the Imperial palace, their brains scooped out to feed von Carstein's ghouls. Felix found it all quite barbaric.

He walked slowly, thinking, planning. One last job. Portable wealth. He knew full well what he intended, a crime so audacious it would live on in the folklore of Altdorf as long as the city itself. The walls above were thick with archers but the streets themselves were virtually deserted. It wasn't like that everywhere in the city, of course: in Amtsbezirk the Tower Prison and Mundsen Keep were surrounded by people desperate to liberate their loved ones so that they might flee, or free the vile murderous scum locked up within their walls so that they might be fed to the count's ghouls as an offering in the belief that it might save the rest of the populace. It was desperate. Hopeless. In Domplatz they stood at the doors of the Tempel Haus begging the handful of Knights of the Fiery Heart to ride out and save them despite the overwhelming odds and the impossibility of their survival or success. In Oberhausen they petitioned at the jet-black building of the Temple of Morr for the god of death to protect their souls.

In Süderich the fish market was long abandoned, the fishmongers with no wares to sell due to looting in the first days of the siege, and in Reikhoch the Ruhstatt Cemetery was the scene of desecration with many of the tombs and crypts of the dead exhumed, the bodies burned and destroyed so that they might not rise up against the living and bring down the city from within.

His wandering took him down narrow alleyways and wider streets to Kaiserplatz on the opposite side of the Imperial palace. The gallows was the only thing left in the vast square. He skirted the edge of the Hofgarde barracks, his feet leading him toward the Imperial mint and counting house. The street was empty so he took the opportunity to really look at the Kaiserliches Kanzleiamt. In this part of Altdorf it was near nigh impossible to tell how the city's population had swollen with thousands of refugees from the surrounding countryside, the road wardens and the militia had crammed them down in the poorer districts of the city, allowing at least the patina of civilisation to remain intact where there was money to appreciate it.

One last job, he promised himself, his smile wide.

In the distance men were barking like dogs, shouting out orders, screaming as the fires caught and burned fiercely, the echoes of flame haunting the empty streets. Felix wasn't surprised the majority of Altdorfers had scurried off into hiding like rats; look at the example their spiritual leader had set – the Grand Theogonist had disappeared into the bowels of the huge Sigmarite cathedral three days ago, though differentiating between day and night had become a thing of the past. Night was eternal. Felix had heard fools blathering about how von Carstein had the power to prevent the sun from rising which was patently absurd but the idiots believed what they saw, and what they saw was night's black heart.

The counting house was a three-tiered masterpiece of stone and wood, as secure as any building ever built. It reminded Felix of a mastiff: squat, determined, stubborn, unbreakable, like some immensely powerful beast that would take every ounce of his nous to tame, but that was what made the game fun. Anything else would have been boring.

With all eyes turned outwards to the Vampire Count's undead on the mud flats the watch patrols had become lax.

A flash of fire whistled overhead, the skull crashing into one of the high towers of the Imperial barracks and showering flame. The fire clung to the stone but it burned itself out quickly. In that moment though the flaming skull was every bit as brilliant as a sun, throwing its light over Kaiserplatz. Felix stood stock still, trapped in its red glare, waiting for a cry that never came. It was amazing how a few days could undo the discipline of years.

More blazing skulls arced high over his head, showering sparks and trailing tails of fire as they lit the night. Despite the horror of what was actually happening there was a curious beauty about the fire set against the black sky.

It was only a matter of time before the dead scaled the city walls and the desperate efforts of the archers and swordsmen along the battlements wouldn't be enough to repel them. Everyone in Altdorf knew it but few were willing to accept it, hence the near anarchy in some parts of the city with shops being looted and stalls stripped of any kind of food that might help some hidden family last another day or two of the siege. It was as though the Vampire Count was deliberately stripping them of their humanity, turning them into rats, scavengers.

The speed with which so called civilised people sacrificed the rule of law and order was dizzying. Thousands turned to Sigmar and the other gods for deliverance but an equal number turned to crime, helping themselves at the cost of others. For an ordinary decent thief like Felix, for whom there was honour and a certain panache to their criminality, this descent of mankind into the pits of degradation and despair was sickening. He wanted to shake people and force them to see that their selfishness was only accelerating von Carstein's victory.

Signs of the dead were everywhere he looked. Von Carstein was playing with them, like a cat playing with a rat before feeding time. Felix knew the stories of how Middenheim had fallen to the wraiths, and how the Ottilia's army had been swept away by the zombie tide. There was no magic that made Altdorf immune. Cities could fall. Empires could fall.

He needed to get out before the walls came crumbling down and the dead flooded the cramped streets. The instincts of civilisation wouldn't stand up to more than a few hours of that heinous horror before it succumbed to the dark side of its own nature. He wasn't a fighter. He lived by his wits, by the sharpness of his tongue, not his sword. He was a rogue.

Felix turned his attention back to the counting house. He wasn't interested in money – a vast sum of coins would be impossible to ship out in a hurry. What he wanted was gems, pure cut and uncut pieces of flawless quality: a fortune that could be carried in his pocket. The value of precious stones was universal.

The guardhouse outside the courtyard was empty where ordinarily there would have been five skilled swordsmen patrolling the courtyard alone.

Felix walked casually across the street, resisting the urge to look to the right and left first. The secret was in making it look as though he had every right to be there. He peered in through the glass of the guardhouse window. The fire in the hearth had burned out and there was no sign that the guards had been there for days. Probably manning the walls, Felix reasoned, liking the way his train of thought was leading him. It was logical of course that with such a visible threat on the other side of the wall few eyes would be turned inwards.

He walked a slow circuit around the counting house, looking for points of ingress and egress. 'There are more ways to skin a dead cat,' Felix said to himself, rounding the corner back into Kaiserplatz. A good thief always knew all the options available to him, and didn't merely rely on the front and back doors, or even first or second floor windows. He craned his neck to measure the distance between rooftops in various places, several of which were probably jumpable. People tended to forget about rooftops when planning the security of their houses. Of course, given the heavy manning of the battlements, entry via the roof was not the most secluded of the options available to him. He had no wish to be seen by some distracted guard who just happened to turn to look back longingly at his home, or needed spiritual strength so turned to the spires of Altdorf's cathedral.

There were too many opportunities for things to go wrong for his liking so he turned his eyes to lower, less overlooked ledges and the darker crannies where the building butted up against others.

And then there was always underground, but Sigmar alone knew how many of the denizens of the once fair city had taken to living like rats underground in the sewers believing themselves safe. Out of sight out of mind was not, as far as Felix knew, relevant when it came to fleeing the hordes of death.

It was, he decided, far from impregnable. But then, it wasn't supposed to be a fortress. It relied upon manpower to keep even the most ardent thief out, which was an act of hubris Felix was sure that the chancellor of the Imperial counting house would come to regret over the coming days.

There would be patrolling guards, and alarms; that was a given considering the nature of the building. The question was what the alarms would do. A literal alarm would summon help but given the paranoia of the extremely rich he half-expected some kind of lethal payback for having the temerity to rob the Imperial counting house.

He needed someone on the inside.

Unfortunately time was against the kind of subtlety that kind of infiltration required. His hands were proverbially tied. He needed to get in without taking the time for the niceties of the con. The job would be lacking the element of finesse a good caper had but it would be efficient and no one would get hurt. That was important. Thugs used brute force; a decent thief used his brain and left the brawn at home. The alarms, Felix rationalised, would be located around the sewers, and the ground and first floors. If he had been designing the security that is what he would have done. There were very few good second storey thieves working the city nowadays. It was an art long forgotten. Coarse crimes like muggings and pickpocketing were the vogue. The skill had gone out of the grift. People weren't prepared to work for their money. They wanted it easy and quick.

Not Felix Mann though, he belonged to the old school. He was a gentleman thief. A connoisseur of crime. He was a throwback, one of the last of the true grifters. His skill lay in making his society believe he didn't exist. In Middenheim he was known as Reinard Kohl. In Talabheim he was Florian Schneider. In Bogenhafen his name was Ahren Leher. In Kemperbad he was Stefan Meyer, and in Marienburg, Ralf Bekker.

In any given city in the Old World he had countless names and countless dowagers and wealthy widows eating out of the palm of his hand, showering him with trinkets for favours, desperate for even a few minutes of his attention. He made them feel special, reminded them what it felt like to be young, to be loved. He broke their hearts but in doing so he gave them something back, pride, a sense of self-worth, his gift was making them fall in love with themselves once more, and he made a pretty penny in the process. Wealthy merchants wined and dined him believing him to be of their ilk. His successes were the talk of every town, and his lies so big everyone just had to believe them.

Carrion birds had settled along the crenellated roof of the barracks. Their beady eyes unnerved him.

He needed to think.

Any weaknesses for him to exploit would more likely than not be on the second and third storeys. There had to be a way in. Had to be.

He walked slowly back towards the Domplatz district trying to clear his mind.

It was like one of those elaborate Cathayan finger traps, the more he worried and pulled at the problem the more the small details sprang out to snare him, which of course had him wrestling all the details which stubbornly refused to be solved. The secret was to draw his fingers out slowly and smoothly. Or in other words to empty his mind; think about something else.

The problem was if he wasn't thinking about the job, the reality of the undead army crowding the Meadows Gate swamped his mind and the instinct to run became overwhelming. As with so many others, the fact that the Grand Theogonist had disappeared into the vaults of the great cathedral did nothing to comfort him. The priest had told the congregation he was retreating to pray for wisdom and enlightenment in this dark time.

The crowds were still gathered before the great doors of the cathedral, waiting patiently for their spiritual father to emerge.

Felix was sure the man had retreated into the bowels of Altdorf and used the complex warren of catacombs and the sewers to escape the city. Without his robes of office few would recognise the man. It certainly wasn't impossible that he might have made his way as far as Reiksport unmolested and taken a ship from there to anywhere in the known world.

It was, after all, what he would have done.

He had expected to find a few stragglers still camped outside of the octagonal cathedral. Hundreds had converged on the place of worship: penitents, worshippers, the fearful and the desperate. To his left a group of women who looked as though they had just crawled out of the sewers knelt in huddled prayer.

There was an almost hysterical reaction from the crowd as the doors of the cathedral began to open, and then a huge sigh of disappointment as they saw it was the lector, not the Grand Theogonist himself who emerged. The man was older by a few years and had the bearing of a scholar and the body to match. His face, however, was plain and open; a face you could instinctively trust. He moved stiffly, as though each step cost him heavily. The hubbub grew.

He gestured for silence.

A gentle murmur whispered through the crowd. He was going to address them. Felix could read the excitement in the rows of faces. As one they all thought the same thing: surely this meant Sigmar had spoken! An air of anticipation rippled through the onlookers. Felix caught it and moved closer, curious to hear what the lector had to say.

The lector coughed, clearing his throat.

'Three days gone our benevolent brother descended into the vaults to pray for guidance. He abstained food and water believing his faith in the lord our god would sustain him. He emerged this morning with the words we have longed to hear: beloved Sigmar has granted our holy father wisdom. With this knowledge our soldiers can slay the beast! He has given us the key to our survival!' The lector raised his hands in benediction.

A huge cheer rang out as people hugged each other, believing themselves saved.

Felix grinned. It was difficult not to be carried away by the lector's enthusiasm. Now he understood why it was the lector addressing the crowd and not Wilhelm himself. Wilhelm's sharp nose and narrow eyes were harder than the lector's, less forgiving, but then he had seen things the lector could not even imagine in the darkest corners of his heart. The lector breaking the news of Sigmar's intervention was a stroke of genius. Felix's grin spread. He knew a good grift when he saw one. This was no case of divine intervention; on the contrary, it was a divine con. But that was the magic of the best grifts, convincing the rubes to believe the impossible. The bigger the lies, the more outrageous the lies, the more desperate the masses were to be gulled by them, especially if there was a little divinity thrown into the mix. This was a new angle for him to think about.

A ripple of movement in the shadows behind the lector caught his eye.

He was about to dismiss it when he saw it again, ten feet away from where he had first seen it: a crease in the shadows, a slight blurring of the wall as something passed in front of it. He wouldn't have been able to see it if he hadn't been looking for it, but now he knew what to look for it was not particularly difficult to follow. He knew what it was: the first layer of the divine grift peeling away before his very eyes. There was someone in the shadows, creeping away from the cathedral. He wasn't sure how the deceit worked, a glamour perhaps?

Curiosity piqued, he followed, keeping close to the shadows cast by the scant moonlight. The peculiar light anomaly moved slowly. He matched its pace, dampening the sound of his footsteps on the cobbles. He knew what he was doing was stupid. It was none of his business. The Sigmarites could pull the scam to end all scams for all he cared. He'd be gone in forty-eight hours. But he was curious. It was what made him a good thief. He didn't take things at face value. He didn't swallow the easy lie. There was a grift going down here and curiosity be damned, he wanted to know what it was all about.

'Killed the cat, though didn't it?' Felix muttered, disgusted with himself as, in the darkness of an alleyway two streets over from the Sigmar cathedral, the figure of a tall, thin man took shape within the shimmering dark. The stranger peeled back the hood of his cloak and stopped mid-step. He had obviously heard Felix. He turned and stared directly at him. Felix winced. They were barely fifteen feet apart. Felix had been careless, gotten too close. He had been so caught up in trying to unravel the sting that he had walked right into one of the central players. He tried to look casually lost, like an innocent passer-by but it was a pointless ruse. They both knew why he was there.

The look the stranger gave Felix sent a shiver soul deep. It was the man's eyes. They were ancient, knowing, and so, so cold. They stripped away the layers of lies and identity and delved deep into the core of who he was. They *knew* him.

'You would do well to forget you ever saw me,' the stranger said, and strode away into the everlasting night.

CHAPTER TWENTY-TWO

Answered Prayers

ALTDORF
Winter, 2051

CURSING HIMSELF FOR a fool Felix Mann retreated to his house in the Obereik district.

His heart was hammering. His hands were trembling. The encounter had shaken him badly.

He couldn't get over the way the man's eyes had dissected his soul. That was exactly what it had felt like: as though the man had taken a chirurgeon's blade to his very sense of self and stripped it with brutal efficacy, slice after bloody slice.

'Forty-eight hours,' he promised himself. Forty-eight hours. One last job and it would all be over. He looked up at the sky, as though hoping to see validation of his vow in the stars but all he saw was the damned darkness. It was far from reassuring even though he knew, rationally, that it wasn't a natural night, this seemingly endless dark. The sun was blocked, it hadn't disappeared. Von Carstein hadn't spirited it away. He wasn't that powerful. It was up there somewhere blazing with radiant intensity. A few miles away, he was sure, it was bright beautiful daylight. It surprised him how much he missed it. He felt its absence in his blood. It wasn't as though he was a stranger to the night. He lived in the dark. As much as anywhere in this godforsaken city it was his home but it was different now. He couldn't trust it anymore. It held secrets.

The man had used it to cloak himself, moving virtually invisibly through the city. That, more than anything else, scared the thief. He didn't like things he couldn't explain and grift or not he knew he was standing on the fringe of a very dangerous game. He couldn't even begin to imagine the stakes but he knew the smart money was on running for the hills. He who turns and runs away lives to fight another day, and all of that.

'Forty-eight hours,' he promised himself again, knowing full well he wasn't going anywhere until the counting house job was done.

A new, horrific dimension was added to von Carstein's bombing of the city during his walk home. Limbs, arms, hands, whole legs, feet, rotten and gangrenous, rancid with plague and other sickness, were catapulted into the city along with the flaming skulls. Felix picked a path through the detritus of human flesh, wondering how long they would be left there to fester, and how long it would take for the disease to spread.

He shot the bolts on the door, locking himself in, but even knowing he was secure, he couldn't sleep. He lay for an hour in the darkness, staring at the ceiling, thinking.

The man hadn't been human, he realised with something akin to dread settling in the pit of his stomach. It was the eyes. They gave him away. There had been no trace of humanity in them, only the ruthless cunning of a killer. Felix held his face in his hands. The Sigmarite priests were treating with the enemy; that was how desperate things had become, that was how much trouble he was in.

'Forty-eight hours,' he said again, knowing that he didn't have forty-eight hours. Time was a luxury he could ill afford.

He pushed himself out of bed and paced around the room restlessly. He didn't like it. He didn't like it one little bit. Circumstance was manipulating him into going faster than he felt comfortable. Rushing a job meant taking risks, taking risks meant making mistakes. The question wasn't if he was going to make mistakes, it was if he was going to get away with them.

A great thief wasn't defined by skill alone, a great thief was lucky. The greatest thieves of all time rode their luck like a dockside doxy.

'To hell with it,' Felix Mann said. He dressed quickly, in dark colours, but not blacks. He avoided black because the darkness wasn't pure, black stood out against it more than deep homespun browns and forest greens. He knelt, sliding two long thin dirks into their sheaths in his boots. He felt beneath the mattress for the canvas wrap and pulled it out. The case was a little smaller than his hand and it contained the tools of his trade. Felix unwrapped the canvas, checking through each pick and sawtoothed metal file methodically before wrapping the small canvas case back up and securing it to his belt. A second canvas wrap contained three coils of copper wire, wax and tallow as well as the fixings for tinder.

He smeared an oil-based salve across his face, the components of the salve rendering his skin dark, in patches deep brown, in others almost olive green with hints of a purer black around the eyes, and tied his hair back with a thin strip of black leather. He greased the toes of his supple leather boots in sticky tar. Next he blacked up any exposed skin he could see in the full length body mirror, including the backs of his hands, smoothing the salve up past his wrists and well under the cuffs of his shirt so that even when he stretched and the fabric rode up there would be no telltale white skin to betray him. His palms he left white. He pulled on a supple pair of leather gloves, stretching his fingers deep into them. He drew a series of deep breaths, regulating his breathing.

He was tense.

Every muscle felt uncomfortably tight.

He ran through a series of relaxation exercises, working from his fingertips inwards. He concentrated on the flow of blood through his body, using it to draw the tension out like a panacea.

He left the house, but not by the door.

He took to the thieves' highway, travelling across the rooftops of the city, keeping low, and sticking to the lower buildings so that he wouldn't be exposed to the guards on the city walls. He couldn't risk a light, which meant he had to go more slowly than he might have liked, giving his eyes time to adjust.

The fourth bell after midnight tolled sonorously through the dark city, echoing down the abandoned streets. A light drizzle began as Felix traversed the rooftops along the banks of the dry gulch that had only a few days earlier been the Reik River. Without water to drive it the huge mill wheels were no longer turning. He hunkered down on the slate roof of the old stone mill house. The drizzle made the slates treacherous. It also wet the tar on his toes. He prayed fervently that they would be sticky enough when he needed them. Coupled with the web of clothes lines and forgotten laundry that criss-crossed the rooftops the slick tiles were a hazard he could have lived without. Occasional lights bobbed by below, carried by watchmen. The light broke the shadows. He waited patiently for the torchbearers and lantern carriers to move on. Now he had committed himself to the job his sense of overwhelming urgency had gone.

He moved on, ducking under a hemp rope that had been stretched between two chimneybreasts and hunkered down again beside a third, using it to keep him out of sight of the archers on the city wall while he scanned the nearby rooftops, picking out the best path between where he was and the Imperial counting house.

The boarded-up windows of many of the surrounding houses made his job so much easier. No prying eyes to worry about and more than a few wrought metal balconies that could be borrowed if the rooftop traverse was interrupted. He picked his path and started to move, keeping low by habit even though there wasn't a moon to silhouette him. Peripheral vision had a way of noticing movement that direct line of sight would often miss. There was no point in taking risks he didn't have to.

Felix moved almost entirely on instinct; he had been a thief long enough to know when to trust his gut feelings about something. He scuttled forward, right up to the edge of an overhanging eave. The next building was a three-storey house, but both the second and third floors had wide wrought iron balconies. Neither, thankfully, was cluttered with plant pots or other potentially noisy bric-a-brac and shutters had been secured over the large windows. The gap between the buildings was ten feet at most, but it was a jump that he really didn't want to make. Felix backed away from the edge and moved carefully along the roof until he had convinced himself there was no alternative. He moved back into place, taking a moment to judge the jump.

It was far from easy.

The second floor balcony interfered with what otherwise would have been a fairly straightforward jump and catch because any kind of impact with his lower legs could easily dislodge his grip on the railings above.

It was a long way down.

He took two steps back, and with a short run-up launched himself off the roof. For one sickening second Felix thought he had misjudged the distance then his wrists slammed into the metal filigree of the upper balcony as his legs continued to swing. He barely managed to catch a hold with one hand, fingers slipping down the iron spike as he hung there precariously, dangling high above the street. He kicked his legs, giving his body the momentum he needed to reach up and grab a firm hold on the trelliswork and hand over hand haul himself up onto the balcony. Sweat beaded on his forehead.

The balcony overlooked a baker's dozen of flat roofs, one of them crowding close to the rough-hewn walls of the barracks across the street from the Imperial counting house. The shadow of the counting house hulked just beyond it. One glance was enough to confirm that the rooftop security was minimal. He clambered up to stand on the balcony's handrail and reached up to grab the guttering, praying silently that it was secure enough to bear his weight for the few seconds he needed. The metal drainage pipe groaned and began to pull away from the wall as he scrambled up it, the tar on his toes sticking and giving Felix the purchase he needed to drag himself up onto the roof.

He lay flat on his stomach, listening to the sounds of the night.

He rolled over onto his back.

Altdorf was oblivious to his roaming. Felix rose in one fluid motion and stalked cat-like across the flat roof. His foot dislodged a tile, which fell forty feet to the cobbles below and shattered with a sound that could have been thunder. He froze, waiting for cries of alarm that didn't come. Thanking Ranald the Night Prowler for small mercies, Felix scaled the outer wall of the Imperial barracks, his boots slipping occasionally despite the tar on them as he pulled himself up. There were plenty of handholds in the pitted stone of the wall where the rain and wind had weathered them and the cement joining them.

And there it was, in all its dark splendour: the Imperial counting house. Among the criss-crossing washing lines a single thick hemp rope had caught his attention earlier in the day. It ran from the roof of the barracks to the roof of the counting house opposite. Smiling despite himself, Felix tested the rope, seeing what kind of strain it could take. It was secure. He knelt beside it, ready to lower himself and traverse the small gap between the two buildings.

The sensation that crept over him was unmistakable. He was being watched. Staying stock still, Felix scanned the rooftops opposite and the walls, then turned slowly, taking in the sweeping rooftop panorama of the city. He couldn't see his stalker but he knew better than to believe that meant they weren't there. He could feel their eyes on him. A good thief soon learned to trust his instincts. In this case his gut reaction was to turn around and go home, better to be alive and poor, than weighed down with treasures and very, very dead. There was always another job. Skills like his didn't just fade away. Thievery was a mindset. 'One last job,' he promised himself. 'It will be all over in an hour.' He swallowed, struggling to ignore every instinct that told him what he was about to do was a very bad idea, and lowered himself onto the rope.

It sagged slightly under his weight, but held firm as he swung himself forward hand over hand. He made it to the other side. He could still feel the eyes on his back.

He knew his way in. There was a ledge above the courtyard, and beneath the ledge a small balcony. By coming to it from above he kept himself out of line of sight of the guardhouse. Felix crept up to the edge, and then shuffled forward a few steps, readjusting his position so that he could lower himself and drop soundlessly onto the ceramic tiles. Working quickly now, he examined the lock, then selected the appropriate pick from his canvas wrap. It only took a second to pop the lock.

Grinning, Felix Mann opened the door and stepped through.

Something hit him in the chest, punching the wind out of him and knocking him off his feet. He tried to get up, but he was somehow being pressed to the floor. Dazed and disorientated, Felix tried to look around – but couldn't move his head. The air around him sparked blue as he struggled to break free of the trap. No net was holding him, no paralysing darts had struck him.

Magic! It was the only answer... But the practice of magic was outlawed. All sorcerers were hunted down by witch hunters, and destroyed. And witch hunters got their authority from... received their orders from...

His thoughts swam. He had been trapped. Him, the greatest thief the Empire had ever known. 'Stupid, stupid, stupid,' he cursed himself for a fool, a stupid bloody fool. The fact that he could talk through the spell did nothing to calm him. The subtlety of the magic only helped convince Felix that he was in deep, deep trouble. The kind of trouble you woke up dead from – or rather didn't wake up at all from. The lack of guards, the convenient rope from the roof of the barracks. Someone had grifted the grifter. He had been set up and fallen for it, hook, line and sinker. A groan slipped from his lips.

All he could do was wait and see what kind of mess he had gotten himself into.

The grating sound of a chain being drawn though brass handles carried up to Felix. It sounded like a death sentence in his ears. At least they weren't going to make him wait long.

Footsteps: two pairs, one heavier and more laboured than the other, echoed in the stairway. The footsteps stopped as one of the people approaching gave in to a fit of convulsive coughing. It didn't sound good at all. Three more steps and then the coughing began again; deep, tubercular hacks.

Flickering yellow light announced the pair long before they were at the top of the stairs. The light cast its jaundiced glow over the room's dark green wallpaper and rows of equally dark oil paintings. Each depicted a grim faced and forbidding chancellor long since buried. The guardians of Kaiserliches Kanzleiamt met Felix's predicament with blank stoicism. He was an invader in their house and judgement was coming slowly up the narrow stairs.

The methodical climb and the bobbing taunts of the light only served to increase his discomfort. Felix wanted it over.

'If you intend to kill me, get it over with would you?' he called out, but he knew they wouldn't, whoever they were. They wouldn't have gone to such lengths to snare him if death was all they had in mind;

a quarrel in the back would have seen to that. They had had plenty of opportunities while he negotiated the treacherous rooftops. No, they had plans.

Which was worse, by far.

He couldn't even close his eyes.

The pair walked along the landing and into the green room. They were as mismatched a couple as their footsteps suggested. One was tall, emaciated, his hair drawn up in a topknot, the sides shaved high above his ears, the other was considerably shorter and moved with the arrogance of a natural born fighter but wore the robes of a priest.

'Felix, Felix, Felix,' the priest said, something approaching a smile on his ruddy face. It didn't last. The climb had taken its toll. He broke off into another fit of coughing. Felix saw the flecks of blood that spattered the priest's handkerchief as he took it away from his mouth. He secreted it in his robes, his smile returning. The priest's obvious delight at Felix's predicament had a cold chill quickening in his gut. He was face to face with the divine grifter, the Grand Theogonist himself. 'This is a pretty little pickle you've gotten yourself into, isn't it?'

Even if he had wanted to, Felix couldn't look away from the priest's scrutiny. He felt like a slab of meat being weighed out on the butcher's block.

He waited for the cleaver to fall.

'You could say that, but you could also say that it is getting more interesting by the minute,' Felix said finally, filling the uncomfortable silence. 'I mean, not so long ago I was all alone up here in the dark, thinking I'd probably rot here for months while the vampires had their fill below, and now look at me, blessed with an audience with the Grand Theogonist of Sigmar himself. Not what I would have expected, given the circumstances.'

'Well, my friend, desperate days call for desperate acts, isn't that what they say?'

'The grift,' Felix said, as though that explained everything.

'I'm sorry?'

'The grift, that's what this is all about isn't it?'

'I'm not sure I understand,' the priest said but the manner with which he said it gave lie to his words. He knew full well what Felix was talking about.

'The grift, the con, the big fat lie you just sold to half the people in this damned city.'

'Interesting, don't you think?' the priest said quite matter-of-factly to his partner. 'How our good thief here is in such an uncomfortable situation and yet he manages to turn the whole thing around so we appear to be the malcontents in this little scenario. It is quite a skill.' His smile fell away. What Felix saw was the face of a very, very tired man. Almost four days locked in the darkness beneath the cathedral had done nothing to help him and he obviously hadn't slept more than a handful of hours, if that.

'You're dying, aren't you?' he said, taking a wild guess: the tubercular coughing fits, the sallow skin, lack of sleep evidenced in the eyes, maybe it wasn't so wild after all.

'Aren't we all?' the priest offered, the flicker of a smile returning to his face.

'Some faster than others.'

'Indeed.'

'Never grift a grifter, that's what my old mum used to say, but that's what you are doing, isn't it?'

'Indeed,' the priest admitted. 'But quite irrelevant to the current situation we find ourselves in, wouldn't you agree?' Felix would have nodded, if he could have. 'I believe, and my friend here can confirm this, that the punishment for being caught *in flagrante delicto* as you have been, is quite steep.'

'You have seen the gallows outside,' the second man said, leaving Felix to put two and two together.

'And, alas, a defence of "I was tricked, yer honour" won't cut it. You're here, and your intentions are pretty plain. Once a thief, always a thief. You can dress up in fancy clothes and attend the society parties but that doesn't make you a gentleman, Felix. You're a thief.'

'And a damned good one,' Felix said.

'Well, present circumstances excluded, eh?'

'Can't really argue with that, can I? So, priest, what do you need a thief for? That is what this is all about, isn't it? You're hiring me for part of your grift.'

The Grand Theogonist bowed slightly. 'Very good, very good indeed. I can see why you come so highly recommended, Herr Mann. The price I am offering is an official pardon for all of your previous transgressions, including this one, and enough wealth in gemstones to reinvent yourself somewhere you are less well known, and live well for years to come. A small fortune, you might say. In addition, you are never to return to Altdorf, understood?'

'Sounds too good to be true so far, priest. Let's say I am waiting for the inevitable knife between the shoulder blades. No offence meant, but you religious types, well you aren't exactly trustworthy, far as I'm concerned.'

'A colourful way of putting it, but on the contrary the charge is a very simple one. I need you to steal a ring for me.'

'Steal a ring?' Felix repeated doubtfully. 'Whose?'

'Ah cutting to the quick of the matter, good, good. This is the situation: four days ago I retreated into the vaults of the cathedral, ostensibly to pray for wisdom. I was waiting for a very earthly sign though. This morning my visitor arrived with precious information. His message might very well save our beloved city from the beast at our doors.'

'And that secret was a ring?'

'So it would seem. I want that ring. I would have asked you out of public spiritedness, but this arrangement seemed far more practical. I do hope you will forgive me for taking advantage of your natural, ah, shall we say curiosity rather than greed? Greed is such an ugly word don't you think?'

'How did you know I would come in through this window?'

'Oh, I didn't. But all the other ways in have been blocked up, or are obviously guarded. This was the most obvious way in. Desperate times require desperate measures, and my colleagues convinced me that a man in their custody – Nevin? – could be "persusaded" to help us catch you. All I needed to do was sit and wait for word of your capture. Sometimes, I have found, it helps to think like the scum around you. I did not take long to deduce that in the citywide panic we find ourselves in, a profiteer like you would look to score an otherwise impossible job. I forced myself to think big. After that, the secret was to make a few of the plum pickings appear tastier – and easier – than the rest and let your – ah – curiosity do the rest.'

'So we could have been having this conversation almost anywhere in Altdorf?'

The priest nodded. 'Under identical circumstances.'

'I am impressed,' Felix said.

'Thank you. So to the crux of the matter: I want you to steal me a ring, a very special ring, tonight. If you agree, you will be freed from your bonds and given safe passage out of the city. If not, well, we won't go there just yet. So, do we have an agreement?'

'There's something you aren't saying, priest. It all sounds too easy. I can't work out why you need me, any one of your holy goons could steal a ring for you.'

'Ah, not quite. You see it is this ring that grants the vampire von Carstein his immortality. Without it, he can die like the rest of his filthy horde. You will find it, along with von Carstein, in his coffin in the white pavilions that have been erected on the mud flats before the Meadows Gate.'

'You have got to be out of your bloody mind!'

'Oh no, no. Think of it this way, Felix: the ultimate theft. No one but the very greatest could even dare, never mind achieve it. The next few hours offer you your very own slice of immortality. Imagine: Felix Mann, the greatest thief of all time, stole a ring of immortality from the hand of the Vampire Count while he slept in his coffin – in the middle of one of the largest armies the world has ever known. Come on, Felix, you have to admit that the notion intrigues you.'

'Scares the bloody life out of me, you mean. You'd have to be a fool to step out into the middle of that lot.'

'Or a dead man,' the Grand Theogonist said, bluntly. Suddenly, with that one sentence, Felix understood the full horror of the priest's threat. The gallows was more than just a death sentence for his crime, it was the promise of resurrection into the ranks of the Vampire Count's mindless undead. Damned if he did, very much damned if he didn't. What they were doing to him was monstrous.

'My god, there's no difference between you, is there? You're as bad as each other. How could you? How?'

'In the face of great evil, the end justifies, always, the means,' the priest said, sympathetically. 'I am sorry, Felix, but that is the reality of your situation. Now, you won't be alone out there. You will have help though most likely you will not be aware of it. My visitor is even now making arrangements to ease your passage through the enemy forces. According to him von Carstein ought to be sleeping for hours to come. I suggest we do not waste any more time.'

He had no choice.

CHAPTER TWENTY-THREE
The Left Hand of Darkness

ALTDORF
Winter, 2051

FELIX MANN WAS in hell.

He lay in the thick undergrowth beyond the city wall, watching von Carstein's men secure the perimeter of their huge encampment. Their torches burned, throwing hellish shadows over the scene. The dead lay where they had fallen when the Vampire Count had retreated to his coffin; the mud flats were covered with thousands and thousands of rotting bodies and bones.

The Grand Theogonist had given Felix a small double quarrel hand-held crossbow and directions to an inn on the outskirts of Altdorf, owned by the temple. It was surprising how far Sigmar's financial influence spread but it made sense that they would want some kind of back door out of the city to hide the comings and goings of their flock when necessary. The cellars connected to a subterranean labyrinth that offered escape from the city away from prying eyes. The tunnel came out two hundred yards beyond the wall, opening out into a cleft in the riverbank, a few feet above the fast flowing Reik. The cleft was sheltered from sight. It was perfect for what he had in mind.

He had been there for twenty minutes studying the movements of the enemy's soldiers. Already he had seen things he didn't want to believe.

They weren't all dead, nor were they all monsters.

There were normal people swelling the ranks of the undead.

Normal people. The idea that men would willingly choose to ally with the Vampire Count troubled him deeply. It was one thing to fight against monsters and lose, becoming one of them, but quite another to willingly align yourself with them. Felix had no idea how many living – breathing – humans he faced. The few he had seen strutted around the mud flats arrogantly. It would have been nice to see their smug grins slip when von Carstein realised he had been robbed of his precious ring. If the Grand Theogonist were right about the ring's nature, those traitors would be the first to face the vampire's wrath.

Felix saw a body swinging from a silver birch. It had been stripped and a sack had been put over its head. Something moved inside the sack. He stared for a moment, sickened by the slick, almost sinewy movement of the thing in there with the man. A ferret? A rat? Felix thought sickly. They had put vermin in the sack. It would have eaten half of the man's face before he died. It was a ghastly punishment.

How could they not understand that alive or dead they were worth as much to their twisted master?

Come dawn the zombie would tear the sack from its ruined head and rejoin the fight.

Felix shuddered.

Four of von Carstein's men stood talking less then fifteen feet away from his hiding place in the undergrowth.

'I tell ya, I heard summink, Berrin.'

'Nah, it's in yer head, lad. We're all alone with the dead out here.'

'That's what I'm saying, man. I heard summink and I'm thinking we should tell someone, because it might be important.'

'An' what good will that do, lad? They'll thank you kindly 'n then they'll wet themselves laughing 'bout you jumpin' at ghosts. Ain't none of us happy we're shacked up wif the dear departed so I say keep yer trap shut 'n wait for some other bugger to tell 'em about it's my advice.'

Good advice, Felix thought with a smile. *Now be a good boy and listen to it.* He lay very still but his fingers itched to nock an arrow and make sure the boy wouldn't live long enough to tell a soul.

'What if one of them's out there?'

'Then most likely he's running scared and no danger to anyone, right?'

'I ain't sure, Berrin. I mean–'

'You think too much lad, that's yer problem. Life ain't all mystery and intrigue. We's soldiers. Soldierin' is what we do and that means we do what we're told, no questions, even if it means we hafta do our business in a field a long way from home and don't get to feel them warm legs of our women wrapped around us when we go to sleep. It's our life, lad. You don't want the vampires thinking yer frightened of yer own shadow, now do ya? They'll just make yer life hell for it.'

Felix smiled at the veteran's logic. *What you don't see doesn't hurt you,* he added silently, willing the boy to let it drop.

The boy mumbled something that he couldn't make out and then started to wander off. The others followed. Felix watched them leave and didn't move until they were out of sight. He rose slowly into a tight crouch, scanning the line of white pavilions to make certain no one was watching. Satisfied, he crept along the rim of the riverbank.

He knew what he had to do. It was suicide, he knew, but the priest knew how to play his ego. Not for the first time that night he cursed his stupidity. The Grand Theogonist was taking a massive gamble, but if it worked... On the humiliating walk down through the counting house the priest talked about an army being like an animal.

And what do you do to a wild animal? You cut its head off, Felix thought, the voice in his head sounding very much like the priest's.

He didn't have much of a plan beyond sneaking in to the Vampire Count's tent, taking the ring and running for his life. Felix had already reconciled himself to the fact that he was unlikely to reach the third step of the plan.

In a way, that didn't matter.

The first few fat drops of rain fell. In five minutes it was pouring from the heavens. The moon was a thin silver sliver in the cloudy sky.

He counted forty-three fires scattered across the mud flats, and guessed there were a dozen men per fire out there warming themselves on the flames. These were the living contingent. About five hundred men, give or take. He didn't want to think about the rest of the Vampire Count's malignant army.

He waited, giving them time to get tired.

Tired men made mistakes.

He closed his eyes and pictured himself walking among them. Cutting their throats while they slept. The image wrapped a chill around his heart not because it was murder but because it was useless. Dead or alive they served the count.

Dead or alive.

The camp had been quiet for more than an hour, soldiers lying in their bedrolls around the dwindling fires.

Felix laid his crossbow in the tall grass and rested the quiver with his extra bolts in it across the wooden shaft. He wouldn't need it where he was going. He took first one dagger and then the other from his boot sheaths and tested their edge with his thumb. Satisfied, he kissed both blades and slipped them back into their sheaths and rose into a crouch, creeping forward a dozen paces through the litter of corpses, his eyes on the nearest fire.

Carrion birds picked at the dead.

He moved slowly. His heart hammered as he lowered himself to the ground again and scanned the circle of fires. It was so loud in his ears it was a wonder von Carstein's soldiers didn't hear it. He didn't move a muscle. The soldiers there were oblivious to his presence. Some slept, others talked, their conversations muted. He couldn't make out what they were saying but as long as no one was yelling and pointing in his direction they could say whatever the hell they wanted for all he cared.

He knew what he had to do even though it revolted him. He looked around for some particularly wretched corpse, ripped his clothes and smeared himself in its blood and rotting flesh until he looked like one of the count's disgusting flesh-eating ghouls.

The darkness was his strongest ally. He clung to it as he crossed the no-man's land between the dry river and the officers' pavilion. To his left, someone moved, rolling over in his bedroll. Felix stood still.

'What you doin'?' the soldier grumbled sleepily.

'Takin' a leak, man,' Felix muttered, hoping he sounded aggrieved enough to mask the sudden swell of fear he felt rising.

'Well, hurry up about, would ya, some of us are tryin' to get some shut-eye. Next time drain the snake before ya hit the hay.'

He waited. Sweat ran down into the palms of his clenched fists. He felt so exposed and vulnerable his skin itched. He looked up into the rain and savoured the feel of it on his face. The kiss of the rain was seductive. He could have stayed there savouring the sensation of it running down his face because he knew it could so easily be the last pleasant sensation he ever felt.

Felix started to move, quietly. The soldiers slept on.

Von Carstein's pavilion was in the centre of the camp, ringed by smaller tents, but none of them were close enough fall into the pavilion's shadow.

A slow grin spread across Felix's face when he saw that there was no one guarding the entrance and the oil light in front of the opening had been left to burn low enough that even the peripheral shadows remained untouched. The rain masked the sound of his footsteps. Instinct told him to be wary. It was too easy. This time he listened to it. The spot of skin between his shoulder blades prickled. It was almost as though von Carstein's men were being deliberately sloppy, letting the lights burn low so that the unguarded flaps of the count's pavilion were nothing more than the bait on a trap set to lure him out into the open and into their steel jaws.

He stopped dead in his tracks.

The figure of a tall, thin man stepped out from between two of the pavilions. The man was hooded but Felix recognised him from the way he moved. It was the stranger from the alleyway; the one who had told the priest about the ring's supposed powers.

The priest had promised help. Felix understood the seemingly lax defences around the count's tent now. The stranger had had a hand in it, he was sure.

The stranger nodded, but said nothing before he strode away into the heart of the darkness beyond the flickering lanterns.

The stranger moved with grace, barely making a sound, barely even disturbing the air with his passage. It was, Felix knew, unnatural.

A priest and a vampire, strange bedfellows indeed, Felix thought, gliding between the canvas walls of two pavilions. He could hear the muted sounds of conversation coming from inside. Rain drummed on the canvas. He walked slowly toward the count's pavilion, waiting for the challenge that never came. He looked over his shoulder, towards the dark shadows of the spires of Altdorf, and slipped through the opening into the tent.

It was darker inside without the lantern to illuminate anything beyond the vaguest of outlines. Felix drew the tent flap closed behind him again. The soft regular sound of his breathing filled the darkness.

He couldn't allow himself to think about what he was doing or he wouldn't be able to do it.

Reaching out, Felix felt his way through the darkness toward the coffins at the rear of the tent. There were two: one had to be the count's, the other his wife's.

The air had a strange tang to it. Some kind of perfumed wood had been burned in the makeshift hearth and the residue still clung to the air.

Felix knelt beside the first coffin as though in prayer. It was consid erably larger than the other, decorated with black iron clasps that were open. Steeling himself against the sudden swell of fear, Felix eased back the coffin lid.

The rain was loud on the roof of the tent.

He looked down at the dead man in the coffin. In the flickering light he appeared surprisingly young. Lush dark hair spilled loosely around his shoulders. He was handsome, his smooth, almost aquiline features giving no hint of the depravity that had replaced his soul.

The Vampire Count's hands were folded across his chest. He wore an extravagant signet ring on his right hand, with a garish gem set amid what looked like wings, the tips studded with precious stones. It was ostentatious. On his left hand the count wore a dull band of what looked like black iron.

Felix didn't dare move.

He stared at the ornate ring with its dark gemstone setting for a full five minutes, barely sparing a second glance for the plain iron ring, before he reached into the coffin and began to prize the signet ring off the count's cold dead flesh.

Von Carstein didn't stir.

Felix weighed the ring in his hand. It was undoubtedly worth an Emperor's ransom but... something about it nagged at the back of his mind. It didn't make sense. Surely the priest wasn't thinking of collecting treasures – and the best grift is the one you don't see. Felix smiled to himself and pried the plain black iron ring from the count's other hand. He laid signet ring on the vampire's chest.

Felix caught himself in the process of slipping the ring onto his index finger. 'Stupid,' he muttered, realising he hadn't brought a pouch or purse to carry the stolen trinket. If it was magic who knew what kind of damage wearing it could do? He had sudden flashes of being paralyzed and being held helpless in von Carstein's pavilion until the count rose.

He closed his fist about the ring and backed cautiously out of the pavilion.

He stared at the coffin, expecting the vampire to come raging out of it at any second, fear hammering against his breastbone as he crept toward the tent flaps, conjuring a mass of putrefied zombies to swarm over him as he slipped out of the tent into the everlasting night, but, mercifully, the dead didn't rise.

He ran for his life.

CHAPTER TWENTY-FOUR

Out of the Darkness, Rising

ALTDORF
Winter, 2051

IT WAS A night for ghosts, ghouls and wraiths, for zombies, ghasts and wights.

It was a night for the dead.

The theft of his ring had unleashed von Carstein's wrath. The Vampire Count stood on mud flats before Altdorf, gripped by a feverish, wild rage. His fury had summoned a blizzard, the elements buckling beneath his black madness.

The rain turned to snow, the snow fell thick and fast without settling on the sodden ground. Jon Skellan and Jerek von Carstein stood beside the count as he raged against the heavens and threatened to tear down the walls of Altdorf with his bare hands. Neither had ever seen the count so utterly devoid of reason or control. It was truly frightening. Von Carstein stood in the centre of the mud flats, his hands raised and head thrown back, shrieking as the wind and snow buffeted him. It was as though his furious incantation drew the storm to him.

Lightning appeared to dance across the tips of the Vampire Count's fingers before it clawed its way back up into the heavens, piercing the dark heart of the night with its ribbons of jagged blue.

Thunder cracked.

The ground beneath their feet and all around them rippled with unnatural life. Small tremors and their aftershocks ran in concentric circles out from von Carstein's feet as the summoning took shape. Drawing strength from nature and all that grew around him, Vlad von Carstein channelled his raw anger into the pattern being formed by his fingers, feeding it to the fallen buried beneath the snow and dirt.

'RISE!' he shrieked. 'RISE!'

All around them the dead were rising.

The trees along the riverbank nearest Skellan had already begun to wither, the needles of the evergreens tinged brown as the life was leached out of them to feed the count's black magic.

The dead lurched and staggered to their feet, even as the ground beneath them buckled and trembled with revulsion. Ghouls cried out in anguish. Wights shrieked as they wound themselves around the rising corpses and tore off into the night sky.

Von Carstein's fury was terrifying.

A moment later the first dead fingers breached the wet surface of the mud flats, clawing at the air for the life that had already been taken from them once.

'Here they come,' Skellan said unnecessarily. His awe at von Carstein's strength resonated in his voice. That the Vampire Count could draw the long dead of Altdorf out from beneath the damned city and onto the plains was incredible. Even fuelled by von Carstein's wrath it was an agonizingly slow process. Bone by bone the dead crawled out of their graves, impelled by von Carstein's ranting spell. At first they came out of the earth one or two at a time, but then they clawed their way free of the dirt in their tens and twenties, all the poor souls who had fallen on the fields before the greatest city of the Empire. Friend or foe, it no longer mattered as they were born again into von Carstein's army.

And they weren't all whole.

Some of the dead rose in pieces, an arm clawing the surface, torso and head dragged up behind it, without legs to support itself where the rot of decay had eaten through it. More and more body parts rose, drawn by von Carstein's hateful summons.

The snow swirled around the mud flats, whipped around by the bluster of the wind. Gradually the snow turned to hail. Hard pellets pelted the dead as they rose.

The Vampire Count's face was taut, his lips moving as though with a purpose of their own, reciting over and over again a litany of pain and anguish as he drew the dead from the dirt.

When he was done close to five thousand dead had risen to swell the ranks of his pestilential force, looking once more with amazement upon the walls of their beloved city. Their bodies were in various states of decay, from the stripped and yellowed bones of the long dead to the rotted flesh of the newly deceased. Von Carstein screamed at the heavens, his voice ringing out the death of a thousand seasons as it duelled another thunderclap.

'Look upon the fall of mankind! See death before your walls. The dead rise. The dead reclaim what once was theirs. Look around you. Behold the Kingdom of the Dead! Behold. Behold! Tremble before its majesty. Fear its might. Fall to your knees. The dead rise and the living fall!'

When his gaze came down, Skellan saw Vlad's eyes were glazed with a wild staring madness.

'The dead are crawling out of their graves, even Morr can't hold them back,' Jerek seethed. 'Ten thousand today, another ten thousand tomorrow? Next week? A world full of dead men and cattle.'

'I know,' Skellan said, savouring the delicious thought. 'The Kingdom of the Dead. Who could possibly stand against it?'

Von Carstein pointed his finger at the wall and the bone siege engines rolled forward. The dead screamed and yelled and shrieked and wailed, and threw themselves at the huge stone wall. Others clung to the towers, riding them as they rolled remorselessly toward the high walls, sixty feet high, twenty feet wide, ballistae, catapults, and ladders. Suddenly von Carstein was the calm amongst the storm.

Frightened archers fired wild arrows from the battlements.

Skellan watched it all in mute admiration, though at times it was difficult to see through the driving hail.

Along the walls the defenders set up notched poles to help repel the siege ladders while others lined up hundreds of clay jars filled with oil as soul-searing screams rent the darkness.

Skellan's mind was icy calm as he took it all in. He let von Carstein waste his energies with fury. Wrath, vengeance, they were all human emotions. Surely the Vampire Count understood that? It was nothing more than pride and arrogance.

The siege engines lumbered toward the walls, straddling the mud flats like something out of myth, colossal giants of flesh fused with living bone. Fires burned at their tops, casting ghastly shadows down the lengths of the infernal machines. The dead clustered around them, heaving them relentlessly toward the high walls.

The city would fall, Skellan knew. It had no choice.

That was the apocalyptic reality of the Risen Dead. Nothing would ever be the same again. The skeletal arms of the onagers cranked back and released scores of flaming and rotting skulls, catapulting them high over the walls. The second volley was different. The buckets of the catapults were loaded with huge chunks of granite, basalt and other hard stones that the dead had scavenged from the land around Altdorf.

The archers on the walls looked on in frozen horror as the sky filled with deadly stone rain that hammered down all around them, shattering the stones, fracturing the walls of buildings and caving in slates and roof tiles as though they were tissue paper. The third volley was, again, fire. The flaming skulls whistled as they swooped through the air. This time, they burned where they hit, the fires catching inside buildings as well as outside. The fourth volley was stone.

The boulders crashed into the battlements and arced over the walls in a monstrous rain of rock and debris.

The noise was horrific.

But the silence that followed it was twice as terrifying as the carnage revealed itself from beneath the clouds of smoke and dust the bombardment had caused. Fifteen archers and another thirty pikemen died beneath the crushing weight of the gate tower as it collapsed beneath the onslaught of huge granite boulders. Moments later their broken and battered bodies were jerking around awkwardly trying to stand on shattered bones as they answered von Carstein's summons to undeath. With the enemy suddenly risen within their midst the defenders along the wall fought for their lives as their brothers in arms turned on them in death. Silver blades flashed in the firelight as they threw themselves at friends they had been talking to only moments before. Von Carstein's curse was sick. It shattered the morale of the defenders to see their friends fall only to rise again as puppets of the beast. There was no safe place. Death could come from any side, in any guise.

Skellan couldn't begin to wonder what they were thinking as they threw the broken corpses over the crenulated wall as though they were garbage.

Still the pile of broken bones writhed at the foot of the city wall, desperate to rejoin the fighting.

The walls withstood the first wave of horror.

For five hours the deadly rain of stone and fire continued, smashing the bodies of the defenders to bloody wrecks, powdering huge segments of the city walls, completely obliterating the spires of three temples and setting light to hundreds of houses. It was merciless. The hail ceased but it was still bitterly cold out there. Stretcher-bearers had two grisly jobs, to tend to the wounded and hack up and burn the dead. They couldn't allow sentimentality to get in the way. They built massive funeral pyres in the squares across the city, dragging the fallen into the flames before they could turn on them and attack the defenders on the wall from behind.

The city reeked of burnt flesh.

Skellan breathed deeply of the smell.

He stood silently, watching the smoke billowing up from the city. The city would fall, broken, like the bodies of its defenders crushed beneath the rain of boulders.

The siege towers rocked into place snug up against the high walls and the dead poured from them, zombies burning and falling away where the Altdorfers soaked them with oils and ignited them with flaming arrows, and skeletons shattered beneath the battery of warhammers and maces as the defenders fought desperately for their lives.

Their desperation gave them strength; they fought like savages.

And still, fresh horrors came, mocking their defence. The onagers and mangonels launched rotting body parts riddled with plague and pestilence over the walls, and the dead followed them with hideous battle-cries, throwing themselves at the city walls as arrows and oil and fire rained down on them. The dead hauled themselves up the giant siege engines and onto the battlements where they were met by Altdorfer's steel. Swords clashed with bone and steel, the archers were joined by axmen on the wall-walk. They fought side by side. Men screamed and cried out, fell and were sickeningly raised again by the dark magic von Carstein had woven over the battlefield, parts of their bodies smashed beyond all recognition, bloodied, cut, ruined.

Vengeful death descended on the city of Altdorf and all along the walls the exhausted men knew dawn offered no respite. The sun would not rise to save them.

This was the last stand.

Already the battlements were slippery with blood and the foot of the wall cluttered with bodies. As the defenders threw the fallen off the battlements they poured oil onto the corpses and lit them with flaming arrows, the oil and flame searing the flesh from the bones of the dead. And still the skeletons rose, charred, lumps of flesh clinging to the bones where it hadn't burned away.

It was a glimpse of hell on earth.

Bloody hour followed bloody hour as the dead surged up the ladders of flesh and bone and the siege engines lobbed horrors from the sky. It was endless: hacking, slashing, tearing, rending, clawing, biting, flaying, dying and burning. As more and more zombies spilled onto the wall-walk more and more of the dead went unburned and rose jerkily to join forces with them. Always though, they were beaten back, albeit barely. Sheer weight of numbers, coupled with the exhaustion of the Altdorfers, would drag the city down eventually. Skellan judged the defenders had perhaps another few hours worth of spirited resistance left in them as it stood, but von Carstein had held back his vampires. Unleashed now, the humans wouldn't stand a chance.

The hours were filled with agony and the screams of death.

The siege engines were ablaze, the living dead fused in the skeletal towers crying out in agony as the flames consumed them. The defenders poured hot oil on the towers, stoking the fire. It made no difference. The towers were only constructs, the day had yielded enough deaths to build twenty more towers if von Carstein so desired.

One by one the towers collapsed in on themselves and toppled over, giving the defenders precious minutes to catch their breath before the onslaught redoubled.

One man strode like a giant along the battlements though, clad in the white of Sigmar, his huge axe bloodied, defying the dead, encouraging the defenders to stand and fight once more even when exhaustion threatened to betray them, tapping on reserves of strength they didn't know they had: the Grand Theogonist, Wilhelm III. The man had a warrior's soul. He may have taken to prayers but he was a fighter. Two decades older than some of the men at his side, the priest shamed them with his stamina and determination.

'Vampires! To me!' von Carstein commanded. It was almost as though he had read Skellan's mind but of course he hadn't, the count was a supreme tactician and an excellent reader of men. He knew the defenders were weakening.

He pointed at the walls.

Skellan grinned wolfishly. Beside him Jerek nodded.

It was time.

Finally there would be blood enough to satisfy even his darkest thirst.

Skellan threw his head back and howled at the flawless black sky.

The others took up his cry as their features twisted and mutated into the bestial muzzles and elongated jaw-line of the beasts they carried within them.

The vampires answered Vlad von Carstein's call.

CHAPTER TWENTY-FIVE
The Fallen

ALTDORF
Winter, 2051

'THEY'RE COMING AGAIN!' someone yelled.

The men were beaten. Exhaustion lay heavy on them. The damned dark would never lift. The respite had been pitifully brief. The Grand Theogonist hefted his axe and walked along the allure, offering words of encouragement to the men in the face of the nameless death swarming up the ladders and over the battlements. He braced himself against a splintered merlon and watched the dead charge.

'Sweet Sigmar...' an archer beside him said, seeing the bestial faces of the vampires as they swept forward, von Carstein himself in their midst.

'Stand tall, soldier. The next few hours determine whether we live or die today.'

The archer nodded sickly. 'Aye, we'll fight the devils 'til we drop, an' then...' he let the thought trail away bitterly.

The priest's shoulder burned and his knees were aflame; every step cost him but he couldn't afford to let the men see his weakness. That was why he had worn the white of his god over his mail, so that every man along the wall-walk could see him and take heart from his presence even as the darkness overwhelmed them. He was an old man and he was dying. Both were irrefutable facts, yet when they looked at him they saw Sigmar himself striding down the battlements, smiting foes and lifting hearts.

He would not fail them.

Blood spattered his white tabard and the silver rings of his mail. None of it, blessedly, was his.

He looked at the archer. The man's eyes were red-rimmed with tiredness. He looked like a beaten dog. Along the line men sat with their backs to the wall, recovering what little strength they could. A few had closed their eyes and dozed, taking advantage of the lull in the fighting. With the siege engines buckled and destroyed they believed themselves safe for the moment. Others stood, staring out at the vampires as they swarmed toward them, looks of sheer horror frozen on their faces as they squared up ready for the fighting to begin again in earnest.

'Look at them, tell me what you see?' the priest said, resting a steadying hand on the archer's shoulder.

'The end of the world.'

'Not while I live and breathe lad, not while I live and breathe. Look again.'

The archer scanned the lines of the vampires, his gaze drawn back to von Carstein himself. 'He looks… like a daemon possessed.'

'Better. It is the blood lust. That and fear. We've done that to him, soldier. He looks up at us and he knows fear.'

'You think?'

'Oh, I know, believe me.'

The vampires reached the wall and began scrambling up it like flies swarming over a corpse. They scuttled up the stonework.

The priest laughed bitterly.

'What's so funny?' the archer asked. It was obvious the priest's lack of fear horrified him.

'My own stupidity,' the priest said. 'I thought we had bought ourselves a few hours. Instead we face death again, grown faster and more lethal even as we have tired and weakened. So be it. Up, soldier, let's make them earn our corpses, shall we?'

The priest sent a runner down the stairs to warn the reserves that the fighting was about to begin again, and had them divided into three groups, ready to plug any gap in the wall should it be breached. There would be no escape from the wall for him or the men around him. He had resigned himself to dying on the walls, the only comfort being that he would be dying free and that had to be enough for him. He coughed, a hacking tubercular rattle, and spat out a wad of blood and phlegm. The bout of coughing served as a wake-up call; he wasn't going to live forever, instead he had to make his death count. Make it meaningful.

'Oil!' he yelled, sending the message down the line. In seconds the last few clay jars were being thrown down at the monsters scaling the city walls, some bounced while others broke. The thick black oil splashed down the stonework and covered some of the vampires. 'Fire!' Arrows dripping flame skidded down the wall, igniting the oil with a dull *crump*. A dozen of the vampires fell away from the wall blazing like human torches as the oil caught light and seared away their flesh. Their screams were terrible as the flames engulfed their bodies. The others came on, like demented spiders, faster, stronger.

The priest drew himself to his full height and hefted his huge double-headed axe.

'Come on then, my beauties, sooner you get up the wall sooner we send you back to hell.'

The men around him stood, bracing themselves for the attack.

They knew what was coming and yet not one of them gave in to the instinct to run. He was more proud of them then than he had been for a thousand days through a thousand different circumstances. They were good men. They were going to die like heroes. Each and every one of them. He felt a swell of grief and pride at knowing them, being part of this with them. It was one thing to share your life with someone, it was quite another to willingly share your death.

'For Sigmar!' he bellowed suddenly, holding his axe overhead.

'Altdorf!' someone answered down the wall-walk. The cry went up: 'Altdorf! Altdorf! Altdorf!'

They might not have been spiritual men but their words shook the foundations of the city wall. Spear butts and sword hilts clanged off the stonework adding to the chant.

'Sigmar help us,' the young archer said as the first of the beasts crested the battlements. A spear thrust in its face sent the creature spinning away from the wall, clutching the bloody weapon where it stuck between soft flesh and hard bone.

The next vampire over the wall was one he knew, a man he thought dead. In another life Jerek Kruger had been a friend. Now the priest stared at the lord of the White Wolves, still dressed in his ceremonial armour and furs, huge warhammer in hand, his face pallid and tinged blue, and knew that his friend was gone. The thing that stood in his place was a cold-blooded killer. The Wolf howled and threw himself into the thick of the fighting, his warhammer cracking the skull of the first man to get in its way. More vampires surged over the walls even as the defenders hacked and slashed at them, trying desperately to drive them back.

The preternatural speed of the vampires coupled with their awesome strength made them a deadly foe. On the narrow wall-walk where the press of bodies made it almost impossible to swing a sword, they were overwhelming. They fought like daemons possessed. For every one vampire slain eight, ten, twelve, defenders fell.

The priest swallowed back his rising horror.

This was why Sigmar had chosen him. He was a fighter first, a man of god second. He threw himself into the fray. Against the fury of the vampires he fought with curious detachment, instinct governing his actions; he caught a sword blow on the shaft of his axe, turned it against his would be killer and drove the flat of his axe head into the vampire's face, bursting the cartilage of the creature's nose and staggering it back the step he needed to roll his wrists and deliver a killing blow, slamming the honed edge of the axe blade into the vampire's throat. It was a massive blow, the priest's full strength behind it. The metal sheared through dead flesh and crunched into the bone vertebrae. The creature's head rolled back, half decapitated, hands fluttering up weakly to clutch at its throat even as its body collapsed under it.

He kicked the monster from the wall and met the next attack head on.

Around him good men died.

He couldn't allow himself to mourn them.

The wall had to hold. If they lost ground here von Carstein would be inside the city. Images of slaughter filled the priest's mind as he hammered the twin-headed blade of his axe into the chest of another fiend, opening the creature up from throat to sternum. The vampire's guts spilled onto the wall-walk. The beast clung to the handle of the priest's axe as it died, its face shifting back to that of a handsome young man. The priest fancied he saw, in that death mask, a look of peace that defied the vampire's violent death. A third vampire fell beneath his axe, its head splitting like an overripe pumpkin as the axe bit into it.

Ducking beneath a slashing sword, he turned and disembowelled a leering vampire with a staggering backhanded sweep of his massive axe.

He stepped over the dead body and moved in to support part of the wall's defence that was crumbling under constant assault from the dead.

A flaming skull shattered at his feet, splashing fire up in front of his face.

The priest backed up a step, waiting for the flames to abate.

The sounds and the stench of death were terrible. It was a bloodbath.

Defenders fell from the wall, broken and bloody, their bodies torn to shreds by tooth and claw, slit open by cold steel, shattered by the crushing blows of warhammers and smashed by falling stones as the catapults renewed their barrage.

Here, at the end of his life, on the walls of Altdorf, he was returning to what he had been before Sigmar saved him and raised him up: a killer. He had come full circle. Though not quite, in taking the name Wilhelm III he had left behind the brute he had been, a drunk, shunned by family and friends, given to rage and violence. He had been shaped by the will of Sigmar, forged by the fires of worship and atonement, to die here, giving his life in defence of the greatest city mankind had ever known. He was Sigmar's hammer made flesh.

'I will not fail you,' he pledged, stepping over the dying flames.

He saw von Carstein.

If ever he had wondered about the lord of the dead's humanity, this ended it. Von Carstein was no man; he was everything the priest had feared, a daemon possessed.

A killing machine.

The enraged Vampire Count was fighting his way along the battlements to face him.

The sounds of battle crystallised in his ears. He remembered them, each and every one, as though they were the last he would hear: cries, screams, curses, pleas, steel on steel, steel on flesh. Another blast of fire roared around his head, black smoke curdling his vision. The priest forced himself to go through it. As the smoke cleared he saw he was standing in a swath of burned and blistered flesh as men lay wounded and bleeding. They had been caught in the fire. Smoke curled up off their bodies. Strips of their flesh were charred black. The priest shielded his nose with his arm. Still it smelled sickeningly of roasted meat.

A scorched face, weeping blood and pus, cracked and completely unrecognisable, reared up in front of his, a ruined hand reaching out imploringly for his help.

He stepped over the fallen. There was nothing he could do for them.

Von Carstein cut down two defenders, his wailing blade cleaving through the right arm of one, severing it just below the elbow, and the head of another.

'I see you, priest!' he yelled above the tumult.

Out of the cacophony the priest heard a whistling shrillness followed by shattering impacts and screaming. Below the wall-walk men were running, shields over their heads. Some had already fallen. Others were trying to reach them, drag them away, destroy them, before they could rise and turn against them. Small fires burned everywhere.

'Come to me then! Come and face your doom, vampire!' the priest rasped, trying to stop his voice shaking as he moved to meet the vampire.

Flying splinters of rock and dirt sprayed him; he felt their sting as they cut his face.

The vampire barged another soldier aside.

They were fifteen feet apart on the wall-walk, the allure slick with blood and dust. The Grand Theogonist hefted his axe, feeling its reassuring heaviness in his hands.

Behind him, a chunk of masonry fell, cracking the wall-walk. More rocks and stones followed as the machicolations caved in beneath the barrage of debris. Part of the wall-walk broke away.

Ten feet apart.

The Vampire Count's mouth opened; he roared his anger and hurled himself at the priest. The priest let the monster's momentum carry him through as he brought his axe up to anticipation of the savage blow. The beast hit him full on, staggering him back four steps. He drove the butt of the axe handle up toward von Carstein's face, catching the vampire a glancing blow on the cheek. Von Carstein bellowed, driving the priest back with the sheer force of his anger as he hit the man, three times, with dizzying speed. The blows snapped the priest's head back three times in quick succession. The Vampire Count was rabid.

The Grand Theogonist shook his head. His own blood from his ruined nose sprayed his arms. He winced, tasting blood where it spilled into his mouth.

'Time to die, holy man,' von Carstein rasped vehemently.

The vampire launched a double attack, swinging the wailing sword high and wide with his right hand and slamming his left into the priest's face. It was a punishing blow but physical pain didn't follow. He was numb to it. There was no feeling. The priest grunted at the impact and cracked the shaft of his axe off the vampire's elbow, bringing the flat head of the axe round to hammer into the side of von Carstein's head. The vampire vaulted backwards, easily avoiding the wild blow – but it bought the priest precious breathing space.

'You talk a lot for a dead man.'

'The same could be said about you.'

The priest pressed his offensive, windmilling his axe forward. Von Carstein ducked under two blows but two more rocked him, one cracking against his jaw the other crunching into his left shoulder. The vampire rubbed a hand across his mouth; it came away slick with blood. He countered with a lightning-fast jab that nearly took the priest's eye out. Blood ran from the gash in his brow, into his left eye. The eye socket itself swelled up purple and bloody quickly. Half the world blurred as he lost most of his vision from it.

'How does it feel to be mortal?' von Carstein goaded. The count laughed deeply and whipped his blade out in a slashing arc, keeping the priest on his back foot.

'You tell me?' the priest said contemptuously. He swatted away the vampire's lunge with the butt of his axe. 'Without that damned ring of yours how are you going to come back this time?'

Lunatic rage flared in the count's dead eyes. He held up his right hand contemptuously, showing the priest the ornate signet ring on his middle finger.

'Your man failed, priest.'

The priest raised his head high, catching the first fresh flakes of white as the snow returned, whirling in the air. Life, hope, drained from him. Mann had failed. They were doomed, all of them.

Von Carstein hit him.

He felt as if he had been slammed face first into a stone wall. A pang of fear went through him, rising up from his gut to his throat, a desperate urge to vomit. Terror dried his mouth, seized his body. Cold specks of snow kissed his face, melted and slid down his neck and beneath his armour.

The darkness closed around him.

He was an old man, his strength slowly fading with each blow given and received, whereas his enemy was immortal, strengthened by the blood and death all around him. He knew deep down in his bones his death was inevitable. They traded blows, hard blows. Fits of coughing shook him. The vampire was merciless, driving his advantage home. His blade whipped out again and again, nicking the priest, shallow cuts that stung more than they bled. Two cuts were bad though, slicing deep into his upper left arm and low on his left side. Both bled profusely, yet still he faced von Carstein, defying him with sheer bloody determination.

He winced at another stabbing pain as the wailing blade slammed into his left side, forcing the rings of his mail into the deep cut. The pain was incredible. His vision blacked out for a heartbeat, his head filled with the sheer agony of the blow. He staggered but refused to buckle. The priest lifted his head up.

'Come on, vampire. Is this it? Is this the might of Vlad von Carstein? Stealer of souls, king of the dead?' He shook his head. 'I am an old man. I haven't lifted a weapon in thirty years. You are *nothing*, vampire. Nothing. It ends here.'

The fighting raged on around the two combatants, death a constant companion on the battlements and the streets below. Screams of anger and pain met the clash of steel and the insidious rasp of fire.

He was dying. He was bleeding out his strength ounce by red ounce.

'You're a fool, priest, like all of your kind. You talk of good, of evil,' von Carstein said, advancing once more. His eyes blazed with naked savagery. 'There is no good, there is no evil. I have passed beyond death, priest. Understand that, there is nothing. I have been there. I have seen the lie of your promised land. My body died a long time ago, far, far away from here, yet here I am. Living. There are things – powers, priest, powers – so far removed from your philosophy they would dwarf your mind, things so old death no longer touches them. Death no longer weakens them. Look at yourself, priest, and then look at me. You can feel it in you, can't you? You can feel it creeping through your limbs, from the cuts in your side and your arm reaching down through the tiring flesh into your soul. Into you. Death. It's in your eyes.'

A huge boulder smashed into the wall-walk; the floor didn't split but it shivered beneath his feet and the existing cracks began to tear themselves apart under the strain.

The priest ignored the rumbling. He did not look down. He only had eyes for the vampire.

'Cling to your half-life, fiend. Live in an eternal dark, for all the good it will do you. You have failed. Here, this is where it ends. Look around you. Altdorf stands defiant. Through the smoke and the dust the people are already beginning the process of healing. They go on living, it is what people do.'

'They go on dying,' von Carstein rasped, slicing a cut deep into the priest's right arm. The steel chain linked rings splintered and broke, gouging deep into his flesh.

He bit back on the pain.

With an immense effort he hefted his huge axe. He could barely see though the veil of pain the vampire's cuts had pulled down over his eyes.

'You can burn us and bleed us, von Carstein, but you won't crush us. Cut me down, another will rise up in my stead. You have failed, vampire. An old man and some brave-hearted boys have beaten you.'

'Hardly, fool. You can barely stand, let alone fight on. You're done. It's over... but,' the Vampire Count added, almost as an afterthought, 'you would make a good vampire, priest. I have never taken a priest.'

The priest tilted his neck, exposing the hard pulse of his jugular. His hands clenched around the shaft of the axe. He straightened his head up and snorted. 'I thought not.'

Wilhelm III, Grand Theogonist, drew himself erect. It took all of his will and strength not to cry out against the biting pain of his wounds. His head swam. He didn't have long left and he knew it.

Von Carstein cut him again, a slash that sliced through his ear and buried itself deep in his shoulder.

He staggered a step forward, barely keeping his feet under him. The pain was unbearable. His vision misted momentarily, then cleared, and he saw with stunning clarity what he had to do.

Tears stung his cheeks.

Von Carstein rammed his sword into the priest's left shoulder; the pain of withdrawal as the vampire wrenched the wailing blade out of his flesh was blinding. A second thrust plunged into his chest, between his ribs, and into his lung. He had felt nothing like it in his life. He was dead, living on borrowed seconds, a final gift from Sigmar. He knew what he had to do. The axe weighed heavily in his hands. He dropped it.

Von Carstein laughed, a bitter mocking sound.

'It seems you were wrong, priest, when you promised me I would die here. This is my city now. Mine, priest! It is you who has failed, you sanctimonious fool. Look at you. Look at you! You are a wreck of a human being. You shame your god do you know that? You shame your god.'

The priest swallowed the pain even as it consumed him. He looked at his lifeblood leaking out of him. There was nothing left. Nothing. He could barely raise his head to face the monster.

Instead of wasting his life on words the priest screamed, embracing the rawness of it, using the blistering pain to drive him on, and in that scream he became like an animal, primal and deadly.

He threw himself at the Vampire Count, his body slamming into von Carstein, his staggering momentum carrying them both back into the bracing wall of the machicolations.

They hung there for a heartbeat, balanced precariously between the wall-walk and thin air, von Carstein using every ounce of his incredible strength to push back against the priest but even as it looked as though the priest's last desperate lunge would end in futility his foot stumbled into a deep fissure in the stone floor. With the full weight of the priest pressing down on him von Carstein couldn't recover his balance. He was helpless. The priest had his arms pinned. He couldn't even reach out to grab hold of something. The priest's grip was iron.

The priest couldn't make out more than a blurred outline of black where von Carstein was trapped in front of him.

With a massive grunt and the very last ounce of his strength, the priest pushed. The vampire strained, struggling to keep his footing but there was nothing he could do. In desperation the priest found the strength to take them both off the battlements.

They fell, locked together in a deadly embrace.

Neither screamed, even as their bodies were broken by the fall. The arc of their descent carried them out into the closest of the shallow ditches, behind the fast flowing moat of the Reik.

The ditches lined with sharpened stakes.

The stake pierced von Carstein's back, bursting out of his chest even as it sank into the priest's. The vampire's eyes flared open in shock even as the weight of the priest drove him deeper onto the spike.

A sound like thunder cracked through the world. He felt it bone-deep.

The vampire gagged, blood leaking out of his mouth as he tried to speak. The priest couldn't make out a word. It didn't matter. The blood told him all he needed to know. He could walk the path of souls now to Sigmar's side.

'I did not fail you…' And though no one heard him, it didn't matter.

There was no pain, only blessed relief.

He bowed his head and let his life go.

The first chink of sunlight broke through the black sky, the ray of light a column of gold on the black of the battlefield.

They died there, trapped together in the sun, vampire and holy man.

CHAPTER TWENTY-SIX

Streets of Ash and Hope

ALTDORF
Winter, 2051

CITIES, UNLIKE MEN, are immortal.

A scholar had said that. Felix couldn't remember whom – Reitzeiger perhaps? He agreed with the sentiments completely. Where flesh and blood failed stone stood firm, and when bricks and mortar failed, well it could always be rebuilt surpassing its former glory. That was how cities flourished. They healed themselves and in doing so they rose like phoenixes from the ashes, resplendent. Those early dark days would slip from the memory as moments of beauty and ingenuity replaced the ruins.

Over the last few days, with the rebirth of the sun, Altdorf had begun the long painful process of survival. Those left behind had said their goodbyes to loved ones fallen defending their right to freedom; normal men who neither wanted nor asked to fight were buried alongside soldiers who had given their lives willingly. That was the cost of survival. Innocent blood.

It weighed heavy on the populace.

An innocence had died among the people of the city. Safety, the most basic of liberties, had been stripped from them. They no longer took the sanctity of their homes for granted. This was a double-edged sword. Good, because it meant they suddenly appreciated what they had. Bad, because the lesson it taught was that anything good could be taken away without a moment's thought. It heightened the grief the city felt. Buildings could be rebuilt, fortified. People would survive, but that sense of comfort, of being protected once the door closed at night, that took a long time to recover. Some would never get over it.

The city was in ruins. It would be a long time before the spires of Altdorf commanded the majesty they once had; broken slates exposed the burnt timbers and gaping holes where homes had stood. The architects of necessity and desire would fix that of course, roofs and walls were only stone, but the wounds betrayed the true hurt Altdorf had suffered. It wasn't about bricks and mortar, it was about children growing up orphans, about wives kneeling at grave markers unable to think beyond what might have been, about mothers wondering if they had enough love, enough strength, enough hope to face the world each day. It was about people.

Felix Mann walked through the ruined streets, listening to the dawn chorus breaking out all over the city.

This was his home. These were his people.

Despite the fact that days ago he had been ready to abandon them to their lot he hurt with them. In the last few days he had become a part of this great city, and soon he would be leaving it never to return. That was his loss to bear. For the first time, emerging from the vampire's tent carrying the iron ring, he had found a sense of belonging, and now he was turning his back on it.

He looked up at the windows of his house. He couldn't go home. That was the crux of it. Things had changed. He couldn't go home. He found himself clutching von Carstein's ring all the harder, pressing it into his palm. Was it truly possible that a trinket had kept the vampire alive?

The talk on the streets, of course, was far more miraculous. The Grand Theogonist's holiness and the grace of Sigmar, they said, had finally undone the monster. They were far more willing to believe the ridiculous than they were to accept the mundane.

Felix loved that about people.

The bigger the lie the happier they were to embrace it. Already they spoke of Wilhelm III with the reverential tones normally reserved for a saint or a martyr. Felix was sure the old man would have approved; it was the icing on the cake as far as his grift was concerned. And, surprising himself, Felix didn't begrudge the holy man in the slightest. The people of Altdorf needed heroes now and magic or not, that was exactly what the priest was, an honest to gods hero.

He walked away from his apartment. He knew where he was going: the Sigmarite cathedral. This morning it felt as though every street led there. The press of people was claustrophobic compared with the emptiness the last time he had walked these self-same streets. Even the smallest avenues were teeming with life.

Felix looked around as he walked, bumping between people. Their relief was palpable. They were talking. Laughing. A few days ago the thought of laughter ever ringing out again in Kaiserplatz had been inconceivable. But there it was. People survived. Adapted. Found joy in the smallest of things.

Still, it would be a long time before anything even remotely resembling normality returned.

Indeed, so heavy were the losses to the men of Altdorf that even with Vlad himself dead, and more than half of his damned vampires vanquished, the rest were able to flee without serious pursuit. It was difficult to watch the enemy flee without giving chase but to do so in their condition was suicide. Reluctantly, the heroes of Altdorf had manned the walls, jeering as their enemy fled the light.

Felix walked slowly, not in a hurry to get to where he was going. He would say his own quiet goodbye after the pomp and circumstance of the state funeral. It was a matter of practicality. He had a price to collect from the lector before he headed north to Reiksport and took the boat. He wondered if it would be difficult to disappear and decided it probably wouldn't. He knew the lies he needed to say for people to accept him as someone else; he had been lying most of his life. He would miss the city though, and the house, but both were just stones that could be rebuilt elsewhere. It was time to start thinking about a different kind of life: a scholar's. Perhaps. He could picture himself locked away in dusty libraries growing old surrounded by even older books.

Then again, he was a thief, and there was a reason for the adage once a thief, always a thief.

No matter what he called himself he knew in his heart he would still be Felix Mann, thief, even though he wouldn't be able to take credit for the greatest job of his career. It didn't matter. He knew and he would take the secret to the grave with him.

It was his second funeral in as many days, though very different to yesterday's, a quiet affair within the walls of the cathedral grounds that he wasn't actually invited to, when the lector had interred von Carstein. Curiosity had Felix taking up residency among the rooftops where he had a good view of the cemetery grounds. The creature's grave had been dug beneath the holy ground they intended to use for Wilhelm, a last defence against the beast's rising.

The lector had decapitated von Carstein's corpse, taking the head and scooping the grey matter and soft tissue out to burn, and buried the rest of the head in an unmarked grave, a white rose in its mouth, his eyes replaced by cloves of garlic.

There were only four people at the vampire's burial, Mann, the lector, Ludwig the Pretender and lastly, Reynard Grimm, the new captain of the Altdorf guard. The body was buried face down, the arms bound behind its back with wire, kneecaps shattered, von Carstein's black heart cut out of his chest and burned along with his brain. He was not coming back. Not this time.

They levelled the inside of his grave and prepared it to receive Wilhelm's body. The Holy Father would serve one last duty for Sigmar, as eternal guardian watching over the Vampire Count even in death.

Felix had expected tears but the outpouring of grief as he entered Domplatz was unlike anything he had ever witnessed. Mourners lined the streets. They sobbed hysterically, a babble of voices choked between gulps and hiccoughs:

'He saved us.'

'Without him we'd be living in the dark.'

'You have to believe... You have to... He was sent by Sigmar to save us.'

'The way he looked at you, he saw into your soul.'

'He was special. There will never be another man like him.'

'He wasn't a man at all, I tell you, he was Sigmar himself.'

'He shone out as a beacon against the dark times!'

'He was the light of our lives!'

'He was our saviour.'

And to them it was all true, to degrees. It didn't surprise Felix to hear talk of the Grand Theogonist's sainthood. It was the perfect end cap to the greatest grift of all time. He had sold a miracle to the entire world and they bought it.

Some had wrapped themselves in flags of Altdorf and banners of Sigmar, others sat quietly on the cobbles weeping openly as though they had just lost their best friend. Felix pushed between them, working his way toward the side door into the cathedral. He wouldn't be going in through the gates.

A young novitiate answered his knocking, obviously expecting the thief, nodded and ushered him inside.

'The lector is in the vaults, dealing with the... ah... prisoner. Captain Grimm has yet to return from the field with his finds from the vampire's pavilion. Would you care for a drink while you wait? The interment will be a few hours, no doubt. You could of course avail yourself of the chapel.'

The novitiate scurried away down the cold corridor gesturing for Felix to follow. The cathedral was surprisingly simple, lacking in ostentation. It had none of the gilt-edges or plush velvets he expected from the priesthood. It was simple, bare, even austere. It was a place for worship without the trappings of the material world. Felix liked it. It reflected well on the personality of the Grand Theogonist. It was unassuming. Down to earth. Of course the public face of the cathedral was anything but, but back here, out of sight of the common man, the hand of Wilhelm III was most noticeable.

'He was a good man,' Felix said to the novitiate's back.

'He was. He listened, you know. He cared. He truly cared.'

'I'm sorry for your loss.' And he was.

'We do not mourn his passing, we celebrate the time we shared with him.'

He led Felix to a small chamber, barely large enough for it to be considered a room at all. There was a hard wooden chair, a small table and a jug of water. Felix couldn't help but smile to himself; the young man had led him to what looked like a penitent's cell.

'Wait here.' With that he left Felix alone.

With time on his hands to think, the thief was forced to do just that.

The last few days had been a strain. He had learned some things about himself he wasn't entirely comfortable knowing.

He heard footsteps a while later, and the flickering light of a candle lit the corridor outside the small room. A man appeared in the doorway, his long shadow reaching deep into the room. He was dressed in the formal robes of the clergy, and did not look pleased to have been dragged away from whatever it was he had been doing.

'Yes?'

The curtness put Felix off balance slightly. He had expected to come, be paid and leave. Business was business, after all.

'I've come for my price.'

'What are you blathering on about, man?'

'My pardon and the money I was promised. I've come to collect.'

'Is this some kind of joke?'

'Hardly. I was... ah... hired... by the Grand Theogonist to do a job for him. I held up my side of the bargain, and now I want you to hold up yours.'

'No such bargains were made, I assure you. Our most benevolent brother did not treat with thieves.'

'No, he walked with hand in hand with Sigmar. Yes, yes, very well, I am scum. I know that. Now give me my money, priest, a deal is a deal. Where's the lector?'

'He's detained currently, now, I suggest it is time for you to leave. Whatever business you believe you had with our beloved holy father, I assure you does not continue with this office today. Good day.'

Felix bristled. He stood, the wooden chair grating back on its legs as he pushed it out of the way. 'I don't think so, priest. A deal is a deal and I intend to collect, with your blessing our without. You do know who I am, don't you?' His lips twisted into a grim parody of a smile.

'I know who you are and I know that you will be leaving here empty-handed.'

He grabbed the priest, throwing him up against the wall. His fists bunched in the priest's cassock, pressing up hard into the man's Adam's apple. The man gagged, his arms flapping ineffectually at Felix's, unable to break the thief's grip.

'I don't make a habit of hurting priests but in your case I'm willing to make an exception. Now, where's the lector?'

'In the vaults,' the priest gasped. 'With the captain.'

'Take me to them.'

'No.'

'I said take me to them. I am not in the habit of asking twice.'

'I can't,' the priest pleaded.

'Don't make me hurt you, man.'

'I can't.'

Felix hit him, once, hard, driving a fist into his gut. The priest doubled up in pain. Felix slammed him up against the wall again. 'I could lie and tell you that hurt me almost as much as it hurt you but it didn't. Actually it felt pretty good. Now, we'll try this one last time, priest, take me to them.'

The man's head came up defiantly. 'They are in the vaults with the prisoner, you can wait or you can leave.' Felix raised his fist again. 'They are not to be disturbed. Hit me again, my answer will be the same no matter how many times you do so.'

Disgusted, he pushed the priest out of his way and walked out of the room.

'Where are you going?' the priest shouted after him.

'Where do you think?'

He stalked down the chill corridor, listening but only hearing the echo of his own footsteps. The entrance to the vaults would, he reasoned, be off the main chapel, assuming that the vaults were part of the crypt or could be reached through the mausoleum. The other logical choice was the kitchens. There was no guarantee of course. With these old buildings the vaults could actually be some long forgotten dungeon with a secluded stairwell hidden away somewhere. He stopped at a corner as a whiff of nutmeg and cinnamon hit him. He followed his nose and found the kitchens, but more importantly, he found a staircase leading down to the depths of the cathedral's cold stone heart.

The air was noticeably colder as he descended, prickling his skin. Even the texture and quality of it changed. It was older air. Stale.

He paused at the bottom of the stairs, listening. He could hear muted voices from deeper in the darkness. He followed the sounds. Warm orange light suffused the corridor.

They were torturing the prisoner when he walked into the cell. The priest and the captain, Grimm, stood over a man who was bound by thick chains to a chair in the centre of the room. The prisoner's head was down so Felix couldn't see his face but it was obvious he had taken severe punishment. His clothes were stained darkly by blood, his hair matted with the stuff. The cell smelled of vomit and urine.

'What in Sigmar's name are you doing here!' the lector spat, seeing Felix in the doorway.

'I've come to collect the money promised to me, then I will be on my way.'

'Get out, fool!'

The prisoner's head came up. It was bruise-purple, swollen and bloody from the beating he had taken. Felix stared at the wretched man. The beating had rendered him barely recognisable as a human being. The sheer brutality of it shook Felix. His eyes darted about the small cell, saw instruments of torture, tongs and pincers, a brazier of hot coals. Grimm held a bar of red iron to the prisoner's throat, the skin sizzling blackly even before the kiss of the metal seared away the top layers of flesh. The prisoner's scream was harrowing. The man bucked and writhed against his chains.

Felix backed out of the room. This was wrong. War drove men to extremes, he knew, but they were extremes of necessity, not wanton acts of evil. The torturing of a prisoner moved very definitely into the realms of evil.

The prisoner's screams haunted the passageway.

The lector came out to join him, sweat blackening his forehead. The man was clearly exhausted.

'This is not for your eyes,' he said, closing his own as the prisoner cried out once more. When he opened them again Felix was surprised at the depth and intensity of grief he saw in them.

'I made a deal with the Grand Theogonist, I rendered him a service, ah, appropriating a piece of jewellery he desired. In return I was promised a pardon and coin enough to begin a new life away from here. I want what is my due.'

'Impossible,' the lector said bluntly.

'I really do urge you to reconsider. I have a feeling that someone would pay very handsomely for this trinket, and in the wrong hands it could almost certainly prove to be far more trouble than it's worth.'

'Are you threatening me, thief?'

'Not at all, threats are idle. I will have my due, priest. Your temple owes me. A deal is a deal.'

'So you say, but I see no evidence of any such deal. Do you have a notarised contract? Do you have a shred of evidentiary proof to support your word? No, I thought not. So as far as I am concerned, thief, you are also a liar. You are wasting my time.'

'You would be dead if it wasn't for me!'

The priest laughed at that. 'I think not, thief. We are all alive by the grace of Sigmar and his divine hammer, Wilhelm III. Now leave before you try my patience further.'

Felix turned on his heel, disgusted, and left them to torture the prisoner. He wanted to be as far away from this godforsaken place as possible. He would take his price and be damned. He didn't need their permission, a deal was a deal. Their coffers would open long enough for him to take his due. He took the stairs two and three at a time, almost running up them. He was seething. At the top, he looked left, then right, and plunged into the heart of the cathedral, following a narrow passage as it opened into the grand chapel. The huge vaulted dome was magnificent, humbling, with its murals and gilt décor. Marble statues of the beatific Man-God Sigmar stood watch over the holiest of holies, impassive to the comings and goings his chosen sons. A scattering of the devout knelt at prayer in the wooden pews. Felix walked through the middle of them, looking left and right for something of value to take.

He saw nothing. For all the obvious wealth on display it was art, sculpture, the decoration itself. In frustration he overturned a pew and lashed out at one of the multi-pronged iron candelabra lighting the room. It fell, the candles snuffed out as the rolled across the stone floor. Felix stalked out of the chapel, slamming the huge oaken door behind him.

The first dark blush of dusk was drawing in. He had lost all track of time while he waited inside the house of Sigmar.

Three novitiates were tending what looked like a funeral pyre in the cathedral garden. There was no body; they were feeding the fire with scraps of paper, drawn one sheet at a time from the old tomes spread out by their feet.

The flames sparked and hissed as the sheets were fed to them, blazing blue in the instant of immolation before being consumed by the red flames.

Felix barged through them in his hurry to be away, kicking aside one of the books. It fell open on a vicious scrawl of unintelligible black ink. His eyes were drawn immediately to the brittle pages that so obviously weren't paper. He was an intelligent man. He could read and write but even a cursory glance was enough to know this was no language he had ever seen before. Instinctively, he knew it to be a grimoire.

He would have his price.

Whatever secrets the book contained they were dangerous enough for the Sigmarites to be burning them. That made them the kind of secrets someone would pay a lot of money for.

Without thinking he grabbed the book from the floor and ran for the street.

CHAPTER TWENTY-SEVEN

Let Us Not Go Gently Into That Endless Winter Night

DRAKWALD FOREST
Winter, 2051

THEY WERE LOST within the dark heart of the old wood.

They were the last. It was hard to believe.

A few days ago they had been part of the most awesome fighting force the world had ever seen.

They had been invincible. They had been immortal. Warriors of the Blood!

What were they now? A few stragglers, beaten, driven from the field of battle, forced to run, to flee, to cling to the shreds of their unlife as their world unravelled. The von Carstein bloodline was all but extinguished, those few that remained pale shadows of the great vampires that had fallen. They were third, fourth, even fifth generation gets. They were not their sires. They lacked the awesome strength of those who had fallen. They were shadows. They were weak.

A spent force.

The Kingdom of the Dead had crumbled on its foundations of dust. The horrors of von Carstein's army, the skeletons and the zombies that had ravaged the country, had sunk slowly back into the dirt as the necromantic magic of Nagash binding their bones came undone with the count's death, transforming the ground before the bleak stone ramparts of Altdorf into one vast garden of bones.

Jerek von Carstein blundered through the undergrowth, dead leaves mulching beneath his feet as he drove himself on, slapping aside the cut and sting of withered branches even as exhaustion suffused his limbs and muddied his mind. They followed him blindly even though he was lost both physically and metaphorically.

All was quiet save for the passage of the dead.

A single raven sat on a skeletal branch, watching them pityingly. The castle's ill-omened birds had followed them from Drakenhof itself, feasting on the offal and carrion the army left trailing in its wake. They scavenged the fields of blood beneath the walls of Altdorf, cawing and shrieking and picking at the rotting flesh of the fallen. While the others lingered to feed this lone bird haunted them. It was always there on the edge of his vision, black wings blurring as he tried to focus on them. He had seen the bird four times since they had entered Drak Wald.

He didn't know if they were following the bird or it was following them.

It didn't matter.

They were all dead.

It was only a matter of time before the humans abandoned the security of their walls and set about finishing what they had begun. They had days, a week or two at best while the enemy regrouped and healed, then the bloodline would be wiped out in one almighty purge.

In a way it was a relief – an end to it.

Jerek was finding it harder and harder to remember who he had been. At times, like now, it saddened him that his personality had slipped, been subsumed by the monstrous beast von Carstein had sired, though these moments were fleeting and few and far between. A pang. Nothing more. Hour by hour he lost himself. Facing von Carstein in the bell tower he had imagined it would all be over in a heartbeat, that his mortal soul would be wiped out, he had never considered the possibility that he might remember what it was like to be Jerek Kruger. The torment was pulling him apart. The need to feed went against everything he had been, and yet it represented everything he had become. Jerek loathed himself and the monster von Carstein had made him.

But that was who he was: Jerek von Carstein. Kruger was dead and gone but for a few rogue memories.

There had been a dark presence inside Jerek, ever-present like a second heartbeat, an echo that tied him to his sire. It had been a comfort of sorts, binding him to von Carstein's twisted mockery of a family. Now nothing lived on. The vampires had lost and in doing so became hollow creatures. The link had been severed brutally and suddenly they were bereft. They all felt it: the ache of loss. The emptiness engulfed them all. They had lost their father and without him, suddenly, they were nothing. It seemed inconceivable. In a few hours the Kingdom of the Dead had come undone. Vlad had fallen, returned to dust by a rag-tag army of humans.

'We need to feed,' Pieter said, sniffing the air for even the faintest trace of humanity, his teeth bared. He had regressed almost to the point of becoming animalistic. Grief brought out his base nature. The man was a weasel: a dangerous creature not to be trusted despite its innocent appearance. 'We need blood and I smell cattle.'

The others crowded around, their faces betraying their desperate need.

'Then go hunt,' Jerek said. 'The woods are filled with trappers' cottages and tiny settlements. All of you, go hunt, feed. Do what you need to. Leave me alone.'

No one moved.

'You heard me,' he said, turning his back on their hungry faces. Their expectancy disgusted him. He hefted his warhammer, felt a thrill course through his fingers as his flesh came into contact with the weapon. It sang in his blood.

Still none of them moved to follow Pieter.

They looked to him for guidance, he realised, because for all their finery and sophisticated ruthlessness, he was the only true warrior left amongst them. He understood their enemy better than any of them because he had led them. They were rats, weasels, ferrets, and stoats, animals used to sneaking, hiding, fighting from the dark, striking fast and moving on. In contrast, he was a White Wolf, fearless, powerful, a majestic beast. They grasped and grasped at the twin illusions of strength and power, desperate to cloak themselves in the stuff, to wear the trappings they offered. Avarice pumped the dead blood through their veins. Hunger for power and hunger for blood, were, he knew, the twin dimensions of the vampire's world. Jerek von Carstein might have been Vlad's get but before his birth into the Kingdom of the Dead he had been born and raised in a world of fear and violence. Raised a warrior from birth, he was a knight, but more than anything else he was a survivor. Their diffidence wouldn't last. He knew that.

Once they were safe the murderous succession would begin. They were liars, cheats, thieves and killers, each and every one of them. There was no honour in their dead hearts. They feared power. They respected ruthlessness. They coveted everything they lacked. Some, no doubt, were already planning his downfall simply because he was Vlad's get and in terms of the blood his claim was stronger than all of theirs.

'Go!'

They scattered, some transforming into their lupine aspects, others loosing the beast within.

He was alone. He sat on an old tree stump, rotten to the core. He heard them crashing through the trees, heard the screams when they came. They were animals.

'You should have forced her to return with us.'

Jerek turned to see Emmanuelle, Pieter's wife, standing behind him. She had come up on him without him hearing a sound. Blood dribbled down her chin. Her porcelain skin looked so fragile in the gloom. In contrast her eyes were flint.

'She was beyond that. To leave would have robbed Isabella of the man she loved. In her madness she believed that staying there, where he fell, she could somehow keep his memory pure, alive, but to return to the castle without him, he would weaken, fade and eventually cease to be the man she loved.'

'So instead you left her there to die.'

'I took pity on her.'

'Pity is for dogs.'

'So what would you have had me do? Drag her kicking and screaming to Drakenhof?'

'If needs be, yes. She is one of us, we don't abandon our own to the cattle. We owe her. We owe Vlad.'

'We owe no one!' Jerek said vehemently. His ferocity surprised him. He mastered his anger quickly. 'We didn't ask to be sired, they chose us, we did not choose them. Now we start fighting for our lives because behind us the humans are coming and they intend to exterminate us like vermin.'

'Humans,' Emmanuelle said contemptuously.

'Yes, humans. Like it or not, the cattle stand on the verge of wiping us out.'

In the distance a woman screamed. Her cries died out quickly.

Emmanuelle's smile was cold. 'Did you hear that? That is how we deal with humans.'

'I know,' he said, afraid of himself, afraid of what he had become, afraid of what his future held. 'I know.'

CHAPTER TWENTY-EIGHT

The Stalking Ground

ALTDORF
Winter, 2051

FELIX MANN CRADLED the book to his chest as he ran.

He pumped his one free arm hard, mouth open as he ran. The spine of the book banged into his chin. His heart hammered in his chest.

He skidded around a corner into one of the seedier districts of the city. Two dogs fought over scraps still on the bone. They snarled as he dodged around them, nearly tripping over the foot still attached to the shinbone they were fighting over.

Two of the Sigmarite novitiates gave chase while the third raised the alarm. Cries of: 'Stop! Thief!' rang through the narrow back alleys but they didn't slow him. People heard and turned and by the time they did he was past them and careening down the street, around the corner and away.

He ran on, through the narrow warren of streets, crashing through laundry hung so low it almost dragged on the cobbles as the wind stirred it.

The sky shifted into dusk, clouds obscuring what little was left of the sun. Night, for the first time in what felt like forever, was his friend again. It promised shadows – places to hide. It was his time.

People stared at him. They would remember the way he had come. He stopped, breathless and gasping, back pressed against a wall, listening for the sounds of pursuit.

He began to understand what he had done.

It wasn't just a book, he knew. He could feel it. The thing was vile. Corrupt. He felt its taint wherever his skin touched the skin of the binding. He didn't want to hold onto it any longer than he had to. It had seemed like a good idea, a means of securing payment and forcing the Sigmarites to keep the old man's word, but like so many good ideas it was not as simple as that. Felix tore a strip out of a laundered sheet and wrapped the book in it. He tucked the book under his arm. The cloth did little to shield him from the book's taint but at least he didn't have to feel the dead skin.

He hurried away from the wall, pushing aside another sheet. He heard footsteps behind him. When he turned there was no one there. He carried on through the alleyway. He didn't know where he was going to go. None of his usual fences would handle something like this. Despite the fact that the ring looked like a worthless trinket, it wasn't. Like the book, it had power – of that he had no doubt. He would need to find a specialised seller but who in the Old World would be prepared to traffic in dark magic. And that is what it was, Felix reasoned. It had to be, judging by the way the Sigmarites had been tearing the books apart page by page and feeding them to the fire. Even the fire hadn't been natural – it had burned blue with the taint of the accursed pages. He put two and two together: von Carstein had animated an army of the damned, bringing them back from beyond the grave to do his bidding. Was that was this was, some dark grimoire containing the secrets of reanimation?

Felix shuddered and cast a frightened look back over his shoulder.

As much as he wanted to think otherwise, raising the dead wasn't outside the realms of possibility. The Vampire Count's war had proved that. If the book he had stolen contained anything close to dark magic powerful enough to raise the dead that made it dangerous in so many ways, not least of which was to him.

He had to think. He wanted to move it on quickly, get his price and leave Altdorf. He could try Albrecht's down by the Reiksport, or Müllers in Amtsbezirk, though that would mean working his way back along the west bank of the Reik to the Emperor's Bridge and then over the Three Toll Bridge. There were a lot of dangerous places for a thief along that road, governmental ministries and influential nobles, and of course Schuldturm, the debtors prison. The prison would be guarded. A cry of alarm could see the chase become a lot more deadly that a pair of blathering priests shouting, 'Stop! Thief!'

No, Müller's was out of the question; too many opportunities for things to go wrong. That left Albrecht. Rumour had it he had a taste for the outré. Perhaps he would know someone interested in the book *and* the ring. A collector perhaps? A lover of antiquities or a scholar with a taste for the obscure. Together they had to be worth a small fortune. Hell, if the book was even half as dangerous as he believed it was, it was priceless.

He paused at an intersection between two streets. Looked left, where an old maid was on her knees scrubbing down the stoop of her tenement house, and right, where children chased each other in circles in the street. He nodded to the woman when she looked his way and scuttled across the street.

He could of course smuggle both items out of the city and sell them to the surviving vampires. They would know the true worth of the book and von Carstein's signet ring. He was angry enough to consider betraying the city and just walking away, leaving them to their greedy fate. The anger would wear off, he knew, and be replaced by bitterness. Without the righteous anger fuelling him Felix knew he wouldn't be capable of selling the lives of friends and neighbours for a few coins, no matter how much he detested the priests.

He would have to hope Albrecht knew someone interested in the kind of arcane curiosities he was peddling, and if not, knew a man who knew a man whose brother's neighbour's nephew knew a man who might be.

His thief sense tingled, the hairs along the nape of his neck bristling as his skin crawled.

Someone was watching him.

He had no idea how long they had been following him. He slowed his walk, giving a chance for them to catch up or reveal themselves by slipping into a shadowy doorway.

He felt their eyes on his back. He had been a thief long enough to know to trust his instincts. He had gone against them once already this week.

'Fool me once,' he muttered. 'Shame on you. Fool me twice, shame on me.'

He looked left and right furtively, scanning the streets.

There was no sign of anyone but that didn't mean there was no one there. It paid to be paranoid in his line of work. He waited, counting to eleven, concentrating as he listened. He tried to pick out any out of place sounds.

Nothing.

He knew that if he stalled much longer his hesitation would tip off the watcher. He needed to move. His instinct was to make for the Reikmarkt but there was no guarantee it would be anywhere near busy enough to lose the watcher in. The siege had decimated trade. The Süderich Marketplatz was closer, and now that a few trawlers had started arriving again, the chances of there being some fresh fish to sell increased, meaning the chances of there being people to disappear amongst increased. Fresh produce was at a premium still, with the trade caravans only just beginning to arrive in the city.

He moved away from the wall. It was difficult not to look around. He was conscious of his every move. Felix pictured himself as he walked, visualising the street in his head, the points of access, places where it was overlooked, places where he would have hidden if the roles were reversed. There were three obvious vantage points but two were useless because they offered little or no chance of pursuit. The third though was a gem, good cover to see without being seen and it covered any number of possible escape routes. Felix had a philosophy: he always considered the predator at least three degrees more prepared and therefore more dangerous than the prey. He was in trouble here and he knew it. Whoever was following him knew about the ring; that was the only logical explanation he could think of. They couldn't have known about the grimoire, the theft had been far too spontaneous and his stalker was far too skilled in the hunt to be one of the novitiates from the temple. So it was the ring they were after.

He knew then who it was.

The stranger with the ancient eyes he had followed out of the Sigmar cathedral before all hell broke loose. The one who had materialised out of thin air and told him to forget what he thought he'd seen. It made sense, of course. He had suspected that the stranger was one of the major players in the Grand Theogonist's grift. This proved it. It stood to reason that he knew about the ring, Morr's teeth, the man had probably told the priest of its existence. That was the Grand Theogonist's divine intervention. Extrapolating the thought, it made sense that if anyone in Altdorf knew the signet ring's true nature it was the stranger.

Felix couldn't fault his reasoning, which didn't make him any happier with the mess he was in.

He couldn't help himself; he cast a worried look back over his shoulder. His eyes instinctively sought out the best of the three vantage points available to the hunter. It only took a fraction of a second to see that the hiding place was empty. The man wasn't as skilled in the hunt as he feared. Felix smiled, a wave of relief washing over him.

He had a chance of getting out of this alive.

He turned to check the remaining vantage points – which of the two the stranger had chosen decided his escape route for him.

Both were empty.

Doubt flooded through him.

Had he misjudged the street?

Had the stranger somehow worked his way around in front of him without him realising?

And then it hit him: the cold hard realisation of just how much trouble he was in. The stranger could have been anywhere, stood right at his shoulder even, and without the slight shifting of the shadows to give him away Felix wouldn't be able to tell until it was too late and the assassin's blade was slipping into his chest or his back or his throat.

He bolted.

He didn't care if the stranger knew he'd been rumbled, he just wanted out of there, away, somewhere less exposed. Somewhere he could dictate the terms of the encounter, though of course Felix knew no such place existed. He ran because it was a matter of survival.

His heart hammered against his breastbone. Adrenaline coursed through his body. He ran – really ran. He didn't look where he was going. It wasn't important. All that mattered was getting away. Within two minutes he was breathing hard. His head swam. He crashed into an old woman on the corner of Rosenstrasse, sending her sprawling. He tumbled and rolled and was up again and running as though nothing had happened even as her curses chased him down the street.

The sounds of pursuit haunted him, the slap of running feet on the cobbles, the ragged breathing, but every second Felix wasted looking back over his shoulder revealed nothing but empty streets. Occasionally he thought he saw a glimmer, a peculiar refraction of light, a snatch of shadow moving oddly but he daren't risk slowing to look properly. He ran because anything else meant almost certain death.

He ducked down a narrow alleyway and scrambled over a low wall into an overrun garden, weeds and junk sprouting out of every nook and cranny. He scrambled over the next dividing wall and the next into another back yard full of weeds and broken planks. The back door of the house was open.

He didn't think about it. He ran inside, through the kitchen and down the hall before anyone had even noticed he was inside. An emaciated stick of a man with greasy hair and sweat stains ringing his tunic stood between Felix and the door, a scowl set on his bony face. He crossed his arms.

'What do you think you're doing?'

'Move!' Felix didn't wait. He hit the man full on, slamming him into the door. The man buckled. Felix dropped the grimoire and drove a fist into the man's gut, doubling him up, then a vicious uppercut with his left. The man went down and Felix put the boot in, kicking him once, twice, three times in the stomach and a fourth time between the legs. The man writhed on the floor in agony. Felix stepped over him and opened the door. The fight had lost him precious seconds.

He turned back to pick up the book and saw the light coming through the kitchen door shimmer strangely, the doorframe bowing as though bending around something that plainly wasn't there.

He didn't wait. He grabbed the book and ran.

Behind him, the hunter laughed: cold mocking laughter.

He was being driven further and further away from the busy streets into the slums of the city.

Worse though, by far, he could feel himself tiring. His legs burned. His knees felt it worst; the impact of each frantic step triggered another fiery burst of pain. He cast a desperate look back over his shoulder and his legs betrayed him. He stumbled and fell, sprawling across the cobbles.

The laughter was close: almost on top of him.

Felix scrambled back to his feet and managed five more steps before he stumbled again, sheer exhaustion tying his legs up. He didn't fall this time and he didn't look back. He ran on expecting the stranger's blade to slam into his back at any moment. In desperation he ran into a gap between two houses; it was too narrow to be called an alleyway. It was barely a passage. Halfway down it he realised sickly that he had run himself into a dead end.

This is where I die, he thought desperately. *Here in a piss-stinking alleyway. For a stupid lousy ring.* The irony of it wasn't lost on him. All the distance he'd put between the slums of his childhood and all the privileges of the life he had stolen for himself, the fancy clothes, the gourmet dinners, the pretty women – and the ugly for that matter – and here he was, returned to the filth and stench to die.

He turned to face the hunter as the man shimmered into solidity right before his eyes. The effect was disconcerting. It was as though the stranger simply stepped out of the shadows where he hadn't been a moment before.

Felix backed up a step, shaking his head as though trying to dislodge the stranger from his eyes.

The man's expression was somewhat pitying as a black-edged blade whispered clear of its sheath. He held the sword naturally, with all the assurance of skilled swordsman; as though there was only one way in his mind this encounter could play out. His balance was good; he moved lightly on his toes, narrowing the gap between them.

'You want the ring?' Felix said holding the grimoire out in front of him like a shield. He hated the way his voice sounded: weak, frightened. But he couldn't master his fear.

'Yes,' the stranger said coldly, eyeing his clenched fist. 'And the book.'

'Take them. They're yours. I-I don't need them.'

'No I suppose you don't,' the stranger agreed matter-of-factly. 'Here–'

Before he could finish the sentence the stranger rocked forward on his toes and the black sword lashed out, snakelike, slicing clean through his wrist. The pain was staggering. Hand and book fell to the ground as Felix screamed in agonised shock. The ring chimed on the cold stone as it rolled away. Blood gouted from the stump of his wrist, spraying everywhere.

Felix screamed, insensate, his shrieks a babble of wretched pleas and curses that rose in an agonised spiral. He staggered forward clutching at the stump, every trace of colour gone from his face as his lifeblood spewed from the wound.

There was a reason the stranger had shepherded him into the heart of the slums: violence was a way of life. People could scream blue murder without the locals raising an eyebrow.

'Hold out your other hand,' the stranger commanded.

Felix shook his head stupidly, the world span wildly out of focus. The pain was overwhelming. Sunbursts of pure white agony flared behind his eyes. The street was gone. There was only a world of pain. He lurched forward another step and slipped on cobbles slick with his own blood, stumbled and fell to his knees. He held his hand up to cover his face and saw only blood red darkness as the stranger's black blade severed it mercilessly.

Felix fell the rest of the way to the floor. He felt his blood, warm, on his face. The cobbles swam in and out of focus.

He saw the man's shoes as he knelt to pick up the ring.

'You don't look good, Felix,' the stranger said conversationally. 'The way I see it, if you live, your days as a thief are over, but I believe beggars can scratch a living on the streets of most cities in the Empire. So that is a small mercy. It would obviously be better if you died, because, well, your legend is assured. Your name shall live long into the future, when they realise what you have done they will laud you as the greatest thief of all time. The fact that you simply disappeared, well that only adds to the enigma. It makes it into a story. For my own part, I am indebted to you for securing my... ahh... inheritance. And the book, such a wonderful, wonderful surprise. Who could have known Vlad had such treasures? I cannot thank you enough. The night, however, is running away from us and I must, alas, leave you to the whim of Morr. Farewell, thief.'

The stranger walked away and he was alone, bleeding out onto the cobbles.

He couldn't move. He felt warm liquid trickle down the inside of his trousers and didn't know if it was blood or urine – and didn't care.

He just wanted the pain to end.

'Help... me.' It was barely more than a croak. It didn't matter; no one would come to his aid.

He lost all track of time, all sense of self. It just slipped away from him in the pain.

Felix tried to crawl towards the mouth of the narrow passage but he blacked out long before he reached the light waiting at the end.

CHAPTER TWENTY-NINE
All That Remains

ALTDORF
Winter, 2051

CAPTAIN GRIMM WAS torturing the prisoner when the novitiate hammered on the cell door.

The lector was glad for the interruption.

He had no stomach for Grimm's brutality or the obvious gusto with which the man went about his task; it made him sick to the core. His head swam. More than once he thought he was about to pass out. And still the prisoner wasn't talking. The man stared straight ahead, the madness of pain blazing in his eyes as Grimm applied red-hot tongs and other instruments of torture to his flesh.

The stench of burned meat clung to the small chamber. The sizzle of hot metal on skin would haunt the lector for years, he knew. He struggled to rationalise it with thoughts of the greater good; one monster's pain set against the suffering of his entire congregation. It was difficult.

He answered the door.

'Yes? What is it?'

The young priest in the doorway was pale, shaken.

'Your holiness... things... you need to come up stairs. The guards have taken a prisoner... a woman. She was raving and trying to dig up the Grand Theogonist's grave. They have her in the tower. The chirurgeon sedated her with laudanum. She is most disturbed, your grace. Her face... she is one of *them*. The creature tears out of her face as her grip on reality slips, your grace. She is incoherent. Before the drugs she was throwing herself at the walls. She tore her fingernails bloody trying to claw through the stone. She was ranting and raving about her beloved. Now she merely whimpers. There is no talking to her. Her sanity is gone.'

'I see,' the lector said thoughtfully. It was possible then that the damned creatures shared similar bonds to the living, love, friendship, the ties that bind brother to brother. Could it be that the woman was in some way tied to the dead count? 'Come, walk with me. I have no liking for the business of torture. It is time I saw the light of day. Now, you say she was found trying to disinter the Grand Theogonist? Perhaps you have read the situation wrong. Think about it. Is it not more probable that she was trying to get to von Carstein's remains?' The lector closed the heavy cell door on the prisoner's screams and walked the dank corridors back toward the sun.

He had no idea whether it was day or night. Time and hours and minutes had lost rhyme and reason in the vaults beneath the cathedral.

The novitiate said nothing until they reached the stairway back up to the surface.

'There is more, your grace.'

The lector stopped, one foot on the stair and turned.

'Tell me, lad.'

'The books given to us to destroy...'

'What about them?'

'The thief... stole one.'

'Then find him and recover it. Those damned books cannot be allowed to stain the world any longer than they already have. There was a reason I bade you destroy them, lad. They are dangerous books. I have no idea if they were original or copies, but I do know they contained the necromancer Nagash's dark wisdom, his incantations, and his defilements. Their presence in the Vampire Count's horde explains his army of living dead. This kind of power cannot be let loose in the world again. Find Mann and get that book back.'

'We have... ahhh... Mann was found in the slums of Drecksack in the shadow of the Muckrakers' Guildhall.'

'Then I see no problem. Mann is caught, the book is returned. We were lucky this time. See to it that the book is destroyed immediately, lad. We can't risk any more mistakes.'

'Ahhh... but... you see... the thief didn't have the book, your grace. He had been attacked. Both of his hands lay on the cobbles beside his body, severed. He was barely alive when they brought him back to the cathedral. Whoever attacked him has the book.'

'Then let us pray they do not know what it is.'

'We will know more if the thief ever regains consciousness, your grace, but I fear his fate is an ill omen. The attack was made to look like natural comeuppance for his thievery but according to the muck-raker who brought him to us the only words Mann uttered before slipping into unconsciousness were: "Shadows... shadows... he walks in shadows." It could be a thief turning on his own, I suppose. The whole concept of honour amongst thieves is ridiculous, after all, but it doesn't ring true.'

He walks in shadows.

Those words froze the lector's blood in his veins. He knew.

There was no doubt in his mind.

Wilhelm had bargained with the devil and the devil had already claimed his due. It wasn't over. Far from it, it was just beginning in earnest. His mind's eye swam with visions of slaughter, fields of blood, corpses being picked over by carrion birds even as they stirred back to unnatural life. How many more would die?

'If you are fool enough to treat with daemons, you get what you deserve, I suppose.'

'Your grace?'

'Just talking to myself, lad. Just talking to myself.' He suppressed a shudder. 'So, one problem at a time. Take me to her.'

Together they climbed the stairs to the highest spire in the cathedral, the Tower of the Living Saints, to the barred door. Two guards stood watch. Both as wooden as the door, both distinctly ill at ease with the task they had been charged with. The lector nodded to the bar. 'Open it.'

'Your grace, the prisoner was drugged incoherent an hour back by the apothecary because she was a danger to herself and to those near her.'

'I will take my chances, soldier. Open the door.'

The man nodded and slipped the bar out of place. The door opened on a threadbare cell. Once, in a past life, the room might have been majestic with its vibrant red velvet drapes and its sumptuous divan but the moths had been at the fabric and decay lay heavy on the furnishings. The woman was huddled in the far corner of the room, a wild animal cornered. Her black hair fell in lank ringlets across her face. She craned her neck to look at him. Her eyes ached with the pure madness of grief.

'Do you know where my pretty one is?' Her voice was painfully childlike in the way it trembled. The hope in her eyes was heart-breaking. And then, as quickly as it came, the innocence was gone and the woman's face was split and stretched by a ferocious animalistic howl as the beast within tore free for a split second before being harnessed again. She twisted and writhed, slapping at her own face, clawing at her eyes fiercely enough to draw runnels that ran like bloody tears down her cheeks. Gasping and panting, the woman looked up at him beseechingly. It was difficult to reconcile the beast and the beauty owning the same form.

The lector made the sign of Sigmar in the air before stepping across the threshold.

'He is dead.'

The woman thrashed about wildly as though being beaten. He saw then that she was shackled and chained to the bedstead.

'No he is immortal! He cannot die! You are a liar!'

The chains jerked and gouged at the wood but they held.

He knelt before her. There was nothing but pity in his voice when he told her: 'I am many things, woman, but I promise you this, the Vampire Count is no more. He is gone.'

She pressed herself up against the wall, shaking her head, drawing her knees up to her chin, wrapping her arms around them and rocking. The chains dug into her bare legs. 'No, no, nonono. No. Not my pretty one. Not my love. He wouldn't leave me here like this. He loves me. He does. He wouldn't leave me.'

'He had no choice in the matter,' the lector said, resting a hand on her knee. She laid her hand on his. It was a moment of false tenderness. She snarled and gouged long claw-like fingernails through the back of his hand, tearing the skin before he could pull away. The wound stung. Blood dribbled between his fingers as he clenched his fist.

Someone entered the room behind him.

'Put the bitch out of her misery, priest,' the newcomer said, harshly.

The lector turned to see Ludwig, pretender to the Imperial throne, both craven and coward, with his personal bodyguard.

'You are not welcome in the temple of Sigmar, pretender,' the lector said, turning his back on the pair. 'Neither is your thug.'

'You forget yourself, priest. Remember, in your secular world I have considerable sway, including for instance, the power to confer the title of Grand Theogonist on whomsoever I see as a valid recipient. If you have any ambitions in that quarter I suggest you remember yourself quickly. Now, I say again, put von Carstein's whore out of her misery and let's be done with it.'

The lector ignored the Pretender and reached out for the woman's chains. With great compassion, in part triggered by the fact that she looked so vulnerable, in part through the survivor's guilt of still being alive when others better than him had gone, and, no doubt because of the atrocities he himself had been party to in the dungeon, he took her hands in his. Despite the revulsion her daemonic aspect inspired he held her hand for a long moment. 'Let me release you, you are not an animal and should not be treated as such.'

'Do you know where my love is?' she asked again, real tears mixing with the blood streaming down her cheeks as she held out her wrists. 'Will you help me find him? I need to bring him home. If I can bring him home everything will be all right.' Without the keys there was nothing the lector could do.

'Use this,' Ludwig said, holding out a sharpened wooden stake. 'Put the beast out of its misery. We have more important things to concern ourselves with. These things must be exterminated.'

The lector stared at the piece of wood uncomprehendingly.

'Do it man. She's not a woman. It's all lies. She is an animal. Worse, she is an animal that has gone rabid.'

'Murder is never the answer,' the lector said.

'Don't think of it as murder, priest. Think of it as offering her salvation.' The Pretender rationalised. 'You are giving her a way back to your precious Sigmar, or at least a path into Morr's underworld.' He pressed the stake into the lector's hands, his face implacable.

The transformation of Isabella von Carstein was both immediate and shocking. Her face contorted in a feral snarl. The snarl betrayed other subtle changes; her rich full lips peeled back on sharp incisors that grew into brutal fangs, her back arched and her brow and bone ridges elongated, thickening. Her nostrils flared and her eyes radiated sheer hatred. She lashed out at him, claws raking down his cheek, drawing blood.

The lector reeled back, falling on his backside and scuttling away from the beast that was the countess. She could, he realised, easily kill him. She wasn't an innocent to be saved, she was a monster to be slain. It was the nature of the beast. She couldn't be tamed. She couldn't be brought back to the light with the love of benevolent Sigmar. Moreover, she didn't *want* to be saved. The woman she had been was long gone; all that remained was an abomination of nature, a by-blow of death, a daemon.

He knew what he had to do but still his hand trembled.

'Do it man, drive it into her heart, kill her.'

He stared at the stake in his hands: a tool of death. He held it poised to strike. Despite her bestial strength the woman was helpless. It was nothing short of butchery. Cold-blooded slaughter. The thought stayed his hand. He was a priest – he cherished life, creation, and all things holy. He did not bring death. He was not some filthy servant of the murder god. He had given his life in service of Sigmar. His nature was to nurture, to treasure, and to save, not to wipe out.

'Are you a coward, man? She isn't human. She is everything your faith abhors! You can feel her taint beneath your skin. She is evil! Do it! Purge the world of her vile existence.'

'She is not the one demanding murder, Pretender.'

'How dare you!'

'I dare because I am not a killer,' he said softly. He couldn't do it. He let the stake slip through his fingers and pushed himself slowly to his feet. 'You though, I could make an exception for.'

Ludwig the Pretender was apoplectic. His face was purple with rage. A vein pulsed in his forehead dangerously. Spit frothed at his mouth as he swore and cursed at the priest. Beside him his bodyguard remained curiously impassive, as though he were used to his master's fits of pique.

'As I remember it you were the one who suggested ceding Altdorf to the vampires and begged the Grand Theogonist to open the gates to save your own precious hide. So, I believe of the two of us, life has cast you in the role of coward, Pretender.'

'You will pay for your insolence, priest!'

'No doubt,' the lector agreed. 'But not with my immortal soul.'

'Where is he?' the woman shrieked then, her anger more than a match for the Pretender's as she fought against her chains. She pulled, twisting and kicking, lashing out again and again until the bed leg cracked with a sound like breaking bone. 'Where is my husband?' She had grabbed the stake from where the lector had discarded it and held it to her own breast. Tears streamed down her face. The blood made her look like something spawned from the blackest of nightmares. She knew the answer but she needed to hear it out loud.

'Gone! Dead! Rotting in the dirt!' the pretender yelled. Ludwig backed off a step behind the safety of his bodyguard. For all his anger he was still a coward at heart. 'Which is where you should be!'

For a split second it was impossible to tell which of the two was inhuman. The anger in the Pretender was vile to see.

Her voice broke, barely a whisper: 'Where is he?'

'He is gone,' the lector said.

'Where is he?'

'Gone,' the lector repeated but there was no getting through to the woman. 'He is dead. Truly dead. He is dust.'

'No... I don't believe that... He is immortal.'

'All things must die.'

'No.'

'Yes,' he said sadly. 'That is the indifference of the world. It doesn't care. We are mere motes, specks in the eye of time. We are all born of dust and to dust we return. He is gone, woman.'

'He wouldn't leave me!' and softer, with less confidence: 'He wouldn't leave me...'

'He had no choice,' the lector said for the second time since entering the room, his tone of voice more than anything conveying his mixed emotions. 'He was destroyed. There is no way he can return for you.'

'Then I have nothing,' Isabella von Carstein said.

The lector nodded. He made to reach out and brush away the hair from her face but she was too quick, ramming the sharp end of the stake into her own breast. There was a sickening sound, the tearing of wet flesh, and the splintering of bone being forced apart as she impaled herself on the wooden stake. Her eyes flared open as the pain registered in her brain and in them he pretended he saw relief.

She couldn't finish what she had begun. The wooden stake protruded from a shallow wound in her chest, not deep enough to finish her.

'Please...' she mouthed, the word barely audible. Her hands still clutched the shaft of the stake. The lector closed his hands over hers and pushed, forcing the point deeper and deeper until he felt her body yield beneath it and it plunged into her heart, stilling it once and for all. Her tainted blood leaked from the wound, over his hands and down his arms.

He backed away, staring at the woman's blood on his hands. He had killed. No matter that there was mercy in it. He had killed.

Isabella slumped to the floor, her skin already beginning to desiccate as the years of unnatural life gave way to accelerated decay. The skin crumbled, the flesh beneath rotting and collapsing in on itself as the air itself seemed to strip away the flesh from the bones. In the end there would be nothing but dust.

The lector turned away only to see the Pretender gloating.

'You have got your way.'

'As I always do. You are a strange man, priest. You grieve for a monster and yet thousands of our own lie dead and buried at her hand. I cannot pretend to understand your loyalties.'

'She was a girl once. I grieve not for the monster she is but the girl she was, the woman she might have been.'

Behind him the dissolution continued apace. Isabella von Carstein's face crumbled and powdered. The sound was sickening, like a plague of insects feasting on flesh, skittering and chittering. And then she was nothing more than dust.

The lector pushed past the Pretender and left the tower room. He made a decision halfway down the narrow winding stair. He looked in on the thief. 'The man is to be cared for, and when he is recovered he is to be offered a new life, here, in the cathedral. He does not deserve the life of a beggar. The man is a hero, one of the last, I fear. We shall treat him as we would any brother.'

The young priest tending to Felix Mann nodded understanding and returned to his tender ministrations.

That left the monster in the vaults.

Steeling himself, the lector descended deep into the darkness.

Captain Grimm was still about his work when the lector pushed open the heavy door. The prisoner was barely recognisable as human, which of course it wasn't, not any more. Blood had swollen one eye shut and the man's flesh was a mess of charred streaks and burns. A single deep bloody gouge ran from throat to groin, almost a hand's breadth, in places burned through to the bone. The room stank of seared meat and fat.

Grimm looked up from his labour.

'End it, I have no stomach for this, captain. Don't you see what we have become? How we have fallen? In a matter of days we have reduced ourselves to the level of animals. We have stripped ourselves of the dignity and compassion that served as our humanity more effectively than von Carstein's brood ever could have hoped. We have looked into the abyss, Grimm, and instead of conquering the beasts within we have embraced them and become monsters ourselves. That is our reward for surviving. We have become more monstrous than the things we were fighting.'

Grimm ran a sweaty hand over his brow, his eyes blazed in the reflected sickness of the brazier.

'He is stubborn, I'll give the beast that,' he said, as though he hadn't heard a word the lector had said. 'But I'll break him. Mark my words, your grace. I'll break the beast.'

'No, Grimm. No more torture. No more death. I'll have no part of it.'

'But the beast is breaking, I have him!'

'At what cost, man? At what cost?'

'It costs me nothing!'

'It costs you everything, you fool. Everything.'

'You have no idea what you are talking about, priest. This thing has no right to life. It doesn't breathe. Its heart doesn't beat. The blood in its veins is rank. It isn't alive. It doesn't deserve your compassion. It is evil. Pure evil, plain and simple, priest. Save your sorrow and regret for something that deserves it. The beast is an abomination. If we can learn from it before it dies then it has served its purpose. No matter how weak your stomach is the beast must die. There can be no reprieve. You cannot save the man he was. The man is dead, long gone. Now only the beast remains. And believe me, priest, the beast must die. Good men died for us and they deserve nothing less.'

The prisoner laughed then, a sick dead rattle. 'Deserve, deserve, deserve. You speak a lot of deserving, soldier. Now listen to me. The beast has a name,' he said, his voice cracked and broken almost beyond understanding. There was madness in his one open eye. 'It is Jon... Skellan. And believe me, I have no intention of dying, not for a very, very long time.'

THE COURT OF THE CRIMSON QUEEN

The Spring of Falsehoods and Blood Debts, 1808

Love lay dying on the rumpled divan.

It wasn't glorious or addictive. There was no revelling in this collapse of the flesh. This death was a tragedy he had thought himself immune to. He looked at his wife's pale face, only made more beautiful by the sickness that tore her body apart. Emotions he believed long dead warred within the emptiness of Vlad von Carstein's soul.

'Please,' she whispered, barely giving life to the sound.

He knew what she wanted, and what she was offering not to die.

But he resisted. He could not explain why.

'I will call the physician back. Perhaps Schliemann can soothe your passage with some root,' he said, resting his own cold hand against the chill-fever of her cheek. Her eyelids fluttered weakly and closed, and for a moment he thought she was gone and that he was bereft. Then he felt the faintest flutter of her pulse against his hand and he knew he could not abide losing this troubled woman who completed him. He felt her life against his palm. The blood was erratic.

Her kind were so short-lived, their presence in the world occasionally glorious, always fleeting. They were like his beloved birds in that respect, their tiny little hearts beating wildly, wasting their life away in fear.

She looked at him, pleading. Eleven years was not enough.

He did not know if the thought was his own, or his wife's. Eleven years had passed since he first walked into the cold halls of Drakenhof and defenestrated his only rival for rule of the province.

He took away his hand, unable to endure the coldness of her.

He gathered the folds of his thick cloak across his chest and turned his back on the woman in the bed. He did not love her. There was nothing left within him capable of the emotion. Yet something in his body resonated to the frequency of her. They were mated in more ways than the physical. There was completeness to their bonding. He found it hard to imagine the protracted loneliness that would accompany her parting.

Outside, the night was dark. It ought to have been raining. That was all he could think of for the longest time. It ought to have been raining.

Behind him, she coughed. It was a pitiful sound.

He had resisted for so long, believing Isabella capable of overcoming the ill-humours of the blood plague, but looking at her now he knew she was failing. The irony of this death of hers did not amuse him. So many superstitious fools had called the curse of his kind the same thing, and yet this most human of sicknesses, a weakness in the blood was anything but supernatural in origin. It had nothing to do with the thirst of his kind.

But it did not change the fact that she would leave him before dawn.

He knew it should not bother him; she was a convenience, a means to an end, a foothold into this forsaken territory but... by dawn he would be a widower and he would be reduced by her loss. He knew that for the truth.

Was it love?

She was most assuredly more to him than a bridge between the old cruelties and the new, but could it be called love?

Were any of his kind capable of such a human folly?

'Please,' she begged again.

He wanted to leave her but could not. He had never been one for rash action, that had never been a part of his philosophies of death. He found himself taking her hand and asking, 'Are you sure you would give up the immortality of your soul for me, my love?'

And perhaps she did love him, at least, because she opened her eyes and said, softer than a prayer, 'You cannot join me in the life hereafter, so why should I wish to abide there alone?'

'The physician waits outside the door, he–'

'Cannot help me now,' Isabella sank back into her sweat-stained bolster, sucking at the air desperately for a breath she couldn't catch.

It hurt him to watch her thus. Frustration burned within his black blood. He was master of death and yet here he knelt at this woman's bedside as helpless as any other.

'Please,' she begged again. 'If this is death I do not want to go into it without you.'

'Yet I cannot join you, Isabella. Your light has burned out and mine, well mine casts only shadow.'

'It... need not... be so,' she managed between raking coughs. Blood and phlegm flecked her chin and cheek.

'But it must,' he said, sorrow in his voice. He looked down at her, this frail little woman who had always had such fire, such fight, and knew she was already dead in all the ways that mattered.

'Then let me taste you, this once, let–'

She broke off, hacking up blood as her entire body convulsed through the coughs. She wiped the blood away with a trembling hand, then held it out, offering it to him. There was no fear in her eyes. He leaned in and placed the tenderest of kisses on her feverish palm, his tongue laving the lifeblood from her fingers. He closed his eyes, savouring its tang. He could taste the sickness in her. It made every ounce of his flesh ache but he licked the last drop from her palm. 'Let me open a vein and drink of my love. Let that be the last thing that I do. Please.'

He shook his head. 'It cannot be so.'

'Then drink of me, drain me, end it now, not this vile sickness.'

That he could do. That one small mercy. It was not as though he had never killed.

'Is that what you want, my love?'

'There is no other way I would rather die,' she said, tilting her head slightly on the stained pillow to offer up the vein in her throat.

He leaned in close enough to feel her pulse on his slightly parted lips, and let his teeth rest there, pressed either side of the vein hard enough to draw the salt from her skin but not so hard as to puncture her flesh. Not yet. He savoured the taste of her, his mortal wife, his love, his folly, and then bit down, drawing the blood out of her.

It was a tragic feast.

Isabella's body stiffened in his arms, a single strong convulsion pressing her up against him. He could feel the frailty of her beautiful corpse through the bed sheets.

'Take me,' she whispered in his ear, a desperate breath.

He closed his eyes as he drank her in, remembering all of the bitter-sweet moments they had shared in their short time together. She was, he had always known, quite unlike any mortal girl he had tasted – and he had drunk from hundreds, thousands, decanting their passion with a tender kiss or tearing it from their flesh with savage thirst. She was the mirror of the darkness in him. That first whisper, claiming her uncle's life as a wedding boon, had told him all he needed to know. Isabella van Drak was a predator. Even now she was more dangerous than a cornered she-wolf. He knew that instinctively, yet he let his guard down in grief and allowed himself to mourn her even as he fed.

Her breath quickened in his ear. 'I choose this pain,' she said, digging her fingernails into the nape of his neck hard enough to draw blood had he been the kind of creature that bled.

'Go now,' he said, hesitating a moment before drawing that final fatal swallow.

'Look at me, one last time,' she whispered, her voice a husk of humanity.

She tangled her fingers in his hair, and drew his head up. He did as she bade him; how could he not? And their lips locked in blood, hers and his, as she opened him up with hungry teeth so that their darkness might at last mingle.

She suckled at his lips hungrily, taking from him what he had sworn he would not give.

He pulled away from her punishing kiss.

'More,' she gasped. 'I need more.'

'It won't be enough,' Vlad said, pushing her back down into the pillows as his ardour rose. 'You want this life? You *really* want it?'

She nodded hungrily, her eyes alight with the fever of death.

'Then I will give it to you.' He held out his wrist, tantalisingly close to her lips, and then drew it away, biting out the thick veins with his own teeth. He held the ragged wound over his wife's lips as she licked and slurped at the dripping blood, desperately trying to sink her teeth into the wound itself. Her mouth opened wider and wider, his tainted blood pooling in her mouth before she swallowed him down.

Her body shuddered against his, revolting against his blood as it spread through her veins, replenishing what he had stolen. The irony of his healthy blood mixing with her sick blood was not lost on Vlad, nor the fact that it could only restore her to unlife, not somehow transfuse her with life.

She looked at him then, pleading for more, with eyes he knew he would never be able to resist.

He had played the dutiful husband, never leaving her bedside as she prepared to cross that final threshold between life and its last great mystery, but in that moment, looking down into her eyes and seeing the emptiness, she owned him.

He took her hand in his and raised it to his lips, sinking his teeth into the last flutter of pulse at her wrist, and drained her.

She died in his arms that night, and he wept for what he had done to both of them.

Come dawn he laid her corpse out on the bed, making it around her, and banished her handmaidens while he waited for her to come back to him. He kissed her brow and said an old prayer in the tongue of his people that ended with the admission that all words were dust. Then, as one last farewell to the flesh, he drew the sheet up over her face.

He knew there were things in his protectorate that he had allowed to fester for too long.

Meinard Vogler, for one.

The man was a thorn.

A thorn with a reputation for malice and murder.

Few transitions were smooth, especially those that involved allegiances and devotions. Ambitions, more often than not, had a way of interfering with what ought to have been common sense. Vlad had sent two emissaries to Vogler's court. The first had returned with the message that the baron, Meinard Vogler, did not recognise the right of succession, the second did not return at all. Vlad understood the message Vogler had sent him. He would not send a third. Men like Vogler only understood strength so while the game of kings was a subtle one at times in some instances it required brutality. Vogler had tried his patience one time too many, he would be forced to bend the knee. Defiance was viral; where one man pulled at the reins of power others would invariably follow, unless their petty rebellion was crushed, ruthlessly and quickly.

Vogler was no fool, he knew precisely what his refusal to bend the knee would cost him, yet still he stubbornly refused to accept Vlad's right to the title his marriage to van Drak's girl inferred, even now, eleven years after the deathbed ceremony. Vlad did not hurry vengeance; time was the one thing the immortal count was not short of.

That refusal was an insult the Vampire Count could not brook. This invite now to the man's stronghold was an interesting gambit. It suggested Vogler was prepared to see reason, but something about it rankled. Vlad had worried away at the invitation for two weeks since it had arrived via messenger. The timing of it almost certainly meant Vogler had been relying upon his wife's illness to distract him. With the invite refused he could hold up his hands and say 'I tried'. But what the rebellious baron could not have known was that Isabella's health had past beyond mortal concerns. She would need to feed when she awoke, and Vogler's people needed to be taught a lesson. There was a coincidence of needs there that could be played to his advantage. It was almost… poetic. He smiled coldly at the realisation.

He left Isabella at peace and set about the business of politics and power.

He found his man, Kail, skulking about the ramparts. He joined him there, coming up beside him silently.

'How is she, my lord?' Kail asked without looking around.

'At peace,' Vlad said. The sun was rising on what would most certainly be a glorious day.

'I am sorry.'

'Do not be. Her peace will not last.'

'Then you...?' This time Ansard Kail did turn, his face twisted with jealousy as he faced his master. The man had made no secret of his desire to join their kind and serve Vlad in death, but while he was useful he was not a face the vampire wanted haunting him for millennia.

'We will be leaving the castle tonight. My love must feed and as you know, I have pressing business with Meinard Vogler. They say,' Vlad said, with the wryest of smiles playing with his bloodless lips, 'that you can judge the strength of a man by the enemies he makes.'

'Then Vogler must be a very powerful man indeed,' Kail said, matching his master's mirthless grin. 'Shall I make arrangements for your visit to Vogler's protectorate?'

'Indeed. We shall need a coach, and a pliable maid to see to my wife's needs, and perhaps another for food should those needs overwhelm her restraint.'

'I shall see to it,' Kail assured him. 'Should I also inform Posner that you will be requiring his services? I am sure his pack are straining at the leash and ready for a run out.'

'There is no need. I will bring our errant baron to heel. One man, even with a few swords at his disposal, does not concern me. There is no uprising, the other nobles are generally cowed. One man will not undermine my rule. I shall crush him.'

Power was an accumulation of subtle strengths – he had been slowly gathering the trust and respect of the other counts and men of power throughout the province. Few had held out against his sweet words, promises, or, finally, his might. Those that had, one by one, met with tragic fates. That was the way of it: no outright fighting, no display of might, merely an unfortunate accident here, a streak of foul luck there. Vogler was one of the few who still resisted – and almost certainly because he believed himself to be beyond the awareness of the Vampire Count, too far removed from his seat of power to be a true threat. Out of sight, out of mind as the old adage went.

'Very good, my lord.'

Vlad laid a hand on his man's shoulder; it was not a gesture of affection. His fingers curled tightly through the fabric of his coat, Vlad's immaculately manicured nails digging into the bone. 'Do not be jealous of her fate, there are worse things than death, my friend. Many, many worse things.'

But Kail did not answer him. He watched a raven in the sky, banking and swooping low after some unseen prey down in the valley below. Vlad left the man alone, trusting that he would do what he had to. Other things pressed on his time. He wanted to be the first thing his wife saw when she returned to this life. There would be much within her that she did not understand and could not hope to cope with alone.

SWEEPING THROUGH THE dusty corridors of the castle, Vlad cursed himself for a fool. Her mirror still rested atop the dresser. It was one thing to wish for a new life, and to think you grasped the constraints of it, but quite another to pick up a mirror out of vanity and habit and not be reflected in the looking glass. Servants balked as he brushed by them. He took the stairs two and three at a time, barely making a sound as he whisked through the galleries and back to his wife's room. Vlad threw the door open and stalked inside.

The sheet over Isabella's face was undisturbed.

He snatched up the mirror, then moved quickly around the room, seeking out anything that had a reflective surface. He took her mother of pearl hairbrush as well as a copper bowl she kept her hair pins in, a twin-stalked pewter candlestick and a blown-glass trinket. He almost forgot the locket at her throat. Pulling back the blanket he snapped the chain and pocketed the jewellery. Only when he was satisfied there was nothing left within the room that might offer Isabella an accidental glance of a reflection that was no longer there did Vlad leave the chamber, intent on disposing the things he had confiscated.

He found Herman Posner's men, Dade and Belew, coming out of the duelling hall. He ushered them over. 'Every reflective surface, anything that catches an image, I want it gone from this place before dusk.'

'So the whispers are true, then,' Belew said, an undertone of disapproval in his voice. 'The lady's light has not truly burned out. Was it wise to bring her over to the night?'

'Do you question me?' Vlad said, his voice dangerously restrained. He inclined his head slightly.

Belew knew better than to push his master. 'What would you have us do?'

'Empty the castle of reflections, that will suffice. These first few days are difficult enough without the constant mocking of looking glasses and half-glimpsed reflections. She is a woman remember, a creature of beauty and vanity. The shell on the outside is important to her sex. We men cast it off, become the beast with pleasure, but it is different for women. Waking into unlife is painful, they shed the skins of their past lives but hold to the memory of their faces. There is identity in the angle of a cheekbone and the curve of a lip, they are us, after all, in so many ways. And yet the memory fades and after a year, two, a hundred of solitude and loneliness those lines and imperfections have left us and we remember nothing. Better to let them slip away than face the shock of having them stolen away by one careless glance.'

'We shall see to it.'

Belew turned to Dade. 'Round up the others, we shall denude the castle one floor at a time.' To Vlad he said, 'Perhaps a portrait, to help her remember herself, sire? Something she could gaze upon at will. There are precious few paintings around the castle, and none of the lady herself save the cherubic daub her father had commissioned for her birth. Old Otto was not a patron of the arts.'

The notion appealed to Vlad.

'That would be a suitable gift for her unveiling, my thanks for your thoughtfulness, Belew. As you say, her father's home has always been austere. A portrait to capture her undying beauty would be no bad thing. Let me think on it. Dispose of these, please. I would be at her side when she wakes.'

Posner's wolf nodded, taking Isabella's few possessions from him.

Vlad returned to Isabella's room, content to sit out the rest of the day at her bedside. He stood at the window, surprised to see so many peasants gathered in the courtyard. It stymied him at first, then he realised they were waiting on word of their countess. Smiling softly, he threw open the hinged wooden shutters, and gave them the word they so desperately wanted to hear.

'My people,' he called down, spreading his arms wide in greeting to encompass all of the gathering. So many faces, washed out and wan, looked up at him with wretched expectation. So many women had fallen to the blood plague already. They knew he was about to tell them she was dead. That was the only way this story could end: the death of a maiden. 'I thank you, we thank you, for your vigil and your prayers. The gods themselves have chosen to answer, this morning, when we feared all was lost, my sweet Isabella's fever broke. She is resting now, but rest assured, friends, she is well and will recover fully. The fates have smiled sweetly upon us.'

His words were greeted by disbelieving silence; these people knew well enough the debilitating nature of the blood plague – and more importantly that few if any survived. That he proclaimed Isabella well was a small miracle to these people whose lives were bereft of the divine.

And then someone down there shouted, 'Merciful Shallya!' and the cry was taken up by others.

'Indeed,' said Vlad. 'Now please, she is weak and we are all tired. We would sleep now. Go home safe in the knowledge that your countess is whole and eager to return to you.'

They cheered again, the cries muffled by the wood as Vlad drew closed the hinged shutters.

He closed the thick curtains and sat a while in utter darkness without even the sound of breathing for companionship.

Isabella awoke with a gasp and nearly choked on the sudden intake of air.

The sheet fell from her face as she sat up in the bed. He could see the disorientation in her face as she looked around the room trying to fix on something real to focus on. He could not remember his own death dreams now, they had been so long ago time had all but erased them, leaving a vague memory of discomfort and choking. They were still writ fresh in his wife's mind. Blood would slake them... eventually.

'Have I come back to you?' she asked. 'Or is this more fever dreams come to taunt me?'

Vlad sat on the edge of the mattress beside her. 'You have returned to this world, my sweet.' He took her hand in his, marvelling at the delicate bones and veins just beneath the skin.

'How can I know? I feel so... weak. The air smells of dust. Can you smell that? Such an unfamiliar perfume. Dust. And unburied dead. That sour-sweetness is my own smell, isn't it? My flesh has turned.'

'It is the stench of rigor, in those first few hours between death and unlife your flesh corrupts just as all flesh corrupts. Musks will mask it and in time it will fade.'

'And the thirst?' she asked, touching her fingers to her lips.

'That will never fade, though you will learn to master it.'

'And this dreadful arousal that courses through my body? Will that too fade, or will it burn within me for eternity?'

'That is the blood.' He held up his wounded hand. Though the wrist had already begun to heal, dried blood still crusted the scars where he had opened himself up for her. 'Our bodies thrill to the fragrance of life. It is more than mere arousal, it is the serenity of life, and all of our ancestors inhaled in one heady aroma. The blood you drank – my blood – contains traces of every woman and man I have fed upon, their lives and their stories, and my sire, and all the lives he fed upon and his sire, and so on into time immemorial. The blood is the life.'

'I feel...' she touched the sides of her face, then mirrored the explorations on his face. 'Nothing, neither happiness nor hope, sadness no despair... I feel... empty.'

'That is our curse,' Vlad admitted. 'There is nothing within that we would recognise as human. We are husks.'

'Then how…?' Isabella began, but did not want to continue the thought. 'You never did, did you? You never fell in love with me.'

Vlad said nothing. That was all the answer he could give.

Her eyes were dark with deep smudges and her breathing ragged. The first moments of the transition were always difficult.

'I can have meat brought to you, raw and bloody. It helps but it is not the same as a first feeding.'

She looked at him then, as though seeing a stranger. 'When must I feed? How soon? I feel weak as a lamb.'

'We will go out tonight, when the moon is up. We will find you something docile for that first blood. There is much for you to learn yet about this new life you have brought on yourself, if you hope to survive it.'

She reached out for him, clasping his wrist. 'Give me more blood.'

Her nostrils flared as she breathed him in. 'I hunger.'

He pulled his hand away. 'There is no sustenance in my blood now,' he lied. 'It is dead. You crave the blood of life.'

It was not true; she had tasted the power of his bloodline, in essence the might of the man himself. To allow her to drink more would weaken him and unduly strengthen her. He would be a fool to consider either.

'Give it to me!'

Vlad slapped her, a stinging blow across the cheek. 'You are no maiden whose chastity I dream of stealing away with pretty words, and there is nothing within me capable of cherishing what I take. Do not make the mistake of thinking I am bound at your side by some kind of mythic adoration. You are my blood now. I could break you if I so chose, and cast you aside if the whim so strikes.'

She looked at him then, horror in her face as she understood the same hungers she felt still burned within him. He released her hand. He could smell the fire in her body now, the reek of the blood soaking into the organs beneath her skin, and into her meat, steeping it in its succulent juice. And though he remembered the tang of her on his taste buds, she was already more potent now, freshly born into the unlife. And yet she was different, wrong. There was no fear in her awakening, no panic. She was calm, almost rational. He had not seen the like before. Those others he had sired had, at first at least, wrestled with the loss of their humanity and the ensuing emptiness that opened up where their essence had been. Isabella simply accepted it. Welcomed it, even.

'You would feed on me?' She offered her own wrist, the gesture a parody of erotica as she held it up to his lips. 'Drink your fill, empty me. I chose to walk forever by your side, my Vlad. I did not know you were incapable of love. I always thought…' she let her words trail off into silence.

'That we were soul mates, the blood drinker and his mate, yet now you understand that there is no soul within the shell and feel lost because the world you thought you understood is not as you imagined it. I do not need to drink you, but soon you will need to feed. Rouse yourself, dress, my queen of the blood, then let us find you fresh blood.'

'Tell me this one thing, why do I still love you if there is nothing?'

And for that he had no answer.

VLAD TOOK BOTH of Isabella's hands in his. 'It is time to unleash the beast, there is a monster within you now that needs to be let live. Reach inside with your mind, can you feel it?'

He had taken her out into the forests beyond Drakenhof for her first hunt. It was imperative that she taste fresh blood, and soon after being sired, for the transition to be complete. His man, Kail, had set six cattle loose, giving them the chance to run for their lives. They wound hunt them one at a time, giving Isabella the chance to bring down helpless prey and savour her first kill.

'I do not know what you mean,' she said, but he saw the flicker of recognition in her eyes. He could sense her uncertainty. She was sickened by the notion of killing, and yet simultaneously excited by it, hungry for it. She itched to run free in the forest and bring down the prey he had released. It was all part of the great game.

'You do,' he said. 'I want you to focus your thoughts inward. Search with your mind. There is another presence within you, a third if you like. The first is the old you that is dying out, the second is this new you born into the unlife, but the third, the third is the most potent of all. The third is the she-wolf, the huntress. She is a savage beast. Find her within yourself. Embrace her. Call her forward.'

Her face began to shift, the muscles around her throat stretching, the softness of her brow shivering and elongating as the beast came forward. And then it lost its shape and her face returned to the simply wan beauty of the dead woman. 'What is happening to me?' There was no fear in her voice, as he had expected, she relished the transformation.

'You are becoming the she-wolf. In that form you shall be able to scent the living aura of your prey. Embrace the hunger. Now, again,' he encouraged. 'Unleash the beast.'

And she did.

Her spine arched, her hands clawing at the side of her face, fingers becoming claws, the fine hairs along her arms growing thick and coarse as her jaw distended, becoming a snout and her teeth sharpened. Her eyes shifted colour, deepening to a dark grey. She howled her pain, an inhuman cry.

Beside her Vlad shifted shape, mirroring her change.

In a moment two majestic wolves stood side by side on the forest road. He looked at the moon, then answered her, baying with a howl of his own, announcing his bride to the children of the night.

They ran, an easy lope at first, then more spirited as they scented game. Occasionally the she-wolf would catch another sent and take off after it, driven by her hunger to feed. Vlad gave Isabella her head, allowing her to bring down her first kill. He knew her scent, she could not stray far.

He shifted back to the shape of a man, and sat a while listening to the sounds of the night, enjoying the solitude for a while before he walked after her. As he neared, he could hear the sounds of her feeding as she tore at the flesh of whatever forest dweller she had brought down. He sniffed the air, catching the fragrance of blood – but it was wrong, it was not the fit healthy wine of some frightened peasant girl, it bore the taint of animal, wolf or fox, blood without the sustenance of human life. He began to run, pushing through the skeletal branches of the trees as they snagged and pulled at his cloak, fear pounding in the place where his heart used to hammer.

He found her sitting cross-legged, the body of a wolf in her lap. She was no longer in bestial form but had reverted back to a vulnerable nakedness. Blood smeared her lips and chin and streaked down her chest where she had succumbed to the frenzy of feeding. That was not what brought him up cold. There was madness in her eyes as she looked up at him, desperate for approval, the head of the wolf in her lap. As Isabella shifted her weight the wolf's body fell onto its side, exposing the shattered cage of his ribs and the ragged hole where she had reached in with her feral teeth and chewed out the animal's withered heart.

She had drained the wretched creature dry.

'It tastes... like... nothing I have ever tasted,' Isabella's voice was drunk with the potency of the wolf's blood. She dipped a hand back into the open cavity of her victim's chest and teased out a string of muscle, lifting it to her lips. She breathed it in before taking the meat into her mouth and chewing it.

It was wrong, the first feeding should not be on some wild animal. She needed blood filled with the vitality of mortality. There was madness in an animal's blood. Vlad knelt beside her, looking into her face, afraid of what he would see in her eyes as she looked back at him. She reached up, taking his face in her bloody hands and drawing him into a crimson kiss, her tongue lingering in the melange of blood and saliva their contact shared.

He broke the kiss.

The blood was good, rich. But it was not strong. He had told her the truth: all of their yesterdays were locked away within the blood, like secrets never to be told. But some stories bled to the surface. On another night he might have knelt beside her and finished the beast. But such intimacy was denied by the all-consuming look of hunger in his woman's face.

'No more,' Vlad said, grabbing a handful of hair and hauling her away from the dead wolf.

She did not fight him. She gazed up at her sire, a curious look of detachment on her pale face. 'It tastes divine,' she said, then craned her neck to look up at him. 'I frighten you. I can see it in your face. I am not the woman you–' She was obviously about to say loved, but caught herself. There was no love between them, not then, not now. 'Eat with me, husband. There is plenty to go around.'

'Do not vex me, woman. Clean the blood from your face. We shall leave this wretched beast for the birds. There is more suitable blood out there in the woods, do you not smell it? Virgin maids, frightened cattle.'

He needed to remove her from this place. As she said, she was his wife, damned to walk forever by his side.

She smiled at him then. 'My handsome protector. They shall call me the Crimson Queen, Queen of the Blood, Mistress of the Shadows.' There was both power and the first glimpse of uncertainty in her voice, as though she needed his approval. 'Do you think they will worship me?'

THE BLACK BROUGHAM coach waited down in the courtyard. The driver swathed in black sat on the bench, whip in gloved hand. No inch of the man's skin was exposed to the dusk. There was no farewell cortège. The courtyard was quiet, the peasants of Drakenhof having returned to their hovels in the town below, content to believe in miracles. Vlad led Isabella by the hand, opening the door and waiting as she clambered inside. She moved with an awkwardness she had never known in life, the stiffness of death still to be worked out of her muscles. He sat himself beside her and drew the thick velvet curtain so that no one would see the carriage's mysterious passengers. He rapped once smartly on the roof and the coach lurched forward.

For an hour the only sounds between them was the sparking of horses hooves on the small granite cobbles that lined the road, and then even that small familiarity faded as the road became hard-packed mud.

All around them shadows made their allegiance with the moon, creating emaciated spectres to haunt the trees.

The first stage of the journey took four nights, following the roads that wound due south through Pfaffbach and then bore west from the ancient township of Nachthafen. The second stage took considerably longer, taking them across the Draken and into the skeletal woods of the ghouls before emerging on the far side, in the Bylorhof marshes and the territories that bordered the furthest western edges of his land. They travelled only by night, sleeping in the coaches by day. The leather banquettes rested over a thin layer of grave dirt, providing the comfort of the familiar for the vampires that sheltered within the coaches.

BARON MEINARD VOGLER's castle was not so much a fortress as a ruin in the shadow of Grimspike, a great tooth of mountain that pierced the bog and marsh of the countryside – a single spar of rock in an otherwise sodden territory. But it was a huge ruin, almost as vast in scope as Drakenhof itself, with parts of it recently restored and fortified.

It was, Vlad had to admit, an impressive sight.

Oil lamps burned in the windows of some of the upper rooms. the light from their dipped wicks flickering fitfully.

As the brougham rolled into the courtyard, Vlad felt a shiver of trepidation. Where he had expected a petulant fop with his few flunkies in tow, he was greeted by an honour guard of forty heavily armoured men. Banners and pennons flapped and snapped in the evening air. Across the courtyard another fifty men ran drills, swords clashing with organised precision. The display of strength was obviously for his benefit. Eyes along the road had obviously noted their approach. Ninety men in the yard, in full regalia going through their paces could hardly be coincidence. It was almost certainly a glimpse at the home of a man with his eyes on greater prizes. No matter; greater men had fallen to the vampire.

Servants bustled left and right: chambermaids, scullery maids, cooks, game keepers, wardens and more, all moving with purpose, bowing and scraping as they came within the baron's orbit.

Meinard Vogler himself was gracious, effusive in his compliments and well-wishes for the countess's health as he helped her out of the carriage. He did not once look Vlad himself in the eye. The vampire was no fool, he knew within minutes of setting foot within the castle this arrogant mortal had no intention of letting them leave his home alive. The irony that neither of them had arrived in that precarious mortal state amused the count.

'Welcome to my humble home, von Carstein,' Vogler said, finally addressing Vlad as he swept open the thick wooden door. The word 'humble' was the last one von Carstein would have chosen to describe the lavish splendour of the castle. The hallway was draped with thick tapestries and rugs. Vogler was obviously a throwback to the mindset of Otto van Drak and those other robber barons who bled their people metaphorically. The new baron was, at least, literal, in his bleeding – and his people would benefit from kindnesses they had never previously known, for a little bit of the crimson juice. 'I am so glad you were in a position to take up my invitation. I must admit I was concerned when I heard of your lady's plight.'

'As you can see, she is quite well.'

'Indeed. Now, You must have worked up a fearful thirst on your journey. Mannheim will see to your luggage and make sure your chamber is ready and your horses stabled. Let us go to my study and talk over a nice glass of red like civilised souls.'

They ghosted across the plane of a huge silvered mirror, only Vogler himself casting a reflection. Their host did not appear to notice. Vlad, though, cursed his thoughtlessness. Such a simple thing could undo them both.

Vogler was a beast of a man, the alpha male of the family litter, with wide-set black eyes and a hooked nose that flared excitedly as he made a point of leading them down the corridors that showed off his wealth, and up the stairway to the study. He dressed with all the civility of a pig, draped with petty embellishments meant to prove his prowess and fearsomeness. The metal brocade of his gown was a fine line of skulls in various states of agony, his hair a wild unkempt mess of curls. Chains hung from his belt, ivory casts of bones dangling like trophies. His face bore the scars of battle – they did not make him any uglier than he already was. Vogler was no doubt used to being obeyed; big men often were, backing up their words with their physicality.

Vogler led them into his study. Again, like the lower rooms this one was opulent to the point of excess, the taste on display vulgar but then, the house was a match for its master. He walked with an arrogance that irked the vampire, but soon enough the man would be humbled for his hubris.

Ancient leather-bound tomes lined the walls alongside oil paintings of the landscape of ruin. A huge oak desk stood in the centre of the room, with three gilt armchairs set before it, arranged in a neat circle. The rug they walked across was worth more than a petty duchy alone. Behind the desk a beautiful brass cast of a skull rested on a wall plaque like a hunter's prize kill.

'Well, here we are,' Vogler said, gesturing for his guests to sit. 'Let us toast your wife's good health, shall we?' Vogler said, turning his back on Vlad as he decanted three crystal goblets of thick red liquid.

'You intend to make the pledge then?' Vlad said, folding his cloak around himself as he sank into one of the chamber's three carefully arranged armchairs. They were a weak man's chairs, Vlad thought, as their softness cushioned him.

'To interrupt is vulgar, von Carstein,' Vogler chastised. 'Before we talk of unpleasant business let us at least pretend civility.'

'Very well,' Vlad said, disliking the man more by the moment. He would enjoy killing him. Slowly.

'Now, a toast, if I might make so bold.'

Meinard Vogler handed the goblets out between them. Vlad did not rise from his seat. He took the drink in his hand.

Vogler had offered them a rich vintage of Bretonnian claret. It was an expensive drink, but he expected no less of the man.

'To new friends,' Isabella answered, raising the goblet to her lips.

She spat the liquid out, throwing the goblet across the room, a look of abject revulsion on her wan face. She rose in a fury. 'What is this foul stuff?'

'Not to your taste, countess?' Meinard Vogler said smoothly. 'Perhaps you like a younger vintage?'

'I like blood,' Isabella rasped, forgetting herself.

'Don't we all,' Vogler said, raising a mocking eyebrow.

The man's casual confidence set Vlad's danger-sense to prickling. The fetishes ought to have been clue enough for him to realise Vogler's predilections and peculiarities went beyond the norm. So, he shared a taste for blood or was he trying to be provocative?

'Shall we cut the pleasantries?' Vlad said. 'They are quite tiresome. Isabella, dear, perhaps you would like to go and freshen up? You have made rather a mess of your gown. It would be only right to dress for dinner. Assuming Vogler intends to feed us.'

'Indeed,' Vogler said.

She nodded, less than eagerly, and left them alone.

Vogler paced back and forth. 'Now,' he said finally, 'let us drop this pretence, shall we?'

'I am all for dropping things,' Vlad said, remembering Leopold van Drak's pitiful screaming.

'Good. You will cede your control over my protectorate, von Carstein. We shall be neighbours, and while it suits, allies.'

The arrogance of the man shocked Vlad. He had expected something: treachery, treason, but not blatant idiocy.

'I think not,' he said.

'Then you shall die and the issue of your rule or my rule shall be moot,' said the baron. 'Which would be a pity. Together, I think, we could bring about death on an unprecedented scale.'

Vlad stared at his posturing host, wondering if he truly were arrogant enough to believe his petty protectorate could ever be a match for the might of his undead kingdom? 'You think to threaten me?'

'Did you not see the might of swords just waiting to answer my beck and call when you entered, *alone*?' He stressed the last word, lingering on what he obviously believed were the implications of Vlad's solitude.

Vlad smiled, cold and cunning. 'I saw a few blades but nothing that inspires fear, Vogler. Men doing drills are not something I think to concern myself with. A pile of corpses at their feet would no more turn them into ruthless killers worth fearing. They are cattle. No more, no less, no matter how you dress them up.'

'Then you are a bigger fool than I thought, von Carstein.'

Vogler walked across to his desk and reached down, lifting a brass bell. He rang it, twice, sharply. It was answered in different parts of the castle, bells ringing out the summons. Within moments Vlad heard running feet and the clatter of steel as Vogler sprung his trap.

Cursing himself for a fool, the vampire wheeled on Vogler, fury drawing the animal from within his face, and grabbed the man by the throat. 'You mock me, little man. Do not,' he rasped, his voice dropping to a cold whisper, 'make the mistake of thinking yourself superior. You and all of your armies are not. I have outlived better foes than you. You will leave this life before I do. Do we understand each other?'

Vogler nodded once, sharply, as he twisted savagely against the vampire's iron grip.

'Good,' said Vlad. 'I would kill you, here and now, for the insults you have given me – but I will not, not yet. I will kill those around you. I will deprive you of everything you believe you love, the people and the finery you hold dear, I will take it all. I will destroy it all. And I will keep you alive to see it all leave you. Then perhaps I will kill you. Or perhaps you will see life with new eyes and we will become those firm friends you talked of. Now I think I shall whet my appetite with a mouthful of traitor's blood.'

Vlad pushed the man away from him, catching him by the wrist as he fell. He raised his hand to his mouth, fangs bared, but Vogler surprised him with almost supernatural speed, and a strength that far outstripped anything a mere mortal ought to have commanded. With a single, arrogant, twist of the wrist and push Vlad went sprawling from his feet. He hit the floor hard. He looked up at the Vogler and saw that he was more than some mere trumped-up petty upstart. He saw a thirst for power in the man's eyes. And a strength that had no right to be there.

Vogler had pledged his soul to a new master.

A fearful foe stared back at the vampire.

Laying his hands flat against the floor, Vlad sprang. With no blade, he was reduced to cunning and claws. Matching the fierce grin of Meinard Vogler, Vlad unleashed the beast within, allowing the savage to tear out of his skin. He roared, throwing himself at the man – only to be thrown from his feet again by a savage roundhouse of a punch that cannoned into his jaw.

Shaking himself, Vlad rose slowly this time.

'I did not think you would be so weak, von Carstein,' Vogler's voice changed, arrogance subsumed by a well of power that resonated within Vlad's bones.

'You talk a lot for a dead man,' Vlad said.

'The same might be said for you,' Meinard replied.

'Ah, but I like to play with my food,' Vlad said, a smile twisting his bloodied lips. He flew at Vogler, tooth and claw, his jaw distending wolfishly as his teeth snapped at Vogler's throat.

Six thunderous blows drove him back again, each landing with superhuman ferocity, speed and precision, hammering into his guts and lifting him bodily from the floor. Vlad fell to his knees, shaking his head in disbelief as he tried to dislodge the fugue of shock that locked his muscles.

'You are weak, von Carstein. I shall take no pleasure in killing you.'

Vogler clapped his hands, and the door flew open, more men spilling into the chamber. A blow to the side of the head sent the vampire reeling, his face sliced open from the bite of an iron blade. He did not bleed.

Vlad circled, his mind still working like the pack animal his instinct fled to, seeking to draw Vogler into a mistake. Four men came into the room, each dressed in the regalia of a vile warrior bedecked in skulls and gore. They moved to circle him, seeking to trap him in the centre and make easy work of him. He needed to surprise them, though how he could do such a thing trapped within their circle of blades, he had no idea.

'Flesh corrupts,' Vlad whispered, raising a hand as though to accuse the man before him. Vogler laughed, but the laugh mutated to a scream, a sound that lost all coherence as the tongue in his vile throat rotted, decaying in a matter of seconds until maggots of flesh spilled forth from his gaping mouth.

The men around him moved as one, their weapons slicing in high and low. With no blade to parry the weapons, Vlad hurled himself from his feet, rolling and coming up in a tight crouch beyond their circle. He cast about quickly, pulling down the row of bookcases and sending Vogler's precious leather tomes spilling across the floor. He picked one up and threw it into the face of the nearest man as his attacker moved in for the kill. The spine of the book hit him across the brow of the nose, shattering the cartilage. He kicked the man's knees out savagely. The man screamed as his legs buckled and he hit the floor. Vlad charged by him, five lightning fast paces, and launched himself off the desk at the face of the second man. Before the warrior could raise his deadly blade Vlad's teeth had torn his throat out. The count hit the floor hard, spinning.

Three men faced him.

Three became two as Vlad snatched up a letter opener from Vogler's desk and rammed it into the third swordsman's eye. The warrior crumpled without a sound.

Two became one as Vlad charged at the last of the warriors, lifting him and impaling him bodily on the great brass skull so that the teeth and jaw of metal protruded through his armour.

Finally he turned on Meinard Vogler who stood calm in the centre of the chaos of death, a smile spread across the ruination of his mouth. He did not try and speak.

There was no laughter from Vlad this time.

'Beg me, mortal. Grovel. Throw yourself at my feet and beg for mercy before I end your life,' he goaded, drunk on the violence of killing.

With a single smooth motion Vlad grabbed Vogler as, incensed at the taunts, the man threw himself at him again. With a single savage twist Vlad snapped the man's neck. Vogler shuddered once and went limp in Vlad's arms. There was rage in the lifeless face that gazed up at him. It was almost daemonic.

He found some small joy in that. He leant in close, inhaling the man's essence, savouring the power of his blood. He had been more than a mere man, that much Vlad knew now, but not how much more – not until Vogler's head lolled and he saw the intersecting lines of the tattoo at the nape of the man's neck. He knew the mark; three parallel lines, one thicker than the rest, crossed by two more lines, making the mark of Khorne.

Cursing his own hubris, Vlad hurled Vogler's corpse aside and left the study, going in search of his wife.

The castle had been a trap, baited by his own arrogance.

How well the dead man had known him.

That single thought burned Vlad but he cast it aside. Isabella was alone within the castle, newborn and weak with the power of undeath only just stirring within her veins.

The burgeoning fear he felt for her was quenched with a single step into the grand ballroom Vogler used as his throne room. Isabella sat on the elaborately carved throne in the centre of the room, bathed head to toe in the blood of Vogler's court. Around the room thirty people, Vogler's cooks and cleaners, maids and men were arranged like dolls in an insane playhouse, posed for Isabella's amusement. They embraced, they lay at one and another's feet in worship, they held their hands to their faces in horror. At their feet, the blood she could not swallow pooled thickly. She sat there, the queen in her crimson court, regal, wan and serene. She was, beyond any pale shadow, worthy of being called his wife.

'Aren't they pretty?' she said, seeing him. She held in her lap the face of a woman she had torn away. She lifted it in front of her own as he walked toward her and asked, 'Which do you prefer? I think she is pretty. I would like her. Do you want me to look like her, my love?'

And in that moment, he knew that she was lost.

He had never loved her more.

DOMINION

PROLOGUE

The Eye of the Hurricane

GRUNBERG
Late winter, 2052

IT WAS DESPERATE.

Kallad Stormwarden knew the tide of the battle had turned. Still, the young dwarf prince stood side by side with his father, matching the gruff dwarf blow for blow as Kellus's axe hewed through the swarm of dead storming the walls of Grunberg Keep. The dwarfs of Karak Sadra had chosen to make their last stand against the Vampire Count together with the manlings.

The walkway was slick with rain.

Kallad slammed the edge of his great axe, Ruinthorn, into the grinning face of a woman with worms where her eyes ought to have been. The blade split her skull cleanly in two. Still the woman came on, clawing desperately at his face. He staggered back a step beneath the ferocity of her attack, wrenching the axe head free. Grunting, he delivered a second, killer blow. The dead woman staggered and fell lifelessly from the wall.

He knuckled the rain from his eyes.

There was no blood and the dead didn't scream. Their silence was more frightening than any of the many horrors on the field of combat. They surged forwards mercilessly as axes crunched into brittle bones, splintering shoulders and cracking skulls. They lurched and lumbered on as arrows thudded into chest cavities, piercing taut skin and powdering it like vellum, and still they came on relentlessly as heads rolled and limbs were severed.

'Grimna!' Kallad bellowed, kicking the woman's head from the wall. His rallying cry echoed down the line as the dead shuffled forwards. Grimna. Courage. It was all they had in the face of death. It was all they needed. Grimna gave them strength while the stubbornness of the mountain gave them courage. With strength and courage, and their white-haired king beside them, they could withstand anything.

There was an air of greatness about Kellus Ironhand. More than merely prowess or skill, the dwarf embodied the sheer iron will of his people. He was the mountain, indefatigable, unconquerable, and giant.

And yet there was a chill worming its way deeper into Kallad Stormwarden's heart.

Only in death did moans escape their broken teeth, but these weren't real sounds. They weren't battlefield sounds. They were sussurant whispers. They weren't human. They weren't alive. They belonged to the gathering storm and they were terrifying in their wrongness.

It didn't matter how hard the defenders fought, how many they killed, they were trapped in a losing battle. The ranks of the undead army were endless, their bloodlust unquenchable.

Bodies surfaced in the moat, rising slowly to the surface, their flesh bloated and their faces stripped away by the leeches that fed on them.

Kallad stared at the tide of corpses as one by one they began to twitch and jerk like loose-limbed puppets, brought violently to life. The first few clawed their way up the side of the dirt embankment. More followed behind them: a seemingly endless swell of death surfacing from beneath the black water.

The futility of fighting hit him hard. It was pointless. Death only swelled the ranks of the enemy. The sons of Karak Sadra would be dining in the Hall of the Ancestors by sunrise.

Kallad slapped the blade of Ruinthorn against his boot and brought it to bear on a one-armed corpse as it lumbered into range. The bottom half of its jaw hung slackly where the skin and muscle had rotted away. Kallad took the miserable wretch's head clean off with a single vicious swing. The fighting was harsh. Despite their greater prowess, the dwarfs were tiring. Defeat was inevitable.

Behind Kallad, someone yelled a warning, and a cauldron of blazing naphtha arced high over the wall, crashing into the ranks of the dead. The fire bit and burned bright as dead flesh seared, tufts of hair shrivelled and bones charred. The pouring rain only intensified the burning, the naphtha reacting violently to the water.

The stench was sickening as the corpses burned.

Kellus brought his axe round in a vicious arc, the rune of Grimna slicing into a dead man's gut. The blow cracked the man's ribcage open. His entrails spilled out like slick loops of grey rope, unravelling in his hands even as he struggled to hold them in. The dead man didn't bleed. His head came up, a look of bewilderment frozen on his features as Kellus put the thing out of its misery.

Kallad moved to stand beside his father.

'There's no better place to die,' he said in all seriousness.

'Aye there is lad, in a bed with a score of grand bairns running around and yapping, and your woman looking down at you lovingly. This here's second best. Not that I'm complaining, mind.'

Three shambling corpses came at them at once, almost dragging Kellus down in their hunger to feast on his brains. Kallad barged one off the walkway and split another stem to sternum with a savage blow from Ruinthorn. He grinned as his father dispatched the third creature. The grin died on his face as down below one of his kin fell to the reaching hands of the dead and was dragged down into the mud of the field where they set about stripping flesh from bone with savage hunger. The dwarf's screams died a moment before he did.

His death spurred the defenders on, firing their blood with a surge of stubborn strength, until the desperation itself became suffocating and closed around their hearts like some black iron fist, squeezing the hope out of them. On the field below, another dwarf fell to the dead. Kallad watched, frozen, as the creatures ripped and tore at his comrade's throat, the fiends choking on his blood in their urgency to slake their vile thirst.

Kallad hawked and spat, wrapping his hands around the thick shaft of Ruinthorn and planting the axe-head between his feet. The last prince of Karak Sadra felt fear then, with the understanding that his wouldn't be a clean death. Whatever honour he won on the walls of Grunberg Keep would be stripped from his bones by von Carstein's vermin. There would be no glory in it.

The rain intensified, matting Kallad's hair flat to his scalp and running between the chinks in his armour and down his back. No one said it was going to be like this. None of the storytellers talked about the reality of dying in combat. They spun tales of honour and heroism, not mud and rain, and the sheer bloody fear of it.

He turned to his father, looking to draw courage from the old king, but Kellus was shivering against the rain and had the deadened look of defeat in his old eyes. There was no comfort to be drawn from him. The mountain was crumbling. It was a humbling experience, to stand at the foot of the mountain and witness the rock crack and fall, nothing more than scree where once the mountain had stood tall and proud. In that one look Kallad saw the death of a legend at its most mundane.

Kallad looked out across the fields where countless hundreds of the dead shuffled and milled aimlessly among the piles of bones, waiting to be manipulated into the fray, and beyond them the black tents of Vlad von Carstein and his pet necromancers. They were the true power behind the dead, the puppet masters. The corpses were nothing more than dead meat. The necromancers were the monsters in every sense of the word. They had abandoned every last trace of humanity and given themselves to the dark magic willingly.

Kallad watched as five more fiends clawed their way up the wall of the keep to the walkway. Would these be the ones who sent him to the Hall of Ancestors?

'They need you down there,' Kellus said, breaking the spell of the creeping dead. 'Get the women and children out of this place. The keep's fallen and with it the city. I'll have no one dying who can be saved. No arguments, lad. Take them through the mountain into the deep mines. I'm counting on you.'

Kallad didn't move. He couldn't abandon his father on the wall; it was as good as murdering him.

'Go!' King Kellus commanded, bringing his own axe around in a savage arc and backhanding its head into the face of the first zombie. The blow brought the creature to its knees. Kellus planted a boot on its chest and wrenched the axe free. The creature slumped sideways and fell from the walkway.

Still Kallad didn't move, even as Kellus risked his balance to slam a fist into his breastplate, staggering him back two steps.

'I am still your king, boy, not just your father. They need you more than I do. I'll not have their deaths on my honour!'

'You can't win... not on your own.'

'And I've got no intention of doing so, lad. I'll be supping ale with your grandfather come sunrise, trading stories of valour with your grandfather's father and boasting about my boy saving hundreds of lives even though he knew to do so would be damning this old dwarf. Now go lad, get the manlings out of here. There's more than one kind of sacrifice. Make me proud, lad, and remember there's honour in death. I'll see you on the other side.' With that, the old dwarf turned his back on Kallad and hurled himself into the thick of the fight with vengeful fury, his first blow splitting a leering skull, the second severing a gangrenous arm as King Kellus, King of Karak Sadra, made his last glorious stand on the walls of Grunberg Keep.

More dead emerged from the moat. It was a nightmarish scene: the creatures moving remorselessly up the embankment, brackish water clinging to their skin. Cauldrons of naphtha ignited on the dark water, blue tinged flames racing across the surface and wreathing the corpses. And still they were silent, even as they charred to ash and bone.

The slick black bodies of hundreds of rats eddied across the blazing water, the rodents racing the bite of flame to dry land.

Kallad turned reluctantly and stomped along the stone walkway. He barrelled down the ramp, slick with rain, and skidded to a halt as the screams of women and children tore the night.

Heart racing, Kallad looked around frantically for the source of the screams. It took him a moment to see past the fighting, but when he did, he found what he was looking for: a petrified woman staggering out of the temple of Sigmar. She clutched a young baby in her arms and cast panicked glances back over her shoulder.

A moment later, the bones of one of Grunberg's long dead emerged from the temple. Dust and cobwebs clung to the bones. It took Kallad a moment to grasp the truth of the situation: their own dead were coming up from the dirt and the cold crypts, and were turning on them. Across the city, the dead were stirring. In cemeteries and tombs loved ones were returning from beyond the veil of death. The effect on those left behind would be devastating. To lose their loved ones once was hard enough, but to be forced to burn or behead them to save your own life... few could live through that kind of horror untouched.

It made sense, now that he could see the pattern of the enemy's logic. The necromancers were content to waste their peons in a useless assault on the walls. It didn't matter. They had all the dead they needed *inside* the city already.

The impossibility of the situation sank in, but instead of giving in to it, Kallad cried, 'To me!' and brandished Ruinthorn above his head.

He would make his father's sacrifice worthwhile, and then, when the women and children of Grunberg were safe, he would avenge the King of Karak Sadra.

The terrified woman saw Kallad and ran towards him, her skirts dragging as she struggled through the mud. The baby's shrieks were muffled as she pressed the poor child's face into her breasts. Kallad stepped between the woman and the skeleton hunter, and slammed a fist into the skull. The sounds of metal on bone and the subsequent crunch of bones breaking were sickening. The blow shattered the hinge on the right side of the fiend's head, making its jaw hang slackly, broken teeth like tombstones. Kallad thundered a second punch into the skeleton's head, his gauntlet caving in the entire left side of the monstrosity's skull. It didn't slow the skeleton so much as a step.

The twin moons, Mannslieb and Morrslieb, hung low in the sky and the combatants were gripped in a curious time between times, neither the true darkness of night nor the first blush of daylight owning the sky. The fusion of the moons' anaemic light cast fitful shadows across the nightmarish scene.

'Are there more in there?' Kallad demanded.

The woman nodded, eyes wide with terror.

Kallad stepped into the temple of Sigmar expecting to find more refugees from the fighting. Instead, he was greeted by the sight of shuffling skeletons in various states of decay and decomposition trying to negotiate the rows of pews between the door down to the crypt and the battle raging outside. He backed up quickly and slammed the door. There was no means of securing it. Why would there be? Kallad thought bitterly. It was never meant to be a prison.

'More *manlings*, woman, not monsters!' he said, bracing himself against the door.

'In the great hall,' she said. The overwhelming relief of her rescue had already begun to mutate into violent tremors as the reality of her situation sank in. There was no salvation.

Kallad grunted.

'Good. What's your name, lass?'

'Gretchen.'

'All right, Gretchen. Fetch one of the naphtha burners and a torch.'

'But... but...' she stammered, understanding exactly what he intended. Her wild-eyed stare betrayed the truth: the thought of razing Sigmar's house to the ground was more horrifying than any of the creatures trapped inside.

'Go!'

A moment later, the dead threw themselves at the door, fists of bone splintering and shattering beneath the sheer ferocity of the assault. The huge doors buckled and bowed. It took every ounce of Kallad's strength to hold the dead back.

'Go!' he rasped, slamming his shoulder up against the wood as fingers crept through the crack in the door that the dead had managed to force open. The door slammed closed on the fingers, crushing the bone to a coarse powder.

Without another word, the woman fled in the direction of the naphtha burners.

Kallad manoeuvred himself around until he braced the huge door with his back, and dug his heels in stubbornly. He could see his father on the wall. The white-haired king matched the enemy blow for savage blow. With his axe shining silver in the moonlight, Kellus might have been immortal, an incarnation of Grimna himself. He fought with an economy of movement, his axe hewing through the corpses with lethal precision. Kellus's sacrifice was buying Kallad precious minutes to lead the women and children of Grunberg to safety. He would not fail. He owed the old dwarf that much.

The dead hammered on the temple door, demanding to be set free.

Gretchen returned with three men, dragging between them a huge black iron cauldron of naphtha. There was a grim stoicism to their actions as the four of them set about dousing the timber frame of the temple in the flammable liquid while Kallad held back the dead. A fourth man set a blazing torch to the temple wall and stepped back as the naphtha ignited in a cold blue flame.

The fires tore around the temple's façade, searing into the timber frame. Amid the screams and the clash of steel on bone, the conflagration caught and the holy temple went up in smoke and flames. It took less than a minute for the building to be consumed by fire. The heat from the blaze drove Kallad back from the door, allowing the dead to spill out of the temple.

The abominations were met with hatchet, axe and spear as the handful of defenders drove them back mercilessly into the flames. It was nothing short of slaughter. Kallad couldn't allow himself the luxury of even a moment's relief – the battle was far from won. His brow was smeared with soot, and his breathing came in ragged gasps, as the heat of the blaze seared into his lungs. Yet, in his heart, he understood that the worst of it was only just beginning.

Kallad grabbed the woman. He yelled over the crackle and hiss of the flames, 'We have to get everyone out of here! The city is falling!'

Gretchen nodded dumbly and stumbled away towards the great hall. The flames spread from the temple, licking up the length of the keep's stone walls, and arcing across the rooftops to ignite the barracks and beyond that the stables. The rain was nowhere near heavy enough to douse the flames. In moments, the straw roof of the stables was ablaze and the timber walls were caving in beneath the blistering heat. The panicked horses bolted, kicking down the stable doors and charging recklessly into the muddy street. The stench of blood coupled with the burning flesh of the dead terrified the animals. Even the quietest of them shied and kicked out at those seeking to calm them.

The dead came through the flames, pouring over the walls in vast numbers, lurching forwards, ablaze as they stumbled to their knees and reached up, clawing the flames from their skin even as the fires consumed their flesh.

Still they came on.

The dead surrounded them on all sides.

The horses kicked out in panic.

The conflagration spread, eating through the timber framed buildings as if the walls were made of nothing more substantial than straw.

Kallad dragged Gretchen towards the central tower of the keep, forcing his way through the horses and the grooms trying to bring the frightened beasts under control. The flames chased along the rooftops. No matter how valiant the defenders' efforts, in a few hours Grunberg would cease to be. The fire they had lit would see to that. The dead wouldn't destroy Grunberg; the living had managed that all by themselves. All that remained was a desperate race to beat the fire.

No direct path to the great hall lay open, although one row of ramshackle buildings appeared to be acting as a kind of temporary firewall. Kallad ran towards the row of houses, racing the flames to the doors at the centre. The hovels of the poor quarter buckled and caved in beneath the heat, and caught like tinder. Kallad was driven towards the three doors in the centre of the street; the intensity of the blaze forced him to skirt the heart of the fire. Only minutes before, the crackling pile of wood before him had been a bakery.

Kallad swallowed a huge lungful of searing air and, taking the middle door, plunged through the collapsing shell of an apothecary's as demijohns of peculiarities cracked and exploded. Gretchen followed behind him, the child silent in her arms.

The lintel over the back door had collapsed under the strain, filling the way out with rubble. Kallad stared hard at the obstacle, hefted Ruinthorn and slammed it into the centre of the debris. Behind them, a ceiling joist groaned. Kallad slammed the axe-head into the guts of the debris again and worked it free. Above them, the groaning joist cracked sharply, the heat pulling it apart. A moment later, the ceiling collapsed, effectively trapping them inside the burning building. Cursing, Kallad redoubled his efforts to hack a path through the debris blocking the back door. He had no time to think. In the minutes it took to chop through the barricade, thick black smoke suffocated the cramped passage. Over and over, he slammed Ruinthorn's keen edge into the clutter of debris, and as chinks of moonlight and fire began to wriggle through, he kicked at the criss-cross of wooden beams. The smoke stung his eyes.

'Cover the child's mouth, woman, and stay low. Lie on your belly. The best air's down by the floor.' The thickening pall of smoke made it impossible to tell if she'd done as she was told.

He backed up two steps and hurled himself at the wooden barrier, breaking through. His momentum carried him sprawling out into the street.

Coughing and retching, Gretchen crawled out of the burning building as the gable collapsed and the roof came down. She cradled the child close to her breast, soothing it as she struggled to swallow a lungful of fresh air. The flames crackled and popped all around them. Inside the apothecary's, a series of small but violent detonations exploded as the cabinets stuffed full of chemicals and curiosities swelled and shattered in the intense heat.

Kallad struggled to his feet. He had been right, the row of buildings acted as a kind of firebreak, holding the flames back from this quarter of the walled city. The respite they offered wouldn't last. All he could do was pray to Grimna that it would last long enough for him to get the women and children out of the great hall.

He ran across the courtyard to the huge iron-banded doors of the keep and beat on them with the butt of his axe until they cracked open an inch and the frightened eyes of a young boy peeked through.

'Come on, lad. We're getting you out of here. Open up.'

A smile spread across the boy's face. It was obvious that he thought the fighting was over. Then, behind Kallad and Gretchen, he saw the fire destroying the shambles of his city. He let go of the heavy door. It swung open on itself, leaving him standing in the doorway, a length of wood in his trembling hand: a toy sword. The lad couldn't have been more than nine or ten summers old, but he had the courage to put himself between the women of Grunberg and the dead. That kind of courage made the dwarf proud to fight beside the manlings; courage could be found in the most unlikely of places.

Kallad clapped the lad on the shoulder, 'Let's fetch the women and children, shall we, lad?'

They followed the boy down a lavish passage, the walls decorated with huge tapestries and impractical weaponry. The hallway opened onto an antechamber where frightened women and children huddled, pressing themselves into the shadows and dark recesses. Kallad wanted to promise them all that they were saved, that everything was going to be all right, but it wasn't. Their city was in ruins. Their husbands and brothers were dead or dying, conquered by the dead. Everything was far from all right.

Instead of lies, he offered them the bitter truth, 'Grunberg's falling. There's nothing anyone can do to save it. The city's ablaze. The dead are swarming over the walls. Your loved ones are out there dying to give you the chance of life. You owe it to them to take that chance.'

'If they are dying, why are you here? You should be out there with them.'

'Aye, I should, but I'm not. I'm here, trying to make their deaths mean something.'

'We can fight alongside our men,' another woman said, standing up.

'Aye, and die alongside them.'

'Let the bastards come, they'll not find us easy to kill.'

One woman reached up, dragging a huge two-handed sword from the wall display. She could barely raise the tip. Another pulled down an ornate breastplate while a third took gauntlets and a flail. In their hands, these weapons of death looked faintly ridiculous, but the look in their eyes and the set of the jaws was far from comical.

'You can't hope to–'

'You've said that already, we can't hope. Our lives are destroyed, our homes, our families. Give us the choice at least. Let us decide if we are to run like rats from a sinking ship or stand up and be judged by Morr, side by side with our men. Give us that, at least.'

Kallad shook his head. A little girl stood crying beside the woman demanding the right to die. Behind her, a boy barely old enough to walk buried his face in his mother's skirts.

'No,' he said bluntly, 'and no arguments, this isn't a game. Grunberg burns. If we stand here arguing like idiots we'll all be dead in minutes. Look at that girl. Are you prepared to say when she should die? Are you?

For all that your men are laying down their lives knowing that in doing so they are saving yours?' Kallad shook his head. 'No. No you're not. We're going to leave here and travel into the mountains. There are caverns that lead into the deep mines and stretch as far away as Axebite Pass. The dead won't follow us there.'

In truth he had no idea if that was the case or not, but it didn't matter, he only needed the women to believe him long enough to get them moving. Safety or the illusion of safety, at that moment it amounted to the same thing. 'Now come on!'

His words galvanized them. They began to stand and gather their things together, tying cloth into bundles and stuffing the bundles with all that remained of their worldly goods. Kallad shook his head, 'There's no time for that! Come ON!'

The boy ran ahead, the toy sword slapping at his leg.

'That stays here,' Kallad said, dipping Ruinthorn's head towards an ornate jewellery box that one woman clutched in her hands. 'The only things leaving this place are living and breathing. Forget your pretty trinkets, they aren't worth dying for. Understood?'

No one argued with him.

He counted heads as they filed out through the wide door: forty-nine women and almost double that number of children. Each one looked at the dwarf as if he was some kind of saviour, sent by Sigmar to deliver them to salvation. Gretchen stood beside him, the child cradled in her arms. She had eased the blanket down from over the child's face, and Kallad saw at last the reason for the child's silence. Its skin bore the bluish cast of death. Still, the woman smoothed its cheek as if hoping to give some of her warmth to her dead baby. Kallad couldn't allow this one small tragedy to affect him – hundreds of people had died today. Hundreds. What was one baby against this senseless massacre? But he knew full well why the sight of the dead child was different. The child was innocent. It hadn't chosen to fight the dead. It represented everything that they had given their lives to save. More than anything else, it showed what a failure their sacrifice had been.

Then, the baby started to move, its small hand wriggling free of the blankets. The child's eyes roved blankly, still trapped in death, even as its body answered the call of the Vampire Count.

Sickness welled in Kallad's gut. The child had to die.

He couldn't do it.

He didn't have a choice. The thing in Gretchen's arms wasn't her baby. It was a shell.

'Give me the baby,' he said, holding out his hands.

Gretchen shook her head, backing up a step as if she understood what he intended, even though she couldn't possibly know. Kallad could barely grasp the thoughts going through his head they were so utterly alien. 'Give me the baby,' he repeated.

She shook her head stubbornly.

'It isn't your child, not any more,' he said, as calmly as he could manage. He took a step closer and took the child from her. The child was a parasite, but despite the wrongness of it, the woman's instinct was still to nurture her baby.

'Go,' Kallad said, unable to look her in the eye. 'You don't need to see this.'

But she wouldn't leave him.

He couldn't do it, not here in the street, not with her watching.

He moved away from her, urging the refugees of Grunberg to follow. He held the child close, its face pressed into the chain links of his mail shirt. Glancing back down the street to the ruin of the stables, Kallad saw the dead gathering, the last of the moonlight bathing their rotten flesh in silver. They had breached the wall and were pouring over in greater and greater numbers. The fire blazed on all sides of them, but they showed neither sense of fear nor understanding of what the flames might do to their dead flesh. The last of the men were lining up in a ragged phalanx to charge the dead. Their spears and shields were pitiful against the ranks of the dead. Even the sun wouldn't rise in time to save them. Like their enemy, they were dead, only Morr had yet to claim their souls.

Kallad led the women and children away; he had no wish for them to see their men fall. The fires made it difficult to navigate the streets. Alleyways dead-ended in sheets of roaring flame. Passageways collapsed beneath the detritus of houses, their shells burned out.

'Look!' One of the women cried, pointing at part of the wall that had collapsed. The dead were clambering slowly over the debris, stumbling and falling, and climbing over the fallen.

'To the mountains!' Kallad shouted over the cries of panic.

Avoiding the pockets of burning heat became ever more difficult as the fire spread, the isolated pockets becoming unbroken walls of flame.

Kallad set off at a run towards the safety of the mountainside and the caverns that led down into the warren of deep mines, across the open ground of the green, and down a narrow alleyway that led to the entrance to the caves. The wriggling child didn't slow him. 'Come on!' he yelled, urging the women to move faster. There would be precious little time to get them all into the caves before the fire claimed the alleyway. 'Come on!' Some dragged their children, others cradled them. None looked back.

'Where do we go?' the young boy asked. He'd drawn his toy sword and looked ready to stab any shadow that moved in the firelight.

'Take the third fork in the central tunnel, lad. Follow it down. It goes deep beneath the mountain. I'll find you. From there, we're going home.'

'This is my home.'

'We're going to my home, lad: Karak Sadra. You'll be safe there.'

The boy nodded grimly and disappeared into the darkness. Kallad counted them all into the caverns. As the last of them disappeared into the tunnels, he turned to look up at the city walls.

Through the dancing flames, he saw the battle still raging. The dead had claimed huge parts of the city, but the manlings were fighting on to the bitter end. He scanned the battlements looking for his father. Then he saw him. Kellus was locked in a mortal struggle. From this distance, it was impossible to tell, but it looked as if his axe was gone. He shifted onto the back foot, the flames licking the stones around him, and was forced further back into the flames as the dead poured over the wall. The last vestiges of Grunberg's defences were breached. The white-haired King of Karak Sadra fought desperately, hurling the dead flesh of mindless zombies from the wall.

A cloaked figure sprang forwards, unbalancing the king. His cloak played around his body like wings in the wind. Kallad knew the beast for what it was, a vampire. Probably not the undead count himself, but one of von Carstein's gets, so close as to be almost identical, but nothing more than a pale imitation at the same time.

The vampire tossed its head back and howled at the moon, exhorting the dead to rise.

For a moment, it seemed to Kallad as if his father could see him through the black smoke and the raging flame. Every bone and every fibre of Kallad's being cried out to run to the old king's aid, but he had been charged with another duty. He had to see these women and children to safety, giving worth to the great king's sacrifice. He couldn't abandon them when he was their only hope. Down there in the deep, they would die as surely as they would have if he had left them in the great hall.

The creature dragged Kellus close in the parody of an embrace and for a moment, it appeared as if the two were kissing. The illusion was shattered as the vampire tossed the dead dwarf aside and leapt gracefully from the high wall.

Kallad turned his back, silent tears rolling down his impassive face.

The babe writhed in his arms. He laid the child on the floor, face down because he couldn't bear the accusation that he imagined he saw in its dead eyes. Sobbing, he took the axe and ended the child's unnatural life.

Smoke, flame and grief stung the dwarf's eyes as he knelt down over the corpse and pressed a coin into the child's mouth, an offering to Morr, the humans' god of death. 'This innocent has suffered enough hell for three lifetimes, Lord of the Dead. Have pity on those you claimed today.'

One day, he promised himself, rising. One day the beast responsible for all this useless suffering will know my name; that will be the day it dies!

CHAPTER ONE

Kaiser, König, Edelmann, Bürger, Bauer, Bettelmann

DRAKENHOF, SYLVANIA
The cold heart of winter, 2055

TWO OF KONRAD'S Hamaya dragged the old man into the cell between them. Von Carstein didn't deign to turn. He made the man wait. It was a delicious sensation and he fully intended to savour the final moments before the kill. There was nothing in the world like bringing death where moments before there had been life. It was such a fleeting thing, life: so transient in nature, so fragile.

He smiled as he turned, although there was no humour in his eyes, and nodded.

The Hamaya served as the Vampire Count's personal bodyguard, his most trusted men, his right and left hands depending upon the darkness of the deed he desired done. They released their grip on the prisoner, kicking him as he sank to his knees so that he sprawled across the cold stones of the cell floor. There was no fight left in the old man. He barely had the strength to hold his head up. He had been beaten repeatedly and tortured to the extremes of what his heart would bear. It was so like the cowards to send an old man to do their dirty work.

'So, are you ready to talk, Herr Köln? Or must we continue with all this unsavoury nonsense? We both know the outcome so why subject yourself to the pain? You will tell me what I want to hear. Your kind always does. It's one of the many weaknesses of humanity. No threshold for pain.'

The old man lifted his head, meeting the vampire's gaze, 'I have nothing to say to you.'

Konrad sighed, 'Very well. Constantin, would you be so kind as to remind our guest of his manners?'

The Hamaya backhanded Köln across the face, splitting his already swollen lip. Blood ran into his beard.

'Thank you, Constantin. Now, Herr Köln, perhaps we can dispense with the charade? As much as I enjoy the tang of blood in the air, yours is sadly past its best. You are the much-vaunted Silver Fox of Bogenhafen, are you not? The *Silberfuchs,* I believe they call you? I assume your paymaster is Ludwig von Holzkrug, although where the loyalties of a man like yourself lie is always up for debate. The Untermensch witch perhaps? Or maybe some other lesser schemer. The Empire is so full of petty politickers, one so much the same as any other that it is difficult to keep track of who is stabbing whom in the back at any given time. No matter. You are what you are and what you are is, without question, a spy.'

'Why don't you kill me and have done with it?'

'I could,' the vampire conceded. He circled the old man. It was the act of a predator. He moved slowly, savouring the helplessness of his prisoner. 'But that would hardly do you justice, Herr Köln. The... ah... notoriety of the *Silberfuchs* demands a certain... respect. Your head must be filled with such interesting truths it would be a crying shame to lose them. Act in haste, repent at leisure, no?'

'What would you have me tell you, vampire? That your people love you? That you are worshipped? Adored? You are not. Believe me. You are hated. Your *kingdom* is fit only for robber barons and fools. It is held together by fear. Fear of the Vampire Count, Vlad von Carstein.' The old man smiled. 'You are not loved. You are not even feared. None of that is of any consequence, of course, because, more than anything, you are not your sire. The only fear around you is the fear that drives you. Compared to Vlad you are a pale shadow.'

'Fascinating,' Konrad said. 'Is that what you intended to tell your paymaster? That the von Carstein threat is vanquished? That there is nothing left to fear?'

'I will tell him the truth: that the scum is rising to the surface, as it always does. That everywhere in Sylvania there is disorder, that the fetid stink of corruption clings to the swamps. I will say that the streets crumble while the parasites suck the lifeblood out of the people, that the peasants despise you for the blight that afflicts their farms, that you are loathed for the famine that cripples the livestock, and blamed for the exorbitant rents you demand from them in return for pox-ridden ground. I will tell him that if they fail to please you with tributes you let your cursed Hamaya feast on their carcasses. Oh, I could tell them that and so much more. I could tell them that your so-called court is infested with sharks that would feast on your royal blood. That Drakenhof is a cesspit of liars, thieves, murderers, spies, and worst of all backstabbing sycophants who whisper sweet nothings in your ear while plotting behind your back. That you are loathed by your own kind, and that you are a fool for believing that they love you.'

Konrad's own grin matched the old man's. 'You are indeed enlightened, Herr Köln. Obviously you are privy to the deepest, darkest secrets of my kind. Yes they would have me dead, it is the nature of the beast to seek out weakness and exploit it. They have not brought me down, as you can see. Drakenhof is mine by right of strength and blood. I am von Carstein. I do not merely call myself such, as others do.' He turned his attention to the two Hamaya who had stepped back from the old man and waited silently. 'Take Jerek, for instance, he understands his place. His loyalty is unquestioning. The blood of our father sings in his veins. He is pure, unlike Constantin, who has claimed the name by right of... what was it, Constantin?'

'Conquest,' the Hamaya supplied.

'Conquest, that's right. Conquest is another word for murder in our world. He earned the title von Carstein by killing another. Our kind survives by strength alone. Strength breeds loyalty. Like Jerek, his loyalty is pure, and yet you have the audacity to tell me that my truth isn't *the* truth? That my world does not work the way I believe? Should I be flattered or furious, Herr Köln?'

'I say what I see. If you do not like what you hear, well, with respect, all you can do is kill me.'

'Not so, killing you is the very least that I can do. I could drag your soul kicking and screaming back from the comfort of Morr's underworld and consign you to the unlife of the living dead, for instance. I could slay you and raise your corpse to dance to my whims like a puppet, or I could leave you to rot. Don't underestimate the torments beyond death that I could inflict on you if I so choose. Now, tell me about the lands you left behind, spy. Tell me about your beloved Empire.'

The old man's head dropped. He lapsed into silence.

'Oh, do speak up while you still can, Herr Köln. The cat hasn't gotten your tongue yet.'

'I am no traitor.'

'But I think you will be before the sun rises on the new morning, if that is any consolation? I think you'll be delighted to spill your guts. Jerek and Constantin will no doubt be sick of the sound of your voice.'

Konrad stopped his pacing, drawing his sword, a blade of bone with a skeletal wyrm carved into its hilt, from its sheath. The blade's edge whickered as it slid free. Konrad rested it against Deitmar Köln's left ear.

The old man screamed as the vampire sliced his ear off with a single smooth stroke. Blood flowed freely through Köln's fingers as he clutched at the ragged hole in the side of his head. He didn't stop screaming as Konrad raised the severed ear to his lips and sucked the blood from it.

The vampire tossed the ruined ear aside.

'Now, where were we? Oh yes, you were telling me nothing I didn't already know, how those around me are untrustworthy. How I have surrounded myself with fools and traitors and those who are loyal now could be traitors tomorrow. How loyalty can be bought with fear. How fear can inspire treachery. You speak in vagaries meant to inspire paranoia. I am nobody's fool, Herr Köln. How does anyone know whom to trust or who to kill? Tell me that, *Silberfuchs*, and then, when you are through answering the unanswerable, tell me all about dear old Ludwig and the squabbles of the Empire. I yearn for a good story and it would be an honour to hear the Silver Fox of Bogenhafen's last lament.'

The old man slumped against the wall, his bloody hand pressed up against the side of his head. What remained of his life could be counted out in moments, and yet despite the sure and certain knowledge of his fate, he tapped some inner well of strength that allowed him dignity in death.

Konrad resumed his pacing, his slow, measured footsteps echoing hollowly on the stone floor. He didn't say a word, but a smile twitched at his lips as the old man suffered.

'Do we really have to take this to its logical conclusion, Herr Köln? I had hoped you would see sense before my patience finally wore thin. It seems I was wrong.' With that Konrad lashed out a second time with the bone sword, cutting deep into the hand Köln threw up before his face to ward off the blow. Bone cleaved bone, although Konrad pulled the blow before it completely severed the old man's wrist, leaving the hand hanging uselessly by a single tendon. Blood pumped from the ragged wound, at first it came in a huge gush that sprayed like a fountain, but it quickly dwindled as shock set in.

The old man gibbered through the pain, his eyes glazed over. It was doubtful whether a single coherent word would escape his lips before his body finally succumbed to the shock, and he died.

Konrad knelt, taking the old man's chin in his hand and tilting his head until their eyes met. Köln tried to say something. His lips moved and sounds gurgled out of his mouth, but Konrad couldn't make any sense out of them.

'Is this the way it ends? Not with a bang but with a whimper? Tragic, utterly tragic, but so be it.'

Konrad rose, lifting the wyrm-hilted blade above his head, poised to grant death and end the old man's torment. Instead, very deliberately and very slowly, he sheathed the sword and hoisted Deitmar Köln to his feet. The old man's legs refused to hold him. Konrad nodded to his two Hamaya, who peeled away from the shadows to support the spy between them. His body sagged as if he was being crucified.

Konrad slammed a fist into his gut. The old man folded in on himself until the Hamaya straightened him up. Konrad hit him again.

'I could tell you that this hurts me more than it hurts you. I would, of course, be lying. This doesn't hurt me at all. Between you and me, I quite enjoy it actually. Now, before I get carried away, I'm going to offer you one last chance to spill your guts before I spill them for you. Do we understand each other, Herr Köln?'

Deitmar Köln lifted his head. Blood smeared across his face and into his mouth. His eyes were glazed and his skin had taken on a sickly grey cast. The old man's tongue licked along his lips as he tried to form a word. Konrad allowed himself a self-indulgent smirk. 'They all talk eventually,' he said, leaning in close to hear what the dying man had to confess.

Köln spat in his face.

An elbow in the base of the neck from the Hamaya Constantin drove the old man to his knees.

Konrad kicked him in the face. It was brutal. The sound of bone and cartilage breaking was sickening. He kicked the old man over and over until Jerek's reassuring voice cut through the fugue that violence had wrapped around him.

'It's over.'

It was. The Silver Fox of Bogenhafen was dead, his secrets taken to the grave.

Konrad's fury dissipated, leaving him standing over the bloody corpse of the old man, none the wiser, and ruing the cost of giving in to his anger.

'Fool,' he muttered, toeing the dead man under the chin to bring his sightless eyes up to meet his gaze. 'All you had to do was talk. The feuding of the would-be emperors is common knowledge. A few choice comments about the Sigmarites sparring with the self-proclaimed Emperor Ludwig could have bought your life, or at least your death.' He turned to Constantin. 'Still, waste not want not. Take him down to Immoliah Fey. I am sure she will appreciate the gift.'

'As you wish, lord.' The Hamaya gathered the dead man into his arms as if he weighed nothing and carried him out of the cell, leaving Konrad and Jerek von Carstein alone.

'Walk with me a while, my friend. This place brings depresses me.'

'It is understandable,' Jerek said. 'Being trapped in this cloying dark is no way to live.'

The pair wandered the labyrinthine halls of Drakenhof Castle, working their way slowly toward the rooftops. The castle was a curious mix of decay and renewal: certain corridors were wreathed in cobwebs and dank with mildew, and one entire wing of the castle had been abandoned to the ghosts of the dead and was buried by dust. Some warmer chambers in what had once been the van Drak tower were darkened by thick velvet drapes, and danced to the shadows of guttering torches and freshly laid fires.

The tower itself had suffered the most complete transformation, to the extent of owning a new name. Vlad's birds had overrun the spire of the old tower, transforming it into the Rookery. Gone was the opulence of Vlad's reign. Konrad and the new breed of von Carsteins offered austerity; their world was one of decay. There was no place for the redeeming love of beauty Vlad cherished.

'We owe our lives to you, Wolf, don't think that I have forgotten,' Konrad said, finally. He pushed open a heavy wooden door and stepped out into the night. The winds cradled him, wrapping his cloak around his thin frame. He breathed deeply of the night air as he looked around the battlements. Only, of course, they weren't battlements anymore. This place had become a haven for Vlad's birds. Even the servants called it the Rookery now. He took solace in the company of the birds.

'Nonsense,' Jerek said.

'Don't be so quick to dismiss the importance of what you did. When others lost their heads and surrendered to bloodlust, you kept yours. You didn't give in to panic. You didn't flee in mindless terror. You thought a way out of death. You brought us back from the point of extinction, but more than that, you brought us home. We are here now because of you, my friend. You are a good man.'

'Hardly,' Jerek grunted, uncomfortable with the vampire's praise. Vlad's ravens scattered as he walked among them. 'I'm not a good man. Perhaps I was once, it is difficult to remember now, but whatever I was in life, I'm not even a shadow of it in death. I have changed to the point that I don't even know who I am. I have cravings that I don't understand, longings and desires that even a few years ago would have disgusted me, and yet somehow I have become a "good man"? No. I am not a good man. Everything has changed. The sun no longer shines for me, lord. I miss that more than anything.'

'You speak as if you are not who you were. That is a lie. We are all who we were, but we are all more complicated than simply being good men or bad men. We all have countless identities inside us. We have the savage who would rip out a man's heart and feed on it greedily, we have the friend whose nobility of heart is pure, we have the lover who sings to us the sins of the flesh and worships the pale alabaster skin of our woman, we have the child we once were, the lad whose fears have never left him, and we have the man we might have become.

'All these and more live inside our skin, my friend. We listen to all their voices when they cry out. We are truly the sum of our life, of who we were. That is who we are, not some newborn dead thing. We are in every way ourselves, and yet we are more than that. We remember all the fears, all the dreams we shared, we remember and they make us stronger. They do not simply disappear. We carry the joys we knew in life, the compassion, and the love – if we were blessed enough to know it – and equally we carry the hatred and horrors of our existence. The difference is that now we draw pleasure from both aspects of our twin souls. You are still the White Wolf of Middenheim, but you are so much more as well. You find yourself enjoying death in a way that you never did before, but my friend, believe me, that capacity for joy was always within you.'

'Perhaps you are right, although I cannot find myself in here anymore, Konrad. I am selfish. I would live in the sun once more. That is the truth of it.'

'Ah, but the truth is like an expensive whore, Jerek. She comes dressed in many pretty dresses and will bend over for any with the money to pamper her. Your truth is not my truth and my truth was not Vlad's. We each shape the world as we walk through it. We write the "truth" with our actions, if we are victorious, then others come to accept our truth, whereas if we are defeated those same people will vilify our truth as damnable lies. Do not overcomplicate life with the search for one unifying truth, it does not exist, my friend.'

'Concubine, courtesan, whore, they're all words that mean the same thing, she lies with anyone with the coin to have her.'

Konrad knelt to cradle a beady-eyed raven in his hand. The bird didn't react to his touch. 'My point exactly. Now, I think we've done this dance long enough. What is bothering you?'

Jerek stared out over the moonlight town far below, imagining the laughter and life around the hearths, and the simple delight those unseen people found in their pitiful existence. He envied them their ignorance. He envied them their happiness. A mass of black winged birds took flight, banking high in the sky to block out the moon as they circled as one.

'An omen?'

'Birds are always an omen, Jerek. It is whether we chose to pay them heed or not that is important. The psychopomps deliver their messages of foreboding, it is why they exist; they are nothing more than playthings of the gods. We see them now, but, tell me, should we take heed of their warning?'

Jerek turned his back on the birds.

'Do you trust me, Konrad?'

It was a simple question and deserved a simple answer, despite the fact that the answer itself was far from simple. 'Yes,' Konrad said, resting a hand on Jerek's muscular shoulder. 'Yes, I do.'

Jerek nodded, 'Which makes what I am going to say easier and more difficult at the same time.'

'Speak freely.'

'Ah, if only it were that easy. I fear there is a traitor amongst us, my lord.'

Konrad laughed. 'I am surrounded by traitors and assassins, my friend. That is why I bid you gather the Hamaya, the best of the best, the most trusted. With them as a shield, I am at least protected from the more overt manipulations of my kin. They have saved me once from my beloved kin's back-stabbing knives, they will no doubt save me again.'

'That is why the betrayal hurts the most. I believe the traitor lies within the ranks of your bodyguard and feeds information to one or more of Vlad's gets, conspiring against your leadership.'

'A traitor in the Hamaya? Are you sure?'

'No,' Jerek admitted, 'not sure, but suspicious.'

'Then I must trust your suspicions, my friend. I would be a fool to ignore you and the birds. The vultures are cycling, it would seem, and as ever they are hungry to feed on weakness. I am not weak. There will be blood in the water, much blood, but it will not be mine. Their fall from grace will be a lesson to all. No one crosses me. Find the traitor, Jerek. Find them, skin them and roast them on a spit until only their ashes remain. I want everyone to know the cost of betrayal.'

CHAPTER TWO
Shadow of the Vampire

THE SIGMARITE CATHEDRAL, ALTDORF
The bleak midwinter, 2055

Kallad Stormwarden had been in Altdorf for three soul-destroying weeks. This wasn't his home. He missed the mountains. The cold stone of the buildings was soulless stuff. He dreamed at nights of the stone halls of Karak Sadra.

He was here because of the vampires of Grunberg. As long as the vampires lived, his own life had but a single purpose: retribution.

The path of vengeance had led to Altdorf before it had cracked and broken, and finally died out.

The war of the Vampire Count had taken a heavy toll. Cities live, and like people, cities die. The pulse of Altdorf had weakened and become erratic, the life choked out of the place. It was a shadow of its former glorious self, although the inhabitants did their damnedest to carry on their everyday lives as if nothing had happened. The dwarf found it fascinating and tragic at the same time. Denial it seemed was the primary characteristic of the human condition.

Not for the first time, he wondered how they could do it. There was no miracle to it though; it was a case of necessity. They had to foster denial, or they would drown in self-pity and be as dead as if the Vampire Count had sucked them dry. That would have been the biggest tragedy of all: for the survivors to give up living because of the high price of victory. Their stubborn determination was a way of honouring those who had paid the ultimate price for their freedom.

In truth, there was little difference between this and the way Kallad lived his life. The memory of Grunberg and those who had fallen there overshadowed each day he lived. Days and weeks, and months could pass, it didn't matter, the passage of time had lost its meaning to the dwarf.

If anything, the Altdorfers losing themselves in the mundane tasks of rebuilding their lives was healthier than the grudge he nursed. They at least were looking to the future, not living in the past where the anger only festered.

'When they're dead,' he promised himself, 'and honour's served, then we start living again, right lad?'

Beside him, Sammy Krauss, the butcher's boy, sat whittling at a curiously shaped stick with his bone-handled knife. Sammy was simpleminded. They had been almost constant companions since his arrival in the city. The boy, it seemed, had taken a shine to him. Kallad didn't mind. He enjoyed the company. It had been too long since he'd enjoyed the simple pleasure of conversation. Given the city's recent history, it wasn't hard to imagine why the boy had attached himself to the dwarf. It wasn't for his rapier wit and philosophical insight: the finely crafted gromril discs beneath the chain links of mail and his double-headed axe, Ruinthorn, were far more reassuring. Kallad was a fighter. With his parents dead, that was what the boy truly needed.

'Do you really remember where all them dents come from?' Sammy asked, marvelling at the idea that each dent told a story.

'Aye,' Kallad said with a reassuring grin. 'This one here,' he tapped one of the layered discs covering his left side, above his fourth rib, 'was a spear thrust from a skaven. It was a long time ago. I wasn't much older than you. Do you know what skaven are, lad?'

Sammy shook his head, wide-eyed with wonder, 'No. I never heard of him.'

'Rats as tall as you. Vicious things, they are.'

Sammy thought for a moment. 'But rats are small, even big ones.'

'Not all rats, Sammy, some can walk and talk.'

'You mean like them from fairy tales?'

Kallad grinned, 'That's the ones. Ugly little bleeders, giant rats that walk like men. They're tainted creatures, for sure. Well, there were four of them ganged up on me. One didn't stand a chance, and two, well it still wouldn't have been a fair fight. Cursed by Chaos or not, the devils weren't stupid. They knew they'd need to take me by surprise to stand even half a chance. Cunning little beasts they are. Vermin. Would have had me for sure but for the armour. See lad, that's why I remember each dent and ding in these old plates, because without them, well, who's to say I'd even be here today?'

'You mean them dents kept you alive?' The awe in Sammy's voice was unmistakable.

Kallad smiled and patted the dented gromril disc. 'That's exactly what I mean, lad. This metal is tough, tougher than almost anything except gomril.'

'Blimey. You mean if'n the Vampire Count'd had your armour he might still be alive?' Sammy shuddered visibly at the thought.

'Ah, no lad, even my armour couldn't have kept that monster alive. It was his time to die, see. A lot of good people gave their lives to make sure his evil ended here. That makes this city special, lad. This is the place the Vampire Count fell.'

'I saw it, you know. I saw the priest fighting 'im on the wall. I wasn't supposed to. Ma had made us all go down to the cellars, but it was frightening down there so I snuck back upstairs and hid in my room. I could see the wall from my window. It was scary because of all the fires and the explosions, but it wasn't scary like the cellar, because it wasn't dark. I don't like the dark, see. Ma says I'm a big boy and I shoulda grown up out of it by now, but I ain't.'

'There's nothing wrong with being afraid of the dark, lad. All our fears come from there. Did you know that? Everything we're frightened of comes to life in the dark, see. That's why we use torches and light fires, to drive the dark back, because deep down it *still* frightens us. That's why in the backwaters so many revere the sun and the moon. The sun drives away the night. It brings renewal, rebirth. It gives us hope. So don't you worry about what your Ma says, we're all a little bit afraid of the dark, it's good for us.'

'Well I'm a *big* bit afraid.' Sammy said, grinning lopsidedly.

'I'll let you in on a secret... me too.' Kallad said.

'It was a different kind of scary watching through the window. People who come into Pa's shop fell off the wall and didn't get up again. Strangers too. I kept looking at 'em, waiting for them to get up again, but they didn't. And the bad men were throwing things over the wall and making fires and explosions, and I didn't think it was ever going to end.'

'You shouldn't have had to see something like that, lad. No one should. But you know what?'

'What?'

'It's over now and life, well life is going on as normal, isn't it? People still come into your Pa's shop for meat, don't they?'

'Well yes, but we ain't got much meat to sell 'em.'

'Not yet, but you will have. Life goes on. Look around you. Everyone is putting their life back together bit by bit.'

'Not everyone,' Sammy Krauss said solemnly. 'Not the priest, he died. Not the soldiers.'

And that was the truth of it. Those left behind struggled to hold the pieces of their fractured lives together, trying to fill the spaces left by their loved ones who had fallen protecting the once great city. How could he explain that to a boy like Sammy? He couldn't, so he didn't try.

'Come on, lad, time to go for a wander.'

Kallad hauled himself up. He didn't know where he was going to go, but he couldn't just sit on the steps waiting for the answers to come and find him. If he wanted to find the monster that slaughtered Grunberg, he would have to walk in the shadow of the vampire, retracing the fiend's every bloody step.

'Show me where the priest's buried, would you lad? I'd like to pay my respects, one fighter to another.'

Sammy nodded and jumped to his feet, eager to be of use. 'He's in the cathedral. It ain't far. I know the way.'

'I'm sure you do, lad, that's why I asked.'

'I could be your guide, an' if I'm really good at it, maybe I could be your squire, you know?'

'Ah but I'm not a knight, Sammy. I don't need a squire.' The youngster looked crestfallen. 'But you know, you could be my friend, that's a much more important job.'

'I can do that!'

'Excellent, now let's go pay our respects shall we, my friend?'

Grinning, Sammy led the way through the narrow warren of streets. Women washed their sheets and beat the dust from heavy rugs with paddles, young children clinging to their ankles. Washing was hung up to dry on lines that strung buildings together.

The boy loved to smile. It was one of the things the dwarf liked most about the lad.

Altdorf was a city rediscovering its own identity. The moneylenders and pawnbrokers were out on street corners, promising shillings now in return for a few extra pfennigs later. They made Kallad sick, profiting from the hardship of ordinary decent people. It was immoral. It went against the idea of people pulling together in times of trouble. Across the old square, queues of hungry people lined up, soup bowls in hand for handouts from the church. Poverty was a new thing to a lot of these people, but the look of quiet desperation in so many eyes proved that even the proudest man could grow accustomed to taking handouts when it was the difference between going hungry or not.

In the long line, Kallad saw a woman weeping in despair, no bravery left in her eyes, only sadness. He didn't want to think what great loss had brought her to this sad fate. The city had drowned in the hate of the Vampire Count. It was amazing that any of them had the fight to face another day without food, alone, reminded of what they had lost, in the happiness of strangers who could still do the simplest of things like beat the dust out of their rugs with their children clinging to their legs. It was people like her who hurt the most, people for whom there was no escape, even in the most mundane acts of every day living.

The militia patrolled the streets in gangs of six and eight, their presence enough to keep order in the more run down districts of the city.

Few spared the unlikely pair a second glance as Kallad and Sammy skirted the fringe of Reiksport. The smell of brine stung Kallad's nostrils. Large stretches of water weren't something he ever wanted to become accustomed to. It was unnatural. It was hard to imagine that people actually enjoyed having the world constantly tilting and rolling beneath them. He shook his head. It had its uses, he couldn't deny that, but given a choice, he'd always keep a few mountains between himself and the sea. The ships were in, bringing with them much needed produce, but even with the influx of food the city was still slowly starving to death. It would be years before things returned to normal. Von Carstein's undead army was a scourge on the landscape. They left sickness and blight in their wake. Calves and lambs were stillborn, cheeses curdled, and grain stores rotted. The dead were more deadly to the land than a plague. The superstitious blamed the dead; the more practically minded cursed and blamed the living for their failings, while knowing that apportioning blame was a pointless activity. It wouldn't feed anyone.

Kallad and Sammy stood on the dockside, watching the Marshall of the Waters guide the unloading of a huge six rigger. His crew wrestled with ropes and guidelines as they hauled crates out of the ship's hold, climbing nimbly up and down the ropes, hanging from the yardarm and dangling perilously in the rigging. They moved like a colony of ants, busy with purpose and yet completely independent of one another. It was fascinating to see. Indeed, Kallad and Sammy were not alone in their interest. People gathered around, curious as to what the ships were bringing in, desperate to discover that it was, indeed, food.

One of the sailors tossed a small orange ball the size of his clenched fist to the marshall, who looked at it quizzically.

'What am I supposed to do with this?'

'Eat it, what do you think?'

The marshall shrugged, sank his teeth into the orange fruit and spat a mouthful of rind and bits of pulp out. 'It's disgusting!' The marshall wiped his mouth, spitting and rubbing at his tongue to try and get rid of the taste. 'How can you eat something like this? I think I'd rather starve.'

'Not like that. You peel the skin off and eat the fruit. It's good,' the sailor explained, miming the act of stripping the orange's thick skin. The marshall looked uncertain. Seeing Sammy and Kallad loitering on the dockside, he tossed the orange to Sammy underarm. The lad skipped forwards and caught it.

'What do you say?' Kallad asked.

'Thank you, sir!' Sammy shouted. His fingers were already wet with the juice of the fruit as he dug them into the soft flesh.

The sailor laughed and saluted Sammy, 'Take all the skin off, lad, and then tear it into segments. It's like nothing you ever tasted before.'

'I won't argue with *that*,' the Marshall of the Waters said with a wry smile, 'but then so's dung, and happy as flies are to eat the stuff, well it ain't necessarily a delicacy if you know what I mean.'

Sammy moaned with pleasure as he crammed the segments of orange into his mouth, sucking the juice off his fingers. 'Good,' he said around a mouthful of food. 'It's good.'

'Told you!' the sailor called down.

'I'll take your word for it, sonny,' the marshall said dubiously. 'Give me a nice sweet cake of oatmeal dripping with honey and a nice warm bitter ale, and I'm a happy man.'

'It's really good.' Sammy repeated, cramming two wedges of orange into his already full mouth.

Kallad nodded his thanks to the sailor and the marshall. It was good to see the ships back in the Reiksport. Even a couple of weeks without them had turned the dockside into a ghost town. Little by little, the ships promised a return to some semblance of normality. The people needed it. A few exotic fruits wouldn't do much in practical terms, but they would do wonders for morale. The captain of that ship was a canny man, Kallad realised, for understanding the value of a few luxuries over necessities that would run out soon enough.

Sammy Krauss, for instance, would remember his first orange all his life. It was hard to imagine that something as simple as a piece of fruit had made today an extraordinary day for the boy, but it had. That extraordinary day would keep him alive ten times as long as a bowl of grain would. It was all about hope.

Of course, the ships would bring more than produce with them, they would bring sailors, and sailors brought coin and a healthy dose of lust that the local establishments were more than happy to cater for. After a long time at sea, a sailor and his coins were easily parted, and there were places aplenty around the Reiksport that catered for every conceivable desire a sailor on shore leave could need sating. It was a mutually parasitic relationship – the sailors came with their pent-up frustration, needing girls, drink and games of chance to throw their hard-earned money away on, and the city needed the sailors with their drunken lusts every bit as much.

Sammy smacked his lips and licked his fingers all the way to the Sigmarite cathedral. The gates to the grounds were closed. Something about that disturbed Kallad more than the food queues and the moneylenders. The door of Sigmar was always open, or at least it was supposed to be. He hammered on the wrought iron railings until an acolyte came to answer the clanging.

'The world has changed for the worse, it seems,' Kallad said. 'When the House of Sigmar takes to locking itself up like a prison come nightfall it is a sorry state of affairs.'

'Indeed,' the young acolyte said smoothly, 'the world has changed, master dwarf. That is its nature. To stand still is to stagnate. To stagnate is to die. Change is the only way to survive. So, how can we be of service to you?'

'We have come to pay our respects to the priest that fell saving this city.'

The young man nodded thoughtfully. 'As an ambassador of the dwarf folk you are more than welcome to post a vigil at Grand Theogonist Wilhelm III's graveside. It would be our honour. It might be best, however, if your companion waits elsewhere. There can be little of interest for the boy at an old man's tomb.'

'Aye, but then it might be best if the lad can say his thanks to the man as well. After all, it was for boys like Sammy that your priest gave his life, wasn't it?'

'Indeed,' the young acolyte agreed, with a slight nod. 'You are *both* welcome to hold vigil. Will there be anything you need?'

'Shouldn't think so, lad.'

'Then please, follow me.' The acolyte opened the gate and led them through a neatly tended rose garden to a secluded grove on the far side of the cathedral, where the shadows of a weeping willow touched the simple stone of the holy man's grave. A second, smaller gate led through the wall to the street. The dwarf and the boy stood beneath the trailing willow branches. The grave was nothing more than a simple headstone that had already begun to seed over with lichen where the shadows of the willow lingered. A white rose bush grew beside the headstone, the thorns scraping against the words of the prayer carved into the stone.

The acolyte withdrew a step, but didn't leave them.

Kallad whispered a quiet prayer to Grimna before he knelt beside the Grand Theogonist's grave and pressed a small metallic disc into the dirt. The disc was carved with a protective rune of blessing meant to ward off the evil spirits. It was a relic from his home, Karak Sadra. How apt that name was now: Sorrow's Stone. His father, Kellus, had crafted the rune himself in the days before the march from the stronghold beneath Axebite Pass to Grunberg, and had given it to Kallad. The token had kept him alive during the slaughter of that city. Perhaps it would offer some protection to the priest's spirit in death.

'What's that?' Sammy asked, curious.

'My father gave it to me. It's a charm meant to protect the wearer from evil.'

The young acolyte nodded his approval at the offering. 'A suitable token,' he said quietly, making the sign of Sigmar across his heart.

'There are ninety-seven windows in this side of the cathedral,' Sammy said suddenly. 'I counted them. Ninety-seven and only one has someone in it.' The non-sequitur threw Kallad, but he followed the direction in which the boy's hand pointed. A pale face stared down from one of the highest windows. The boy was right: every other window was empty. Curious, Kallad moved to get a better look at the high window where the sun didn't reflect off the glass. The watcher didn't shrink back from the window, despite the fact that he was obviously aware he had been seen. Instead, he matched the dwarf's scrutiny with a detached study of his own.

Kallad turned to the acolyte. 'Who's that?'

The young priest looked up at the face in the window. 'That's the thief,' he said with obvious distaste.

'The thief?'

'Felix Mann, a thoroughly dislikeable man, if you ask me.'

'Aye? An' yet he finds himself inside the cathedral of Sigmar when the gates are locked? I have to say I find that a mite interesting, considering how difficult it is for a normal person to come pay his respects to your god.'

'His presence is... tolerated,' the young acolyte said, grudgingly.

'You could be tempted to wonder if your man is a guest or a prisoner,' the dwarf said.

The young priest didn't have an answer to that, at least not one he could give in words. His eyes shifted involuntarily towards the headstone. People with something to hide tended to give their secrets away with the stupidest of tells. The thief wasn't a prisoner, at least not in the traditional sense, even if the four walls of the cathedral had become his dungeon. There was only one reasonable explanation for why the priests had offered the protection of the temple to a thief: he had friends.

'The edicts of our god require us to tend to the weak and needy, and to protect those that cannot protect themselves. The thief would be dead without us. He cannot so much as fend for himself. He wouldn't last a week on the streets.'

Kallad didn't buy into the priest's rationalisation. It was too convenient by far. Plenty of other people were starving and barely living at a subsistence level, with no homes after the siege, no husbands, and no hope of life ever really returning to normal. Broth lines and prayers for broken souls were not the same as offering Felix Mann sanctuary.

'Neither would a thousand others. They aren't surviving, so what makes Mann special?'

'The thief's curse,' the acolyte said. Seeing the dwarf didn't understand he elaborated, 'No hands.'

That aspect at least made sense: it was a vindictive punishment for petty crimes. Admittedly, it was barbaric and taking both hands was almost unheard of, but what didn't make sense was why the Sigmarites had taken an interest in the thief, instead of just turning him over to the almoners or leaving him to beg? It wasn't as if the city didn't have its share of cripples and beggars, panhandling in the streets for scraps of food and the odd coin that might come their way. There were beggars on every street corner, each with a tale more wretched than the last. That the priests of Sigmar had singled this one out meant that he was marked in some way. He had done something to deserve their charity beyond simply being crippled.

'That's not what makes him special, priest, you and I both know it. Why not turn him over to the almoners?'

'He ahh well his affliction... shall we say that some feel he was maimed in the service of the church, and as such we carry the weight of guilt, which is, of course, preposterous.'

'A thief losing his hands in the service of Sigmar? Are you being serious?'

'Not at all,' the priest assured him.

As if sensing that he was the topic of conversation, the man finally moved away from the window.

A few minutes later, the huge iron banded doors flew open and Felix Mann staggered out of the temple gasping and out of breath from running through the vast cathedral. He was not in a good way. His face had begun to collapse in on itself, his cheeks and eyes waxy sunken hollows, his nose sharp and angular. He was gaunt beyond the point of malnutrition. The waste of a man was shocking to see. What remained were the remnants of Felix Mann. He was less than human.

The thief staggered forwards on shaky legs and debased himself at Kallad's feet, the bandaged stumps of his wrists up in front of his face. Kallad had to imagine the ghosts of hands clenched, begging.

'Just put me out of my damned misery, dwarf! Do it! Crush my skull. Cut my head off my shoulders. Slice my throat, open my gizzards, just do something to finish it, please. I... I don't want to live like this anymore. I don't want to be a prisoner, a freak fed and watered and forced to give thanks for being a cripple to a god who hasn't done a damned thing for me except see to it that I wound up like this. Have pity on me, dwarf. Finish what the vampire started. Do that for me. Do that!'

'You are not a prisoner here. Far from it,' the acolyte said coldly. 'We have made you welcome, fed and cared for you. You could have been left to beg in the gutter like a common criminal. You are free to leave at any time. Remember that before you call us your gaolers.'

'I am not free. If I were there would not be men outside my door at night.'

'We would not have you harm yourself. Sadness over your, ahhh, affliction, might undo reason. We seek only to help you.'

Sammy had backed away behind Kallad, and the acolyte looked distinctly disappointed at the thief's ravings.

'Stand up, man.'

'Look at me. I'm a cripple.'

'Aye, but it ain't the end of the world. I ain't one for judging a man by his looks or his name, better to judge him by what he does. He can curl up an' die or he can get up an' start living again. So stand up.'

'Damn you,' Felix Mann said, but there was no strength in his curse. He spat in the priest's direction and then sagged and folded in on himself, beaten.

'I already am,' Kallad said calmly. 'I am Kallad Stormwarden, the last dwarf of Karak Sadra. The vampires destroyed my people.'

'Then you understand,' Mann said flatly.

'No, I don't. I took their beating and I stood up again. Now, I hunt them. I will not rest until every last vampire is purged from the face of the Empire.'

'Then you'll be joining your people wherever your dead go. You cannot win.'

'Don't grieve for me just yet.'

Felix Mann shook his head violently, 'You don't get it, do you? You're dead already, you just don't know it. I've seen the daemon you are stalking. He did this to me.' Felix held up the stumps where his hands had been severed. 'You can't beat it. It can hide in plain sight. It lives in the shadows. You can't fight it, because you can't *see* it.' His voice took on a hysterical quality, the words beginning to tumble into each other in their rush to be out of his mouth. 'You can't beat it. It isn't alive. It's immortal. It's got the ring. It can't die. It can't die, dwarf. It can't die. Do you understand that? You can hunt it, but you can't kill it. Cut off its head and it will come back. Cut out its heart and it will come back. Burn it and it will rise from the ashes. It will come back and it will keep coming back. Do you understand that? Do you?'

Mann's daemons were like no vampires Kallad had ever heard of, invisible, invincible, they sounded like something invented to scare children. However fanciful, the thief's hysteria had the ring of truth to it. Something had driven the thief to the point of madness. It wasn't hard to imagine that something being the same monster behind the unnecessary evil of the slaughter of Grunberg. That made Felix Mann's story the first real lead Kallad had found since coming to Altdorf, and by necessity that made Felix Mann the missing link that he had been searching so long to find. He just had to bring him back from the edge.

'Rubbish,' the acolyte sneered. 'You're fully of fanciful nonsense. Down to the trauma, no doubt. The Grand Theogonist himself laid down his life to save us from these daemons you rave on about. The threat is gone.'

He was one crucial step closer to finding the fiend that had butchered his people.

'I understand,' Kallad said, 'that the thing has frightened the life out of you, and I understand why the priests have taken pity on you. All I can say is, that way lies madness. This is no way to live.'

'Don't mock me, dwarf,' Mann said, the edge of reason creeping back into his voice. 'Kill me or be done with it and leave me to rot in peace would you?'

Kallad shook his head.

'That's not the way it's going to happen. If you want to live again, help me to kill the beast. If not, well maybe I should crack your skull and put you out of your misery.'

Felix Mann held up his ruined wrist stumps. 'What can I do?' and again, this time more a question than a statement of uselessness: 'What can I do?'

'I can help you, thief, if you are willing to help yourself. Given a forge to work in I can craft hands. Well not real hands. They'll be more like gauntlets than real hands and they'll have to fasten to some kind of shoulder brace. They won't be pretty, and they won't move or have any kind of grip, but they'll be better than nothing. I'm no master smith, but I can make one like it's holding a cup and give the other a kind of hook attachment. They'll give you your life back. You'll be able to feed yourself and start living again. The rest is up to you.'

Silence hung between man and dwarf.

'Why?'

'Because you fought it and you lived.'

'Only because it let me.'

'That doesn't matter. You know it. I'll give you your hands back and in return I want you to talk. Tell me everything you can remember about the vampires. Everything. A good hunter knows his prey. There are less surprises and they die easier that way.'

'They just don't *stay* dead,' Felix Mann said, bleakly.

'This one will,' Kallad promised. 'Believe me, this one will.'

CHAPTER THREE
Voice of Shadows

BENEATH THE SIGMARITE CATHEDRAL, ALTDORF
The bleak midwinter, 2055

JON SKELLAN SNEERED as the soldier's fist thundered into his face. He spat blood. He was beyond pain. They could beat him, burn him and brand him, but they couldn't break him. They cuffed him with silver bonds that seared into his flesh, burning it raw. It didn't matter. He was immune.

'Is that all you've got, soldier?' Skellan mocked. The soldier back-handed him twice, hard, knocking the wind out of him. Skellan rolled his head with the blows.

At first his captors' abuse had verged on the inhumane, but as the days had faded into weeks and the weeks into months so their appetite for his suffering had faded. The beatings became more mundane. They lacked imagination. They lacked the hatred that made torture so terrible. They weren't cold or emotionless. They were... benign. Skellan drew strength from the fact that they toyed with him, testing the limits of his endurance. Day after day they beat him savagely, but it only served to make him stronger. He lived. They didn't dare kill him, but they suffered no such restraint when it came to beating him bloody. Skellan was no fool. If the Sigmarites had wanted him dead they could have killed him on any number of occasions. He was under no illusions. He was at their mercy. No, the simple truth was that they wanted him alive.

That meant they needed him.

For all the taunts, for all the experiments with devices of torture meant to break him, they needed their pet vampire.

It gave him the strength to resist them.

Behind the bars of his cage Skellan had few comforts. Soiled reeds were spread across the floor to insulate it from the cold and damp, and he had a blanket. Rats kept him company, creeping in through the cracks in the stone walls and working their way up from the subterranean sewers of the capital as the rains came, flooding out their lairs. Those he could catch, he killed and fed off. It was no way to live, but it was fresh blood, and blood renewed him.

The soldier moved around behind him and delivered a crushing blow to the back of Skellan's neck. The force of it sent the vampire sprawling across the reeds. With his hands cuffed, he had no way to catch himself as he fell. Skellan lay on his stomach as the soldier delivered a solid kick to his ribs. The kick was savage enough to lift him six inches off the ground. Gasping, Skellan drew his knees up towards his chest. Jagged strands of reed dug into his face.

'Better?'

The soldier said nothing.

The vampire wasn't worth his words.

Skellan knew what they thought of him.

He crawled towards the small mound of dried reeds that he had gathered to form a crude mattress. His gaolers had taken his chair away after Skellan had broken the leg off and beaten one of his captors to death with it in an attempt to provoke his own death in return. They let him live, but stripped his cell, leaving him a pot to relieve himself in and little else. The pot was useless, of course. His body didn't process the usual liquids or toxins as a living man's did.

The worst thing, by far, was that knowing he needed blood to survive, the priests brought it to him.

They fed him with it as they would a suckling babe.

They bled themselves and brought it down to his cellar dungeon, still warm, but already congealing as the heat left it. The blood was vital, but had little restorative value after being drawn from the donor. Little was better than none. Although it only took a few minutes for it to lose the life that Skellan needed to survive, the priests didn't trust their prisoner to feed off the living – with good reason.

His pitiful diet meant that hunger tormented him constantly. The need to feed drove Skellan to the verge of madness and hallucination. He began to believe that he could smell the Sigmarites' lifeblood pulsing through their veins as they prowled the corridors beyond his prison.

In the darkness, he closed his eyes and sent his mind out, imagining that he could actually hear each and every distinctive pulse that filled the chambers of the cathedral above him, despite the layers of stone and mortar. He savoured the rhythmic dub-dub beat of a hundred hearts in a hundred bodies that knelt in prayer; the way they missed an occasional beat or raced as the emotions demanded. In the darkest hours, Skellan allowed himself the fantasy of feeding properly. He played with images of white flesh and blue veins rising to the surface of the pale skin as he sucked hungrily at the throats of the priests.

There was nothing like fresh blood drawn from the still living. It was ambrosia. Skellan fantasised himself running amok in the cathedral, draining the priests one by one in a mindless orgy of blood, paying them back for every last one of the torments they had inflicted since his capture.

It was a sweet fantasy, and it would be fulfilled. He promised himself that.

They would age and weaken. He wouldn't.

He would live, and one day he would be free. When that day came they would know the nature of the beast they caged in their cellars, until then he would suffer their beatings.

The bolt on the door slid back and Reynard Grimm, Guard Captain of Altdorf, entered Skellan's prison. The man was a curious contradiction. Trapped in his skin were two distinct men, one a brutal sadist and the other a weaselly sycophant who clung to the Sigmarite gospels as an excuse for his cruelty. Grimm drew far too much pleasure from the pains he inflicted on his captive to be the guardian of righteousness his swaggering pretended.

The shadows shifted curiously around Grimm as he pushed the door closed, as if something hid within them, invisible to the naked eye. Skellan followed the peculiar blur as it merged into the darkness in the corner of the cell. It must be was a trick of the guttering light. There was nothing there. He turned his attention to the soldier.

'Nothing better to do with your life, Grimm?' Skellan asked. The fear was gone. An uneasy contempt rested in its place. The reverse, however, was not true. The Grimm Skellan had come to know was a coward.

'What could be better than listening to you scream, vampire?'

'Oh, I can think of any number of things, but then, I have an imagination. It is both a blessing and a curse, believe me,' Skellan said, letting the corner of his lips curl into a derisive smile.

'Save your breath, vampire, you'll need it to scream soon enough.'

Skellan shook his head. 'You still don't understand do you, Grimm? I don't have breath to hold. I don't have a heart that beats. I don't have those weak human emotions like love and fear. I am kin to the damned. I am a vampire. I am purged of all the weaknesses of your kind. I shall walk amongst the living long after *you* have become dust and slipped from memory. But you, Grimm, you are nothing, less than nothing. You are a child in a man's skin. You are afraid. You fear me. I can smell it. Your cowardice clings to your skin, it infects your sweat. It cries out to every predator in creation: Kill me! Kill me!'

Behind Grimm's shoulder, the cell door opened once more. The Lector looked troubled as he walked into the small prison cell.

'I begged you, guard captain, no more torture. I speak with Sigmar's mouth, do his words mean nothing to you?' the Lector laid a hand on Grimm's shoulder.

'Shut up, priest.' Grimm shook the priest's hand off.

A ripple of movement in the shadows behind the Lector caught Skellan's eye. He was about to dismiss it when he saw it again, a few feet away from where he had first seen it, much closer to the Lector now: a crease in the shadows, a slight blurring of the wall as something passed in front of it. He wouldn't have been able to see it if he hadn't been looking for it, but now he knew what to look for it was not particularly difficult to follow. There was someone – or something – in the shadows, creeping up behind his two captors.

Skellan forced himself up from the reeds, to kneel before his jailors. It was anything but a gesture of subservience. He was defying them. He met Grimm's eye. The soldier was demented. There was no rationale in his gaze, no thought. He hated Skellan, not for who he was, but for what he was. The guard captain had lived through the Siege of Altdorf. He had seen friends and comrades die at the hands of the vampires. He had reason to fear and reason to hate all that Skellan represented. Those reasons drove the man. He was avenging ghosts every time he laid a hand on Skellan. And every time Skellan dragged himself back to his feet he was mocking the man, reminding him that his dead were still dead and that there could be no revenge for the living.

Grimm lashed out, but his blow never connected.

The outline of a tall, thin man gathered substance within the shimmering dark. The stranger threw back his hood and grabbed Grimm by the hair, tugging back hard on his scalp to unbalance him. The surprise and sudden ferocity of the attack meant that Grimm fell back into the stranger's deadly embrace. He was utterly helpless. In the moment before the stranger sank his teeth into Reynard Grimm's throat, his eyes met Skellan's. Recognition passed between them sending a shiver soul deep. For the first time, Skellan believed he was truly insane. He wanted desperately to believe that Vlad von Carstein had materialised out of the shadows to save him, but it was impossible.

The Vampire Count was beyond resurrection, and yet Skellan saw the Count's eyes. They were ancient, knowing, and so, so cold. They stripped away the layers of lies and identity, and delved deep into the core of who he was. They *knew* him.

The stranger sank his teeth into the soldier's throat, pinning his arms to his side as he kicked out helplessly. He drank hungrily and then snapped Grimm's neck with a sickening economy of movement.

Grimm's body crumpled and collapsed on the floor in a lifeless heap.

Skellan sprang forward, launching himself from his knees like a cannonball. He arched his back and used the full momentum of his body to hammer his forehead into the Lector's chin. He connected with a sickening crunch of bone, his weight bowling the priest off his feet. The priest sprawled across the floor, insensate.

The stranger, Vlad, smacked his lips as he toed Grimm's unmoving corpse. 'Rather like drinking vinegar when rich Bretonnian claret is so near by, but it slakes the thirst. Still, we'll sample some of that vintage before we make good our escape. No doubt you have a debt or two to settle with the priests.' He saw the way Skellan was looking at him, partly in awe, partly in fear and with unmistakable recognition. 'I'm not him,' he said.

'But you look–'

'Similar,' the stranger conceded. 'We are, after all, similar monsters, are we not?'

'But you are his aren't you? I can smell him inside you.'

'I am von Carstein, if that is what you mean. There is some of him in me, as there is some of your sire in you. Vlad brought me into this life. It was a long time ago, longer than I care to remember, and a long way from this ruined burg. He saw something in me he liked, a ghost of himself perhaps? Only he could say for sure. He may not have loved me the most – that honour I feel sure went to Isabella – but he most certainly loved me longest. Now feed, and then we leave.'

'What about these?' Skellan held up his manacled hands. The silver had cut deep wounds into his flesh.

The stranger nodded once and spun on his heel, drawing the cloak around his head and disappearing into the shadows. The cell door opened and closed on nothing as the vampire slipped out. A moment later, the stifled cry of a guard echoed back to Skellan as he knelt over the Lector's corpse, his chin slick with the priest's blood. The killing had begun.

When he looked up, the stranger stood in the doorway, holding the key to his manacles.

'Care to join me in a feast?'

Skellan nodded. 'I will taste their blood,' he said, simply.

'Good. Hold out your hands.'

The stranger manipulated the key in the tiny lock mechanism until it sprang and the silver cuffs fell to the floor.

Skellan rubbed at his ruined wrists. 'Who are you?'

'Come with me and find out.' The stranger turned his back and disappeared through the door.

Skellan had no choice but to follow him.

CHAPTER FOUR
The Night of the Daemon

THE SIGMARITE CATHEDRAL, ALTDORF
The bleak midwinter, 2055

Screaming priests shattered the peace of the secluded graveyard.

For a moment, none of them moved, frozen by the arcane magic of the unexpected scream, unwilling to believe it was actually a scream and not some distant memory, risen to haunt them – a ghost of the past or some revenant shade stirred by their presence amongst the graves. They had all heard enough screams and seen enough horrors for such a basic trick of the mind to unnerve them. It was a curse of the age. This, however, *was* a blood-curdling scream that clawed out of the confines of the cathedral's underbelly. It wasn't the imagination playing tricks. More powerful than any of the eight winds, the scream drew its strength from the most primitive of sources, that primal fear deep in every man. It held the priest, the thief, the dwarf and the simpleton wrapped in its fragile spell. Then the spell shattered as a second scream strangled off into wretched silence.

Whatever had caused the first scream had silenced the second.

Kallad felt the chill touch of premonition as his hands closed around the leather-wrapped shaft of Ruinthorn.

Felix Mann was the first to react. His face crumbled, his newfound resolve short-lived. 'See... see...' he moaned. 'They won't die... they won't die. They won't.'

'Quit your blithering, man.' Kallad Stormwarden dragged Ruinthorn clear and hoisted it over his shoulder. He hadn't gone two steps towards the doors of the temple before the young acolyte grabbed at his shoulder.

'No!' The dwarf spun around. 'For Sigmar's sake, no weapons in the house of our god!'

'With all due respect, you stick with your prayers for comfort and I'll stick with Ruinthorn. Sammy, get out of here.'

The youngster shook his head.

'We're friends.'

That said it all.

Kallad nodded. There was no argument. The lad had used his own words back at him.

'Aye, we are lad, but I can't be worrying about you in a fight. You do as you're told.'

Sammy Krauss bunched up his knuckles, ready to fight, and stubbornly refused to move. 'I can fight.'

None of them had time for an argument. There had been no more screams in the last few seconds, but that didn't mean dying wasn't still going on inside the cathedral. In Kallad's experience, death was silent more often than not.

'Come on, priest,' Kallad urged. Ruinthorn was a reassuring weight in his calloused hands. 'This is your house, let's go find out what all the ruckus is about.'

Like Mann, the acolyte looked more than simply shocked by the screams: his eyes were filled with growing terror. The pair knew something he didn't, that much was obvious, and what they knew troubled them deeply.

The acolyte was hesitant to enter the cathedral.

Kallad gave him a none too gentle shove and followed him in.

At first, the smell reminded Kallad of the deep mines beneath Karak Sadra, the tang of iron sharp in the foetid air, but the priests burned incense and an assortment of powders to take away the reek of unwashed bodies. Blood smelled like iron. What they smelled as they entered the cathedral was blood. It was a cloying out of place stench, acrid against the closed-in musk of the priests.

It didn't bode well.

Kallad kissed the mark of Grimna on Ruinthorn's head and stepped into what he feared would be a charnel house of slaughter.

There were no more screams.

He felt his gorge rise as he walked down the narrow passage. It was quiet: too quiet.

'Something's wrong here. This place stinks of death. What do you know, priest? What are you hiding from me?' Kallad growled at the acolyte. The young priest shuddered and made the sign of Sigmar in the air before him. The man was a nervous wreck.

Kallad pushed past him. The corridor divided into three, a truncated passageway that led to two massive oak doors, and two longer passages that curled left and right. Kallad sniffed the air. The reek of blood was redolent. It was impossible to tell where the concentration was strongest. He listened, but there was nothing, no sign of life within the great cathedral. A hundred priests and countless penitents should have been inside the cathedral's walls. There shouldn't be any place for silence among so many souls. It sent a bone deep chill through the dwarf.

'Taal's teeth, I don't like this,' Felix Mann said, behind him. 'It's too damned quiet. Where is everyone?' The thief had a gift for stating the obvious. 'It's out, isn't it?'

Kallad turned to see that Mann had pushed the young acolyte up against the wall and was forcing the ruined stub of his wrist into the man's throat.

'You let it escape. You fools. You bloody stupid fools!' His voice escalated into hysteria. His accusation echoed through the passageway, the word 'fool' folding in on itself over and over again.

Kallad dropped his axe, grabbed Mann by the shoulder and pulled the pair apart. He slammed the thief up against the wall. Mann's breath leaked out of him in a slow moan. His eyes were wild and wide with terror. Kallad had no idea what the thief was seeing in the dark, but whatever it was clearly had the man frightened.

'You let it escape,' Mann repeated, his voice flat and subdued. He was trembling violently.

'What?' Kallad pressed. 'Let *what* escape?'

'The thing in the cellar.'

'No,' the acolyte whimpered. 'No. They couldn't... it couldn't escape.'

They all heard it: the sound of running feet. For a moment, Kallad believed that the sound belonged to the ghosts of this place, the dead locked in a never-ending cycle of flight and death. He shook his head, trying to dislodge the uncomfortable malaise that had settled about him since entering the cathedral.

He pressed Mann up against the wall. 'Let *what* escape?'

He didn't need the thief to answer. He knew. It made a sick kind of sense. The Sigmarites had taken one of von Carstein's brood prisoner after the siege, it was the only reasonable explanation for their fear. Now the beast was free and they had nothing to restrain it with. The holier-than-thou idiots believed that their god would protect them come what may. That kind of blind faith was dangerous.

'You didn't... tell me you didn't try to cage a vampire down there. Don't you people ever learn? Look at what the creatures did to your city–' Kallad was almost knocked from his feet by a frightened-faced priest as he came hurtling out of the kitchens. The priest's ceremonial robes were up around his knees and his sandalled feet slapped on the cold stone floor. The man looked as if he had come face to face with every daemon his faith had ever imagined into being. For a fleeting moment, Kallad pitied the fool, before he remembered that they had done it to themselves.

'The beast is free! Run! Run for your lives!'

Kallad bent down and picked up his axe. Ruinthorn was an extension of his soul, not merely a weapon. With it in his hands, Kallad Stormwarden was complete. Anger surged through his veins. The fools had tried to harness a daemon. The arrogance of manlings never ceased to amaze him.

He turned his back on the thief and the priest, and loosing a mighty war cry charged in the direction the frightened-faced priest had come from. He didn't care if the others followed him or not. A vampire was loose in the cathedral. One of the stinking creatures that had slain his family was within spitting distance. His thoughts glazed over with a veil of hatred. He would find the creature and he would rip its dead heart out with his bare hands and ram it down its gaping throat.

He stalked down the chill corridor, listening, but only hearing the echo of his own footsteps. The entrance to the vaults would, he reasoned, be off the main chapel, assuming that the vaults were part of the crypt or could be reached through the mausoleum. The other logical choice was the kitchens, since they would no doubt have access to either cold storage or a wine cellar. Either of these might link into the vaults. There was no guarantee of course. With these old buildings, the vaults could actually be some long forgotten dungeon with a secluded stairwell hidden away somewhere. He stopped at a corner as a whiff of cider and roses hit him, but laid over it was the unmistakable tang of blood. He followed his nose and found the kitchens. Knives had been abandoned in the middle of cutting a succulent shank of ham. Pots of vegetables stewed on the fire. There was no starvation in the house of this god. More importantly, he found a staircase leading down to the depths of the cathedral's cold stone heart: the cellars.

From there, he followed a narrow passage down until he found a fork that offered two choices, one to the depths of the crypts and the makeshift dungeons, the other back up to the House of Sigmar. The staircase down was thick with dust. Although it had been disturbed recently, it was definitely the path less travelled. He took the stairs down.

The air grew noticeably colder as he descended, prickling Kallad's skin. There was a peculiar quality about it. It wasn't like the air of the deep mines, there was no vitality to it. It was starved.

The smell of blood hung heavy in the air, richer and stronger than anywhere else in the cathedral.

It was a slaughterhouse reek.

The torches along the walls were dead, burned out. Kallad paused at the bottom of the stairs, listening. He could hear moans from deeper in the darkness. He followed the sounds through a maze of passages until he saw an open door.

Two priests were huddled over the dead bodies when he walked into the cell. He couldn't make out what they were saying – some kind of last rites for the dead, perhaps.

'Where is it?' Kallad asked, making sure the holy men saw Ruinthorn and were left in no doubt as to the meaning of his question.

Sammy Krauss stepped into the cell behind him. Neither Mann nor the Sigmarite had followed. Sammy looked scared but resolute. The lad had guts. Kallad hoped he'd get to keep them after the day was out.

'It's daylight,' Kallad pressed. 'The creature can't be far. Talk to me, damn it!'

He looked at the two bodies sprawled out across the floor, and the silver cuffs laid almost ceremoniously between them: one soldier, one priest. He couldn't understand how the beast had slipped its bonds, but it didn't matter. The creature was free and at least two men were dead for their foolishness.

The dead priest's robes were different to those worn by the others, marking him as special. His head hung back unnaturally on his broken neck, exposing puncture wounds where the beast had drained every last ounce of blood from his body. A crust had dried around the wounds. The soldier had shared a similarly grisly fate of a broken neck and bloody punctures.

Death was death, ugly and dirty no matter whom it befell. There was no special sanitised death for the devout. They bled and soiled themselves exactly the same as the thieves, whores and beggars. When it came, death was the greatest of all levellers. All men left the world equal no matter their station in life.

The tableau of butchery confirmed Kallad's worst fears. Instead of frightening him, the knowledge galvanised the dwarf.

The elder of the two priests looked up from ministering to the dead, the fallen priest's hand cupped in his. 'The beast is free.' His voice was as dead as the men sprawled out at his feet.

'Tell me,' Kallad urged.

'There is nothing to tell you, dwarf. The Lector believed he could trap a daemon. He was wrong. He paid for his error with his life. Now the beast is free and others will pay the same price, Sigmar save their souls.' The way that last, part plea part prayer, came out of the priest's mouth left Kallad in no doubt that the man's faith had been deeply shaken. Violence had a way of making weak men lose their religion and strong men find theirs.

'What are you doing here?' the second priest challenged, finally looking up. His eyes were red-rimmed with tears, his young face deeply scarred from the pox or some such youthful disease.

'Saving your life. Now, help me, instead of asking stupid questions.'

The sound of breathless running had them all looking towards the door as Felix Mann stumbled through it. 'It's killed dozens up there, dwarf. Bodies are everywhere.'

'Is it still here?'

'How the hell should I know? I came to find you because you've got an axe. The way I see things, you're my best chance of making it out of here alive so I am sticking about two steps behind you.'

'Show me,' Kallad said.

Kallad followed him through the vaults, up to the cellar and finally into the main floor of the cathedral. Neither spoke.

It was true. The pews were strewn with broken bodies, necks snapped and hanging impossibly, throats opened, blood congealing in the gaping wounds. Kallad counted twenty corpses littering the aisles of the great domed cathedral. The naked savagery of the attack was shocking. That it should have happened in the House of Sigmar made it doubly so.

They found fifteen more corpses scattered around the many rooms of the cathedral, left where they had fallen, necks broken, flesh tinged blue where the blood had been drained from them.

'How could one creature do this?' Mann asked, looking down at another ruined corpse. In death, the brothers of Sigmar looked distressingly alike, rigor ridding their features of any individuality.

Kallad didn't have a chance to answer, but like the thief, there was something about the scale of the slaughter that disturbed him. He couldn't see how one creature could wreak so much devastation unchecked. Surely someone should have raised an alarm. Nothing about the escape rang true. It was too... clinical.

A cold stone of certainty sank in Kallad's gut.

The creature wasn't alone.

Its escape wasn't some spur of the moment opportunity. Someone, or something, had freed the beast.

That led to the disturbing possibility that there was a traitor inside the cathedral.

Who could he trust? Could he trust *anyone*?

The answer was no. He couldn't trust anyone.

Kallad searched the library. The same instinct that told him the escape was not some random happening nagged him when he looked at the chaos that had been the cathedral's library. He picked up one of the damaged tomes, reading the words off the spine as best he could.

The frightened young acolyte that had met them at the gate found them in the library. The place was a mess. It had been ransacked, books ripped open, spines torn, pages scattered across the table. The librarian sat at the head of the table, his head lolling impossibly on his broken neck. Impossibly, well, impossibly for the living, not for the dead it seemed. The killer had taken the time to mock them, putting a book in the dead man's hands. The beast had gouged the old librarian's eyes out to complete the irony.

The young acolyte slumped into a chair across the table from the dead librarian, his head in his hands.

'They were my friends,' he said simply.

'They were fools for thinking that they could cage a vampire and make it dance to their tune.'

'It wasn't like that.'

'No?'

'No. The Lector thought that if we could study the beast we could learn its weaknesses. You can't beat an enemy you don't know, that's what he said.'

'Well the man was an idiot. Believe me, you can fight anything and anything can fight you, and only a complete idiot would let a blood-sucking monster into his home and not expect it to cause bloody murder.'

'But he–'

'Ain't no buts about it. How long was the thing here?'

'Since the siege.'

'But that was *years* ago.'

The young acolyte nodded.

'But you'd have had to feed it... blood.'

The young acolyte nodded again.

'Grimna's balls, man. Didn't you see what it was doing? Just by being here it was turning you all into monsters. You fed the thing blood?'

'Our own. We bled ourselves to feed the thing.'

'You gave it a taste for your own blood? Your own blood? And you kept the thing caged less than fifty feet beneath you as you just prayed to your precious god. Listen to yourself, even Sammy here wouldn't be naïve enough to think that was a good idea. Now you're paying the price for your stupidity. Ask yourself if it was worth it. When the beast is breaking your neck to get at the big fat vein pulsing in your throat, ask yourself if it was worth it.'

Silence stretched out between them, the truth of the dwarf's words heavy in the air. You couldn't cage a beast forever. At some point it would break free.

The young acolyte walked around behind the dead librarian, treading on pages of ancient texts. Kallad looked at the earnest young man. The light spilling in from the vast stained glass window of the library's far wall fragmented his face into yellows, reds and greens, and vast hues of sickly colours between.

Tears stood out in his eyes when he spoke.

'Kill it,' he said, simply. 'Find the monster and kill it. We have money. We can pay you. Find it and kill it before it causes more death.'

'Aye, that I will, but not for your coin. your money's no good to me. I want four good swords, reliable men, not the kind who lose their heads to panic in a tight spot and some kind of mage or sorcerer, and I'm thinkin' four clerics of Sigmar. We'll set out at dawn and have all day to hunt the beasts. They can't get far.'

'A sorcerer? We couldn't. Magic... it is outlawed. We couldn't sanction such a flagrant sin. It cannot be the only way, surely?'

'Do you want to catch the beast, man? We need magic, and I don't care a whit about your sensibilities. Without a magician we could be chasing round like blue-arsed flies, there's a huge world out there with places to hide, but any dead thing leaves the reek of corruption in the air. It ain't natural, see. What happens is the world cries out against it. Now, a good magician can smell the stink of a vampire on the winds of magic as the beast passes. With a magician, we can track the beasts from their own stench, and holy men are better for fighting the dead than even the best swordsmen. They've got faith *and* weapons.'

The young acolyte nodded sickly. His eyes were haunted. His hand hovered an inch above the librarian's shoulder, unable to rest on the dead man's shell. It was painfully obvious that he was remembering the countless times he had spent with the old man, talking, learning, and thinking about a better world. The events of the last hour had corroded a part of his soul. He would never be the same again. Kallad knew full well what was happening to the priest, it was the forge of life, he was being tempered by the evils of the world. He would either shatter or come out of the fire hardened and able to deal with the very worst the world had to throw at him.

'Nevin Kantor,' the acolyte said at last, turning his back on the others. 'The church holds his life forfeit for the abomination of petty magics. He is due to be executed by Grimm's guards I believe. Perhaps I can barter his freedom in return for him serving you? No promises, dwarf. Be ready at dawn. I will do what I can.'

When he had gone, Mann dragged out a chair and sank into it. 'The vampire wasn't alone.'

'No, he wasn't.' Kallad agreed. 'Someone helped the beast to escape.'

'Who would do such a thing?'

'Or what?' And that was what disturbed the dwarf. The violence was inhuman.

'You think another one of them did it?'

'Tell me, thief, could you deliver someone you hated to this kind of death? I mean truly hated, not just disliked. Feel the blackness of it in your gut and tell me, could you do this?'

Mann thought about it for a moment and shook his head. 'No. There's no humanity in it.'

'Exactly. Manlings may kill, no denying that. They're inventive when it comes to death. Sometimes they dress it up an' make like it is all noble, with rituals and duels, and sometimes it is vindictive, a knife in the night driven home by spite. But this, well I don't know about you, but this goes beyond any notion of spite I've ever known. Makes me think that maybe there's something to that story of yours, truth be told.'

Slowly, all trace of colour drained from the thief's face. He cast a fretful glance at the blinded corpse of the librarian as he laid his wrists on the table. 'You think it is him, don't you?'

Kallad Stormwarden nodded. 'Aye, I think it's him.'

'He's come to finish me because I know about the ring. Oh, sweet Sigmar!'

'Don't look to your god. This is your chance to reclaim your life. Stand up and fight or roll over and play dead, it's your choice and only you can make it. You're alive now, even when all these others aren't. That means it's not about you, not this time. Now, I'll only ask once, come with us in the morning. Slay the beast and get your life back.'

Mann stared at the dwarf, and even before he opened his mouth Kallad could hear the excuses shaping on his tongue.

'But what can I do? I'm a cripple, not some hero. I can't even wipe my own... How can I slay a vampire? Tell me what I can do.'

'Anything you want. Anything you want. Think about it.'

With the invitation hanging between them, Kallad left the library.

The priests had done a sweep of the cathedral, in every chamber, every storeroom, through the mausoleums and the crypts, even up in the vaults and on the rooftops. The beast was gone.

The long process of gathering the dead had begun. Grimm's guards had been summoned and word of the murders was out. Every bustle of movement was tinged with panic. It would take a long time for these people to recover from this invasive death. It was one thing to experience death, after all, Morr came for everyone eventually, but it was quite another to experience this kind of slaughter. Hardened soldiers weren't expected to face a cathedral more akin to a charnel house, and those that did lived with nightmares for the rest of their lives. Simple men like these would never be the same again. They had lost more than their brothers to the butchery, they had lost a part of themselves: their innocence.

That night could easily have been any of many nights from the dark days of the siege. The shadow of the vampires hung over the city once more, a grim shade that dredged up the worst and most painful memories of those desperate times. Kallad wasn't immune. He sat alone, removed from the soldiers as they fought to impose order over the panic of the clerics, remembering Grunberg.

'Will I never be free of these daemons?' he asked himself, staring at the dancing flames of the bonfire. The soldiers were burning the dead men's clothes.

'None of us will, dwarf,' the thief said, coming up to stand beside him. 'Our dreams will never be as empty again. We will never know the love of a good woman or the companionship of good friends. Our love now is vengeance, our friends: hatchet, axe and sword.'

'You are not as thoughtless as you would have others believe, are you, thief?'

'It would seem not. I'll not be coming with you, dwarf. Our roads go in different directions come dawn. That doesn't mean I intend to give up on life. There is something I need to do. Who knows, perhaps our roads will cross once more, some place far from here.'

'That saddens me, manling. Intelligent company is hard to come by. Still, I hope you find what you're looking for at the road's end.'

'Personally, I hope I never find the road's end. That's where we differ, dwarf. I'm not looking for the end. I thought I was. I thought I was looking for an end to life, because I didn't want to live it. What I should have been looking for was a turning point, a fork stuck in the road to show me where my new life began. There are so many directions we can go. We don't need to be in a hurry to get where we are going. Sometimes we need to remember that the journey itself is as important as getting to the destination.'

'And you're ready to start travelling again?'

'I'm ready to start travelling again.'

'And you're not just running away because your daemons scare you?'

'Of course I am, dwarf.' Felix Mann smiled. 'I'm getting the hell out of here and running as far away as I can, any half-wit would. If I am lucky I'll find somewhere I can start living again without being reminded of the beast every waking moment of every god-damned day. I want to die old and happy, dwarf. Metal hands or not, if I come with you that won't happen. Think of it as self-preservation.'

Kallad nodded, the flames reflected in his eyes. A soldier cast a bloodstained robe into the fire.

'Sometimes all we need to do is forget. Thing is, we can burn every last memory and we still can't manage it. Some old ghosts don't like to be laid to rest. You do what you have to. Anything's better than being left here to rot. May your god go with you, manling.'

'And yours, you.'

'Aye, I'll be needing all the help I can get.'

The priests left Kallad alone. Word had spread among them that he was leaving in the morning to hunt the vampire that had shattered the serenity of their cathedral. It hadn't turned him into their hero. There were no hearty slaps on the back, no unending flagons of ale to dampen his fears and wish him well on his way. Their looks left him in no doubt as to how they judged him. To them, he was a killer, just as the beast he hunted was a killer: there was no intrinsic difference in their eyes. He was the second bringer of death to walk the passageways of their home that day. It didn't so much puzzle him as sadden him.

Kallad *was* a killer, he knew that, he had killed many many times in his life, but he slew monsters. He protected those that couldn't protect themselves, people like the priests of Sigmar. He avenged those who had fallen, people like the priests of Sigmar. His kind of death was no arbitrary thing. Only the young acolyte was different, he was the only one that saw that Kallad wasn't a monster.

'Not yet, at least.' Kallad said to himself.

There was always the possibility, however, that a killer like Kallad could cross the line without ever realising it, becoming judge, jury and father confessor to the damned. It was a thin dark line to tread, with either side falling away into madness. The dwarf knew that. He was intensely aware that Ruinthorn brought death, and fiercely determined that it should only deliver to those deserving it. He had, after all, earned the name Stormwarden. It wasn't his people's way to easily grant names.

Kallad didn't want to be around the priests and the soldiers as they buried their own, so he retreated into the cathedral in search of an empty cell. A few hours sleep would do him good.

There was a chill about the place that hadn't been there during the day, as if the soul of the place had iced over come sundown. He found a room with a simple cot and blanket, and lay down to catch a few hours' sleep.

The thief had the right of it: the chance of Kallad growing old was slim at best. It was never something he had worried unduly over. He had sworn an oath to avenge his people. He would do that or die trying. From the moment he had stepped into the tunnels that led into the mountains around Grunberg he had ceased to be his own person and become an instrument of fate. On nights like these he felt the weight of it, but it was his burden to carry, and carry it he would.

Too tired to care, Kallad climbed into the cot fully clothed, drawing the blanket up over his chest, and closing his eyes. Despite his exhaustion, sleep was slow in coming, and when it did, it was fitful and disturbed. Scattered dreams were plagued with memories of Grunberg, the woman Gretchen and her baby. He dreamed of them often, wracked by guilt over his own actions. Even now, he was unable to come to terms with the fact that he had killed a child – even though the child was dead and turned, and was nothing more than a parasite feeding on its mother's tit. It didn't matter that he had had no choice. It didn't matter that it had become a monster. When he slept, he saw only a child, an innocent baby, dead at his feet, his axe bloody in his clenched fists. Kallad tossed and turned, Gretchen's screams bringing him back to jarring consciousness. Only they weren't Gretchen's screams. A priest somewhere in the labyrinth of the cathedral wept while another cried out, and another keened for the dead while others chanted, their lament far more unnerving than any tears. Together, the sounds had become the screams of his dream. He listened to the outpouring of grief. These people would never be the same again.

Long before the night was out, he gave up trying to sleep and went to sit in the secluded grove beside the Grand Theogonist's grave.

There, at last, he found peace.

The token he had pressed into the dirt reflected the twin glows of Morrslieb and Mannslieb.

'Peace be with you, brothers,' he said to the ghosts of the dead, knowing that their souls would have begun the long journey to Morr's underworld.

Come the first blush of dawn, the acolyte found the dwarf sitting beneath the weeping tree, eyes closed, Ruinthorn balanced across his lap. The young priest wasn't alone. Two more nervous-looking Sigmarites accompanied him.

'I talked to my brothers after prayers last night, urging them to help. It seems my request fell on deaf ears, or frightened ones. I could not get your fighters. However, we would come with you, master dwarf. These are my brothers, Joachim Akeman and Korin Reth.' The two men nodded to the dwarf. 'And my name is Reimer Schmidt. I have been assured that three of Captain Grimm's guards will meet us at the postern gate. Here at least I have not failed you. I am told the guards are most eager to avenge their leader. These are good men, brave, unflinching in battle, veterans of the siege. They know what they are hunting better than most.'

'And what of the mage?' Kallad asked without opening his eyes.

'His parole has been agreed, on condition.'

'I don't like the sounds of that.'

'No, I didn't imagine you would. The magician's life is forfeit, but the witch hunter Helmut van Hal has agreed that the freak can serve your quest as it feeds the greater good, but in return, when his usefulness to the quest is over he is to be... neutralised.'

'I don't kill in cold blood. It's what separates me from the monsters I hunt.'

'Then Kantor will stay here and die as is fitting for a soul touched by Chaos.'

'It must be good to be you, priest, content in your world of absolutes,' Felix Mann muttered, coming up behind the priests. He was packed to travel, a small satchel slung over his shoulder. 'Personally, I couldn't care less what happens to the magician. I'm pretty damned sure it's his fault that I ever ended up in this mess, so I can't pretend that it would worry me unduly if he fell off the end of the world in some tragic accident.'

'Are you coming with us, thief?' the young acolyte, Reimer Schmidt, asked. Kallad grinned at the holy man's discomfort. Travelling with killers *and* thieves was probably more than his principles could bear.

'Hardly. Only a fool would follow the dwarf where he's going, and I stopped being a fool sometime last night. What can I say? Better a live cripple than a dead hero.'

'You disgust me, thief.'

'I'm rather proud of him, myself,' Kallad said. 'Well men, let's wish Herr Mann well on his journeys, wherever the road might take him, and go fetch us a magician, shall we?'

'So you agree to the terms of his release?'

'I never said that. It's a long road and things can happen, let's leave it at that shall we?'

'Then van Hal won't release him into your custody.'

'We'll cross that bridge when we come to it, eh? Me and Ruinthorn here can be *very* persuasive when we have to be.'

CHAPTER FIVE
The Curse of the White Wolf

THE CITY OF THE WHITE WOLF, MIDDENHEIM
The dead of winter, 2055

IT WAS AN impossible task.

Jerek von Carstein knew it the moment that Konrad had confided in him, but the new Count would not be dissuaded. Konrad could not deny that the vampire nation needed rebuilding if it was to survive the scourge that was mankind, but the humans were hardly the sole enemy of the dead. They were their own worst enemies. The truth of it was all around him. The livestock around the castle were pitifully weak, drained to the point of anaemic uselessness by the few surviving vampires that had made it back to Drakenhof – restraint was not in their nature. They fed as they needed to feed. These were the last of their kind. Gone was the noblesse of Vlad von Carstein, and with it the wisdom of the Vampire Count. Vlad had known better than to exhaust the fresh blood around his castle. He cultivated the cattle, raising them for food, not slaughter.

Not so this new breed.

They understood only the most basic of urges. They hungered, so they fed. They didn't care that they were killing more and more humans, they were only cattle after all. They didn't care that there were none to replace the dead. There would always be more humans. That was their purpose: to be slaughtered for food to sate the never-ending hunger of the beast. Their lives were inconsequential.

Jerek had walked amongst them during the nights that followed Konrad's visit. It took no great wisdom to see that the remaining cattle would not make strong vampires. He had argued passionately with the new Count, trying to make him see how unsound his reasoning was. Better the few vampires that they had than swelling their ranks with the dregs of humanity. The weak would always fail, it was in their nature. A weak human would become a weak vampire. Weakening the bloodline was a mistake.

Konrad listened, but in listening twisted everything Jerek said to fit his own idea. All he succeeded in doing was convincing Konrad that the Hamaya must go abroad in search of new blood, blood worthy of being sired into the unlife. Each of the five Hamaya must seek out and sire five gets.

Jerek had argued against it because it would weaken the vampires, but Konrad had insisted. He had a vision of a new breed: the deadliest of the species come together as his people. That in turn demanded that their choices be careful ones. Konrad was right: these new gets were the future of their people. In turn, every new get would be forced to sire five of their own, and so on, making unlife a plague amongst the living once more. He couldn't deny that the plan had strategic merits.

The Hamaya were hand-picked from the survivors of Altdorf, the best of the best, most loyal to Konrad's claim to the title Count, strategists and bladesmen forged into an elite band of brothers. The bond between them was as close, Jerek swore, as any he had experienced in his other life as the White Wolf of Middenheim. They were not simply ruthless killers devoid of conscience and scruple. They were not undisciplined beasts driven by the base needs of their kin. They were more than that. They still had something – a spark of humanity that made them so much more than simply mindless beasts.

Jerek had picked them himself for exactly that reason. He knew that left to his own devices Konrad would have simply culled a handful of the most ruthless creatures from within his menagerie of monsters and erected a cordon of fangs around himself, hoping it was enough to ward off the inevitable. That was by far the biggest difference between the two: where Konrad saw weakness in humanity Jerek saw strength. That, perhaps, said more about the Wolf than it did about his master.

'Every leader needs one truth speaker amongst the gaggle of flatterers. Never be afraid to speak your mind, my friend,' Konrad had said. Never be afraid to speak your mind. They were easy words to say, but far from easy ones to live by in the court of the new Vampire Count. 'Few have the courage to stand behind their own words. I am no fool, Wolf. I know I have my share of flatterers, but I would be a fool if I ignored my one truth speaker.'

Therefore, Jerek had bent the knee and sworn always to offer his lord the truth as he saw it, not wrapped up in pretty words meant to flatter into deception. Even as he made the pledge, he knew that he would come to regret it.

With that promise spoken, he had returned to his home and taken to haunting the survivors he had left behind. At night, he roamed the Palast District, hugging the shadows along the north wall of the city. He prowled the Middenpalaz and its warren of buildings crowded in around the Graf's palace, he even stole into the ducal mausoleum to stare at the tombs of the men he had served in life.

He watched ladies walk beside their beaux in the Konigsgarten, and when he could put it off no more, he returned to the Square of Martials, descending the small flight of stairs into the great square to sit on the wooden benches and remember the days when he had drilled his men beneath the watchful gaze of Gunther Todbringer's statue. Sitting there brought back more ghosts than he cared to remember. This cobbled square was as much his home as any place in the world. He heard them all, the clatter of hammers, the buckling of shields, the curses and the cheers, and over and over the chant: 'Ulric! Ulric! Ulric!'

It was that memory that took him to the great bronze statue on the corner of West Weg and Sudentenweg.

'How did you find the strength to do it?' he asked the man of bronze. He didn't expect an answer, because there were no answers. Two children balanced on the statue's broad shoulders and a broken-backed rat was crushed beneath its foot. At the height of the Black Plague, Graf Gunthar had sealed the city gates for six long months, condemning thousands to die. It must have taken incredible fortitude to resist the temptation to open the gates when so many innocent people were dying, but Gunthar had had no choice, the gates had to stay closed to save Middenheim. It was an old story, but one worth remembering: from great sacrifices, great victories are born.

Jerek bowed his head and turned to enter the spectacular Temple of Ulric, the very heart of the city itself. Doubt touched him. Could the creature he had become walk into a holy place? Did enough of his self, enough of the White Wolf, remain to allow him to enter? He steeled himself.

This was it, his last farewell to the person he had been. It was true what they said, you could not go home again. It was only to be expected that a city changed, moved on. Like Graf Gunthar, Jerek was a thing of the past. Few, if any, would remember him. It was one thing for a child to return home a man and find that the streets he knew had grown smaller, but it was quite another for a dead man to return to a city only to find it so fragile and mortal. Everything about the place, even the stone walls that had seemed so resolute and unchanging, owned an air of transience, as if they knew their time was fleeting.

'I am a man,' he told himself, 'beloved of Ulric. That is what I am, not the beast von Carstein made me.'

He believed it, and his belief was so sincere that he stepped through the doors and stood still beneath the vast vaulted roof, amazed once more at the architecture that defied gravity's pull. He wasn't struck down for his temerity. In the centre of the temple, the sacred flame burned brightly. This was why he had returned home: a final test of himself.

He felt an unfamiliar sickness gnawing at his belly as knelt before the eternal flame. In his mind, he held the thought that had been with him since Konrad first issued the order for the Hamaya to breed.

The god had prophesied that so long as the flame burned the city would endure. The flame still burned and the city had withstood plague and the ravages of the Vampire Count's undead host, so perhaps there was an element of truth to the legend. If that was the case, then perhaps more of the old stories held true. One in particular rose in Jerek's mind: the sacred flame would not harm a true follower of Ulric.

Twisting the words of Magnus the Pious, Jerek whispered, 'If I am wrong then the flames will surely consume me,' and thrust his hand into the fire.

He stared at the flame and his flesh, feeling the agonising heat as it seared at his hand, but the flame did not burn him. Jerek withdrew his unblemished hand.

'Then perhaps I am not damned,' he said, turning his hand over to examine the perfect skin.

Despite the sickness in his gut, Jerek left the temple convinced that the Wolf God had given his blessing.

THE SIGN OF a hangman's gibbet and noose swung in the night breeze. The Last Drop was not the kind of establishment that Jerek Kruger had frequented in life. In death, it was made for Jerek von Carstein. Its iniquities were many and varied, and for that reason soldiers and thieves alike loved it. Jerek pushed open the door and stepped into the thick pall of smoke and stale ale that filled the taproom.

No one looked up; no one challenged him. The Last Drop was that kind of place. Patrons kept themselves to themselves. There was nothing to be gained by idle curiosity, but there was everything to lose.

Roth Mehlinger sat alone beside the fire, his gnarled hand closed around a tankard. Five years had worn hard on the soldier. After all that he had seen, it was no surprise he had sought solace in his cups.

Jerek sat himself at the table beside the man who had, in life, been his right hand, the Grand Master's Shadow.

Mehlinger had always been a loner, dour and taciturn.

The man's guilt at their failure was etched deep into his face. Black hair hung lank and greasy over his eyes. The Knights of the White Wolf had failed him, or he had failed them. It didn't matter. He was alone, and as Jerek had drummed into them over and over, alone they were weak, only when they stood together were they giants.

It was difficult to see the man like this.

'Hello, old friend.'

Mehlinger looked up from his drink. He didn't seem unduly surprised to see the dead man. 'Come to haunt me have you, Wolf?' He raised the tankard in a toast, 'Here's to the dead who won't stay dead, eh?'

The man was drunk. Jerek pitied him. It wasn't an emotion he was used to feeling. Indeed its wrongness only reinforced the message of the sacred flame – his humanity had not yet been expunged. There was some good in him, enough, at least, to feel pity for a friend.

'It doesn't have to be this way,' Jerek said.

'No? You mean I don't have to live through it day after day, drinking myself into oblivion and *still* unable to escape my damned daemons? You think I come here for fun?' Mehlinger waved expansively, his gesture taking in the whole taproom. 'You think these people are my new friends? I don't and they aren't. I come here to drink myself to death, maybe then I can escape, eh? Maybe then...' The irony of his own words was lost on the drunk Mehlinger.

'Come with me, Roth. Be my shadow once more.'

'Nah, got good drinking still to be done. You go haunt one of the others for a while, leave me in peace.'

'Come with me,' Jerek said again, pushing his chair back and standing.

'Can you make it all go away? Can you make it disappear? Can you take the things I lived through from my head and make me forget them?'

'I can,' Jerek promised.

'Ah, what the hell,' Mehlinger muttered, dragging his chair back. He staggered and almost fell, but Jerek reached out and steadied him. 'Let's go then. Look at me, going for a walk with my ghosts and leaving half a tankard of ale on the table to boot. Must be losing my mind.'

They left the alehouse together, Mehlinger leaning heavily on Jerek's shoulder for support. He led the old soldier away from the front door and the softly sighing sign, and down a narrow alleyway. Jerek pushed the soldier up against the wall, hard, and forced his head back to expose the pulsing vein at his throat. He sank his teeth in, drinking hungrily from his last living friend, gorging himself until Mehlinger was seconds from succumbing to death, and then he relinquished his bite, the soldier sagging in his arms.

'Join me, Roth. Feed on me.'

They shared the Blood Kiss.

He had fed on humans before, but this was different. This was intoxicating. This was exhilarating, but even as he felt his tainted blood mingle with Mehlinger's, he tasted the last shreds of vibrancy that had been the man's life. As it faded his gut twisted and clenched, the last vestiges of his humanity rebelling against the siring. Jerek gagged, coughing up Mehlinger's blood, but it was too late. The kiss had been shared.

In that instant, Jerek von Carstein hated the man that had been Kruger and Jerek Kruger loathed the beast that had become von Carstein.

'Why?' Mehlinger gasped, the vampire's blood running from his mouth. 'Why did you do this to me?' Hatred blazed in his eyes as he sank to his knees, dying.

Jerek couldn't answer him, but he knew then that he couldn't do it, he couldn't sire another soul into this unlife he lived.

'I am sorry,' he whispered into his friend's ear as the last breath of life escaped his lips. 'I am so sorry. I will be here when you wake,' he promised.

He saw out the night cradling the dead man in his arms. He hated the thing von Carstein had made him, but that was who he was now: the Wolf was dead and in his place walked a monster.

An hour before dawn, Mehlinger awoke.

CHAPTER SIX

All on a Summer's Night

NULN

The dog days of summer, 2056

A NATURAL BALANCE asserted itself between Skellan and the stranger as they travelled. By night, they ran as wolves, sharing their kills and feeding off the beasts of the field, but the blood of the lamb and fox and deer was no substitute for the blood of virgins or whores.

The hunger for real blood, the thick, intoxicating stuff of life, lured them into the villages and towns along the roadside.

The richness of it was impossible to resist.

It was in their nature to hunt and feed, but both revelled in the bringing of death and the intimacy of feeding. Any flesh, any blood, would have sufficed, but the pair developed a preference when it came to their kills. They liked them young and ripe for the taking, not soiled old hags. So they hunted the daughters and sisters, coming up on them in the dark, dragging them down into the dirt, tearing at their skirts as they kicked and struggled. Their desperation heightened the thrill of the kill. It didn't matter if they were farmer's daughters or the porcelain-skinned brats of the aristocracy, they begged and pleaded just the same as the vampires sank their teeth into them and they tasted every bit as delicious.

In Kemperbad they feasted on the blood of sixteen virgins in the shrine of the goddess Shallya while the statue of the goddess herself wept her perpetual stony tears.

They delighted in the profanity of it, defiling a holy place, ravaging the little mothers of the shrine while they cried out. It was more than death, more than merely taking lives. It was a ritual. It was a twisted glorification of all things beautiful, since they took only those closest to perfection, those who exemplified the feminine ideal. They dined on exquisite corpses. They sated their hunger on innocent meat, and they worshipped at the divine altar of sex, with passion.

They didn't just kill: they devoured.

They discarded the dead one by one, tossing them aside as they moved on to the next. The dead women sprawled across the cold stone floor, arms and legs akimbo, necks broken, the only colour on their otherwise alabaster-pure complexion the twin rivulets of blood that dribbled from the puncture wounds in their throats.

They became a plague on the countryside, leaving a trail of death in their wake.

In Striessen they savoured the kills, taking several nights to seek out the few jewels in the town's crown: three girls, the daughter of a pawnbroker, the sister of the silversmith and the young wife of a chandler. They were by far the most delicious of Striessen's offerings. Where Skellan was hungry for the kill the stranger urged him to take it slowly and savour it.

'Anticipation serves to heighten the sweetness of the feast,' he explained, standing on a street corner beneath the chandler's sign. A candle burned in the window above invitingly.

'Let me take her.'

'No, my eager young friend, we wait. We draw it out slowly, ounce by precious ounce, tasting it as it drips down our throats like the sweetest elixir.'

'I am hungry.'

'And you will be hungry again tomorrow. We wait. We are not savages. There should be beauty in all that we do, even killing.'

'You sound like *him*.'

'In many ways he was the best of us all, anyone who would be ruler of the vampire nation would do well to study his philosophies.'

'He was weak. At the death, when it came down to it, he was weak.'

The stranger shook his head, like a teacher disappointed in an otherwise apt pupil.

'It takes great strength to rule wisely. All it needs is a hint of weakness to succumb to your most base desires. Think on it.'

'I will, and you know what else? Tonight I will feed.'

With that, Skellan had scaled the outside of the building, climbing the clematis and other vines that clung to the façade of the old house, and tapped at the window.

His smile had opened the window. Her screams had been heard across the town.

The following night, he had claimed the silversmith's sister. This time they had sat on the thatch of her roof, deliberating the effect the chandler's wife's death had had on the small town. Skellan savoured the panic it had injected, while the stranger saw it as the death knell on their brief sojourn amongst the cattle. They would have to move on instead of being left alone to graze selectively for weeks and months more.

The girl's death was a bloody affair. She died in the window, shattered glass digging into her breast even as she sank down onto the wooden frame, the life leaking out of her as Skellan fed.

The pawnbroker's daughter was the last of the true beauties of Striessen to die.

'This one is mine,' had the stranger said as Skellan stood on the threshold.

'Is she now?'

'Yes.' And the way he said it left Skellan in no doubt that he was serious. 'Wait outside. Go find a goat or something.'

He left Skellan at the bottom of the stairs. The girl didn't scream once, although she was far from silent. By the sound of it, she gave herself willingly to the stranger, urging him to take her life.

It was too easy.

They left Striessen before dawn. The stranger urged caution, but Skellan was buoyed up on the adrenaline of the feast and argued for one last stop on the way home: Nuln.

They had to wait before they could enter the old capital. The wooden bridge had been drawn up to allow a three-mast schooner passage down the Reik. In places, the wall that ringed the city was low enough so that raiders would only need carts to scale them, not ladders.

It was easy to see why Nuln had fallen at the feet of Vlad von Carstein, where Altdorf had stood in stubborn defiance. The cities were not comparable. Nuln itself was a city within a city, an ancient core at the heart of the new city, still ringed by the crumbling walls that marked the boundary of Nuln's old town. The old streets of the Old City were so narrow that the two could barely walk side by side, so naturally, this was the busiest district of the city. The place was a curious hodgepodge of architecture. Each new generation had crowded in its own peculiar buildings, cramming them into spaces where there weren't really spaces, making the streets claustrophobic and unpleasant. Even as night gathered, the air was thick with the smoke of blacksmith's fires and the acrid tang of the tanner's newly treated hides.

Women of dubious repute congregated around the streets between the Merchants Gate and the City Gate, calling out to passers-by who looked as if they had coin to spare on a bit of rough and tumble.

Skellan drank in the many and varied pleasures of Nuln with relish. The lure of the big city called to him. On every corner there was a feast to devour. Every night for two weeks, Skellan stepped out, walking amongst the prostitutes as they worked the streets, feeding in the dark alleys before dawn, and disappearing into the remnants of the night while the stranger watched, biding his time, being careful to select the finest blood rather than the vinegar that Skellan drank so greedily.

It was no surprise that the spires of the great city inspired the pair to new heights of cruelty.

In the course of a single night, they changed the city forever. The ruling family, Liebowitz, was more than merely ousted, it was defenestrated, despoiled and degraded. Their deaths became the thing of legend.

'The Family Liebowitz will mourn this night for centuries to come.'

'You give the cattle credit for a long memory. In my experience, they fart, roll over and forget it ever happened,' Skellan said. They stood in the centre of Reiks Platz, listening to the chestnut vendor struggling to sell the last of his wares. The smell of caramelised sugar was a tantalising counterpoint to the all-pervading reek of leather.

'That, my friend, is because you do not give them something worth remembering. It's all petty pain with you. Back alleys, brothels, and smoke houses. It lacks any panache. Who cares if a prostitute dies? Who cares if some fool strung out on laudanum winds up dead in a gutter? Tonight, we walk into the houses of the rich and the beautiful, bringing death to the fore. We show the city that no one is safe, not even in their own home. The death we offer can find them anywhere. That is how you make them remember. You make death visible. You make it *frightening*.'

'I still don't see what they have done to deserve such thorough extermination? In every other killing you preach caution, but now you would have us throw it to the wind.'

'It is personal, a debt to be repaid, in full. I will say no more on it. Tonight, we sup on the blood of the aristocracy and see if it is truly blue. No more back street whores. The Family Liebowitz may rule the city for a few hours more, but their fall will be spectacular, and the people of Nuln will remember this night like no other. Tonight, we dine in a style befitting who we are, my friend.'

And they did. They killed both men and women, but they only fed on the women.

Two men died in their beds, fat with the gluttony of the truly rich, another had his neck broken and was thrown down the stairs, two more were given lessons in flight that they failed to master and died sprawled out across the cobbled streets.

The dead were not left to rot.

Together, Skellan and the stranger hauled them up to the rooftops where they impaled the corpses on thatching spikes and lightning rods, making scarecrows out of them. Seventeen more men died that night, only to be mounted like stuffed animals along the rooftops of the old town, but it wasn't about the men. The women suffered fates worse than death and degradation.

In all, they dined on eleven Liebowitz women.

As with their men, the corpses were stripped and impaled, upside down, through the mouth and down the throat, and left to feed the birds on the rooftops, but not before the pair had savoured their flesh to the fullest.

Even in the grip of the blood frenzy, the stranger was ruthlessly selective in his treatment of the cattle. He took only the best meat for himself, leaving Skellan to please himself with his cast-offs even as he moved on in search of better game.

Skellan followed him into the last house, the one the stranger had claimed for himself, into the woman's bedchamber, to where she lay beneath the sumptuous scarlet covers of her divan. The stranger moved silently to the bedside and knelt, whispering something in her ear that caused her lips to part and a forlorn sigh to slip between them.

Skellan lurked in the shadows, tasting his own blood as he bit into his lip. The stranger captivated him as he guided the woman, little by little, towards a willing death, until she finally loosed a single primal scream as the vampire's teeth found her pulse and penetrated her supple flesh.

The woman's blood fresh on his lips, the stranger held her beautiful corpse in his arms, and turned to where Skellan lurked in the shadows. His smile was cold. He touched his fingers to her blood where it ran down his chin and began to daub his name, in her blood, on the wall above her bed.

Three words, written in blood: Mannfred von Carstein.

In that moment, Skellan understood the nature of the stranger's power and the terror that this hidden message would inspire, claiming ownership of the slaughter as it did.

She was the one they didn't carry up to the roof. Instead they arranged her corpse so that it looked as if she merely slept deeply. It was a fragile illusion destroyed by the blood on the wall above her head.

Part of Skellan resented the way the vampire treated him like some stupid lackey, but a bigger part of him admired the stranger's economy of slaughter and the ritual aspect of it. The cattle would wake in the morning to find thirty-three naked corpses impaled on the rooftops of Nuln. It was a message that would be impossible to ignore.

As Skellan walked away from the last of the Liebowitz houses, he wondered how many of the onlookers would understand the full irony of the message: that these deaths mirrored the fall of Vlad himself. It was not only savage: it was beautiful.

The stranger was right: the cattle of Nuln would remember this night.

The stranger. He had to stop thinking of him as that.

The stranger had a name now: Mannfred von Carstein.

Mannfred, Vlad's firstborn.

The moons were still high in the sky, shining their silver on the streets as Skellan and Mannfred shifted into lupine form and bounded away from the city. After the frenzy of blood, the fresh air was intoxicating. They ran on into the night, taking shelter before dawn in a hermit's cave once they made certain the old man had no more use for it.

They slept the whole day through, only waking deep into the following night. Despite the feast, they were both starving and cold.

Skellan banked up a bundle of dry sticks and lit a small fire in the mouth of the cave. Outside, wolves howled, insects preened, their mating calls another layer to the music of the night, and bats flitted about the treeline.

'I know who you are,' Skellan said, turning his back on the night.

'I never tried to hide it,' Mannfred said, toying with the ring that he wore on his right hand. It was his only concession to adornment; he wore no other jewellery, no chains or broaches or other trinkets, only this solitary ring, which, Skellan had noticed, whenever he grew pensive he toyed with.

'But you never told me.'

'Oh, but I did, my young friend. I did. I told you many times, but you were not listening. I was his first, I said. He may not have loved me most, but he loved me longest, I said. I never hid who I was.'

Skellan poked at the flames with a stick. He watched as the ashes scattered, conjuring a short-lived flame sprite. Finally he said what was on his mind.

'Why are you here? Why are you hunting with me? Why aren't you in Drakenhof claiming your kingdom? It's rightfully yours.'

'Indeed it is. I am here because there is nowhere else at this moment that I would rather be. I am not embroiled in a bitter war with our own kind because it is not time yet. Believe me, there is a time for everything.'

Skellan looked sceptical.

'You have spent time in the form of a wolf, I know, but how much time have you actually spent as a wolf?'

'Is there a difference?'

'Oh yes, in the form of a wolf, you shroud yourself in wolf's clothing – it is merely for appearance's sake. If you surrender yourself, relinquish your grip on your identity and truly *become* a wolf, the petty concerns of this life cease to be important. You live to hunt and feed. You cease to be you and in turn take on the identity of the pack.'

Skellan nodded.

'What happens when the alpha male dies and the pack is left leaderless?'

'The survivors fight for dominance.'

Mannfred nodded. 'They fight amongst themselves, the contenders asserting their right to rule by strength and cunning. What some don't realise is that sometimes the fight needs more cunning than it does brute strength. Remember that every wolf is potentially deadly, even the runt of the litter. They circle and circle, looking for a moment to strike, and when that weakness arises they are bloodthirsty and brutal. They descend as one, bringing the opposition down, and pick the corpse clean. In any pack, the fight for leadership is bitter, and make no mistake, it could easily cripple the pack if too many males lock themselves into the fight for dominance.'

'Is that what you are doing? Using your cunning instead of your strength?'

'Fights are won by strength of arms, young bucks lock horns, it is all about bravado, swaggering and intimidating your enemy, but wars aren't won that way. Wars are a long game won by strategy. Answer me this: why wrestle all of my brothers, Pieter, Hans, Fritz and Konrad, when I need only fight one of them? The others will have weakened that one. You see, my friend, there are times when it is better to stand back and watch them struggle, and then challenge the winner when the others are dead and gone, don't you think?'

Skellan couldn't fault the logic.

'It makes sense. So while you sit by idly, they give in to the wolf and strive for dominance, not for a moment suspecting that you are waiting in the wings to dethrone the victor.'

'Something like that, yes.'

'It sounds exactly like that.'

'Only I have no intention of waiting idly in the wings, as you so elegantly put it. There are things I must do, preparations that involve me going away for a while. They will be occupied, no doubt, chasing their own tails.' Mannfred reached inside his pack, drew out an oilskin-wrapped package and began loosening the ties that bound it together. Tenderly, he peeled back the skin to reveal a book. Laying it on the ground between them, he turned to the first page.

Skellan couldn't read the scratchy symbols that scrawled across the top sheet – the ink had faded, soaking into whatever it was the book's maker had used for paper. It wasn't parchment, that much Skellan *could* tell.

Mannfred traced his finger over the crude design, lingering almost lovingly over the tail of what appeared to be a comet drawn in the centre of the page.

'There is power in this. More power than a fool like Konrad or an oaf like Pieter could ever dream of. While they strut and preen, and try to impress the lesser breed, let *us* learn from those long since departed. It was in this book, and in nine others like it, that Vlad found his strength. The wisdom of this book is unparalleled, but then its author was a genius. This is a distillation of power. The glimpse these pages give into the Dark Arts is unlike anything you can imagine, Skellan. With these words alone Vlad raised an army from the bowels of the earth: words, not swords. Words.'

'And you would use them?'

'I'd be a fool not to, and I may be many things, but I am no man's fool. These are only the tip, like a berg of ice. These incantations offer a hint of the power that lies below the waterline. It is intoxicating, my friend, and I admit, I want it all, but I am not ready for it, not yet. I'd drown before I'd even tapped an ounce of this power.'

'Then what good are they? All the spells in the world and you can't use them.'

'Oh I could use them, I could raise a great nation of the dead, I could despoil the lands of the living, turning it into a vast waste. With this power, I could shape the world to my whim, but in the process, I would lose myself. With great power comes far greater danger. Already I crave the power these offer. The temptation is huge to simply absorb all they have to offer and avenge our people, becoming a scourge on the Empire. It is already a canker in my unbeating heart. The thirst is unquenchable. I could destroy them. I could raise a glorious army with myself at its head. I could be worshipped and feared. The cattle would bow down at my feet and my enemies would tremble at my might. I want all of this and more – so much more. I dream of it at the height of day, and I dream of it as the shadows stretch towards dusk, I dream of it and I taste it, so real are my dreams. This world is mine, Skellan, mine for the taking. In my dreams I hold dominion. I rule.

'But, I am no fool. This power would consume me. I couldn't hope to contain it, not as I am. A wise man knows his limitations and weighs them against his ambitions. I know mine. I am no match for the maker of this book or the dark wisdom he imparted. Not yet, but I will be... I will be.'

'I believe you,' Skellan said, and he did.

'And yet, you have no idea what it is you see before you. Blind faith. Well, my blind friend, let me open your eyes: these incantations were crafted by the first and greatest of the necromancers, the supreme lord of the dead himself. Now do you see?'

'Nagash,' Skellan hissed through clenched teeth, the name as ephemeral as a dying breath as it faded into the flames.

'Nagash,' Mannfred agreed. 'With this power I could rule the world of the living, metamorphosing it into a land of the dead. With this power I would be unstoppable. However, with this power, I would condemn the thing I am, I would banish whatever it is that passes for my soul, and become *him*. I have seen how his magic works, seen the traps woven into the spells to draw the reader deeper and deeper into the darkness until it is too dark for him to find his way back to himself. I would not sacrifice myself for all the power in the world.'

'We have no souls. We are empty.'

'Do you believe that? Do you feel empty?'

Skellan didn't have an answer for that. He stirred the fire again, thinking about it. The power for revenge, for dominion over the Empire of the Cattle was there, before them, ripe for the taking. All he had to do was reach out and take it, but he couldn't.

As much as he wanted to, he couldn't bring himself to accept the gifts that the book promised.

'Then the book is useless,' he said, casting the stick into the heart of the flames.

'Today, yes, but who knows about tomorrow? Our paths, for the moment, lie in different directions, but they will merge again, of that I have no doubt. At dusk, I will leave you.' He raised his hand as if to forestall any argument. 'I must walk this road alone. While I am gone, though, I would have your help. I will need eyes and ears in the court of the Vampire Count so that when the time comes I will be able to claim what is rightfully mine.'

'You would have me be your spy?'

'Not only my spy, but so much more than that. The new Count will need friends. I would have you be one of them. I would have you get close to him, close enough to feed his uncertainty and bolster his ego. We have hunted together, Skellan. I know you as I know all of my brothers. Play to your strengths, make yourself indispensable and you'll have the pack dancing to your tune.'

'What is to stop me, then, from turning my back on you, using this influence to betray the surviving von Carstein's and taking the pack for myself? They know me. They have fought beside me. They have hunted with me, but, more than anything, they fear me because I have none of their weakness.'

'Yet, you were captured and they run free. You may not have their weaknesses, but you have your own, believe me. What stops you from claiming the pack? Two things: first, the sure and certain knowledge that when I return from the Lands of the Dead you will have to face me. I suffer no compunction when killing to get what I want, even when I have hunted with the victim. Second, the fear that will eat away at you that when I do return I will be both the Mannfred you know, and so much more. That will suffice. Be my instrument in the Court of the Blood Count. Be the voice in the night that drives my enemies to madness or be my enemy. It is your choice, Skellan.'

CHAPTER SEVEN

In the Court of the Blood Count

DRAKENHOF, SYLVANIA
The dying light of autumn, 2056

KONRAD VON CARSTEIN had surrounded himself with sycophants and fools, and he knew as much, but his need for platitudes and praise outweighed his need for forthright speaking. For that he had Jerek and his Hamaya. For everything else, he had the fools with their forked tongues.

He understood the nature of battle. He understood the need for wise council and truth speakers. He understood the need for strength and the need for cunning, but most of all, he understood that he was alone, and could trust no one.

He had seen men die – he had killed them. There was a natural order to it: the wolves slaughtered the lambs. It had always been that way, and it always would be that way. It was a simple philosophy, but its simplicity made it no less telling. Konrad knew better than most that the difference between life and death was a single heartbeat. He knew that the others would bring him down if they could, if they thought for a moment that he was a lamb. It was the nature of the beast: the strongest survived, and in strength became godlike, forcing those weaker to bow and scrape before them.

He felt the stirrings of fear as he prowled the passages of the castle. There were reminders of his heritage everywhere, of who he was, and what he was. The portraits of Vlad and Isabella had been vandalised, slashed with knives, the gilt frames bent out of shape. Some lay splintered on the floor while others hung on the wall still, a gallery of tattered canvases mocking the dead. He took no pride in being Vlad's get. Vlad had failed. He had succumbed to the most basic of all human weaknesses: love. It had been his undoing. Konrad would not fail. That was the only promise he made to himself. He would not fail.

Fear was good, it gave strength to the man who held it in his heart. It was a peculiar truth. He often heard others talk of fear as weakness, and every time, found himself believing the speaker to be a fool. A lack of fear was as potentially lethal as, say, panic or arrogance. Panic undermined a fighter, leaching away at the warrior's muscles, whereas arrogance left the warrior open to carelessness. No, no matter what they said, there was no shame in fear.

Konrad stared at the ruined face of his progenitor hanging from a broken frame. The knife had sliced through the canvas in a vicious X, dividing the face into four broken diamonds. In his vanity, Vlad had surrounded himself with his own likeness, needing the oils to remind him that he existed. They were not the same beast. Vlad had worn his cold arrogance like a shroud, but at the last, faced with the taunting of a simple mortal, he had surrendered to rage, and that anger had been his undoing. The dead Count had forgotten the simple lesson of fear. Had he harboured even an ounce of it for his enemy, he would never have fallen to the Grand Theogonist. His cardinal sin was in believing himself immortal. It was his vanity that led to it. He allowed himself to believe that he was special.

He had forgotten the truth: even the dead could die, and true death, *that* was worthy of fear.

Konrad turned his back on the man and continued on his lonely rounds of the ancient castle.

There were ghosts, of course, trace memories that lingered. He fancied he heard the laughter of Vlad's minions echoing from more than one chamber, only to open the door on an empty room and dust – so much dust. The sounds of women giggling and lusty calls of men in heat faded to nothing as he closed the doors and moved on.

He was alone, yes, but never truly alone. The ghosts of the conquered resided still in the old castle, clinging to the stones they had called home. Of course, people also surrounded him almost constantly, servants and sycophants ready to bend and scrape to his every whim.

It was a curious dichotomy. Konrad craved the very company that left him feeling so isolated and alone.

Then there were the cattle with their petty problems. They crawled like lice out of the woodwork, looking to him for salvation.

He was no one's saviour.

So, while they begged for mercy and petitioned for his wisdom to settle disputed land rights and grazing, or sought redress for the stupid thefts of loaves of bread and milk, he felt himself going slowly mad. He didn't care about them or their problems. They were cattle. They existed to be fed upon.

Why Vlad had thought them worthy of his time, Konrad had no idea. Perhaps it amused the dead Count to play lord and master? Konrad found no such amusement in the game, at least not when it was played straight. Changing the rules offered some possibilities. Improvisation was the secret to entertainment. Many of the petitioners he simply had thrown to the wolves, not caring if they were the wronged party or the wrongdoers. Their deaths were poor sport. They fell on their knees and begged and wept, a few even put up a fight, but in the end their bare hands were no match for the wolves' teeth. He saved a few special victims as treats for his necromancers to experiment on. It would teach the others a lesson: not to bother him with trifles.

Konrad savoured his reputation as a cruel count, even cultivated it: it kept the cattle in their place and sent out a clear message of dominance to his kin.

Konrad swept down the marble stairs of the grand staircase and through the great hall with its crush of penitents, ignoring the pleas and grubbing hands that reached out to touch him. He was in no mood for the smell of unwashed cattle – they stank and they made his home reek of bodily fluids. He paused, halfway through the hall, imagining the place aflame, the cattle burning away to nothing. There was something to be said for a cleansing fire. Smiling, he continued on his way.

The room he was looking for was buried deep within the bones of the old castle, beneath the cellars and the dungeons, even beneath the crypts. Once, it might have been a treasure house, but now it was a macabre gallery of sorts. The heads of thirty dead men, in various states of decay, were set on three, tiered rows of spikes. He knew every one of them, or had known every one of them well enough to kill them. Over the years, he had taken to collecting, as trophies, the heads of those that wronged him. It gave him grim satisfaction to know that in death they were his.

He visited the room regularly, using the captive audience to talk through his thoughts, looking for flaws in his reasoning. Talking aloud helped, and having an audience made the talking easier.

Only recently, they had started talking back to him.

It was nothing more than a word or two at first, little enough that he had doubted he had heard it in the first place. However, those precious few words soon grew into full sentences. He stopped hearing whispers of: 'murderer' and 'fiend' and found himself eavesdropping on conversations of treachery and betrayal as the heads argued amongst themselves.

'Still alive then?' the head of Johannes Schafer asked.

'Yes,' Konrad said, closing the door.

'We're surprised, considering,' the skull of Bernholdt Brecht mocked. Brecht was the oldest, his skin stretched like leather and smooth where the burns had taken his life. 'We hear things, you know, even down here.'

'You keep us locked in the dark, but we still hear whispers.'

The voices were a maddening chorus, their words interchangeable, their voices insubstantial and indistinct as they blurred around one another. Konrad could barely tell them apart as they became more animated.

'We know the darkest secrets of those around you.'

'You surround yourself with people who say what you want to hear, but behind your back they plot and scheme away, planning your downfall.'

'You place too much trust in those who say what you want them to say instead of giving you good council. You love the flatterers and ignore those who would serve you well. It will bring about your end.'

'You will not walk so tall then, dead man. Oh no, you'll be like us, stuck on a spike and left to rot, Morr take your soul to keep.'

'He already has it,' Konrad said, no hint of irony in his voice.

'No, it walks the long dark road searching for rest. It is locked in eternal torment, trapped between waking and sleep. There can be no rest, not for the killer in you, not for the boy in you or the man in you. Your soul withers in denial. The boy you were burns. The man you were burns. It never ends. The fire never ends. It consumes all that you were and all that you could have been.' The voices were in such a rush to talk that their words tumbled into a single demented voice, losing all separation and identity as they filtered through the thickness of Morr's veil.

'You aren't real. You think I don't know this? You are all in my head.'

'And you are in all of ours.'

'All of ours.'

'Yes. In all of ours.'

'If we are in your head our words must be the truth as you believe it to be. Welcome to your truth, Konrad. Welcome to your truth, a soul damned to the fires of hell, no rest for you, not when they send you on your way. Oh no. Not when the knife in the night cuts out your rotten heart and feeds it to you. No rest for you. Trust no one, not even your closest. Oh no, in the land of the blind, who can see the invisible threat? Who will remember you when you are gone and turned to dust? They circle around you, they are looking for a weakness to exploit, and they will find it. They will, because you are weak.'

'I am not weak.' Konrad lashed out, taking the head clean off the spike and sending it rolling across the floor.

The others laughed, a horrible mocking sound that threatened to deafen him.

He kicked the head viciously into the wet stone wall and walked down the line, hand drawn back to strike any head that goaded him.

'He will be first,' the last head said.

'Who will be?'

'The golden one, the one that shines brightest, the one that burns. All that glitters is fakery to lull the fool. To trust him is to die.'

Konrad paced the small chamber, clutching at his head as he tried to clear it, to think straight. The heads had never let him down before, in that regard their council was not easily discarded.

'How can I know?'

'Look in the mirror and see the lies reflected in the glass.'

Konrad laughed bitterly. 'I am surrounded by lies and liars, and none of them cast reflections. That is your wisdom? It is the curse of our kind to be invisible.'

'The invisible threat is the one that the wise man fears most, because they are like you. They are weak and their weakness drives them. They are not to be trusted, like snakes. Snakes, yes. They are snakes, not to be trusted. Oh no, not to be trusted.'

Konrad knelt, gathering the fallen head in his hands. Slowly and deliberately he impaled it back on its spike.

'This is insanity.'

'These are your thoughts, aren't they? This is your wisdom, spoken aloud. Trust no one. That is the wisdom we offer you. Heed it. You should. It could save your life.'

The voices fell silent as one.

There was nothing left to say.

Someone would betray him, someone close to him. Someone he thought of as a friend: the Golden One.

Konrad walked along the line of faces, studying them one at a time. None spoke.

He prodded them with a finger, poked them, held either side of their jaws and tried to force them to speak, but they had nothing to say.

They had imparted their wisdom.

He wanted to dismiss what they had said, but he couldn't. They knew things they couldn't know. They knew things *he* didn't know.

And still they came to pass.

He sat a while in silence, thinking about what they had said. There was no great trick to it. All men of power surround themselves with advisors of ambition and hunger. Treachery is a part of their hearts. Few who strive for power are pure. To say that the seeds of his downfall were all around him was nothing more than his own paranoia talking, sowing the seeds of doubt.

Yet even the paranoid man can have good reason to fear those around him.

He was not von Carstein's only heir, but for now, he had the support that gave him power enough to hold off the threat of the others.

That might not always be the case. He would have to be a complete fool to think otherwise. Loyalties shifted. People could be bought and sold.

He was playing the long game. He needed to cement his power, become the undeniable master of the vampire nation.

While the others lived there was always the threat of usurpation. They were strong, among the strongest of Vlad's remaining kin. They were von Carsteins. The legacy of Vlad's tainted blood flowed in their veins. The irony was that he needed to build up the strength of his people, yet his paranoia would have him tear out the heart of them to save his own skin. Given the chance, they would kill him. He knew that. He couldn't allow them the chance.

However, before the game played out, he would have to deal with them.

It was the only reasonable solution.

Konrad left the room of heads. He found Constantin in the library. In another life, the vampire had been a scholar with an uncanny grasp on the histories of the Old World.

'How goes it?'

'It goes,' Constantin said, scratching the back of his head with ink-stained fingers. Papers were spread out on the desk before him.

Konrad settled into a chair beside the first of his own gets. He felt an acute bond with Constantin. It was almost fatherly in nature, and like any father, he had high expectations and higher hopes for his son. He steepled his fingers and feigned interest in the peculiar sigils scrawled across the papers laid out in front of him.

The new library was just a small part of Konrad's legacy, but it was a vital part. With knowledge came power. By surrounding himself with great knowledge gathered from the four corners of the world, Konrad hoped to secure even greater power. He ached when he thought of the wealth of knowledge that his sire had lost in his folly. No doubt the damned Sigmarites had burned everything and Nagash's genius was lost to the world forever. It was a sickening thought. With a single spell, Vlad had raised an army from the dirt. What could he, Konrad, have done with that power at his disposal? That was Vlad's other sin: he had lacked imagination. Power existed to be unleashed.

'I see you are making progress.' Konrad gestured at the spread of papers.

'Cataloguing this would take twice my lifespan,' the scholar said, and then seemed to remember that his world had changed and he had time enough at last to read all of the books in this vast library, and then more. 'I suppose you are most interested in the histories?'

With Constantin's care, Konrad's library would rival any house of learning across the world when it came to tomes of magic and ancient knowledge. The histories were Konrad's own addition. With the scholar's aid, a new version of his life was being fed into the history of the old world. It didn't matter if the stories were lies, given time they would merge into truth. Konrad could create his own dynasty, tracing his blood back to Vashanesh, the first great vampire, and eventually enough people would believe the lies and the lies would become accepted truth. That was the wonder of knowledge; it was fluid, malleable.

Konrad had studied the history of the Empire as much as father, mother and circumstance forced upon any aristocratic boy – it didn't do to be ignorant amongst your peers. He knew of the plagues and the wars, the triumphs of spirit and the darkest days when all, it seemed, would come to an end. The dates and details had lost their clarity, but it didn't matter. With Constantin, he was slowly rewriting the world, one page at a time.

'And the... ah... other matters?'

Konrad had no gift for the arcane and so, of course, found himself utterly fascinated by it. He sought to learn everything he could from the likes of Constantin who had a natural grasp of it, but the more they explained, the less he understood.

'When documents of interest surface they are taken down to Immoliah Fey. She is most grateful for your sponsorship, my lord, and hopes to repay your trust when the time is most pressing.'

There was that word again: trust.

'Indeed, nothing in this world is given freely, Constantin. She knows that I expect something in return for my generosity. The day will come when I extract my price, whatever it may be. There is no trust involved in our relationship. I command her, master to servant. Tell me Constantin, is there trust in our relationship?'

'My lord?'

'Do you trust me, and more to the point, should I trust you?'

The scholar thought about it for a moment, which pleased Konrad. It wasn't an automatic response. He wasn't kow-towing to his lord. He was weighing up the various aspects of their relationship. If that was not a sign of trust, what was?

'No, my lord. I fear there is little or no trust between us. For my part, I live in fear that I shall displease you and suffer the fate so many others have. You brought me into this life, and blood aside, this life is not such a bad place to be, but there is no trust there, only fear. For your part, I suspect that you covet that which you do not have, in this case, that would be knowledge. You see these papers and you despise the fact that they mean nothing to you. You hate the weakness that highlights in you. It means, despite your strength, that you are the lesser man in at least one regard, so, you intend to leach out what you can, and then crush me when you have bled me dry. There is no trust there, only bitterness.'

'You are a perceptive man, Constantin.'

'For all the good it does me, my lord.'

'Ah, but you see, ours is a healthy relationship, is it not? We have a respect for one another, founded on fear perhaps, but it is a mutual respect. We need each other.'

'One day my usefulness will come to an end,' Constantin said, picking up his quill and dipping it in the inkwell beside the open book, 'and that is the day that I die.'

'Then it is up to you to make yourself useful, is it not?'

'I try, my lord,' Constantin said.

'I would have you write a ballad, something heroic. It would be good to have troubadours singing of my triumphs, don't you think?'

'It shall be done,' Constantin said. 'Your legend shall be sung across the land.'

'You are a good man, Constantin. I hope you will always be as useful to me.'

'As do I, my lord.'

Konrad pushed his chair back and rose, pausing midway as if struck by an impromptu thought. He nodded to himself. 'At tonight's feast I would have you join the top table.'

'It would be an honour, my lord.'

'See if you can't have something to perform, there's a good man.'

'As you wish, my lord, although it may be a little... ah... hurried.'

'I have full confidence in you, Constantin. You won't let me down.'

The scholar began to scratch hastily at the page in front of him, only to score out the line he had written. Konrad left him to work in peace.

THE FEAST ITSELF was a drab affair, unlike the banquets he had enjoyed in life. The Hamaya had selected ten lucky penitents to be the centrepiece of the feast. They were stripped and bled slowly, one by one, their thick red blood decanted into goblets and passed among the creatures at the top table, still warm. Jongleurs juggled and took pratfalls, but it was all rather dull. Konrad was bored by the whole affair. He gave a lazy wave and the performers were dragged from the stage, joining the delicacies on offer. Their deaths raised a smile from the Vampire Count.

'Some entertainment at last,' he said, leaning over to Pieter.

His brother grunted.

'You always were easily entertained.'

Pieter had been changed by his days in the Drak Wald. They all had, but Pieter more so than the rest of his twisted mockery of a family. He had regressed, become almost animalistic in his mannerisms, and he fed as though every meal might be his last. It was disgusting.

He had made his play for power in the forest, challenging Jerek's right to lead them to safety. The Wolf had slapped down the challenge, effectively emasculating Pieter. He was by far the weakest of them now, reduced to sneaking around, sniffing for victims in the dark like some low hunter, a ferret or a stoat, or some such animal used to living in the filth of humankind.

Emmanuelle, Pieter's wife, was a different monster altogether. He could see why Pieter had chosen to sire her. It was not for beauty; she was interesting more than attractive and the angles of her face were all slightly askew. No, Pieter had sired her for the woman she had been. Even now, the mortal shone through, eclipsing the immortal. With her lips rouged by fresh blood and her eyes wells of lost souls, it was easy to see that in life the woman must have been enchanting. In death, she was magnificent.

Beside her, Hans looked less than amused. Of them all, he was perhaps most like his sire. There was an edge of detachment about him, but it cracked easily beneath his vile temper.

Jerek lurked in the shadows, not joining them at the top table. He never did. Hans could not stand the Wolf. He made no secret of his disgust that Vlad should have soiled the bloodline with a brute like Jerek. In mock deference, Jerek chose to put himself as close to Hans as he could at any given time, stoking the embers of the vampire's temper. He would serve as Hans's personal bodyguard at feasts, knowing it riled Hans. He felt, Konrad was certain, that his own place in the family was threatened by the last of Vlad's gets. It was difficult for Hans to be the bigger man. At times, he was curiously childish, like a brat that had been spoiled and subsequently found it maddening not to get his own way.

Fritz, the last of the brothers, sat beside Constantin; he was the sun to Hans's moon. Where Hans was sullen and took to brooding, Fritz was gregarious and garrulous. He surrounded himself with a coven of gets, seven glorious women who crawled all over each other to satisfy even his most basic whim. In life he had been a hedonist, in death he satisfied his every desire, no matter how extreme.

Lesser vampires sat at benches around the walls, where they satisfied themselves with some of the local meat.

'Bring on the dancing girls,' Fritz said, clapping his hands. His seven gets moved to centre stage, dancing with veils of finest silk, their movements supple and erotic as they danced for their father-in-death. Fritz crossed his hands across his belly and sat back to enjoy the show.

Konrad stared at the women. They made him uncomfortable with their provocative dance. He saw his mother's disapproving shade behind them, her twisted face shattering the frisson of intensity for him. Still, he watched as they moved, bringing out curved swords that they placed on the floor and adopted into the dance, bringing a dangerous edge to the sensuality of their movements.

Breathless, Konrad watched as the swords flashed and the skin tantalised, and then it was over and the seven women threw themselves to the floor to the rapturous applause of Fritz. Others joined in as the women rose, and soon the great hall was full of appreciative applause. Konrad stood, bringing his hand down for silence. His control over the crowd was complete. He nodded.

'I think it is time we partook of another delight, having stuffed our faces with fresh meat, and satisfied our eyes with these young ladies. It is time to look to the future. After that, I believe young Constantin wants to treat us to a ballad of his own creation. First though, the soothsayer, please.'

Two of Konrad's Hamaya escorted a filthy little man between them. He led a goat on a rope up to the top table and bowed stiffly. The goat was little more than skin and bones, and its master looked no healthier.

Pieter stifled his giggles.

Hans shook his head in disgust.

Fritz clapped delightedly, while Constantin, at the end of the table, looked decidedly uncomfortable.

Emmanuelle was looking at Konrad, not the curious little man and his goat. He found it impossible to look away. Was it wrong to covet his brother's get? He was sure it was, but then, so much of the very best things in life were wrong. That didn't stop him from wanting them.

'My dark lord,' the soothsayer muttered, trying to claim Konrad's attention. 'Speak what you would know, and we will consult the omens.' He pulled a slim, gem-studded ceremonial dagger from the rope band cinched around his waist. He brought it to his lips and kissed the blade's edge. 'What is it to be, lord? What questions burn in your heart?'

The word 'burn' jarred in Konrad's head. It seemed to haunt him today. He turned to take in the little man. His skin was dark, although it was dirt not tan that muddied it, he was thinning on top and his beard was scraggy.

'I would know the future for House von Carstein, fortuneteller. Speak to me, man. You have us all on tenterhooks. What is the wisdom of the gods?'

Two of Konrad's loyal Hamaya lifted the goat onto the central table and held the beast by the scruff of the neck, covering its eyes with a hand until it calmed. The animal was understandably skittish. The thick tang of blood was heavy in the air.

'Hear our words, oh goddesses of discord, oh gods of dissension, show what the fates have in store for this great house, peel back the dark shadows, illuminate the path to wisdom, show us the clefts where failure lurks in wait, we ask this of you. Show us.' With that, the little man thrust the ceremonial dagger deep into the goat's belly, tugging on the blade until the animal's guts spilled out across the table, black and bloody as they slopped over the diners and their food, and spilled down onto the floor. The goat convulsed in his arms, its hooves kicking and sliding through the reeking string of guts. When the beast's death throes subsided, the soothsayer dumped its carcass on the floor and knelt to study the omens offered up by the animal's entrails still smeared across the table.

The soothsayer looked up, fear written bold in his ugly face. 'The omens are not good, lord.'

'Not good?' Konrad said, raising an eyebrow. 'Explain.'

The little man swallowed and rose to his feet. Even standing, he was no match for the Vampire Count. 'The guts are rotten, lord. The beast's flesh is putrid. This is a bad omen.'

'Indeed, perhaps we have another beast to hand that you can divine some mystical insight from its disembowelling.'

'This is ludicrous,' Hans objected. 'Must we sit through this chicanery? I for one have better things to do.'

'You will sit down,' Konrad said calmly.

Hans stood.

'I said you will sit down,' Konrad repeated, an edge creeping into his voice as he rose to meet Hans.

'I will do no such thing.'

'Brothers, brothers, let's just enjoy the show, shall we. Look, they're bringing in a sheep to gut. This ought to prove most entertaining, as our frightened little soothsayer looks to predict a glorious future to save his own skin.' Fritz stood between the pair. 'This really is unnecessary. Show some decorum, please.'

Grunting, Hans sank back into his seat. He made a show of teasing off his gloves one finger at a time and cleaning his nails with the tip of his knife, studiously not looking at the soothsayer as he gutted the sheep.

The animal's entrails were putrid.

Terrified, the little man looked up at the row of vampires sitting at the table before him. His tongue cleaved to the roof of his mouth as he struggled to speak the doom he read in the spilled guts.

'Betrayal lurks on every corner. Betrayal will be your downfall. Friends cannot be trusted.'

'Give me your knife, man,' Konrad said, coming round from behind the table.

He held out his hand.

'Now.'

The little man passed the vampire his thin-bladed knife, his eyes alert, darting with fear. Konrad enjoyed the momentary thrill of power that coursed through his body as he drove the point of the knife into the soothsayer's stomach. He opened the man up, even as the soothsayer screamed and tried to hold in the ropes of blue intestine as they spilled between his fingers.

'Now, I am no magician, but I suspect, looking at the signs here, that the future is bright for House von Carstein. Very bright indeed.' He kicked the dead man. 'I am equally sure that if he could speak, our soothsayer would agree. Alas, it seems the divination took rather a lot out of him.'

'Oh, this is preposterous,' Hans said, in disgust. He rose, picking up the leather gloves from the table. 'You are a disgrace to the family. Everything about you is vile. You are an aberration. You strut and pose, and act as if you are superior. You act as if you are *him*, but I have news for you, brother: you are not him. You are not worthy of his name. You are a disgrace. You always have been, you always will be. The soothsayer is right, if we follow you, we march willingly to our own doom!'

'How dare you,' Konrad said.

No one else moved as Hans came around the table and slapped Konrad across the face with one of the gloves.

'A duel!' Fritz cried out delightedly.

No one listened to him.

Still holding the bloody knife, Konrad, sneered and pressed the keen edge of the blade up against Hans's cheek. 'I could gut you here and now,' he rasped. He applied pressure to the blade, enough to cut the skin. It drew no blood. Konrad licked at the blade, tasting the soothsayer's blood. His smile was filled with predatory cunning.

'You could try,' Hans said coldly.

'Our brother is right, you have called me out. Your bloody sense of honour will be served in the last minutes before first light. We will settle this once and for all, *brother*. I will give you a few hours to regret the rashness of your actions, and then I will meet you in the duelling hall where your gets can watch me cut your heart out. Now get out of my sight.'

It was Fritz's idea to add fire to the spectacle.

They banked timbers up along both sides of the duelling hall and doused it in oil. As the duellists faced off, they would apply a torch to the wood and make things interesting.

'This is all so childish,' Emmanuelle said, taking her seat in the gallery. For all that she obviously disapproved, she was more than happy to partake in the proceedings.

'On the contrary,' Constantin said, leaning in to talk quietly. The duelling hall had odd acoustics. Words had a way of carrying further and louder than intended. 'A duel of honour is the last bastion of civilization, my lady. The situation might be contrived, but it is designed to maximise fairness of combat. It is likely that either Hans or Konrad will die in just a few moments, and in their death will prove the right of the victor. Scholars call it the last resort of law. It is a fascinating process.'

'It is barbaric.'

'On the surface, perhaps,' Constantin conceded, 'as all forms of war are, but beneath the surface it is immensely cultured. Consider the phrase "throwing down the gauntlet". This comes from the ritual of the duel. One accepts the challenge by picking up the gauntlet or glove, and there are, of course, many alternatives that could provide satisfaction. First blood, which of course means the first man to bleed would lose, but given our nature that is rather inappropriate, I am sure you would agree. Hans could of course have chosen to demand the ultimate price, to the death, in which there is no satisfaction until the other party is mortally wounded. He would equally have been within his rights to cease the duel when either of them is incapacitated, albeit not yet fatally.'

'You know a lot about fighting for a man who locks himself away with his books day and night.'

'It is precisely for that reason, my lady. There are things of interest in every book. The word "duel", for instance, could have derived from the old Imperial word for war, "duellum"; but it could equally have originated from the word "duo", giving new meaning to one-to-one combat. My personal favourite is actually much older, coming from Reikspiel, "teona": "to burn", "to destroy". The gauntlet of fire is a fitting addition to the proceedings. It certainly adds an element of danger to both participants. Only the strongest of our kind can resist fire. Many peasants still believe the way to destroy a vampire is to burn it.'

On the duelling floor, Konrad turned to stare at the pair in the gallery. Constantin lapsed into silence, assuming his constant chatter had disturbed his sire's preparation.

Grinning, Fritz leaned in from behind the pair. 'You know, Constantin, you really do need to get out more. I could send some of my girls to your library to... ah... help you forget about those books of yours for a while if you like? If nothing else, they could most certainly offer you a unique avenue of study for a while.'

'Fritz, you are incorrigible. Now, stop trying to corrupt young Constantin.'

'Yes, sister-mine. You take all the fun out of life, Emmanuelle, do you know that?'

On the floor, Konrad ran through a series of stretching exercises, both with and without his daemon sword in his hand. He moved with the grace of a natural gymnast, supple and lithe in the way he shifted from pose to pose. His balance complemented his graceful movement. The speed with which he ran through the exercises turned them into a beautiful kind of dance. The fluidity of the dance was hypnotic. There was an arrogance to it that was almost brutal. He took a silk cloth, tossing it into the air, and spun, bringing the sword to bear. The silk parted into two on either side of the blade and fell to the floor as Konrad sheathed the sword.

He looked up as Hans entered the duelling hall.

'I had begun to think you had come to your senses, brother. I am glad to see that I was mistaken. I will give you a moment to prepare. I would hate to be accused of foul play.'

Hans rolled his shoulders and then turned to bow to the gallery. He turned back to Konrad.

'You are an insufferable windbag, Konrad. It's time you were cut down to size.'

'Ah, but are you the man to do it, brother?' Konrad sneered. 'Personally, I think not. We shall see, soon enough. Seconds, light the fires, if you would.'

Two of Konrad's Hamaya touched their torches to the oil soaked wood, and a tunnel of fire was born.

The heat was staggering.

At either side of the duelling hall, a necromancer tapped the winds of magic, channelling the flame to make sure it didn't rage out of control. A single word from either of them would douse the conflagration before it could spread further into the castle.

Konrad drew his sword and stepped into the tunnel of flame.

At the other end, Hans matched him, his own sword a slim, slightly curved, blade that was unique to his native land. He touched the sword to his lips and stepped into the flames.

The duel was not graceful.

Hans launched a reckless lunge, the flames pressing in around his shoulders, which Konrad easily sidestepped and countered with a cuff from the pommel of the daemonic blade, and with an easy laugh meant purely to goad Hans into even more recklessness. It succeeded.

Konrad swatted aside two more thrusts from his brother, his smile broadening with each.

The only sounds in the duelling hall were the clash of blade on blade and the snap and crackle of the flames building into a genuine blaze.

Konrad allowed Hans a moment's respite, trading parries before he countered with his first serious attack. Hans was no match for either Konrad's reflexes or his swordsmanship. He had no intention of allowing his brother dignity in true death. He wanted the vampires in the gallery to see him for what he was: their better. He took three steps forwards, and rather than launch a feinted move, a combination of blows ending in a high cut, which Hans would have expected, he thrust hard, driving the daemonic blade into his opponent's upper arm. The blade pierced deep into the muscle, causing Hans to lose his grip on his own blade. The curved sword clattered to the floor. In that moment, Hans knew that he was dead.

Konrad showed no mercy.

Untouched by the flames licking around his feet, Konrad stepped in close, drawing Hans into a deadly embrace.

'You're dead,' he rasped, and then pushed his foe back so that he stumbled trying to catch his balance. With dizzying speed, the daemonic blade swept around in a vicious arc, cleaving Hans's head from his shoulders in a single cut.

Konrad didn't stop there.

He cut his fallen brother up, and piece by piece fed him to the flames, while the others looked on.

'He who burns brightest...' Konrad said, laughing. 'So much for the Golden One.' With the fire blazing around him, Konrad walked from the hall.

In the gallery, Fritz rose to his feet and applauded.

'That, my friends, is a true von Carstein.'

'That,' Emmanuelle said, 'you idiot, is a true monster.'

'One and the same, my dear: one and the same.'

'Your ignorance is dazzling, Fritz. Don't tell me you can't see what just happened.'

'Hans was a fool. He allowed himself to be manipulated into a fight that he had no hope of winning.'

'And next time it could be you, or Pieter, or me, or whoever, dear Konrad believes is a threat to his blessed reign.'

'I am no fool, sister-mine.'

'Oh, I think you have just proved that you are, Fritz.'

CHAPTER EIGHT
Slouching Towards Sylvania

THE BORDERLANDS OF SYLVANIA
The first kiss of snow, winter, 2056

THERE WAS SOMETHING about the magician that made Kallad Stormwarden distinctly uncomfortable.

He was not like other manlings he had encountered. It wasn't that he was distracted and seemed to spend most of his waking hours lost inside his own head. It was not that the man was unreadable where most manlings wore their allegiances proudly, like badges of honour. It was not that the man spoke in cryptic rhymes of things that made little or no sense to the dwarf.

It was much more simple than that. Kallad did not *like* Nevin Kantor.

Still, he was necessary. Without the sorcerer, their pursuit would have been next to impossible. Kantor paused on the rise just ahead, apparently sniffing the air. The dwarf knew that the unnatural passage of the dead left a stink on the winds of magic, rich enough to be followed by a deaf, dumb and blind adept. Kantor had explained it to them on that first night, so many moons ago. The dead were an abomination and as such were reviled by nature. The winds were sensitive to the nuances of the world they flowed over, and picked up traces of nature's revulsion, fashioning a tainted ribbon that could, in theory, be tracked on Shyish, the sixth wind, all the way to the beasts themselves.

Kantor disappeared over the rise without looking back to see if the rest of the party followed.

Grunting, Kallad shouldered his pack and set off after the magician.

Kantor was tall, even for his kind, although it seemed that he possessed no more flesh than the soldiers that journeyed with them, which left him looking gaunt and emaciated by comparison. His hair was drawn up in a topknot and the sides had been shaved high above his ears, in the fashion of the corsairs.

The magician had led them to Nuln as the month slipped into Vorhexen. The butcheries of the vampire, Jon Skellan, were all too apparent inside the walls of the old town. The streets teemed with gossipmongers, and charlatans offering protection from the vampires with their gewgaws and talismans. The charms were of course useless, but the peasants were willing accomplices in the trickery, needing to believe that they offered some form of protection. Every other person they met in the streets wore the sigil of Sigmar on a chain around his neck. The rest carried more practical forms of defence: stakes, garlic cloves, bloodwort, wolfsbane, vials of water blessed from the temple fonts of their chosen deities, and silver. Merchants traded their share of the season's harvest for the silver to fashion into daggers and amulets. Superstitious fear gripped the city.

The conversations on every street corner returned again and again to the bloody fate of the ruling family, the Liebowitzes. Their bodies had been buried in the family mausoleum, face down, their coffins sealed over with huge slabs of stone.

No one was prepared to risk their return.

They had stayed in the city for four days, learning what they could from the gossips, but it was next to useless. Reports varied from Vlad von Carstein himself having returned to savage their city, to a vast horde of the undead descending in a single night's depravity. There were stories that informers working with the beasts had walked through the city during the day marking the houses for slaughter and making sure that members of the blue-blooded aristocracy were singled out.

In a peculiar way, the locals had come to think of the beasts as liberators as well as monsters.

This was a revelation to Kallad.

Nuln had a marked effect on the others. The sense of urgency that had gradually dwindled during the long weeks of walking returned. Memories of the butchery of the priests in the cathedral were fresh in the mind once more. Even Sammy, who had been a continuous chatterer, grew solemn and withdrew into himself during the days they spent in the old town. It gave Kallad another reason to hate the beasts they stalked.

They left Nuln with renewed purpose.

What none of them had expected was for the magician to tell them that the spoor he followed divided into two. It confirmed Kallad's greatest fear – they were tracking two vampires, not one: Skellan and the creature that had rescued him from the depths of the Sigmarite cathedral.

'The spoors are different,' Kantor explained. 'One is much more potent than the other. It is impossible to say which is our creature, meaning the one imprisoned by the priests, but of the two, the greater evil took the path leading south. The other, I would hazard, is returning to Sylvania.'

'So we have a choice,' Reimer Schmidt said, the young acolyte obviously not liking either of the options they faced. 'We track one beast back to its lair, where more of its kind will undoubtedly be waiting, or we follow the other south, wherever its path may lead. The other being the obvious master of the pair.'

'That's no choice at all,' Joachim Akeman said quite matter-of-factly. It was obvious that the cleric was resigned to meeting Morr along whichever road he travelled.

'We could return home,' Nevin Kantor suggested. 'We have seen what the beasts are capable of. What chance do we stand? We few against monsters capable of such savagery?'

'Aye, you could all run off home like cowards with your tails stuck between your legs. There's nothing stopping you, but I won't.' Kallad said. 'The only thing evil like this needs to flourish is for good men like us to do nothing. You can go home and hide if you like, but I won't. I'll walk into the belly of the beast if I have to. I'm killing that creature, or it's killing me. Make no bones about it.'

Korin Reth nodded. 'I'm in no great rush to meet my maker, but the dwarf has the right of it. I'll stand with him wherever he leads us.'

'Good man,' Kallad said. 'And' what about the rest of you?'

'I'm with you,' Akeman said.

'Me too,' said Reimer Schmidt.

Grimm's soldiers nodded one after the other, pledging themselves to the hunt.

'And what about you, magician?'

'One death is much the same as another,' Nevin Kantor said, without enthusiasm.

'Then it's settled. We go on. It dies, or we do. There's no going home. So tell us what you can, magician.'

'Not much more to tell, dwarf. The greater evil has taken the path south, the lesser monster has turned for home. Both, as far as I can tell, travel alone.'

'Well, that's something. Now then, we've got us two roads to choose from. Magician, what's your gut say? Which way did *our* vampire go?'

The sallow-faced mage gathered up a handful of grass and tossed it into the air. The blades fanned out and drifted on the breeze, each one following its own unique path.

'Pick a blade of grass, dwarf, any one, and toss it into the air. Then do it again, and again, and one last time, just to make the point.'

Kallad did as he was told. His green stems followed yet more trajectories. 'I'm guessing there's some kind of wisdom in the demonstration?'

'Indeed. How can we tell which way the next blade of grass will blow?'

'We can't.'

'Obviously. Each blade takes its own path. Like destiny, if you like. It is fated to fall precisely so, but we can predict its path, to an extent. We can test the wind,' Kantor moistened his finger and held it in the air for a moment. 'Wind's coming from the south-south-east, so there's a better than average chance that our blade of grass will drift this way.' He sketched a rough path with his finger. 'The wind isn't strong, but the grass is light, so it could well travel further than we'd expect. I'd guess it'll land around... here.' He marked out a spot with a small white stone. 'Another stem, if you would, dwarf.'

'What's this got to do with anything?' Korin Reth asked.

'Patience, priest. You'll see soon enough.'

Kallad tossed the stem into the air. It caught on the breeze and twisted, landing less than a hand span from the sorcerer's stone.

'Impressive,' Kallad conceded. 'So how does this help us, because I assume it does?'

'Oh, it does. It most certainly does. You see, we can apply the same logic to determining which path we should take.'

'What? Throw ourselves in the air and see which way we are blown?' Reimer Schmidt chuckled.

'Not quite, if we assume that Skellan is the weaker of the pair, we can deduce that he was the one who returned to the safety of that cursed country.'

'And why would we assume Skellan is the weak one?'

'Because he was caged for the best part of two years, whereas the other one has been at liberty all this time, feeding properly and building its strength. From the disturbance in the winds, it is obvious that the stronger of the beasts went south. It isn't random at all, it is logic.'

'So you're sure the creature that killed them priests went across the border into Sylvania?'

'As sure as I can be, yes.'

'Then we head south.'

That surprised them.

'You mean east, surely?'

'No, I mean south. We don't want the runt of the litter, we want the master.'

'But if Skellan went east–'

'We go south,' Kallad insisted. 'Your man's right. Skellan must have been near helpless when the other one rescued him. That means the other one has to have been behind most of the killing in the cathedral. Stands to reason.' It wasn't a convincing reasoning, however, and Kallad knew it.

He had his own reasons for wanting to head south.

He knew that Skellan was a link between him and his father's killer, but he wasn't the murderer. Kallad's gut told him that this newcomer was more important to his continuing search, which meant going south.

It was a matter of strength; it always was with wild animals. These beasts were no different.

'Like I said, one death is as terminal as another, dwarf. You say we go south, we go south,' Nevin Kantor said, picking up the white pebble and dropkicking it into the distance.

Now, almost a month after that parting of the ways, they were close to exhaustion, short on rations and water, and a long way from home. The animals were tired and they were reduced to taking turns riding in the cart.

Kantor led, as he had done every day since they had left Altdorf. Kallad and the others trudged along ten paces behind the sorcerer.

They had long since dispensed with the idle chatter of the road. Now, they walked on in silence. It had been that way for weeks. They had nothing left to talk about so they fixated instead on the road as it opened up ahead of them. Sammy trudged on at the dwarf's side without complaint, but it was obvious that he was missing the familiar streets of Altdorf, even without his parents there to take care of him.

As Kallad crested the rise, he saw that the sorcerer had stopped a short distance ahead. It was obvious something bothered him. Kallad turned and gestured for the others to hurry up.

'I can smell him.'

'How close?'

'As close as we've ever been, dwarf. It's less than a day since he came through here, the stink is *that* strong.'

'That would mean he bedded down somewhere around here.'

Kantor nodded towards a stand of trees less than a mile distant. It was dense enough to provide cover from the sun. 'That's my guess, right there.'

Kallad squinted as he surveyed the landscape that stretched out before them. He couldn't fault the sorcerer's reasoning.

They were close.

After all this time, they were close.

Sunset was still a good hour away, meaning that the vampire had nowhere to run. All they had to do was flush it out into the sun and the beast would burn.

'This is it, we've got it cornered.' He shouldered Ruinthorn. 'The bastard's down there and he's got nowhere to run, and if he so much as steps outta the trees the sun'll fry 'im.'

'Are you willing to risk your life on an old wives' tale, dwarf?' Kantor asked, pointing up at the setting sun. 'There's nothing to say he *will* burn except stories. I'd rather have something more substantial if I am going to be staking my life on its veracity.'

'Doesn't matter, last thing we want to do is flush him out. If we're lucky, he'll be sleepin' the sleep of the damned an' we'll be right on top of him before he even opens his eyes.'

'Or he's wide awake and waiting for us to walk into a trap,' Reth said, staring at the trees as if by sheer force of will he might see right through them to the dark heart of the wood where the vampire waited.

'Or he's wide awake and waiting for us,' Kallad agreed. 'Either way, it ends here.'

It wasn't a reassuring thought.

After months of searching there was no time left to prepare. They all knew what they had to do. There were only so many ways you could kill a vampire: beheading, burning, cutting its black heart out or dismembering the beast. It would be a bloody struggle, Kallad knew, and given the strength of the enemy, more than one of them would fall before the day was through.

It was a price he was willing to pay if it brought some satisfaction for the victims of Grunberg. The beast was accumulating a huge life-debt. Grunberg, the Sigmarite priests, the thief. Too many had suffered. Kallad thought of the thief, Felix Mann, and the courage he had shown facing up to his crippling. It was humbling in a way, to see such courage. It was almost easy to face death on a battlefield, to run headlong toward it matching skill for skill with the enemy but to leave the safety of the cathedral and try to find a new place for himself within the world was bravery beyond measure. Kallad wondered how the thief would cope without being reduced to begging; he had faith the thief would find a way. His resourcefulness would be tested, for sure, but Mann was a survivor. His encounter with the beast proved that.

It was time to start repaying the life-debt.

He set off across the field to the trees. The others followed.

With Ruinthorn in his hands he felt whole. On another day it might have disturbed him that he needed his axe to feel complete. Today it felt natural.

The vampire sat on an upturned stump of tree, waiting for them as they stepped into the clearing. There was no doubting that it *was* a vampire. The creature's face was aquiline, its features sharp, hard, but it was the eyes that gave the lie to the creature's vile nature. They were utterly soulless.

The vampire rose with deceptive grace and inclined his head towards Kallad.

'You were looking for me?'

'Aye, if you're the one responsible for the dead priests, we're looking for you.'

'Well, it seems that you have found me, dwarf. Now what do you and your merry band of misfits intend to do about it?'

Kallad bristled. The creature's arrogance was aimed at goading him into doing something stupid, he knew that, but knowing it didn't stop him from wanting to gut the fiend with his bare hands. He brought his axe to bear.

As one, the three soldiers from Grimm's guard drew their swords. The metal sang as it slid free of the sheaths.

'Eight against one, hardly a fair fight.' The vampire said, a wry smile playing over his lips. 'Let's do something to redress the balance shall we?' He bent, and in one fluid motion drew two wickedly pointed daggers from sheaths concealed in his left boot, and sent them end over end into two of the soldiers' throats. The men were dead before they hit the ground. The vampire tumbled to the left and came up on his right leg, flinging a third dagger into the eye of the last soldier. 'Now, that's better,' he said, rising smoothly.

In that moment Kallad froze.

The young acolyte, Reimer Schmidt, reacted first, hurling himself across the clearing at the vampire.

The creature didn't move as the young man brought his fist around and smashed a vial of blessed water from the font in the Sigmarite cathedral. The glass cut into the creature's cheek, but the water did nothing except wet his face.

'Your faith is weak, priest. You don't believe, do you?' Before the young acolyte could answer, the vampire had him in a deadly embrace and snapped his neck savagely. He tossed Reimer Schmidt's body aside and launched himself at the dwarf.

Kallad barely managed to block the creature's first strike, bringing the butt of Ruinthorn up and slamming it into the vampire's jaw as the beast sank his fangs into his forearm. The blow sent the vampire reeling and bought Kallad a few precious seconds.

The naked savagery of the beast was staggering. It had torn through them in seconds. Kallad stood side by side with Sammy Krauss,

Joachim Akeman and Korin Reth. Behind them, Kantor screamed. It was a sound of pure, wretched, panic.

It was over before it had even begun. Despair threatened to overwhelm Kallad. This was it. He had failed. There would be no avenging the tragedies of Grunberg, no satisfaction for his people, and no rest.

The magician turned and fled the clearing.

Kallad let him go. He wouldn't get far if the beast chose to hunt him down, that much was obvious.

It was over for all of them and the vampire hadn't even drawn its blade.

'Well, well,' the beast said, rubbing a hand across its jaw, 'I think I should save you until last, don't you, dwarf? Let you see your friends die.' The vampire dropped into a tight crouch, its body seeming to contort and stretch, tearing its clothes from its back as its body elongated. The leather of its sword belt snapped and the sheathed blade fell to the floor. The thing – because it wasn't a vampire anymore, it was something between human and wolf – threw back its head and howled before it sprang forward, huge jaws tearing at the throats of the terrified Sigmarites as the vampire's form shifted into that of a massive dire wolf.

Kallad hurled Ruinthorn. The axe flew end over end and embedded itself in the beast's arched back. The vampire roared in pain, and fell, sprawling in the dirt. It drew itself back to its feet, face contorted in rage as it turned. Ruinthorn had hurt the thing, but not badly enough, nowhere near badly enough. It was too late for Akeman and Reth. The creature had torn the flesh out of their throats. Their blood soaked its muzzle as the wolf turned on Sammy.

It came forward cautiously, protecting its wounded side. Even wounded, the beast was lethal.

'Run, boy!' Kallad yelled at Sammy, but Sammy stood rooted to the spot, too frightened to move. 'Run!'

The spell holding Sammy shattered and suddenly the boy screamed, stumbled back a step, tripped, and fell, sprawling across the dirt.

The wolf was on top on him in a second, huge teeth tearing at the flesh of his arms as he threw them up to defend himself. His screams were terrible as the wolf took off half of his face with one savage bite.

Then the screaming stopped, and the silence was twice as terrible.

Kallad threw himself at the creature, trying to wrench his axe from its back, but the beast twisted and threw him across the clearing. Somehow, Kallad kept his grip on Ruinthorn, tearing the axe from the beast's back. He scrambled to his feet.

The wolf circled him cautiously.

Despite the massive wound in the beast's arched back there was no blood.

For a moment, he wondered what it would take to kill the creature – but he knew. Less than a quarter of an hour ago he had told the men exactly what they needed to do to slay the vampire, in whatever form it took: burning, beheading, dismembering. There was no fire, but Ruinthorn was more than capable of meting out the other deaths.

The creature was hurting, that much was obvious by the way it moved.

It wasn't invincible.

'Time to die, vampire,' Kallad said through gritted teeth.

The wolf growled deep in its throat, keeping a distance between itself and the dwarf's axe.

Kallad took a single step back, rocking on his heel and raising Ruinthorn above his head. Loosing a savage cry, he launched himself into a spinning step forwards. The momentum of the axe carried him through the arc faster than any normal blow, but it missed its mark. The wolf's head was still planted firmly on its shoulders.

The massive swing left Kallad dangerously open, but the wolf failed to take advantage of the opportunity that Kallad's miss had gifted it.

The dwarf surged forwards again, swinging wildly. There was no finesse or subtlety to the attack, but it was as brutal as it was ugly. The wolf went up on its hind legs as the axe thundered into its side. Bone crunched, splintering under the impact. The dwarf's momentum sent them both tumbling and rolling across the dirt floor. The wolf's jaws snapped at Kallad's face, scoring deep cuts down his left cheek and biting clean through half of his ear.

His head swam. The pain was blinding.

The clearing blurred in and out of focus.

He tried to stay focused on the dark shape of the wolf prowling in front of him.

The wolf growled low in its throat and lunged. Kallad sidestepped and slammed a gauntleted fist into the side of the beast's head. The wolf's teeth sank into his shoulder.

Can the beast feed in this form? The thought flashed through his head as they rolled together, locked in a deadly embrace.

He broke the beast's hold, but only for a moment. The wolf's teeth bit into Kallad's forearm. The surge of pain as the fangs sank into his flesh was excruciating, and was made much worse as Kallad yanked his arm forwards, dragging the wolf close enough for him to thunder his forehead into the beast's muzzle.

Snarling, the wolf rolled away from him.

Kallad scrambled to his knees, planted the axe in the dirt and hauled himself to his feet.

The world swam dangerously.

Kallad stumbled back two steps and righted himself. When he looked up, the wolf had begun to change.

'Fun,' the vampire growled, caught halfway between his own form and that of the wolf. The beast stood on two legs once more, its skeletal structure hideously malformed. Two huge wounds gaped in his torso, one in his side, the other scored deeply along the line of his spine. The beast's skin writhed with unnatural life as beneath it the bones cracked and reshaped until the metamorphosis was complete. 'But not so much that I want it to last all night.'

'Then stop your yapping and finish it.'

'My pleasure.' The vampire dropped into a crouch, its face twisting with rage as it sprang sideways, rolling and coming up with the discarded sword belt in its left hand. It drew the blade, and threw the scabbard aside. The blade sang as it rasped free. The vampire brought it round in a vicious arc, cutting low and high in a single sweep before returning to guard.

Kallad stepped in to meet the beast's attack when it came.

He stumbled, tripping over Sammy Krauss's outstretched arm, and in that instant the vampire was on him.

Kallad felt a searing pain across his chest as the vampire's blade plunged into his side, working its way up between the dented discs beneath his mail, seeking out his heart.

The world faded into black. The last thing he saw: the cold eyes of the vampire. The last thought: that he had failed his people. That the grudge would go to the grave with him.

Then he slipped into the blackness.

CHAPTER NINE
Ring of Fire

THE BORDERLANDS OF SYLVANIA
The first kiss of snow, winter, 2056

MANNFRED STOOD OVER the dwarf.

The wounds in his back and side were deep, the pain debilitating, but far from lethal for one of his kind. Even so, he owed the dwarf a more painful death than he was able to offer. He left him to bleed out into the dirt.

He opened himself up and breathed in the winds.

It was as he thought: the magician had opened himself up to Shyish, the death wind. That was how they had tracked him. It would be the fool's undoing. Only the strongest sorcerer could bear any kind of exposure to Shyish without being blackened by it. The man was already doomed. It would be eating away at his immortal soul even now, burrowing its way into every crease and fold of his humanity and stamping it out.

Mannfred reached out, touching Shyish.

The wind was invigorating. He savoured it as he drew it into himself.

'I'm coming for you, little man,' he said, knowing that Shyish would carry the taunt to his victim's ears no matter how far away he had managed to flee. It wasn't far enough. 'Run, run as fast as you can. It isn't fast enough. I will find you. Maybe today, maybe tomorrow, but someday, I promise, and it will be the end of your life. So run, coward, while your comrades rot.'

He walked amongst the dead, but there was no sustenance to be had from them. Their blood had already begun to lose its vitality. It was about the life-essences in the blood, not the blood itself. To drink now would be poison. Pity, because thanks to the damned dwarf he needed to feed.

They carried nothing of worth, a few petty trinkets and holy marks of Sigmar, hammers and swords. By far the most interesting thing was the dwarf's hammer, but he had no intention of touching it. He could feel the silver threads that the dwarf had had woven into the leather grip. It was a fine weapon, a match for any axe he had ever seen.

What he needed was clothing. His own clothes were left in tatters after the transformation.

He stripped the dead, taking what would fit.

The wound in his side troubled him. He could feel it burn where it had opened up. It would take time to knit. In the meantime, it made walking uncomfortable where the raw flesh rubbed.

He had time.

Mannfred returned to the tree stump and sat. He found himself toying with the ring he wore on his left hand, turning it around his middle finger.

The wound in his side was really beginning to burn. He touched it with curious fingers, feeling out the true extent of the damage, and he found that it was much smaller than he had at first thought. The sides of the gash were hot, which explained the fire he felt. He reached around awkwardly, probing the deep cut that ran parallel to his spine. Only it wasn't deep anymore. It was a shallow cut.

Neither wound was as damaging as he had first thought, although both burned with a hellish fury.

A sudden jag of pain lanced from his side into his heart. Mannfred cried out against it, sinking to his knees. He threw his head back and roared.

As the black agony subsided, Mannfred touched the wound in his side, dreading what he might discover.

The gash had almost sealed. Already the burning was beginning to ease.

It made no sense, until he thought of the times, when, with his own eyes, he had seen Vlad fall only to return, rejuvenated. He looked at the signet ring, the plain little trinket that he had claimed as his inheritance from the thief, Felix Mann, and began, finally, to understand.

'Thank you, father,' he said, standing.

He dressed himself in the dead men's clothes. There were no boots that fit, so he resigned himself to going barefoot as he set off after the magician.

Mannfred moved carefully, but the wounds had already healed over. After a few minutes, he broke into an easy ground-eating lope. The magician was easy to follow. He had blazed a panicked trail that even a blind man could have followed.

He caught up with the man in the middle of the open field. The man scrabbled about in the dirt, begging for his life. It was quite pitiful.

Mannfred could smell Chaos taint on the magician, already. He had tasted Shyish, and now he was addicted.

'Spare me,' the magician begged. 'Please, sweet Sigmar save me.' It was a pathetic whimper.

Mannfred smiled coldly, his face shifting as he released the beast within, and reached towards him.

CHAPTER TEN
The Unforgettable Fire

THE SUBTERRANEAN CATHEDRAL,
BENEATH DRAKENHOF, SYLVANIA
The darkling buds of Pflugzeit, spring, 2057

MIESHA'S WORDS HAUNTED him, even now.

She may have been Hans's get, but she was also Hamaya, chosen by Jerek for her loyalty to the vampire nation. With her sire dead, she had suffered. It had taken every ounce of her will to reclaim some sense of herself, and with it she had become stronger.

For that, he had promised her a commendation, an elevation in the ranks of the Hamaya. She would be rewarded.

Whether he wanted to or not, Konrad believed her when she said that his brothers Pieter and Fritz were scheming behind his back. He had always known they would.

The fact that they had chosen to band together to see him beaten, however, was like a stake through the heart. Although he was loath to admit it, the fact that they could hate and fear him so much was curiously gratifying.

Konrad had always known what he would have to do, but their petty scheming had forced his hand far sooner than he would have liked.

He stood on the stone dais, his brothers flanking him on either side. Behind them, Konrad's loyal Hamaya had arranged themselves in a tight cordon.

They were nearly a mile beneath the surface, in the subterranean cathedral that his thralls had mined out of the very earth itself. Down here, they were immune to the whims of the sun and the moon, and other such inconveniences. Around the vast cathedral with its ceiling of stalactites as a warren of cells and chambers that made up the war rooms and Immoliah Fey's vault. The necromancer had built a sprawling underground kingdom for her research into the dark arts, including a black library that far exceeded anything from the rooms above. She had assembled treasures dating back to Nehekhara, and perhaps even Neferata herself, holy books and unholy ones, artefacts of power, masks, some renditions of familiar animal faces and other far stranger creatures, charms, icons, rods, staves, wands, and a vast arsenal of weapons.

There was even a caged pit for gladiatorial death matches, all in the name of amusement. The cage fights were brutal and bloody, with the new vampires thirsting to be a part of the kill as they looked on.

Death was good for morale.

In the galleries, a thousand flickering torches illuminated the upturned faces of his new vampires. Their faces were tainted a sickly green by the luminescence given off by the lichen that grew on the walls. Some wore expressions of idolisation, others outright hatred. Both were vital to the future of his people.

There were hundreds of them, all tied in some way to the bloodline. These were *his* people: he was their father-in-death, their lord, their master, their god.

He turned to Miesha.

'Come forward, girl,' he said, quietly. Then louder, to the gallery: 'Hear me, my family.' His voice carried easily, the acoustics of the domed vault amplifying his words. 'Our people have suffered since the fall of our beloved father-in-death. We were beaten, forced into submission, the lands around us stripped and useless, our cattle drained and our spirit broken.

'It is not so now. In each and every one of you we have been reborn. In ways that the living cannot comprehend, we are kindred. We are merely the beginning. We stood against the might of the Empire in the war and we suffered years of loss as a result, struggling merely to subsist. As our people slept, so did their dreams of dominion. Now, take a look at the faces around you. Do you see the hunger there? Do you see the fire to take back what is rightfully ours? Has it woken in the face of each and every one of you?

'You are servants of the vampires, but you alone are nothing. As part of the organic whole you are everything.'

Konrad paused, giving his words a moment to sink in.

'We are one, you and I. Nothing separates us. If you suffer hurts, I suffer with you, and if I suffer hurts, you, in turn, will suffer with me.

'Miesha, my love, kneel.'

She came forward and knelt at Konrad's feet, her smile one of satisfaction. Her loyalty was being rewarded, her position of influence cemented. She bowed her head, going along with Konrad's mockery of the knighting ceremony, and waited.

'If one amongst us betrays one of us, they betray all of us. If one harbours deceit in their heart, if one would scheme for their own gain, understand that they are scheming against all of us, understand that they are lying to all of us, and believe me, I will not stand for that.'

He drew his sword.

'Miesha, one of my trusted Hamaya came to me. She spoke of my brothers, my beloved brothers Pieter and Fritz,' he gestured with the sword towards first Pieter, and then Fritz. 'She claimed that they plotted treachery behind my back. I know my brothers, they would do no such thing, for like me, they have only the best interests of the vampire nation in their hearts. So why would Miesha do such a thing? Because she sought to profit from it.'

Konrad nodded to the flanking Hamaya, and one, Onursal, a dark-skinned giant, stepped forwards, laying a hand on Miesha's shoulder, claws sinking into her flesh and holding her in place.

She looked up at Konrad, and the first flickerings of fear registered in her eyes.

'There can be no other reason. She came to me with outright lies about my brothers. So here, my people, I make an example of those who conspire against *my* rule.'

Konrad brought the blade down with an executioner's precision, cleaving the woman's head from her body in a single smooth blow. Her body held its position for a moment before collapsing in nervous convulsions. Konrad sheathed his sword. Miesha's head rolled across the dais, the look of shock frozen on her face as it came to a stop.

He turned and bowed to each of his brothers.

They understood the point of the demonstration. It was not for the assembly of vampires, it was for them.

The message was plain: those who stand against me can expect no less a fate. The ruthlessness of it was shocking.

He had sacrificed one of his own to reinforce the point.

'Let us speak of this no more. We have more important things to consider by far. Together we stand before you, brothers, united.

'You,' he spread his arms wide to encompass the entire gallery, 'are the results of my desire to rebuild our great nation. You are here because of *my* will. I have a vision for our people. You were but the first stage of that great vision. It is time now to put the second stage into practice.

'Some of you may say: "He has brought us another plan. When he had completed the first, why couldn't he leave us in peace to feed and grow at our own rate? Why the haste, why run before we can walk?"

'The truth is our enemies do not stagnate, they move forwards every day.

'Now that we are restored, it is time to take the fight to our enemy's door. They shall tremble once more as they peer out into the darkness, knowing that we walk in the night. It will be a war fought on three fronts, the first a guerrilla assault on their societal structure. You are to go abroad in search of those with peculiar gifts. You are to scour the land for any with even the slightest aptitude for magic, not just known practitioners, but folk with unusual luck, men surrounded by uncanny stories. You will seek out midwifes who have never lost a child, soldiers who have survived terrible campaigns and tell tales of their fortune while other suffered, and people, who might, in some way, have touched one of the Eight Winds. They are to be brought back here to Immoliah Fey, who will drain them of their talents, creating a second tier of what will be our unstoppable force: a corps of magicians skilled in the Lore of Death.

'To show how little store I put in the gossiping of that traitor,' he inclined his head towards Miesha's corpse, 'the second assault, a force of purebloods led by my brother Pieter, will sack Nuln, spreading discord amongst the humans. We will not give them the luxury of sleeping easily in their beds. The third, a force of equal measure, will be under the command of my brother, Fritz. I trust him to make Middenheim bend its knee before the year is out.

'It is time for us to reclaim the night and teach these humans the true meaning of fear.'

It was done. He had trapped his brothers into exile whilst making them into heroes. In sending them away, he had shown the assembly who was in charge, and made it difficult, if not impossible for Fritz and Pieter to continue to plot his downfall in tandem. He had meant what he said; alone they were nothing. He smiled coldly as he turned to face them.

Their exile was only his first move in a long and drawn out dance of death.

A part of him looked forward to their response. It would keep life interesting.

'The fate of our people is in your hands, my brothers, do not fail us.'

With that he dismissed the assembly, bidding his brothers take their pick of whichever subordinates they would take into battle.

He looked down at poor Miesha. He was proud of her, and proud of himself for giving her death meaning.

'Stay,' he said to Jerek as the Hamaya turned to leave. 'All of you, stay.'

The six took up positions around their master.

'What would you have us do with her body?' Onursal asked.

'Dispose of it as befits a traitor.'

The vampire nodded. The fate of a traitor in the new vampire nation was gruesome. The corpse was spitted and roasted, and then stripped, and the meat was fed to the birds up in the Rookery.

'I find it hard to believe.' The Wolf's gaze drifted towards Miesha's corpse. Konrad had known Jerek would take her death personally. He had chosen her. He had helped her through the insanity that threatened to overwhelm her in the wake of Hans's death. Seeing her die branded a traitor must have galled him.

'It is not so hard to believe, my friend,' Konrad said, smoothly. 'The madness had obviously rooted itself deeper than you were able to reach. Without question she was still spoiled by her master's evil. You cannot hold yourself responsible. You did all that you could, but we always knew there was a chance she would not come back to us.'

Jerek remained unconvinced.

'She had weathered the worst of the withdrawal.' He shook his head. 'She was getting stronger and stronger. It makes no sense.'

'Then perhaps she had a relapse,' Konrad said, his irritation flashing through. 'I suggest, my friend, that you let it go.'

He refused to allow himself to get worked up during his hour of victory. No, this was a moment to be savoured, not lost in a blur of anger. Konrad took a moment to compose himself.

'There is someone I would have you meet. He came to me last night, having escaped from the belly of the beast itself. Vlad placed great store in his talents. Wolf, I believe you and he are acquainted?'

Konrad gestured for the newcomer to join them.

All eyes turned to see Jon Skellan step out of the shadows. He came to stand beside Konrad.

'With the... ah... sudden vacancy, I have asked Skellan to join us. He has unique skills. Now, there is something I have no wish to talk of, but alas must. Despite our best efforts, I believe that at least one of you is loyal to my brothers. This pains me greatly. I do not ask much from those around me, only loyalty. In return you are privileged above all others. This is my reward, to learn that there are vipers in my nest.'

No one argued with him. No one claimed that he was wrong. They knew better than to try to dissuade him when he had his mind set on something.

'Well, my little schemers, take this to your masters, and let them stew on it. They aren't coming home.'

He looked at them all, one by one, judging them. Then he gave the assassination orders for Fritz and Pieter.

CHAPTER ELEVEN

The Ravens Left the Tower

KONRAD'S TOWER, DRAKENHOF, SYLVANIA
The long dark night of the soul, spring, 2057

HE KNEW THEY would come for him. It was only a matter of time. That was why he had challenged them so openly, proclaiming their death sentence before the Hamaya.

He had expected it to goad either Pieter or Fritz into some rash action, some obvious treason that he could punish with impunity.

He had taken measures to protect himself, of course. He was no fool.

Konrad no longer slept in his own coffin. While it was empty, the coffin was set up to look as if the new Count slumbered within. Instead of the coffin, Konrad preferred the solitude of the rooftops when Morrslieb and Mannslieb held sway, or the subterranean seclusion of the cathedral when the sun was at its zenith. This night, he held a lonely vigil on the balcony outside his bedchamber.

The armies had gathered, billeting the city below.

The differences between Konrad's new army and the last army that had marched to the banner of the von Carsteins were marked. Where Vlad had enjoyed the portability of tents, Konrad chose to stamp his authority on the land, claiming ownership of houses and leaving families begging for scraps. For him, there were no banners or pennons snapping in the wind, no black pavilions for the marshals, and no supply wagons. The dead had no need of such accoutrements. There was movement, however: black coaches rumbled through the streets bearing the seal of the von Carsteins.

Hundreds of small fires burned in the fields between the castle and the city. He didn't look directly at them, knowing their dance would slowly mesmerise him. He needed to be alert, watchful. He kept his gaze moving over the countryside without allowing it to settle on anything for too long. Every once in a while, he glanced up towards the green aura of Morrslieb and the brighter silver corona of Mannslieb; it all served to break up the monotony of waiting for the inevitable.

He listened to the nocturnal chorus: the insects, the hoot of an owl, the mournful cry of a wolf, and the wind in the gutters of the tower.

Ravens gathered along the balustrade, their beady eyes surveying the night world. At times like these the birds kept him company. Their presence also held the ghosts at bay.

The chamber door creaked open. The wait was over. They had come for him.

With the torches lit, the room was fully illuminated, although the glass between them effectively rendered Konrad invisible. He watched as the three men, wrapped in dark cloaks, crept up on the coffin, standing at the head and on either side of the wooden box. It was a measure of how little his brothers regarded him. Three assassins. Three humans. Insult aside, it was fascinating to see his own murder taking place, or what they thought would be his murder.

The attack when it came was shocking in its savagery.

The body in the coffin was butchered.

He suffered a curious sense of disassociation, watching his would-be murderers hacking away at the corpse in the coffin. It was like watching his own death through the eyes of a stranger.

He would have to thank Immoliah Fey for the corpse, and for the glamour that disguised it.

Konrad watched until their frenzied cutting subsided into exhaustion, and then pushed open the balcony door and walked into his bedroom.

'Sorry to disappoint you, but it seems I am still very much alive.'

One of the assassins dropped his blade in fright. It clattered on the floor.

'You, on the other hand, well, forgive me if I am wrong, but I think you could very well be dead.'

He came at them in a vengeful fury, his fist bursting through the ribcage of the first assassin and wrenching the dead man's heart out of his chest with one vicious tug. Spinning on his heel, he lunged out with his hand extended and rammed clawed fingers into the second assassin's throat, rupturing his windpipe. The man dropped his sword, gagging, and stumbled back, clutching at his throat as he suffocated.

Konrad turned on the last assassin.

'Which of my brothers sent you?'

The man said nothing.

Konrad moved in closer. He reached out. His hand closed around the man's jaw.

'I'll ask you again, which of my brother's sent you?'

He squeezed, hard.

'Fritz.'

He had got what he wanted. Not what he expected, but what he wanted. He still didn't relent, even as he felt the bone crush beneath his fingers. The man's screams were silenced abruptly as Konrad snapped his neck.

He stripped the dead man of his hood. He recognised him. It was one of his own. He stared at the man's twisted face. The recognition was galling.

Quickly, Konrad stripped the hoods from the remaining assassins. Again, both were, or had been, his own thralls. They should have been bound to him, and as such incapable of rising against him. They should have been subservient, existing solely to do his bidding. The evidence to the contrary lay dead at his feet.

Somehow, Fritz had turned them against him. That fact was more disturbing than the botched assassination attempt. Fritz had found a way to break his hold on his own servants.

Konrad had been sure that the fop was only interested in his hedonistic pursuit of pleasure, but obviously, the whole harmless philanderer persona was an act, one he played perfectly. He surrounded himself with whores and doxies to help keep up the act, but obviously the Fritz he thought he knew was not who Fritz really was. This would bear thinking about.

In that moment, cold-blooded fury overwhelmed him. All rational thought burned up within his anger. Had he been his sire, he would have dragged their souls back from the abyss, kicking and screaming, and raised them again, as mindless zombies. He wasn't his sire, however, and his impotence maddened him all the more.

He lashed out, splintering the side of his coffin with his fist.

He upturned the box, spilling parts of the dismembered corpse across the bloody floor. He tore down the portraits from the wall. He splintered the back of the chair on the open door and, raging, pulled the books from the shelves. He shredded the spines and ripped out the pages, scattering them around him like confetti. Blood soaked into the pages where they fell around the bodies.

His rage consumed him. It was blinding. Then, as quickly as it had come, it was spent. All that remained was slow smouldering fury.

He looked at the assassins with thinly veiled hatred. He *would* extract his price for this insult. Fritz would pay.

He stood in the doorway, calling for a servant to fetch the Hamaya.

'I want these,' he gestured at the bodies, 'delivered to my brother Fritz's chambers immediately.'

Onursal bowed. The Hamaya betrayed no expression upon seeing the devastation that Konrad had wrought in his own chamber. 'It will be done.'

He gathered the body of the last assassin in his arms.

'I know this man. He was no assassin.'

'Until today,' Konrad said, the implication obvious. Something had turned the man into a hopeless assassin. Onursal was no fool, the fact that he was being asked to deliver the bodies to Fritz was a clear indication of where the responsibility for the man's conversion lay.

Jerek von Carstein stood in the doorway.

'Are you sure this is wise, Konrad?'

'Are you questioning me, Wolf?'

Jerek shook his head. 'Not at all, just urging caution. Once you deliver these to Fritz's door there can be no turning back. You know that.'

'Take one of the damned bodies, Jerek. You are not my conscience, so stop acting like it. I'll carry the third myself. I want to see his face when his filth washes up on his own doorstep.'

Only he didn't carry the third, he beheaded it and carried the head by a bloody tangle of hair.

Together, they swept through the cold passages of the castle, climbing the hundreds of stairs to Fritz's high chamber. Konrad threw the door open and sneered at Fritz's surprise as he bowled the assassin's head into the room. The head cracked off the doorway as he threw it. It landed at his brother's feet.

Konrad stepped into the room. The Hamaya didn't cross the threshold.

'What do you have to say for yourself, *brother-mine*?' Konrad asked, cruelly mimicking Fritz's intonation.

'If you want something done right, do it yourself would seem to be appropriate.'

'Indeed, that would be why I am here.'

Konrad drew his daemon blade, feeling the vibrations course through him as the blade sang out, demanding blood.

Fritz was unarmed.

'It seems you have me at a disadvantage,' Fritz said, stalling. He cast his gaze left and right, looking for something that could be used as an impromptu weapon. There was nothing.

'I don't really care, brother,' Konrad said, moving closer, 'but more to the point, I don't see why I should.'

'We're family,' Fritz offered, a smile spreading across his face as he spread his arms.

The smile incensed Konrad, as he knew it was calculated to. He did his best to stifle the anger he felt building, but it was difficult.

The need of the daemon blade sang in his tainted blood. It demanded a death, demanded sating. It fed off the heat of his rage, stoking it even as he battled for control.

Slowly and deliberately, Konrad brought the dark blade to his lips and kissed it before shifting into a fighting stance.

'So be it, brother-mine.' Fritz clapped his hands sharply, twice. Doors on either side of his chamber opened, and his women entered, hunkering down and giving themselves over to the form of she-wolves. They circled around Konrad, jowls curled back in feral snarls. 'Seven angry young women, Konrad, I would call this an even match.'

'You've miscalculated, brother. I don't need to kill them, only you. They can snap and snarl all they like. It doesn't matter. They are all tied to you. Your death will be enough to put an end to any threat they might pose, pretty though they might be with their shiny pelts. I would have thought swords would have been more your style, Fritz. They are so terribly... suggestive, after all. Now, I am taking what is mine, by eternal right. Say your goodbyes. I am sure your bitches will miss you.'

Kicking a wolf aside, Konrad launched a blistering attack, the sheer ferocity of it driving Fritz towards the window. He ignored the howling wolves as they snapped at him. They were insects, annoying, but inconsequential. He only had eyes for Fritz. The traitor would pay.

Lunging, he buried the bone blade deep in Fritz's stomach. The sheer momentum of the attack carried the pair out through the huge window, spraying glass everywhere, and for a moment, they were falling, locked together by the daemonic sword. Their black cloaks wrapped around the pair as they wrestled then flared out wildly as the wind ripped them away. For a moment, they became the silhouette of vast black wings as Konrad lost his grip on the sword and Fritz fell away, the sword still impaled in his gut.

He fell soundlessly, threw his arms wide and burst upwards suddenly, his body going through a hideous transformation, the cloak fusing to his arms like leathery wings, his bones breaking and metamorphosing into the shape and form of a huge black bat.

The sword tumbled away harmlessly, chased by the black ghost of Fritz's shed clothing.

Konrad spread his arms wide, focusing on the form of a bat in his head. He gave himself to it, feeling his body respond. He stopped freefalling, and was flying.

As a bat, he was blind.

He reached out with his remaining senses, using the displacement of the air caused by the panicked flapping of his brother's wings to build a picture in his mind, and chased Fritz out into the darkness.

They banked high, arcing back towards Konrad's Tower – what used to be called the Raven Tower in Vlad's day – and swooped low along the castellations, scattering the birds. He lost Fritz in the chaos of wings.

Konrad scoured the sky for a quarter of an hour, but what seemed like thousands of the black birds had taken flight, blinding him in the sheer volume of wing beats and caws.

Cursing himself for a fool, he went to ground, dressed and collected his sword. Its hunger was far from sated, but its longing would be answered before the night was over.

He could, at last, sleep. There would be no more attacks tonight. Fritz was beaten, and Emmanuelle would prevent Pieter from giving in to any kind of rash stupidity.

First, he had one thing to do.

He climbed the several hundred stairs to Fritz's chamber and, revelling in their screams, butchered his brother's harem while Jerek and Onursal looked on dispassionately. He didn't care that their true deaths weakened the vampires as a whole. Losing seven gets in a single night would virtually cripple Fritz, which was what mattered.

He left the corpses littering the floor for Fritz to find if he was foolish enough to return.

That would not be for a long time yet.

The link between sire and get was a powerful one, and Konrad knew that Fritz would be lying somewhere in a gutter, stinking with fear, and sure, beyond a shadow of a doubt, that he was dying.

'He will not cross me again,' Konrad said to the Hamaya as they returned to his tower.

'He would be a fool to,' Onursal said, opening the heavy wooden door.

'We will stand guard at your door tonight, all the same.' Jerek said as Konrad entered the chamber. The room looked as if a tornado had blown through it. Jerek stooped and righted the toppled coffin. The side of the box was splintered where Konrad had hit it, but it would do for a few hours more. 'Sleep well, my lord.'

And sleep he did, the sleep of the damned.

He dreamed he was walking the streets of the city below, loitering in the seedier districts of Drakenhof. On a corner, he saw the indistinct shape of a woman, blurred as is the nature of dreams.

* * *

SHE LURKS IN the darker shadows of the alleyway. He can see that she is wearing an exquisite gown of flowing silks and a veil that covers the lower half of her face. Even so, he knows that she is beautiful.

'Do you think I am beautiful?' she asks, as he approaches.

All he knows is that he must possess her.

Up close, she is even more attractive.

She reminds him, in almost every way, of his sire's bride, Isabella.

'Of course you are,' he says.

'Liar!' she screams, tearing away the veil that covers her mutilation. Her mouth has been ripped open, her unnatural smile spreading from ear to ear, her tongue lolling horribly through the gash. 'Tell me again, now that you see me, am I beautiful?'

Konrad stares at the ruin of Vlad von Carstein's bride, screams and tries to flee, but she is too fast. She snares him in claws that he cannot escape and draws him up close to whisper: 'I want to do to you what was done to me,' in his ear as she pulls a sharpened stake from the many folds of her gown and plunges it into his heart.

As he dies in her arms, her face blurred, losing focus and form, shifting into the face of Jerek, into the face of Vlad, into the face of Skellan, of Miesha, of Pieter, of Hans, of Fritz, Onursal, Immoliah Fey, Constantin, Emmanuelle.

The faces of those he once called friends.

HE AWOKE IN a cold sweat, trapped inside the confines of his coffin. He lashed out, hammering at the wooden lid until it shattered, and surged out of the wooden box, gasping even though he had tasted his last breath more than a century earlier.

He rose, trembling, as Jerek and Onursal burst into the room. Their expressions said they expected the worst. Konrad was not about to confess his dream.

'Leave me.' The manner in which he said it brooked no argument. The Hamaya backed out of the room.

He didn't know who he could trust.

Trust, he laughed bitterly. The truth was that he could trust no one.

He couldn't stand to be cooped up in the castle anymore. He needed to feel the wind on his face, to feel the illusion at least of freedom. He wondered if this was how Vlad had felt. Thinking of his sire made him think of the hundreds of nights when the ancient vampire had haunted the rooftops of this very tower. That decided it for him. He gathered his cloak up, fastening the gold chain around his throat, and swept out of the chamber and past the Hamaya.

'Stay!' he commanded, as if he was talking to a pair of dogs.

He climbed the stairs to the roof at a run, taking them two and three at a time in his need to be out beneath the bruise purple sky.

He pushed open the door.

The wind sucked and pulled at his cloak, folding it around him and billowing it out behind him in turns as it funnelled around the rooftop. Konrad strode right out to the edge, standing on the brickwork of the castellation itself, nothing between him and a fall of a thousand feet.

He looked down.

For a moment, it was as if he was suspended out in the black heart of the night. It was breathtaking, that sense of liberation.

The rush of vertigo was dizzying, but there was no fear.

He could willingly have given himself to the fall if he had wanted to, even one thousand feet was not enough to kill him.

Indeed, he wanted to jump, to fly free in the sky.

The ravens gathered around his feet, pecking at his toes and worrying at the leather of his boots. He let them.

'He's not the only one,' the largest of the ravens said, its voice a raucous caw as it craned its neck to peer up at him with its beady yellow eyes.

'I know,' Konrad said, still looking out over the world below.

'They all want you dead,' the creature's voice cut deep into his nerves, the words like nails on glass, as it coughed them up.

'I know.'

'There are enemies on every corner.'

'I know.'

'Your brothers would rise in your place.'

'I know all of this, bird.'

'You do, you do, but know you Pieter? That he plots your downfall? That he dreams of dominion?'

'Then I shall have to see that his dreams become nightmares.'

'Oh yes, yes, yes, nightmares. Before he dies – nightmares. Kill them, Konrad. Kill them. They would kill you.'

Konrad looked down at the carrion bird. It looked positively enraptured by the prospect of more death in the old castle.

'You are your master's creature, aren't you, bird?'

'Oh, yesss.'

'There will be more blood, take that message to your master in whatever Hell he is in.'

'Yes, yes, yes, yes,' the raven cawed. 'Trick Pieter, see him dead, before he tricks you. They scheme and scheme, your lying kin, they would see you rot, cut you into pieces and feed you to us birds, yes they would, yes, yes, yes.'

'Then perhaps that is what I should do for them. Make their dreams come true. Call it my gift. Konrad, the Blood Count.'

'Bringer of death, this immortal,' quoth the raven.

Konrad heard movement on the stairs and retreated quickly into the shadows thrown by one of the tower's many gables, dark enough and deep enough to conceal him.

Jon Skellan walked out onto the rooftop. Bending, he began to feed a few of the birds with small strings of meat. They ate out of his hand.

Konrad watched the spectacle with growing curiosity, gradually becoming certain that the birds were talking to the new Hamaya, even though he wasn't close enough to make out what they were saying.

'So, they talk to you as well?' he asked, stepping out of the shadows.

Skellan scattered the ravens, cawing and flapping his arms to drive them off, and turned to face his master. 'They make good companions,' he said, a sly grin spreading across his face. 'They ask no questions, and tell no lies. What more can you ask for from a friend?'

'Yes,' Konrad agreed. 'There is something almost noble about them, isn't there?'

'Unlike your brothers,' Skellan said.

The frankness of his words surprised Konrad. He was unaccustomed to his servants being so bold. It made a refreshing change. He knew he had chosen well in Skellan. Like Jerek, he was a truth speaker. Konrad had had enough of sycophants to last him several lifetimes. 'From what I have seen of the pair, they lack any semblance of nobility.'

'Guttersnipes, the pair of them,' Konrad agreed. A raven settled by his feet. Utterly unafraid of them, it pecked and scuffed at the scraps of meat that Skellan had dropped.

'Yet they hold great power in your court, and you honour them by giving them command of your forces going to war on the morrow. One would think they have some hold over you. A fop and a whore-whipped fool, not the greatest of vampires ever sired.'

'Well, if any of the gods are paying the blindest bit of notice, we'll both be honouring their gravesides before the war is out.'

'Keep your friends close, and your brothers closer, eh?' Skellan said.

'Or send them away and hope they drop off the end of the world.'

Konrad felt a kinship with this vampire, one that he had not felt with any of Vlad's gets. Perhaps it was because he knew his place in the hierarchy, that as Posner's get he could never rival a true von Carstein for power, perhaps it was his plain speaking, perhaps it was just a remnant of that foul dream. He didn't know, but he felt an affinity between them. It was something he had little experience of. Throughout his life, he had been forced to fight for everything he had. Even before, in his old life, he had had no true friends. Mother had seen to that. Now, he knew, people sought him out for their own interests. Skellan was different. He was like Konrad. They were both outsiders. They didn't fit comfortably into this world of the dead, and they both carried their ghosts close to their chest.

'Of course, it never hurts to give them a push,' Skellan said.

'Indeed, we owe it to ourselves to weed out the weak. In death, as in life, only the strongest should survive.'

'Couldn't agree more.'

'In which case, my new friend, I have a task for you.'

'I am yours to command.' Skellan's smile was predatory in the extreme.

'Travel with Fritz. Become his shadow. See that he does not return to Drakenhof.' Even in his own ears, Konrad could hear the echo of the raven's broken-up cadences.

'You can trust me,' Skellan said, no hint of irony in his voice.

Konrad felt a great peace settle around his shoulders. Yes, yes he could trust Skellan.

CHAPTER TWELVE
Up from the Ashes, in Flames

THE BORDERLANDS, SYLVANIA
The last rites of spring, 2057

THE BEAST HAD left him for dead.

It was a mistake the fiend would come to rue, Kallad vowed, even as his world was consumed with pain and he slipped into darkness once more.

He had no way of knowing how long he had been unconscious.

Awareness returned, the world revealing itself in hallucinatory fragments: the caw of the carrion birds, the rustle of leaves, the smell of blood thick on the breeze, and with them came the pains of his wounds, but for the most part the world was a meaningless wash of colour. He couldn't focus.

He was lying on his back. He didn't have the strength to move.

I am not going to die.

He felt the muscles in his left arm quiver. He was burning up from the inside out.

Despite his determination to live, he knew he was dying, and that there was nothing he could do to change the fact.

Gritting his teeth against the sudden flare of pain, he tried to move. Blackness rose up to claim him.

When he came to again he was alone. The vampire had disappeared into the trees. Kallad bit down on his lip, beads of perspiration running down into his eyes as he tried again to force his body to move. He succeeded in craning his head enough to see that the vampire had stripped the dead of anything it could use.

The slight movement caused his vision to swim, blur and dissolve into a blackness of agony.

He was alone. He couldn't move, couldn't think.

He knew that death was close. The splotches of light leaking through the trees lay like silver coins scattered across the ground. His dead were offering Morr the price of his passage. There silver was no good to him. He lay in the dirt, staring at the canopy of leaves blocking out the sky, and imagined what it would be like.

Who would come to guide him to the Hall of Ancestors? His father? He had failed his people so he had no right to a hero's welcome. Perhaps there would be no emissary. Would that be the ultimate price he paid for his failure? Being left to find his own way home?

'I am not going to die.' His defiance was less than a whisper, but he meant it. He wasn't going to die – not yet.

He still had breath in his lungs. He focused on the pain, used it to remember that he was still alive.

Across the clearing, carrion birds picked at the corpses of Sammy and the soldiers.

Kallad Stormwarden lay in the dirt. He would have laughed, but there was little of amusement in his predicament. He had lost a lot of blood and even his prodigious strength was failing. The arrogance of the vampire rankled. The beast hadn't bothered to finish him off, instead choosing to allow this slow lingering death. 'Well, I'll not give you the satisfaction,' Kallad rasped, biting back on the pain as he finally managed to roll onto his side and push himself up against a tree bole. He screamed in agony as he worked himself into the sitting position. He slumped against the tree, counting the minutes until the pain finally ebbed.

The worst of the pain was in his shoulder and left side, where he had taken two deep cuts. A slow fire burned in the wounds. He had almost no manoeuvrability in his arm. The slightest change of position sent a sharp dagger of pain lancing through him.

He felt out the wounds. Blood had dried into his armour where the rings and plates had been broken and dug into the gaping wounds left by the vampire's blade. The blood had congealed around the metal, fusing skin and armour together. Kallad was going to have to separate it, and not kill himself in the process, if he was going to have any hope of making it out of the clearing.

His screams ought to have been enough to raise the dead.

The dwarf clung stubbornly to consciousness, focusing on the bodies of the dead, and the fact that they had been stripped, and were nothing more than food for the crows. He was determined not to go the same way.

The wound in his side began to bleed again where he had torn it open, but at least it was clean of the stink of gangrene. It was a small mercy. How long it would stay that way if he didn't clean it and tend to it, well that was a different matter. He had seen too many good men die from infected wounds. While he burned, he knew that his body was still fighting off whatever sickness the wounds had caused. He needed to tend to the wounds before he blacked out again.

Forcing himself into action, Kallad shrugged off his pack and took out his water flask.

He took a swallow, and then biting back against the sheer agony of movement, drew the mail shirt off over his head, and dribbled a little of the water onto the wound, wincing against the sting. He tore a strip of cloth from the muslin wrapping around his rations and used it to tenderly flake away the blood that had crusted around the wounds. They were worse than he had thought. Cleaning the gash was agonisingly slow, and used most of the water in his canteen, but it had to be done.

He clung to consciousness as he poked and prodded the wounds to be sure that they were free of anything that might cause infection. He wished he had some liquor, the alcohol would had been excellent for killing any lingering bacteria that might have gotten into the wound, but if he was going to waste his time lingering over wishes like that then he might as well wish for bigger miracles. He could wish that Nagash's black books had been destroyed before they fell into the Vampire Count's hands, or for his father to have slain the beast on the Grunberg's wall and not fallen. He could wish for his clan to be beside him now, instead of these few dead boys. There were bigger miracles worth wishing for.

Next, he rummaged around in the pack for the thin needle of bone and the seamstress's thread wrapped around it. He threaded the needle and, drawing the lips of the gash together, pushed the tip of the needle through the flap of skin and began to sew the wound shut. It was basic field surgery. It wasn't pretty, but it would hold until he could get to a chirurgeon. More importantly, it would give him a chance to heal.

Twice during the stitching Kallad found his focus swimming and the world tilting beneath him, but he stubbornly refused to give in to it. The thread burned as he drew it through his flesh, but he welcomed the pain as a reminder that he was alive.

Only when he was finished did the dwarf allow himself to slump against the tree trunk and give in to unconsciousness.

A none too gentle boot in the side brought him sharply back around.

Kallad's head came up. In his disorientation he still half-expected to see some emissary of the dead come to escort him to the Halls. Instead, he saw a young dirt-smeared face grinning down at him. The grin disappeared as the boy realised that Kallad was still in the land of the living. Flustered, he stuffed his hands in his pockets, obviously trying to hide whatever he had taken from the bodies of the dead.

Kallad grunted and reached out, trying to grab the boy. The exertion had the world swimming out of focus again. As it settled, he saw that the boy held a blunt-edged knife in his trembling hand, and was obviously torn between helping him up and sticking the knife in his gut to finish him off.

Biting down on the pain, Kallad grabbed the boy's hand and pulled him close enough to taste his sour breath. 'Don't make me kill you, boy.'

The boy nodded quickly, trying to pull away.

Despite the fire in his shoulder Kallad's grip was iron.

'Wouldn't dream of it. I'm rather fond of breathing.'

'I'm glad to hear it. Now, tell me your name.'

'Allie du Bek.'

'And where are you from, Allie du Bek?'

'Vierstein.'

'Well Allie du Bek from Vierstein, just between the two of us, there'll be no easy pickings from the dead, if you take my meaning?' Kallad inclined his head towards the boy's hands where they were stuffed in his trouser pockets. 'Empty 'em, there's a good lad.'

Du Bek turned out his pockets. He had taken two rings and a Sigmarite talisman. The silver hammer was tied on a leather thong. It had belonged to the young acolyte, Reimer Schmidt. He had no more use for it where he was.

'Put the rings back, but if you want to wear the hammer, I don't think the priest would begrudge you.'

Du Bek fastened the talisman around his neck before returning the rings to the dead.

Kallad watched him. He moved awkwardly, favouring his left side as if his hip had dropped or some such skeletal deformity hampered him. He coped well with it though, proving once again the resilience of youth.

He really didn't want to get the boy involved, not after what had happened to Sammy, but he didn't see that he had a choice. Kallad promised himself that he wouldn't let Allie du Bek get too close. Part of him actually hoped that the lad would just run off and not come back, even if that meant his own chances of survival dwindled considerably. He was a fighter. He would make it. He wouldn't have more deaths on his conscience.

'When you're done, bring me some food from one of the packs, and then go find someone from that village of yours to help me. Your father, maybe. Another night out here in the dirt doesn't appeal. Those birds might just get fed up of waiting.'

Du Bek nodded and crouched beside Korin Reth's body. He pulled the pack out from beneath the fallen holy man and rifled through it. He rescued a muslin-wrapped chunk of pumpernickel bread, a browning apple and a hunk of pungent cheese, and gave them to Kallad.

Allie du Bek touched the talisman at his throat and grinned. 'I'll go fetch me pa, he's a border warden,' he said, and ran off into the trees, leaving Kallad alone with the dead.

THE HEALING PROCESS was frustratingly slow.

Every morning, Kallad woke in agony, fearful of exploring his wounds in case the tenderness of the day before had succumbed to infection during the night. For the first few weeks, even his own light touch was enough to make him wince.

The village of Vierstein was barely bigger than the four stones its name suggested – a double row of buildings clustered close along the sides of a brackish river. The villagers made him welcome, although many stared openly as he went through his gentle morning exercises, trying to recapture some of the strength and manoeuvrability his wounds had cost him. They had never seen a dwarf before so he bore their curiosity with good grace. Kallad chopped wood and moved grain, and laboured, stretching his endurance daily, until his strength began to return.

LOTHAR DU BEK, Allie's father, was a good man. He helped Kallad by burying the bones of his comrades, and saw to it that Kallad was fed and had a roof over his head for the weeks he needed to recover.

He didn't know how to tell the dwarf the magician had not been among the dead.

The border warden was skilled at reading the play of a battle out of the dirt, discerning the signs and getting a mental picture of how the fight had unfolded. He had followed the magician to the point where the vampire had overwhelmed him, but there had been no corpse. There *had* been a one-sided struggle. The lack of a body had disturbed both the border warden and the dwarf. Was the magician the vampire's prisoner? Was he lying dead in a ditch somewhere?

If he was the beast's captive then, day by day, the magician was getting further and further away from them.

Less than a month had passed since he had vowed that there would be no more deaths on his conscience.

Kantor was turning it into an impossible promise to keep.

Kallad and the border warden talked often at daybreak when Lothar returned from his nightly patrols. The hinterland was becoming more dangerous by the day. Lothar talked regularly about huge black wolves the size of men prowling in the dark, picking off game. He regularly found the carcasses of deer and venison, mauled, throats ripped out, hides torn open, ribs cracked apart, and the innards gone, having served as a feast for the beasts.

The black wolves disturbed du Bek, not only because they were unnaturally large, or because they were more powerful than any wolf he'd been forced to hunt in his life as a border warden, but because they showed no fear of him. They didn't retreat from his scent. They howled into the night, as if they were talking to one another, and circled him, shepherding him away from wherever they fed. The animals showed surprising cunning, and truly were pack creatures. They were never alone.

Du Bek sat down heavily at the table and pulled his gloves off. 'I killed one,' he told the dwarf. They had discussed the unnatural creatures often enough for Kallad to know what du Bek meant. 'I caught it shadowing me, I don't know if it was trying to draw me away from something or lead me to somewhere. It didn't feel right. My skin crawled whenever I felt its gaze upon me. I couldn't shake the feeling that it was *hunting* me. I couldn't have that. I brought it down with a silver-tipped arrow through the throat.'

The border wardens had taken to using silver-tipped arrows during the time of the first vampire wars when Vlad von Carstein had tormented the settlements along the River Stir. They had seen a lot of unnatural things, including loved ones rising from the grave to terrorise the night. In defence they clutched every superstition they knew, including silver and garlic, white roses, relics and blessed water.

Tinkers and vagabonds were still doing a brisk trade in pseudo-religious artefacts. It was all about faith. People wanted to believe, so people were gulled out of their money. It gave them a warm, false sense of protection.

'I saw it go down with my own eyes, dwarf, but when I went over to reclaim the shaft the beast's carcass was gone. The corpse of a naked man lay sprawled out in the dirt, Kallad. There was no wolf! As Morr is my witness, there was no trace of blood on the arrow's tip as I pulled it out of the fallen man. He didn't bleed, not a drop. I tell you, dark things are gathering over there,' Lothar du Bek said, shaking his head as he tore off a chunk of bread and dipped it into the steaming bowl of broth that his wife had ladled out a few moments earlier.

The dwarf wasn't about to argue. He had seen enough to know that evil was abroad once more. Lothar's stories of strangers travelling only at night, black coaches on the highways, restless wildlife, and now huge dire wolves that were really men stalking the borderlands, didn't leave much to the imagination. After years of relative quiet, the enemy was amassing its forces once more.

'You did well, my friend.'

'But to what end? Every night there are more of them. What is one death amongst their number? A nuisance, no more, surely. They are like a black wave of death ready to bear down on the country, and all that stands between them and the honest decent ordinary folk of the Empire are a few border wardens and men like you.'

'Well, I'm no man, but I'll forgive you. I get your meaning, but you're wrong. We aren't alone, far from it. Every one of those ordinary decent folk will take up arms against the beast. Don't sell them short, they're good people.'

'Aye, and good people die, Kallad, and much more easily than those beasts, at that. You know that as well as I do. Andreas returned last night. That accursed land has changed him. He used to laugh, but not yesterday. All he would say was that he had seen things no living man was meant to see. I didn't want to force him, he'll talk when he's ready. The little that he did share though was grim indeed. A woman was taken by force. A black carriage bearing the crest of von Carstein came into her village and three men snatched her. The day before, strangers had been asking about folk in the village, peculiar questions.'

'Such as?'

'If anyone had unusual luck, say was always lucky at cards, or dice.'

'I see.'

'The woman was the midwife. She'd saved several babes, including more than one breech where the child came out upside down.'

'What would the Vampire Count want with her? It isn't as if the dead fall pregnant.'

'This isn't the first time the black coaches have taken someone from around here. It's happening more and more, as if someone, or something, is collecting people like her: people who have a certain something about them, something that sets them apart, be it luck, a gift or a talent. It don't bode well, mark my words.'

Kallad lay on his back in the dirt straining to press a sack stuffed with rocks and scraps of metal and other rubbish off his chest. His arms shook with violent tremors as he strained against the weight of it, forcing his elbows to lock. He gasped out a count of ten and slowly brought the sack back down to rest on his chest, counted once again to ten, and then repeated the press, forcing a scream between his clenched teeth as he lifted the huge weight.

His shoulder, back and sides burned, but for the first time in months, the pain was brought on by honest exertion, not his wounds. He still favoured his left side a little, taking the extra strain on his right, but he was mending, finally, and he was strong enough to help out around the farms, doing manual labour for those in need, in return for food and lodging.

Sweat beaded on his forehead and gathered in the valley where his throat met his torso.

Allie du Bek sat cross-legged on the floor, hefting a smaller stone, first in his right hand, five times, and then repeating the exercise with his left. The boy was fascinated by Kallad's stubborn refusal to bow to his wounds.

'What news have you got for me?' Kallad asked, heaving the sack aside and sitting up. He towelled the sweat off with a rag.

'None good, Kallad,' Allie said, tossing the stone over his shoulder. It hit the wooden wall of the wood shack and bounced away.

'Tell me anyway.'

Kallad walked over to the barrel that collected rainwater as it ran from the wood shack's guttering, and sank his head and shoulders into it. He came up spluttering, gasped three times, drawing deep breaths, and plunged his head back into the water again.

He was under for a long time.

Allie counted to twenty before Kallad came up for air.

'More of the same, really: three reports of kidnappings in the last week, lots of sightings of the black coaches, a few rumbles of the sleeping sickness striking some of the younger girls up and down the border. Father's been hellishly busy with the border wardens. He gave me a message for you: the wardens have killed three more wolves, and each one went the same way as the last one he told you about. He said you'd know what that meant.'

Of course, he did – wolves that died as men.

'Keep talking, lad,' Kallad said, hefting his axe and burying it in a chunk of wood. He split it in half on the chopping block, and then in half again, and tossed the quarters onto the grass up against the side of the wood shack. He grabbed another piece, and split it, rolling his shoulders afterwards. It was good to feel the blood circulating again. He felt stronger than he had in months.

'Father's gone out hunting with Jared and Klein. Why does it have to be this way?'

That was something that Kallad didn't have an answer for. He wasn't comfortable trying to pass off evil as some part of nature, and wasn't any more at peace with the idea that the world needed evil to attain balance within itself. Telling Allie that good men and women died just because, well that was no answer at all. So he let his silence answer for him.

'Father says that ignorance breeds fear,' the boy said after a while.

'He's right, but in this case, even knowing your enemy won't help lessen the fear. The more you know about the monster, the more frightening it becomes. These things are like parasites that crawl into the mattress of your bed at night and hide there quietly, coming out when you are asleep, to feed on you, bloating themselves on your blood. They need you to survive, and yet their very nature is obsessed with destruction. They are their own worst enemies, but it's still right to be frightened of them. Let the fear give you strength, but don't allow it to overwhelm you. That's the trick.'

Kallad swung his axe again, slamming it into the log on the chopping block and splitting it clean in two. With each stroke his determination to heal intensified. The monsters could not be left to ravage the countryside. Good people were dying. They didn't deserve to disappear into the bowels of Drakenhof to feed the vampire's bloody hunger.

He wiped off his sweat, and planted the double-headed axe at his feet.

'Come on, boy. It's time I said my goodbyes to some old friends. I've put it off long enough.'

Allie du Bek hopped down from his perch and skipped towards the trees. He waved for Kallad to follow.

Splitting logs and pressing sacks of coal only took him so far towards regaining mastery of his limbs. The simplest of things, walking, lying down, still caused incendiary pains to flare if he moved even slightly awkwardly. It galled Kallad that while he struggled like some newly hatched bird, the vampire moved further and further away from him. He was not used to feeling so utterly helpless. He was Kallad Stormwarden, the last survivor of Karak Sadra. He was not about to roll over and play dead. Instead, he stubbornly drove the feeling off, and trudged after Allie as he plunged into the forest.

They were going to the graves.

He had always known that the day would come when he was strong enough to move on, and this small respite would be over. Kallad had struggled to convince himself that that was the reason why he hadn't made his peace with the dead. It wasn't, of course. It was guilt.

Guilt had prevented him from returning to the clearing where they had fallen, although he went there when he slept, traitorous dreams dragging him back night after night to relive his failure.

TIME HAD DESTROYED every last physical reminder of the fight with the vampire. The grove was pitted with the shallow graves of a few good men. Nature had already begun the slow process of reclaiming the slight mounds that marked their final resting places.

None of them were marked. They deserved better. Every soldier who died fighting evil did.

Kallad bent his head and offered a prayer to the God of the Underworld to look after the souls of his travelling companions, and took the time to remember them one at a time: Sammy Krauss, Joachim Akeman, Reimer Schmidt, Korin Reth, the renegade magician, Nevin Kantor and the three soldiers from Grimm's guard.

His eyes were red-rimmed with tears when he looked up. He breathed in deeply, ready to turn his back on the dead, when it stuck him – there weren't eight shallow graves in the clearing, there were seven.

'Where's your father?'

'I told you, he's gone out hunting with Jared and Klein. Why?'

'Because something's wrong here, boy, the numbers don't add up. There's a grave missing.'

'We buried all the dead, I helped him.'

'I believe you, but I need to talk to your father.'

'He won't be home 'til sunrise at the earliest.'

'Grimna's balls… You saw the dead?'

'Yes.'

'All right, now think, boy. This is important. Did one of the corpses have its hair drawn up in a topknot, the sides shaved high above its ears?'

'Like a corsair?'

'Exactly like that, yes.'

Allie du Bek shook his head.

Kallad cursed himself for a fool. It had never even occurred to him that Kantor wouldn't be amongst the dead. He looked back in the direction that the magician had fled all those months ago. It was impossible to tell which way he had gone. An all too familiar wave of helplessness rose up to engulf Kallad. The dwarf needed more than just a skilled tracker, he needed a miracle worker. Whatever tracks the magician had blazed in his panicked flight were long gone.

'I need your father and I need him *now*.'

'But it's getting dark.'

For a second, Kallad felt the cold hand of doubt close around his heart. He brushed it off.

'Find him.'

Allie du Bek nodded nervously.

'I don't know where he is, not really, he could be anywhere along the ranges.'

'It doesn't matter how long it takes, I'll be here.'

* * *

IT WAS LONG into the night when Allie returned with his father and the two other border wardens.

That they had been in a lethal fight against the dark hunters was obvious.

Lothar had long raking scratches down the side of his face where claws had dug in, and his shirt was torn at the shoulder and soaked black with dried blood. He'd ripped one sleeve off and wadded it up to staunch the wound, but it was obvious, even ill-lit by the moonlight, that he had lost a lot of blood and was ghastly pale.

Both Klein and Jared bore wounds of their own, but none as substantial as du Bek's.

The man moved awkwardly, favouring his wounded side. It was no surprise that it had taken Allie the better part of the night to return with them.

'It's worse than it looks,' Lothar said, grinning and almost simultaneously wincing.

'Aye, I don't doubt you.'

'The boy said that you think someone survived, or at least isn't buried here.'

Kallad nodded. 'A magician, he turned coward and ran when the fighting began.'

'Then he must have run like the wind, because believe me these beasts can *move*. If he made it, he's long gone, dwarf, you know that.'

'Aye, but that'd also make him my only link to the vampires. If he's alive, I need to find him, Lothar.'

'The trail will be dead by now.'

'I know. After a couple of days it's almost impossible to follow a trail. There won't be footprints to follow, but maybe he got clumsy. It happens. Like as not nothing made it through the winter, but I can't leave it like that, not when there might be a hint somewhere that'd at least point me in the right direction.'

'Well if there is, it's nothing that we'll find in the dark.'

'Good job it took you the best part of the night to get here then, eh?'

The border warden turned gingerly to scan the glade. The sun was beginning to rise redly through the trees, but the darkness remained fiercely determined to keep its secrets close to its heart for a while longer. He had been right, there was little to see.

'What do you remember of the fight, Kallad?'

'Too much, truth be told. Kantor, the magician, ran off that way.' He pointed towards a break in the trees. 'That was the last time I saw him.'

'Then that would be a good place to start, but, understand, after we step through the trees every step is guesswork. No promises, dwarf. Most likely, he's long gone, or we'll find a corpse that we missed first time.'

Kallad nodded.

It was a slow, painstaking search, the three wardens pausing often to examine the ground, or the break of a fine branch that had gone rotten over the winter, but which could, conceivably, have been a sign of the magician's flight. He had no idea how they could do it. To the dwarf, a snapped twig was a snapped twig. There was no distinguishable difference between any of the many bits of deadfall they negotiated, and a leaf trodden into the dirt was nothing more than nature taking its course.

'Here,' Jared called. He'd split off from the others and was running a parallel path off the beaten track. They fought their way through the undergrowth to join him. Bracken and some kind of nettled fruit bushes had grown up around the mossy tree trunks, building a natural wall that stung and pulled at their skin and clothing as they beat a path through it.

Kallad couldn't tell what he was supposed to be looking at, but Lothar and Klein became quite animated, kneeling to examine the dirt and the broken branches.

'There was a fight here,' Jared explained.

'Not much of one, either,' Klein said.

'How can you tell?' Kallad couldn't see anything that could possibly indicate that a fight had taken place.

Lothar knelt, examining something trodden into the ground. He took a phial from his pocket and dripped a dribble of clear liquid onto it. There was a sizzle and a small wisp of smoke, and then it was gone. 'Good find, Jared. I'd stake my life on the fact that this is where the beast caught up with your magician,' Lothar du Bek said. 'The good news is that there's no body.'

'So he's alive?' Kallad asked. He had no idea what the warden had just done, and he didn't really want to know what magic it was, either. If it served to make du Bek certain that the magician had survived, he wasn't going to waste time arguing.

'Well, the signs of the fight are all but gone, but there most definitely was a struggle here, and my guess is that two people walked away from it.'

'So the vampire has the magician?'

'I didn't say that. I said two people walked away from this fight.'

'What do you mean?'

'They didn't leave together. The tracks have all but been obliterated, but my gut feeling is that one set leads off in the direction of the blasted ruins that mark the border with Sylvania, you can see what looks like a heel print pressed into the hardened mulch of the dead leaves, it isn't much, but it is something. The other heads south, into halfling territory. This one is easier to follow.'

'We followed the vampire south.'

'Then it is reasonably safe to assume that the beast carried on its merry way without your magician. That doesn't explain why it let him live, or why he chose to head into Sylvania alone, but those are riddles that can't be solved by me. You know the magician, dwarf. Is he the kind of man to walk alone into the belly of the beast?'

'Not unless the coward found his courage,' Kallad said, shaking his head.

'Frightened men do peculiar things,' Klein observed. 'It is conceivable that he could have made some kind of pact with the creature, striking a bargain to save his life.'

Jared shook his head. 'Unlikely, what does a magician have to offer a vampire lord? The beasts aren't inclined to strike bargains.'

'True,' Lothar agreed. 'You either get lucky or you die. For some reason he's alive, or at least lived long enough to walk out of this forest. It's likely the beast left him for dead, as he did you, Kallad, only we didn't find him. He could be lying twenty feet away, rotting.'

'Or he could be halfway across the world,' Kallad said. 'If he drove the beast off where we failed, well, who knows, eh? The only thing that makes any sense to me is that he's running. He knows that his life is forfeit if he stays in the Empire. That was a condition of his release by the Sigmarites. He was to serve the quest, and when his usefulness was done, so was his time for breathing.'

'Are you sure he knew this?' Lothar asked.

'He would have been a fool if he didn't. The witch hunters don't give up their prisoners lightly.'

'Well then, I think you're right and we have at least one answer to the riddles we've found this morning. The man is running for his life, in the only direction he can – into von Carstein's foul realm. So, he's beaten, perhaps close to death, and he comes to. His instinct is to run. He can't go back to the Empire, so he has to go forwards. It's likely he'll keep on running 'til he falls off the world.'

'Perhaps he hopes to redeem himself by slaying the beast in his lair, after all, he faced one vampire and lived to tell the tale, which is more than can be said for most men. If it was me, I know I'd be trying to find a way to go home. You can't run forever.'

'I have to find him,' Kallad said, knowing it was the truth. Together, his axe and the magician's sorcery stood a chance against the fell beasts.

Alone they were doomed.

'Then we best return home for supplies and make ready to hunt down this magician of yours.'

'We?'

'No offence, Kallad, but you couldn't find your arse with a map and a mirror. So yes, we. Jared and Klein are more than capable of patrolling the border for a few nights without me, and Allie will keep his mother company. It'll keep the boy out of trouble.'

'What about?' He gestured towards the blood and the ragged cuts.

'They should slow me down enough to move at your pace for a while,' Lothar du Bek chuckled.

CHAPTER THIRTEEN
Vado Mori

MIDDENHEIM, CITY OF THE WHITE WOLF
The blistering heart of summer, 2057

THE WALLS OF Middenheim couldn't hope to withstand them. The city would fall.

Hope, they said, was the last thing to die.

They were wrong. Hope died long before desperation, pain and fear had relinquished their hold on the living.

Even then, death was no escape: not when the dead could be pulled out of the earth and puppeted by the malicious finger of a necromancer like Immoliah Fey.

Skellan watched as Fey drew the dead out of the dirt. She lacked the grace of Vlad von Carstein, but what she lacked in grace, she more than made up for with power. The winds of magic howled around her, the air itself crackling with the intensity of the magic she wove. The incantations tripped off her tongue, staining the air around her with the putrescence of death. The necromancer revelled in it, throwing her head back, her voice spiralling in a discordant chorus as the dead danced at her beck and call.

He had seen this before, but it still unnerved him. With Vlad, it had been an awesome display of his strength and mastery over the nations of the living and the nations of the dead. He commanded the skies and the dirt, and both jerked around readily to his whims. With Fey it was different. Her magic lacked the ferocity of Vlad's. It was subtle, toying with the fabric of the universe and cajoling it to respond to her demands. In some ways it was more unnatural.

They came slowly at first, bones clawing out of the dirt, broken and rotting, emerging in a second bizarre birth into the unlife. Then, with increasing regularity, they were drawn from the earth's shallow graves and ditches where they had been left to rot.

Skellan could not abide the woman, but her usefulness was undeniable. As a magician, she was hardly the equal of Vlad, but what had started as a fledgling army almost certainly destined to fail, had grown into an unstoppable force of nature, because of the necromancer.

Fritz von Carstein stood two paces behind Fey, his eyes aglow with the fire of hunger. Skellan had a grudging admiration for Fritz. The vampire cultivated the image of the carefree Lothario with his harem of nubile young vixens, but Skellan had quickly come to realise that it was all an elaborate act. Beneath the foppish exterior lurked a cold ruthless cunning that outstripped anything Skellan had seen in the unstable Konrad or the earnest Pieter. Fritz was an enigma. He played the fool beautifully, so well in fact, that it became second nature, a mask to be drawn down, that rarely slipped, but for all his talk of decadence and decay there was an underlying current of dark wisdom and steely determination to Fritz that betrayed the act. Skellan harboured no illusions: the vampire played the fool to encourage those around him to underestimate him. It was a useful ploy, one that no doubt had considerable mileage in it.

Fritz was playing the long game. His plans were subtle and would no doubt have been successful, if left to root and fester.

Which is what made the assassination attempt on Konrad so out of character for the cautious Fritz. It was reckless. Three thralls against a vampire of Konrad's strength was blatant stupidity. Fritz couldn't have expected it to succeed, which meant that the scheme had another aim, something that wasn't readily apparent to Skellan.

What did Fritz have to gain from driving Konrad into a murderous frenzy?

Nothing – or perhaps everything.

After Konrad's assault, Skellan hadn't expected to see Fritz again, but as Konrad blustered and strutted with all the pomposity of a man possessed, dishing out orders for the gathered men, Fritz had walked calmly in through the castle gates to claim his place at the front of his army. It was all Konrad could do to restrain himself. This petty act of defiance was the best laugh Skellan had had in months. He thought Konrad had been about to burst a blood vessel; the vampire was apoplectic. The wolf, Jerek, had laid a restraining hand on Konrad's shoulder and, surprisingly, rather than brushing it off von Carstein had succumbed to it.

'You made it, I see.'

'Nothing could have kept me away, brother-mine. This is a great honour, and I intend to see your faith in me repaid manifold.'

Skellan had almost laughed out loud at that. It was a subtle threat, but it was a threat nonetheless. It was a pity that Fritz had to die, because it could have been interesting to see their little power play run its course. It would have been entertaining, if nothing else. So little of life – death – offered any amusement.

In one sly act of defiance, Fritz had turned his banishment into a not so silent act of rebellion, and a promise of retribution.

That was something Skellan could respect.

He had come to know the vampire over the months they had travelled together. The transformation was subtly stunning as Fritz came out of his brother's shadow. He was everything Konrad was not. He was articulate, thoughtful and ruthless without the callous cruelty of his kin. Villages fell at their feet, but where Konrad would have razed them to the ground and revelled in a blood feast, Fritz used death to inspire fear. He farmed the women, bleeding them a little at a time, taking them prisoner and exerting a curious mesmerism over them, so that they willingly pandered to his whims and came to him night after night to satisfy his hungers. He kept the most beautiful for himself, rebuilding his harem one beauty at a time. All but a few of the men, he had put down, with a few survivors encouraged to flee for their lives, thus ensuring that the horrors of the vampiric horde would spread like flames across the parched countryside.

The dead were coming. There would be no mercy. None could resist.

Long before their arrival, word had reached Middenheim, ensuring that the City of the White Wolf knew fear, and that those dark imaginings had had time to fester and grow. Its inhabitants remembered the time before, when the dead had all but destroyed the city, ghosts, wraiths, wights and other ethereal dreads descending on its cobbled streets.

Unlike his father-in-death, Fritz took no great joy in the destruction. It was merely a means to an end, and that end was his ascension to power.

Mannfred was right to be wary of Fritz.

It was Fritz who had taught Skellan the greatest of truths – that sunlight need hold no fear. He hadn't believed the older vampire at first, not until he had reached out into the sunlight itself, turning his hand slowly left and right, offering the palm and back to the sun's glare. Even with the evidence of his own eyes, Skellan couldn't get past the probability that it was some kind of trick, and that if he tried to replicate Fritz's casual exposure, he would burn.

'It's in the mind,' Fritz had assured him, stepping out into the light. 'Only the weak need fear the sun. The strongest of us can move abroad even under a full sun.'

'But–'

Fritz tilted his head up to face the sun, relishing its warm kiss.

'Are you afraid, Jon Skellan?'

'Of nothing,' Skellan said, joining von Carstein in the light. It felt peculiar at first, more intense than he remembered it ever being when he was alive. His skin prickled and he felt sure that he was about to be consumed by unholy fire.

'Concentrate. You have nothing to fear. Focus on the feelings spreading through your skin and dampen them down. Do it now.'

Skellan held his hand before his face. The skin had turned an ugly red.

'What's happening to me?'

'You are burning from the inside out, now concentrate.'

'Or?' The angry red blush had spread the length of his arm. He could feel the intensity of the fire swelling beneath his skin.

'Or you burn.' The brutal matter-of-factness of von Carstein's answer was all he needed. Skellan focused on the searing heat beneath his skin and willed it to subside.

For a moment, he feared the worst as he felt a sudden flare in the glands beneath his arms and between his legs. Then there was nothing, no sense of feeling at all. The fire had died.

'You see?' Fritz asked.

'Can we all do this?'

'Our kind? Yes, we all have the power to master the heat. Few choose to, though, drawing comfort from the shadow world of night.'

'I pity the fools.'

'Don't. Pity is something to be left behind in your old life, Skellan. Savour this triumph and know that the day holds nothing worth fearing. Let that knowledge set you free.'

It had, in more ways than von Carstein could ever have imagined.

Still, as Fritz had said they would, the others clung to the darkness when they could have walked proudly through the day. It disgusted him.

Immoliah Fey brought her hands down and slumped, exhaustion taking its toll. Five hundred corpses in various states of decay and wholeness crowded around the necromancer, bugs crawled over strips of rotten flesh and flies swarmed around the corpses, drawn to the filth of the grave. They shambled and lurched to Fey's danse macabre.

Very soon, the people of Middenheim would know the true meaning of the word fear. Theirs would be a painful lesson, learned in the hardest of ways. Then, with the White Wolves humbled, the vampires would descend with bloody fury.

'Ready?' Skellan asked the dark-skinned man at his side.

'I was born ready.'

'A shame you weren't ready when you died, eh?' Skellan said without a hint of irony. 'We go in the second wave, behind the corpses. Torch the temples and meeting halls to drive out the living. Kill the men and any children that get in the way, but leave the women for von Carstein.'

'As you wish.'

'It isn't as I wish. If it were, I'd loose the beast within and have us go in with a vengeance. Just this once, I would give the vampires free rein. Let the world know what it is like when the aristocracy of the night feed.'

His dark-skinned companion smiled a cold smile.

'Indeed. Such cruel wonders we could unleash. Pity the cattle, then.'

'Pity? No, no, no.' Skellan said, echoing von Carstein's admonition. 'Why waste your time with something so... banal? Pity is for the life you left behind. Focus on yourself, feed on the joy their suffering brings.'

Pressed up against the portcullis, her face pale with fear, Skellan saw a woman clutching a child to her breast. From this distance, she bore an uncanny resemblance to Lizbet. The similarity didn't touch him. When the time for it came, she would burn like his dead wife had. It mattered nothing to him.

THE BATTLE WAS brutal and bloody.

The White Wolves sallied forth, hooves sparking on the cobbled street as they passed beneath the keystone of the massive arch that housed the city gates, two and three at a time. War horns bugled a fanfare. The White Wolves fanned out across the plain into a rolling wall of death as their war cries sang out. This was combat at its most primal. Pennons snapped in the air. Horses stamped, impatient, smelling blood on the air.

The bugle sounded again, a single short violent bray, and the Wolves charged.

The young wolf at the head of the riders threw back his head and howled, his flame-red hair streaming out behind him in the wind as he raised his warhammer above his head and whipped it around in a savage arc.

They hit the dead at full glorious gallop, splintering their ranks, and the battle was joined. The iron heads of warhammers cracked the brittle bones of the dead.

Immoliah Fey puppetted her corpses expertly, sacrificing them beneath the hooves of the Wolves' horses, causing the beasts to shy and fall. Blood spilled, the vampires unleashed the beasts within, and joined the battle.

Infantry followed the charging horses, dogs loping at their sides.

Arrows rained down from the walls of the city, cutting down friend and foe alike. The archers possessed no particular skills, but what skills were necessary to fill the sky with a rain of death? What was important was that the deadly rain never ceased.

Even with their forces bolstered by Fey's zombies, the battle was hard on the forces of the dead. The White Wolves fought with the desperation of the condemned. They knew they stood to lose more than their lives if they failed. They knew that they were fighting for the lives – and deaths – of every one sheltering behind the towering walls of the City of the White Wolf. The intimacy of the battle added steely determination to their fearsome combat rage. This was their fight, their home, and they would not fail this time. They owed the dead that much.

Skellan fought like a daemon, taking the fight to the Wolves. His blade cut and cleaved and stabbed, opening guts and slicing throats indiscriminately, while he kept Fritz von Carstein in his line of sight as the vampire waged his own bloody war on the living of Middenheim. Whether drawn by recognition or merely sensing that the man had risen to replace Jerek and therefore held a pivotal position amid the ranks of the enemy, Fritz fought his way mercilessly towards the Hamaya's kin. Blades clashed on bone. Men screamed. It was carnage.

Then the two met, the young wolf and the immortal beast, and it was over before it could become a fight, the shaft of an arrow jutted from his horse, bringing the beast down and crushing its rider's legs, pinning the young wolf helplessly in the mud of the battlefield.

Von Carstein leaned in close enough to breathe foetid breath into the rider's face as his hands closed around his neck.

Skellan moved quickly, disengaging the soldier he faced, shifting his weight onto his back leg and pivoting, bringing his sword around in a low arc that hamstrung his opponent, and rolling away, ducking beneath a wildly swinging hammer and coming to his feet. A thrust gutted the only soldier between him, and Fritz and the young wolf. He slipped in the mud, but still managed to cover the ground between himself and von Carstein in the time it would have taken a living man's heart to beat once – and for the young wolf trapped beneath his dead horse that single beat was the difference between life and death.

It had to be now.

Skellan came up behind the gloating Fritz, and in one smooth move drew the arrow from the dead horse's neck and rammed its silver tip into the vampire's neck. The bloodless tip punched out of Fritz's throat and suddenly, instead of strangling the young wolf, the vampire's hands were at his own throat, clawing at the silver arrowhead that had killed him, even as the unlife spilled out of his body.

There was no dignity in Fritz's second death.

Skellan leaned in close and, not caring that the young wolf overheard, whispered in von Carstein's ear, 'A gift from Mannfred. Nothing personal, you understand, but there can be only one heir to Vlad. Your continued existence was an irritant. It complicated things. So you see, we couldn't allow you to live. Not that it matters any, but I liked you, Fritz. Of all of them, you were perhaps the most dangerous, the most worthy. Such is life, my friend.'

Fritz's eyes had begun to glaze over as the unnatural ties binding him to the land of the living severed one by one.

'Soon, your brothers will be rotting in the underworld beside you. Take some comfort in that last thought, eh? You won't be alone for long.'

Fritz tried to speak. His mouth opened and closed uselessly. He managed a pathetic gurgle before he slumped forward over the young wolf's horse and died.

'Our lord has fallen!' Skellan cried, brandishing his sword over his head. 'Retreat! Sound the retreat!' The news of von Carstein's death spread across the battlefield like wildfire. These vampires had not stood beside the first Vampire Count, they harboured no illusions that their immortality was in fact true immortality. That their leader had fallen sent shockwaves through the survivors, crippling them with panic.

It was all Skellan could have hoped for, and more.

Fey's zombies collapsed where they stood as panic undermined the necromancer's hold on them. She fled, while the vampires surrendered the field, leaving the White Wolves with nothing left to slay.

Skellan loitered on the field, watching from a distance as, freed from beneath his dead horse, the young wolf hosted up Fritz's corpse, preparing it to be dismembered. The man cut Fritz von Carstein's dead heart from his chest and tossed it to the dogs at his feet.

Smiling to himself, Skellan turned away from the slaughter.

CHAPTER FOURTEEN
Victis Honor

NULN BESIEGED
The blistering heart of summer, 2057

JEREK VON CARSTEIN'S HUMANITY refused to be snuffed out.

It lingered, haunting him, a living ghost in the kingdom of the dead. The irony was repulsive.

Instead of revelling in the dark world of unlife, Jerek found himself clinging to the tatters of memory that belonged to his life before. Inconsequential things that hadn't mattered then, but had become more and more vital since his fall from Middenheim spire. He found himself remembering the faces of people he had barely known. They came to him in sudden flashes, accompanied by hints of what they had meant at the time, scents, accents and tiny hallucinations that drew him back towards the man he had been.

Worst of all, he welcomed them. He welcomed the pain that came with remembering. He welcomed the guilt that threatened to consume him. He welcomed the anger that smouldered beneath the memories. He welcomed them all because they were all reminders that he might be a monster, but that he hadn't surrendered his soul. Some tiny spark of it still flickered within him. He hadn't surrendered to the darkness and the cold. He found no comfort in pain. He took no joy in suffering.

The companionship of the dead repelled him.

Instead, he clung to his living ghost, knowing that to do so was to invite madness.

In Roth Mehlinger he saw all the world's sickness made flesh. Even in the few months since his siring, Mehlinger had completely surrendered to the beast within. He savoured the hunt and the kill, and being Jerek's first, he was strong, stronger than he had any right to be. He walked abroad in daylight without any fear of the sun. He infiltrated the city, not caring about the high walls and the iron gates meant to keep the wolves from the door. He took wing, metamorphosing into a ravenlike black bird. No walls ever constructed could bar a bird. Mehlinger came and went as he pleased, feeding on the young and beautiful of the city – and stupidly the peasants suspected nothing, because Mehlinger had a taste for young men and cared nothing for the pretty little bakers' daughters or the temptations of the more worldly barmaids.

He haunted the slums, taking pleasure in the screams of otherwise strong men as he forced them to submit bodily to him, and then he fed.

In death, Mehlinger was everything the man had hated in life.

'You made me, father,' Mehlinger had sneered, seeing Jerek's distaste for the first time. 'Never forget that. I was happily drinking myself to death before you decided to play god and do this to me. Every death is on your hands as surely as if you had killed them yourself, only this way is more fun for me. For once, I don't have to be content to live half a life in your shadow. I can be my own man, Jerek, and you know what? I like the man I have become.'

'You stopped being a man a long time ago, Roth. What you are now, well, that is not a man.'

'I'm whatever the hell I want to be, wolf. I don't need your permission anymore. You did that much for me when you took my life.'

'I'm sorry, Roth, more than you can ever know.'

'Don't be. This death is not such a bad place to be.'

Mehlinger was drawn to Pieter von Carstein. They were similar beasts, ruthless, callous, deadly, and suffered no compunction in killing for fun and amusement. They hunted together at night, Mehlinger feeding while Pieter played with his food. Von Carstein did not share Mehlinger's passion for boys, but he more than made up for it by creatively torturing the cattle before offering the succulent flesh up for Mehlinger to suck greedily on. Their relationship was parasitic. They fed off each other's sickness, exacerbating it, driving each other to acts of fouler and fouler depravity.

Jerek had turned his back on his get.

The thought of putting Mehlinger down had crossed his mind, taking responsibility for the monster he had sired and finishing what he started, but it wasn't easy. Their bond was stronger than sire and get. There was all that went before: the wolf and his right hand. They had a history.

That he couldn't turn his back on that history was another sign that Jerek von Carstein was still, in part, Jerek Kruger, the White Wolf. So, Mehlinger lived on, his corruption growing more and more complete by the day.

Together with Pieter, Mehlinger had rejoiced as one of Konrad's pet necromancers, Katja von Seirt, had touched the winds of magic, drawing on Shyish, the sixth wind, to raise a horde of dead that counted in the tens of thousands. The taint of Chaos hung over their conquering army. It was the ultimate vampiric essence, bleeding the land dry as it swarmed towards Nuln, devastation trailing in its wake. The blight inflicted by Pieter's army rivalled anything caused by his sire, Vlad. The sickness that had for so long afflicted Sylvania seeped into the Empire. Nature itself, the greens and golds of summer, withered and died, trampled beneath the shuffling feet of the dead.

In many ways, Jerek knew, an army was like a snake. It depended upon cunning against greater foes, and its body was impotent against enemies if its fangs were not kept sharp. Pieter was the head of this army, the necromancer Katja von Seirt and the wolf, Jerek, its fangs. Von Seirt was venomous, certainly, but her bites were proving ineffective because of von Carstein's ineptitude. The vampire was no tactician. He had little grasp of the art of war. He was nothing more than a pale forgery, replicating things that he had seen done before, but without the ruthlessness that had made them successful. Like all classically insecure leaders, he ignored Jerek's battle-hardened wisdom in favour of his own council. The siege of Nuln had lasted four months already, rendering the most basic of their weapons, fear, redundant. The citizens of the city had grown familiar with the dead at their door. They were inured to the fear that such a force ought to have inspired.

Without fear to undermine the enemy, they needed to resort to deviousness. Unfortunately, Pieter took to posturing before the city walls, demanding the living bow down before him or die, but he lacked the wherewithal to follow through. His words were little more than empty threats, or so it seemed. The corpses surged at the walls, only to be beaten back with flames and oil.

The defenders did not surrender meekly. They met his demands of servitude with jeers, throwing rotten fruit and vegetables from the battlements, which in turn only served to cause Pieter's anger to spiral out of control. The vampire ranted and raved, cursing all humanity for the vile scum that they were, unable to distance himself from the haranguing. He spat curses as the defenders threw refuse from the walls. Three farmers struggled with the rotten carcass of a dead cow, sending it toppling from the high wall. The animal fell, stiff with rigor.

'HAVE YOU THOUGHT more about my puzzle, Katja?' Jerek asked the necromancer.

'I have thought of little else, wolf. So much so that I have come to think of it more as a curse than a question, it haunts me so.'

'Have you come to any conclusions?'

'Many and none, if that makes a blind bit of sense.'

'Not in the slightest.'

'There is nothing to prove the veracity of your assumption that your sire's power lay in his signet ring.'

'I know it to be true, the cattle talk. The ring was stolen through treachery.' He had heard the story in Middenheim as he hunted Mehlinger. The Sigmarites had turned to thievery to bring about the fall of Vlad von Carstein. In desperate times, humanity was capable of stooping to the most desperate of measures. How they could have known of the ring's restorative magic he had no idea, but he didn't doubt for a moment that they were right. It explained his sire's irrational anger as he had thrown everything he had at Altdorf in an uncharacteristic rage, and it explained why he had fallen.

The ring was the key to it all. He had to find it, Find it and destroy it before others could possess it. He had long since begun to suspect that the ring's existence was the reason for his lingering humanity. It had become a smouldering obsession. He thought of Mehlinger, the callousness of the monster he had become, the pure blooded vampire, and of Pieter with his all-consuming hatred for the living, even Konrad with his capricious whims and fragile instability. Any one of them with the ring on his finger could rise as the ultimate dark lord. The thought chilled Jerek to the marrow.

'Indeed, in which case a magic greater than mine has fused within it some form of regenerative magic. This would not, in theory, be impossible, but it would be beyond the ken of any adept of magic that I have ever encountered.'

'So you couldn't replicate it?'

'Forge a new ring to make you truly immortal? No.'

'That is some small mercy,' Jerek said. 'Do you know anyone capable of it?'

'As I said, I've yet to encounter a sorcerer with the kind of mastery necessary to craft such an artefact. Fey, perhaps, but I doubt it. This is old magic, wolf. Such knowledge has slipped into darkness. The von Carstein ring is irreplaceable, and lost.'

'If Pieter has his way we march on, to Altdorf. He intends to tear the city apart looking for the ring.'

'He's a fool.'

'Worse, he's a desperate fool.'

'Does he imagine that the Sigmarites have buried the old Count with it still on his finger? The ring's gone. Destroyed.'

'Who knows what he thinks – if he actually thinks. It's a mess,' Jerek said to the necromancer, von Seirt. 'The man makes fools of us all.'

'So, what would you have me do, wolf?'

'Humble the fool.'

'The living are doing a fine job of that from where I am standing.'

'This cannot be allowed to continue, woman. They are making a mockery of us. It is a shambles.' He looked up at the wall where a man mimicked Pieter's posturing, strutting backwards and forwards along the wall walk. 'They even have a fool pretending to be descended from the vampire slayer, van Hal. They need to learn humility. They need to remember fear.'

'And how do you propose to teach those lessons, wolf?'

'It is not my place to propose, Pieter has made that plain enough.'

'Rubbish, you are Hamaya. You answer only to the new Count. If you will it, I will have my dead tear the walls apart, stone by stone and feast on the living. You need only say the word and it will be done.'

'And if *I* say the word?' Pieter von Carstein came up behind them, Roth Mehlinger at his side like some fawning lapdog. His honeyed voice dripped with loathing. 'Tell me, I am curious, magician. Would you show me the same loyalty you afford this grizzled old fool?'

'I serve but one master,' Katja said coldly.

'Ah, yes, my beloved brother, we shall have to see about that. Now, answer my question, would you have your dead tear the walls down stone by blessed stone if *I* willed it?'

'Unquestionably.'

'I don't believe you, magician,' Pieter sneered.

'Then ask me, my lord, and find out for yourself.' The necromancer inclined her head slightly, a condescending gesture meant to rile Pieter.

'Perhaps I will.'

'Do it,' Mehlinger said, a sly smiling spreading across his hateful face, 'and then take a leaf from the old wolf's book and turn the vampires loose, let them feed, all of them. Let them drink their fill. No more hiding behind the zombies. Unleash the beasts, Pieter. You know you want to.'

Von Carstein's grin was truly repulsive. He looked beyond them, to the man on the wall, the one who claimed to be Helmut van Hal. 'You will know suffering like no other mortal,' he promised, not caring that the man couldn't hear him, 'and when you are finally dead and think yourself safe from pain, I will bring you back and kill you all over again.' He turned to Katja. 'Come, sister in shadow, there are things I would know before I turn you loose.'

'You need only ask.'

'Ah yes, ask my little dark deceiver. That is exactly what I intend to do, although I doubt that I will enjoy your answers.'

'The truth is seldom uttered for the sake of enjoyment, lord.'

Jerek watched the pair leave, von Carstein linking arms with the necromancer. It was an intimate gesture that spoke of lovers not enemies. Jerek noticed Mehlinger's discomfort at the sight.

'Jealousy doesn't become you,' he said, turning his back on his old friend. Pieter and Katja had neared the wall. Jerek moved close enough to hear the vampire call up to the defenders:

'Your determination to die is impressive, mortal. However, your prancing and preening has lost its edge of entertainment. Frankly, it has become boorish. So, little man, I am here to tell you that you've won, but before all your stupid followers start getting excited, what I mean to say is that I will grant your wish. Tonight you die, all of you. Every last man, woman and child, unless you bow down to serve me, in life, or death. There will be no mercy!' This last Pieter screamed at the top of his lungs, his voice dissolving into hysteria.

The man on the wall smiled, which was not at all what Jerek had expected from a man hearing his own death sentence being delivered. He assayed a theatrical bow, seemingly oblivious to the undead host amassed at his door. This was a blind, Jerek realised, a ruse, misdirection. Pieter was being goaded into making an even bigger idiot of himself than he already was. The gambit put the wolf in mind of a sideshow trickster's misdirection. They wanted von Carstein's eyes fixed firmly on the wall, so what was it they weren't supposed to be seeing? Where was the real threat?

He contented himself with the knowledge that he would know soon enough, and if Pieter and Mehlinger suffered as a result, well, he wouldn't mourn either one of them. He was conflicted. Von Seirt was right, he was Hamaya, but he was also human, or at least some small part of him was. As Hamaya, he served a different master, and had no loyalty to Pieter, Konrad wanted him disposed of, after all, and as a human, he found himself praying for the same outcome, but for very different reasons.

Pieter von Carstein was dangerous.

The men on the walls knew that, the living hiding behind them most certainly did. Their game was obviously intended to blind the vampire to the obvious, like a scorpion backed into a corner, the humans were at their most dangerous when they appeared trapped.

The next few hours would be fascinating for the impartial observer, Jerek knew. Pieter's tactical naiveté and his horde of the damned, matched up against the posturings of the man on the wall and the puppeteer playing his strings. Given the desperation of the situation, few could claim to be impartial. Both factions had a vested interest in the other's failure. It was fascinating to Jerek, who found himself looking for the sting in the tail. It had to be there. What did the defenders have to gain by driving Pieter into a fury?

Apart from the obvious, that mad men don't think straight, he could see no great advantage to incensing the enemy.

Instead, Jerek turned his attention closer to home. He studied Pieter and the woman at his side. Were the two lovers? He thought perhaps they were. There was an intimacy between them, a familiarity of movements, of bodies used to being close together, but there was no obvious affection. He suspected that neither cared very much for the other. For Mehlinger, their easy proximity was like a stake through the heart. The vampire's seething was almost palpable.

Mehlinger's rise amongst the aristocracy of the night would no doubt be spectacular. He embodied the darkness.

A flicker of movement drew Jerek's gaze to the top of the high wall. More men had joined van Hal. They stood beside him on the wall walk, their numbers swelling, fifty, sixty, then a hundred, and more, until finally the wall was crammed with soldiers, who all turned their backs on Pieter von Carstein. Puzzled, Jerek watched as, as one, the defenders of Nuln pulled down their trousers.

The old wolf burst out laughing.

He found himself liking these unknown men. They were his kind of people. They had guts. They were real soldiers. Good men, not shambling corpses dancing to the tune of some madman. They didn't deserve to die any more than anyone else did, but this petty act of defiance had sealed their fate. Forgiveness was not a von Carstein family trait.

THEY WERE DEAD before dawn.

Von Carstein unleashed the beasts, ordering his vampires over the walls. They had no ladders to climb, those were for the lumbering dead that von Seirt had swarming over one another, making ladders out of their own corpses, until they breached the walls in thirty places, bringing them down one stone at a time, just as the necromancer had promised. A cloud of bats filled the night, flitting and darting high over the streets of the city, their song an unbearable chorus of excitement and hunger. The creatures settled on rooftops and gutters, transforming as they did into their feral forms, the beast within released and ready to feast.

Nuln fell in a frenzy of feeding.

The screams were sickening. The creatures chased the living through the streets, hunting them down, tearing the clothes from their victims' backs even as they tore flesh from the bones, and gorged themselves on so much fresh meat.

Jerek took no part in the slaughter.

He walked through the streets strewn with broken bodies and cobbles slick with blood, detached from it all.

Whatever it was the men of Nuln had hoped to achieve by angering Pieter had obviously failed. In a matter of hours, the city had become a necropolis. Death walked the streets of the Imperial city, and stalked the living, welcoming them into Morr's dark embrace. Age, creed, colour, it didn't matter, all were reduced to one single absolute: they were meat for the beasts.

They wallowed in the splendour of the city. They dined in the palaces and in the paupers' hovels, and each meal tasted divine. Virgins offered up their throats and legs, and crones crawled on the floor, bleeding and dying as they debased themselves for the vampires.

It went beyond war. It went beyond death. It was an orgy of blood lust and depravity. It was sickening in the extent of its thoroughness. The vampires drove the living out of their hiding places, torching houses, and smoking them out of the temples where they had clustered begging their gods for salvation. Only there was no salvation from the dead. There was no light to guide or save them. The darkness was all consuming, the creatures of the dark invincible.

Sated, finally, after hours of gorging themselves, the vampires fell into a kind of drunken slumber. Jerek saw them lying side by side with the corpses that they had drained so that it was impossible to tell them apart from their victims. He stepped over them and walked around them. He looked up at the sky. The sun would be rising soon, not that it mattered to the inhabitants of this once great city. Light, dark, it was all the same to the dead. Come dusk, the ranks of von Seirt's horde would swell by the thousands and Nuln would be left to the rats. It beggared belief.

He hadn't done this. He hadn't been a part of it. There was no blood on his hands, but that didn't matter. It didn't absolve him of the slaughter. He was a beast now. Even the smell of the blood had his heart racing and his mouth salivating with disgusting hunger. He wanted to feed, to join in the killing, and that was enough to damn him in his own mind.

The depravity of it revolted the wolf. The sheer scale of the killing was incredible. It outstripped anything he had ever experienced, every battlefield he had ever fought on, it was worse, even, than the fall of Middenheim, because this was different: this was inhuman, monstrous. It was butchery. The dead weren't soldiers, they were women and children, they hadn't taken up arms or bared their arses, they hadn't made the fight their own, it had been forced down their throats until it choked them to death.

After months of seeming impotence, the dead surrounding the city in a lake of rotting flesh, it had become a war of attrition. The living needed to feed, so the dead choked off their farmland and their livestock, polluted their water and waited, seemingly content to let disease and starvation have their way before they stormed the walls. Then suddenly this.

There was no honour in this victory.

It sickened Jerek.

Carrion birds settled on the rooftops and window ledges, drawn to the stink of the slaughter. They were legion.

They came down to feed, even as the sun began to rise slowly, red on the dead city.

Hating himself, hating the need he felt settling on his shoulders and the surety that he *would* succumb to it and feed, Jerek walked out of the killing ground in time to see the trap sprung.

JEREK SAW THE men hunched low and moving swiftly across the ground. Even from a distance he recognised the front man as the supposed descendent of van Hal. He gesticulated wildly, directing men left and right. It was all done silently. They split into smaller groups with impressive discipline, three clusters of ten apiece angling back towards the city, two more groups of ten fanning out across the undead camp, making for the black pavilions of Pieter and his loyal vampires – the same vampires who had gorged themselves senseless in the city and lay in sated slumber like stuffed pigs.

Jerek dropped down on all fours and gave himself over to the change. Focusing on the wolf inside his skin, the lupine form, the grace and power of the beast, he felt himself changing, his curiosity giving way to the most basic, primal, instincts: preservation and hunger. The bones in his shoulders broke and remoulded themselves, larger and more powerful, as the vertebrae of his spine stretched and arched, his wild mane becoming a pelt.

The wolf moved carefully across the field, his easy lope silent beneath the crackling and spitting of the burning city. The smoke masked the pungent reek of fear, but it didn't bury it away. The soldiers stank of it: fear and faeces. Moving close to Pieter's pavilion, he saw the red-rimmed eyes of the lookout and realised what they had done. They had traded their own, gambling that the sacrifice would be worth it, that it would give these last few men the chance to slay the beasts. It was the supreme sacrifice: not their own lives, but the lives of everyone they knew and loved. There was no way that these fifty men would be able to live with themselves come sunrise. Then, inevitably, the blood of more good men would stain the field.

Van Hal emerged from the pavilion, clutching a blackened heart in his hand: Pieter's.

He saw the wolf and nodded, throwing the beast the dead meat.

Jerek fed.

A second soldier stepped out through the tent flaps, the fingers of his left hand tangled in Roth Mehlinger's hair. A stump of white bone jutted out of the ragged flesh where the neck should have met the body. The vampire's face was frozen into a death mask of ridiculous surprise.

'The beasts are dead,' van Hal said, his voice empty. There was no triumph in his victory. The cost had been too high. 'Now we pray for our brothers. May Sigmar guide their swords, for tomorrow, we die.'

Behind him, moving like the ghosts they truly were, the three groups of soldiers re-entered the city through the main gates. With von Carstein's so-called protectors wallowing in the afterglow of murder, these thirty would be more than enough to cut out the canker that was the undead in their city.

Jerek sensed movement, a shape rising beside the canvas pavilion. He knew that the fight was not over for these few, not while von Seirt had breath to command the dead. The wolf tensed and sprang, bowling aside the soldier clutching Mehlinger's severed head. A moment later, they saw what he had seen: the dead rising. Steel rang out as the defenders of Nuln drew their swords, ready, eager, to die now that their final die was cast, the game played out.

The wolf tossed back his head, sniffing out the necromancer's reek, her bodily fluids, the sickly sweet tang of her secretions that were so uniquely female, and then he found traces of her on the wind. She was close. He followed the smell of her. Death aroused her, making it easy.

She had taken refuge amid the cages where von Carstein kept the kidnapped villagers that he used to sate his vampire's thirst. She was pretending to be one of them.

Jerek bounded into the enclosed circle of wagons, his momentum taking him through the wooden bars of the cage, splintering them and cutting him in the process. Snarling and feral, his teeth snapped and tore at the necromancer's throat as she tried to ward off the attack, but the sheer ferocity of the wolf's assault drove her back further into the corner of the cage.

Her screams were desperate, but her death was no more savage than she deserved.

Jerek tore Katja von Seirt's throat out and fed on her.

Her corpse jerked and spasmed beneath him as her nerves fired off random triggers before relaxing into death. Still, Jerek drank greedily, savouring the rank corruption of the necromancer's lifeblood as it trickled down his throat.

When the soldiers came to free the prisoners, he had returned to his human form. Van Hal stood at the broken wooden bars of the cage, peering into the darkness within. He saw Jerek, naked, standing over the woman's corpse.

They shared a moment of mutual recognition. The soldier understood.

'I should kill you,' van Hal said.

'And I should kill you, but I have no desire to, soldier. You have paid enough this day for a hundred lifetimes.'

'Indeed, but I cannot let you leave.'

'You can,' Jerek said. 'This woman,' he toed the corpse of von Seirt with his bare foot, 'would have killed you all. The dead collapsed did they not, even as they rose up to strike you down?'

Van Hal nodded.

'Her hold over them died as she did.'

'You're the wolf I fed?'

'I am, but more importantly I was, once, the wolf. Now I am not sure what I am, but I am not one of *them*.'

'Nor are you one of us.'

'No, but we, I think, want the same thing.'

'I want the beasts destroyed. I want the dead driven back to the hell they came from. I want my family back. I want my world to know peace.'

'Then we are not so different, soldier.'

'Here's what's going to happen, I am going to leave to check on the other prisoners. When I return in a quarter of an hour, I am going to put you out of your misery. Use these fifteen minutes to make your peace with your god.'

'Thank you, soldier.'

'Don't thank me, wolf, I am tired of being thanked for doing the wrong thing.'

With that van Hal left.

Jerek was gone long before he returned.

CHAPTER FIFTEEN
The Sins of the Father

DRAKENHOF, SYLVANIA
The drawn-out dog days of autumn, 2057

JARED AND KLEIN left them at the border.

Twice, they had encountered the huge dire wolves hunting, and twice they had slain the beasts. Lothar du Bek was a dichotomy in battle. While his eyes blazed with righteous fury, his every action was calm to the point of detachment. He nocked the silver tipped arrows and drew back on the bowstring, holding, waiting, judging the wind, the distance, and keeping the beast in his sight before loosing shaft after shaft with skill and precision. The arrows took the beasts between the eyes, in the throat and heart. It was over quickly.

'You're a dangerous man, Lothar,' Kallad had observed, shouldering his axe as they stood over the corpse of a man who had, moments before, been a huge wolf.

'These are dangerous times, my friend. I am nothing more than a child of the times.'

Kallad and Lothar du Bek travelled on through the barren lands of Sylvania. The folks they passed wore the same harsh signs of malnutrition and superstition, bellies distended, bones pressed out starkly against emaciated skin. They were the physical embodiment of the land they lived in with its dead trees and infertile soil. These were haunted people. They huddled on the sides of the road as the pair passed, clutching their talismans and casting frightened gazes over their shoulders to see that they had moved on down the road. They didn't talk. Kallad was used to trading information about the road with fellow travellers met on the journey, but not so in this hellish place. They kept themselves very much to themselves. They had no time for others.

A signpost on the roadside marked another two miles to the next village.

With night drawing in, the pair would need to find somewhere to sleep. The village would no doubt have a tavern or inn, and hopefully a room to spare, or a common room where they could bed down for the night. The cold nights were drawing in and bivouacking down on the roadside was becoming less and less appealing. A night in a warm bed sounded good to both of them.

'Let's push on,' Lothar suggested. 'Right now I'd trade another half an hour on the road for a night by a warm fire, a minstrel and a jug of mulled wine.'

'Aye, reckon I'd trade half an hour on the road for a decent bite to eat.'

'Fed up of my cooking already, eh, dwarf?'

'Oh aye.'

A mile outside the village they past three cairns piled up by the roadside, the stone mounds marked with the sign of Morr. One of the cairns was considerably smaller than the others, and obviously covered a young child.

They paused for a moment to pay their respects to the dead before walking down into the village.

The windows of every house they passed were shuttered, although glimmers of warm light seeped through the cracks. The doors were likewise closed. There was no livestock in the fields, and no dogs or cats running wild.

It felt to Kallad as if they had walked into the village of the damned.

'I've got a bad feeling about this place.'

'Couldn't agree more. It feels like the life's been sucked out of it.'

'Aye, that's it exactly. It's been drained dry.'

The tavern was no different from any of the other buildings. The windows had been shuttered and barred, although smoke drifted lazily from the chimney, evidence at least that there was life inside. The door, however, was locked.

Kallad rapped on the door. No one answered.

He looked at the border warden, who shrugged, and banged again, hammering on the wood with his gauntleted fist.

'Do we have to batter the damned door down?' Kallad shouted.

'Go away,' a voice answered. 'We don't want your sort here.'

'Open the door, man.'

'Go away,' the voice repeated stubbornly.

'Grimna's balls, just open the damned door before I kick it in and start pounding on your head instead.'

He slammed his fist into a wooden panel above the brace, once, twice, three times, causing the wood to splinter.

'For pity's sake!' the voice behind the door pleaded. 'Leave us be.'

'This is ridiculous, dwarf. Let's just leave these people alone. They've obviously got a good reason for not opening the door. We can sleep in the stable,' Lothar du Bek said.

'All I want is a warm meal and a place to lay my bones. It doesn't seem too much to ask from an inn.'

They heard the sound of a bolt being drawn back.

The door cracked open an inch.

'You're not one of them?'

'What're you blatherin' on about, man?'

'You're not...' he peered out at the dwarf and the hulking figure of the warden beside him. 'No, you're obviously not. Inside, quickly.' The innkeeper threw open the door and ushered the pair in. No sooner had they crossed the threshold than he was slamming and bolting the door behind them.

The taproom was dead. A small fire burned in the hearth. There were no other customers.

'Business is boomin', eh? Not a surprise if you won't let people in, I reckon.'

'People don't want to be outside, not after dark, not if they know what's good for them,' the innkeeper said, locking the final bolt into place. 'Now, we ain't got much in the way of food, but there's some broth, a bit of yesterday's bread left and ale enough to get you blind drunk, if that's what you're hankering for.'

'Sounds like a feast compared to what we've been living off for the last few weeks.'

'Well then, you're welcome to it. I'll see to the drink first. Sit yourselves by the fire.'

'My thanks.' Kallad drew off his gauntlet and held out his right hand. 'I'm Kallad Stormwarden, and this lanky fellow is Lothar.'

The innkeeper shook hands with the dwarf. 'Mathias Gesner. Make yourself at home, Kallad Stormwarden.'

'Are you alone here, Mathias?' Lothar asked, unclasping the hasp of his travel cloak and draping it over the back of a threadbare armchair beside the fire. He sank into the seat and planted his feet on the footstool.

'Yes.' The pain of loss was etched into Mathias Gesner's plain face. He was obviously a simple man, not given to lying. He wore his hurt on his sleeve, as the old Reikspiel saying went. It didn't take any great intelligence to know that it hadn't always been this way. At some point not so very long ago, this inn had no doubt been the heart of a thriving village. Things changed quickly in this godforsaken country. That, at least, accounted for the bolts and the shuttered windows. Kallad remembered the cairns on the roadside. He had been right in thinking that they had stumbled into a village of the damned. These people were living in the dark through fear: fear that the light would draw attention to them, and with it, more death would come their way. They had given up believing that the light would keep the monsters at bay, such were the depths of their despair.

The food, when it came, was far from delicious, but it filled a hole. Mathias joined them at the fire. They ate a while in silence, all three men locked away with their own thoughts. The bread was hard, the broth bland, but after travel fare it smelled almost heavenly. The ale was good, better than it had any right to be in this out of the way corner of Sylvania.

Lothar smacked his lips appreciatively as he banged the tankard down on the table.

'Not bad at all.'

'Aye, it's a tasty drop, for sure,' the dwarf agreed, foam thick in his beard. He backhanded his mouth dry and smacked his lips appreciatively.

'We brew it here, me and…' the innkeeper stopped mid sentence.

Kallad didn't press him. He knew where the sentence had been going: into the territory of the dead.

Outside, a howling wolf greeted the gibbous moon.

It was a sad lament.

The cry was taken up somewhere in the distance, a faint and haunting, familiar response.

Knowing what he knew of the beasts abroad, it chilled Kallad's blood.

Beside him, Mathias had gone pale. His hand trembled. 'Soon,' he said, closing his eyes.

As if in response to the innkeeper's prediction, the door rattled in its frame and a moment later, whoever it was out there was hammering and pleading in a pitiful voice:

'Open up, gods alive man, open up! Please.'

Lothar began to rise, but Gesner stayed the warden with a firm hand and a single shake of the head.

'Please! For pity's sake, please. I'm begging you, man. Please.'

'Sit,' Gesner said, his face blank. 'It isn't what you think.'

'But–'

'I said sit.' The steel in Gesner's voice was surprising.

'Oh, sweet Morr, they're coming! I can see them! Open the door! Please, I beg you! Open the door.'

Then the begging ceased. It was replaced by thick cackling laughter. 'Next time, father! Next time!'

For the next few minutes the only sound was the snap and crackle of the fire in the hearth.

'My son,' Mathias Gesner said finally, his eyes red with unshed tears. 'They took him two moons ago. I buried him with my own hands, alongside his mother, Rahel, and our little girl, Elsa. He returns every night, banging on the damned door to be let in as if he thinks that this time I might unbar the door and he'll be saved.'

'I'm sorry,' Kallad said.

'It's all rubbish,' Gesner continued. 'He's one of them now. He'd feed off me just as contentedly as he would a whore. He's right though, one day I will be too tired to keep him out and the whole charade will be over once and for all.'

'Aye, it's easy enough to die if'n that's what you want,' Kallad said.

'What else is there, really?'

'Life,' Kallad said. 'That's all there ever is.'

'Sometimes it isn't enough.'

'I won't argue with you there, Mathias, but when it comes to this, the beasts turning father against son, well, this is where good men have to draw the line.'

'What do you mean?' The innkeeper sniffed, the first tears salty on his cheek.

'I mean it ends now, here, tonight,' Kallad promised.

He stood up, shouldering Ruinthorn, and strode over to the door. He pulled back the bolts one at a time and raised the bar.

The door burst open before he could get out of the way. It knocked him back, spinning him into du Bek. Kallad barely had the time to turn before Gesner's son was through the door and on them. 'Hello father, I'm home!' The beast mocked, hurling himself at the dwarf. 'Did you miss me?'

Kallad saw his own weakness reflected in the creature's lifeless eyes: his failure to protect his companions from the vampire they hunted, his inability to save Sammy Kraus, his inability to save his own people, and his guilt at his father's death on the wall. In that moment, Kallad Stormwarden knew hatred.

He thundered the butt of Ruinthorn into creature's gut and then reversed the blow, bringing the butterfly head of the axe around in a brutal arc that came within a whisker of decapitating the beast. Gesner's son moved with lupine grace, rolling beneath the axe-head, back arched to the point of breaking, and then flipped, planting the flat of his hand on the floor and springing up off it. He clapped his hands delightedly as he landed.

Kallad hurled himself forwards, matching the beast's grace with stubborn determination. He planted his feet and let Ruinthorn do his dancing for him. The twin-headed blade sliced through the air, once, twice, three times, four, blurring into insubstantiality as it pared the air. The beast mocked him, moving aside from Ruinthorn as easily as if he was dodging a drunk's wildly swinging blows. The blade of the axe cut close to the vampire's skin twice, drawing the thinnest tears in the fabric of his grubby shirt. The beast raised an eye, and Kallad put it out, slamming the butt of Ruinthorn into the vampire's face, the silver hook he had screwed into the shaft ripping up the monster's cheek and splitting its eye wetly.

Gesner's son howled, but the old man didn't move.

Kallad delivered a second and a third crunching blow, bringing the creature to its knees. Then, with one mighty blow, he sheared the vampire's head from its shoulders, and stood over the twitching corpse as true death claimed it.

'Turn away,' he told Gesner, and waited until the innkeeper had done just that before he split the fiend's ribcage with the sharp end of his axe and cracked open its chest to pull the beast's rotten heart out.

Kallad tossed the blackened organ into the flames of the fire and watched it spit and hiss as it shrivelled in the heat.

'Come first light, bury your son, Mathias. He won't rise again. You have my word on that.'

The innkeeper didn't say a word. He shuffled forwards and knelt, cradling the dead boy's body in his arms.

Kallad left him alone to grieve.

Du Bek followed him upstairs. They closed the door on a small bedroom to shut out Gesner's stifled sobs.

'Why did you do it?' Lothar asked, still at the door. Kallad didn't have an easy answer for him. 'We could have slept the night out in the safety of the room and moved on in the morning. You didn't have to make this your fight, Kallad. So why? Why risk everything for an old man in a damned village?'

'It's in my blood, laddy. What would have happened if we'd gone on our way tomorrow, eh? Gesner would be dead. Hell, the whole village would be nowt more than food for the bloodsucking parasites. By moving on, we'd have condemned every living soul in this place as thoroughly and completely as if we'd driven the stake through them ourselves. Could you live with that?'

'No,' du Bek admitted.

'No, me neither. So there was no choice, not really, see? It became our fight the moment the lad started banging on the door.'

The border warden nodded thoughtfully.

'But that's not it, is it? That's not the truth. It's noble and it's the right thing to say, but it isn't the truth, is it? I mean, it's like saying the fight was yours the moment you opened the door. It's right, but it isn't the truth. So tell me.'

Kallad was silent for a moment. He turned away from du Bek, unable to meet the warden's eye. He stared out through the window, at the darkness and the mirror of their room reflected on it in the glass.

'No,' he said at last. 'It's not the truth.'

'What is?'

Kallad grunted. 'The truth. What can I tell you? All that evil needs to flourish is for good men to do nothing. Every fight is my fight. They killed my father. Cut him down in cold blood as he fought to save wives and children in Grunberg. They killed my people, not just one or two: all of them. I'm the last dwarf of Karak Sadra, the last. My family died fighting for humans, in a fight that wasn't theirs, but they did it, 'cause that's our way. We fight for what we believe in, and I made a promise on the dead. I swore, even as the monster cut my father down, that I would bring every last one of these vile creatures to their knees and make them beg for their worthless carcasses even as I cut their dead hearts out. That means somethin' to me. I'll purge the old world of them single-handed if I have to, or die trying. That's why I need the magician. He can smell their dead stink on the wind. With him, I can turn defence into attack. I can hunt them down and kill them in their lairs.'

'That, dwarf, is a grudge worth having.' Lothar moved away from the door, drew his sword and knelt at Kallad's feet. He lowered his head and offered the blade out across his palms. 'My sword is yours if you would have it.'

CHAPTER SIXTEEN
The Black Library

CASTLE DRAKENHOF, SYLVANIA
Season's end

A THIN PATINA of frost rimed the stalactites dripping from the ceiling of the vast subterranean library.

Library – Nevin Kantor laughed at that.

The place was no more a library than Konrad's so-called cathedral was a place of worship. Both had all the trappings of their names, but lacked the soul that was so integral to the originals. They were little more than pale copies, like so much of the second Vampire Count's realm.

Konrad's library was a huge dome-shaped chamber hollowed out of the rock beneath Drakenhof, the stalactites hanging down like stony swords of doom some sixty feet above the magician's head while he studied, an ever-present reminder of the capricious count. The walls were lined with dusty shelves that were crammed to overflowing with books, obscure arcane texts, diaries, prophecies, codices, sacred ramblings and incantations of dark wisdom, interspersed with bell jars filled with blind eyes floating in saline, salamander skins, cockroach carapaces, pigs' bladders, spider eggs and snake venom. It was a veritable treasure trove of arcana, some nothing more than superstitious claptrap, but the rest, rare and coveted wisdom.

Unlike a real library, it was also a prison.

Thugs stood guard. Their allegiance to the clan van Carstein went beyond a simple loyalty to Konrad. The flat-headed bullies had emerged from the east with his sire, Vlad. Long-lived and yet not pure-blood vampires, speculation about the swarthy thugs was rife. Clubs hung loosely in their fists. Sneers were permanently pasted on their thick lips. Their bare arms were like ham hocks, big and fleshy, and covered with a scrawl of tattoos. Hidden within the tattoos was the key to their arrogance, sigils designed to make them impervious to all but the most insidious of magics, tattooed on their flesh by Vlad himself.

The cells behind the library were filled with yokels and superstitious morons who somehow managed to tap one of the winds, with luck or latent talent, but not genuine skill. Whether or not the sigils would have actually deterred a sorcerous attack was irrelevant – few of the denizens of this dark pit had any real magical gift. They were as likely to try and club the guards to death with heavy books as they were to evaporate the water in their bodies and leave a baked pile of human paste on the stone floor.

There were few true magicians in Konrad's school. Tapping the winds accidentally was by no means the same as possessing true power. The bumpkins could coo about the mystical talents of the midwife who brought a brat out from a breech birth, and marvel at the soldier whose lucky trinket deflected an arrow tip destined for his heart. It wasn't magic, not in the pure sense. It wasn't worthy of awe.

So yes, they were prisoners, but it was the physical stature of the thugs that held them in fearful check, not the magical wards on their gaolers.

Nevin Kantor harboured no illusions: he was as much a prisoner as those poor fools were. The difference was that he was a willing prisoner. In magic, Nevin Kantor believed he would find his own immortality.

The resources that Konrad had gathered in his library surpassed Kantor's wildest imaginings. He pored over the books, absorbing every word, every mark in the margins, every explanatory diagram, every supposition and superstition.

He also heard whispers.

Leverkuhn and Fey were thick as thieves, scouring the shelves and recessed stacks for decayed pages and spineless tomes, picking through the incantations and reassembling the knowledge therein. He heard them when they thought no one was listening. At first, it had plagued him: a doubt gnawing at his skull incessantly, and so, he ingratiated himself with Immoliah Fey. The seduction was easy. It always is when you hold to one basic truth: women, even women like Fey, have the same base urges for contact and skin as men do. They need it in the same way. They want it in the same way. Kantor said things, intimate things, drawing her into his confidence with pillow talk and promises. It wasn't love, it was physical and practical, a means to an end, nothing more. The passion paid off. She told him their secret: they believed that somewhere in this vast uncatalogued horde of arcana were pages from Nagash's lost books, incantations from the *Liber Mortis*. How else, she reasoned, sleepy after their frenzied coupling, could Vlad have raised the dead?

Their reasoning was sound in one aspect, but deeply flawed in another. Kantor knew that Vlad had indeed possessed some pages from Nagash's lost books, in that much they were right, but Kantor had seen the same irreplaceable knowledge go up in smoke as the Sigmarites burned the dead Count's possessions in a cleansing fire. Only self-righteous fools like the priests would have done something so unmitigatingly stupid. Wisdom, Kantor believed, should be protected not purged – even the wisdom you disagreed with. Burning books was an act of sacrilege. It stank of smug Sigmarite stupidity.

Fey and Leverkuhn ought to have been his allies in his quest for understanding, but the two shunned him.

He shouldn't have been surprised. He had lived a life on the fringe, not accepted by the people around him. The Sigmarites had imprisoned him, intent on snuffing out his life once his usefulness to them had ended. Oh, yes, they were happy enough to bleed him dry if it suited them, and they made no secret of the fact that they were willing to sell his flesh cheaply enough – indeed, they had, for the princely sum of two vampires.

That was the value they had placed on him. Even then, the dwarf had only bought him because of his usefulness. He could sniff out the beasts, and in doing so could help the dwarf commit suicide by tracking the monsters back to their lairs. Kallad Stormwarden had talked of nobility, of the eternal struggle against evil, of buying freedom with courage. It was all hyperbole: rubbish. The dwarf was dead, killed by a stronger foe. There was no nobility in it. Death didn't consider eternal struggles and courage when it weighed out lives. It valued only strength, cunning, and power. He felt no regret over it. The dwarf would have seen him dead before the end of their shared road, so why should he shed a tear for his own would-be murderer?

He had long ago come to terms with the fact that he was shunned and reviled for what he was.

He had even come to accept the reasons. It was because he was different, because was he was attuned to the earth itself, because the music of it sang in his veins, because it bent to his will, and because he had power.

The only acceptance he felt came in the soothing caress of Shyish. The wind knew him. It savoured his flesh as he drew it into him. It delighted in his existence. It sang in his blood. It *loved* him.

In return, it was only natural that he loved it, and that he gave himself to it, body and soul.

He felt Shyish inside him even when he wasn't consciously drawing on it. The wind was a soothing presence, a calming one. A friend. A lover. It filled him: completed him.

He knew that he was changing. The flesh he wore was nothing more than an imago, a shell that he would crack his way out of to emerge as a new, beautiful, beast. He could feel the changes taking place inside him. He could feel his blood purifying, his organs being strengthened by Shyish, and the black wind making him its perfect servant. He welcomed the changes. With von Seirt dead, the only true talents were Immoliah Fey, Aloysius Leverkuhn and himself, and he would be the greatest of them all. He embraced the black wind. That, in itself, gave Kantor a position of power in the mad vampire's court.

Nevin Kantor understood Konrad von Carstein, probably better than the vampire understood himself, because they were not that different. He craved what he lacked. He coveted their magic to make up for his own shortcomings. They snickered behind his back and called him the Blood Count.

Kantor hunched over the desk, dipped the quill's nib into the inkpot and scratched out the curve of a 'C' on the vellum stretched out on the tabletop. It was painstaking work, laborious and frustrating. The ink splashed as he drew the nib down with a flourish, giving the letter 'H' an elaborate tail. Muttering a curse, Kantor took a blotting cloth and cleaned up the smear of black.

He heard footsteps, but didn't look up, expecting them to fade away into the stacks.

They didn't. They approached his desk, slow, measured, and echoing curiously in the vast vaulted room.

Kantor looked up as Konrad dropped a bloody rag on his desk. Anger flared, but the magician battled it down. Stupidity would only damage his situation. He wanted to bleed the Vampire Count dry of every ounce of knowledge that his black library possessed. The image brought an ironic smile to his lips, which Konrad mistook for gratitude.

It wasn't a rag, Kantor realised. It had the texture and consistency of vellum, but it wasn't vellum either. He touched it, spreading it thin on the desk. Black blood smeared across his work, ruining everything that he had set down over the last week. He barely noticed. The feel was immediately familiar, and yet utterly foreign. It was skin: human skin.

He looked up at the Blood Count.

Konrad's face split in an easy grin.

'A gift, my pet. Cure it. Make a book out of it. Use it as the binding for your grand grimoire.' He held up a hand, staying Kantor. 'No, no, don't thank me. It's nothing really. It belonged to a rather uncooperative fellow. He has no use for it now, so best not let it go to waste, eh?'

'I don't know quite what to say.' There was a mild edge of distaste to Kantor's voice, but his fingers played almost lovingly over the various textures of the stripped skin. The thing was both revolting and curiously compelling at the same time. He lingered over the softer areas, the undersides of the arm and the throat, and the coarse skin of the heels, the palms and the elbows.

'Tell me you'll put it to good use. You have no idea how difficult it is to skin a corpse without ruining the thing. Painstaking, well more like pain *giving* actually, but you get the idea.'

'Indeed, rather vividly,' Kantor said. He pushed the skin to the side. In his mind, he was already imagining the secrets it would bind: his first book of magic. He lifted his fingers to his lips, tasting the tang of iron that was the dead man's blood, smelling it, stark in his nose. It was still warm.

The vampire smiled, perching on the corner of Kantor's desk. 'Good, good, good. Now tell me, how goes your research, my pet? I have high hopes for what miracles you might conjure.'

'Slowly,' Kantor said, avoiding the truth. He didn't want Konrad even vaguely intrigued with his discoveries. The knowledge he'd unearthed was his. There were things he needed to do without the ever-present shadow of the vampire lurking in the background all the time. Obfuscation, that was the secret. To give a little, without so much as hinting as to its true worth. 'There is a wealth of fact and ten times as much fantasy in these books, my lord. Sifting through the dross for nuggets of gold is tiresome. So much of it is useless.'

'Ah, well, that's a shame. I had to go to considerable lengths to acquire my collection. I am sure everything my heart desires is hidden away here on one page or another. What can I say? Don't let fear of failure get under your skin.' Konrad chuckled, enjoying his own droll sense of humour.

'Given the usefulness of your latest gift, I'll make a point of it, my lord Konrad.'

'I knew you were a clever boy, even when you knocked on my door begging to be let in and allowed to serve me.'

'Shyish guided my feet, my lord. The black wind wishes to aid you in any way it can.' It was easy to lie. The vampire's vanity blinded him to anything approaching the truth. Part of the magician wanted to tell him, to whisper the name 'Mannfred' and have done with it, but another part of him enjoyed the game too much to give it up so easily. The time for revelation would come, but it wasn't now. He needed to be patient.

'Yet it mocks me, Nevin, by shutting itself off to me when all I would do is unleash its blessed darkness into the world. I would be a dark destroyer. I would bring the world to its knees, if only it would open itself up to me. If only I could be like you... You know, I could be forgiven for thinking that *you* mock me as well.'

'Who can understand the whims of magic, my lord?'

'Not I, it would seem,' Konrad said, bitterly.

The irony of it was delicious, but he didn't want to spoil the Blood Count's good humour. It was hardly surprising that since the demise of his brothers – and in Mannfred's continued absence – Konrad had been almost cheerful, but his humour was an unstable beast. One wrong word could quite easily see that goodwill vanish. Then, who knew what desk Kantor's skin would end up being deposited on as a so-called gift? The vampire owned his life and could, at a whim, snuff it out. The threat was implicit.

Oh what a tangled web we weave when first we flatter to deceive. Kantor picked up the dead suit of skin once more, turning it over in his hands. He found the face. He recognised the donor. He would not mourn the man. He would, however, make good use of his remains, crafting a book of blood and magic to rival anything seen in millennia. He also knew exactly which ensorcellment he would refine and record first: Diabolisch Leichnam.

'I am expecting great things of you, don't disappoint me, my pet. I don't handle disappointment well.' With that, Konrad left him.

Nevin looked at his hands. They were covered in blood. He was trembling, not with fear, but with exhilaration. The time was ripe. Konrad had given him the excuse he needed to assemble the incantations that he had already begun secreting in various hidey-holes. He laid his hands down flat on the table.

Let the madman posture, he thought bitterly. Give the fool his day, for tomorrow is mine.

That was the truth of it.

Nevin Kantor was a liar, and an accomplished one at that. It wasn't Shyish that had guided his feet to Drakenhof Castle. Mannfred von Carstein, the true heir of Vlad's Kingdom of the Dead, had bartered his life for servitude. When he could have struck Nevin Kantor down, he spared him, making a pact. It was Mannfred who owned his life, not Konrad. At Mannfred's bidding, he bent and scraped to the lunatic, but he did not *serve* him. He had bought his life with a single promise: that he would infiltrate the court of the mad count and pave the way for Mannfred's return. *Let the others fight and swagger, and ultimately destroy each other,* Mannfred's words echoed in his mind. *They are a devious backstabbing bunch of degenerates incapable of seeing the long game. Let them destroy themselves, and when the time is right, when all is said and done, then I shall return, not a moment before. You are to be my eyes and ears in the madman's court. Serve me well and you will be rewarded; fail me and we will finish what we started here today.*

As the ghost of Konrad's footsteps disappeared, the magician pushed back his chair and walked through the stacks of books and other curiosities. He knew what he was looking for, but was in no hurry to reclaim it. The place reeked of lonely death. He waited, fingering the spines of dusty books, and easing them out of the stacks to turn reverently through their brittle pages. Silence settled over the library. Still he waited. The books fascinated him. In more than half of them, the scrawl was unintelligible. In hundreds more the inks, and bloods, had faded, so much so that the words barely stained the page, but the smell as he cracked the spines and opened them was a heady rush of must, decay and genius. It was ambrosia for the hungry magician.

It took a moment to find what he was looking for, a single sheet of yellowed parchment woven out of pressed reeds, slipped inside a mildewed tome of folklore. On it, written in a flaking rust of blood was the incantation *Diabolisch Leichnam*. Beside it on the shelf lay an elaborately carved six inch-long bone case. Kantor rolled the sheet like a scroll and stuffed it inside the bone case before slipping that, in turn, inside his shirt.

Convinced, finally, that he was alone, Kantor left the stacks. He could have sneaked out, there were ways, but that wouldn't buy him long enough. He needed the best part of the night, not a few stolen minutes, so he walked towards the stairs.

Before he was even halfway there, a lantern-jawed thug blocked his way, huge ham-hock arms folded across his barrel chest. 'I don't think so.'

Kantor squared up to the man, half his size and no match for the thug's brawn, he nonetheless knew he had to play the game. There could be no fear. 'You aren't kept around for your depth of thought, though, are you? So move,' he said.

'I said I don't think so.'

'Let's put this another way, shall we? Words of one syllable: let me go or die. There, even your thick head should be able to absorb that.'

The thug didn't seem particularly disturbed by the threat, although the beginnings of a grin played across his lips. He was obviously enjoying the game. 'You ain't going anywhere 'cept back to your cell.'

Slowly and deliberately the magician withdrew the bone scroll case from within the folds of his shirt and pressed it into the guard's cheek. 'Do you know what's in here? Do you have any idea what this magic is capable of? Well, do you?'

'I'm sure it's supposed to turn my body inside out, ripping the bones right through my skin and dumping my guts on the floor at your feet, right?'

'Close,' Kantor agreed. 'Very close indeed.'

'Shame it's in that little box then isn't it? I mean, it isn't a lot of use in there is it? Especially not against my little babies.' The thug tapped the spiral of tattoos on his flexed bicep.

'It's a game isn't it? Always a game.'

'More of a dance, I'd say. You want summink I've got, I want summink you've got. We dance around it for a while, threaten to do unspeakable things to each other, and make a deal that keeps both of us sweet.'

'You're scum, do you know that?' Kantor was enjoying himself. 'Now, believe me, there's nothing I want to do in the world right now more than I want to rip your innards out in a most spectacular fashion, but I am rather hoping it doesn't come to that.'

''Cause of the mess, right?'

'Something like that, yes.'

'It's more than my life's worth to let you leave, you know that, don't you?'

Kantor nodded, taking them into the next stage of the dance.

'Damned if you do, damned if you don't. All things considered, it's not your lucky day, is it?'

'Luckier than yours, to my way of thinkin',' the thug said. He hadn't flinched so much as an inch since the bone case touched his cheek, not to twitch a smile, nor to sneer his distaste.

'How so?' Kantor asked, genuinely curious.

'Ah, it's like my old man used to say, a fool and his money are easily parted. Show me your money, fool. You want out, and me, I'm supposed to wait 'til I'm relieved, but I reckon I could meet him on the way, for the right incentive.'

That was what it always came down to with the dregs of humanity. Kantor smiled widely, pocketing the scroll case. Not, of course, that he would have wasted the *Diabolisch Leichnam* on the trollish thug.

'What, pray tell, would you consider the right "incentive"?'

The thug made a show of scratching his scalp and furrowing his brow, as if lost in thought. His eyes lit up, as if he had just stumbled upon the idea: 'Shillings.'

'Because there's a vast supply of coin down here, I suppose? Something else, perhaps? Something I might actually *have*?'

'Ah but you've got 'em, ain't ya? Show me your money,' the thug grinned, rubbing thumb and forefinger together. 'S'all about money. You pay me, I do you a favour. It's the way of the world.'

Nevin Kantor wanted, for just a moment, to flatten the leering fool all across the wall. Instead, he matched the thug's grin.

'Indeed. Well, you know, I might have something to interest you.' The magician slipped a carnelian-studded ring from his finger and palmed it. He noticed the way the gem drew the thug's eye. 'Perhaps we can come to some sort of accommodation? Let's say out tonight, back when you change shifts tomorrow? No one any the wiser that I've wandered. How much might such an accommodation cost?'

The thug shook his head. 'Cost? That pretty ring you've just hidden, but it's impossible, you know that don't ya? You'll never get away with it. The Hamaya'll sniff you out, and you'll be banged up in a proper cell without your precious books before you can say Johannes Eisblume.'

'Let's just say it is a risk I'm willing to take. So, do we have a deal?'

'It's your funeral.'

'So, we have a deal?'

'Aye, we have a deal.' The thug held his meaty hand out. Kantor pressed the ring into it and closed his fingers, making a fist.

'Sunrise,' the thug said. 'That's when I'm back. I'll be less than a quarter of an hour late, but not much less. Make sure you're back and tucked up in your cell or I'll be forced to hunt you down and break you into tiny pieces of bone and gristle. You wouldn't want that, now would ya?'

'As much as I wouldn't want to take all the fun out of your life, I think we'll try to avoid that little scenario, eh?' the magician said, turning on his heel and walking back towards the discarded skin.

CIRCUMSTANCE HAD TURNED Nevin Kantor into an expert at biding his time.

Drakenhof was a warren of disused rooms and desolate corridors that spread out like cavernous fingers into the mountain beneath the castle itself. Deep in these, Kantor had claimed his own room, utterly remarkable in every way, except one: to the casual passer-by, the room did not exist. The magician had woven a glyph around the doorframe masking it from casual discovery. Someone would have to know about the room to find it. It was a small security, but even a tiny bit of privacy was better than none.

Kantor paced the room.

A woman lay bound and gagged in the centre of the room. He had taken her from the slave pens. She wouldn't be missed, and even if she was, people would simply assume that one of the vampires had grown hungry. That was the beauty of having a ready supply of fresh meat.

'Oh, do stop whimpering, girl. You're driving me up the damned wall.'

The woman kicked and writhed, fighting against her bonds. She had woken a few minutes earlier, before he had finished preparing the incantation. Kantor walked into the centre of the bloody pentagram daubed on the stone floor and clubbed her across the side of the face with his fist.

'The more you fight the worse it will be for you, I promise you that.'

Doing his best to ignore her moans, the magician set tallow candles on the points of the pentagram, sealing them with melted wax to the stone so that they wouldn't topple during the ceremony itself.

He drew a second summoning circle for himself, pinning it out with silver thread to ensure that it remained unbroken. He harboured no illusions about the nature of the sorcery he was dabbling in. *Diabolisch Leichnam*, the diabolical corpse, was old magic, dating back, he believed, to the court of Neferata. It was magic of the blackest nature. In the common Reikspiel, it was known as *The Vessel*, an incantation capable of stripping the soul from the flesh, leaving behind an empty vessel capable of being occupied by a cuckoo, a lost spirit. It was, in a manner of speaking, a way for the necromancer to prepare a host to accept his own essence, should the need arise.

It was a fallback, an ace in the hole as the gamblers liked to call it. Kantor wasn't fond of risks and most certainly wasn't a gambler by design. The answer lay in strategy, in careful planning and forethought. It was possible to pre-empt an enemy's actions if you knew him well enough. The secret was to know your enemy, and armed with that knowledge, to minimise potential failings long before they became a problem.

Only a fool went into a fight blind.

One by one, he lit the candles. The flames guttered slightly as he began to speak, although no natural wind stirred. Excitement flooded Kantor's veins as he embraced the touch of Shyish.

The woman's eyes flared with terror. She was screaming behind her gag, but not even as much as a whisper made it through. Her back arched as she struggled to roll herself out of the bloody pentagram. It was useless of course, he had seen to it that she wouldn't be leaving the circle until he was ready to carry her empty shell out.

Kantor raised his hands in supplication, forming the words of the incantation with precision.

The light flared and almost failed, the black wind surging around the tallow candles. The sulphurous reek of brimstone filled the air, sickly sweet and cloying. It burned at the back of his throat, making it difficult to shape the words.

He sank to his knees, refusing to misshape even a syllable, threw his head back and forced the sealing line of the incantation through his lips. The skin of his hands, spreading up his arms, glowed darkly, the black wind seeping out of his veins and staining his skin.

Then the candles died.

He stopped mid-word, his heart hammering in his chest.

You dare, mortal?

He had no way of knowing if the question was in his imagination or if it was real, in the room with him.

The next line of the incantation, what was it? His mind was blank. No, not blank, filled with fear. He had to reach behind the fear, had to find the words he had spent so long memorising. There was nothing but darkness. Black.

He stared in horror at the daemon manifesting before him, drawing substance out of the air itself to make itself whole. The thing was like nothing he had ever seen: silver horns, one complete, one broken down to a stump, skin like the stone wall behind it, mould and rot shrivelling around its empty eyes, teeth like tombstones, chipped and broken and breath like brimstone.

It reached out for him, but couldn't pass beyond the barrier formed by the silver thread. The urge to run was almost irresistible, almost.

Kantor closed his eyes. Still he could see it, blazing in his minds eye.

He licked his lips.

The next word...

The next...

The last:

'Cadaver!' The word dripped from his tongue like venom. A triumphant grin split the necromancer's face.

He opened his eyes.

The daemon, half-materialised, matched the grin.

This marks you, magician. You are aware of that, are you not? This marks your soul indelibly. You are mine now, my tool to wield.

'Giving on both sides, daemon – you are mine. That is the pact of bonding, is it not?' He was shaking, adrenaline coursing through his body. He could taste the power in the air. It thrilled through him. He was alive with it.

Until I sever it, yes. Then I will feed, although there is barely enough flesh on your bones to make a decent meal. Your soul however, your soul is fat and corrupt, deliciously so.

'And you will feed, essence of the winds, I have seen to that. Take her, not her flesh mind, only her soul. You can gorge yourself on her sweet meat at another time.'

The daemon fed, stripping the woman's soul from her flesh, even as she screamed for her life, begging, whimpering and finally falling silent, lifeless, in the centre of the pentagram.

Come claim the flesh, magician, the daemon goaded, spiritual residue dribbling down its chin. It licked its talons clean, slurping up the drool with glee.

Instinctively, Nevin Kantor took a step forwards. The daemon couldn't help itself: in hunger, its eyes darted to the silver thread. Kantor drew up sharply, his toe less than a finger's width from breaching the protective circle.

Ahhh almost too easy, magician.

'But not quite. The woman is gone yes?'

No trace of her essence is left within the shell.

'Good, then your work here is done, essence of the winds, begone.' He clapped his hands and was alone with the corpse of the dead woman at his feet, the stink of brimstone strong in the air.

He had to work quickly now to bind the empty vessel to him so that it would withstand the onslaught of decay and corruption that had already begun to set in with the banishment of the host's immortal soul.

Soon, he would have a place to flee, should his master's schemes fail.

CHAPTER SEVENTEEN

Bring out your Dead

THE IMPERIAL CAPITAL, ALTDORF
The birth of the New Year

THE WOLF ENTERED the capital at dusk.

Jerek moved silently, with the grace of a predator, through the darkening streets. It felt like so long ago that he had last walked amongst the living, like a man. It was a lifetime ago.

The denizens of the city lived with new caution, casting suspicious glances back over their shoulders as they walked from shadow to deeper shadow, doorway to alley to doorway, expecting at any moment the claws and teeth of death to drag them down and revel in the slaughter of their flesh. Von Carstein's war had carved this new world.

They had no idea that the wolf could dress in human clothing, that the monster could walk unnoticed in their midst, looking for all the world just like any one of them. He did not enjoy the deception.

Jerek pushed open the door to the Crooked Crone and walked into the taproom.

No one turned to stare. No one cried, 'Fiend!'

Licking his lips, the wolf called over a serving girl and ordered a pint of the house brew.

He handed her a bruised shilling and took a seat by the fire, tempted by the warmth.

Jerek didn't know where to begin. By rights, in the wake of Pieter's spectacular failure at Nuln, he should have returned to Drakenhof. He hadn't. He had come to Altdorf, city of spires, in search of von Carstein's signet ring. It had become an obsession, a disease. To his way of thinking, if he could find it, so could anyone else, and he couldn't allow them to. That meant he had to find it, and he had to destroy it.

Only it wasn't that easy.

The last glimmer of humanity in the wolf might have wanted to shatter the promise of dominion that the ring offered, but that was nothing against the hunger of the damned beast within him. The beast craved it. Inheritance: the word gnawed away at him. Like hunger, it saturated his corpse. He wanted it destroyed, yet all the while, he hungered for it.

The beast was growing more powerful by the day, demanding its right to eternity.

Soon it would be impossible to deny, and then he would be forever damned.

He warmed himself by the fire.

The taproom of the Crooked Crone was busy, women with easy smiles worked the long tables, while men with loose purse strings spent their shillings and pfennigs as if they believed that tomorrow wouldn't come, and who could blame them in these uncertain times? Let them take their pleasure when and where they could.

Men, deep in their cups, hunched over a rickety table playing knucklebones. They cursed, money changed hands, they rolled, cursed some more and more money moved across the table. Win some, lose some, the drinkers didn't seem to care. They laughed, talked of life and love, and pulled occasionally at the serving girl's skirts as she wove a path around them. Jerek sat awhile, enjoying the easy camaraderie.

Constellations of conversation moved around him. He closed his eyes and let them all wash over him. Still, he heard snippets. The shadow of the vampires hung heavy over the city. Much of the talk had moved on from the evils of war and its depravations, and grown more introverted and personal. Few had forgotten the butchery at the Sigmarites' cathedral. Those horrors were somehow more real now, given the years between the war and the fall of Vlad von Carstein at the hand of Wilhelm III.

It was amazing how humanity coped with tragedy. They could brush aside the devastation of thousands, in sympathy for the tragedy of a few. In that way, they were much like the other creatures of nature, the pack animals that put the welfare of the pack ahead of their own. Tens of thousands had died under the choking hold of the

Vampire Count, through starvation and privation, rather than to more ruthless killers like steel and talons.

The conversations barely even remembered the sacrifice of the Grand Theogonist. The priests themselves might have sought to canonise the man, but the commoners had already begun to forget his sacrifice. That was another miracle of humanity, short memories.

How many years was it since he had stood on the city walls, defiant? Surely not long enough for his bravery to have become as nothing?

Jerek found himself thinking of humanity in terms of the beast that he had become, not the man he was. Years had passed, more years than many would care to remember. They hadn't forgotten. They had become removed from it. Other tragedies had befallen their lives, and gradually von Carstein had become a monster consigned to a dark time. That was the final miracle of mankind, the ability to move on.

Of course, this last miracle was as much a curse, forced on them by the fleeting nature of their lives. This second life had framed his perspective in ways he would never have been able to understand before.

He doubted that anyone here would know his sire's final resting place. He had thought they might share some kind of bond, even now, that would allow him to sense Vlad, six feet under and riddled with worms. There was nothing.

He sank back into his chair and tried to think like a Sigmarite. How would they dispose of an evil they could barely comprehend? A cleansing fire? Ritual purification? Or would they set their blessed Sigmar to watch over the fiend, even in death?

Perhaps there was a bond, after all. Jerek smiled to himself. Given the mindset of the priests, it was obvious what they had done with the vampire's mortal remains. They had buried them, and where better to inter the beast than beneath the watchful gaze of the man who slew it?

That was the truth, he was sure. It was the Sigmarite way, to cover the darkness with light as they sought to sanitise it and make it safe.

He knew where he would find von Carstein. More importantly, he knew where he would find the ring that gifted the beast his incredible restorative powers: in the dirt beneath the holy man's grave.

Jerek raised the jug to his lips and drank deeply, imagining that he could actually savour the bitter-sharp taste of the brew as it rolled down his throat.

He smacked his lips and called the serving girl over. She had her hands full, juggling mugs and tankards and sidestepping groping hands. In another life the wolf would have taught those pups a lesson in manners, but not today. Today it was important that he was one of them.

'Bonny lass,' he called, snagging the girl's apron as she breezed by. He held her firm. She looked down at him, a smile on her lips, but nothing in her eyes. 'I'll take another.' She nodded. 'And thank you for smiling for me, love. It's made this lecherous old wolf's day.'

For just a moment her eyes brightened. That was enough for him. He closed his eyes again.

The ale came, and went down his throat. He tuned out the hubbub, even when a piss-poor minstrel struck up a ragged tune that had the locals joining in enthusiastically. He let the noise wash over him. All he needed to do was wait it out. They all had homes and beds to go to.

The singer butchered just about every tune out of his mouth, but the punters didn't care. They slammed tankards down on beer-soaked tabletops and cried out for more, joining in reels and shanties with noisy appreciation.

Finally, the landlord rang the bell over the bar, signifying the end of the revels with a call for last orders. A few of the hardened drinkers downed one last ale, but most began their wobbly journeys home to sleep off the worst effects of the drink. Jerek wouldn't envy any of them come morning.

As the last of the drinkers drifted out, the wolf left his fireside seat and joined them, stumbling slightly to mirror their own unsteady gaits.

'Which way's the cathedral?' he asked, bumping into the shoulder of the man beside him. Grinning, the man pointed off in the direction of one of the many spires.

'Had a few too many, eh?'

'Jus' enough to forget what the woman looks like 'n where she's waitin',' Jerek slurred, a lopsided grin pasted across his face.

'Ah, you knows what they say fella: ain't a woman in the world who ain't made pretty by enough alcohol.'

'Ain't that the truth! Jus' a pity us fellas need to drink to make a sows purse outta the pig's ear, eh?' Jerek agreed with a hearty chuckle and staggered on his merry way.

For the sake of appearances, Jerek walked a little unsteadily – not the exaggerated drunken lurch that would be remembered by the casual observer on his way home, but the occasional misstep that made him look like just another one of them.

He leaned against the wall on the street corner, and then pushed off again, repeating the pattern street after street until he saw the dome of the grand cathedral.

The iron railings were barred, but it didn't matter. The surrounding wall was low enough for him to scale it, easily. Jerek scrambled over the wall, his feet scuffing up the stone as he hauled himself over the top. He dropped down to the other side with a grunt.

The grounds of the cathedral were well kept. A small glade of trees sheltering a single grave caught his eye. He walked through a neatly tended rose garden to the secluded grove and into the moonlight shadows cast by a weeping willow. There was a simple stone marking the holy man's grave. A second smaller gate led through the wall to the street. The headstone was seeded over with lichen where the shadows of the willow lingered. A white rose bush grew beside the headstone, the thorns scraping against the words of the prayer carved into the stone.

He knelt at the graveside, but there was nothing remotely reverential about it. He reached out to claw at the dirt with his bare hands, but stopped, his fingers only inches from a curious metal disc set into the grass. He didn't recognise the rune embossed on it, but he felt the heat of its power even before his hand closed on it. The disc seared into his skin with shocking force, hurling the wolf back bodily from the grave.

Jerek staggered back to his feet, shaking his head. He felt the residual power of the rune in every fibre of his being, as if it was somehow attuned to his dead flesh. He turned his hand over and stared at his blackened palm and the negative image of the rune that had been branded on it. Tentatively, he reached out again. He felt the fiery pain of the burn swell, long before his hand came close to touching the dirt. He tested its limits, pushing to the point of agony, and still he couldn't lay so much as a finger on the dirt of the Grand Theogonist's grave.

It made sense, of course, that the place would be protected.

Indeed, the talisman told him all he needed to know about the dual nature of the priest's final resting place. Why else would it need a warding against dead flesh, if not to keep Vlad beneath the ground and the living dead from being able to reach down and bring him back?

It meant that he needed to exhume the holy man to get to the body beneath it and, ultimately, to the ring.

Only, he couldn't, *he* couldn't.

There was, however, more than one way to skin a cat. Just because he couldn't, didn't mean that someone else wouldn't be able to.

Jerek looked around. He knew if he didn't act quickly even this slim hope would be undone by the simple fact that his presence would be felt within the walls of the great cathedral, the sickness of unlife causing nightmares and heart tremors, stomach cramps and nausea, and countless other side effects within the holy men.

A beggar perhaps? He could drag one off the street and force him to do his bidding.

No. It had to be someone above suspicion if seen by watchers inside the cathedral.

Who then?

On the far side of the rose garden there was a small cemetery. A cemetery needed a gravedigger. What was more natural than a gravedigger abroad during the dark hours, preparing for the day ahead?

He could breathe the fear of unlife into the man, bullying him into this vile act of desecration. Could? He would have to.

Jerek knew then what he had to do. Stripping down until he was naked, his clothes folded beneath the willow, he drew on the wolf, giving himself over to the change. As the agony of the transformation took him, he screamed, the scream giving way to the protracted howl of a wolf baying at the moon.

No lights came on within the cathedral.

The wolf padded easily through the rose garden towards the lines of graves, and the small gravedigger's hovel beyond them. His skin crawled this close to so many idols and effigies of the Man-God planted in the earth. He wove a path through the graves to the gravedigger's door. Thirty feet shy of the door, the wolf sprang, hurling itself bodily at the barrier, breaking its flimsy lock open and tumbling into the small room.

He smelled the man before he saw him, cowering in his blankets, grey hair stuck up in stalks, skin sickly pale with fear.

The wolf padded slowly over to the gravedigger's bedside, jowls slack, saliva drooling around sharp teeth.

'Mercy, no,' the old man pleaded as the beast pressed its muzzle up to within inches of his face. Then he began to change, the monster withdrawing in favour of the man. The wolf's low-throated growl shifted into the more natural rhythms of Jerek's breathing. His bones shifted and re-formed until he stood naked before the old man. Instead of diminishing it, his nudity only served to reinforce the old man's fear.

'Up, gravedigger, as of now, your life is mine. You live and breathe at my whim, understand?' He baited the gravedigger.

The old man nodded so hard that Jerek almost laughed… almost.

He scrambled out of bed, his scrawny body all slack skin, bone and cavernous shadow in the moonlight, desperately eager to please the monster that had invaded his home if it meant staying alive.

'What… what?'

'What do I want?'

The gravedigger nodded again, 'Yes.' The old man was shaking uncontrollably. The last thing Jerek wanted to do was cause his heart to give out in fear.

He felt remorse for what he was about to do, but the beast was still fresh in his blood, suffocating his defiant humanity. It was a sign that the monster was winning the fight. Soon he would feel no compunction in slaughter or desecration, but for now, the bitter tang of guilt reminded him of what it meant to be alive.

He stifled it because, for once, it had no place in what he was about to do. He needed to surrender to the beast's baser nature.

'I want you to do a job for me. I want you to dig up a grave.'

It took a moment for his words to register through the old man's fear. 'You want me to dig a grave for you?'

'No, I want you to dig *up* a grave for me. The grave has already been dug once before.'

'I can't–'

'Oh, but I think you'll find you *can* and what's more, you *will*.' Jerek curled back his lip to make sure that his meaning wasn't lost on the old man. He needn't have worried, it wasn't. 'Get dressed, pick up your shovel and follow me. I don't want to hurt you, but that doesn't mean I won't. Do we understand each other?'

The gravedigger nodded again, grabbing and dropping a grubby shirt from the back of a wooden chair. He bent and picked it up from the floor, staring at Jerek the entire time as if, by looking away, he might incite the beast to attack.

Jerek walked out of the tiny hovel. The air felt good on his skin, cold enough to raise the prickle of goose pimples, but not so cold as to shrivel his skin.

A moment later, the gravedigger emerged, a bulls-eye lantern lighting the path at his feet. His expression was grim.

Without a word, Jerek set off into the graves. He wondered how long it would take the old man to realise which grave he wanted exhumed. Not long, surely. Then what? Would he resist? Fight? Raise the alarm? Or would he simply dig?

Behind him, the old man whimpered as they entered the rose garden. There was only one grave beyond this point.

'I can't...'

Jerek stopped beneath the trailing leaves of the weeping willow. 'Dig,' He said simply and with utter finality.

'I can't,' the gravedigger repeated, even as he planted his shovel in the dirt.

His suspicion had been right: the peculiar metal talisman didn't affect the old man.

'Dig,' Jerek repeated, sickened by himself even as he said it. It was easy to pretend that he felt nothing, but then lies were always believable – only not to the liar himself.

The old man dug, for his life. He turned the shovel through the soil, opening up the grave.

Jerek dressed again while the gravedigger toiled.

It took most of the long night just to reach the depth of the first corpse that the grave harboured. Tears streamed down the gravedigger's face as he dug, begging for forgiveness even as his shovel struck the wood of the Grand Theogonist's coffin. He shovelled away the dirt, until the silver clasps of the box were visible.

'Open it,' Jerek said. It was unreasonable to expect the pair to be actually buried together, but it would have been stupid not to check.

The gravedigger used the butt of the shovel's handle to crack the seals and open the metal clasps. The air sucked into the wooden box as the lid cracked open and the stench poured out of it. Time and maggots had reduced the holy man to loosely assembled bones and strings of gristle. He was alone in the coffin.

'Seal it and lift it out, we're digging deeper,' Jerek said.

The old man did as he was told. Using the edge of the shovel, he dug around the coffin, freeing it so that he could angle it upwards, and lift it out of the ground, although the task was far from easy.

Jerek had been right in his reasoning. Less then a foot beneath the Grand Theogonist's coffin, the gravedigger unearthed Vlad's remains. Without the luxury of a box, the Vampire Count had been picked clean by the grubs, his bones stripped completely of flesh, muscle and gristle. Only strips of rag remained of his once fine clothing, but the gold chains and more importantly, the ring, remained.

The Vampire Count's hands were folded across his ribcage, the extravagant signet ring on his right hand. It was gold with a garish gem set amid what looked like wings, the tips studded with precious stones.

Jerek didn't dare move.

He stared at the ornate ring with its dark gemstone setting for a full five minutes.

He couldn't believe that the Sigmarites could be so stupid as to leave the ring – the key to the Vampire Count's power – in place.

Exhilarated, he eased the ring off the finger of bone and slipped it onto his own finger. He expected to feel something, the tingle of power flooding into this tainted veins, the answering cry of immortality, but there was nothing. He held his hand up before his face, staring at the metal wings as they spread over his knuckled fist: nothing.

Did he need to cut himself? Would blood seal the bond between vampire and ring? Would he feel its power then?

That was when his stupidity sank in, finally. For all its ostentation, the winged ring wasn't the fabled von Carstein ring, it wasn't blessed with awesome powers of recuperation, it was nothing more than a pretty trinket. Why would the ring be on his finger at all? It was true: the priests had stolen it to rob von Carstein of his unearthly powers.

He couldn't bring himself to believe that.

He dropped into the hole in the ground, scrabbling about in the dirt, grunting and scraping, pushing aside the bones.

Nothing.

The ring could be anywhere.

Without knowing who took it, there was no way of knowing where it might be.

He had no choice but to return to Konrad's court, empty-handed, praying against reason that the trail ended here in this desolate garden of Morr. He knew that it didn't. It *began* with the thief who had stolen it, and even knowing that, it was beyond his ability to track it. He could only hope to wrest it from its wielder when it resurfaced, because it would, he harboured no illusions about that. An artefact so vile could not remain lost for long.

Better to let any who came looking, sniffing around and asking questions, think he had found Vlad's precious secret and made away with it.

Jerek dragged himself out of the grave and stood, dusting the dirt off his clothes.

He made sure the gravedigger knew what he had retrieved from the grave, making a fist around the winged ring, and cracking his knuckles. He reached a hand down to help the old man out of the hole, but then changed his mind, and left him knee deep in the bones of the dead to excuse his desecration.

'Your lucky day, old man. You get to live, at least until sunrise, when the priests will string you up for messing with the bones of their blessed saint.'

CHAPTER EIGHTEEN

The Taking of the Virgin and the Hag

THE COURT OF THE BLOOD COUNT, SYLVANIA
The Night of the Ravens

WOMEN LINED THE walls.

Konrad, Vampire Count of Sylvania, reclined luxuriantly in his sire's obsidian throne, savouring the heady aromas of the feast. Vlad had surrounded himself with beauty, like many beasts, drawn to the darkness within the soulless art, as if it somehow filled the void shaped by their death. Konrad despised such stupidity. There was beauty in the taking, not in admiring something unattainable: in the taking.

Konrad sighed and waved airily in the direction of a flaxen-haired beauty chained up against the wall. Her skin was as dusky as her almond-shaped eyes. She shook her head violently, writhing around against her captors' grip as they unlocked her manacles. The woman sobbed, begged, kicked and screamed. Oh yes, the beauty was most certainly in taking what you wanted, Konrad thought. The girl's fear was exhilarating. It was so much more passionate than quiet acquiescence. It was always better when they fought back. It added a sense of theft to the feeding.

One hundred and eleven women were chained, naked to the walls of the great hall, for his delectation. Their blood sang to him. He could sniff out their uniqueness, the virgins and the crones, the mothers and the whores. They all had their own unique stink. He looked at them, and at the rest of his court, coveting them.

'This,' he said grandly, 'is what separates us, what sets us apart. What you want is in my power to give. Come, let us feed!'

The woman shrieked as she was thrown down at his feet, the strength of the thralls driving her to her knees. Onursal, the Hamaya, stepped up and grabbed a fistful of her hair, tangling it in his fist as he pulled her across the floor. Her bare feet scrambled and her hands slapped at the cold stone as she tried to stop the pain, even as it soared inside her.

This was power, and it was intoxicating.

It was natural that others craved what he had, and sought to take it from him.

The beauty was in the taking.

He would have been a fool to believe that he was safe. Pieter, Fritz and Hans might be dead, but treachery still lurked in every shadow, waiting to undo him. It was the nature of the beast: he surrounded himself with predators. To show weakness was to invite death. There wasn't a creature in the room that wouldn't have delighted in bringing him down and feasting on his corpse as a way of raising themselves up in his stead.

He looked around the room, at the naked and the dead.

He had no friends among them and could afford no trusts or confidences. They looked at him the same way, he was certain: they wanted him dead.

Well let them want, Konrad thought bitterly. He wouldn't give them the satisfaction of seeing even a hint of weakness. He would be the complete vampire, lord of his people, master of his house, cruel and callous, driven and decadent, inviolable and immortal.

He clapped his hands and the two thralls bled the woman, eager to satisfy their master's desire.

He sniffed, nostrils flared, the tang of her fresh blood was heady.

He would deny himself no more.

The pleasure was in the taking.

Konrad fed first, the thralls grabbing her hands, slitting her forearms from her wrists, deep into the hollow of her elbow, dripping the rich nectar down his throat in a luscious fountain. He savoured it as it spilled over his lips and ran down his chin.

'Another!' he commanded, even before this one was bled dry, eager for another flavour to bleed onto his palate. That was the beauty of the human cattle: they all tasted different, their blood reflecting the richness and vitality of their lives, against the youth and inexperience.

The thralls dragged the woman away to satisfy the ghoulish flesh eaters of the undead Count's hall.

A younger girl replaced her. She was barely a child, her blood innocent, and full of temptation. It was a delicacy that he had come to appreciate.

Konrad leaned back, his mouth open as the leering thrall drew a knife across her wrist.

She screamed as her blood dripped into his mouth. He nodded, and the thrall tossed the girl aside. He had barely tasted her, preferring to give her as a gift to one of his chosen ones. He knew their weaknesses, knew what they hungered for, be it young, old, boy, woman. It paid to know those closest to him, and know them intimately. Those weaknesses could always be turned against him. Onursal, the dark-skinned giant, caught and drained the girl, sidestepping her corpse as it slumped to the floor. He bowed to Konrad. 'My thanks, master.'

Konrad indulged the vampire with a wry smile. Yes, he knew his people and their weaknesses.

Around the great hall, other Hamaya feasted with their master.

Not all, Konrad amended, seeing that Jerek had not joined in the feeding.

Jerek.

The Hamaya was not himself, and hadn't been since returning from the debacle at Nuln. Konrad wanted to believe that his loyalty was not in question, that his youngest brother knew his place, but how could he know for sure? Jerek was von Carstein as much as Fritz or Pieter, or Hans had ever been, as he himself was. The taint of Vlad soiled the Hamaya's veins. How could he not crave Konrad's power? It was his blood right: his inheritance. He was von Carstein and now that, of his brothers-in-death, only Konrad remained, how could he not look at the count and crave more? In his place, Konrad knew that it would have been impossible to resist the pull of power. That left him with a problem.

The wolf was the consummate predator, ruthless with its enemies.

Was the wolf his enemy? How could he not be, given what was at stake?

The beauty was in the taking. That was the only truth to life.

Konrad turned away from the traitor, glad to see Skellan drinking hungrily. Over the course of a few minutes, Skellan gorged himself on every flavour of blood available. Konrad watched as he moved in close to an old woman, skin loose and mottled on her frail bones, and tangled his fingers in the woman's hair, yanking her head back. Seeing Konrad's intent scrutiny, Skellan laughed and called, 'Doesn't she remind you of your mother?' as he drew the hag close enough to sink his teeth into her leathery throat.

'Only in as much as she's just as dead as the bitch, otherwise no,' Konrad snarled. There was no humour in his expression as he sank his teeth into a dead-eyed blonde who had staggered too close to him for her own good. He spun her around and let her fall. 'Music!' the Vampire Count proclaimed. 'A party needs music. Someone play! I want someone to play for me!'

There were no musicians in his court. They had fed on them when he had decided their tunes did not fit his mood.

'Will someone sing for me? Jerek?'

The wolf could not mask his revulsion. He pushed past one of Konrad's thralls struggling with a fat-bellied sow of a woman. Both went sprawling across the blood-slicked floor as Jerek left the great hall.

'I think perhaps you have lost your mind, my lord,' Skellan interjected smoothly, halting Jerek mid-step. Skellan let his words hang for longer than was wise. 'The old wolf is tone deaf and is incapable of carrying a tune. Better, surely, that we make these women scream, as one, and let their terror be music to our ears as we revel in their deaths.'

'As it should be!' Konrad agreed. 'Let us savour the agonies of our fodder! Let us drink, not only their blood, for even a bug can do that, let us devour their fear! Let us lose ourselves in their fear. Truly, let us feast!'

And they did, in an orgy suffering. The screams of the dying women shook the hall, folding in on themselves in a spiralling chorus of suffering. It was delicious, dizzying.

It was a rhapsody of murder, and Konrad stood in the centre of it all, lord of his domain, master in his own house, and drunk on the music of death.

He claimed the last for his own, whispering almost tenderly in her ear as he sucked the lifeblood out of her ruined face. There was no simple death for her. He chewed off her nose and sucked the mucus and blood with equal abandon.

Sated, he held her still, surveying the carnage. This was power, here, made flesh.

Dead flesh.

This was the power of death over life.

He caressed her cheek, looking for the one face he couldn't see: Jerek's.

Skellan moved up beside him.

'He's gone, hasn't he?' Konrad asked. He didn't need to say who.

'In more ways than one,' Skellan said. 'I have marked a change in him since Nuln. Something happened to him there, I fear, and he's not the same man as a result. Not the same *wolf*. He's lost his taste for the kill. You've noticed it as well, haven't you?'

Konrad nodded. 'He didn't feed tonight. Not once.'

'That is troubling, but not surprising.'

'No?'

'No. It was something he said a few weeks ago, "A wise man does not drink from the cup of his enemy", that was it, I think.'

'His enemy,' Konrad mused. He didn't want to believe it, but all the signs were there: the shift in personality, the introspection and reclusion, the late return weeks behind the few survivors of Nuln, the unwillingness to share blood with his brothers. These were all precursors of the cold hand that was betrayal. 'No one, not even the wolf, can offer such a slight and believe himself immune from retribution. I will have his apology and his loyalty, or I will have his tongue.'

Skellan inclined his head as if weighing two equally worthy options. 'As it should be, my lord. There is wisdom to such thinking, although I wonder if it will have the desired effect on Jerek, or if your brother is too far gone for such a clean solution. I must confess I rather fear the worst.'

HE FOUND JEREK on the roof.

The wind was savage, and the night black. Jerek stood amid a murder of glossy feathered ravens, the birds flocking around him as if he was their messiah. The wolf's face was grave.

Konrad stepped out onto the roof.

'So my company offends you, wolf?'

Jerek did not deny him.

A black knot of hatred twisted in Konrad's gut. The Hamaya lacked even the courtesy to lie to him.

Jerek turned his back on Konrad, feigning interest in the chimneys of Drakenhof far below.

'Who is master here, Jerek? Answer me that.'

'I did not choose this life, Konrad, and worse, I do not like what I have become. I look about me and see life that I cannot be a part of. I see the people I fought to save from the evil I now am. I am lost, caught between two worlds, but not part of either one. Tell me where the crime is in that? It is not a slight to you. Not everything is about you.'

'You did not answer my question.'

Jerek turned slightly, his wild mane of hair streaming in the wind, 'I should not need to.'

'But you do,' Konrad said coldly.

Hatred blazed in the wolf's eyes as his lips curled into a sneer. 'You are a fool, Konrad. You see enemies where there are none. You make enemies where there were only friends. You don't know when to hold out your hand, and when others do, you slap them away. Look around you, look at the birds, they fight and squabble over scraps. That is your kingdom, Konrad, a bloody fight for scraps. Your magical new world is built on fear, and fear is like sand, it shifts.

'You revere strength, or at least claim to, although it is obvious that it scares you. Make no mistake: strength does scare you, no matter what you would have others believe. Strength in others terrifies you, so you stamp it out, betraying your own weakness, while thinking it makes you strong. A strong man surrounds himself with strong men. A weak man postures in the centre of a circus of simpering fools.

'Believe me, *Blood Count*, there is always something more frightening to be discovered in this world, if you look hard enough. The secret is, coming to terms with the fact that the daemons you know are always less fearful than the daemons you don't know.

'You are your own worst enemy, *my lord*.'

'How dare you?' Konrad said.

There was no anger in his voice, no bluster. Indeed, it was almost a question as opposed to statement, as if the wolf's defiance bewildered him.

Jerek took a step forwards, closing the gap between them.

'How dare I? Where is the dare in telling the truth, Konrad?'

Konrad stiffened. 'You risk much, speaking to me this way, wolf. If we were not alone I would be forced to bring you into line.'

'You mean silence me, Konrad. No more lies between us.'

'I still could, wolf.'

'And in doing so, prove my point. Yes, you would be stupid enough to do just that, wouldn't you?'

Instinctively, Konrad raised his hand, ready to strike.

Jerek did not flinch. He stared at Konrad's fist as if daring him to do it, to lash out.

Konrad held himself in check, barely. A muscle beneath his cheek twitched. His fist clenched, fingernails digging into his palm. Had the stuff flowed through his veins, his fingernails would have drawn blood.

'That's what you want, isn't it, wolf? You want to goad me into attacking you. You want me to fall into a rage and throw myself at you.' A look of puzzlement spread over the Vampire Count's face. He lowered his fist slowly. 'Well, you will have no satisfaction from me.'

The wolf shook his head in disgust.

'You think I have lured you up here to fight you? You truly are a fool, Konrad. My being here has nothing to do with you, but everything to do with what you are.' Jerek laughed, a bitter, bleak sound that was ripped away by the wind. 'What we both are.' He looked over his shoulder, back towards the sheer drop down the mountainside to the jagged rocks below. 'I haven't come here to challenge you. I have come here to die, Konrad. I have come here to put an end to my own suffering once and for all, but I lack the strength to do it.'

'Oh, it can be arranged,' Konrad goaded, taking a step to match Jerek's, so there was nothing between them.

The ravens scattered, cawing raucously as they burst into the sky in a flurry of black wings that blotted out the slice of silver moon. The birds buffeted the pair, wings slapping at them, bullying them closer to the edge. Konrad took another step, unclasping his cloak. It fell behind him, only to be lifted by the wind. Billowing out, it sailed over the parapet like his own discarded wings.

'I favoured you wolf, I trusted you. I treated you like the brother you are.'

Jerek shook his head in disgust. 'You mean you used me as a tool to do what you were incapable of. You had me remove those you feared and cement your authority by becoming your personal assassin? That's no act of brotherhood in my world.'

'In your world? You talk as if we exist in different realities. We don't, Jerek. Your world is *my* world.' Jerek shook his head, denying the truth of Konrad's words. 'You are more like me than you realise, brother. Together we could have achieved great things.'

'There is no greatness in murder.'

'At my side you could have had the world.'

'At your side I could have butchered the world, there is a difference.'

And there it was, the truth.

'So it is true what Skellan said, you have lost your taste for killing. What kind of beast have you become, Jerek? Because you are surely a wolf no longer.'

'I am not the wolf I was, but nor am I the wolf you would have me be. I am torn in two.'

'Then you are a fool, Jerek, because you can only ever be the killer, as the scorpion can only ever be the scorpion, the lamb the lamb, and the raven the raven. It is your nature just as it is theirs. To deny it is to deny your essence, to deny your soul.'

'I have no soul, our bastard of a father stole it from me!' Jerek's sudden anger was shocking.

Konrad understood. 'You hate him, don't you? You hate him for what he did, and would undo it if you could. You would renounce his gift, you would sacrifice the power he blessed you with, the life he gave you, and go back to grubbing in the dirt like some pathetic pig.'

'I don't hate him. I want to hate him, but hate is an emotion, and even something as basic as that is lost to me. I would kill him if I could. I would see the curse of his existence purged from the land, if I could.'

'You would kill me.' It wasn't a question. 'Well, wolf, I was right when I called you my truth speaker, although I have little liking for the truth that you offer now. There can be no easy forgiveness, it seems, and there can be no trust, not now. You know what it means, don't you?' Konrad's face shifted in the moonlight, his features contorting harshly as the beast within rose to the surface.

He was on Jerek before the wolf had a chance to react, tearing at his face with his claws. Jerek threw his hands up to ward off the attack, the flat of his hand – his burned hand, branded with the rune from the protective talisman that sealed the Grand Theogonist's grave – connecting with the side of Konrad's face. The Vampire Count reeled back is if he had been stung, his cry rending the night in two. He dropped into a crouch, snarling, as Jerek surrendered to his own primal monster and wore its face. Only then did the dance begin in earnest.

The birds cackled and shrieked appreciatively, circling overhead.

Konrad lashed out, driving Jerek back towards the roof's edge. Jerek met the blow and matched it, catching Konrad's fist in his own, stepping in close enough so that the mad Count's graveolent breath stung his face, and slammed his other fist into his throat. It would have killed a living man slowly, suffocating the life out of him as his windpipe collapsed in on itself and starved him of precious air. Konrad's head snapped forwards, fangs scoring across Jerek's wrist as he pulled it back.

Konrad twisted his arm, breaking the wolf's grip on his fist, and even as Jerek struggled to reassert his dominance, the Vampire Count surged forwards, cannoning his forehead into Jerek's face. The blow shattered the wolf's nose. The wolf staggered back under the sheer ferocity of the blow. Konrad followed it up with a dizzying combination of high left, to the temple, a savage low right, to the kidney, and a devastating second left in the centre of the gaping wound that had been the wolf's face.

Jerek stumbled back, his hands held up desperately in front of his face to ward off another blow.

Konrad spun and kicked downwards, his heel snapping the links between ligament and bone beneath the wolf's knee. Jerek stumbled back, perilously close to the roof's edge.

There could be no mercy for the wolf.

Konrad threw himself forwards.

The birds drove themselves into a frenzy, swarming around the pair.

The slate beneath his feet cracked and broke away, leaving Jerek's back leg hanging over nothing. Through the ruin of his face, the wolf grinned, and in a last act of defiance, took the victory away from Konrad. His smile never wavered. He looked at his would-be killer, and of all things Konrad saw pity in the wolf's eyes. Then Jerek fell back silently into the endless black and was snatched away by the battering wings of Vlad's ravens.

Rage seethed within Konrad as he moved up to the edge. He half expected to see the erratic flight of a bat trying to mask itself in the murder of birds, but the birds had all settled on the mountainside, filling every crevice and cranny. He strained to see beyond the ravens, to the teeth of the rocks below. Jerek's body was little more than a dark stain as it lay unmoving on a splinter of jagged rock. He refused to believe what had just happened. The wolf hadn't fought for his life, he had thrown it away! That last grin, the deliberate lurch backwards, giving himself to the fall instead of trying to save himself, it had been one final act of defiance, done out of spite and stupidity.

It galled him.

'How dare you?' he yelled down at his fallen brother, the manic pitch of his voice scattering a few of the more nervous birds. They circled the dark stain like vultures. Ravens were carrion eaters. Soon they would descend on the wolf and strip his carcass clean. Konrad watched for an age, while the sun rose and his rage subsided, until the remaining birds gave up their vigil. Still, the wolf lay there broken, at the base of the crag. Then and only then did a savage smile spread across Konrad's face, even as he reined in the beast and shifted back to human form. He might have been robbed of the thrill of the actual taking, but it didn't matter. What did matter was that he was alone. The Golden One, whoever the hell that might have been, was dead. He was the last von Carstein.

Triumphant, Konrad left the ravens to feed on the wolf's broken body.

CHAPTER NINETEEN
Ghost World

ACROSS THE OLD WORLD
Winter

THERE WAS NO evil that Jon Skellan was incapable of.

It was a game that offered only mild amusement, but it was a game that he loved to play just the same.

With his bare hands, he took a dark land and reshaped it into a ghost world.

His beasts ruled by tyranny. There was no justice. There was no fairness. There was no *humanity*. The world was reduced to two absolutes, pain and death, death and pain.

Skellan revelled in it. He revelled in the fear that his beasts inspired, and savoured the pain they delivered.

HE WALKED THE line of crucified corpses along the roadside. Upside down, the dead served as food for the birds and reminders to those left behind of the price of rebellion. It was a savage lesson, one the cattle took to heart.

The dead faces, drained of blood, stared back at him. More than half of their eyes were gone, pecked away by the flock of black ravens that trailed Skellan's force, scavenging carrion where the dead meat was discarded and left to rot.

They brought with them the return of the blood plague, but this time it was indiscriminate in its slaughter. Old, young, male, female, none were immune to the insidious illness, as Skellan's beasts sought to drain the Old World dry of every decent drop of blood that pumped through its veins. The pandemic spread, striking the largest cities of the Empire and wreaking as much devastation there as it did in the smallest villages. They started calling it the Season of the Dead.

The living barred their doors and windows, barricading themselves in, in the vain hope that the dead would pass them by. The dead did pass, and in their wake they left empty buildings and more than their fair share of ghosts.

Word had come that Lutwig had ousted his ineffectual father, the Pretender, Ludwig. The succession was irrelevant. Skellan didn't care who led the cattle. They existed for one purpose, to be hunted, brought down and feasted on.

With so many of Konrad's trusted Hamaya gone, it was only natural that Skellan should rise in both influence and power. Like his sire before him, he rose to be von Carstein's right hand, but unlike Posner, he would not make the mistake of getting himself slaughtered for ambition. He would bide his time. There was little to be gained by moving hastily and everything to be won by cautious strength. It was a long game, and a long game called for cunning and guile, not posturing and posing.

He watched and he learned, taking the tricks of others and turning them to his advantage. Where Vlad had offered his victims the choice of serving him in life or in death, Skellan was less prosaic. The choice he offered was an immediate death or a painful one. Few willingly chose pain. Those that did were not disappointed.

For months, the vampire's legion of the damned had savaged the land of the living, the necromancers adding fresh impetus to the sport by inventing cruel and unusual punishments for the living who were foolish enough to resist them. Skellan couldn't deny that he enjoyed their perversions, even encouraged them, but Nevin Kantor concerned him.

Even a fool could see that the necromancer was growing in strength, outstripping those around him as he opened himself up to the taint of the black Chaos wind. Death was no longer enough for Nevin Kantor. He consumed Immoliah Fey, owned her. Such was the lure of his power that even a necromancer with Fey's rare gift should fall for his fake endearments. There was no love, even he could see that, just pretty words whispered in the dark, and midnight promises, which were nothing more than midnight lies.

He took the living and violated them in ways that Skellan had never imagined possible. He experimented on them, testing the limits of their endurance, seeking to break the bonds that made them human without actually driving them into Morr's arms. He stripped flesh from bone without allowing his victims to die, forcing them to watch as layer after layer of meat peeled away before their eyes. A few, he delighted in killing, drawing every ounce of moisture from their flesh, leaving only desiccated husks. He turned others into cannibals, feeding them with their own flesh, and had destroyed them so completely that they ate it willingly.

Worse, he turned mother onto son and father onto daughter, by a dark geas, the dead being absorbed back into the family, like some never-ending serpent of consumption, the beast feeding off its own tail. He manipulated their minds, forcing visions of hell to root behind their eyes, with promises of the torments on offer should they fail him. He also raised the dead, not their corpses, but their souls, even as they travelled the long and winding road to the underworld, drawing them back, demanding to know what they saw, in detail. Demanding to know not only what they saw, but also what they felt and heard, all of it, what it was like to be dead.

The intensity of his obsession was unnerving, even to Skellan.

Kantor was a threat, potentially more so than the Blood Count. Since Jerek's betrayal, Konrad's behaviour had become increasingly erratic and unpredictable, as what was undoubtedly madness burrowed away inside him. He had come to rely more and more on Kantor's magic, more so even than Skellan's sword. It made it increasingly difficult for Skellan's gentle nudges and sly whisperings to find their mark, although he continued to goad the unstable von Carstein into fully-fledged paranoia. To that extent, Mannfred had been completely correct when he judged Konrad: his brother possessed the fundamental insecurities of a paranoiac. Kantor had set himself up as a counterbalance to Skellan in the Count's allegiances. Skellan understood Konrad's fascination with Kantor: the necromancer manipulated the winds into miracles. More and more, Konrad sought out the human, and while Skellan had no idea what they actually discussed, it was obvious that Konrad trusted Nevin Kantor's council as much if not more than Skellan's.

Kantor was turning into a problem.

Months of manipulation were coming to fruition, a multitude of small, carefully laid plans playing out, in time for Mannfred's imminent return.

The necromancer could not be allowed to interfere.

Konrad would fall, with Skellan's help, and it would be spectacular.

He knelt beneath the upturned crucifix, scooping up a raven before the birds could frighten and scatter.

'Are you there?' He demanded. His voice was pitched low so it wouldn't carry.

The bird's yellow eyes roved and it cawed harshly, ruffling its feathers and trying to burst out of his grip.

'Always,' the raven cackled as Skellan's grip threatened to crack its delicate bones.

'Your brother's crown is slipping. The fool's slaughtered almost everyone close to him. It's only a matter of time before he turns on the last few who remain loyal to him.'

'Good, good.' The black bird preened.

'But the necromancer is turning into something of a problem.' Skellan confessed his fears to Mannfred. 'He's unpredictable, and growing dangerously powerful. He's become Konrad's crutch, making it increasingly difficult to deliver the coup de grace. I fear he may prove troublesome.'

The bird offered a single piece of advice, 'Keep the necromancer close.' Then it fell silent, its yellow eyes blinking shut.

He felt its heart race, beating hard against his hands as whatever hold Mannfred had on it was relinquished.

Frustrated, Skellan crushed the bird in his hands and dropped it in the dirt beneath the crucified man.

'Something for you to snack on if you grow hungry,' he said, but the dead man didn't laugh.

CHAPTER TWENTY
The Soul Cages

DRAKENHOF, CITY OF THE DEAD, SYLVANIA
The Season of the Dead

THEY WERE IN trouble, but then they had been in trouble from the first moment they set foot in Drakenhof, over a month ago.

It had taken the dead that long to find them, but find them they had, in a derelict corner of the city, grubbing around like rats trying to find hide or hair of the magician. Deserted buildings crowded in over them. The tight alleyway gave them an edge, but whatever hope he had had of taking advantage of it was quashed when the beasts drove them out into one of the smaller squares, pushing them towards the well in the very centre.

Lothar du Bek drew steel, ready to fight for his life.

Adrenaline coursed through him.

Beside him, Kallad Stormwarden shook his head, 'No, you have to learn to pick your fights. This isn't one we can win.'

Eight of the beasts circled them: eight vampires. Three had taken the form of great dire wolves and prowled the circle's perimeter hungrily. The beasts' feral eyes never left the pair. There was a ninth, lurking in the shadows behind them, watching, waiting for the right moment to reveal itself. Lothar had seen it even before the circle had closed fully around them.

The dwarf was right, but he was damned if he was going to simply lay down and die like some sick cow looking to be put out of its misery. He would make them pay for his life. That was the very least he could do.

'You think they'll let us surrender?' du Bek asked in disbelief, steel wavering before his face as he turned and turned, unwilling to expose his back to any of the beasts, and unable to do otherwise. 'They aren't about to take us prisoner, dwarf. Soon as you lower that warhammer, they'll tear your throat out.'

'Aye, it's a gamble,' the dwarf said, 'but if we choose to make a last stand here, it's going to be a *last stand,* make no bones about it. Dunno about you, but dying's not particularly appealing, given what they do to the dead around here.'

The dwarf was up to something – he had to be. His kind didn't lay down their weapons, they fought to the death, making their enemy pay with blood for their lives. He had to trust the dwarf, but that didn't mean he couldn't vent his fear, 'They're animals! All they want to do is feed on us.'

One of the beasts broke the circle, and as he did, his face shifted back into that of a man. His smile was the only thing that gave the lie to his humanity. He was every bit the beast whatever face he chose to wear.

Lothar turned slightly to face him, keeping the blade's edge between them.

'You do us a disservice, human.' The vampire said the word 'human' as if it was a curse. 'Lucky for you, I don't take offence easily.'

'Do you think I care, animal? I'm happy to die here, and just as long as I gut you in the process I'll lose no sleep in the afterlife.'

Shaking its head, the vampire laughed easily, 'As if I'd actually allow you the luxury of eternal sleep. No, it would be much more fun to play with you for a while.' The fiend turned to Kallad. 'You, dwarf, I feel like we are old friends already. Every time I look over my shoulder, you're there. You just never give up, do you?'

'Thought I recognised your stink, even if I didn't recognise your face,' Kallad said.

'Now, now, dwarf. Practise what you preach and all that. You don't want to go getting my friends all excited now do you?'

The wolves bristled, hackles rising, their pacing growing more urgent as they circled the three of them.

The spectre of the Vampire Count's castle loomed over their backs. It sent a shiver running through du Bek, as if someone had just set a heavy foot down on his grave.

'Circumstances just changed,' Kallad growled, reaching back for the leather grip of Ruinthorn's shaft. 'You made your peace with your maker?'

'My maker is dead, no peace needed or wanted, dwarf. Have you made your peace with your own god?'

'Grimnir is ever at my side.'

'Well, he didn't appear to be at your father's side, did he? Finding out our parents aren't immortal can be traumatic at the best of times. Seeing them abandoned by your precious gods, well, that's liable to make an atheist out of even the most devout of us.'

All of the muscles tightened in Kallad Stormwarden's face. The dwarf hawked and spat a thick wad of phlegm into the vampire's face.

His lip curling into a sneer, the vampire wiped it away. 'I had hoped you would walk with me, I would know my hunter before I kill him.' He held his fingers out as if offering the phlegm back. 'I'll take this as your refusal. It matters not, your blood will tell me all I need to know when the time comes.'

'It's him, isn't it?' Lothar said to Kallad.

'Aye, Lothar, it's him,' Kallad said. The circle was truly complete, Lothar realised. Here, in a pox-ridden alleyway in a city starved of humanity. It was a soul-destroying discovery. 'The beast that the Sigmarites thought they had tamed. His name is Jon Skellan. He butchered the priests of the Sigmarite cathedral in Altdorf, murdered the family Liebowitz in Nuln, and burned his way across the western world.'

The vampire sketched a mocking bow.

'The one and only, dwarf, although, you missed out some of what I consider to be the highlights of my career. I must admit, you have me at something of a loss; your fame is not so universal. I imagine you are Gimpy or Wazzock or some such wonderfully evocative name.'

'Kallad Stormwarden, son of King Kellus, last son of Karak Sadra.'

'Well Kallad, son of Kellus, how does it feel to know that it is all going to end like this, after so long looking for justice? I would imagine it must be galling to be so close to your revenge, only to have all hope of it crushed just like that.'

'You and me, beast.' Kallad said. 'Forget the manling, forget your wolves, you and me, last man standing.'

The vampire laughed. 'What do you take me for? Do you think I give a damn about your stupid sense of honour, dwarf? I can't think of one good reason to give you any hope of satisfaction. Do you think your grudge means anything to me? No, eight of us, two of you, those are pleasing numbers.'

'Nine,' du Bek said inclining his head towards the shadows where he knew the final beast hid.

The vampire's smile was cold. 'So you have eyes. Good for you, human.' He gestured towards the shadows. 'I believe this is something of a reunion. Come out, come out, wherever you are.'

Du Bek didn't recognise the man as he emerged from the anonymity of the dark, but Kallad did.

'Kantor.' It was barely a breath, both recognition and denial in one word, as if the world had been pulled out from under his feet.

'The magician?' Lothar asked. This was wrong. It was all going horribly, horribly wrong. They had come to this godforsaken place to free the magician, not to find him turned, and siding with the very enemy they sought to kill.

'One and the same,' the vampire said, clearly enjoying the effect that Nevin Kantor's unveiling was having on the dwarf.

Kantor walked confidently between the wolves – indeed the animals parted slightly, as if in deference to the magician.

'You just refuse to die, don't you, dwarf?'

'I could say the same about you, magician.'

'Indeed.'

'So you sold your soul, eh?'

'Don't be so melodramatic, dwarf. You were supposed to kill me. That was the only way the Sigmarites would allow us to travel together, was it not? The moment my usefulness was over, I was to be put out of my misery like some stinking mutt. Don't bother denying it, I know the truth.'

'I wouldn't have done it. I'm no monster.'

'It's academic really. Last time I saw you, you were lining up to join the ranks of the dead.'

'But as you can see, I didn't die.'

'All things considered, dwarf, it would appear that all you succeeded in doing was delaying death for a little while longer.'

'Well,' the vampire interrupted, 'as much as I am enjoying this little tête à tête, I think its time we got around to the killing, don't you?'

Lothar stiffened. He tried to look every way at once, desperately trying to cover every direction that the attack could possibly come from. It was impossible. His back was always bared to one or more of the beasts.

Beside him, the dwarf knelt, head down as he laid his huge double-headed axe down on the ground at his feet. 'Then kill me now and be done with it. I've got no fight left in me.'

'No!' du Bek yelled, throwing himself forwards. His sword speared out towards the magician's guts, and by rights ought to have spilled them out all over the cobblestones, but Nevin Kantor said a word – a single word – a harsh crack like the booming rumble of thunder answered, and a splinter ran through the folded metal of Lothar du Bek's sword. The splinter opened into a crack, splitting the sword wide open and showering him in jags of hot metal.

His hand recoiled from the hilt as the black magic chased from the sword up his arm and into his heart, sundering the organ as easily as it had the blade.

He was dead before the pieces of him hit the floor.

KALLAD STORMWARDEN CAME to in darkness.

Death would have been a blessed relief from the image of his friend's body tearing itself apart from the inside out, but it wasn't to be.

He was alone in the dark. There was no window and no light source to give even a hint of the room's size.

He fumbled around in the dark, touching stone and rotten reeds. On hands and knees, he tentatively explored the darkness. His hand found the wall and followed it. The cell was small, no more than ten feet by ten.

Kallad's knee upended the water bowl that had been left out for him, spilling its contents across the floor.

He felt out for a second bowl, reasoning that if there was water there could equally be food. There wasn't.

And they had taken his axe.

He curled up in a corner, his back pressed up against the wall.

In the aftermath of bloody ruination of du Bek, the vampire, Skellan, had stepped up and cracked him hard across the skull, turning the world to black. He remembered nothing after that. His head ached, and every time he moved it, a wave of nausea surged through him, twisting his guts inside out. Kallad moaned, the sound a dirge in the dark. He needed the wall at his back, its solidity was reassuring.

'Kallad Stormwarden, you are a fool.' His words barely touched the black. They sounded peculiar in his own ears, as if distant, muffled by a thick wadding of wool. That didn't dilute the truth of them, however. The mistake he made was in thinking that the living would protect them from the dead, when they couldn't even begin to protect themselves.

They had arrived in Drakenhof with their heads full of stories, gathered village by village, and all sharing the same disturbing similarities: housewives, midwives, gamblers, soldiers, farmers, it didn't matter who they were, anyone who owned even a hint of the uncanny had been snatched and dragged to the black castle of Drakenhof. It was more than just distance that separated Sylvania from the Empire. Centuries of oppression had taken their toll on the people. They had been stripped of even the most basic facets of personality, humour and hope. Kallad and du Bek found themselves pitying them, and along the way, they had convinced themselves that the poor downtrodden peasants of Sylvania would embrace them, rise up against their tyrannical master and bring down the beasts, once and for all. Poverty ruled the ruin of a city. The living shuffled like the dead and the damned through its filthy streets. It was stupid, naïve, dangerous, thinking that they had turned the castle itself into an icon for the evil they hunted, and it had killed Lothar du Bek.

Rather than embrace them, the peasants shunned their would-be liberators. They crossed the streets to avoid them and cast fretful glances over their shoulders as if they feared being seen even the width of the street away from the foreigners. Such was the long-reaching arm of their vile master.

It should have been obvious, given the fact that the Vampire Count's cruelty was carved into every gaunt face that stared back at him.

'Two men can't storm a castle,' du Bek had argued across the table in the hovel that they had found abandoned on the edge of town, even as Kallad outlined his plan.

Plan. It wasn't a plan, it wasn't even close. It was a plan's ugly sibling, a barely formed notion. The ruse meant to open the door, but after the door was open, Kallad had known that beyond that point there was nothing. 'Well, they can, but not without winding up very dead.'

'Aye, but we don't need to storm it, we just need to get inside. We don't need to take the walls down or destroy the place. It's a simple kill. Remember, we've got our man in there already.'

'You've got no intention of getting back out alive, have you?' du Bek had said, finally understanding. 'We're talking about suicide.'

'No, not suicide, my friend, it's a trade, a life for a life. Killing the monster that killed my people is enough for me, it has to be.'

'It's still suicide if you aren't planning on walking out of that place alive, dwarf, and you know it.'

Now here he was, his friend dead, trapped in the darkness deep beneath the Blood Count's castle.

He would have done anything to go back just a few days and change things. Allie's face formed in the darkness of his mind's eye. The boy had lost a father and he didn't even know it. He wondered how many days and weeks would pass before Allie du Bek stopped running to the window at the sound of a wagon, horses hooves, even footsteps and muffled conversation? How many months would it take for the lad to accept the truth: that his father wasn't coming home?

It was one thing to plan his own sacrifice, that was a price he was willing to pay if it meant his people would be avenged, but it was quite another to turn it into the murder of his friend. Too many people had died around him, good people, people who hadn't deserved their fate. Lothar du Bek was just one of many. That hurt.

The darkness only served to make the pain worse as his mind taunted him with flashes of memory, and snatches of conversations and long dead voices.

He lost all sense of time as thirst took hold and hunger gripped his gut.

Still no one came.

Was this to be his torture? To be left alone to dwell on his failings and wrestle his ghosts?

In the darkness, he saw Nevin Kantor, the magician, looking down in distaste at the blood on his clothes.

If only it was as easy to exorcise the living as it was the dead.

IT WOULD HAVE been easy to give up, to let the darkness take him, but the grudge burned brighter than ever inside him.

He would live to see it fulfilled.

THEY CAME FOR him.

They were like something out of a nightmare. Huge lumbering things that might have once been human. They dragged him between them. There was nothing comforting in the near dark. He saw things, shadows, shapes, but without the torches flickering he would have been blind to the glimpses of an underworld that didn't bear witnessing. For all that he lived his life below the surface he wasn't blessed with extraordinary sight – and the treacherous light was more than capable of playing tricks on him.

The dead lord of Drakenhof had extended his kingdom far below and beyond the foundations of his castle. The thugs bullied Kallad, stumbling and staggering, through the vast network of tunnels cut into the rock. Lichen and moss grew in the deep cracks and in places a skin of water dribbled over stone.

A familiar smell seeped into the stale air. It took him a while to place it, but when he did, the knowledge stirred the faintest flicker of hope: the Vampire Count's thralls had mined so far that they had broken into the web of deep mines that radiated out from core strongholds beneath the World's Edge Mountains: Karak Varn, Zufbar, Karak Kadrin. He breathed deeply of the air, needing its familiar tang to revitalise himself.

With that vitality came a yearning for what had been, for what he had lost. It hit him hard. He reached out and touched the rough-hewn rock. He made a promise to himself: there would be a reckoning for his people. There would be justice: retribution.

He had no idea where they were taking him until they shoved him through a door and barred it behind him as he stumbled into the holding pen.

'Welcome to the soul cages,' a wizened old man said in a voice as brittle as his bones.

Kallad could hear voices, cheering, banging and stamping feet. There was a narrow door at the far side of the pen, and a bench where the old man sat. Otherwise, the room was bare. Kallad pressed his face up against the bars, straining to see beyond them.

'Opens onto the Long Walk, and then up to the fighting pits,' the old man explained. 'The Count likes his entertainment raw and bloody.'

Kallad listened at the bars. It was impossible to gauge the size of the crowd, but its bloodthirsty nature was all too plain. They bayed for blood.

The clash of steel rang out, and then there was silence.

The sudden surge of noise from the spectators drowned out the screams of the dying man.

Kallad could picture it all too perfectly in his head: the clash of swords, savage cuts and wild slashes raining down, barely being parried in a dizzying fight to overcome death by the sheer strength of the sword arm, or to succumb to its inevitability.

There was an aura of death to the underground chamber. Men, who moments before had strode out to conquer the world, came back on stretchers, dead or dying. There was no glory in the fight. It was a lie, perhaps the greatest one of all.

The door to the pits slammed open and three ghoulish creatures dragged a body into the pen between them.

'Best get out there, dwarf. The Count don't like to be kept waiting.'

He could hear them calling for him, although they didn't know his name. The cry of: *blood, blood, blood* echoed back to him.

Let them wait, Kallad thought bitterly, and let out an abrasive bark of a laugh as he walked through the door.

It was a long walk to the surface, made longer by the haunting echo of footsteps and the muted whispers of dead men, remembered forever by the tunnels sandstone walls.

How many men had walked this same tunnel on the way to their deaths? Too many was the answer. Images of Morr, Lord of the Dead, lined the tunnel walls, whilst nameless souls dominated the floor mosaics.

The Long Walk, the old man had called it. Kallad was fully aware of the duality of the name.

Dark-skinned thralls, the life leached from their eyes, guarded the entrance to the pits.

Kallad strode out into the pit amid roars from the banks of vampiric spectators. The pit was huge, carved out of the bare rock. Stalactites hung down over the killing ground. Huge stone walls ringed the pit. There was no easy way to escape. Banks of seating scaled up the walls, climbing almost as high as the longest of the stalactites dripped low. The seats were filled. Thousands of hungry faces stared down at him as he walked into the centre of the pit.

He stopped and turned, scanning the ranks of the dead for a familiar face. He found Skellan, and beside him, a darker beast with the same mesmeric features as the beast that had slain his father. The blood of other men stained the sand at his feet. The Vampire Count, Konrad von Carstein, sat high up in the stands, most of the seats around him empty. The Count, it appeared, did not like his sycophants getting too close to him.

Kallad waited for the Blood Count to meet his gaze. The creature wouldn't.

As von Carstein rose to his feet, someone shouted, 'Death comes!' The crowd took up the chant: *'The Count! The Count! The Count!'*

Kallad let the sound wash over him. It was nothing more than bluster, meant to instil fear. He would not let it.

In the city, he had heard talk that Konrad could trace his blood back to Vashanesh, the first great vampire, and that he enjoyed thousands of years of vampiric taint in this veins.

The dwarf knew a lie when he heard one. A dynasty of aristocratic blood, or thirty-odd generations of cutthroats, whores, murderers and pirates? The truth was a curious beast in the hands of a ruler like Konrad and, no doubt, those close to him fed the flames of his mad delusion, their worm-tongues worshipping his lineage.

He shrugged it off. It wasn't his problem. He was blessedly immune to the vampire's vanities.

Von Carstein's gaze filled with sick longing as he looked towards the shadowed entrance of the pit. Kallad refused to be drawn into looking for his opponent. He would live or he would die, looking back would do nothing to alter that.

'Do you want to beg for your life, dwarf?' Konrad bellowed. His voice echoed around the subterranean pit.

Kallad hawked and spat into the sand, 'Where's my axe, coward? Frightened I might kill your pets?'

Servants of the Vampire Count moved out onto the killing floor. One of them carried Ruinthorn.

He walked slowly towards Kallad, offering the axe to the dwarf.

Kallad hefted it, felt its reassuringly familiar weight in his hands, and braced himself for the fight of his life.

He would feed them all the dead meat they could handle. As the old dwarf proverb went, 'The time will come when all gods die', and as the traps opened on the lion pits, Kallad felt doubt for the first time in years. It was a strange sensation, a quickening in his chest: the realisation that this flesh, this body, didn't belong to him, that it was a gift from the Creator. Intellectually, he knew what he was feeling: fear. Was this what the others felt when they faced Ruinthorn? He felt a surge of pity for them, the young who had fallen to his axe. Were they somewhere now, in the Halls of the Dead, pitying him in turn?

He saw Skellan smiling down on him, saw Konrad seemingly hypnotised by the creature emerging from the darkness of the pits: a naked beast-faced vampire.

The creature roared, dropping into a fighting crouch. Even as it did so, the beast's back arched and stretched as it transformed into a huge black furred dire wolf.

It was the largest wolf he had ever seen.

Is it that time, Grimna, thought Kallad? Is my life counted now in seconds? Then more bitterly: it is if you think it is, fool. Fight for your damned life!

He brought Ruinthorn to bear, kissing the rune embossed on its huge butterfly blades. His world narrowed down to the axe and the creature he had to kill. His knuckles were white. His hands were shaking.

Skellan leaned over and whispered something to the Vampire Count, but Kallad was in no position to wonder what.

Konrad laughed. His laughter, like his words before, rolled around the cramped subterranean pit, taunting Kallad as he stood down there in the middle of the killing floor.

He would not die here. He would avenge his people. He would find Kantor and wring the life from his body. He *would* live.

The assembly of vampires would not be satisfied by mere blood, had come to witness slaughter, and to a beast they were hungry for it.

The wolf circled warily, jowls curled back, nostrils flared as it smelled blood on the air. It moved slowly, a curious kind of recognition on its twisted face. Kallad studied the monster as he would any other opponent, gauging it for weaknesses, assessing its strengths.

For a second, the world froze, the beast rising out of its crouch, Konrad's mouth wide in laughter. Kallad didn't move as much as a muscle.

He had long since stopped wondering what it would feel like to die. The wolf loosed a baleful howl. Still, Kallad didn't move.

The wolf circled him.

He stood square and watched the creature as he would have watched any other opponent, facing it down, and showing no fear, despite the fact that he was suddenly aware of every drop of blood pumping through his veins and the very real mortality it ensured. It had weaknesses. Everything did. The trick was believing that, and not succumbing to the bone-freezing fear that was doubt.

The wolf circled him, its massive claws raking the wet sand. Kallad's grip on the axe tightened.

He swept Ruinthorn through a dazzling combination of sweeps and arcs, but showmanship had no noticeable effect on the creature, and only served to tire the dwarf. The wolf continued its relentless circling, claws churning through the sand.

A deathly hush settled over the crowd.

Kallad held his ground, content to let the wolf exhaust itself going around and around in circles.

He lunged forwards, shifting his weight onto his front foot and swept the butt of the axe forwards, reversing the blow to test his foe. The wolf swatted the steel blade away as if it was an irritating fly. Still, the force of the impact reverberated down the length of Kallad's arm, giving him a very real idea of the sheer brute strength of the thing he faced.

The wolf let out a roar of rage, reared and lunged forwards. Its claws raked across Kallad's cheek before he could spin away. The wound stung unnaturally as the taint of unlife burned itself into his skin.

Kallad spat at the dirt. Ignoring the fire beneath his skin, the dwarf threw himself at the wolf, Ruinthorn's twin blades ripping into the creature's thick hide. The wolf shrieked: a distressingly human sound as it lost focus on its bestial form and began to shift back into its human guise. The crowd roared, a shockingly animalistic sound.

He looked up at Konrad, and beside him Skellan. The Blood Count's smile was vicious. Kallad spat another wad of bloody phlegm onto the wet sand.

Wounded, and caught between forms, the wolf-man was more dangerous than ever. The echo of human cunning blazed behind its eyes. Somehow, it retained the natural abilities of both forms, making it twice as deadly.

The wolf-man slammed its half-formed fists against its chest and leapt.

Kallad threw himself to the floor as the thing's claws raked through the air where his head had been a second before.

It launched a second desperate attack, before Kallad could scrabble to his feet.

The crowd was screaming.

The beast came down on top of Kallad, its powerful jaws closing like a vice around his nose and the side of his face. The pain was incredible. Fifty wounds punctured his ruined face. Kallad screamed, a real full-bellied desperate scream, as he fought the all-consuming blackness that threatened to engulf him. He felt his own piss run down the inside of his legs. This wasn't how he wanted to die. There was no honour in it, no restitution for the dead, and no price for Grunberg, for Kellus, for Sammy and du Bek and all of the others.

He owed them more than this.

Kallad's head swam with sickness.

There was joy in the creature's eyes, Kallad saw, right until the last when he brought Ruinthorn around over its back and split it open at the spine, parting hide, bone and flesh in a killing blow. In that last second of life, a flicker of recognition passed between them, killer and victim, and then the beast was slain. Kallad pushed the monstrosity to the side and struggled out from beneath it.

Struggling to his feet, Kallad felt their sickness wash over him.

He found the beast that had killed his father, met his gaze and did not flinch as he said, 'And now I am coming for you.'

Konrad von Carstein did not look happy, but beside him, Jon Skellan looked positively delighted by Kallad's victory.

Then a wave of dizziness took him. He staggered, but he did not collapse.

Kallad turned away from the Blood Count and walked back towards the soul cages.

The vampire's thralls swarmed over him as he entered the tunnel. They pulled at him, trying to tear Ruinthorn from his grip. Kallad snarled and cracked one of the men's skulls off one of the many images of Morr decorating the wall. The thrall twitched as he slumped to the floor. A bloody red rose blossomed just below his receding hairline. Kallad stepped over the man's legs.

'Who's next? No need to all rush at once, there's plenty to go around.' His grin was manic as he thundered an unforgiving fist into the side of a second thrall's head. He made the mistake of getting in the dwarf's way.

Three more thralls stood between him and the cage door.

Kallad dropped into a fighting crouch. Ruinthorn, held level at his waist, rested easily in his hands. He turned the blade over and over.

'You want to die, lads, then take one step forward, otherwise get the hell out of my way.'

They gave him no choice: as one they charged.

Fighting at close quarters in a cramped tunnel was far from ideal, but against unarmed men with no skill for the game, it was little more than butchery.

They were unarmed and underfed. They didn't stand a chance.

In less than half a minute, Kallad was stepping over their corpses.

The old man looked up as he pushed open the door. He smiled. There was genuine warmth to it, 'You made it back, then, eh? I bet that pleased the Count no end.'

'He didn't look too happy,' Kallad agreed.

'What happened to the guards?'

'Had an accident. It's slippery back there. Stupid buggers fell right on my axe. Made a hell of a mess.'

'They'll send more,' the old man said.

'Then let's hope they're just as clumsy, eh? Now, I dunno about you, but I'm just about ready to get out of this place. Are you with me, human?'

'Look at me, I'm an old man. I can barely make it across this cell without having to sit down for twenty minutes to catch my breath.'

'Then I'll carry you on me back, laddy. I'm not leaving you.' It was guilt, of course, survivors' guilt, as if by helping this one old man he could make up for all the others that he hadn't been able to help.

The old man ratcheted himself up from the bench. 'Sebastian,' he said, holding out a liver-spotted hand. Kallad shook it.

'Kallad.'

The dwarf heard footsteps coming up the Long Walk. He slammed the door and wedged it with the wooden bench that Sebastian had just vacated.

'Well come on, Sebastian, wouldn't want to outstay our welcome.'

The passage divided into three smaller passages, each lined with identical heavily barred wooden doors.

'The soul cages,' the old man said. 'You didn't think you were alone down here, did you? There must be fifty or sixty more just like you, fighters who are thrown out to fight for their lives for the Blood Count's amusement.'

Without a word, Kallad strode purposefully towards the first door and threw back the bolt barring it. He pushed the door open and stepped into the doorway. 'On your feet,' he called into the cell. 'We're going home.'

He moved on to the next cell, and the next, and the next, the message the same for each and every one of von Carstein's prisoners. 'We're goin' home.'

SKELLAN STOOD BETWEEN the dwarf and freedom.

The dwarf had a small army of starving prisoners behind him. Desperation might have made them dangerous, but malnutrition and abuse, and the constant promise of unlife hanging over them had stripped them of spirit as well as strength. They stumbled into each other, stumbled and fell, and lacked even the strength to drag themselves back to their feet before the next one had stumbled over them.

'Going somewhere?' Skellan asked.

He was not alone. The last four of Konrad's loyal Hamaya, including Onursal, backed him up. He raised his hand and was met by low-throated growls as they unleashed the beast within.

Too easy, Skellan savoured the thought. He fully intended to enjoy the killing now that the time had come. The bones were cast, the endgame was playing itself out and, all things considered, there was no way he could lose. It was beautiful watching all of his plans come to together into one perfect glorious whole. That Konrad had demanded Onursal come with him to kill the dwarf was just a delicious irony, and so convenient. It would save hunting the beast down later.

'Out of my way, vampire,' the dwarf barked.

Skellan chuckled. 'Given the circumstances I am not sure you are in any position to be giving orders, little man.'

'I killed your friend back there, and I figure I can kill you just as dead, if I have to. Now move, Ruinthorn is getting thirsty.'

'You really are quite tiresome, dwarf.' Skellan turned to Onursal. 'Kill him.'

He moved aside so that the Hamaya could charge.

The dark skinned beast pounced, throwing himself at Kallad. Onursal staggered the dwarf back into the shambling pack of wretched human beings that were far beyond saving. They scattered, and the dwarf went down beneath the ferocity of the Hamaya's attack.

Skellan grinned and watched for a moment as the dwarf gave every bit as good as he got, battering the beast back in a flurry of blows. It looked as if the dwarf might actually have it in him to kill the Hamaya, the contest was that evenly matched. Skellan held back the remaining Hamaya.

'The fight is his. If he is incapable of killing the dwarf he has no place among us.'

That wasn't the truth, or at least not the whole truth. It was only an aspect of it. Excluding Skellan, Onursal was the strongest of Hamaya, and he was fiercely loyal to Konrad; stubbornly so, even in the face of the Blood Count's madness. His death would be a bitter blow for Konrad.

'Never tasted dwarf blood,' one of the Hamaya said petulantly.

Skellan shook his head. 'Blood's blood. Goes down just the same.'

'So you say.'

As Skellan watched the struggle, his face slipped, the daemon rising to the surface. Cold black anger roared through his veins. He harnessed it.

Satisfied that the dwarf would not fail him, Jon Skellan turned on the three remaining Hamaya.

'You want blood so bad? Here,' he tore out the throat of the beast nearest him in a shocking display of naked savagery. 'Drink this.'

He tossed the corpse at the gaping Hamaya and spun, lashing out. His claws eviscerated the second Hamaya before the creature even saw the danger.

The third, Massika, was more difficult to kill. The creature backed off and turned to run. Skellan surged forwards, arching his body so that he hit the side wall at a run, using the sheer force of his momentum to carry him up it, and propelled himself into the air, arms and legs pistoning as he hammered into the back of the fleeing Hamaya and brought it down.

Skellan grabbed a fistful of hair and yanked the creature's head back.

He hooked the claws of his other hand into the vampire's eyes and ripped the top of its skull away from the bones of its neck. The beast's cries were pitiful. Skellan pulled again, tearing the head free of the spinal column, and a third time, until the skin tore and the head came away in his hands.

When he stood, Skellan saw Kallad Stormwarden staring at him, perplexed by this sudden turn of events. Onursal lay dead at his feet, the dwarf's axe still buried deep in the Hamaya's spine. The first of the twin blades had actually torn open the vampire's chest cavity and spilled his black heart and a rope of greasy intestines across the tunnel floor.

The dwarf planted a boot on the Hamaya's back and wrenched his axe free.

His footsteps echoed chillingly as he advanced on Skellan, ready to kill again.

'Don't make the mistake of believing you know everything, dwarf,' Skellan said, still holding the dead Hamaya's head in his right hand. 'I've bought your life here, make no mistake about it. You wouldn't have lasted another day fighting in the pits. You aren't stupid. You can work out why I'm helping you. I want the monster dead, just as much as you do, but it is about more than that – more than him. You have to understand that, dwarf. The fates of nations of the living and nations of the dead rest in your hands.'

'You don't own anything, least of all my life. The only thing I'm interested in is killing your wretched Count and laying my people's ghosts to rest finally and forever, the rest is going to have to be someone else's problem 'cause it sure ain't mine.'

'Stupid grudges. Do you think it matters if one vampire dies? One bloody vampire? Do you think it will save a hundred other villages? A thousand young girls? You're a bigger fool than I took you for if you do. Cut down one and another arises. You might avenge a few dead, but you'll damn a hell of a lot more living. Is that a price you want to pay, dwarf? Can your conscience live with sacrificing hundreds, thousands, of souls just to satisfy your bloody grudge? Right now you need to live. That's why I'm putting my own throat on the line. You need to get out of here and convince Emperor Lutwig and the Otillia, and whoever else will listen, of the threat Konrad von Carstein and his necromancers pose. You've seen a little of it here. You have an idea of what he is capable of, but this is just the beginning. The damned that marched to Vlad's drum are nothing compared to the nightmare that this madman is raising. He intends to turn the Old World into one vast Kingdom of the Dead, and he won't rest until everyone is rotting and risen into his brave new world.'

Skellan didn't move. He couldn't afford to make a mistake.

He had to work a way around the unreasoning stubbornness of the dwarf's grudge and convince him that there was more to be gained by pushing the boulder that would start the landslide that would bury Konrad von Carstein. Rather than succumbing to the instant gratification to be had from striking down one enemy, with a little patience he could bring down a damned dynasty.

The dwarf shook his head. 'No, I don't buy it. You're selling me a lie. You're a cold-blooded killer, like your master. There's no reason for you to help me, less it helps yourself, too. And let's face it, you being dead helps me a lot more than you being alive. I think we finish this here.'

'You being dead doesn't help either of us, dwarf, and believe me, that's how this little charade would play out. Go, now, get word to your people. Warn the Empire. Tell them what you have seen. Impress it upon them. They *must* be ready when the Blood Count marches!'

The dwarf shouldered his axe and Skellan knew, through all the bluster, his message had found its mark. The dwarf wouldn't just carry the message, he would ensure that the living were prepared.

Skellan turned and walked away, knowing that the dwarf wouldn't strike him.

The dwarf was one of a rare breed: a hero.

Skellan could smell his bleeding heart.

CHAPTER TWENTY-ONE

From the Mountains of Madness

THE WORLDS EDGE MOUNTAINS
Dawn of the Dead

KALLAD LED THE survivors through the endless subterranean world of the deep mines, miles beneath the surface, beneath the light and the air. They stumbled along blindly behind him.

They had no food and no water.

They were dying by the day. The fifty he had rescued were reduced to thirty.

Twice already, Kallad had felt the draught of fresh air leaking into the mine, tasted it, but every turn seemed to lead them deeper into the claustrophobic depths of the Worlds Edge Mountains.

They stumbled on.

A few wanted to scavenge meat from the dead, arguing that the sustenance would keep them alive, buying them precious time to find their way out of this purgatory.

Kallad would have none of it.

For each of the fallen, he delayed, building a makeshift cairn from broken stones littering the tunnel.

The echoes of von Carstein's men ransacking the tunnels, hunting them, haunted them. The sounds of running feet, distant taunts, wolves baying and ringing steel kept them from sleeping, driving them on beyond the point of exhaustion.

Still they stumbled on.

'We're going home.' Kallad said it like a mantra, repeating it over and over.

They had long since stopped believing him.

They had christened the deep mines Sorrow's Heart, and resigned themselves to dying in its depths, but they didn't die, these last few.

Kallad led them out of Sorrow and into daylight for the first time in weeks, months, and for some of them, years. Stepping out into the air felt like being reborn from the darkness of despair into the light of freedom. He threw his head back and laughed, savouring the irony of a dwarf being happier out under an open sky than beneath a mountain. He saw the way they looked at him, but still he laughed. Let them think him mad.

Freedom came at a price. The sky was thick with snow, blowing a blizzard. The cold tore through their scant rags, but still it was the most beautiful moment of release. They gasped and sucked in air, fell on their backs, the snow crusting and powdering around them, and tried to embrace the sky. They were free of Sorrow. They were out of the godforsaken maze of tunnels, and they were going home to wherever home was. It was a long walk, but even Kallad welcomed the snow-laden sky over his head and the wind in his hair. Beside him, Sebastian swore that he would never complain about being stuck outside in the middle of nowhere again, knowing even as he made the vow that he would break it. He was an old man. Complaining about the elements was his lot in life. The day he stopped complaining about the blasted snow or the blessed rain was the day he died.

Kallad looked at the few men he had led out of hell and smiled. He had come to think of them as his lads.

'We're going home,' he said, and this time they believed him. Their cheers could have been heard in von Carstein's grand hall, with the Blood Count himself rooted to his obsidian throne by the ragged jubilation. Every one of the men facing him had resigned himself to dying long ago. Now, they were going home, and it was because of him.

It was a small counterbalance for his Indic scale, lives saved to weigh up against lives lost.

They were going home.

One of the men knelt and scooped handfuls of snow into his mouth, another rolled in it, and others sank down and kissed the ground. More than a few cast a last lingering look back in the direction of Drakenhof, invisible in the distance.

Kallad knew that it wasn't just because of him that they were going home. They owed their freedom to one of the beasts: Skellan.

He didn't understand why the vampire had turned on its own, or why it would want von Carstein toppled, but that didn't matter. The beast had bought their freedom. Kallad was determined to use it to pay Skellan back by wiping his kind off the face of the earth.

He saw that the old man, Sebastian, had moved away from the group and lay, propped up awkwardly against a boulder. The dwarf walked over to sit beside him. Drawing nearer, he could tell that there was something wrong. It was the angle of the old man's head, the way it lolled on his neck. Kallad had seen enough death to recognise it close up.

It wasn't fair, after everything, having made it out, for Sebastian's heart to give in here, now, when they were free. There was no justice in it. Kallad bottled up the sudden surge of anger that he felt rising inside. They were going home.

Kallad knelt at Sebastian's side.

'At least you died free, looking at the sun,' Kallad whispered, his breath conjuring wraiths of mist that hung like a veil between the living and the dead. It was a small consolation. The failing sun was a sickly yellow eye on the horizon. Small mercy that it was, the old man had died with the gentle warmth of the sun on his face.

Kallad closed the old man's eyes.

It was a last act of kindness. Already, the old man's skin was colder than death. His sweat had become a brittle frost that clung to his face like a second skin. A fine dusting of snow had settled on his rags, now that the heat of life had left his body.

Kallad stood, ignoring the icy chill worming its way into his heart.

Behind him, the Worlds Edge Mountains and their snow-capped peaks reared, reaching into the grey sky. Beneath him lay a sweeping bank of forest, the white-laced leaves rustling like living things, while the north wind whispered fragments of the wood's darkest secrets, hints of the hearts it had stilled, the dreams it had buried in its rich soil. The nearness of the forest was oppressive.

The wind cried traitor in his ear. He ignored its mocking voice, knowing that the whispers would be endless and unforgiving. 'I haven't forgotten you,' he promised his ghosts. Guilt was one of the many burdens that came with being a survivor. Guilt and ghosts. He had ghosts, ghosts that whispered and taunted with the voice of his own guilt, ghosts that could never forgive him for being alive, because he couldn't forgive himself.

'I COULD LIE down now.' He barely breathed the words, knowing that he couldn't. That he didn't have it in him to give up. 'I could close my eyes like Sebastian, sleep and never wake up. The cold would take me before dawn. Is that what you want?' But the wind had stopped listening to his lies. It knew he could no more lie down and die than the sun could cease to shine or the seasons stop turning. It was a survivor's nature to survive, to go on living no matter the costs to those around him. A survivor would find a way.

Kallad Stormwarden was a survivor.

He would carry the message to the living.

Von Carstein would be stopped.

He wiped the sweat from his brow before it could freeze there. His lips were chapped from the wind's perpetual kiss. The others were feeling it too, the intense cold that came with their freedom. Their rags were no defence against it. The cold was their enemy, just as lethal and immediate as the soul cages had ever been. Kallad hadn't realised just how thirsty he was until he knelt and brushed away the thin coating of snow from the surface of a small frozen tarn. Quickly, he used the wooden handle of his axe to crack the ice. Kneeling over the tarn, he scooped a handful of water to his lips. It tasted heavily of minerals and dirt, but it could have been wine to the lips of a drunk. He drank deeply, wiping at his beard where the water ran down his chin, and scooped up another mouthful.

'Over here, lads! Water!' he called. Those desperate enough came running, staggering over the mountainside, stumbling, falling and pushing themselves on for fear that they would be too late and the water would have run dry by the time they arrived.

In the distance, movement caught his eye. He pushed himself to his feet and squinted towards a thin line of picked-clean trees that spotted the horizon. Shapes moved across the whiteness. He counted three figures. They moved with the surety born of life on the mountain. It took a moment to realise that they were dwarfs: a scouting party.

'Grimna's balls, we're saved!' Kallad said, slapping one of the few survivors on the back.

The youngster grinned back at him.

They walked awhile to shelter: an abandoned bear cave beyond the trees. Despite the blizzard and the blinding snow, many of the survivors were reluctant to re-enter the earth.

Kallad didn't have the heart to bully them back underground, so those that wanted to freeze were left to shiver and huddle up against the trees as they tried to light a fire with damp wood. Truth be told, he wasn't too enamoured of the idea of going back underground either, but he wasn't about to freeze to death out of stubbornness.

It wasn't merely pragmatism. He *had* to survive this final ordeal. He had no choice in the matter. He had to deliver his warning to everyone capable of standing against the vampires, and convince them that their only hope of survival lay in putting aside their arguments and joining together. By dying here, he would damn them all.

The dwarfs were a short range scouting party from a nearby stronghold, Karak Raziac, although it still served under the aegis of Karak Kadrin far to the north.

The cave was stocked with game that had been skinned and dried, and it was obviously something of a permanent base for the dwarf scouts.

'Hunting greenskins,' Grufbad Steelfist explained. 'The beasts have been causing hell over the last few months. Getting braver and braver with their raids. Stealing cattle, burning down homesteads. Razzak wants them stamped out good and proper, so we're out looking for the rat hole they crawled outta.'

Steelfist was the leader of the small troop, an unflinching soul hewed out of the very stuff of the mountain he ranged.

Kallad knew the story well enough. He could have been listening to his father, Kellus, declaring that the greenskins had gotten out of hand and needed to be put in their place. He nodded.

'What about yerself? By the sounds of it you're a long way from home, Kallad son of Kellus.'

'Aye, long way for sure, Steelfist, and I'm just talking about distance,' Kallad said sourly. 'We got thirty refugees from the dungeons of the Vampire Count here, and barely a lick of grub between us. The manlings have been through hell and back, and instead of being safe, now they're up against the elements. I doubt even half of them will make it back to their families.'

'That's them, I asked about you.'

Kallad looked at the hard-faced dwarf. Twin scars ran down Steelfist's cheeks where he had been in an argument with a wicked blade and lost, badly. He was perhaps twice Kallad's age, if not more, but then, in eyes of his people, Kallad was little more than a child, for all that he had lived more than sixty years.

'There are things I have to do,' Kallad conceded. 'For my people, and for others.'

Steelfist nodded, 'You have the mark of a grudge bearer.'

'Aye, but I'm coming to understand that the grudge isn't all, that there's more I have to do to earn my rest.'

'It never ends,' Grufbad Steelfist agreed. 'So, for now, share the burden a while. Tell me your story, Kallad Stormwarden.'

And so he did.

Kallad talked of abandoning his home, the march to Grunberg, the fall of Kellus and the suckling baby dead in its mother's arms, feeding off her like some ungodly parasite until he killed it a second time. He couldn't remember her name, and it hurt him that she had slipped from his memory so easily. He talked of the slaughter of the Sigmarites in Altdorf, hunting Skellan and his unnamed master, the death of his companions at the hands of the beast, and his own bitter wounds. He told Steelfist of the villages with their barred windows where fathers locked out their own sons because the plague of unlife had claimed them, the traitorous vampire who had freed them in return for the promise that they would raise a force to stand against the Blood Count, and he painted a bleak picture of the days to come.

'We must get word to Razzak,' Steelfist said, 'convince him to dispatch emissaries to Karak Kadrin, Zufbar, Karak Varn and every stronghold the length of the Worlds Edge Mountains. It won't be easy, he's dour at the best of times, but he's not stupid. This threat goes beyond the manlings. The undead curse is one that even a thickhead like him cannae ignore for long.'

'You think he'll march?'

'Aye, if you plead your case like you just did, youngling. I think he'll answer the call, and the dwarfs of the deep will march to war at the side of the humans once again.' There was an edge of pride in Steelfist's voice as he wrapped a fatherly arm around Kallad's shoulder. 'Come on, let's round your boys up for a feed, and then get on our way. Time's running out. It'll be day after the morrow before we're in sight of Karak Raziac. 'Nother day after that before you can talk to Razzak.'

Kallad felt the uncomfortable sensation of eyes watching him. He twisted. There was no one there. Then he saw a black raven, perched on an overburdened bough less than ten feet beyond the mouth of the cave, studying them intently. He trusted his instincts. The bird was unnaturally curious. Kallad knelt and picked up a rock, throwing it at the carrion bird. The stone whistled past the raven, cannoning off the tree trunk and causing a flurry of snow to spill. The raven cawed once, a deep guttural sound, and took flight.

Something about the bird disturbed Kallad Stormwarden profoundly. He sensed, in fact, that he was witnessing the first rumblings of the storm of the century.

CHAPTER TWENTY-TWO

Torn

THE RAVEN TOWER, DRAKENHOF CASTLE, SYLVANIA

The Winter of Discontent

JON SKELLAN JUGGLED the knife easily, tossing it from hand to hand, the silver blade turning end over end lazily as it passed through the air.

Konrad was raving.

He wasn't listening. He didn't actually need to, he had heard it all before: the paranoia, the deep-seated insecurity, and, surprisingly the suspicion of all animals around the castle. He had ordered all of the dogs butchered, cats gutted and nailed up around the city, drove the ravens from the tower and had poisons laid down to kill any foolish enough to return. He did the same with people he grew suspicious of, gutted them, poisoned them or drove them off.

The Blood Count went off on these random rants regularly, losing all sense of self in his tirade, and one was very much like another.

'Konrad doesn't like it! Oh, no he doesn't. Not at all. No, can't trust them. No. They would destroy Konrad if they could, but they can't. No, they can't.'

'No,' Skellan agreed, 'they can't.' Whoever they were, Konrad had developed a wonderful habit of railing against imaginary foes recently, seeing conspiracies where there weren't even people to conspire. He liked to take credit for the mild erosion of von Carstein's sense of self. He had wormed his way into the Blood Count's confidence, dislodging the others he trusted, those who supported his reign.

The prize was the necromancer, Nevin Kantor. The magician had been a thorn in Skellan's side ever since his arrival at the black castle. He had worked his way close to the Count, ingratiating himself into Konrad's favour by reinventing himself as the Blood Count's pet.

For a while it had worked. Kantor offered Konrad the gift of magic.

It was something Skellan couldn't hope to compete with. The hunger for magic had, for years, been the Blood Count's obsession. The secret was to turn the magic itself into something sinister and untrustworthy, like the Hamaya who had betrayed their master, like his treacherous kin, like all who had a reason to covet Konrad's power. It was as ingenious as it was simple. He had to play on Konrad's ignorance and turn the magic into something to be feared instead of adored.

The whispers were simple enough at first, snatches of gossip overhead below ground, in the subterranean necromancer's library, from the soul cages and the fighting pits. Magic had been used in the dwarf's escape. Skellan hinted that he believed the necromancers had engineered the whole thing, after all, the dwarf had been Kantor's travelling companion. They had a shared loyalty, a bond older than Kantor and Konrad's. The web of lies he spun was almost believable, and the beauty of it was that with Konrad's mind so torn, there was far more material than necessary.

He told Konrad that his precious necromancers were looting his gold, using his own coin to raise armies of their own, loyal to the black magicians, merging their skeletal horde with ghoulish humans.

In the end, Skellan had broken Kantor's hold over von Carstein with the simplest of arguments: the magician could not be trusted. It was in his nature to manipulate the truth of the universe and reshape it in the guise of one of his lies. It wasn't that Nevin Kantor manipulated the winds, it was the nature of magic itself to corrupt the practitioner. If it were natural, honest, then Konrad would have been able to do it, but he couldn't. So it wasn't Konrad's failing. On the contrary, it was Konrad's strength. The winds could not twist him.

Skellan also promised him protection, of course.

He looked around the room, at the gibberish that he had forced a peasant to scrawl in a tight spidery hand across the walls. He lied to Konrad and told him that they were wards against incantations, shields against the evil thoughts of those who would do him harm, and that the peasant was actually a hedge mage. He cemented the lie with another, promising Konrad that if he fed on the blood of the mage he would make the gibberish unbreachable. Konrad drank greedily and fed the corpse to his dogs, the same dogs that he butchered a week later.

The delicious irony was that the protection itself terrified the Blood Count. He paced the room, never at rest, never able to relax for fear that there was more to the scrawls than the dead hedge mage had admitted – that perhaps the peasant had actually been in the employ of the necromancers, and that it was no protection at all, rather a form of entrapment.

The Blood Count turned to Skellan, his anchor in a sea of chaos.

'But you love Konrad, don't you Skellan? You are loyal to him. You understand that Konrad is great.'

'I worship him,' Skellan said, knowing that the wry humour was lost on Konrad, 'for Konrad is the most monstrous and powerful of all the children of the night. Konrad is Vashanesh reborn.'

Konrad is also stark raving mad, he added silently.

'Yes,' Konrad said. 'Yes, yes, yes. You understand Konrad. You are loyal. You are the only one, Skellan, the only one that Konrad can trust.'

'I am the Golden One,' Skellan said.

The secret was in the way the web supported itself with its own fabrications. Enough lies had been proven true in the Blood Count's eyes to make even the most outrageous new ones seem plausible.

The Hamaya were his now, freely given by Konrad. With Onursal implicated in the escape from the slave pens – he had, according to Skellan, turned on his fellow vampires. It was only good fortune for Skellan that the dwarf's axe had brought the dark-skinned Hamaya down before he could turn on him. Konrad, at Skellan's insistence, demanded the Hamaya purged. Then, summoning the remainder of the vampiric aristocracy to the subterranean cathedral, he urged Skellan to fulfil the role of father to the Hamaya, as the wolf, Jerek once had, and choose only those that could be implicitly trusted, so that once more the Hamaya were proud to serve Konrad, the Blood Count.

This winnowing gave Skellan the perfect opportunity to cull the few lynchpins of Konrad's precarious Empire, isolating Konrad in his own court.

It was all so subtly perfect. There was a synergy to the lies. They fed off one another.

Where others trod on eggshells around the madman, Skellan masked his own role in the dwarf's escape with the confession of failure. He begged Konrad's forgiveness for his own shortcomings. He hadn't seen the traitors in their midst. He had allowed himself to be gulled by them and as such it was his fault as much as it was Onursal's and Kantor's.

It was a stroke of genius. His own cowardice had allowed the dwarf to escape. Indeed, he was only alive because the dwarf chose to allow it. In confessing his own failings, Skellan showed himself to be the true inheritor of the wolf's place at Konrad's side. With one beautiful lie, he became Konrad's new truth speaker. In a court of lies and paranoia few would own up to failure for fear of bringing von Carstein's wrath down upon their own heads. It was a self-preservation instinct. Skellan set himself apart by owning his failure.

He had knelt before the Blood Count, asked forgiveness, and awaited judgement. It had been a risk, but he had played it right. By offering up his own head, Skellan had proved, beyond a shadow of a doubt in the madman's torn mind, that he was the only one that Konrad could truly trust.

The improbability of the dwarf sparing the vampire never occurred to him.

'Konrad will see them now,' Konrad said, suddenly.

Finally.

'You understand what you must do?'

'Konrad is not a fool. Oh, no, no, no. Konrad is not a fool. He will not allow them to treat him like one. They will learn their lesson well today. Konrad will teach them with steel.'

'Well said, my lord.'

Skellan sheathed the knife.

It had taken little prodding to convince Konrad that the time had come to go to war, it was all part of the web of deceit that he had spun. The beauty of it was how it all came together so flawlessly to support itself. The dwarf, freed by the faithless necromancers, was out there, warning the humans, galvanising them into resistance. Because of the necromancers, the Empire's defences would be strong, stronger perhaps than anything his sire had ever faced. It was fitting that the traitors should lead the line. The necromancers should be made to fight, not merely raise zombies to hide behind. They must fight, *and die*.

Skellan opened the door to the necromancers, Fey, Leverkuhn and Kantor.

He was looking forward to seeing their faces as he delivered their death sentences.

CHAPTER TWENTY-THREE
Ruinthorn and Runefang

THE BATTLE OF THE FOUR ARMIES
The Season of Rot

THE RELENTLESS STAMP of ten thousand feet reverberated around the hills. The sound folded in on itself, becoming an endless rolling thunder that washed across the Empire. Hammers and axes banged on shield bosses, and gruff song drove the dwarfs on. They were a tidal wave of righteous fury to come crashing down mercilessly on the heads of the dead.

They bore the weight of vengeance on their shoulders.

The world had suffered enough.

It ended here, with the coalition of the living, ready to purge the land of the unnatural plague of von Carstein's kith and kin.

'We'll not fail you, Kellus,' Kallad Stormwarden swore, hoisting the banner of Karak Sadra. He bore the burden of the banner himself, proud to bear it into battle one final time. He fully intended to plant it in the Blood Count's skull and make his final stand beneath the pennon as it tore in the wind. 'Not while there's breath in our lungs and iron in our arms.'

The dwarfs marched to war united under the banners of the great strongholds. They had mustered six moons ago, in the shadow of the blighted towers where the Stir crossed the Silver Road. Five thousand was less than Kallad had hoped for, but more than he had dared expect. He prayed it would be enough.

At the muster, King Razzak and his counterparts from Karak Norn and Karak Hirn had urged Kallad to claim his birthright and allow them to name him king before the great battle so that he might march towards whatever fate Grimna held in store for him as the last ruler of the fallen karak.

'Nay, your kingship, it isn't right,' said Kallad. 'Kellus was the last king of the stronghold. There is no Karak Sadra now. I'll not be proclaimed king over a pile of rubble and ghosts. It's not right.'

That had ended the discussion, and the royal line of Karak Sadra would end with Kellus, last true King of the Karak, slain by the very monster that they were marching to fight. It was a fitting tribute that his son should carry the banner of Karak Sadra alongside the banners of Karak Raziac, Karak Kadrin, Karak Hirn and Karak Norn.

The vampire's evil had spread deep into the Empire. Instead of uniting, the forces of the Empire were in complete disarray. Runners had returned at dusk with stories of bitter conflicts amid the forces of the living, with both Lutwig and the Otillia claiming the right to lead the army. Helmut of Marienburg, on the other hand, strove to council patience and cooperation, arguing that in fact each of the three of them should be figureheads for their own forces, as Razzak should be for the dwarfs, in a grand army of equals.

They shouted him down as an idealistic fool.

So, all three declared themselves master and commander of the four armies, and retreated to discuss tactics with their own men, ignoring emissaries from the other camps. Instead of cooperating, they were tearing their armies apart, issuing conflicting orders, preparing conflicting contingencies, and expecting non-existent support.

It would be a massacre.

'Fools!' the dwarf king spat. 'The Blood Count won't need to defeat them, they'll do it for him.'

The stars hung radiant silver in the darkening sky, casting their pure light down onto the cracked and broken path that led to the battlefield. Most of the bloodsucking flies of the mountain's moss had retreated into the night, but Kallad felt the sting of the occasional stubborn insect feeding on his flesh. He slapped his neck, bursting the bloodfly between his fingers.

The winds blew incessantly down the Silver Road, funnelling down between the mountains and along the path of the river.

'The curse of power, Razzak. Much wants more,' Kallad said, shaking his head sadly.

'It was ever the way,' the king agreed. 'Your few years have brought you wisdom, Kallad son of Kellus. That's a rare thing.'

'In worse things, aye,' Kallad agreed, accepting the compliment. He scuffed his feet. The brittle grass had been worn away by trampling boots. 'But in other things, in better things, I'm woefully ignorant, your kingship. It is my curse. I know peace only with my axe in me hand.'

'Such are the times,' Razzak agreed.

Far to the south, the camp of the pretenders' three armies was a wall of glowing light against the backdrop of night. It was impossible to judge how many souls camped out under the stars, making their peace with Morr before the dawn's early light banished the little respite they knew.

Kallad had faced enough battles to know what was going through the mind of each and every manling down there: thoughts of home, faces and smells, making connections inside their heads, bringing back memories of childhood and first love, of intimacy, and beneath them all, a black undermining undercurrent: fear.

Fear was the hidden enemy, capable of infiltrating even the stoutest heart. Stark cold fear brought on by the sure and certain knowledge of what they faced across the field, by the inhuman nature of the enemy.

Fear could make even a strong man weak.

There would be desertions as fear got the better of some men. The lull before the storm broke was always the worst time, when fear was at its most deadly. Things would happen in the glow of the night's fire that would be regretted, should the participants live long enough to have the luxury of regret. Mistakes would be made. All they could do was pray that they would not prove fatal.

Kallad made his excuses and withdrew, choosing to walk alone for a while. He sought the calm centre of his being, the pacific core where he was the rock around which the storm broke. There was no peace. He could hear his own heart, the steady rhythm of it, so absolute was the calm here, removed from the killing ground. There was a mindless quality to it, an eternal reminder of mortality.

There, alone on the mountainside, surrounded by his kin, it began to haunt him.

THE BATTLEFIELD WAS littered with wasted life.

The dwarfs had turned the tide of the skirmish, the Hammerers and Ironbreakers charging down from the low lying hills and crashing into the bones and lichen-smeared carcasses being puppeted across the field of death by von Carstein's necromancers. Kallad planted the standard in the dirt and threw himself into the thick of the fighting, his double-headed axe hewing through rotten flesh and brittle bone with ruthless efficiency. He was a tightly controlled whirlwind of death on the battlefield, Ruinthorn hacking and slashing, cleaving limbs, stoving in dead skulls and gutting his ghoulish foes. He fought with the manic intensity of a true slayer. The dead lay in pools at his feet. He cut down fifty, sixty, more, losing count to the endless press of the enemy surging forwards, wave after wave of the dead and the damned.

He took a battering, was dragged down twice by clutching hands, and twice managed to fight his way back to his feet and drive the dead off.

The dead relinquished the field only when Razzak ordered the full might of the engineer's war machines to be wheeled into the fight. The war machines were huge chariots, equipped with bolt throwers and fire breathers that belched a cocktail of liquid fire, and of rolling artillery flankers and organ grinders that fired silver shot instead of arrows, burning the dead where it sizzled into their flesh. Ballistae launched fragile demijohns of blessed water into the front ranks of the dead and huge stones that skittled through the skeletons.

The legions of the dead restrained themselves. The winds rose, biting and blowing hard across the field. Thick storm clouds drew in, heavy with the threat of rain.

The next few hours saw several small, relatively ineffectual raiding parties driven off by the living. It exposed them for the shambles they were. Twice the Otillia and Lutwig clashed, their own men turning on each other in frustration. The Blood Count was testing their mettle, gauging the effectiveness of their response. Already, after only a few days of trying to coexist, the living were in disarray. They undermined each other at every turn.

Chirurgeons tended to the wounded, but the living were too late to reclaim their dead. The necromancers wove their dark magics, breathing black life back into the fallen and drawing them into the ranks of the dead, swelling von Carstein's unnatural horde with dwarfs and humans. Kallad took a savage blow to the side, crushing the plates of his mail shirt. His breathing was laboured, drawing a fresh breath was an effort. The dour faced chirurgeon poked and prodded the wound.

'You've bruised your lungs and it feels like you've cracked a couple of ribs. Y'll live.' He pressed a poultice up against the wound. 'Keep this in place for an hour, it'll ease the swelling from the ribs and take the pressure off your lungs.'

'Aye, if you know who gives us a minute's respite,' Kallad said. He left the chirurgeons' tent and headed towards the dwarf encampment, away from the bickering manlings. He saw Lutwig, the Altdorfers' pretender to the Imperial throne, deep in conversation with two unsavoury looking sorts. He was whisper thin, with lank, greasy hair that spilled over the right side of his face, and gaunt cheeks. The stresses of the war were taking it out of the man. The last time he had heard speak of Ludwig's successor he had been deemed striking, handsome and commanding, but none of these adjectives suited the tired man that stood across the field from him. Kallad's sharp eyes spotted a pouch changing hands. It was surreptitiously pocketed.

'Tonight,' one of the others said, his voice just loud enough to carry to where Kallad stood, rooted to the spot. To make sure there was no misunderstanding, the soldier drew a finger across his throat, signing the execution order with the promise that it would be done.

Who would Lutwig want dead so badly that he would pay soldiers to be assassins?

That of course was only half of the question, the full question was slightly different: who *here* would Lutwig want dead so badly that he would pay to have him killed?

There was only one answer: the Otillia.

The Otillia directly opposed Lutwig's every move and was making a mockery of his leadership. That kind of slight would burn a man of singular ambition.

Was this so-called hero of the Empire such a coward that he would resort to assassination?

'There's a storm coming,' Grufbad Steelfist said, coming up behind Kallad.

Kallad looked at the thick rolling thunderheads in the sky, and then back at Lutwig and the assassins.

'You're not wrong, my friend. You're not wrong.'

THE CRIES RANG out before dawn:

'The Otillia is slain!'

'Murder!'

Her throat had been cut while she slept. Her chamberlain had found her in a bed of blood-soaked sheets. The old man had been roused by the sounds of struggle from within her pavilion.

The fiends had not escaped justice, one lay dead, slumped over her magnificence as if in worship, and the other had stumbled into a dawn patrol, her blood still on his hands. The assassin had denied nothing, he had merely smiled and looked at the rising sun. 'It is not over,' was all he would say for an hour. Then, with the sun high in the sky, he changed his statement, 'It is over now. The day is lost, the day is found, and bodies there are, all around.' They executed the assassin at noon, during the highest point of the sun, but not before he had confessed his sins and named his paymaster. Few could believe it, even when Kallad Stormwarden came forward and confirmed that indeed, the assassin was one of the pair he had seen trading gold for promises with the Pretender, Lutwig.

Gossip was rife. Lutwig of Altdorf, Pretender to the Imperial Throne, had sanctioned the assassination of one of his greatest political rivals, the Otillia of Talabecland. Fears rose for Helmut of Marienburg, the third pretender. Could Lutwig be so bold as to shatter their fragile peace now of all times, and push his claim for sovereignty?

Talabheimers declared the murder a vile act of cowardice, yet still there were whispers from certain quarters to the contrary, that it was a stroke of genius and would have taken great courage from Lutwig, as, finally, the forces of the four armies could be united under one commander, and two deaths would assure thousands of lives saved. Talk of the greater good was a dangerous thing.

Shockwaves ran through the camps. Driven by fears of resurrection, those loyal to the Otillia hacked her corpse to pieces and burned it. It was far from a fitting burial for an empress. Even as her pieces burned down to embers, tempers rose and fights broke out. At close quarters it was turning ugly. Vigilantes seeking their own justice turned on stragglers from other camps who had wandered too far from their own people, bludgeoning them to death with sticks and stones. It wasn't enough for them. The Talabheimers demanded restitution. It was like a sickness within the mob. From one raised voice came the cry, 'Death to Lutwig!' and the hatred of the others was inflamed. They marched on the Altdorfers' camp, intent on ramming the pretender's head onto a pike, turning the man who would be Emperor into food for the ravens.

Torches blazing, they raised arms, turning on their allies as they forced their way through the tent city to Lutwig's pavilion.

They were greeted by an angry mob, armed with hatchet, axe and sword, and equally hungry to taste the blood of their master and commander's murderers. There were two murders that night, but Helmut of Marienburg was not the unfortunate second victim, Lutwig of Altdorf was.

Physicians emerged from Lutwig's pavilion, faces grave. The pretender had succumbed to the poison on the assassin's blade. There was nothing even their considerable skills could do, Lutwig was dead.

'The pretender is dead!'

'Murderers!'

The Altdorfers surged towards the Talabheimers, demanding their own bloody justice.

In a bizarre twist, King Razzak's dwarfs and Marienburg's men found themselves between a rock and hard place, trying to keep the peace and root out the truth among so much wild speculation and flared tempers. Two of the three pretenders to the Imperial Throne were dead, that much was undeniable. The uneasy peace was shattered. The four armies were disintegrating, and now, of course, was the perfect time for the dead to rise up and destroy what little remained of their resistance.

They came quietly, fiends rising from between the trampling feet to claw down the mob, dragging them down into death. They came loudly, on nightmare steeds, brandishing unholy blades, banshees shrieking in their wake as they charged.

Even the threat of extinction couldn't reunite the armies of the living.

It was cold-blooded slaughter.

Without the dwarfs it would have been so much worse.

As it was, thousands fell in the hour that turned the field into a Morr's paradise on earth.

Razzak ordered the organ grinders to spray bullets of silver across the field, indiscriminately. The engineers used up every last flake of metal in their arsenals to drive off the dead and earn a few minutes of respite.

The screams of the dying were hideous. The screams of the living were worse.

The necromancers pulled every last corpse from the mud and threw it at the living.

Kallad stood in the middle of it, swamped by the press of humanity as it strove to tear the throats out of its traitorous allies, while it all but succumbed to the crush of the dead.

In resisting the dead, the dwarfs bought the living precious time to unravel the treacheries of the night before. Too exhausted to fight, and drained by having to dismember friends and sword brothers to save them from a fate far worse than death, the men rallied around the banner of Helmut of Marienburg so that the third pretender could impose some kind of order.

The truth, when it emerged was as bitter as it was ironic: Lutwig had ordered the Otillia's murder, hoping to rise himself up as rightful leader of the armies of the living, and likewise, the Otillia had paid good coin to assassins to dispose of Lutwig, who she saw as nothing more than a thorn in her side.

In one way the whisperers had been right, however, with only one figurehead to rally behind, the living were more than fit to match the dead on the field of combat.

They buried their dead and their hatreds with them, and clung to Helmut of Marienburg, as they would have to Sigmar himself had the Man-God descended from the clouds to fight beside them.

THE BATTLE RAGED on day and night for a week.

There was no give on either side: no weakness.

The dead fought for dominion.
The living fought for salvation.

The dead had called a parlay and come out under the flag of truce. It was unexpected, and not welcomed by the survivors.

The soil steamed, the rocks and dirt hissing with heat where the liquid fire had burned itself out.

Kallad stood in the middle of the scorched earth, the banner of Karak Sadra gripped firmly in his hand. He forced it deep down into the sizzling soil, ramming the point home, and shouldered Ruinthorn, keeping the faithful axe close to hand should he need it.

The carnage was laid bare across the killing ground, skulls set on sword pommels, carrion birds haunting the skulls. Ravens circled overhead, swooping low to pick worms of flesh from the newly dead. They were a numbing reminder of war's cost and its futility. Kallad knew that in a few hours those bones would begin to stir again, twitching back into unnatural life as the necromancers reanimated them.

Only Morr himself could take any satisfaction in this day's work, and only then if the necromancers didn't succeed in robbing him of the souls that were rightfully his.

The contempt this enemy had for life was staggering.

Four vampires walked across the steaming earth. They squared up to the living. He recognised Skellan as one of them. One of the creatures was female, but that was not the only difference that marked her as special in this group of the dead. Indeed, despite her chalk-white complexion and red red lips, there was something distinctly *alive* about her.

Helmut of Marienburg, his son Helmar, Kallad, and the dwarf king, Razzak, met the dead halfway across the burned earth. They were all that remained of the leaders of the four armies.

The woman spoke: 'Our master wants to speak with you.'

A distant howling caught Kallad's attention: wolves.

'He would now, would he?' Helmut said, his voice thick with utter contempt.

'It is not a request, human,' the second vampire interceded smoothly. 'Konrad *commands* an audience with the leaders of the living. There will be no discussion.'

'Your master's arrogance is outstanding.'

'As is your stupidity.'

Kallad studied Skellan's face during the exchange. A flicker of a smile touched the vampire's lips as insults were traded. He was enjoying himself. He obviously hoped to provoke the pretender into saying or doing something rash.

'Konrad would speak with von Holzkrug as he believes the Untermensch witch and the pretty pretender are no more,' the fourth vampire said, stepping forwards. He swept his cloak aside, resting his delicate fingers on the wyrm-hilted blade at his side. 'Konrad gets what Konrad wants, always.'

'Konrad does,' Skellan said, speaking up for the first time. 'Gentlemen,' He inclined his head slightly to Razzak, 'and dwarfs, may I present von Carstein's rightful heir, the Blood Count himself, Konrad, Vashanesh reborn.'

It burned Kallad to be so close to the beast that had murdered his father. He tugged unconsciously at the standard, lifting it six inches out of the dirt.

'Konrad gets what Konrad wants,' the Blood Count repeated, the wyrm-hilted sword singing as it slid clear of its sheath, 'and Konrad wants…' He turned in a circle, pointing the tip of the blade at each of the living in turn. It passed over Kallad and stopped on Helmut of Marienburg. Konrad's grin was sly. 'You! Or are you craven?'

'What are you talking about, man?' Marienburg blustered. 'You want me for what?'

Kallad could feel the rain on his face as the skies broke: a drop at first, then harder, more insistent.

'Konrad would make a king of you. Yes he would, a true king, not some petty pretender. Konrad would raise you up and honour you, as you deserve. Konrad would have men worship you. Konrad would turn you into a legend among the dead. A dead king. Yes, that is what Konrad wants with you, Helmut of Marienburg. Konrad wants to make you immortal, human. Konrad wants to bless you.'

The ground beneath their feet sizzled as the first raindrops evaporated.

'Konrad is mad,' Helmut barked, drawing his sword and slapping away the Blood Count's blade with it. For a moment, the two swords locked. The steel serration along the edges of Marienburg's monstrous Runefang caught Konrad's bone blade. The last of the pretenders rolled his wrist and drew his blade back with a smooth tug. It was a simple manoeuvre that would have disarmed a weaker foe with ease, but von Carstein's grip never wavered. His blade slipped free of Runefang's teeth.

Kallad launched himself into the fight, only for Skellan to intercede. 'This is not our fight, little man,' Skellan hissed, catching hold of Ruinthorn with both hands and forcing the dwarf back.

'Konrad is glad you have decided to accept his offer, your majesty. Konrad is delighted.'

'Father!' Helmar cried as Konrad launched a blistering attack that finished with his sword slicing Helmut's chest. His ringmail saved him from having to scoop up his entrails. Marienburg staggered back under the frenzied attack, barely getting his sword up to deflect three more staggering blows aimed at removing his head from his shoulders.

Steel clashed loudly with steel-hard bone.

Still, Skellan would not release his hold on Ruinthorn. 'Stop the boy from getting himself killed,' the vampire said, pushing back and sending the dwarf sprawling.

Helmut stumbled over a smouldering chunk of rock protruding from the steaming mud.

It was all Konrad needed.

The vampire threw himself into a forward roll, coming up on his left shoulder, sword snaking out like some pit viper's tongue. The wyrm-hilted blade slipped easily through the muscle of his calf and up into his hamstring. Konrad came out of his roll, towering over the fallen pretender.

Negligently, he cut the ties binding Helmut of Marienburg's soul to his flesh.

'Now Konrad is as good as his word. Yes he is. So to make you a king! Immoliah!'

Kallad was back on his feet quickly enough to restrain Helmar.

'Now's not the time, man. Fight when you can kill them. Don't make the mistake of giving up your life cheaply,' he rasped, clamping a hand on the newly orphaned boy. Helmar shook it off and stumbled forwards, his legs buckling as his body betrayed him. He didn't scream or cry as he fell to his knees. He collapsed in on himself. His grief was absolute. He opened his mouth to moan and sickness swept over him. Helmar threw up as the woman moved easily to her master's side.

The rain streamed down her face, matting her luxuriant raven black hair flat to her face. She looked up as if to savour it, raising her hands above her head. The wind swarmed around them. At the far sides of the battlefield the dead stirred, pulled closer to the necromancer by her silent call. She breathed the wind in, Shyish merging with nature's own cold, wet wind, in her lungs, and she breathed out magic.

The corpse of Helmut of Marienburg shuddered as unlife touched it.

The dread Kallad felt was all too real. Around him, he saw dark shadows moving on the battlefield and heard the low, keening moan, of the dead shuffling forward, effectively isolating them from the rest of the armies of the living.

'Rise!' Konrad screamed. 'Rise my new king of all the dead, rise!'

The corpse rose, gracelessly. Its legs betrayed it, collapsing where there was no muscle to support the bone.

Immoliah Fey reached out a hand to steady the newly risen corpse, bleeding the black wind into its bones to give it the strength to stand.

Neither Immoliah Fey nor Konrad saw Helmar of Marienburg gather up his father's Runefang, and lurch forwards, sobbing. The first they saw was the wicked teeth of the sword cutting into his father's neck. It took Helmar three swings to decapitate his father's corpse.

CHAPTER TWENTY-FOUR

Sometimes They Come Back

THE BATTLE OF THE FOUR ARMIES
The Season of Rot

SKELLAN FACED THE dwarf, Kallad Stormwarden, across the mutilated corpse of the third pretender, Marienburg.

'This is better than I could have dared hope, dwarf. You have excelled yourself.' Skellan kicked the corpse at his feet, 'So much death, so meaningless in its brutality. The Blood Count could never have wrought so much destruction alone, but you know that, don't you, dwarf? You understand the sickness of the living, don't you, dwarf? But, as with all good things, it must come to an end. All those cravings, all those personal weaknesses, greed, ambition, lust and other base hungers. Humans are the worst sort of monster, so dwarf, my thanks. You have served your purpose admirably, but now that you've served, I regret to say that you're nothing more exciting than a loose end. It's time to tie you off.'

'You talk too much, vampire. Shut your yapping and fight. I'll kill you first, and then I'll take your damned master into the dirt if that's the way its gotta be.'

Beside the dwarf, Marienburg's son turned on Konrad, brandishing the bloody sword, Runefang.

'I'll have your head, murderer!'

'Oh, Konrad likes this. It's grand. Lots of blood to be spilled, lots indeed, starting with the little man's.' The vampire's smile was quite mad.

Helmar lunged forwards, but again the dwarf restrained him.

'This is not the place. Go, your people need your leadership. A lot depends on you. More than just your anger is at stake here, manling. You have your people to think about. You're theirs now, not your own. Be the man you have to be.' The dwarf levelled a finger at Skellan, singling him out. 'This here is my fight. Me and the vampires. This is what it comes down to: payment of old debts. It was you on the wall at Grunberg, beside your sire. You killed my father that day, you butchered my people, those're debts that need accounting for, Konrad von Carstein. It's time for the reckoning, a life for a life.' Kallad stepped forwards, axe in hand.

'Konrad killed your father as well?' the Blood Count asked, relishing the thought. 'How delicious. Well Konrad has killed a lot of enemies in his life, so why not two fathers? You have a bond now, you two. Thank Konrad, yes, thank Konrad for making you brothers through grief. Konrad is irresistible. Konrad is Vashanesh reborn. All should tremble before his might. Fall at his feet and beg for Konrad's mercy. Yes, beg!'

'Oh, shut your yapping, your madness,' Skellan growled, mimicking the dwarf's colourful dialect and economy of words. His patience for the mad Count's ravings had long since worn thin.

'You serve a fool, Skellan. In my books that makes you the bigger fool,' Kallad said. The dwarf pumped himself up and swung his huge axe in an explosive arc aimed squarely at lopping Skellan's grinning head from his shoulders. The axe screamed through the air. Skellan didn't move until the wicked silver edge was less than a foot from his throat, and even then he barely moved. Rocking back on his heels, he watched the axe slice through the air a fingertip's width from this nose. His grin didn't falter for a moment.

'Predictable, dwarf,' he said, stepping in close and thundering a clap off the side of Kallad's helm that would ring in his ears for hours to come.

The dwarf launched three successive scything attacks, the third of which stung Skellan across the left arm as he turned his ankle on a jag of stone, causing him to miss-step and almost not make the dodge.

The wound smarted. He backed up a step further, feeling out the gash.

'You'll pay for that, little man,' Skellan promised, and the world exploded with violence.

Skellan hurled himself forwards, unleashing the beast within, his face contorting with rage as he roared at the dwarf, hammering him back step after brutal step. The dwarf had no defence for it. His axe flashed and cut, wide of the mark. Skellan drove him back, slamming a fist into the dwarf's nose and shattering the gristle, and again above the eye, spilling blood.

Around them, the battlefield came alive with the sounds of war. The living had seen von Carstein's treachery, seen their last liege lord fall, and had united, turning their combined fury on the dead. The Blood Count's necromancers matched their might with black magic. The clouds parted, but instead of a brilliant beam of light shining down from the heavens, they unleashed the might of Shyish, the black wind leaching all light and colour out of the world. Thunder cracked and the rain came down. There was no first drop, it was a deluge, turning the field into mud, and drawing sheets of steam from the scorched earth.

Next came the flies.

Thick clouds of bloodflies swarmed over the living, getting into their noses and eyes, into their mouths and down their throats, choking them and making it impossible to see, as the dead descended. The armies of the living stumbled on blindly into the shambling dead, rotten claws tearing at their armour, dragging them down as they slipped and slithered in the oozing mud.

Konrad was swept up in the fighting and carried away on a rising tide of death as his wyrm-hilted blade hacked a path of blood and steaming entrails through the living. Immoliah Fey was at his back, her whispered incantations bringing them back in time to see their own guts unravel in their hands painlessly.

Bubbles of mud burst as the ground roiled, coalescing into straining arms and the curves of skulls as the long dead crawled back up from far below the battlefield, the bones of animals and men answering the necromancers' call. Broken antlers breached the surface, followed by the black sockets of a wolf's elongated snout and eyes, and the skeletal remains of a horse's fetlocks. More beasts rose with the remains of the men, most rotten and incomplete, but that did not stop the dead animals from trying to answer the call back to unlife.

Skellan's world narrowed to just the two of them, the dwarf and him. The rest could go to hell, blazing every inch of the way with brimstone and the very stuff of the earth, the rocks, the dirt and the grasses melting beneath the intensity of the unholy fire as they went.

He threw himself at Kallad, driving the dwarf to his knees with the fury of his blows, jumping and seeming to hang suspended in the air for half a second before arcing his spine and delivering a massive kick to the side of Kallad's head. He felt the bone give beneath his foot. The dwarf slumped in the mud, axe spilling from his hands. The fight left his eyes as he looked up, dazed and beaten.

Steel sang as Skellan drew his sword and stood over the dwarf, poised to deliver the killing blow.

He drew back his arm and swung, but the blow never landed.

A crippling blow slammed into the base of Skellan's spine, and a second one into the nape of his neck. The sword tumbled out of his hand as his fingers sprang open. Before he could turn, a fourth and fifth blow had crunched into his spine and ear with crippling force. Pain exploded behind his eyes.

He staggered away and fell, his legs buckling. He sprawled in the mud beside the dwarf and slithered around onto his back so that he could see the face of his attacker.

He saw a ghost looking down at him.

Although the ghost's face was ruined, it was still hauntingly familiar. For a moment, the only thing Skellan could think was that the dead had truly answered the necromancer's call. A rush of doubt filled him. It was an emotion that he had almost forgotten the taste of, and he didn't appreciate being reminded of its bitter tang.

He tried to rise, but the ghost pressed him back down into the mud with an all too substantial foot.

'I should have known your being dead was too good to be true, wolf.'

'Go,' JEREK URGED the dwarf.

He didn't allow himself the luxury of seeing if the dwarf heeded his advice. He kicked Skellan hard, hammering a blow into his side that almost lifted him out of the sucking mud.

In the long months of his exile, Skellan's had become the one face that haunted the wolf, not Konrad's, not Vlad's: Skellan's. His evil was subtle and far-reaching.

He kicked Skellan again, in the face this time, below the right eye. A brutal blow that split the skin and cracked the bone, sending a sliver into the milky orb. Skellan pitched sideways and fell back. Jerek lifted him bodily and slammed him down again in a backbreaking crunch.

'Nice to see you too,' Skellan coughed between gasps, his hand pressed up against his ruined eye.

'Give me a reason, Skellan, just one, to finish you and it is done.'

'You're going to keep an eye on me, are you?'

The unnatural darkness hanging over the battlefield slowly dissipated as the living drove back the dead.

'You mock me at your peril, Skellan,' Jerek said coldly.

'I know, but what can I do? It is in my nature. Why have you come back, wolf?'

Skellan started to rise, only to have Jerek's heel crunch into the bridge of his nose. He sprawled backwards in the mud, head cracking off a jagged edge of rock. 'I've killed men for less, wolf, remember that.' His face was a mess, his nose smeared halfway across his cheek, and the twin white bones of his brow exposed where the flesh had curled away from it. The splinter lodged deep in his blind eye completed the ruin.

'Him,' the wolf said, inclining his head to indicate the manically laughing Blood Count cutting a red swathe through the scattering humans. 'He must be stopped.'

'Couldn't agree more,' Skellan said. He picked at the bone in his blind eye, 'but time and again that isn't enough, is it? We cling to our foolish ideas that simple solutions exist. You want him gone, I want him gone, and yet here we are, enemies once more.' Skellan drew the sliver of bone out of his right eye, the jelly of its vitreous humour spilling down his cheek. 'So while I work quietly to destroy everything that he is, you disappear only to return claiming that our mad Count is your sworn enemy? It's all very... melodramatic, isn't it, wolf?' He held the jagged splinter of bone between thumb and forefinger, examining it with his good eye. 'Have you learned nothing from the von Carsteins? There is beauty in all things, even betrayal. A little more forcefully and you could have really hurt me, you know. As it is, I think it will leave a nasty little scar.'

Skellan tossed the bone away.

Jerek looked at the man he had come to hate. Until that moment, he truly believed that he had gone as far into the vampiric aspect of his nature as it was humanly possible to do.

He was wrong.

'Show me your hands.'

'What?'

'Just do it. Show me your hands.'

Skellan held out his hands.

There were no rings.

Frustration consumed Jerek. He surrendered totally and completely to the black surge of anger, channelling it through his fists as he pummelled them into Skellan's face, wiping the grin off it by destroying the vampire's mouth. Over and over, he pounded his fist into the smug grin, ruining Skellan's mouth by shredding his lips against his teeth.

He didn't stop until Skellan was incapable of fighting back. He kicked and beat Skellan into the ground and then stood over him. It would be so easy to finish it, to slay Skellan and rid the world of his taint, but he couldn't do it. He wanted to, there was no doubt about that in his mind, but he couldn't physically do it. Skellan's words stayed his hand. What if it was true? What if Skellan truly wanted Konrad dead, and not merely to usurp his throne?

What if for all the crimes the man had committed, for all the atrocities carried out by his hand, he had come to realise the unnatural threat the dead posed to the very fabric of the world itself? What if? What if? What if? He couldn't answer any of the questions flying round like blind ravens inside his head, colliding, crashing, falling into and over each other, wings flapping desperately, the cacophony of caws drowning out all hope of rational thought. What if Skellan offered the most unlikely alliance?

He couldn't do it. He couldn't deliver the killing blow, even though he knew that if the roles were reversed, Skellan would have suffered no compunction in his place.

Jerek left Skellan in the dirt.

The battle raged on.

He didn't know where to turn. So much of his life had been given over to the hunt for von Carstein's signet ring. After the fight with Konrad, it had been easier to disappear than to go home.

Home? That was a joke. He had no home.

He was trapped between two worlds, human and undead, and not welcome in either.

Jerek was a ghost, cursed to haunt the Old World until he found the damned ring and could finally rest. Until then, he could only torment himself by haunting the living and the dead, lurking on the outside of their realms, looking in.

He saw the dwarf staggering back towards the safety of the pavilions and felt the pull of the necromancers' magic. He didn't know which way to turn. Neither camp would welcome him. He cursed himself for a fool for being drawn to this foreign field, but he had always known that he had no choice but to be here. He had to walk amongst the dead. He had to find the ring. It had to be destroyed. He couldn't allow it to fall into a madman like Konrad's hands, or worse, an amoral killer like Skellan's.

Jerek walked away from the killing.

He followed the dwarf towards the chirurgeons' tents. War was not one battle: it was continuous attrition, grinding down the enemy over and over again. Von Carstein would surrender the field. The signs were there to be read. A sunburst of light threw its yellow glow across the fighting, scattering the shadows. They returned a moment later to smother the light, but it didn't matter, the darkness had shown weakness, vulnerability. That in turn gave the light hope. The living rallied, throwing themselves at the dead.

Then, from between the cracks in the hillside, came salvation: a long rippling snake of movement coming out of the valley of darkness and spilling out onto the plain, dwarfs bearing the banner of Zufbar, another thousand at least.

Wooping around them, human riders bore the banner of Marienburg, their burnished armour catching that fleeting burst of light and magnifying it. They swarmed onto the field, lances levelled, skewering the mindless dead who were too slow or too clumsy to get out of their way. Their chargers' hooves crushed skulls beneath the stampede, and the dwarfs cleaned up after them.

The dead were routed.

This day, at least, was won.

Drive a foe from the field one day and he returns the next, renewed, more desperate to be your doom.

As much as he was loath to involve himself, to expose himself, Jerek knew that his only hope lay with the dwarf and his people. They were committed to exterminating his kind, in that common cause they were united. They were his best chance of destroying Konrad, even if it meant sacrificing himself.

Cheers went up from the living, but they were not the exuberant cheers of victory, they were the desperate cries of relief. They had been saved; they hadn't won. There was a difference, and they knew it.

JEREK WATCHED THE dwarf. He haunted the camp. It was surprisingly easy, considering his nature, to move unnoticed.

He wasn't sure exactly how he was going to befriend the dwarf. He had thought about claiming that he was owed a life debt for saving the dwarf from Skellan, and while it might be enough to keep him alive, it wasn't exactly something that he *wanted* to do.

Would the dwarf throw his lot in with the dead, trading one evil for another? Moreover, when the deed was done, would the dwarf turn on him?

The surprising truth of it was that after living through the torments of this unlife, Jerek welcomed the prospect of that final rest. It held no fear for him, even if dying again did mean the destruction of all that he was. Here, now, he would have welcomed a complete cessation of existence with arms wide open. If the ring was destroyed, then it was a price worth paying.

Years of fighting against his nature could finally end here, on this field.

That was why he had returned, that was the truth he was hiding from himself.

He knew this was the first move in the endgame.

He knew that by saving the dwarf and making his presence known to Skellan, he had accelerated everything. He *could* have lurked in the shadows, hunting for clues, following the path of the ring, but by coming forward, he had chosen to become a catalyst. Things would happen around him. Mistakes would be made, hands played too early, secrets betrayed. One of them would lead to the ring, he felt sure. One of them *had* to.

As the dwarf passed, Jerek stepped out of the shadows and grabbed him from behind, pressing his hand over the dwarf's mouth and hissing, 'Shhhhhh,' before the dwarf could fight back. 'I am a friend.' He removed his hand.

'You're no friend of mine, freak.'

'Then let's hope that by the end of the night I am,' Jerek said.

THE DWARF HEARD him out.

'Why in hell should I trust you?'

Jerek had wondered that himself and the truth of it was far from convincing. 'Because of who I was, not who I am,' he said, hoping it was enough. 'Because, as the White Wolf of Middenheim, I gave my life trying to protect the same thing that you are trying to protect, and because, for some reason, a spark of whatever it was that made me *me* still burns inside me. How long it will last, I don't know, but while it does I am a ghost, trapped between the land of the living and the nations of rot and decay. I am nothing in either world, and because of that, I can pass unnoticed in both. I can get where you can't, close enough to Konrad to kill him if that is how it must end. I do not want to end up like *them*.'

'And what are you proposing I give you in return?'

'Help.'

'Go on.'

'You know the story of the first war?'

'I was there, yes.'

'Then you know that it was won by guile, not force. Von Carstein had a talisman of incredible power that enabled his dead form to regenerate. The talisman was stolen during the Siege of Altdorf, allowing the Sigmarite priest to slay him once and forever.'

'I know the story,' the dwarf said. 'The Vampire Count's ring. The thief stole it and gave it to the priests.'

'Yes, the von Carstein ring – only I don't for one minute believe that the thief gave it to the priests. Put it this way, it wasn't in either grave and I can't see them leaving it in a jewellery box on a nightstand, can you?

I need to find the thief who took it. I need to make sure that the damned thing is destroyed. That is what I need your help for.'

'And who told you I know anything about any ring?'

'You did, just now. I said talisman, you said ring.'

'I could have heard that in a taproom just about anywhere in the Empire.'

'Yes, you could have, but you didn't, did you?'

'No, I met the thief. I saw with me own eyes the price he paid for his heroics. He ain't got that ring though, you can take my word for that. One of your kind took it. Cut his hands off in the process and left him for dead, only he didn't die.'

Jerek didn't say a word for the longest time. When he finally spoke, it was as if he hadn't heard the dwarf's words. 'I saw the banner you bore into battle. I recognised the device: Karak Sadra. I know what happened to that stronghold, dwarf. I know who was responsible for destroying it. That means I know what you are, or who you are, rather. You are the last of your clan.

'Knowing that gives me the key to you, how you work. I know what drives you. I understand the anger festering inside you, the need for vengeance, better than any other you will meet. You bear a grudge against the monster that slew your people.

'I bear one as well, against the monsters that made me into what I am. I will not lie down and let them swallow my world whole. I will not stand by and watch it plunge into eternal night. I will not watch it become a place of blood and sorrow. No, dwarf, that cannot be allowed to happen, but it falls to people like us to prevent it. That is what will happen if what you say is true. That ring cannot be allowed to adorn the finger of a vampire. It cannot. The world cannot withstand another dread lord of my sire's ilk.'

That confession went against every instinct the wolf possessed, still it felt important to have no lies between them, not if he was going to sway the dwarf to his side.

'You're saying you and him... you and the mad one... you're brothers?'

'Of a sort, dwarf, but not in any meaningful way, there is no kinship between us, no bond. He is vermin and should be treated as such.'

'You're brothers though, in blood. Brothers with the monster that killed my father.'

There was no way he could deny the truth so he didn't.

'You see a beast gone rabid what do you do?' Jerek asked.

'Put it out of its misery.'

'That's my brother, dwarf. A beast that needs to be put out of its misery, that is all he is.

'Now, guile won the last war, not strength of arms, not the supreme sacrifice of one man. That stinks like the effulgence it is. The thief won the war by taking away the one thing that von Carstein had – his invulnerability. Once he was stripped of it and made mortal, the war was as good as over. Any blade could have struck him down. It didn't have to be Sigmar sent or Ulric blessed. This war could be won the same way. The Blood Count has no talent, and so long as the von Carstein ring hasn't found its way into his possession, he isn't blessed with that infuriating knack of coming back and coming back and coming back. All he is is a madman who demands that his few pet magicians raise his armies for him. He is a shadow of his sire and he knows it, self-loathing and doubt consume him. He strives to reinvent himself as more than he is. He is trying to build a legend, but those men he relies upon, well, they have no such immortality – in other words, they aren't particularly difficult to kill. Hit them and the war is essentially over.'

'I've got no liking for this and I don't mind saying,' the dwarf grunted, cracking the bones in his neck as he twisted, 'but there's no denying what you're getting at. Well, it makes a fair deal of sense.'

'You don't need to like it, dwarf, just accept that it is so. I am less than human, more than vampire, something else entirely and nothing completely. I have no loyalty to the dead. I would do what I have always done, all my life. I would protect the living. I'm not claiming the life debt you owe me for saving you from Skellan back there, although I could. I know your culture. I know what it means to save a dwarf from certain death. I know that you are beholden to me, but I don't care. I want your help given willingly or not at all. I cannot risk you suffering a change of heart. No, what I am asking for is nothing more than your help in preventing a dark and hungry god from arising in our time, in our children's time. I am asking you to do the right thing. You have already proven that you know more about this thief and the ring than I have unearthed in long months of searching. Together, we can do things that alone we can't. So, dwarf, do we have a pact?'

He studied the dwarf, saw him struggling to get past his natural hatred of the beast he had become, the betrayal he felt knowing he faced a blood relative of the beast that had slaughtered his people, trying to grasp that something of the man he was still remained, and that he could in fact be trusted.

Finally, the dwarf nodded.

'Aye, you hold up your end, get close to the necromancers and kill them if you can, but the mad vampire is mine,' Kallad Stormwarden said, spitting on his palm and holding his hand out. 'When that's done we'll turn our attention to that damned ring of yours.'

They shook, sealing the bargain.

CHAPTER TWENTY-FIVE
To Kill the Mocking Birds

GRIM MOOR
The Season of Decay

DEATH COMES TO all living things, there is no escaping it: death, the great destroyer; death, conqueror, liberator, defiler, despoiler.

Death. It was his gift to the living.

Konrad von Carstein's mind was in turmoil. Thoughts he didn't recognise as his own pulled him every which way. He was torn. He heard voices: they weren't externalised, they were inside him. They taunted him and jeered at his failings. He knew the loudest of them. It belonged to a head from his rotten gallery. Although the head of Johannes Schafer was far, far removed, the man's voice was an incessant yammering in his head, going on and on and on.

He screamed. He hammered at his temples, trying to drive the voices out, but they wouldn't leave him, and they wouldn't leave him alone.

Schafer was dead. Konrad couldn't remember how he had killed the man, only that he had and that the rogue had been a screamer. That he remembered. Now, as penance, he carried the ghost around inside his head.

'Leave Konrad be, leave him!' Konrad yelled, spinning around violently. He tore the map from the table and shredded it. His sword lay on the tabletop beside a goblet of dark liquid. In anger, he lashed out and sent the weapon clattering to floor. His necromancers, Immoliah Fey and Nevin Kantor, backed off a step from his madness. 'Not you! You!' They had no idea whether they were supposed to stay or go. 'You will obey Konrad! You will serve him with your heart or he will feast on it, Understand?'

Neither said a word.

In truth, they had no idea whether the Blood Count was talking to them or raving at some invisible speaker whose words filled his head.

There was an uneasy balance in the room: they could not trust him and he could not trust them. He knew they were scheming behind his back. Skellan kept him informed. Skellan, his last loyal soldier. Skellan, poor, pitiful Skellan. The war had all but destroyed him, but he refused to die.

It was only pity that stayed Konrad's hand, pity for himself, not for Skellan, pity that the wretched beast was the closest he had to a friend, family, or a lover; pity that all around him sought to topple him from his lofty perch. Pity that it had come down to this: kill or be killed.

He had never been afraid of bringing death into the world. Death was his one true talent, his gift.

Konrad heard a cough and turned.

'Whistle up the daemon,' he said as Skellan moved awkwardly into the room. The Hamaya dragged his left leg, and his right arm hung uselessly at his side. The muscles showed signs of atrophy. It had set in with surprising speed, as if Skellan had lost the will to heal himself, and had given in to the natural entropy of all things flesh. The bones twisted around on the shoulder joint, hunching his back uncomfortably.

For all that, it was his face that betrayed the full extent of the toll that the war had taken. It was barely recognisable: a ruin of scars closed up his right eye, the flesh itself merging into a flat plane from nose to brow with only the narrowest slit where his eye had once been.

He refused to say who had done this to him, although Konrad harboured suspicions. There were few great heroes allied to the forces of the living, certainly no more than a handful of men capable of standing up to a vampire of Skellan's lethal cunning.

'You wanted me?' There was no deference in Skellan's voice. His battering had knocked the respect out of him. Konrad would deal with it, in time, but not today. Today, he needed Skellan's devious nature to undo the forces of the living that had rallied behind Helmar of Marienburg's banner. He knew Skellan was devious, that Skellan plotted his own schemes, that his Hamaya desired nothing more than to usurp him, but Konrad was no mere beast, Konrad was Vashanesh reborn. Konrad was supreme. Konrad was immortal!

'Yes, yes, yes. Konrad wants you. Konrad wants to pick your brains. These two pretend loyalty, but they refuse Konrad.'

'Then make them. It is as simple as that. Take something of theirs and threaten to destroy it. What do they love more than anything?'

'They love nothing,' Konrad said, exasperated.

'Wrong, your madness, they love their books. They love the trinkets and treasures you gave them. They love their power. Take it away from them. Take it all away from them unless they do as you demand.'

'You can't!' Fey cried.

Kantor slapped her across the face, hard. She wheeled around on him, her snarl feral.

Skellan laughed harshly. 'See, Konrad. Threaten to take their toys away and they turn on each other fast enough. You didn't need me for this.'

'Konrad would hear the truth, and you are his truth speaker, Jon Skellan, so speak to him. When you look at the field what do you see?'

'What do you want me to say? Bloodshed, devastation, suffering? I see a world of hurt.'

'But is it enough? Does it satisfy you? Will it open the way for the Kingdom of the Dead? Will it?'

'You want the truth?' Skellan asked, shuffling awkwardly to one side so that he could draw the tent flap back. The cold air, heavy with the taint of blood and urine, blew into the pavilion. The sounds of battle rushed in behind it. The sounds of death and dying, the low moaning keen of the zombies, the creaks and groans of the skeletons, the shrieks of the ghouls and the howls of the dire wolves a haunting counterpoint to the agonies of the living, the clash of steel on bone and the wet tearing of flesh.

'Yes, Konrad would hear your truth.'

Skellan stared at him, his one good eye blazing hate. 'I think you are finished, Konrad. I think your pets are turning against you and you can't do a damned thing to stop it. I don't think you even see it, you are that blind. Kantor here, and Fey, have dreams of dominion. They see the world you are carving out and think to themselves: but this is all our doing, not his. And they are right, because without them you are nothing, and out there, on that blasted moor, I think you are being destroyed bit by bloody bit.' His words came out slurred because he couldn't curl his lips around them properly when he grew angry. 'They will not write glorious histories of your life, and they will not fall for the drivel you had Constantin scribble in your honour. They will remember you for what you are, a poor deranged fool. That is my truth.'

'You seek to anger Konrad? You seek to drive him to violence, yes? Konrad understands your pain, understands that you are less than a man, so you lash out at his greatness to appease your own pain. Konrad understands, but Konrad does not forgive. Oh, no, Konrad does not forgive such slights.'

Skellan smiled, as best his ruined mouth would allow.

'It isn't for Konrad to forgive. Konrad matters nothing to me.' He shook his head, as if irritated that the Blood Count's affliction of referring to himself in the third person had transferred itself to him. 'Who controls your Hamaya, your madness? That's a rhetorical question, by the way. I do. We both know it. Every one of the second generation was hand-picked by me. Where does their loyalty lie? You can answer this one, go on, have a guess.'

'You,' Konrad rasped, the beast roaring out from beneath his skin. His brow split, his nose thickened and elongated, stretching his mouth up to bare cruel fangs.

'Me,' Skellan agreed.

He didn't unleash the beast.

'Who is loyal to Konrad? WHO?' the Blood Count raged, spinning around the confines of the tent. He grabbed Immoliah Fey by the throat and drew her close. He saw fear in her eyes and revelled in it, rasping into her face, 'Are you loyal to Konrad, bitch?'

For all her magic, she had no answer for him. She feared him.

That in itself was condemnation. Who had need to fear but a traitor?

He threw her aside and wheeled around on Kantor. The weasel threw up his hands and spat an oath that hit Konrad in the gut, twisting his insides. He didn't understand what he was feeling at first, didn't grasp the seriousness of it as the necromancer continued his malicious incantation. He felt a fire in his blackened heart, felt it spreading out through his left arm and down his left side. He didn't wait to see what was happening to him, he lashed out, sending the necromancer sprawling back over the table and into the pavilion's canvas wall. He stood over Nevin Kantor, poised to deliver judgement.

'You will swear loyalty to Konrad, spirit of Vashanesh reborn. You will swear it or you will die here.'

'I will bring your army to its knees first,' Kantor rasped. 'You ignorant fool, harm me, and your hold over the dead dies. Can you be so far gone that you don't realise it? Your army exists through me, not you. You are not the lord here, Konrad. I am, and she,' he inclined his head towards Immoliah Fey, 'is my dark queen.'

'Build an empire on dust, Konrad, and you have to expect it to sink eventually. It is the way of all things.'

'No,' Konrad said, refusing to believe the truth of his own ears. 'No, no, no, no.'

Kantor struggled to his feet, a contemptuous sneer pasted across his face. 'Do you hear that, Konrad?'

'Konrad hears nothing.'

'Exactly, that silence is ominous isn't it, considering this is a battlefield. Where are the screams of the dying? Where is the clash of sword on sword?'

'What have you done?'

'Only what I promised – I have taken my dead back. They do not fight for you. They await my will, and sense that my anger is directed inwards, focused on you, Konrad. Can you hear them coming? Can you hear the grind of bones, the shuffling feet? They are coming for you.'

Konrad pushed past Skellan and staggered out of the pavilion and into the harsh light of day. The sun burned his skin. He looked up at the sky, at the golden orb hanging above his head, and screamed, 'Where is the darkness? Konrad commands it be night!'

The necromancers emerged from the tent, faces impassive. Skellan came up behind them, something gleaming in his right hand.

'You truly are a fool, aren't you, von Carstein?' Kantor spat. 'You bluster at the heavens and don't even look at the earth. Look, damn you, see your doom as it nears.'

'Betrayal,' Konrad whispered, seeing the dead fighting amongst themselves, the vampires struggling against the endless press of Kantor and Fey's automatons. The dead were coming for him: the dead, his dead. 'Fight!' Konrad roared. 'Butcher the living!' But it was useless.

'Your time of blight is over, Blood Count,' Kantor said smugly.

It was the last thing he ever said. Skellan rammed a thin-bladed dagger into his back, between the third and fourth bones of his ribcage, and buried it deep into the necromancer's heart. His lips moved, but he didn't make a sound. A white mist leaked from Kantor's mouth, coalescing into a wraith-like shadow, gathering form. It was a vile beast. Konrad knew what he saw, just as he knew that he couldn't be seeing it. Kantor's essence, Kantor's soul, and then, even as the winds around the battlefield howled and a massive thunderclap split the clear blue sky, the mist dissipated and an unerring calm settled over Grim Moor.

Then his body collapsed.

The dead under Kantor's thrall echoed his collapse as one, the black thread of Shyish that bound them back to this life cut.

Ravens circled the battlefield, settled on the roofs and guide ropes of the pavilions, on the corpses of the dead and on the stones, and cawed, their mocking cry taking on an uncomfortably human aspect: *he is coming... he is coming...*

Konrad ran at the nearest ravens, scattering them.

They swooped low overhead, cawing, cawing, ceaselessly cawing: *he is coming...*

Immoliah Fey struggled to rally her own zombies while hissing incantations to raise Kantor's dead from the dirt of the field, but the vampires had turned on them.

The dead were destroying themselves. All the living had to do was bear witness.

'Kill them. Kill them all!' Konrad raged, running around the battlefield like a madman possessed, flapping his arms at the black birds.

Skellan allowed himself a satisfied smile.

THE FORCES OF the living rallied, given new strength by the sight of their enemy's collapse.

They brandished swords and spears, and charged into the mud of the field, stumbling and falling, and picking themselves up to charge on, their war cries terrible to hear.

True death came to the dead on the field that day.

KONRAD STOPPED, FROZEN in the act of strangling a raven.

Out of the bloodshed and devastation of Grim Moor strode a face from his past, a ghost.

'Konrad killed you,' he said, even as the bird broke in his hands.

Jerek von Carstein stood before him.

At his side were two grim faced dwarfs and the boy-man, Helmar, clutching his father's sword, Runefang.

Fighting raged around them, the living banishing the dead.

Skellan moved to stop the dwarf, Kallad. Beside him Grufbad shook his head.

'Out of my way, ugly, this is between me and the man that killed my father.'

'Kill him!' Konrad yelled, but to his horror, he saw Skellan shake his head.

'You have to own the consequences of your own actions, Konrad,' Skellan said, grinning. 'Looks to me a lot like the world has come to pay you back.'

'You say no? Konrad will kill you if Konrad must, you will die just the same, little man.' The Blood Count reached down for the wyrm-hilted blade at his side, but it wasn't there. It was inside the pavilion, beneath the table. His anger swept him away. 'Konrad has no need of steel!' He threw himself at the first dwarf, Kallad, who met his charge head on, butting his head full into Konrad's face. Rage deadened all feeling. Konrad lashed out, clawing at the dwarf's face. The dwarf took it without flinching.

Konrad felt fire, in his chest, and looked down to see the blade of a huge double-headed axe buried in his chest.

His scream, as the dwarf yanked the axe clear, was terrible to behold.

His scream, as the dwarf slammed the axe home a second time, was worse.

But still he didn't fall. He caught the dwarf's axe and hurled it away, backhanding a massive blow across the side of Kallad's temple. He roared, pure animalistic rage, and then felt arms take him. He couldn't break the grip. He writhed and twisted and shrieked but there was no way out of these bonds.

Kallad stepped up again, ready to cleave skull from shoulders but Helmar stayed his hand.

'He killed my father as well, dwarf. I would finish this. For me, for my people.'

Kallad looked at the young warrior. There was something in the young pretender's face that told him he needed it more, to find peace, than Kallad did. 'Aye, lad, justice is done whoever lands the blow. Do it.' The dwarf stepped back.

Helmar stood over Konrad while Grufbad held him down.

He raised the Runefang...

KONRAD'S VISION BLURRED. He saw Skellan. He saw the ghost of Jerek. He saw Immoliah Fey dead at his feet, the wolf holding her heart in his fist. He saw the dwarf.

His legs buckled beneath him.

All around, the ravens mocked him. He saw them everywhere, a murder of black birds, and in their eyes, he saw the true source of his betrayal, and knew at the last that he had been undone by one of his own.

'Konrad is betrayed,' Konrad breathed, darkness closing over him. He reached out for the wolf, for his truth speaker.

He never felt the blow that claimed his head.

EPILOGUE
Grim Moor

KALLAD STORMWARDEN STOOD over the corpse of the Blood Count.

He had his revenge. He had justice for his father. He had retribution for his people. And yet... and yet he felt nothing.

There was no satisfaction in delivering death. He was hollow.

'Time to leave this place,' Jon Skellan said, and seemed to unfold his crippled body. He stretched and bent, manipulating his muscles. He drew himself to his full height, forcing his leg to obey him. He gasped, pressing his shoulder back into place. His arm still showed the rigor of atrophy and his face bore all the marks of mutilation from Jerek's beating, but his bearing was powerful once more as he shook off his helpless disguise. 'I am not one for lost causes, eh wolf? I delivered my end of the bargain, now you deliver yours.' He turned to leave and then stopped. 'You did well, dwarf, surprisingly well. I wouldn't have thought you had it in you. Go back to your hole in the ground. The greatest of them all is coming. You do not want to be here when he returns.'

Ravens settled on Skellan's shoulder, one on his left, one on his right, and though the wind tore away their mocking cries, he could have sworn he heard a name:

Mannfred.

RETRIBUTION

CHAPTER ONE

Stranger in a Strange Land
The Lands of the Dead
Before

THE MAN CAST a terrified glance over his shoulder as he ran.

He couldn't *see* anything, but that didn't matter.

He could *feel* it getting closer.

He fled across the desert, staggering up banked dunes and lurching down them again, his legs buckling as the wind buffeted him. Sand burned the soles of his feet. He ran. He fell. He forced himself back to his feet. He ran again. He stumbled. Fell.

It followed.

It was there – no matter how far he ran, how fast – it was always there.

It was relentless.

He clutched the bundle of rags tightly to his chest. The thing wrapped within the rags was repulsive. It reeked of corruption; stank of the dead wind. Paradoxically, it was alive in his arms. He felt it, a pulse beating through the layers of cloth. It craved, hungered. He felt its presence inside his head, the insidious whisper of its need. One word: release. It ached to be free, to be loosed upon the world now that it had stirred.

'Not yet,' he managed, through cracked lips. His voice was raw, thick with grit and sand. The desert heat burned in his lungs. His skin crawled, as though the heat of the sun ate away at his flesh. Blisters chaffed against the course weave of his robes. It was an exquisite form of torture. He clung to the pain. He couldn't remember a time without pain. It was the one constant of his world. As long as there was pain, he was alive.

Long thin tendrils of shadow swelled up around him, like some giant hand snatching him from the desert sands. He spun around, stumbling backwards with the momentum of fear. There was nothing behind him – nothing that could have cast that shadow. He turned away quickly. He fixed his gaze on the heat-shimmer of the horizon.

The sun blazed in the sky, flensing him of all sense of self.

His robes, a dirty-white robe worn threadbare in places, whipped around his legs. He was covered from head to toe. Only his eyes were exposed to the elements. Still the sand bit at them, stung them into tears. The world blurred.

The sand shifted beneath his feet as he staggered on, desperate to be free of this dead place. Dust devils churned around him, surging up from the ground like mystical djinn only to be blown away on the wind, no more threatening than the grains of sand they were.

The tendrils of shadow thickened. The man ran for his life. He didn't dare look back. He didn't need to.

He knew what the shadow was. He had always known.

The claws of the dark lord, reaching out, reaching...

No, that was impossible.

That was the voice of his fear speaking to him, a malaise that had haunted him ever since he had entered this forsaken land. It was paranoia worthy of Konrad.

Konrad.

The name bubbled up inside his head.

He tried to focus on it, to recall the face behind the name, but there was nothing.

Shadows coiled around his blistered feet.

Reaching out from his slumber, woken by your own stupidity, fool.

Your power.

At the back of his mind, the mocking whisper:

Your arrogance.

He clutched the bundle tight to his chest. It weighed heavy in his arms.

Dark shapes began to solidify on the horizon. His mind painted them as daemons come to claim his soul and drag him down to Morr's Underworld. A moment later they coalesced into trees. Oasis or mirage, it mattered little to him. He staggered on, his feet dragging one after the other. He tried to imagine the cool trickle of water down his throat, quenching the fire inside him: the need.

Laughter rang in his ears: hysterical, spiralling, mocking.

The ring on his left hand, a plain unassuming adornment, caught the glare of the scouring sun, dispelling the dark shadows for a moment. His determination to survive grew with each unsteady step. The ring was important to him, but he had no idea why.

His thoughts swam in and out of focus. He tried to focus on the oasis. He walked on. It never appeared to get any closer.

'You're not real,' he croaked, knowing even as he said it that his mind was playing tricks on him.

He walked on.

The world tilted, blurred.

He heard the caw of birds, but saw nothing in the sky, straining to make sense of it as blood came sliding down from the sun, burning the desert red before it faded into the black of night.

Darkness hid the shadows – it didn't banish them. The twin moons of Morrslieb and Mannslieb appeared low in the sky, rising. The desert air grew cold. He stumbled on, staring at the ground as it fell away beneath his feet until he splashed over the water's edge. He fell to his knees, setting aside the bundle, and reached down to scoop up mouthful after mouthful of sun-warmed water.

It did nothing to slake his thirst.

It was an unquenchable fire inside him.

He was burning up from the inside out. It was consuming him and there was nothing he could do to quell it.

A black bird had settled on one of the branches around the oasis. The beady-eyed scavenger had obviously come to feed on his corpse. He looked up at the creature, defying it, defying the fire, the hunger, the all-consuming need inside him. 'I will not die here,' he told the bird, and he meant it.

His defiance didn't impress the bird. Its harsh *caw caw caw* mocked him.

He threw back his head, tore away the wrapping of his headscarf, and screamed, startling the bird into flight. It swooped down out of the tree, clawed feet looking to pluck out his eyes as its wings beat and battered at his face.

The man's hand snaked out with eldritch grace, taking the bird out of the air. He held it for a moment, cradling the creature in his hands. The bird's wings flapped desperately as the force of his grip intensified, crushing its delicate ribcage as though crumpling vellum. He tore the bird's head from its body with a savage twist and raised the still flapping carcass to his lips, sucking greedily at the blood and flesh, feeding.

It tasted *good*.

This was what his body had hungered for.

This was the need driving the maddening cravings he felt tearing at him: Blood.

He savoured the flavours, the thickness of the liquid as it ran down his throat.

The taste stirred a dark memory.

He had tasted blood before.

He tore at the bird with his teeth, spitting out blood-clotted feathers. It wasn't enough. Now that the need had been awoken it demanded sating. He tried to stand, but he lacked the strength.

The world swam out of focus and he lapsed into unconsciousness.

THERE WAS BLOOD on his hands when he came to.

The blood was rust-coloured and caked hard, but it was undeniably blood. He *had* killed the bird. It hadn't been some weird fever dream. He had torn the head off the animal and sucked greedily at the gaping hole, draining the pitiful creature of every precious ounce of blood.

And he had *enjoyed* it.

But rather than quell the pain, the blood only served to intensify it, reminding his body of what it craved.

He looked up.

Where the land and sky met, a swarm of black specks had begun to gather. He watched them solidify, a murder of black-winged birds taking shape out of the dark sky, hundreds of them. They seemed out of place in this wilderness of sand. They took on individual forms as they neared.

He didn't move.

He couldn't.

He lacked the strength even to hold his head up.

The first birds roosted in the branches around the oasis, but soon others settled on his legs and in his lap, crowding around him, their black bodies a bloated swarm. He could *feel* them – not just their nearness. He could feel their pulses: faint, ephemeral beats tripping out the erratic skips of fearful life. He reached down and took one of the birds from his lap, cradling it in his hands.

'It doesn't end here,' he promised the bird. The raven cawed raucously as though it understood. He smiled as he pressed down with his thumbs, splitting the bird's breastbone and pulling the creature open. He raised it to his lips and drank greedily. Draining it, he cast it aside and scooped up another.

He feasted on the ravens and crows, and countless other carrion creatures that had flocked to him.

It wasn't human blood – but it was blood.

It was revitalising.

It gave him strength.

And with the blood came memories of self – a name.

He tore into another and then another, sucking at the wounds. Ribbons of blood trickled down his chin. He tossed his head back and roared his defiance. It was a primal sound, animalistic. The birds cawed and crowed as panic spread through them. A few scattered, taking flight only to be brought down by others in a flurry of wings and violence. They flocked to him, drawn to the bittersweet tang of blood. It was in their nature. They were scavengers, carrion eaters.

He tore into the frail bodies, milking them. It was wanton gluttony. He ripped at the soft meat, splitting open the underbellies and gorging himself on the birds until hundreds became a few. He stopped himself from destroying them all. He took one in his hands, lifted it to his lips and opened his mouth – but instead of feeding, he whispered into the bird's ear. The creature answered with a shrill caw.

Around him the remaining birds echoed the raven in his hands, their caws spiralling into a hysterical chorus – a threat, a promise, the truth.

'Mannfred is coming! Mannfred is coming! Mannfred is coming! Mannfred is coming! Mannfred is coming! Mannfred is coming! Mannfred is coming!'

Their words reverberated through him.

'Mannfred is coming! Mannfred is coming! Mannfred is coming! Mannfred is coming! Mannfred is coming! Mannfred is coming! Mannfred is coming!'

They shrieked through every raven and carrion crow across the Old World.

Mannfred: that was his name.

But it was more than merely his name that had been returned to him. The birds' sacrifice had bought his salvation. He would not perish in the sand and the dirt. He would not be buried beneath the dunes in the Land of the Dead. He would escape. He gathered the bundle into his arms, cradling it close to his chest. The half-life the rag wrapped treasure possessed no longer felt threatening. He welcomed it.

The last of the dread vampire counts of Sylvania surged to his feet and scattered the few remaining birds to the four winds. Their caws rose hysterically as they burst into flight.

'Mannfred is coming! Mannfred is coming! Mannfred is coming! Mannfred is coming! Mannfred is coming! Mannfred is coming! Mannfred is coming!'

The birds would carry word to his most loyal followers. They would prepare for his return.

A lone rook circled above him, its cry a deep-throated rumble.

'Mannfred is coming!'

Mannfred smiled coldly, renewed by the blood of the birds flowing in his veins, and took the first step on the long walk home.

THE BLACK SHIP

I
Navigating the Reik

THE BLACK SHIP ghosted downriver, cutting silently through the heart of the Empire.

Those that knew ships marvelled at the lines of the three-masted barque. She was a spectre on the brackish water. She drew frightened eyes. How could she not? The barque was unlike any ship seen on the Reik in that she appeared to have no crew. The superstitious called the black ship a ghost and whispered that she was crewed by the revenant shades of sailors whose mortal remains had sunk to a watery grave. The ship herself, they breathed, refused to fail them. She would bring the dead home.

Those superstitious fools were almost right.

The Vampire Count stood alone on the deck, enjoying the twin moonlight of Morrslieb and Mannslieb. Ravens circled overhead. He was growing accustomed to the birds. He took a peculiar sort of comfort from their nearness. The black ship sailed on, deeper into the heart of civilisation. The signs of habitation grew more frequent: washed clothing hung out to dry, goats left to graze near the water's edge. At first the homesteads were little more than wooden shacks, but as the black ship sailed deeper into the heart of the old world the buildings grew more sophisticated, built of both wood and stone.

Coils of fog clung to the riverbank. Oil lanterns burned, barely penetrating the fug. Greasy black smears of smoke curled up lazily into the night.

The first chill of winter was in the air.

He savoured it. This was his time. He was the winter of mankind.

The riverbanks reeked of mortality, petty lives and petty squalors crushed together to offer the illusion of safety. Humanity echoed the rats of the bilge tanks, swarming all over each other, revelling in filth and decay, spreading disease.

He turned his back on it, content to let their unseeing eyes look on while the ghost ship sailed past their wretched strip of life as it clung to the riverbank.

He lifted the hatch set into the deck and descended into the belly of the black ship. The crew – for the ship wasn't manned by ghosts or anything quite so fanciful – avoided their peculiar passenger. He knew what they called him: *Allogenes*. In their tongue it meant, literally, 'the stranger'. He enjoyed the epithet. It was fitting. That was, after all, who and what he had always been.

He paused mid-step.

He heard something: grave dirt grinding under the boot of a crewman.

The dirt of unnamed graves had been scattered all across the lower decks. It went some small way to negating the vile pull of the sea on his body. He listened, seeking out the enticing *dub-dub* of the man's heartbeat and the blood flowing in his veins. It was a delicious tattoo. His nostrils flared. He could smell the fool. Living in these cramped confines left no room for hygiene. Every one of them stank, the stench made so much worse, more pungent, by their fear, and those smells were unique in their odour.

He waited for the man to show himself.

The crewman tried to back away into the shadows at his approach, but there was no hiding from Mannfred.

'Come to me, sailor,' he said, gesturing the frightened man forwards. The man's face, trapped in shadow, twisted, betraying the agony he felt trying to control his own limbs. The crewman stumbled forwards against his will and debased himself at the vampire's feet. 'Better. You would do well to remember your place, human.'

The storm lamp hanging from the wall by a rusty nail guttered and died.

'I am hungry.'

The sailor looked up, the veins in his neck protruding as he fought against the vampire's will. Mannfred sneered. Even token resistance was futile. He curled his index finger, beckoning the man to his feet, and tilted his head, lips parting slightly in anticipation of blood. Fear blanched the sailor's face. His entire body shivered violently. Mannfred enjoyed the delicious tang of terror that seeped into the man's stink. He drew him closer and opened his mouth wider, poised to sink his teeth into the soft white flesh of the sailor's throat, only to push him away with a careless wave of the hand.

He sniffed the air, breathing in all the rancid scents of the ship. The hold was alive with the rich heady tang of blood. He closed his eyes, enjoying the lure of the flesh.

'Bring me a body. Make it young, ripe. I don't care for old meat.'

The sailor nodded sickly and scrambled back, feet scuffing at the planking. He shook his head, 'Please don't make me choose.'

'Go before I change my mind and feed on you, man.'

The sailor looked up, eyes wide, black holes of shadow in his fear-blanched face, and scuttled off towards the deeper darkness of the hold.

The barque's timbers groaned as the black ship rode the tide, the hulk shifting and settling around them. Mannfred smiled. It was a cold, pleasureless expression. He waited until there was only the lulling, hypnotic rhythm of the river lapping up against the barque's sides before he retreated into the sanctity of his chamber to wait for his meal. He enjoyed pretending there was some kind of grandeur about the black ship. There wasn't. His chamber was nothing more than a belly hall, stripped bare of ornamentation. It would have been used in the past to store grain and other comestibles on long voyages. Now it housed a makeshift coffin. The bottom of the coffin had been lined with a fine sprinkling of grave dirt gathered from one of the many ports of call along the way. No doubt they regretted fishing him from the sea. Mannfred's nostrils flared as he breathed deeply. Traces of his homeland still clung to the dark loam, though they were barely perceptible beneath the rank odour of the hold.

Rats infested his quarters, fat, bloated, slick furred vermin.

There was a timid knock on the door.

'Come in.'

The door opened slowly. The crewman dragged a young girl in by the hair, pushing her to the floor at the vampire's feet. Her loose cotton shift was torn across the shoulder and down the front, the flesh beneath grey with grime. She hadn't just been plucked off the streets for his delectation, she'd been brought up from down below. The bruises from the chains were still livid, fresh. She'd never stopped fighting, hoping to be free. He wondered, idly, what fate the wretched girl thought lay in store for her. She couldn't possibly have imagined the truth when the sailors of the black ship had snatched her away from her home all those weeks or months ago. Her eyes fixed on the coffin. She opened her mouth to scream. Mannfred back-handed her hard, delivering a stinging blow across the mouth. His hand silenced her. He nodded approvingly.

'Good, good. My dear, it is so good of you to join me for dinner.' He turned to the sailor, mildly amused by the eagerness in the man's jaundiced eyes. 'You can leave us now, man, unless, of course you would prefer to stay, join in the feast?'

The girl whimpered, turning to plead with the sailor, to beg for her life. The sailor shook his head. Instinctively, his hand closed around Manann's talisman, a small black iron trident he wore at his throat. The old wives' tales amused Mannfred. The cattle were so sure that they understood his nature. They clutched their white roses, garlic cloves, Sigmarite hammers and other gewgaws meant to scare him off, took refuge in sunlight and hid behind other seedless superstitions, such as vampires not being able to cross fast-flowing water. They seemed to forget that his kind had minds and were capable of applying them. They were not so easily tied to their domains as they had once been – grave dirt could be moved, the sun could be resisted. It took strength, but he was strong. The notion that the dead must retreat to their coffins come sun-up was quaint but stupid. No such stricture bound him so long as he carried with him a handful of dirt from the site where he had been reborn into the world of the dead. And blood of course. He needed blood.

'Get out,' he told the sailor. The man didn't need to be told a third time. The door grated back into place. Mannfred circled the girl slowly, twice around. He knelt beside her, taking her chin in his hand, gripping it hard enough to make her wince as he forced her to look him in the eye.

'What is your name, girl?' He didn't need to know, didn't care. It was a gesture, a courtesy. She wouldn't thank him for it, but while she spoke it focused her mind, making it easier for him to impose his will on her. It was a simple conjurer's trick. She opened her mouth, and then shook her head as though her name had been there on the tip of her tongue only to escape her. He smiled. 'Don't be shy, my dear. In a moment we shall know each other quite intimately, I promise you.'

'Margarete.'

'Such a sweet name: are you a sweet girl, Margarete?'

'I... I...'

'I am sure you are, come here, let me taste you.' He laid a hand gently on her shoulder. He wanted to enjoy this moment, so he let his hold on her slip, allowing her to feel the agony of his touch as his fingers sank into her shoulder. She screamed and blood followed. Still he forced his fingers in deeper, to the bone. He hauled her up until her feet were three inches above the floor. Her dress, slick with blood across the shoulder and red down the back, fell open on her nakedness. He studied her for a moment, the rapid shallow rise and fall of her breasts, the sudden rash of goose bumps that prickled her otherwise flawless skin, the dark shadows around the curves of flesh.

'Exquisite,' he sighed. With his free hand Mannfred tipped her head back, baring the main artery in her neck, and sank his teeth into her throat. Her legs kicked twice and then dangled lifelessly, the fight sucked out of her. He drank deeply, greedily. Her blood dribbled down his chin as he dropped her corpse. He ran the back of his hand across his lips.

It wasn't enough.

It was never enough.

He turned his back on her, leaving the corpse for the rats. It didn't take them long to come scurrying out of the woodwork. They chittered and squeaked as they burrowed into her body, teeth tearing through her sodden shift to get at the feast. The sound of them eating provided an eerie counterpoint to the constant ebb and flow of the Reik against the barque's hull.

Mannfred lowered himself into the coffin, allowing himself a moment's respite, the calm before the coming storm, while the black ship sailed on, deeper into the heart of the Old World.

CHAPTER TWO

Bridge over the River Aver
The Plains of Stirland,
North of the River Aver

Even an idiot like Dietrich Jaeger had to be aware that the triangulation of land between Brandstadt, Eschendorf and Furtzhausen was strategically important for one reason and one reason alone: bricks and mortar. Not the scattering of houses that were home to the fishermen, farmers and ferrymen, but something else entirely.

Even an idiot...

Vorster Schlagener stopped thinking about it and counted out thirty steps, pushing through the thick grasses along the riverbank. He turned and counted out thirty more, returning to his mark.

It was a lonely duty for his last night. Vorster shook his head. He was calm. He had expected to be frightened, but he wasn't. He had had plenty of time to wonder why the fear wasn't more intense, more paralysing. The truth was black – fear came when the possibility of death neared. Vorster had long since faced up to the grim reality of his plight: come the morning he *would* die. It would take a miracle for the events of the coming day to play out any other way. That was why he wasn't afraid. He had accepted it. Good men sat huddled around the campfires. Their conversation was muted, their spirits low as they too came to terms with the stark reality of their situation.

They would be dead before sundown on the morrow.

And yet, none of them ran.

They sat, warming themselves by the flames, looking over the river at the curls of smoke rising up from the enemy's fires. There were so many fires littering the field. They were outnumbered almost ten to one judging by the campfires. Worse, Ackim Brandt led the Talabeclanders.

Brandt was everything Jaeger wasn't.

War might well have been a collective punishment, but the fate of a battle could still be tied to individuals.

Brandt was a soldier forged in battle, fiercely loyal to his command, blessed with a quick mind and a gift for strategy. He was able to read a battlefield and make split-second decisions capable of turning the tide of any given combat. He was a soldier's soldier.

Yet, the common soldiers like Vorster had to follow the whims of fops like Jaeger, because their families had enough money to buy their commissions. This kind of nepotism was all too common in the new armies. They called them organisations of opportunity, because with so many young men dying so senselessly there was always the chance of advancement for those lucky enough to survive a campaign or two.

Dietrich Jaeger was just one of many, no better or worse than the rest. He lacked the experience to carry out the task he was charged with and worried too much about his own reputation. That, alone, had proved enough to damn those under his command – like Vorster's younger brother, Isidor.

Vorster picked up a small stone and cast it out across the river. It fell short, splashing and disappearing. For a moment, he wished he could have been that stone; that the water could just close over his head...

He turned to look at the bridge.

There was a reason the dwarfs had chosen to build the only stone bridge on the Aver on this strip of land – outside of the cities of Averheim and Nuln – and join Stirland and Averland. It was pivotal to the defence of the entire region. This meant that it was pivotal to any attempted conquest of the region. It wasn't just the only stone bridge, it was the *only* bridge. There were ferries and punts dotted up and down the river, of course, but for an army the bridge at Legenfeld was the only way to cross the Aver in numbers and at speed. Lose the bridge and surely everything else would follow. That was the way of war – one defeat led to another, the enemy gaining momentum day by day, mile by mile of conquered ground, until their forces swept down like a giant wave, relentless and irresistible.

That was the nature of war – the strong came crashing down on the weak.

The fact that pretender had turned upon pretender and the Empire was being ripped apart from the inside out mattered nothing to any of those who would be emperor. With no great evil from the east to keep them occupied it hadn't taken humanity long before, like the great wyrm, it had coiled around to consume its own tail. Treachery and betrayal were the two great constants of mankind. Vorster had joked with his brother, Isidor, that, as a soldier he would never find himself without work – there was always someone to fight even if it was his own mother. Powerful men would always find a way to make normal folk like him die to settle their arguments.

Isidor had died three weeks later, gutted by a marlin pike on a faraway field. He had been running at a blackpowder cannon emplacement with eight other men, ordered to charge by an idiot of a man who was determined to sacrifice them to feed his own vanity. He wanted the cannon. He would have it, at any cost.

That idiot was Dietrich Jaeger.

Vorster hadn't forgiven the man for surviving when better men had fallen to sate his ego.

That, too, was the nature of war.

Idiots and cowards had a tendency to live.

Vorster turned his back on his comrades. He gazed along the river, first towards Nuln, though of course he couldn't see anything but water skaters and the occasional ripple where a vole or water snake slipped into the river, and then back towards Averheim.

The bridge was too wide to be properly defensible with so few men. When Brandt came they would be overwhelmed relatively quickly. Holding the line would be flat out impossible. It wouldn't take more than a handful of riders to cut through their ranks like a knife through rancid butter. With the defenders scattered, the cavalry would swing back and come at them from the behind, causing havoc. Then, and only then, the footmen would come surging in to finish the job. Pandemonium and death would reign. It would be brutal and it would be bloody.

But it would be over quickly.

That was the only mercy to be had from the coming day.

The senseless nature of Jaeger's orders betrayed the fact that the man didn't have so much as the faintest inkling what he was doing. He lacked confidence in his judgement, though he would never own up to it. He covered his doubts with bluster and arrogance. Even now, on the verge of battle, he set himself alone, aloof from the men under his command. He had left Vorster with one instruction: the bridge must be held at all costs.

That was it.

Exactly how the men were to achieve that miracle he didn't share with them. Jaeger made it sound so simple, where in truth that lack of confidence gnawed away at him, creating great holes of doubt. He was constantly second-guessing himself, trying to anticipate where the attack might come from. The man didn't have the common sense to listen to better men when they offered wisdom hard won on the battlefields of the Old World facing the Sylvanian vampires. It didn't matter to him that they were more experienced soldiers. Instead of listening he insisted on posturing and posing and pretending to be a strategic genius.

Well, Vorster thought bitterly, come the morrow that lie will be well and truly put paid to.

It all came down to this: a bridge. They couldn't afford to give the bridge up and they didn't have the strength of numbers to prevent it from being taken from them.

Vorster knew what the orders really meant: buy time and hold the bridge until the reinforcements from Brandstadt and Furtzhausen arrive. Failure would mean that Averland had a precious foothold in their homeland. One they wouldn't give up cheaply. If they failed, hundreds, perhaps even thousands, would die unnecessarily. That was the weight Vorster felt, not his own mortality but theirs, all the other nameless men, women and children of the soon to be dead.

The road to Wollestadt, a few miles to the south of Legenfeld, was a major trade route from the Black Fire Pass to Nuln. It came close to the river in a few places, but none closer than this. The territory on the border was the location of frequent skirmishes, advantage changing hands regularly. It wasn't so long ago that the forces from Stirland had been on the offensive, threatening Averland's trade roads. The trade roads were like arteries all across the Old World. Thanks to them, an army could plunge deep into the heart of Stirland, Talabecland and Middenheim, to Marienburg, Erengrad and as far north as Praag – as far as Pfeildorf, Grenzstadt and Meissen southwards – west to Delberz, Bögenhafen and Carroberg, and east across the Worlds Edge Mountains to places he could barely imagine beyond their strange sounding, exotic names. They were all joined.

For all that, the trade roads were the last place a reasonable man would have expected Averland's forces to attack from. Certainly they were a goal that Averland would strive to achieve if they wanted to push on to the north, consolidating their territorial gain. Jaeger argued passionately with his number two that that was the precise reason the road needed guarding. No man in his right mind would expect an attack from there, so that was where the enemy would strike first. He was prepared to stake his life on it, his life and more importantly, the lives of his men. They would, he reasoned, traverse the river upstream on one of the ferries and seek to work their way around behind his army; not the full force of course, just enough troops to guarantee success for the main body of the army.

It didn't matter for a moment that there was no legitimate reason for Dietrich Jaeger to divide his forces, which was precisely what he had decided to do.

No legitimate reason…

Dietrich Jaeger himself led the thirty riders patrolling the Wollestadt road. The man was a coward; that was the only thing Vorster could think.

He had deliberately placed himself as far away from danger as was humanly possible. It was, to all intents and purposes, desertion, only the idiot was too much of a coward to actually run away. Instead, he'd crawl back to the elector count with some cock and bull story of how he had done his very best, of how valiant he had been. Yet, it had broken his heart because it still wasn't enough. Good men died and they would forever stain his conscience. Jaeger was an inveterate liar, capable of spinning the most self-serving yarns and making them sound convincing. Vorster had heard a few, and even when he had known better, he had found himself *almost* wanting to believe Dietrich Jaeger… almost.

It was hard to feel anything other than loathing when the man's lies condemned ordinary decent soldiers.

A coward was a coward no matter how he chose to dress up his spinelessness. The irony in Stirland's banner, the skeleton wrapped in the proclamation 'Victory or Death', had never been more apparent to Vorster.

And so they were alone, a few good men left to hold the Legenfeld Bridge, come hell or high water.

Of course water was the least of Vorster's problems.

The bridge itself was majestic. Not some low span of stone, its span had a high parabolic camber, the elaborately carved arch tall enough to allow the brisk river traffic to pass easily beneath. It was a wonder: the intricacy of the carvings, the sheer magnitude of the construction and the agelessness of it. Vorster looked at the stones. They had been there before him and would be there long after he was gone. He was in no doubt about that. Vorster couldn't begin to imagine how old the bridge actually was. It was certainly more substantial than any of the houses in the vicinity. Vorster knew the lie of the land better than most of the defenders because he had been born and raised in the village of Furtzhausen, which stood only a few miles down the river from the bridge. He certainly knew it better than their erstwhile commander.

Vorster Schlagener scratched at his head where the chiggers had taken chunks out of his shaved scalp. It itched worse than a dose of the clap. The tiny red insects had had a field day, but only on him. No one else sported so much as a rash. As his old ma always used to say, they went for the bad meat first. He had already picked bloody six of the more livid bites along his forearm. The chiggers thrived in the combination of the heat and humidity, congregating in the tall grasses close to the water. It was typical, he thought bitterly, that Jaeger had chosen him to stand sentry on the riverbank. The man was spiteful. Vorster picked away at the bite behind his left ear, burrowing into the irritation with his grubby fingernails.

The fact that across the river Ackim Brandt and his men made their final preparations for his death while he worried about insect bites was mildly ironic.

There was nothing personal about it. It was war. Lives were reduced to acceptable losses and collateral damage. They stopped being human. The dehumanisation of the enemy was a sad necessity. To think of them in human terms, to give them names and faces and lives, well that way lay madness. Still, for all the hopelessness of his situation, Vorster promised himself, for his wife and his family, that Ackim Brandt would pay for the bridge. Vorster had no intention of dying cheaply. Women he had never met and had no argument with would wake up widows because of him. There was a simplistic eye-for-an-eye kind of justice to it. His wife would be a widow, his son, barely a summer old, would grow up never knowing his father. It wasn't fair and it wasn't a comfortable thought to live with, but then his life was measured out in minutes, so he could bear it for as long as he had to.

He took the top off a chigger bite, scratching so hard he drew blood.

'Damn it,' he muttered, bending down to tear off a handful of grass to staunch the blood. He caught something, a smell on the wind, and then a scurry and a splash as dirt and pebbles spilled back down into the river. He saw the fleeting shape of a shadow loom over him and threw himself to the left, hitting the ground hard.

Brandt's man, soaked from head to toe from the river, carried a wickedly curved dagger.

Vorster saw three more dark shapes emerging from the water: assassins.

He screamed as he hurled himself forwards. The assassin's blade sliced into his shirt, cutting into his left arm. Ignoring the pain, he rammed his own dagger into the man's throat. It was a brutally efficient kill. The assassin clutched at his neck, gargling blood as he tried to hold back the inevitable. Vorster didn't give the man a second thought – he was dead. The others weren't. He drew his sword and charged along the riverbank, yelling himself hoarse as he charged the nearest of the men coming out of the water.

He splashed into the river, slashing at the man's gut. His opponent hissed in pain and countered, a wicked backhand cut that took a chunk out of Vorster's cheek as he reeled away from the blow. He was bleeding but he didn't have time to worry about it. The ground beneath his feet shifted. He slipped. His ankle turned as the riverbed of stones betrayed him and dumped him on his backside. Moving silently, his opponent leaned in for the kill. A black rag covered the man's face. Vorster rolled away, scrabbling back through the long grass. The blade flashed down. He managed to deflect it with the side of his own blade. Before the assassin could finish him he jerked back, a black-fletched shaft protruding from his shoulder. That moment of pained surprise gave Vorster the chance he needed. He rammed his sword straight up between the assassin's legs and buried the blade deep in his gut. The dead man's weight tore the blade from Vorster's hands as he fell across him.

Vorster wriggled out from beneath the corpse in time to see two more assassins taken down by crossbow bolts. The metal tip of one bolt burst out through the back of the first assassin in a spray of arterial blood. The second bolt took its target in the cheek, piercing the man's mouth and burrowing deep into his brain. Both died silently.

Vorster pulled his sword out of the dead man. A horn sounded behind him. He knew what it signified – the oncoming storm. Brandt's main force was gathering. The assassins had been sent to weaken them, paving the way for a quick confrontation. Brandt, like any good leader, obviously hoped to minimise the losses among his men. Chance put paid to that.

A flaming arrow lit up the sky, blazing a trail like a comet.

It was obvious they weren't waiting for sunrise. A second arrow and a third arced high, lighting up the bridge. Dark shadows moved, the men of Averland, creeping up on the stoneworks. Swords danced in the moonlight. They came in a silent rush.

The men of Stirland met them head on in a clash of steel and blood. The first flush of the conflict was savage. Two men fell, three more spilled in through the gap they left. The defenders drove Brandt's men back with brutal efficiency, the first rank of spearmen holding their line against the dirt-smeared black clad warriors, while behind them five crossbowmen ratcheted volley after volley of bolts into the front ranks of their opponents.

It wasn't enough.

Vorster rushed to join his comrades on the bridge. They were outnumbered and it was only going to be a matter of time before they were overwhelmed.

Vorster was not a devout man but he prayed for a miracle. Without one, the battle for Legenfeld Bridge would almost certainly be over before dawn.

His cries were echoed by the defenders.

More flaming arrows lit the sky, streaking down far behind their lines. He saw the blue and red banner of Averland, snapping on a high pole, jostling in the midst of the oncoming tide of men, its once golden sun blanched of all colour by the moon.

Vorster breathed deeply, drawing on the calm centre of his being.

'It begins,' he muttered to himself.

The old soldier beside him hawked and spat a wad of yellow mucus and backhanded his mouth clean. 'Let's hope it ends, too. I'd hate it to go on forever.'

Three men came at him.

One took a crossbow bolt in the groin and fell before he had even taken four paces. He lay convulsing as the remaining two stepped over him.

'Well that evens it up,' the old soldier grinned. 'Let's see if we can't help these boys find their way to Morr, shall we?' The expression was horribly out of place, but if they were going to survive the day it was exactly the kind of black humour that would see them through.

He was a tempest of blind fury as he threw himself into the fight, crying: 'For Stirland! For liberty! For honour! For Martin!'

Vorster fought like a cornered beast, lashing out reflexively. His sword bit into flesh and bone. His injuries burned. He lost his sense of self. Around him steel clashed, people – friends – screamed and fell. The old man fought beside him, matching him blow for blow. He talked incessantly, urging Vorster on, yelling when it looked as though a blow might slip through his guard, cackling when one of their enemies fell. It was desperate, and yet Vorster was dislocated from it, cocooned in the anger he felt at Dietrich Jaeger's abandonment. A commander went down with his men. That was the way of it. He didn't run like a coward.

Time stretched out like molasses. The sun was high in the sky before he realised it had even risen.

The dead lay in pools of blood at his feet.

'What price victory?' he muttered bleakly, taking advantage of a lull in the fighting to catch his breath. As he looked up a blow cuffed him around the ear, staggering him back. He barely deflected a second, more ferocious attack, parrying the blade even as it lunged towards his heart. It was instinctive. Any level of thought between eye and hand would have been a death sentence. Where his enemy would have expected him to remain on the back foot Vorster twisted to the left and lunged forwards, impaling the surprised man. His mouth opened, closed, opened again, sucking air as Vorster wrenched his blade clear. The man's legs buckled and he fell to his knees.

Vorster stepped back and swung, bringing the blade around in a savage arc. It cleaved through the man's neck, severing his head. It hit the floor and rolled to his feet, eyes still wide with shock and fear. Vorster had heard stories from people who had been to beheadings – supposedly the severed head could still think and feel for up to a minute and a half. He looked down at the accusing eyes and kicked the head away. He didn't want to know what the dead man was thinking *after* he had killed him.

There was space around him for the first time in what felt like an age.

A horn sounded, blowing three times, sharply, recalling the attackers and offering Vorster and the others a moment's respite.

He looked around. Where there had been friends there were corpses. Forty-five men had guarded the bridge. He counted ten still standing. They had given a good account of themselves. Averheim had lost as many again and would lose more before the day was out.

But the bridge would fall. It was inevitable.

It seemed like an odd thing to die for: bricks and mortar. It wasn't heroic. It wasn't something to inspire a balladeer. No one would sing songs of their last stand. Now, had it been a woman, a great beauty, the daughter of a nobleman they had been fighting so desperately to save, that would have been different. But it wasn't a beauty. It wasn't anything of real value. It was a damned bridge in the middle of nowhere.

Bitterness clogged his throat.

He had never imagined his life would be traded for a bridge on the hinterlands between Stirland and Averheim.

It felt so utterly pointless, ludicrous really.

That, too, was the nature of war. There was no art or artifice to it. It was kill or be killed, die or die trying and all of those useless clichés. It was a senseless waste.

When the next charge came it would be the end.

'Why are they letting us rest?' It was one of the younger men, blooded for the first time.

'No need for 'em to rush it, lad. We ain't going nowhere and they know it. Ten of us against four hundred of them: it don't matter how narrow the bridge is, we ain't gonna hold 'em up for more than a few minutes, if we're lucky.'

The young soldier said nothing.

Vorster took pity on him. 'What say you and me stand at the front, eh? Meet them head on and make the bastards pay a hefty bleedin' toll to cross our bridge?' He smiled, but even as he did he knew he probably looked manic.

'I'll be right beside you,' the old soldier said, coming up to stand next to him. He spat on his palm and held it out for the younger man to shake. 'Last one to ten gets the beers in when we get back to Wurtbad, deal?'

'Deal,' Vorster agreed, spitting on his own palm and shaking. 'Anyone else want in on this, Elias is throwing his money away.'

'The old fool hasn't got two beans to rub together,' Klemens, a bear of a man, said, coming up behind them. 'I wouldn't trust him to buy the lad's beer. Reckon I better stick close to the boy to make sure Elias coughs up what he owes, come the end of the day.'

Vorster smiled. 'You keep one eye on him and I'll keep another on him. That ought to be enough.'

'You think? Last time Elias promised to get a round in, Sigmar was wet behind the ears.'

'Knowing my bloody luck the old git will get himself killed right as he's about to dip his hand into his pocket,' Ueli said, joining them.

'I'm surprised he's wearing trousers with pockets!' Klemens grunted, laughing at his own joke.

The moment passed quickly. They all knew what this was: the calm before the storm.

The horn would sound again and…

Vorster saw him first – a lone rider under the white flag of truce. The horseman rode into the centre of the great stone bridge and reigned in his mount, waiting.

'Who speaks for you?' the rider called. Vorster knew the man immediately. It was Ackim Brandt himself. He was tempted to order the commander's execution. It would have been an easy thing to do, but he refused to lower himself to that.

'I do,' Vorster said. Klemens nodded, as did Ueli.

He walked out to meet the rider halfway across the bridge.

Brandt dismounted. He teased off his metal gauntlet and offered Vorster his hand. Vorster hesitated a moment before he took it, expecting treachery. It took him a second to remember that Ackim Brandt was not Dietrich Jaeger.

'You have fought well today,' Brandt said.

'For all the good it has done us.'

'By my count enough people have died here today to satisfy Morr for a month. Now I would bury my dead.'

'It would take you a quarter of an hour, less, to finish us off. There are ten of us to your hundreds.'

'Will you lay down your swords? I am a civilised man. You will be given a head start to return to your loved ones.'

Vorster shook his head. 'As much as I am tempted, no; we are all men here and we know what we face. When it comes down to it, we face it with pride. Despite your numbers, you have yet to cross our bridge. We are the reason for that.'

'Indeed you are, soldier. Indeed you are. You have done yourselves proud here. There is honour in that. I have to admit I admire your tenacity. In different circumstances I would have been proud to fight at your side. As it is we find ourselves on different sides of this battle, but that does not mean we have to be barbarians. If you will not surrender, consider this: with your permission, I would collect our dead. In return, I offer you and your men one more night of life in honour of your stand here. You will not be forgotten, soldier. On your word we will stand down 'til dawn.'

'And we live to fight another day.'

'It is a fair offer. As you say, the dead aren't going anywhere. I could easily have you put out of your misery. Instead, one more night with friends, one more sunrise. You deserve that.'

'Another night of dread expectancy? Another night of gnawing fear?'

'One more night to listen to the beauty of the world, to feel cold water on your face, to wake up to bird song,' Brandt countered.

'Another night to make peace with Morr?'

'Indeed, but who couldn't use another night?'

Vorster looked back at his rag-tag group of survivors. How could he deny them one more night of life? He looked at Elias, standing with his arm around the youngster, Zechariah. 'Until sunrise?'

'You have my word.'

'Thank you, commander,' Vorster said.

'Are you sure you won't reconsider surrender? You seem like a good man, I would hate to kill you for nothing.'

Vorster smiled, an echo of Elias's black humour sneaking into his voice as he said, 'Well, just between us, Brandt, I hate to die, but it won't be for nothing. I will promise you that. Victory or death,' he said, nodding back towards the Stirland standard, the flag rippling lazily in the slow breeze.

The Averlander nodded, understanding. 'What is your name, man?'

'Vorster Schlagener.'

'Well, Vorster,' Brandt said, 'fare thee well, soldier. I will say a prayer for you tonight. Let Morr know that you are a good man, and that you and your friends deserve honour in death. May Sigmar have mercy on your soul.'

A flurry of black wings caught Vorster's eye. Three ravens had settled on the stone abutment behind Brandt. It was not unusual, considering the blood spilled already. What was unusual was that these three were the only carrion eaters that had begun to gather.

'And on yours, Brandt. The birds are gathering. Best have your men recover the fallen before they decide to feast.'

The Averlander nodded, spurred his mount around, and cantered away, back towards his waiting army, leaving Vorster alone on the bridge.

He walked back to the others.

'Well, what did he want?' Klemens called before he was even halfway.

'He wants to gather their dead, and in return offered us respite.'

'Taal's teeth!' Elias exclaimed.

'Don't get too excited old man; it's only one more night.'

'Aye, but that might be all we need.'

Vorster had tried not to think about it when Ackim Brandt had made the offer, but Elias was right. One more night could be exactly what they needed for salvation. Reinforcements were on the way from Brandstadt and Furtzhausen.

'Zechariah, I have a job for you. I want you to run like the wind, find Jaeger on the Wollestadt road and get him back here before sunrise. Our lives depend on it lad.'

The young soldier nodded earnestly, not understanding that Vorster was sending him away so that he might live. 'I'll bring him back, sir.'

'No need to call me sir, lad. Now go.'

Zechariah turned and ran, sprinting away towards the trees.

'That was a good thing you just did,' Elias said, resting his hand on Vorster's shoulder.

'Let's hope it helps us.'

'You know that's not what I meant, Vorster.'

'I know,' he shrugged. 'He's just a boy. I couldn't very well damn him.'

'No,' Klemens agreed, 'but you were quite capable of damning the rest of us, eh?' The big man chuckled to show there was no malice in his words.

'Oh, we were damned a long time ago, my friend,' Vorster said, picking away at one of the chigger bites on his arm.

THE BONFIRES BURNED on both sides of the river for the best part of the night. Five huge fires lit up the sky turning night into day. The stink of burning flesh filled the air.

Vorster knelt as close to the flames as the heat would allow. The fire stung his eyes, but it gave him an excuse for the tears of grief he shed. Body by body, they threw old friends onto the fire.

It was hard, harder than dying.

That too was the nature of war, being left behind to mourn.

He didn't hear them at first, because of the snap and crackle of the fire. Klemens came up behind him, clapping his hands vigorously. He looked up from the bodies still lined up, waiting to burn.

Riders.

Five of them.

They had obviously ridden hard. Their mounts looked dead on their feet and the men didn't look much better.

'What's going on?'

'If I was a religious man, I'd say a miracle,' Klemens said, grinning. His grin was infectious. 'They're outriders. Martin's army is less than five hours away.'

'Five hours is after dawn, my friend. Still plenty of time for us to die.'

'Oh it gets better,' Klemens said, obviously enjoying himself. 'They encountered Jaeger prancing around on the road. Let's just say they... ahem... *convinced* him to return. They've made camp just beyond the tree line. No campfires, no noise, but believe me, they're there, waiting. When Brandt comes to take on us few he is going to be in for a hell of a surprise when Jaeger's cavalry come crashing down on his head. While they are still reeling from that, Martin's army is going to stride onto the battlefield. Two thousand men, Vorster. Talk about a morale breaker. I'd love to see Brandt's face when it happens. We did it, my friend, we held the bridge.'

Vorster wanted to smile but couldn't because he was all too aware of the cost of the miracle: the bodies at his feet and those being charred to ash in the fire.

He felt hollow.

That too was the nature of war.

THE BLACK SHIP

II
Navigating the Reik

THEY SAID THAT to see the black ship was to foretell your own death, such was the thrill of fear the barque sparked among the living.

They said it was an omen.

They pointed at the carrion birds following in its wake and muttered oaths and curses as readily as they uttered prayers and begged boons.

No one could deny that death followed the black ship.

In Marienburg three merchants in gaudy silks were left to rend their garments and weep like babes on the waterfront as their women walked willingly onto the black ship, mesmerised by the tall, gaunt figure of Mannfred, on the prow, wind streaming through his long luxurious locks as he beckoned them forwards. Their husbands tried to stop them of course. Their deaths were unpleasant.

He did not consume the women at once. They were taken down to the cages in the hold, to be brought up when the hunger was at its height. Their screams as they were forced below decks sent a thrill of pleasure coursing through the Vampire Count. There was nothing like fear. It was intoxicating.

In Altdorf, under the noses of the holy men, Mannfred disembarked to hunt.

The Shade of Death still hung from the towers around the city wall. He remembered when the citizens of the capital had adopted the mocking banner and the rage it had inspired in his sire. Vlad had not taken resistance well. Neither, it seemed, had the city. Much had changed since Mannfred had last walked her cobbled streets, little of it for the better. There was an air of poverty and desperation about the city. Even the great spires seemed somehow less than they had been before Vlad's reign.

A fool tried to extract a pfennig toll from him to cross a narrow footbridge. Mannfred rummaged in his pocket and pulled out something that flashed silver. The fool leaned in closer, to see better, and wound up clutching the slick ropes of his intestines in his hands as he toppled sideways into the Reik. Mannfred crossed the bridge, moving to one of the older parts of the city. Crossing the river he noticed the shift in smell. The dock side of the city reeked of rotten fish and the sewers where they washed out into the river, whereas this side of the bridge had a more distinct odour, or odours – the mix of sweat and vomit from drunken sailors trying to make their way back to their berths was overlapped by the rich leather tang of the tanneries. There was a marked contrast between the buildings as well. The architecture this side of the river was eclectic to say the least. Adjacent buildings mimicked exotic building styles, Tilean columns supported Kislevite domes. They were tall, at least four storeys, the upper levels hanging out over the streets, throwing the alleyways and streets below into deep shadow. They made it easy for Mannfred to move through the capital. He drew his cloak up over his head, fusing with the darkness and becoming, like the black ship, a ghost.

As with the barque, to catch a glimpse of his black shape was to foretell one's own demise.

He tilted his head slightly to the side, catching the faint whiff of humanity on the wind. He listened, pressed up against the wall, blending almost perfectly into the shadows: voices. They came grubbing down the curb, five children ranging from five years up to a more worldly teenage girl. They were emaciated, slack skin draped over sharp bones. He thought they would pass him by until the girl froze mid-step and turned to look directly at him, as though she knew full well what kind of monster he was.

'Please mister, can you spare us a coin or two? We're starving.' He had no doubt she was telling the truth. She came towards him, holding out a hand thick with a cake of grime.

Mannfred didn't move. He breathed deeply. It was her time; he could smell the blood on her. 'Yes,' he breathed. 'Yes, yes, yes.'

Her face lit up. 'Megan, you look after your brothers for a few minutes. I'll catch up with you by the stage door of Zeigmuller's theatre. We'll eat well tonight, I promise.'

She planted a kiss on her younger sister's forehead and skipped – almost running in her eagerness – across the street to him.

Mannfred opened his arms and folded her into an embrace.

She didn't resist.

Instead she gave herself to him, bringing her hands up to trace the line of his ribs and breathing into his ear: 'Take me somewhere nice mister, two new pennies and you can do whatever you want, but not here, please.'

His smile widened. 'Oh, I don't need to *pay* you, my dear.'

He touched a finger to her ear, craning her neck to the side with the slightest pressure from a nail.

'Please,' she breathed, looking into his hungry eyes. 'You promised.'

'I don't think I did.'

He leaned in, teeth and tongue touching her porcelain flesh. He breathed deeply, letting the breath leak out slowly over her skin. She sighed. It didn't bother him in the slightest that she was faking pleasure at his nearness. He bit. Not hard enough to pierce the skin, but enough to cause her breath to catch in her throat. His hand pressed hard against the small of her back, drawing her to him. He bit a slow teasing path up to her ear. 'Follow me,' he breathed, pulling away.

He knew she would, and not just for want of the coins.

He led her through the narrower streets on to Templestrasse, towards a richer district, letting her think he was some local merchant wandered too far from home. He paused outside the Vargr Breughel Memorial Playhouse, smiling at the artist's rendition of the haunting thespian currently performing the female lead in *Genevieve & Vukotich*. Before them the rooftops of Altdorf rose in tiers, seven and eight high, towards the richest homes of the city, the walled estates of the gentiles. 'Not far now,' he promised. Her hand slipped into his. It was a cruel parody of some lover's intimacy.

He led her towards the gates of Salzbrunnen Park, and through into the confusion of the trees and shrubberies run wild. He paused under the dark shadow of a weeping willow, the long trailing leaves casting daggers against the moonlight. He drew her close. He felt her heart beating hard against his chest. It was... seductive.

'Give yourself to me, dear. It hurts less that way,' he promised.

She touched his face.

Her breathing was shallow, fast, urgent.

'Two pfennigs, mister.'

He smiled indulgently at her. 'Yes, of course.' he took two silver coins and pressed them into her palm. 'There, my dear, happy now?'

She looked down at the coins. She had been expecting brass pennies, not silver coins. Her hand closed quickly around them and secreted them away inside the folds of her frock before he could change his mind and take them back.

'Come to me.'

She hiked up her skirts around her thighs and pressed herself up against Mannfred.

This time he bit her hard, sinking his teeth deep into her sweat-salted skin and sucking greedily at her lifeblood as it pulsed down his throat. She shuddered in his arms but he didn't let her fall, even as the strength drained out of her limbs. He drank, emptying her. Her blood invigorated him. A low sigh escaped her ruined throat, like the wet collapse of a blacksmith's bellows. It dwindled into a blood-clogged gargle and then nothing as the last breath left her. She died in his arms, feeding him.

He lay the girl down tenderly beneath the willow, rummaging within the folds of her frock to find the two silver coins he had given her. He straightened her dress and closed her eyes. It looked for all the world as though a pretty little maid had fallen asleep beneath the tree, until he knelt and placed a silver coin on each eye. Then it looked as though a pretty little maid had died beneath the sad tree.

He left her, knowing there were four more unsuspecting souls waiting for him outside the stage door of Zeigmuller's theatre.

He would feed well as the black ship continued its ghostly passage on to Nuln and beyond.

CHAPTER THREE

Schönheit und das Tier
Nuln, Imperial City on the Reik

JON SKELLAN WAS at play.

The city was his for the taking.

He had shaken off the disguise of a cripple that he had worn in his final days with Konrad, and had come some small way towards recapturing his strength – at least in part. The disguise had served him well, both on the battlefield, and later in retreat, but it felt good to be *powerful* once more.

His face still bore the disfigurements of Jerek's beating. The lacerations around his cheek and eye-socket were still livid. He wore a black leather patch over his ruined right eye, enjoying the look of sinister menace it afforded him as he prowled. He knew he would heal even more, given time, though time was something he felt he had precious little of. It was a curious dichotomy for an immortal, to have all the time in the world and yet to be pressed by such urgency. He could feel it, the oncoming storm, as though the pressures in the air changed to accommodate the coming of Mannfred von Carstein. He had become curiously aware of it since Grim Moor. At first he had put it down to the regeneration his body was undergoing, but it wasn't that. It was true his kind had phenomenal regenerative powers. The scars around his cheek had already hardened and begun the process of re-knitting. The eye itself would take longer, though he was unsure he would ever regain sight in it; but it wasn't that. It was something else: a prescience, his hyper acute senses sparking off at some unseen threat, an awareness, a feeling deep down in his craw. He couldn't explain it.

He stalked the fog-bound streets of Nuln, slaking his thirst for blood on the ample supply of prostitutes and vagrants in the Alt Stadt district. The place was wretched, hidden away behind a high wall, out of sight and mind from the rest of the wealthy city. Skellan enjoyed the anonymity the place offered. Only the sick, the cast out and the homeless resided in the Alt Stadt, and it was a place where the Watch feared to tread, making it the perfect haunt for him to take refuge in while his wounds healed. The food was plentiful, if emaciated and diseased. He hungered for the vitality of youth, a fresh-faced girl in the throes of puberty or a boy in his teens, bursting with hormones and untapped strength, instead of the varicose veined whores and the slack-jowled tramps.

The pure white walls of the great Temple of Shallya seemed to mock the grimy desperation of the city. It stood; pure, commanding, a thing of beauty surrounded by decay and hardship. It was a beacon of hope. Skellan lurked in a recessed doorway across the street from the temple doors, watching the anonymous guards in their rags change shifts. Despite what he hoped, the Sisters of the Dove were not alone. A shame, Skellan mused, as he had a hankering for a fresh, healthy, woman; one that would put up a fight, kick and scream a bit, and make a game of it.

The area around the temple was a maze of shanties. They were hovels. There was no other word for them. He had seen poverty before, but these hastily erected slums went so much beyond poor housing; they were lawless holes where hope was beaten out by desperation and hunger was king. Life was cheap. It was nothing to find a corpse slumped in a gutter, come dawn, beaten to death or having simply given up fighting for life against the adversities of the city.

It was the perfect place for him.

He had spent a month in Nuln, never once venturing out of the Alt Stadt.

For a while, when he had first arrived he had feared discovery. He had clung to the dark spaces, skulked like some rat, picking through the gutter for scraps. That had all changed when he had found the stairwells. They were dotted throughout the Alt Stadt: crooked stairways, narrow twisting flights of cracked and broken stones leading down far below the surface. They clung to the sides of the shanties, existing in the tight crevices between crumbling walls. At first he wasn't sure exactly what he had found, but curiosity led him deeper.

Some of the stairs went far below the street level – one hundred, two hundred feet, leading to layer upon layer of tunnels and dark passages linked and woven one on top of the other in a honeycomb of possibilities. The longest of the tunnels meandered indefinitely, curling up towards the surface and the river. It ended in a tight metal staircase that came out in what looked to be a natural cavity in the side of the Reik, forming a wide stone quay far out of sight of the City Watch. The weed-choked opening was, no doubt, favoured by river pirates and smugglers. Skellan used it several times for mischief-making on nocturnal missions. The secret passages became a second home to him.

They called this *Unterbaunch* – underbelly – of the city the *Zufluchtsort*, a sanctuary, and that was exactly what it was for Jon Skellan. He had crawled down those stairs, the blood of Grim Moor still fresh on his hands, a wretched, contorted half-man, and had dragged himself into a corner amid the dregs of society. Down there he was anonymous, left alone like any other leper, to lick his wounds and fester – only Skellan was healing, getting stronger.

The severity of his wounds was such that it would be a long slow process, and it would *hurt*.

He dragged himself beneath the crypts of an abandoned temple, taking refuge in what had once been the grave dirt of the quarter. It offered some small respite, but even here the pain was unbearable. He would cry out, sleeping only fitfully, his dreams tortured by memories he thought long gone – abandoned along with his mortality. He found the ghost of Lizbet's face returning in the delirium tremens that plagued him. At first his anger ripped through her smile, tearing away to the ephemeral nothing that was the substance of dream, but later, as he succumbed to the tortuous healing process of his kind, Skellan welcomed thoughts of her. They were so much better than the other thoughts he tortured himself with.

When at last he was strong enough to emerge he succumbed to a feeding frenzy. Six women in as many hours found their way into his arms and then fell away into the gutter.

The worst of the Alt Stadt was hidden below the ground, the thieves highways or rather lowways, offering access to the richer areas of Nuln: the Meer district, Gerechtstadt and the Justice Palace with its warren of scribes and petty bureaucrats at work, the Sonder district with its nautical trade, and of course, the Unterhaltungsstadt, the entertainment district with its bordellos and a constant supply of ale from the tap houses along the Drog Strasse.

He turned his back on the temple.

It was time to venture deeper into the city, somewhere his hungers could be sated, while others sought to sate their own: Drog Strasse.

* * *

THE UNTERHALTUNGSSTADT WAS an exercise in overindulgence. It reeked of oversweet perfumes used to mask the sour stench of humanity. Scratch beneath the surface, Skellan thought, and you'd be able to see the worms.

Two women of the night stood side-by-side at the mouth of the street, cheeks rouged and temples powdered white. They were squeezed into their bustiers, laces drawn so tightly the ripples of fat spilled over them. The doxies called him over, but then stopped, mid-beckon, sensing something wrong with him. They backed up physically, pressing themselves into the dark shadows of a recessed doorway, praying fervently that their would-be mark would pass them by.

Skellan savoured their fear.

It didn't matter that they had no idea who or what he was – their most primal urges drove them to hide from him. That was power unlike anything he had tasted in life. It was intoxicating.

Oil lamps flickered as he passed them by, their blue flames guttering. Black horse-drawn carriages rolled down the cobbles of Drog Strasse, their drivers cracking the whip to spur them on. A gaggle of voices laughed, enjoying some private joke as the press of theatregoers came streaming out of the Herrscahft Theatre's side doors. Skellan stopped fifty feet away, stepping back into the door of a red-velvet bordello. He felt a hand on his shoulder, the gentle touch of fine delicate fingers, and snarled. He didn't turn to see the effect it had on the woman. The hand withdrew, that was enough.

Two figures emerged from the theatre.

The man was obviously a fop, worried only about surrounding himself with pretty things. Every gesture and movement was effeminate. His powdered face made him look like a porcelain figurine, something a child could easily break.

Now the woman, she was *mesmerising*.

She had vitality.

She radiated raw sensuality.

She was, Skellan reflected, numinous.

Even from fifty feet away Skellan felt the pull of her presence, and the awe she inspired in passers-by as they moved in and out of her orbit.

She was almost certainly a courtesan, the fop's paid companion for the evening.

Skellan watched, reminded strangely of Vlad von Carstein's brooding charisma. Hers was different. Von Carstein's draw was darker, more nihilistic in nature. The woman was dark, certainly; her hair was a curling cascade of black that spilled halfway down her back. Moonlight froze within the pearls braided into her lush curls, each one no doubt worth a pretender's ransom, but her darkness was physical, not spiritual. For all of von Carstein's brooding intensity she offered the kind of frission that caused grown men to act like slobbering idiots around her, and she was well aware of her power. In that way the courtesan and the vampire were not so different after all.

Skellan studied her as she moved; it was almost luxurious. Where men of steel prided themselves on economy of movement and effort, this she-devil was extravagant with her gestures. She loved the world around her and lavished it with her attention. There were no half-measures, no incomplete or distracted shrugs. She was a lady of committed passions, passionately committed. He envied her that. He envied her a life outside of the gutters and the shadows.

She passed him in a hush of linen and silks. The cloths rubbed against one another to conjure a sussurant river of sound. She had one hand in the fop's. The other held a delicate peacock feather fan that was little more than an artifice. It was useless for cooling her face. The white ruff of her collar gathered around her throat. Her delicate skin was pearlescent in the lamp light, but it was her eyes – strangely knowing in a face so young – that snared him.

He stepped out in front of them, causing the fop to start. The she-devil didn't miss a beat. She lowered her eyes coyly and smiled.

'Sigmar's hairy backside! You scared half the life out of me,' the fop exclaimed. It was such a ridiculous thing to say that Skellan couldn't help but chuckle. No doubt the Man-God did have a few hairs back in his day, but it wasn't an epithet he would have been proud of. It certainly wasn't an all-conquering appellative. 'Are you mocking me, sir?' Then he stopped, seeing Skellan's wounds in the lambent glow of the oil lamp.

Skellan touched his scars, his fingers finding the leather eye patch. 'Ah, this...' he said. 'Got it at Grim Moor,' he dropped his voice to a conspiratorial whisper, 'fighting a vampire.'

His words had the desired effect on the effeminate young man. He backed away a step, his lack of gallantry putting the woman between him and Skellan. Skellan took the opportunity to move in close to the woman. She didn't shy away from him, which intrigued the vampire. On the contrary, she withdrew her hand from her companion's and offered it to Skellan. He took it and kneeling, raised it to his lips. 'Guten abend.'

'Good evening,' she said, smiling slightly at the sight of the scarred, one-eyed man on his bended knee playing the chevalier.

'Das einzige Schöne ist eine bezaubernde Frau,' Skellan said, smoothly. *The only beauty is an enchanting woman.*

'And who are you, flatterer?'

'Skellan, Jon Skellan.'

'Well Jon Skellan, you are quite the charmed one, fighting vampires and living to tell the tale.'

'I like to think of myself as the hero of my own life story,' Skellan said.

'What is this fool blathering on about?' The fop virtually hissed, recovering his courage and trying to push between them.

Skellan ignored him. 'And you are?'

'Narcisa da Vries. My rude companion is Niculai Gaspard. He is, as I am sure you know, an actor of no small repute.'

'Currently treading the boards in Vitas Mortis, a piece I penned myself,' he said with such utter disdain for the other man that Skellan couldn't help but smile. The man was a blowhard *and* a hack.

'Indeed,' Skellan said, never breaking eye contact with Narcisa. 'I shall have to drag myself out of the slums more often if it means I get to rub shoulders with the beautiful and the famous.'

'You should,' she said.

Skellan's smile broadened as her fingers moved, apparently of their own accord, to touch the vein at her throat.

'May the night be kind to you, flatterer.' It was her eyes, Skellan thought again. They were so much older than her face. Narcisa da Vries fascinated him – well fascinated him as much as any prospective meal ever had.

'And to you both. What was your play again, Gaspard? Schönheit und das Tier?' Skellan smirked and walked away before the fop could get his dander up sufficiently to actually say something back to him.

THIRTY FEET DOWN the cobbled street Skellan turned to see Narcisa da Vries looking back over her shoulder directly at him. He couldn't see her expression, but her body language was invitation aplenty.

She knew exactly what he was, and she welcomed it.

He had always imagined there would be those who craved what his kind had to offer – those who hungered for the immortality of the blood kiss. He could not deny that she was enchanting, but that made her more dangerous than any plain beauty. Even as a mortal her numina blazed. What would come of her should she be born again into the unlife? He breathed deeply, trying to recall her scent. Dare he turn her into Schönetod? La Bella Morte? The Beautiful Death? Dare he not? She was mesmerising, he thought again, and yes, he knew he wanted her. He was sick of all the rancid meat, the washed out wretched corpses of the homeless, the starving and the diseased. She was fresh. Vitas Mortis indeed: vitality and death. She promised far more than any dried-up matron from the Sisterhood of the Dove. He licked at the air, wetting his lips. Yes, perhaps he would sire her, perhaps. She would be a trophy, of that there was no doubt.

Schönetod: The Beautiful Death.

With that delicious thought firmly in mind, he followed them.

Narcisa walked slowly, lingering over inviting shop windows where the merchants had displayed their wares, pointing and laughing. Skellan imagined her talking in sweet whispers to her beau. In every way, the fop, Gaspard, seemed to fill her up. Skellan moved behind them, never allowing them out of his sight. To anyone else they probably looked like perfect lovers as they moved arm in arm down the cobbled streets. Skellan's face twisted bitterly. He would feed, he promised himself. Let those same people who smiled and nodded now be the ones that found their corpses in the river come sunrise. The actor and the courtesan, bled dry and bloated by the Reik. Let them cling to their dead smiles then. Let their ghosts talk in sweet whispers until the end of time.

By the river, she tossed her head back and laughed. Her laughter's melodic thrill, like a bird speaking in a language only he understood, reached Skellan. The laughter wasn't for the fop. It was for him. She wanted him to understand how superior to Gaspard she truly was.

He followed the pair from district to district all the way back to their lodging rooms across from the statue of a long-dead noble with a chipped and weathered profile. He settled himself down on the statue's plinth and waited, watching the windows to see which, if any, lit up on their homecoming. There was a bakery near by. The air was filled with the rich scent of freshly baked bread and the more delicate aromas of pastries, cinnamon and chocolate.

He didn't have to wait long before he saw Narcisa, backlit in a sheer linen gown, laces undone on her ample curves. He stared at her in the window on the fourth storey. She knew he was down there, watching. She wanted him to see. It didn't matter that it was a fleeting glimpse. It was enough. He knew what he had to do. Skellan rose to his feet. Heavy vines of ivy, interwoven with clematis crept up the wall to her wrought-iron balcony. He tested them, pulling hard to see how deep their roots had burrowed into the brick wall. Satisfied, he climbed.

Skellan rose, hand over hand.

The stone was coarse beneath his fingers.

Midway up the mortar crumbled and a handful of clematis came away from the ivy with a sickening tear, leaving him dangling precariously over the city street. He hung there for a second, expecting more of the plant to wrench free under the force of his sudden drop. Tendrils of greenery and flowers wrapped themselves around him, the syrupy fragrance of the clematis overpowering. He kicked at the wall, scrabbling around for a toehold to support his weight before gravity undid whatever was holding the last of the clematis to the ivy in the wall. The toe of his shoe scraped over the stone, sticking on the slimmest edge, but it was enough. He shifted his weight and leaned back slightly, looking for a handhold above him. There weren't any. He dragged his fingers down the stone, searching out a weakness. The mortar, undermined where the ivy had rooted, crumbled. It was enough. He forced his fingers into the crack and hauled himself up another foot. He took his time, scaling the wall foot by foot, making handholds where there were none.

Skellan reached out and grabbed the black iron balcony railing and pushed himself away from the wall, hauling himself up onto the balcony. He hunkered down beside a planter overflowing with a riot of night-blooming jasmine and pressed his face up against the window.

The room beyond was opulent: regency stripe on the walls broken up by cameos and oils. An extravagant golden fire dragon had been woven into the huge rug; the workmanship was, even from afar, exquisite. The carpet had almost certainly been imported from some far eastern land at no little expense. A huge four-poster bed dominated the room. Veils of lace were cinched to the elaborately carved posts. Storm lanterns bathed the room in a lush, warm glow. A seven-tier crystal chandelier hung from the ceiling, each of the tiny perfect facets of glass catching the light and scattering it across the enormous bedroom in a kaleidoscope of colour.

And yet Skellan barely registered the finery, because Narcisa lay naked on the bed, more lush and opulent than any mere trinket or tapestry.

The fop lay beside her, his hair matted with sweat, his prissy shirt and waistcoat cast aside in his ardour. Skellan touched the glass. She reached up for Niculai Gaspard, but at the last moment, as she drew him down onto her, her eyes shifted and her smile widened as she met Skellan's gaze. Her face distorted as though a veil passed across it, the hunger rising as her nails dug bloody runnels into the actor's back. She raised her fingers to her lips, one by one licking them clean.

A shiver of delight traced down Skellan's spine as she tangled her hand in the fop's bedraggled locks and drew his head down until his lips brushed her collarbone as though it were the most sacred inch of skin on her body, worshipping her inch by perfect inch.

Then she bit him.

She came up bloody, her teeth ruby. She wiped the back of her hand across her face, smearing the blood across her cheek in the parody of a smile. The beast finally found its way out through her face; her cheeks narrowed, jaw distended, brow planed, as every contour of her grew harsher, more defined, and yet still held to that core of physical beauty. It was not a full transmogrification; she did not fully become the beast in the way that Skellan did when he loosed the animal inside him. She maintained the illusion of humanity even as she fed on the cattle, but she was a kindred beast, of that he was certain. He met her gaze, saw the predatory cunning there and rejoiced in it. Then she lowered her head again, feeding.

It was different though, controlled. She wasn't draining the life out of her lover; she was decanting him, like a fine brandy, just a mouthful of blood and then breaking the contact. Her discipline was extraordinary.

The fop rolled over in her arms, languid in the afterglow of their coupling.

Skellan moved away from the window, spilling the jasmine planter. The sudden flurry of noise betrayed him. He scrambled around, trying to prevent the clay pot from shattering on the balcony floor. It slipped through his fingers and hit the floor hard, shattering. Skellan winced. He pushed himself to his feet and was half way over the railing when, still bleeding, Niculai Gaspard threw open the glass double doors and stood, naked, on the threshold. Gaspard levelled the percussion pistol in his right hand at the centre of Skellan's forehead.

'I know you, sir. Don't think I don't. With a face like that how could I not? Now I suggest you stay right where you are,' Gaspard said, thumbing back the black iron hammer until it *snicked* into place. 'Believe me when I say I won't hesitate in pulling the trigger.'

Skellan didn't move, didn't take his good eye from the black bore of the pistol.

Narcisa da Vries moved in close behind her lover, one arm sliding around his waist. Her fingers traced the lines of his ribs as they caressed his skin.

'My, my, I do believe it is Herr Skellan from Drog Strasse. How peculiar,' the woman said, obviously enjoying the moment. 'One might wonder what you are doing on my balcony in the dead of night.'

'Up to no good, surely,' Gaspard rasped. The pistol wavered in his hand. His free hand covered his genitals. The man had remembered his nakedness and was uncomfortable, and not surprisingly. His nudity left him psychologically vulnerable despite the weapon in his hand. 'No better than a common peeping tom. I should shoot you on the spot, villain; put you out of your misery.'

'And out of my bedroom,' Narcisa said.

Skellan waited, knowing there would be no sudden sunburst of agony in his skull from the shot tearing into him. Gaspard was a windbag. He wasn't man enough to pull the trigger. No, he would pump himself up and preen and bluster but he wouldn't bring an end to it. Few could. It took a special kind of man to kill. Knowing this gave Skellan the upper hand, despite the bizarre nature of the situation. Of course, there was always the possibility that the fool's violent trembling would cause the gun to go off accidentally. More pointless things had happened, to be sure.

Skellan tensed, ready to spring. The pain of the fall would be welcome compared to suffering the black iron shot through the skull.

'What did you intend? To wait for us to sleep and then rob us blind? Murder us in our beds? You cowardly cur! I should wipe the floor with you. You are less than a man!'

'Oh, just shoot me and be done with it, you pompous blowhard,' Skellan muttered. Instead of dropping down he swung his leg over the iron railing and began to lower himself back off the balcony.

'Stay where you are or I'll shoot,' Gaspard said. His nakedness undermined the venom in his voice, making him appear quite ludicrous as he stood there waving the pistol around.

Narcisa leaned in, drawing her arm tighter around his chest, pinning him as she bit into the soft flesh of his neck just hard enough to draw blood. Gaspard let out the smallest of whimpers. The pistol jerked dangerously in his hand as his body convulsed, pleasure coursing through him.

'We should settle this like men,' Skellan said, still half-on, half-off the balcony.

'Like men?' Gaspard said with disbelief. 'You break into my house and expect some kind of leniency? You propose what? Fisticuffs? You deserve nothing short of death, sir!'

'Then,' Skellan said, slapping the fop across the face with the flat of his hand. 'Pistols at dawn, you want satisfaction, I want your woman. That should satisfy your sense of honour.'

'I... I...'

'You ought to kill me, I know, you already said that. Perhaps you will manage it come morning.'

The woman's smile was only enhanced by the small ribbon of the actor's blood that had dribbled down her chin.

THEY MET BESIDE the river before first light.

Gaspard picked the spot and waited beneath one of the many mournful willows. A small dinghy was moored on the riverbank. As with the day before, he was dressed in an elegant coat of red silk and dark flowing breeches that ballooned over the top of knee-length leather boots. His shirt of ivory silk was open. At his throat he wore a silver hammer of Sigmar, for all the good it would do him from twenty paces.

Skellan smiled grimly, the fop had obviously raided the theatre's wardrobe to best look the part.

Beside him, Narcisa looked exquisite in a long flowing skirt of the subtlest blue and a simple white blouse. She curtseyed to Skellan as he approached. He responded with a slight inclination of the head.

Gaspard didn't so much as acknowledge his presence.

Skellan stretched, rolling his shoulders to work the ache out of them. It had been a long night. After the encounter on the balcony he had been forced to retreat to the Alt Stadt empty handed. Luckily, as dawn crept in he had found a baker's boy running errands. The boy tasted sweeter than his pastries smelled.

Skellan picked a strip of gristle from between his teeth.

He saw that the fool had set up a small table and a stool. There was a glass tumbler and a decanter containing amber liqueur on the table.

The actor had gone to great lengths to set the scene. It was a shame his theatrics lacked an audience.

Niculai Gaspard's second walked slowly towards him. Gaspard's man carried a small case fashioned from the finest walnut, lacquered and polished. The case bore the crest of some petty noble long since stamped out by the greed of the ever-expanding Empire. It was fastened with twin gold hasps. The man nodded to Skellan as he approached. Skellan watched as he broke the hasps and opened the velvet-lined case on two identical double-barrelled percussion pistols. The weapons had Tilean curved grips and steel end-caps that were carved with the same crest as the walnut case. The barrels themselves were seven inches long with swivel ramrods. They were beautiful pieces.

Skellan took one, making no effort to mask his smirk, as he knew it would rankle the fop no end. He looked across the field of honour to where the fop was stretching and loosening his muscles up as though he expected the duel to degenerate into a brawl. There was a nervous energy about Gaspard. Skellan supposed it was some form of pent up righteous fury. The pistol was heavy in his hand. He wasn't used to such cowardly tools. He liked his killing intimate, close. Still, he sighted down the barrels. The aim appeared true.

'You have made your decision, sir?' the second asked deferentially.

Skellan nodded.

He knelt, resting the barrel beside a fallen leaf. Pulling the hammer into full-cock he dry fired the pistol into the grass. The leaf moved an inch as the wind from the barrel got beneath it. Skellan nodded appreciatively. It was a well-made piece.

Beside the pistols was a powder flask. Skellan took what he needed, pouring a small measure of the black powder down the muzzle of the pistol. He made a show of checking the pistol to see that everything appeared to be in working order – no obvious blockages that might cause the gun to backfire or the shot to ricochet. He took two of the lead balls from the purse of shot and depressed them into the cylinders one at a time. They fit snugly into the chamber. So exact was the fit that a small ring of lead sheered from each ball as they were tamped down until they sat perfectly beside the black powder. Finally, he greased the inside of the barrels with what smelled like duck fat. He half-cocked the pistol and nodded.

'If you would be so kind as to stand on your mark, sir, I will see to Herr Gaspard's pistol.'

Skellan walked slowly to a point midway between the weeping willow and an imperious royal oak. Gaspard's man had planted a small red flag in the dirt to signify the mark.

Skellan watched the fop go through the same elaborate routine, taking his pistol, loading it, and greasing the barrels to avoid chain fire from the second barrel. Gaspard laboured over it, doing everything as slowly as humanly possible. It was gamesmanship. It was also a ham actor overacting. He wanted to give Skellan time to get nervous, for doubt to worm its way into his mind and undermine his aim when the time came for them to face each other.

The fop walked slowly towards the mark, his man one pace behind him.

'Prepare to die, Herr Skellan,' Gaspard said, coming to stand beside him. The man was sweating profusely despite the relative chill of the morning.

Skellan smiled coldly.

'Oh, I am long since past preparing, little man. Come, I grow weary of waiting to kill you. I want to taste your woman.'

The second coughed politely into his gloved fist. 'The rules of engagement are simple. It is a duel of honour. You each have two shots, to be fired alternately. You will stand back to back, and on my word take ten paces, turn, take aim and fire. Should one or both of you die in this duel, may Morr have mercy upon your soul even as your death proves the right of the other.'

'May the black birds carry your soul swiftly to Morr,' Gaspard said.

Skellan saw then that a handful of crows and a single large raven had settled down on the thin drooping branches of the willow above Narcisa da Vries. The sight of the carrion eaters chilled him to the marrow. More birds settled on the riverbank, another huge raven landing on one of the dinghy's oarlocks.

'On my word... begin!' The second cried.

Skellan counted off six paces, deliberately walking half a step slower than Niculai Gaspard. On the seventh he drew the hammer back to full-cock. On the eighth he vented a primal roar, scattering the birds for a moment. On the ninth he listened for the telltale snick of Gaspard thumbing back the hammer on his own percussion pistol. On the tenth he turned to face down the barrel of the fop's gun. Gaspard drew aim first, levelling his gun. Skellan could hear his breathing, fast and shallow, and could see the muzzle wavering unsteadily. There was a crisp detonation and pain exploded within Skellan's chest. The lead ball had taken him clean between the third and fourth ribs. He looked down at the powder burn where it had torn through his shirt. He dug a finger into the hole, rooting around until he picked the hot lead out of his chest with a grubby fingernail. He dropped it on the ground, shaking his head.

'I'm sure those damnable birds would, if I still possessed a soul,' Skellan said, levelling his own pistol.

Before he could squeeze off his first shot Gaspard triggered his second. Skellan felt the sting of lead as it tore away part of his left ear.

'Well now, that was hardly in the spirit of things, was it?' He said as he squeezed off a single shot, blowing away the lower part of Niculai Gaspard's face and jaw. The man staggered back pitifully, the pistol spilling from his grip as his body slowly began to register the fact that it was dead. Gaspard lurched one step to the side and fell.

Narcisa applauded mockingly. 'You owe me dinner, Herr Skellan,' she said walking towards him.

The birds swooped down, settling on the corpse. They picked away at it even before the man's nerves had ceased their spasms. The raven came to rest on his upturned hand. It tilted its head curiously, beady yellow eyes boring into Skellan.

'Speak then, bird,' Skellan said, knowing this was no ordinary spectator.

'Mannfred is coming!' The raven cawed, its beak stretching hideously wide. 'Mannfred is coming! Prepare for the Count! Mannfred is coming home!'

'Do birds always talk to you?' Narcisa asked, fascinated by the winged messenger. She reached out to stroke its ruffled feathers, but the bird took flight before she could touch it.

'More and more of late,' Skellan confessed.

'And do you always listen?'

'Without question.'

CHAPTER FOUR

The Heart of Darkness
Nuln, Imperial City on the Reik

JEREK REFUSED TO feed.

The Wolf had been plagued by birds for months. The black, slick-feathered carrion eaters were drawn to him. They spoke to him with the voice of madness. He had heard that withdrawal from blood could have that effect. By not feeding he was driving himself to the point of insanity. The madness was incipient. It crawled around inside his head before coming to life in the strangest of ways. It was so specific. The ravens and crows would settle on his lap, their yellow eyes looking up at him as they delivered their message: *Mannfred is coming*. It was always the same message. *Mannfred is coming*. The birds urged him to return to Drakenhof to prepare for the new count's coming. He broke their necks and discarded their convulsing bodies along the roadside, without feeding upon them. They were his madness. Over and over cawing the same message: *Mannfred is coming. Mannfred is coming.*

The more he denied them the more frequently they came.

He had fled Grim Moor, taking the form of the great white wolf, running for days before collapsing with exhaustion. He wandered, lost. The cravings plagued him, but he would not feed. He walked barefoot, wrapped in a blanket he had stolen from a clothes line on the edge of a small hamlet in the middle of nowhere. He slept huddled against the boles of trees and in the dark corners of farmers' barns. Despite his immense will, the old wolf could not completely deny the need for blood. He subsisted on rats and field mice, water voles and once, a fourteen pointed stag that, in wolf form, he had brought down with his teeth. The meat was good; the blood was better, but it wasn't pure. His kind needed more to survive; their cravings sang for the blood of humanity. It was so rich and full of vitality and each body held so much of it. To drink was to sate one's appetite completely.

He had been lying at the roadside, naked and tired in his blanket, when a line of Strigany caravans had slowed to offer him a ride. He had been hesitant at first, expecting a trap, until the leader had introduced himself as Vedas, Guardian of the Old Ways, and offered his hand. The tattoo on his forearm was curiously similar to the von Carstein wolf's head. The feral-faced Vedas had smiled reassuringly and said, 'You are safe now, mulo.' It was an odd word, an old word meaning, literally, dead person. Jerek took his hand and hauled himself up into the wagon. They clothed him and offered sustenance, knowing full well what he was.

Vedas was an entertainer, a mountebank and a tinker of sorts, his vardo caravan filled with pots and pans in need of repair, old boots and other oddities. He liked to talk, as Jerek came to learn over the coming days. He was an endless font of gossip, though with no way to verify the veracity of his wild stories it was impossible to separate fact from fancy.

Still, a lot of what he said supported things that Jerek had witnessed in the months since Grim Moor. The Empire was tearing itself apart, but that was the stupidity of mankind. Such was their blind arrogance that they believed themselves superior to every other creature, including their fellow man. The Strigany caravans skirted minor battlefields and killing grounds still fresh with carrion. The story was always the same. One petty noble with pretensions had thrown away the lives of his subjects, sending them up against another equally petty aristocrat with grand delusions. The play of life was ever the same.

The punishments for the conquered were harsh. Corpses were nailed to stakes as a message to the living: to resist is to die. It had taken years for this to become commonplace once more after the fear of the risen dead. The living had grown bolder, though whether it was through arrogance or stupidity he did not know.

There was a bitter irony to the slaughter. What the cattle did to their own was worse by far than anything Vlad von Carstein could have conceived for them. So they had liberated themselves from the tyranny of the night only to set themselves up as the darkest, most brutal, of all tyrants. He wondered if they would have appreciated the irony in the hallowed halls of Altdorf.

As the Strigany caravans travelled they picked up other whispers. One recurred more and more the closer they ventured to the Reik: a black ship sailed her waters, and where she came death surely followed. Hamlets and towns were alive with gossip. The black ship had been sighted and soon after there had been a spate of disappearances. Few dared give voice to their fears as though by simply naming the black ship they would bring its curse down upon their heads.

They travelled on towards Nuln.

The Strigany caravan was made up of actors, tumblers, acrobats, jugglers and other physical entertainers. They travelled from place to place performing their plays across the old world.

They revered Jerek, or mulo, as they called him because of his nature. They were guardians, living protectors of the dead. They brought him gifts: the electrum figurine of a jaguar, a black obsidian brooch that had once belonged to a lady of wealth and means, a jade funeral mask from Cathay, so exquisitely carved it that appeared almost alive, and so much more. The jaguar fascinated him. It was so detailed, utterly accurate in every way as though the beast had somehow been miniaturised by the craftsman. Its perfection was unnerving.

They also brought him food.

Their proximity, though taunting because of the strength of their pulses, was a blessing for they kept the birds at bay.

They made camp outside the walls of Nuln.

They were not the only ones. The city gates were closed and would remain so until first light. Merchants and travellers alike were forced to wait.

Before they entered the big city Jerek decided he would break away from the caravan, he was uncomfortable with this nearness to humanity. It was tempting fate, asking to be discovered and slain. He moved carefully, leaving the moon as little of himself to illume as he could. He touched a finger to his tongue, the memory of blood still lingering there, its tang strong enough to taste.

He turned his gaze back to the city with its high, defensive walls patrolled by weary bowmen. Behind the walls, rooftops rose in a clutter of slate. A city was a city was a city – narrow streets of cobblestone and filth crowded by buildings carved from the same dull grey stone as the city wall, the high domes of the citadel with its weather-beaten gargoyles, and the masts of the few tall ships and cutters down in the harbour, cluttered by dingy dockside taverns, whorehouses and warehouses: Nuln.

A raven cawed a mournful, haunting cry.

Jerek studied the harbinger as it settled in the branches above his head. A half-smile touched his lips. *An ill-omened bird come to watch over me*, he thought, barely sparing the raven a second glance, even as it shrieked, *Mannfred is coming! Mannfred is coming!*

It had been a long time since he had first heard the bird's message, back on the battlefield of Grim Moor, though he had heard it too often since. The animal blood the gypsies fed him had kept the incipient touch of madness away long enough for him to know that the birds were no figment of his broken mind. That was a small mercy.

A second city of canvas was being hastily erected on the plains to either side of the Kemperbad Road. Amid the tents, the garish swirls and flashes of colour marked the Strigany caravans. Jerek closed his eyes, and abandoned himself to the emptiness curdling inside him.

The bird loosed another cry and took flight. Jerek's gaze followed the harbinger until it was a black spot in the eye of the moon.

'Go tell your master I refuse to bend the knee, little wing. Go warn him that death walks his way... he will not win.'

Jerek moved with deceptive grace, steps sure on the treacherous shale, a fleeting shadow within the dark, ghosting across the plains. He paused again, listening this time to the silken rush of the river, the crackle of the campfires, the lulls in the droning conversations. He slipped his hand inside the folds of his cloak, feeling the reassuringly familiar weight of the old hammer at his hip. The hammer was the last relic of his life as Jerek Kruger, White Wolf of Middenheim. It marked him for what he was. It was a simple double-headed hammer with a worn leather-wrapped hilt, impossibly woven into the fabric of his soul from the moment he had accepted it and joined the ranks of the wolves of Ulric all those lifetimes ago.

Jerek took pains to ensure that the iron head was covered before he set off again, breaking into a steady lope that ate the grass in long, easy, strides. Slowly at first but with steadily more insistency it began to rain. The thin veil of rain stung his face. The elements were a mental rather than physical discomfort. He was always cold. Cold was death.

He skirted the ring of campfires, keeping the shadow's edge between him and the light. The voices were louder here, and the conversations almost understandable. A second-rate minstrel was butchering a commoner's ballad on his mandolin. His voice was weak, the intonations and resonance noticeably off-key and lacking even the simplest melody. For all that, there was a simple magic in the minstrel's tale that captivated his audience, sang to the shadows of their dark souls, their rapt faces dancing in the firelight. Or perhaps it was the fire's warmth that held them still and not the minstrel's song at all.

Jerek moved on, stepping around the back of a tent, careful to avoid tripping over the trailing guide ropes as he edged out of sight. From within he could hear the murmur of voices, more campfire gossip, the grunting of one-night lovers coming to grips. He slipped away from the tent, creeping along the side of a high-wheeled Strigany caravan with gaudy side panels.

The calls from the crowd sparked another song from the minstrel. Jerek waited, loitering on the edge of the gathering until Vedas came up beside him. The gypsy drew on a briarwood pipe, exhaling deeply. Pungent smoke rafted up in front of his face.

'What troubles you, mulo?'

Jerek didn't answer, not at first.

'Spirits are high. They appear happy, no? Yet it is a rare thing for our people to be anything other, no? They are always happy as they tread the unending road. Not so. Strigany do not show their true feelings. Where you see singing and laughter there is sadness and despair. Listen closer to the lyrics of the singer, the shifting chords of his instrument, those low mournful notes he intersperses amid the joyous salutations of the melody. It is all a lie, mulo. Scratch beneath the surface.'

Jerek listened. Vedas was right. There was an air of melancholy to the song that he hadn't appreciated until the Strigany had pointed it out to him.

'We are guardians of the old ways. That is no easy burden. We bear the secrets of our people, and the secrets of those long forgotten. We nurture their wisdom. The world was not always so old, mulo. Once it was young and men were rash. They did things without thinking. They traded on their mortality for gratification. They were hedonistic in their pursuit of pleasure. We are the last keepers of their rituals, the last beneficiaries of their wisdom. They live on through us, and when they return we will be there, waiting.'

Jerek knew who those hedonistic old ones were; his immortality was, after all, the legacy of their blood curse.

'Inside me lie secrets that would break a weaker man. The same, I am sure could be said of you, mulo, no? Come, Chovihani would see you.'

Chovihani, the crone, was the caravan's grandmother. She was a seer, gifted with second-sight. It was traditional for all Strigany caravans to travel with a grandmother, one familiar with the old ways. She was the most pure. Chovihani was a pox-riddled hag. Her face was a rash of warts and wiry black hairs and her eyes without irises were pure white save for the small black pupils in their centres. Vedas led Jerek to the old woman's campfire.

'Little mother? May we join you?' Vedas asked politely.

Jerek had expected a little more reverence for the hag. Vedas, though, treated her as family, no more, no less.

The hag craned her neck, peering up into the darkness beyond the circle of firelight. 'Is that you little Vedas?'

'It is, mother.'

'And you've brought the dead man to me.' Her face broke into something approximating a smile. She rubbed her wizened old hands together briskly. 'Good, good. Yes. Sit, sit awhile. Join me.'

There was a canopy between the tent and one side of the fire, offering shelter from the downpour.

Jerek sat cross-legged across the fire, Vedas beside him. The gypsy took a tin cup from beside the fire and filled it from the pan heating over the flames. He passed it to Jerek. The liquid was tart. It tasted vinegary. Vedas poured himself a cup and drank deeply, swallowing the entire contents of the cup in a single mouthful. He smacked his lips appreciatively. 'Arafulo: few can make it today. The secret of the infusion is lost to all but a few. We are lucky, Chovihani knows her herbs. It is said to heighten the mystical aura of the drinker. Indeed, our spiritwalkers drink Arafulo prior to entering their trance state.' He turned to the witch. 'It is good, little mother.'

'The dead man doesn't agree with you, Vedas.'

Jerek laughed. 'She doesn't miss a thing, does she?'

The old woman pricked her finger and put three drops of her blood into the liquid. Her blood altered the flavour only subtly, but the difference was enough for Jerek to think it tasted like ambrosia.

'She doesn't,' the crone rasped, cackling delightedly, 'but she's not so far into her dotage that you need to talk about her as though she were some feeble-minded cretin.' she tapped her temple with a crooked finger, 'Sharp as a tack, my mind.'

'I am quite sure it is,' Jerek said.

The crone leaned across, taking his hand in hers. 'Oh,' she said. 'Such sorrow, in you, such sorrow. Dark, not dead. Dark, not dead. Such sorrow in the dark. Eternity, surrounded by the dark, not dead. Dark as a crow's wing.'

Jerek pulled his hand away sharply, breaking whatever trance the old woman had slipped into.

Her white eyes turned on him. 'Let me tell you a story, dead man, of Hajnalka and her brother Anaztaz for they are in many ways kin to you.' Jerek began to rise, but Vedas urged him to remain seated. Jerek shifted uncomfortably. He had never been fond of soothsayers or seers. It all smacked of a human need to map out the unknown. He had been around them long enough to know that men made their own destinies. No matter how sage, soothsayers were rarely right. Their prophecies were translated and twisted to match the future the listener wanted. Few were ever able to hear the original prophecies and live long enough to see how the foretold future differed from the days they lived. Jerek had lived his life happily ignorant. He saw no reason for his death to be any different.

'Sweet Anaztaz, nothing more than a boy who failed his sovereign, fell on the field of battle to a bitter blow, his body cleaved in two. His father, his lord, decreed that the boy was not to be buried for he had disgraced the family with his failure. "None shall grace him with sepulchre or lament, but leave him unburied, a corpse for birds and dogs to eat, a ghastly sight of shame," proclaimed his father. It was a curse beyond fathoming. Hajnalka though, pretty Hajnalka, a loving sister, had pity in her heart. She gathered all of her courage and defied their father the king, standing proud. "I owe a longer allegiance to the dead than to the living: in that world I shall abide for ever," she whispered, sprinkling grave dirt over her brother's broken corpse. Livid, her father, the lord, walled her up in his castle for he was a vengeful soul that did not like being shamed in any way. He was mighty. He was king. He was conceited and vain and his vanity incurred the wrath of the gods twofold – one, for trapping the dead amongst the living, refusing the burial of his son, and two for keeping the living, his own daughter, trapped among the dead.

'This is your curse,' Chovihani rasped, 'to be trapped between both worlds: the dead and the living. Listen well, mulo. You must give in to your nature. You are a beast, the man you were is no more. You are a predator, a vampire. You must feed or lose yourself.'

'You don't know me, witch,' Jerek growled as he shrugged off her hand and rose angrily.

'We are your people, mulo. We know you better than you know yourself. Bring him the girl, Vedas. Slit her throat in front of him. The blood will answer everything. Mulo will feed the beast within. He won't be able to resist that hot sweet liquid as it flows. It is his nature. He is a beast.'

'I am not the beast here, witch.'

Jerek stalked away from the campfire.

He loathed himself for the monster he was. He loathed the Strigany more for reminding him of it.

MOROI AND ARMINUS Vamburg were both a long way from home.

The witch hunter and his companion walked the dusk streets of Nuln. Moroi drew the collar of his greatcoat up around his throat and the wide brim of his felt hat down low over his eyes. He had a vile headache. The pressure of the blood against the bones of his skull was intense. His vision blurred as he walked, the rain-slicked cobbles pitching and rolling like the deck of a ship beneath his feet.

Vamburg walked silently beside him. His eyes scanned the rooftops for the slightest untoward movement. The rain made it difficult to see much of anything and it showed no sign of slackening before dawn.

The storm had nothing to do with Moroi's pain.

There was trouble coming. He could feel it in his bones.

The black ship haunted Moroi even as it haunted Nuln, spreading disease and discord through her fusty streets. It was as though a plague had taken root within his mind. Whispers came to him, men's tongues loosened by fear. A weaker man could easily have believed that dead men cursed to sail on black seas for eternity were pacing her decks, but Moroi was cynical. Flesh-and-blood zombie pirates were little more than bogeymen invoked to frighten children.

He knew enough, however, to trust his instincts. Whatever it was, it was close. His prescience was a gift, or a curse, of his profession. Hunting those corrupted by the winds of magic, twisted by the taint of Chaos or defiled by the canker of evil changed a man. To fight evil, one needed weapons. His hand sought the reassuring presence of the repeating six-shot crossbow clipped to his leather belt. The pair of them had been through a lot together. Not every creature earned the right to a trial, sentencing and hanging. More often than not circumstance demanded that Sigmar's justice be dispensed ruthlessly.

He had thought, a few years ago, of replacing the weapon with a percussion pistol but when it came to it he preferred the crossbow. There was something satisfying about its weight and heft. With his back in a corner, he knew he could trust it not to let him down. So the notion of a pistol had been discarded.

The blue-oil lamp on the street corner had burned out, leaving the night darker there. He stepped into the shadow and froze. He had heard something. A single sound: the slow sigh of a breath leaking out. Moroi turned slowly in a full circle, looking for the source of the sound.

He saw someone, the indistinct outline of a man.

'You sir! Hold!' Moroi cried as the man turned and fled. He set off after the panicked stranger, Arminus Vamburg on his heels.

The harsh slap of their footsteps echoed along the street.

Moroi skidded on the rain-slick cobbles, losing his balance. He hit the floor hard but was up and running again without missing a step.

What he saw beggared understanding. The man – for man it most certainly *had* been – dropped to all fours but didn't slow. His spine arched, tearing through the shirt on his back and bursting the waist of his trousers as he tossed his head back and howled at the moon. Before his eyes the man shifted into the form of a great dire wolf, leaving a trail of ruined clothing in its wake.

Moroi dropped to a crouch and unclipped the crossbow, levelling it and sighting down the short stock. He breathed deeply, once, twice, and on the third exhalation squeezed down on the trigger, loosing the bolt. It flew true, taking the werebeast in the hindquarters. The creature howled its agony but didn't slow. Moroi loosed a second bolt but it flew wide, the wolf bucking and thrashing as it sought to dislodge the shaft buried deep in its flesh.

Then it disappeared around a narrow corner, squeezing through little more than a crack between two buildings.

Vamburg charged past Moroi, skidding around the corner after the creature. Moroi rose and gave chase. Coming around the corner the werebeast was nowhere in sight. There was blood though, a telltale drip leading to a crooked spiral staircase that descended into the bones of the Alt Stadt. He knew that the stairwells led down to the Unterbaunch, the underbelly of the city, providing a haven for thieves, murderers, vagabonds and the whole gamut of undesirables. It was ironic that, by most people, the witch hunter would have been judged among that group. The werebeast was wounded, but short of tearing the miles and miles of catacombs and tunnels apart inch by inch there was nothing they could do.

'Do we follow it down there?' Vamburg asked, looking pointedly at the blood. His accent was thick, the words coming between ragged gasps of breath. He had a short silver dirk in his hand. He didn't need to say what he was thinking: it's wounded, it can't get far.

Moroi looked to the moon. It was, as he thought, a gibbous moon. 'That thing was no lycanthrope, my friend. The moon is a week from full.'

'A vampire?'

'Almost certainly.'

'A renegade, then. One of the last.'

'Stop thinking like a true son of the Empire, Arminus. What is the evidence of our eyes? Tell me that which we know and no more.'

Clarity was a good exercise for Arminus. If the apprentice were to become the master he would need to think with logical precision.

'There is a vampire in Nuln.'

'Exactly. And what do we know of the beasts?' Moroi smiled. His friend was learning. The secret was to follow the evidence, not invent it.

'Vampires must feed on the blood of the living.'

'Good. He was undoubtedly out tonight in search of succour. We disturbed him. That means he is hungry and wounded. That in turn means that he is weakened.'

'So we go down then?'

Moroi shook his head. 'We would be fools to walk into the unknown. There could be a nest down there. We have no proof that the creature is alone. No, we use our heads, Arminus. We out-think the beast. We do not rush headlong into the heart of darkness. We bide our time, wait for day when the beast is at its weakest and then we flush it out from its sanctuary and kill it. Now I have a job for you my friend. Go rouse the Bürgomeister. I would have a crew of navvies here within the hour. We might not be able to enter the sewers, but we can most assuredly make it difficult for the beast to evade us in the meantime. I want to seal off as many of these stairways as possible. There are eight I know of in this quarter, but I have no idea how many are spread across the entire district. It doesn't matter, we can't hope to block them all up, but the fewer exits the beast has, the better our chance of snaring him on our terms. It is, as ever, about dictating the manner of engagement. We do not allow our enemy to take us by surprise.'

But take them by surprise the beast did.

The navvies, under Vamburg's supervision, worked through until dawn and deep into the heat of the following day sealing thirty-six stairwells down into the Unterbaunch. For all their toil there were countless other entrances that were overlooked. They bricked up the narrower of the openings and nailed thick wooden planks across the mouths of wider ones.

Moroi did not contradict his companion as he gave his orders. To have done so would have undermined his authority with the city watch. Moroi judged it better to allow his man to learn from his mistakes. They would inevitably come at a price, but lessons paid for were ones remembered.

The watch posted guards, two to a stairwell, although as the day wore on complacency crept in and they grew lax with their patrols. In a moment of sublime stupidity the Bürgomeister ordered their recall three hours before dusk, deeming the threat to have been extinguished by the valiant witch hunter and his companion. Only then did Moroi intervene. He argued hard against this idiocy but, mind made up, there was nothing he could do to dissuade the Bürgomeister from his withdrawal.

Four hours later they were counting the cost.

Vamburg knelt down beside the splintered beams scattered across the mouth of the same stairwell they had chased the werebeast down the night before.

'It took a shocking amount of force to break this,' Arminus Vamburg said, turning the timber over and over in his hands. Moroi agreed. He refrained from the obvious retort. Vamburg was doing exactly as he had been taught, quantifying the known. It had taken a shocking amount of force to splinter the beam. It was three inches thick, solid oak, and it was shredded apart as though it were nothing more substantial than a page of vellum.

'The beast is out there and it is that idiot bureaucrat's fault.' Moroi felt a gnawing sickness in his gut. It was always the same when he was near an abomination. It was a physical reaction to the wrongness of the entity. He felt it now. The blood in his skull pounded against the bone plates. He rubbed at his eyes.

Vamburg saw his friend's distress. 'It's near isn't it?'

Moroi nodded, a pained breath leaking slowly between his lips. 'Close enough.'

He scanned the rows of blind windows and then raised his gaze to the gables and eaves of the crowded houses, looking for the beast. 'It's watching us.'

Vamburg followed the direction of his gaze.

Nothing.

'Sir! Sir! Come quick sir!' A young lad charged up to the witch hunter, grabbing his hand and trying to drag him away.

'What is it, boy?'

'It's my ma, sir. Please come quick.'

'Show me,' Moroi said, that cold stone of certainty sinking sickly to the pit of his stomach. He knew they were too late even before he pushed open the door to the hovel. The cramped room reeked of it, the filth of death. The woman lay in the centre of the floor, her throat torn out. The man at her side wept. Moroi felt wretched as he crossed the threshold. All he could think was that it was yet another death that could have been prevented had the bureaucrat simply listened to him. But then, men in power weren't famous for listening to underlings and outsiders.

The man looked up. Even in the dim light of the foetid room Moroi could see that his eyes were rimmed red with tears. 'My wife...'

'When did you find her?' Moroi asked, ignoring the man's grief. There were facts he needed. The time for mourning would come. He had spoken with widows and widowers too many times to feel pity for their plight. If they had information locked up within them he wanted to prise it out of them. That was the extent of their relationship.

'When I came home... I don't know...'

'Think man, whatever you can tell us could well be the difference between life and death for someone else's wife.'

The man sniffed, snot dribbling down his face. He wiped it away with the back of his hand, succeeding only in smearing it across his cheek. 'I don't know. Thirty minutes, maybe more. I don't know.'

'Thirty minutes is long enough for him to be anywhere in this damned city by now,' Vamburg said, hitting the doorframe in his frustration.

'No,' Moroi said, 'I can feel him. He isn't far away. He's watching, and now he knows we have found her. It is all a part of his game.'

'You give the beast too much credit.'

'And you, my friend, do not give it enough.'

'Beast?' The man asked. He touched the ruin of his wife's throat and held his bloody fingers up for Moroi to see. 'What sort of beast is capable of such...?' He stopped mid-sentence. 'A vampire. Does that mean she...?'

Arminus Vamburg laid a comforting hand on the bereaved man's shoulder. There was nothing either of them could say to ease his pain. Death was no respecter of love or happiness. It didn't care if the deceased was a mother or a wife. It didn't matter if those left behind would never be the same again.

A fly moved sluggishly around the open wound, its presence the most natural and repugnant thing in the world.

Moroi saw it first – the wound on the man's arm. Some of the blood on the woman was his. 'Did you see the murderer? Speak the truth man. Did you see him?'

The man nodded and held out his wrist where he had been cut during his struggle with the vampire. 'She's infected isn't she?' He pushed at the cut, trying to close it, as though by doing so he could undo what had been done to him. 'So am I, aren't I? Don't lie to me. He killed me as well didn't he?'

'No,' the witch hunter said shortly, 'but your woman... I am sorry; there is no way of knowing, so we must perform the ritual for her own sake, lest she be born again into the unlife for our impropriety.'

'Ritual?'

'Arminus, take him outside. Prepare a grave for this poor woman. There are things a husband should not have to see. I will need the roses from the bed beneath the window.'

Vamburg nodded. 'It will be done.' He handed Moroi the canvas satchel that he carried slung across his shoulders. Moroi took it, and began rifling through the bag looking for the instruments he would need to complete the ritual. 'Come with me,' Vamburg said, seeing the witch hunter draw the wooden stake and iron hammer from the satchel. He held out a hand for the man to take.

'I should be here...'

'No, you will be of more use to her and to us preparing a place for burial. Do not remember her this way. You do not need to see more. It will never leave you. Every time you close your eyes and see her face, you will remember the blood instead of the smile. Is that what you want?'

The man shook his head. 'No.'

'No,' Moroi agreed.

Vamburg led the man by the arm.

'Go with them, boy. This is no place for you.'

Vamburg returned a moment later with the heads of fifteen white roses. He closed the door to the hovel, leaving Moroi alone in the charnel house with the dead woman. He walked around her corpse three times, slowly, counter-clockwise, looking at the mess the beast had made. She might have been pretty before, it was impossible to tell. He knelt, gripping her jaw to open her mouth. He filled it with the heads of the white roses and pressed her jaw shut. He had no reason to believe that the beast had given her his blood curse, but unlike the bureaucrat he wasn't about to risk the lives of others by being anything less than meticulous. He had a duty to the living. He had, for that matter, a duty to the dead.

He withdrew a wooden stake, fashioned from the trunk of a hundred year old ash tree, and hammered it through her breastbone, piercing her heart.

His head pounded. The ache had faded for a while but it had returned with savage vengeance. He couldn't allow the beast to undermine his resolve. He rooted around in the satchel for the small diamond-toothed saw he needed to decapitate the woman. It was an ugly business. He looked around the room for a blanket to use as a shroud. Moroi wrapped the corpse in the coarse blanket he found on the pallet that the couple had obviously shared as a bed. He had known too many distraught husbands return, curious, sad or just numb in the head from grief. No man needed to see his wife laid out like a slab of dead meat.

He stuffed her neck with more petals.

She would not rise again.

The pain in his head intensified. The beast was close, arrogantly so. It was mocking him with its nearness and there was nothing he could do.

He pushed himself to his feet and staggered back to the door. His head swam dizzyingly. He opened the door. Vamburg and the husband had dug a shallow grave where the roses had grown. Moroi nodded to his companion. Together they laid the woman to rest beneath the window, face down. They covered her, replanting the denuded roses above where she lay.

The man knelt in the dirt. 'Would you say something? I want to send her to Sigmar, but I don't know what to say?'

Moroi knelt beside the man. 'What was her name?'

'Käthe.'

Moroi took the silver hammer from around his neck and pressed it into the dirt at the foot of the tallest rose bush. 'Sigmar will know her with this, my friend. He needs no pretty words to find his own. Her flesh is part of nature now, joined in the cycle of life. Her soul though is unfettered. She flies with the gods. She would not want you or me to grieve for her. She knows that one day you will be together again. That is the beauty of love. It is eternal, unending.'

'Thank you,' the man said. 'Thank you for everything.'

Again, a fierce stabbing pain lanced through the witch hunter's skull. He couldn't keep the pain from registering on his face. Vamburg put a steadying hand on his friend's shoulder.

The pain came again, brutal this time. Needles of fire speared into his brain, the lancing pain so hot it was blinding. Despite Vamburg's hand, Moroi convulsed and slumped forwards face first into the dirt. His cry died on his lips. The last thing he saw as he fell were the garish colours of a Strigany caravan crossing the mouth of the street not fifty feet away.

THE AIR WAS thick, the night without a sound.

They had gathered outside the Sigmarite temple, firebrands blazing, torches held high, armed with pitchforks and hoes and other makeshift weapons. They wanted blood. There was a beast within the walls of the city. It had slain one of their own.

Moroi stood on a wooden crate.

He had their attention.

It was always difficult to judge the animal that the crowd became, to know when tempers would rise, how quickly and when finally they would go on a rampage.

He held up his right hand for silence.

'It is true,' he said, and then waited for the murmur to subside. 'There is a killer in the city.'

'A vampire!' someone shouted.

Moroi turned on the heckler. 'A killer,' he said coldly. 'I make no claims to its origins.'

'Don't lie to us, witch hunter!' someone else called, disgustedly. 'We aren't children!'

With so few immortal dead still plaguing the living it had been a long time since Moroi had gathered a vampire hunt. He was ashamed to admit that he had missed the thrill. The hunt itself was a familiar thing, but the old passions that accompanied it were addictive. He had forgotten just how much so. Moroi waited out the shouts. 'The creature has a lair beneath the Alt Stadt, though I believe the Strigany are protecting it.'

'Then we make them surrender the beast!'

'And if they don't?' Moroi asked, barely above a whisper. He didn't need to shout. His words carried to every man and woman in the crowd. 'What are we prepared to do?'

'Burn them!'

'Kill them all!'

Moroi shook his head. 'No, for then you would become worse than the beast. It kills to live whereas you would be killing out of retribution.'

'Smoke it out!'

'Make them surrender the beast!'

'Are you prepared to die?' Moroi asked. That silenced them. He looked at them, studying the rows of faces, the hunger in them and the potential for hurt. The difference between the savage and the civilised was whisper thin. It sickened him, and yet he needed them fired up, righteous and angry. Anything else and they would die before nightfall.

A low susurrus of fear whispered through them.

'Good,' Moroi said. 'You should be frightened. This is no game. There is no guarantee that the man beside you will be there tomorrow. You might be faced with a friend, tainted by the beast, forced to ram a stake through his heart and cut his head from his shoulders. Will you be capable of doing that? He won't be your friend anymore. Your friend will be long gone, but the beast will wear his skin. It is unnerving, but the daemons ever were creatures for turning our worst fears in upon us, were they not?'

Feet shuffled uncomfortably. The witch hunter knew he was losing them. They didn't want to hear about mortality. They wanted rousing words to fire their blood along with promises of glory and a great story to tell around the fire in the taproom, of the day they hunted and slew a vampire in their home town. He could not give that to them. He couldn't feed them full of lies and send them unprepared into a fight that could well spell their deaths. He wanted them to know that it wasn't glamorous. He wanted them to know that heroes died as easily as villains outside of the storybooks.

'So if you can live with the truth, that should we fail, your friend could rise again as your mortal enemy, corrupted in death, then stand with me. We hunt the beast at its strongest, at night. Why? For fear that if we don't more good people will die. I cannot have another woman like Käthe stain my conscience, because now, by acting, by standing up, I could stop it. So I will hunt the beast at night. I will bring it down when it is at its strongest. I will, because in this I am the hammer of Sigmar made flesh. If I walk alone, so be it. If you stand at my side, do so knowing the truth: the beast is lethal, a killer. What we are about to do out of need, it does because of its nature. Ten of us alone might not be sufficient to restrain the beast. It is strong, and it is cunning. It is old – who knows how old – for it has outlived others of its kind, those that fell with the von Carstein hordes. It is a survivor, and that makes it all the more dangerous. But we must try, or else tomorrow it could be your wife, your daughter that we are burying beneath your rose garden. Or worse, you might wake in the morning to a loving kiss mere moments before the beast that was your lover tears your throat out with her teeth. Is that a kiss you would have?'

He stepped down from the crate.

There were no cheers. His words had subdued them, and had thinned their number by half, as those not prepared to die had moved away unnoticed. This did not surprise him. Few would willingly risk death, but it was those few who remained, resolute.

He stepped aside, nodding to Vamburg. This was where his companion excelled, whipping up the crowd with rousing words after he had delivered his dire warnings.

Arminus Vamburg stepped up onto the crate and raised his arms for silence. The gesture was redundant. No one was talking. 'We know little of the beast itself save that it is wounded. We know nothing of its origins or bloodline. This means we know nothing of its strengths. What we do know is that the creature walks as a man though it is capable of shifting form. Last night we witnessed its metamorphosis into a dire wolf.'

Moroi nodded.

'It is, without doubt, deadly in both forms. But we are not helpless. Moroi has a gift, a boon from Sigmar himself. Such evil as this is repugnant to his blood. His body rebels at the presence of the abomination. What this means is that he can sense its approach. It cannot sense his. This is our advantage.

'We can lay a trap for the beast. It can be caged. It can be wounded, but most importantly it can be killed. It is not immortal. Anything that died once can die twice. It has had practice,' he said wryly. 'Last night Moroi put a crossbow bolt in the fiend's hide, but that does not mean it will be weakened. They have remarkable regenerative qualities. For all we know it could be healed already.

'When you encounter the beast, do not look it in the eye; it has the power to turn your mind against you, leaving you powerless to resist. Do not for a minute doubt me. I have seen grown men overpowered, turned into thralls to these fiends. No man deserves that fate.

'There are several ways it can die. Mark these well. If you get close enough, a stake of wood through the heart, or decapitating the beast will end its life. Dismemberment will slow if not outright kill the vampire. Fire will shield you. A vampire, even the strongest of its kind, fears the destructive power of flame.' Vamburg lapsed into silence. He had warned them, there was nothing else he could do.

He stepped down from the crate and stood beside Moroi. Together, they marched through the dark streets in search of the Strigany caravan, fifty men of Nuln following in their wake, torches blazing, makeshift weapons burnished in their light.

They walked silently, determined.

The beast sheltered by the Strigany would die.

THE BLACK SHIP

III
Landfall

THE BLACK SHIP made landfall deep in the blighted heart of Sylvania, resting finally in the shadow of the Vampire Count's castle: Drakenhof.

The taint of its past was almost tangible.

Mannfred stood on the deck and breathed deeply of it, savouring the not so sweet air of home.

Home. It was an alien concept but, of all the places in the world, the old castle was as much a part of who he was and his heritage as anywhere else in the world. To look at it, the fortress was like some huge leering gargoyle perched high on the mountaintop. Black specks swarmed around the highest tower, circling ceaselessly. Vlad's precious birds: the same birds that had helped drive Konrad insane. From here the windows in the towers and turrets were blind and the rooftops indistinguishable from level to level, all save one: the Raven Tower, by far the highest point of Drakenhof. Clouds thickened overhead, obscuring the waxing moon. Mannfred watched awhile as the shapes lost definition, coalescing into one giant shadow daemon. It was a fitting image.

There were, he saw, after a moment, lamps burning in some of the castle's higher windows. No doubt his servants were making ready for his return. A black brougham coach waited by the jetty, the von Carstein family crest emblazoned on its door. Four horses, splendid beasts, coal black, steam curling from their nostrils, drew the coach. The coachman sat unmoving, cloak drawn up over his head so that his face was lost completely in black shadow. The man was utterly still.

'Denn die todten reiten schnell,' the steerman beside him said, and it was obviously the truth: the dead did travel fast.

Mannfred waited as the crew lowered the boarding ramps, heaving the huge baseboards into place. They settled with a resounding thunk. Black birds circled overhead, cawing and crowing as four pale-skinned and slack-faced sailors unloaded his coffin. They carried it between them, loading it onto the brougham. More listless sailors dragged the prisoners down the gangplank. Their chains rattled as they shuffled forwards. Mannfred pointed at one of the men, curling his finger in summons. Two sailors pulled him out of the line and dragged him over to the vampire. The man's hair was a mess of grease and knots, his beard grown through in patches, but his eyes retained the vitality Mannfred liked so much. The man was still very much alive. He looked up at the Vampire Count, opening his mouth to beg. Mannfred silenced him with a back handed slap that snapped his neck back, broken.

'Very good.'

The sailors held the man, his head lolling uselessly on his neck, while Mannfred slipped the small black iron razor-cuff over his right thumb. He drew the blade across the man's throat, opening the jugular in a bubble of arterial blood, but with the heart stilled there was no spray. He drank until sated, and then disposed of the corpse over the side.

The dead man floated.

Mannfred watched as the first raven settled on the corpse. A second and third joined it.

In the shade beyond the brougham coach he saw the hulking forms of three dire wolves – his welcoming party from the castle, no doubt. He had expected more, as was fitting for a lord's return.

He was in no hurry to go down to join them.

It was enough that he was coming home.

Gathering the oilskin-wrapped bundle, Mannfred disembarked. At the bottom of the gangplank he turned to the captain. 'My thanks,' Mannfred said. 'Your ship and crew are returned to you, as promised.'

The old sailor didn't say a word. He couldn't. Mannfred had cut his tongue out six days into their journey together.

Mannfred strode over to the coach. The driver dismounted, coming around to open the door. He held a storm lantern in his hand.

Mannfred reached inside and laid the bundle on the red leather banquette. He turned, sensing the approach of the wolves. All three lay supine at his feet. He smiled at their subservience and gestured curtly for them to rise. They bowed their heads to him, noses pressed into the dirt, and turned, loping away. A moment later the night filled with the mournful sound of a wolf howling at the moon.

The last of the black ship's crewmen moved quickly up the gangplank. In a matter of moments the deck became a swarm of movement. One man spider-climbed the rigging as another hoisted the main brace while two more tied off guide ropes. The captain stood at the wheel. Mannfred fancied he could see the hate burning in the man's eyes.

Mannfred held out his hand for the lantern, but instead of taking it he allowed it to fall to the floor, glass shattering, flames rising as the air rushed in to feed them.

He lowered his hand into the heart of the fire, and uttered four short words never intended for human tongues.

The flames appeared to meld with his skin, not burning him, but somehow becoming a part of him. He held his hand before his face, marvelling at the chaotic dance of the fire. A fire sprite arced from his fingertips, crackling through the air until it touched the black cloth of the main sail, burning it. Around Mannfred the air reeked of ozone. Around the sailors on the black ship the air stank of charcoal and burning cloth as first the main sail and then the mast ignited.

Cries went up.

The crewmen ran for pails of water to douse the blaze. Mannfred placed his hands together, allowing the flame from one to consume the other. The fire grew in intensity and purpose. Scarcely audible, he repeated the incantation with a vehemence that was staggering. As the last word tripped off his tongue he drew his hands apart, creating twin balls of flame. Both quickly gathered size and substance until he cast them off, two great balls of fire hurled at the belly of the black ship. The air snapped and cackled around his head as the flames streaked like a twin-tailed comet across the night sky.

They hit the barque in a deafening roar. The beams and decking of the black ship buckled, timber splintered away from the seams, and the very belly of the barque collapsed beneath the explosive force of the detonation. Flames engulfed the ship.

The heat from the conflagration was awesome.

A sailor fell from the rigging, dead before he hit the deck. Another threw himself into the Reik, falling ablaze. His arms windmilled frantically. His screams didn't stop as he hit the water. The captain clasped the wheel, unmoving even as the flames crawled up his legs. He was the one person who couldn't scream.

The lantern burned itself out, but the ship burned on.

Satisfied there would be no survivors, Mannfred turned his back on the burning ship and climbed into the brougham. He rapped on the ceiling and the carriage lurched forwards.

The black coach's departure for Drakenhof was heralded by the shrieks and caws of carrion crows.

Finally, he was going home to claim what was rightfully his by birthright, by strength, by cunning and by grand design: his inheritance, his dominion.

Mannfred interlaced his fingers behind his head, and leaned back. He listened to the birds. They were calling his name. Over and over: *Mannfred is coming! Mannfred is coming!*

His choice of messenger amused him. The ravens were thought by the superstitious to be psychopomps, conductors of souls into Morr's Underworld – birds of ill omen, most certainly. It entertained him to imagine the birds being responsible for guiding him home, warning the living of his return and summoning the dead to fight by his side.

Mannfred reached down for the rag-wrapped bundle on the seat beside him. He felt its pulse through the oilskin as he laid his hand flat on it. The sheer power of the binding coursed the length of his arm as his fingertips felt out the embossed mark on its skin. The thing possessed a repulsive life of its own. He smiled coldly. He knew the origins of the mark without needing to see it. It was the sigil of the greatest of the liche lords – Nagash.

He closed his eyes, enjoying the gentle soothing motion of the coach on the road. The coach rolled on into the night, through the valleys of shadow and despair.

Shadows coiled around the brougham's wheels, reaching out to snare the coach, but the wheels rolled on and the shadows blew away to nothing.

Mannfred dreamed of the dead.

CHAPTER FIVE

Black Isabella
Drakenhof,
The Dark Heart of the Kingdom of the Dead

THE BROUGHAM COACH slowed to a standstill.

The castle was a dark god on the horizon, a sanctuary for mourning souls. Its broken battlements showed a jagged line against the backdrop of the night sky. Mannfred stared. There was a forest where once there had been an empty plain, though there were no ordinary trees in this forest. Mannfred opened the door and climbed out of the coach. He walked slowly towards the first of the 'trees'. It was a man, or had been. Most of its flesh had been picked clean by Vlad's ravens. The corpse had been impaled on a huge stake, driven up from below and long enough to pierce the dead man's jaw, pinning him upright in death like some macabre scarecrow. It was a forest of the impaled. The bone trees were planted thickly, no more than six feet between them. There must have been five hundred, more.

The ravens settled on the yellowed skulls, picking away at worms of flesh they had yet to strip.

Mannfred walked through the bone forest. His fingers trailed across the corpses, brushing up against the dead. There were women and children amongst them. Death was indiscriminate. That, and the lights burning in the castle windows, angered the vampire. He hadn't sanctioned the slaughter of his cattle.

He took the skull of one of the impaled in his hands, leaning forwards to press his forehead against it. He closed his eyes and began to whisper, breathing the words of invocation, pressing the bones harder until they buckled and snapped, demanding the spirit of the dead man return to face him, to explain. The vanquished had no wish to return. The spirit resisted his summons, fighting, but Mannfred was strong, stronger than the dead. He tore down the veil between the two realms, drawing the man back until his lifeforce was trapped once more within his bones. His screams as the pain returned were terrible to behold. Mannfred refused to release him despite his pleading.

'Speak to me,' Mannfred commanded.

The skull shivered in his hands, the jaw working, grinding on the gristle where the flesh and muscle had been rendered down to fat. No sounds emerged.

'I said speak!'

Black Isabella, the dead sighed: a name, an explanation.

'More. What happened here? You will not know rest and there will be no surcease, until you explain.'

A woman… they call her Nadasdy… she is mistress of the castle. She bathes in the blood of the young… she feeds… we came against her… we few… from the city below… we came at night, fools that we were… when her kind is strongest… we came with torches and pitchforks to fight a daemon… we failed… this is our punishment… our reward… I know no rest. I hurt!

'She did this to you? A woman? There are hundreds of you.'

It was… slaughter… she fed on us… drank our blood… I… I… watched my son… die… watched them drive the stake into him… Was forced to hear his screams because he would not die… I tore my own ears off… in desperation… but still I heard him… His screams… Hers was the last name on his lips… Nadasdy… not his mother's name… not his god's… the bitch who took… his life.

Mannfred released his hold on the bones, in turn relinquishing his grip on the man's spirit. The dead man's jaw hung slackly, the wooden spike the only thing preventing it from coming away from the rest of the skull. The spirit was gone, fled back to the comfort of death.

Nadasdy; he did not know the name, but that meant nothing. It could easily be a bastard child of Konrad, a get left to rule the roost when her sire was slain. He was not his companion's keeper. He did not know every wench he had suckled on in his madness. It mattered little. This Black Isabella would learn what it meant to cross him.

He returned to the brougham.

'To the castle,' he told the coachman, closing the door and leaning back out through the open window. 'It is time this Nadasdy learned who is the true heir of Drakenhof.'

The coachman inclined his cloaked head, no expression or emotion in the movement, and yet it reeked of approval. His leather whip cracked in the air, and the horses broke into a gallop.

* * *

MANNFRED EMERGED FROM the black coach, his hood pulled up over his head so that his face fell in shadow.

He swept up to the huge oak and iron-bound doors of the castle. Little had changed since he had last stood before the great door, little that was except for him. He was changed utterly. He reached out for the huge black iron wolf's head knocker on the door and hammered on it three times. The sound reverberated throughout the courtyard and deep inside the castle.

The reek of death still clung to the air, but that was ever the case with killing grounds. The blood could be scrubbed, the bodies buried or burned, it mattered little. The stink permeated the stone and soil and clung stubbornly to the place. It was a physical thing, more real to many than ghosts or revenant shades. It was something they could understand. Mannfred touched the wall of the old place, feeling its grief. The castle had seen much suffering, had witnessed the brutal slaughter of the Totentanz of Geheimnisnacht all those years ago, when Vlad had revealed himself to the world, and before that the casual cruelties of Otto van Drak's capricious reign. Konrad's madness was a blessing beside that, he was sure. It was no surprise that trace elements of it, like memory, had imprinted themselves on the very walls of Drakenhof. The building sorrowed. He felt it all through the stone.

'I am here,' Mannfred said, softly, as though reassuring the great castle.

He heard the massive bolts being drawn back. A moment later the door opened a crack. Musty air leaked out, and on it he smelled the servant's fear as the cadaverous little man peered out through the narrow opening.

'Who is the master of this fortress?' Mannfred's voice was horribly calm as he spoke.

'Nadasdy, lord, and she is mistress of Drakenhof, not master,' the little man wheedled, rubbing his hands together obsequiously. His bald pate beaded with sweat.

'Indeed. Please inform your mistress that I would speak with her.'

'Yes, yes, of course, sir, of course. Though it is late and she will not be happy. I will convey your request, yes, though she may not see you. The mistress is whimsical, her humours change and I cannot predict them.'

'She will see me,' Mannfred said.

'Yes, of course, yes.' The servant scraped his feet, bowing low and backing up, allowing the door to groan open on its rusted hinges. 'Whom shall I say is calling?'

Mannfred said nothing. He pushed back his hood, gratified to see the shock of recognition on the servant's face as he caught sight of the plain bronze ring on his hand. The man bowed even lower. When he straightened, his manner had visibly changed. The weaselly toadying of moments before had been replaced with cunning. The man seemed to grow in stature.

'Welcome home, master. The woman is in your sire's chamber in the Raven Tower. I shall make preparations for her disposal.'

'No. I shall see to her myself.'

'Very good, master.'

Mannfred took a moment to adjust his collar and cuffs, and then moved past the servant. It was a bittersweet homecoming. He savoured the ambience of the old castle for a moment before sweeping through the lower levels, cloak swirling behind him. His footfalls echoed through the halls. There was an air of decadent decay about his ancestral home. The air was rank with the musk of rotting tapestries. A low keening moan whispered in his wake, along with other noises, including the scratch and skitters of rats. How could the heart of Vlad's kingdom have fallen into such disrepair? It would not, Mannfred vowed silently, remain so. He would restore the great castle to its former glory. In the great hall the obsidian throne, the mark of Vlad's dominion, lay on its side, toppled. Mannfred righted it. He turned slowly, surveying the fallen grandeur of the hall. It had been more than a century since he had last walked these hallowed halls – one hundred years of solitude, laying the foundations of his Kingdom of the Damned.

He lingered a while with the ghosts of that Geheimnisnacht, remembering the feeding frenzy that had been the slaughter of the aristocracy. It had been a night unlike any other. It had hinted at the power of his sire, that he dared invite his enemies into his home and had the strength to cull them. It was audacious, brutal, and quite, quite brilliant. The unveiling had sent tremors throughout humanity that were still being felt today. The fear of the black ship was more to do with the fear of that night, the possibility that it might be returning and that such evil might have found a way into their simple lives.

He wandered through many of the old rooms, trying to recall their purpose. He stepped into what had obviously been the library at one time. So much had been destroyed. The vellum had decayed, the skin – not the best thing to bind a book with – crumbled. So much had been lost.

The flash of a silver head caught his eye amid the detritus of life. He crossed the room to investigate. He picked through the rubbish, moving a shredded tome and scrolls where the ink had long since perished. He toed aside a rotten canvas to reveal a cane with a silver wolf's head for a handle.

He stared at it for a full minute before stooping to pick it up.

He had never thought to see this again, and could not begin to imagine how it had ended up here, amid the ruin of this room.

Vlad had carried the wolf cane with him when playing the aristocrat. Mannfred leant on the cane, affecting the pose of the gentleman, and then hefted it, lashing out with the silver head. It swung sweetly, though it stung to grasp. He remembered that Vlad had had a penchant for wearing gloves, all part of the guise of the wealthy man. Mannfred walked back through the library, across decomposed books and blind scrolls, twirling the cane in his hand as he went. It felt natural, adding a certain symmetry to his return.

He took the stone steps of the winding staircase three at a time, the silver head of the cane tapping against the stone wall in time with his steps. The picking and snickering of the rats faded away, the vermin fleeing at his approach.

He crossed the portrait gallery, where a single portrait was left hanging. It was a curious piece, Konrad in the centre, arms wide, decanting the blood of a naked girl – though it could well have been a boy, the artist had given the victim's sexuality a curious ambiguity – into an earthenware chalice. Konrad, messianic in the centre, was surrounded by his loyal disciples, his Hamaya, all twelve of them sharing his feast of blood. It was curious that there was only one cup between them. It was, no doubt, how mad Konrad had seen himself, dispensing favours to his loyal few, a king at his own table. Mannfred recognised the face of Jerek von Carstein depicted at Konrad's left, a betrayer's dagger in his hand, his face twisted as he leaned in beneath the table towards Konrad. It was an amusing piece, and obviously the artist had intended some hidden meaning, including all sorts of symbolism in it that wasn't easily read. It was signed Cornelian Ovidad in a tight scrawl.

He climbed the stairs of the Raven Tower. He threw open the iron-banded door and ascended a second staircase. His sire's scent was long gone. He lifted the cane and rapped sharply three times on the chamber door. He didn't wait for the witch to open it for him. Mannfred tore the door from its huge hinges, the pins shearing off as they were wrenched free of the wooden frame.

He stood in the doorway.

The woman, Nadasdy, was sprawled out naked across the huge divan. The chamber was vulgar, an exercise in decadent excess totally at odds with the rest of the castle. It was lush, opulent. The air hung thick with aromatic spices, crimson shade and more exotic narcotics that overwhelmed the senses.

Mannfred stood in the doorway.

He looked at the woman.

There was something about her that was strangely familiar. She was an old soul though, he thought, so it was unsurprising if their paths had crossed at some time. She came to consciousness slowly, groggy from whatever intoxicant polluted her flesh and blood. Mannfred crossed the room, reaching the bed as she knuckled the sleep from her eyes. There was no anger in his movements, no emotion at all. Emotion was weakness. Mannfred was coldly methodical in the execution of his retribution.

'You are not wanted here, witch.'

She rolled on the bed, lifting her head to look at him. There was something dreadfully familiar about her eyes.

'I waited for you,' the woman crooned, obviously still caught in the failing edge of a dream and thinking he was some lover returned. She reached out to grab at his sleeve. 'I knew you wouldn't leave me alone here. I always knew, so I prepared the way as you wanted.'

She talked as though she knew him – though there was a rambling hallucinatory quality to her words – but he knew with growing certainty he had never met the woman. She was, he assumed, as mad as her sire, for surely she was Konrad's get, her mind addled by the narcotics she indulged in. She would not have been the only one driven insane by the blood kiss. She obviously thought he was his brother-in-death.

'I am not Konrad, woman. Your sire is dead,' Mannfred said, slowly, belabouring the point. 'Do you understand? You are alone.'

'No! You are here!'

'You are all alone,' Mannfred repeated, 'and you have harmed me and mine. I do not look kindly upon your presence in my house, or on your treatment of my subjects. Your forest of the impaled is an abomination, Nadasdy. Our kind has more thought, more cunning, than that. You do not cull the cattle, you cultivate them. You owe me their blood, Nadasdy. I shall start by taking yours.'

'No,' she pleaded. 'No, you don't understand! I did it for you! It was always for you!'

'Hush. Your lies make you ugly, woman.'

'No! No! I am no woman! I am your servant! I prepared the way! I defied death for you! Do you not know me? It is–' Mannfred touched the witch on the forehead and whispered a single word of power. Nadasdy's jaw locked mid-word, her desperate plea silenced. Mannfred stared down at her, enjoying the look of abject fear frozen on her face. He did not care who she claimed to be.

'I am master of Drakenhof, Nadasdy. This is my birthright. You tried to steal from me. I am glad. It gives me an excuse to make a lesson out of your corpse.'

He sat on the edge of the divan beside her, running the edge of the razor-cuff slowly from her throat all the way down to her pubis, paring the flesh. As the blood began to well from the wound he whispered the words, calling her flesh from her bones. The incantation was a cruel one. She could not move, could not scream or whimper, even as the pain grew so severe that she lost consciousness. Mannfred slapped her back awake. He wanted her to feel everything.

He flayed every inch of skin from her corpse, and then pared the muscle and tendon, drawing the bones out. He performed the act slowly, and with surgical precision.

It was a wretched death that took far longer than it had a right to because he held her soul, refusing to let her die until he was done punishing her.

THE WARREN OF subterranean catacombs beneath Drakenhof was Konrad's legacy. The Blood Count had been obsessed with his grand design, digging deep beneath the old castle, and expanding into the mountain range and inevitably into the ancient labyrinth of warrens beneath the old world. The enormity of it was staggering. Mannfred stood alone in the centre of the great subterranean cathedral where Konrad had ruled his empire. It engulfed him. The silence was perfect. There was a quality to the air that made it quite different to the world above. It was purer, unbreathed.

The high vaulted ceiling dripped with long gnarled and gangrenous stalactites. The lichen clinging to the rock shed a repulsive luminescence, lending the subterranean chamber an unearthly quality.

A huge basalt altar commanded the central dais. Twin runnels had been carved along the outer rim of the stone altar. They bore the dark stains of blood where victims had been sacrificed to Konrad's madness.

Blood. Such an amazing thing, blood, that exquisite taste, its perfect colour, that viscous consistency. Everything about it was remarkable, right down to the fact that the trace elements of life itself were there in that thick fluid. It was a living liquid. Even when spilled across the sacrificial altar it would live on, for a while.

He had things to do before he allowed himself the luxury of feeding again.

Behind the altar was the greatest mockery of all, the remains of the façade of a Sigmarite temple. Jagged pieces of stained glass images of the man-god and his miracles remained in the broken windows.

Konrad's vanity was incredible.

Mannfred circled the altar.

Row upon row of tiered benches and walkways had been carved into the hemispherical wall, creating a great stone amphitheatre. It was all pomp and pageantry. A great leader did not need to fall back on such tricks.

Coming full circle Mannfred braced himself against the altar, allowing the trace memories to wash over him. He could see, in his mind's eye, Konrad commanding his army from this very room. He could hear the ghosts of his tirades, the words seared into the memory of the place. It was Konrad's great and secret show. Mannfred felt the echoes of his loathing even now, trapped within this vast room. The stir of echoes was haunting. It would have been easy to lose his sense of self beneath the tide of the past, but Mannfred was strong. He drew what he needed from it and broke contact with the stone before it could in turn begin feeding off him.

'As it is below, so shall it be above,' Mannfred said, stalking out of the cathedral. He swept through the old cages, row after row of prison cells, empty save for a few bones, through into the true library of Drakenhof.

The stacks were immaculately tended, unlike anything else in the old stronghold. Mannfred ran his fingertips over the spines of the old tomes, reading the names off one by one, amazed at the wealth of arcana buried beneath the castle. More so because of the loving care that had obviously gone into maintaining the collection. He walked along aisles of glass cabinets full to bursting with fetishes and gewgaws of faith, fragments of scrolls, shrunken heads, talons of rare birds, onyx and ruby dust, reliquaries and bones of every shape and size from every creature imaginable, seeds, withered husks and shells, pickled faggots of brain in a demijohn, black tulips and black lotus petals, mandrake roots, the wizened heart of a child, dead eyes, bloodstone, a splinter of what looked to be warp stone and cocoons of butterflies along with a colourful spread of wings from the same insects. They were veritable cabinets of curiosities and he knew that each one was in some way vital to a ritual.

Despite his impotence Konrad had chosen to surround himself with all of the accoutrements of magic. For once Mannfred admired his brother-in-death's single-minded obsession.

He wasn't alone.

He paused before the end of the last bookcase in the line, listening intently for the slightest sound out of place. He heard it then, though it was hardly out of place: the slow rustle of a page turning. He waited, listening. He pulled a thick tome from the shelf, dislodging an ungodly amount of dust that billowed up into the musty air. The book was entitled *Die Göttliche Komödie, a Treatise on Morr's Underworld*. He wasn't the least bit interested in the book. It was what lay behind the book that mattered.

A small man sat huddled in the corner of the stacks, a sheaf of vellum on his knee, scratching out words with a quill. A stub of candle burned beside him. His complexion was waxy, his hair matted and lank. He wore a simple scholar's habit. Ink smeared his fingers and the side of his face where he had obviously touched it without thinking.

'It's not ready yet. Soon, I promise. Just a little while longer. It needs to be perfect. So much to write,' the little scholar said without looking up. He scratched out another word, painstakingly re-inking it in a moment later. He looked up from what he was doing, brow furrowing. 'Oh, you're not Konrad. You shouldn't be here.'

Mannfred crouched down beside the scholar. 'Who are you?'

'Constantin.'

'Well, Constantin, what are you doing in my library?'

'Working,' the scholar said earnestly. He clutched the sheets of vellum to his chest. 'But this isn't your library... it is Konrad's.'

'Konrad isn't here any more. That makes this my library and, by extension, whatever you are working on, mine. Let me see.'

Constantin shook his head. 'Where is Konrad? Is this a trick? Are you going to report to him? Tell him that I am loyal, that I will complete my task, that all he needs is a little patience.' At that the little scholar laughed, a bitter barking laugh. 'Patience, does he even know the word? No, no, don't say that!'

'I am master of this castle, Constantin, not my brother.'

'But Konrad is coming back?'

'No, Konrad is not coming back. Konrad is dust and ashes, Constantin.'

'Dust and ashes,' the scholar echoed. 'Is this a joke? Are you trying to trick me into revealing my true feelings? Do you want me to say my master is a mad man? I will. I do not fear him anymore. I am master of my library.'

'When did you last feed, Constantin?'

'I... I don't recall,' the scholar admitted, scratching his head. 'Days, weeks? They have no meaning in the dark.'

Mannfred understood then what had happened to the scholar. Fear had kept him down here working on whatever task Konrad had charged him with, and rather than resurface to feed he had hidden away in the dark and dusty stacks, slowly starving himself into insanity.

Mannfred pried one of the vellum sheets from Constantin's hands, much to the scholar's chagrin. 'Give it back! Mine! That's not for your eyes! No! Not finished.'

Mannfred saw what it was immediately – a ballad, though it made precious little sense, for all of the crossings out and recrossings out. It was about – or seemed to be about – his brother, though it bore no resemblance to the mad one's real life. 'He had you rewriting history? Glorifying his reign?'

'That is my charge... to sow the seed... for he is Vashanesh reborn. He told me so himself.'

'He wasn't, Constantin. He was a miserable paranoid creature unworthy of our sire, and most certainly unworthy of one such as Vashanesh.'

'He could come back... he could be...'

'No,' Mannfred shook his head. 'You are free, Constantin. He is dead, truly dead.'

'Free?' The scholar breathed, as though unfamiliar with the concept.

Mannfred nodded.

He held out a hand for the scholar to take, helping him stand. Constantin was unsteady on his feet. He reeled like a drunk. Flecks of spittle gathered in the corners of his mouth.

'Where are we going? I don't want to see Konrad. I haven't finished. He has a temper. I don't want to anger him.'

'Konrad is dead,' Mannfred said again, as though simple repetition would drum it into the scholar's broken mind. It wouldn't. Not even blood could save him now.

Mannfred wrapped a protective arm around Constantin's shoulder. 'Come, walk with me, I have something wonderful I want to show you.'

'Really?' Constantin asked, his voice full of hope.

'Yes,' Mannfred said, his right hand forcing a way through the scholar's chest and bone, breaking a hole all the way through to his withered heart. For a moment, his hand wrapped around Constantin's ruined heart, Mannfred saw the innocence and openness in the scholar's face, and then it died as he wrenched the organ free, putting the addled vampire out of his misery.

As IT IS below, so shall it be above.

The process of restoring the old castle was monumental. Where Konrad had hidden in the shadows, delving deeper, Mannfred made his own shadows. He was that kind of monster.

Peasants were brought up from the town to toil, serving as hod carriers, bringing the stones to the masons. There was a rhythm to it. They moved like ants marching up and down the ramps to the cries of the overseers. There were casualties, unbalanced by the weight of the stones as they traversed the wooden scaffold to the stonemason. Exhausted men fell. Their stones were collected by other thralls and delivered to the master masons high up on the scaffolds.

As the season turned, the old castle gradually metamorphosed into a thing of majesty spanning the peaks above the city – in effect becoming a city above the city below. Mannfred's Drakenhof was a massive citadel of dark splendour.

Nine towers were added, one a dazzling minaret that speared the sky, three stunted beside the others, flat-topped. Invisible to the world below, Mannfred would retreat to these lower tower tops, where he would drive himself through a series of punishing routines, apparently fighting an invisible opponent. Sometimes he fought open-handed, other times he used weapons, most often swords, though occasionally he trained with a staff carved from black ash.

The work on rebuilding was agonisingly slow. Mannfred chafed at the bit. He wanted the castle restored *beyond* its former glory. It stretched his endurance, but the new count was a patient creature. He could wait, allowing things around him to come to a natural fruition. The rigorous exercise regime was little more than a discipline. He gave himself to it completely, entrusting his chamberlain, Ebrahim, with the day-to-day running of the restoration. The man's understanding of the mathematics of building and the angles of construction was impressive. He was able to predict the curvature of arches, the loads capable of being borne by keystones and the strength of any given foundation based around complicated calculations. He murmured about the sacred geometry underpinning the building – how all the angles came together in a pattern most pleasing to the eye, as though one were looking upon a creation of the divine. Mannfred had to agree there was something awe-inspiring about the castle. It looked less like a gargoyle and more like a majestic black dragon perched upon the mountainside.

The new count was a reclusive beast. He did not impose himself upon his subjects. Runners came with news of strife in neighbouring provinces, the Empire at war, determined to tear itself apart from the inside out. He listened, accumulating knowledge. Knowledge was at the core of everything the new count did. There was no excuse for ignorance. Often he sat alone, poring over obscure arcana in the subterranean library, fathoming another aspect of the esoteric world. He breathed deeply of the wind of magic, savouring the nearness of Shyish in this place. For all his madness Konrad had chosen wisely in bringing his library down here. The old rock was stained with more than just bloodshed. It had an essence of something else, something more. Shyish: the amethyst wind, sixth wind of magic, so dark it appeared almost black as he unravelled it to get at its core. His fascination with the wind was complete. It offered power unlike anything else. To be able to draw from it, weave it into the threads of his desire and create magic was true power.

The two were inextricably joined. One could not draw on the winds without tasting power. One fed the other in an addictive spiral.

Then there was the living book that had escaped with him from the Lands of the Dead. It was unlike anything in the library. He had unwrapped it lovingly, hesitant to touch its corrupt skin, but even as he laid his hand on it he knew, inside, with calm certainty that it was right – that it was his. It always had been, whispered the seductive voice in the back of his mind. As he cracked open the spine a shadow, almost enough to be called a shape of substance, ghosted free, drifting across the wall, though there was no source of light to birth it. Mannfred knew it for what it was. He rose to close the thick velvet drapes and extinguished the single stub of candle that burned, throwing the room into complete darkness. The darkness was no more reassuring. He felt the shadow coil around him seductively. He refused to flinch or recoil. He was stronger than that – he did not jump at shadows.

'Be gone,' he said with such calm authority that the darkness drew away from him with a hiss. A breeze from out of nowhere rifled the vellum pages, turning them quickly. The ambient temperature of the room had dropped considerably. 'I will not repeat myself.' The cover of the living book slammed closed, and he knew, instinctively that he was alone in the room once more.

He kept the living book in the room that Vlad had once shared with his bride Isabella.

It contained such knowledge.

He caressed the binding, turning the page. The words were in no language he could understand, though as he traced his fingers across them he found them making sense, the words awakening some forgotten corner of his brain that linked them all, all of his kind, back to their father Vashanesh. Such was the power of the living book.

It promised such dark delights.

As the castle grew so too did the town below as people were brought in by Ebrahim to serve the new site, and to feed the new count. There was no indiscriminate bloodshed. They came to him willingly, offering their blood, and he drank, though never to the point of death. He cultivated his livestock, leaving them with enough strength to work on the restoration. The needs of Drakenhof came before gluttony.

For when the hunger would not die there was a windowless room, on the seventh floor, where those who would willingly feed the beast lay in narcotic slumber awaiting the return of their master.

MANNFRED SAT ALONE, a raven in his fine-boned hands. The winds were picking up, winter drawing in. There was a chill that hadn't been there even a few weeks before. He sat on the battlements of the Raven Tower overlooking what had been the forest of the impaled. The plain had been turned into a shantytown of lean-to's and shabby tents for the itinerant workers. From his perch the patterns within their movement were all the more obvious.

A distant scream cut off abruptly. He could barely make out the corpse at the foot of the minaret. It lay broken, arms and legs bent in ways their joints were not supposed to allow. He lost interest in the corpse as the birds circled. They would descend, finally, when the corpse was nice and ripe. He was not eager to see it. He took no delight in the savagery of their feeding. Where Vlad had seen a beautifully choreographed dance, Mannfred saw bedlam, every carrion bird prepared to tear the food from the mouth of another should it save them foraging the corpse.

He turned his attention back to the raven in his hands.

The bird was dead, but that was as it had to be for it to work as a conduit. He smoothed back the feathers on its tiny head with his fingers and lifted it so he could see into its dead eyes. He exhaled, his breath ruffling the bird's plumage.

'A woman you say?' he demanded of the dead bird. His words carried halfway around the old world to emerge from the mouth of another dead raven in the hands of Jon Skellan.

'She fed on him, Mannfred,' the bird's beak hung open slackly as the words came out. 'She is one of our kind, but I felt nothing. I stood less than an arm's length from her, and I felt nothing. How can that be?'

'She is not of our blood,' Mannfred told the bird.

'Not of our blood?'

'There are other bloodlines, other families. It was a dark time, the Diaspora, Abhorash, Neferata, Ushoran, Vashanesh, Harakhte, Maatmeses and W'soran all fled the fall of Lahmia, each one seeking safety at the far ends of the world where none might recognise the curse of our kind on them: the stigma. Each one, in time, was progenitor of his own bloodline: Blood Dragon, Lahmian, Strigoi, von Carstein and Necrarch. There are more. It matters little. Some allowed their evil to overwhelm their physical form and are more beast-like than human. Ushoran's Strigoi root around in the dirt of the grave, drinking the turned blood of the long dead. They are quite savage and quite, quite mad. Others, those descended from Neferata, are creatures of exquisite beauty. They cling to what they once were and still call themselves Lahmians. Was she a creature of uncommon beauty this woman of yours?'

'Yes.'

'And she is walking freely through the city?' He marvelled at the thought. 'They do not hunt her?'

'No.'

Mannfred thought about it, about what it meant for a Lahmian to be able to move at will through human society. The possibilities it offered were endless. The temptations...

'I should very much like to meet this woman and her dark mistress.'

'You do not think she is alone?'

'They seldom are. The Lahmians are pack creatures. They congregate. Alone they are weak, but together, together they are strong. There is more to this than meets the eye, my friend. Another piece is in play. I do not like it when I am not in control of the board. It makes me uncomfortable. Things become unpredictable.'

'Well that certainly stops them from becoming boring,' Skellan said through the dead bird. Mannfred did not appreciate the gallows humour.

'There are worse things than facing a predictable enemy, Skellan. Make arrangements. There will be a meeting between our bloodlines. There are things that must be done. Do not fail me.' It was said casually but the threat was implicit. *Do not fail me.*

The bird shuddered once, a final dying breath escaping its fragile corpse, and went still, the communication broken. Mannfred tossed the bird aside.

There were preparations to be made, foundations to be laid.

He looked up at the sky. The first tentative snowflakes of winter turned in the air, melting before they reached the ground.

He opened the door on the seventh floor.

Three women and a man lay on the blood-red divan, the sheets wrapped around their flesh. The man's eyes were glazed, his skin waxen. They were exquisite mortals, all four. The women looked up expectantly. He shook his head slowly, holding out a hand for the man. The man rolled over, still lost in the languid torpor that comes out of the heat of passion. He saw his master in the doorway and rose. Mannfred was selective with those he chose to feed from. There was an intimacy to the act of feeding. It was something to be savoured. The flesh he chose was beautiful. There was no room for ugliness in his menagerie. Why drink from the hag when you can sup on the virgin? Why swallow old, tired blood, when you can get drunk on the innocence of the young?

It reflected his vanity.

The man stood naked before him.

'Come, Rasul,' Mannfred commanded, turning his back on the women's disappointment. All wanted to be favoured by the new count. All were eager to please. He led the man to his own chamber. Neither exchanged a word on the long walk. To those who saw them together, it was curious how one mirrored the other's movements almost perfectly, like a skilled mimic, but it was not just in movement that the two were similar. The man bore an uncanny resemblance to the new count. They were by no means identical, but they were undeniably alike. For that reason and that reason alone, Mannfred tolerated his rudeness.

Mannfred closed the door behind them, and walked over to the window. He looked out over the growing city, amazed once again at the transformation being wrought on his ancestral home. It was his in a way it had never been Vlad or Konrad's. He had stamped his ambition on the very masonry, shaping it in his image.

'Impressive, isn't it?'

The man nodded. It was, though to his eye it looked as though the architects of need and desire had gone to war creating a monstrosity.

'There is so much that still needs to be done, but that is the way of all things. You begin, and it seems from that moment forth you never reach the end. I pity the cattle their short lives at times. How must it feel to never see the completion of one's dreams? Ah, but you would know, Rasul. So tell me, do you ever yearn for time? Do you have dreams of dominion over your own flesh?'

'I do,' the man nodded. 'We all do, I think, at times. We look at our daughters growing up too fast and wish time would stand still for them, holding the moment of their innocence a little longer. Some learn to appreciate the fleeting nature of life, others hunger for more.'

'And you?'

'I hunger for more.'

'Good. That is what I am offering you: more. I will be leaving soon and I would have you look after my interests here, Rasul. I need to have faith that my will shall be done.'

'You have servants my lord, an army who would die for you,' the man grunted, something approaching a laugh. 'They have died for you already, actually. Your will is what binds them to this realm, and you worry that your will shall be done? Have faith.'

Mannfred turned away from the window. He reached out for Rasul, drawing him close. The man came to him willingly, tilting his neck to offer up the vein. A maze of scar tissue had hardened around his throat: puncture wounds that had healed over with time. It was not the first time Mannfred had retreated to this room with the young man, but it had been a while. Of late, Mannfred's tastes had gravitated towards the fulsome young women sprawled naked across the divan, but Rasul was special. There was something almost narcissistic about feeding on the man.

Mannfred ran his tongue across the hard scar tissue before sinking his teeth into Rasul's neck. The blood came into his mouth in a rush. He savoured the delicious shiver that chased through his body and didn't stop. He continued drinking even as the convulsions wracked Rasul's body. Rasul reached up, his hand falling on Mannfred's cheek. A moan of pleasure escaped his lips, as, at the point of death, Mannfred opened his wrist with the razor-cuff and forced the wound into Rasul's mouth. The young man drank greedily. The sharing of blood was exhilarating. Mannfred had to wrench his wrist free of Rasul's suckling. Rasul stared at him, wounded, ragged strips of flesh clogged between his teeth. He licked at his lips, desperate to swallow every last drop of the vampire's astringent blood.

'You will be me,' Mannfred whispered, sinking his teeth back into the young man's throat. 'For all the world you will be me.'

'I will be anything you want me to be,' Rasul breathed, the words leaking out with his last mortal breath.

He died in his sire's arms and was reborn into the world of blood.

CHAPTER SIX

In the Shadow of the Valley of Death
Talabecland, Obelheim in the Färlic Hills

Fate came in the form of a swirling dust devil.

A tiny wisp of smoke like burning parchment appeared on the horizon less than a mile away, the bastard child of a horse and rider rolling like thunder across the dry plain.

They all knew what the rising dust meant. The orders were coming.

Vorster Schlagener pushed back the tent-flap and emerged into the morning. He joined the others watching the rider's approach. Conversations were muted. Silent trepidation rippled through the camp. It was time. There was an air of disbelief. No one breathed a word. No one dared.

Vorster tried to busy himself with some mindless task. Taking out his sword he thought about sharpening it against the whetstone, but he had done exactly that the night before, before turning in for sleep. The blade was as sharp as it had ever been. Instead he oiled his chainmail.

He looked up from the laborious task as the glistening black mare arrived. The rider had almost run the animal into the ground. Foam bubbled from the corners of its mouth and its coat dripped with sweat. Most of the men turned away, unable to watch the rider bring the beast under control and trot up to Vorster. They had been waiting for what felt like forever, but come the hour they were unable to face the course their lives would be forced to take.

The rider was young and surly. He reached into his saddlebag and handed Vorster a sealed dispatch contemptuously. 'You advance to the front,' he said, and jerked on the reins to gather his mare for the return trip. The exhausted horse wheeled around.

'Wait!' Vorster bellowed, tearing off the wax seal and finding nothing of value within.

All too conscious of the fact that the men were looking to him for leadership, Vorster pushed himself to his feet and approached the rider. He lowered his voice, moving close so that his doubt wouldn't carry to them and become contagious. He held up the orders, crushing them in his hand. The details were worryingly thin: *The cavalry to advance rapidly to the front – prevent the enemy carrying away the guns. Talabecland cavalry is on your left. Immediate.* 'Which guns? Where?'

The dispatch rider was derisive. 'What does it matter?' he asked. He waved a dismissive hand at the mouth of the valley. 'There is your enemy. Are you a coward, man? Fight for your master, and do not question him.'

With that he spurred the horse's flanks and rode away.

DIETRICH JAEGER THREW up his hands in sheer delight. 'At last we do *something!*' he said. Vorster did not share his enthusiasm for suicide. 'Too many days sitting on their hands drive the rank and file crazy. Better to keep in the thick of it. Glory, my young friend; that is what it is all about, the glory of war.'

Vorster stood stock still, barely able to keep his temper in check. He felt bitterly aggrieved by the blatant disregard the high command had shown for the lives of his men. He braced his hands on the war table and waited for his superior officer's dresser to finish fumbling about trying to put the preening fop's boots on. The dresser buffed the leather with a rag. He wanted to stuff the idiot's words down his throat so that he choked on them. There was no glory in war. The longer he served men like Dietrich Jaeger the more he realised that their idea of honour was an outmoded concept. What it really meant was dying spectacularly and stupidly.

'Now we'll show those infantry swine a thing or two. They can be the butt of *our* jokes for a change.'

Vorster bit his tongue. He wanted to say something. He wanted to point out the idiocy of the orders, but he knew that Jaeger wouldn't care one whit. The man was a buffoon. He looked at the he map of the battlefield. It was an unmitigated mess and the orders that went with it were suicidal. He looked up from the map, straight at Jaeger. 'Show them what, exactly, sir? That we place no value on human life? Well we could show them that, most certainly. You know as well as I do that no cavalry should ever charge blackpowder gun emplacements. Even just a few cannons and a line of flintlocks are enough to wreak havoc among the horses.'

Jaeger got to his feet dismissively. 'Nonsense! You fuss like an old woman. Just imagine! It will be glorious!'

'I am imagining, sir. It will be slaughter. The horses panic and we're cut off and the entire field becomes pandemonium. Not to mention that we have a weakness on our left flank.'

Jaeger snapped his fingers for a goblet of wine. His dresser moved up smoothly to his side with a fine glass and a decanter filled with ruby red liquid. He poured the officer a glass and then melted back into the shadows in the corner of the command tent. 'What weakness?' Jaeger quipped sauntering over to join Vorster. 'What are you talking about, man? Really, Vorster, you asked for more horses and I found a way to give you horses.'

'I did not ask for stallions, sir, and for good reason.'

Jaeger sighed elaborately, and raised his hands to the heavens as though beseeching Sigmar to intervene on his behalf. 'You really are an impudent son of a bitch, you know that? Let me remind you that you are a junior officer! *My* junior officer. Now, where is Lord Ignatz?' Jaeger sipped his wine, rich, like a goblet of blood. He glanced at his dresser. 'This really is very good, Fredrich. Where did we get this one?'

'Sir, with respect–'

Jaeger slammed his goblet down on the table slopping a deep red stain right across the map of the valley, a foreshadowing of the slaughter to come if the idiots were allowed to run the asylum. 'Good God, Vorster! What does it matter?'

Vorster spoke slowly and carefully, enunciating every word perfectly as though he were talking to a simpleton. 'Because, commander, cavalry horses are either geldings or mares. *Ours* are mares, and our mares are *in heat.*'

Jaeger clapped an amused hand over his mouth and laughed from his belly. 'So we'll breed ourselves a new division!' he chortled, tickled at the notion of his junior's prudishness. 'Let the stallions have their heads, and see the enemy tremble.'

'The strength of our plan is in our swiftness, and surprise,' Lord Ignatz declared melodramatically as he swept into the tent unannounced. 'Mark my words, boys, we'll be on top of them before they can get off their first shot. What good are their cannons then, eh?'

Vorster seized on the glimmer of hope. 'Did the scouts return? I didn't see them.'

Ignatz seemed bemused by the question. 'I can see the range from my tent flap perfectly well. If we pass through the valley here, at Ramius Point,' he said, driving his knife into the map with cold arrogance, 'we ride up over the ridge, and they'll never see us coming.'

The knife was buried right in the darkest part of the spilled wine.

'There!' Jaeger said excitedly, jabbing a finger at Ignatz's chest for Vorster's benefit. 'There is a man who understands strategy.'

Vorster felt the blood drain from his face. Since the battle had begun Dietrich Jaeger had taken no steps to find out what was happening beyond the mounds, hillocks and ridges that cut off their view of the ground that had fallen into the hands of the enemy, none at all.

The worst tactical mistake a commander could make was to assume that the battlefield remained static, that all the pieces of the enemy's forces had remained exactly where they were at their last encounter. The battlefield was dynamic, constantly shifting.

Vorster cast a desperate eye over the battle plans laid out on the table. There was no guarantee that the Talabeclanders were in any of the positions Jaeger had assigned to them. Any idiot ought to know enough to wait for the latest scout reports, but no, not this idiot.

Dietrich Jaeger was determined they should go in blind and no matter what Vorster said he couldn't make the man see that it was suicide. The fool was blinded by promises of glory. No doubt he had already begun drafting something to say when the elector count himself came to laud him with praise for his unsurpassed heroism – arrogant, ignorant fool.

Vorster quietly made his way towards the exit. 'I'll tell the men to get a good night's rest,' he said. 'I assume we go at dawn?'

Jaeger shook his head. 'Oh I don't think so, young man. I didn't put my boots on to go to sleep. Tell them to saddle up. We go in an hour.'

WHEN THE TIME came, three hundred and sixty-five men and bristling horses made a gleaming display spread out across the dead earth of the Hardamin Flats.

It had threatened snow earlier in the day, but the wind had picked up, blowing the clouds through. The afternoon sky was clear – a glorious day, as Jaeger had said, emerging from the command tent. The sun, past its zenith, was still high in the sky and there wasn't a cloud to be seen.

Vorster eyed the afternoon sky with unease, hoping in vain that Jaeger would see sense. By the time they reached the valley floor the sun would be low and in their eyes.

Of course, Dietrich Jaeger was more concerned with clambering up onto an old wooden chest so that he could deliver his little speech, exhorting the men to valour in the name of Martin and freedom. He really was an odious little toad. He didn't care for a minute that the charge represented the single biggest stroke of insanity ever perpetrated on the field of battle, because it, like his stallions, would be glorious.

Vorster let the words wash over him, filling his senses instead with the strong smell of oiled leather, polished steel and anxious horses. He went inside himself, centring his spirit around a calm core. He had no god to pray to, none that he believed capable of intervening as he plunged headlong into the mouth of madness, at any rate.

It wasn't that he was afraid to die; he had made his peace with whatever deity had spawned him a long time ago. Dying on some foreign field was not what worried him, either. It wasn't that he was filled with sudden regrets for the things he hadn't done. It wasn't even that there were so many beautiful and ugly women he had yet to make the acquaintance of. None of that mattered. He would die willingly for freedom. He believed in what Martin of Stirland asked his men to do, and admired the fact that Martin could be seen on the battlefield, not hiding away behind the command line. The man was a natural leader. Unfortunately he was surrounded by a few too many fools, and Vorster didn't suffer fools gladly.

He snapped out of his introspection as the roar went up, the men vaunting their leader. Jaeger and Ignatz thrived on this rubbish; it pandered to their egos.

They moved into position.

When the final command was given, field commander Lord Ignatz dropped his sword in a flashing - and yet cold - salute and the cavalry rode out as one.

THE GROUND TREMBLED under hoof, the advance sending ripples through the earth.

The riders moved across the plain, stalking beasts, the scent of blood in the air, eager to chase the jackals of Talabecland from their turf.

They rode, triumphant, into the mouth of the valley, the banner of Stirland snapping in the breeze. Vorster surveyed the terrain from his mount. The first three quarters of a mile was a gentle descent into a narrow pass between cliffs that rose up like gnashing teeth ready to crush them. It was here that the first sign of trouble came, from the left flank as stallions and mares became pressed together, intoxicated by each other's heady scents. The proximity was too much for one powerful horse and the stallion reared up, attempting to mount the mare before it, throwing the rider from his saddle and smashing another man with its flailing hooves.

A wave of panic rippled out from the chaos.

Vorster rode forwards. There was no time for doubt or hesitation. Panic was a rare beast. Once it took hold in one mount it would spread like wildfire through the others. He steered his own stallion through the press of horses until he was close enough to take charge.

He drew his sword and slit the throat of the frisky stallion. The beast screamed and rolled onto its side causing two more riders to guide their mounts away from the bright red spray of blood that gouted out across parched soil and men alike.

It did not slow their advance even a hoof beat.

As the valley opened out before them the arrowhead shaped tip of the imposing Ramius Point ridge loomed ever closer. Vorster spurred his horse forwards, coming up level with Ignatz. He saw a flash of uncertainty in the man's eyes. The fool had not thought to take the fork into account.

'Which track, sir?' Vorster asked earnestly. 'Left or right?'

Ignatz ignored him, straightening up in the saddle. He rode forwards as if nothing was wrong. 'Left or right, sir?'

The decision was vital. Vorster mapped the battlefield out mentally, placing the landmarks according to what he remembered seeing on the map. The reality was nothing like the map though. Left or right? One track gave limited cover. The other did not. The time for sending out scouts to check the lie of the land was long passed. Ignatz ought to have known immediately which tine of the fork they should take. He could see the conflict in the officer's eyes. He was clueless.

Vorster pressed the point. 'Which track, sir? Left or right?'

Ignatz fumbled with his sword, the sweat from his palm loosening his grip. 'The left – no! The right!'

'Surely the left offers more cover, sir.'

'I said the *right!*' And with that Ignatz spurred his mount hard and surged ahead to lead the way, brandishing his sword above his head and shouting, 'Canter!'

The calvary upped its pace and followed him into the corner.

The hot, sweaty muscle of the warhorses beat out the faster rhythm of their advance. The dust from so many angry hooves, thrown up into the air like a ghostly shroud, announced their approach to all.

The lip of the ridge came into view.

The bowl of the Färlic Hills lay beyond the ridge.

Horses and riders streamed up the incline. It was too late to turn back. They rode out into no-man's land.

FROM THEIR VANTAGE point on the Obelheim Plateau, high above the bowl, the Stirland command watched Lord Ignatz's advance with increasing alarm. It was lunacy in the extreme. They couldn't – in all honesty – believe what they were seeing. Their orders had been simple enough, deliberately so, to avoid the chance of mistakes like this.

It was suicide, nothing more and nothing less.

'Where in Sigmar's name does he think he is going?' Martin breathed in disbelief.

Junior officers scrambled to make sense of Ignatz's manoeuvres as they compared them to the battle plans laid out before them and the orders they had given him, but it was quite impossible to enforce any kind of logic onto the charge. The idiot was taking them the wrong way!

Flustered, Oskar Zenzi, one of Martin's more trusted Kompmeister's hurried over to his marshal's side. 'We've checked the maps, double checked them, sir, and well, we believe he's going the wrong way, sir.'

'I can see the fool is going the wrong way, man! I am not blind! My orders were explicit. He was to outflank the enemy!' The Marshall's voice dropped an octave as the gravity of Ignatz's mistake began to settle in. 'Where does that path lead him?'

Zenzi rubbed at his face. He had gone very pale. 'Right across the enemy cannons, sir, and well within their range.'

The command post descended into bedlam. The chaos was mirrored on the field of battle below. Shouts rang out, officers desperate to apportion and deflect blame for the fiasco. They tripped over themselves in a hurry to address the Marshall's rage until finally one of them had the presence of mind to roar at the dispatch rider.

'Get your arse down there and tell him to pull back, man! Tell him to pull back!'

It was a desperate gallop, the messenger driving his horse into the ground, and even as the beast gave up the ghost and collapsed beneath him he saw it was for nothing.

The cavalry had been engaged.

They were as good as dead.

THE FIRST BLASTS were deafening. They shook the ground with a jarring ferocity, but mercifully they were off target.

Vorster knew they were nothing more than probing round shots to enable the Talabecland gunners to judge their distances. The second volley would be lethal.

Iron cannonballs hit the ground obliquely, skipping over the cavalrymen's heads. The air grew thick with churning dust making it difficult to see where they were going, and in the process transforming the pockmarked soil into a silent death trap. One hit its mark, bringing horse and rider down in a spray of blood and bone. His screams were hideous.

'Listen to me! It's not too late to turn back! There's no cowardice in it!' Vorster pleaded, but Ignatz was having none of it. He held his sword arm firmly aloft, keeping the men at canter and crying, 'Steady…! *Steady…!*'

'We're too exposed, sir! This is insane! Get your head out of your arse and think for once, sir!'

'Damn you, man, we ride!' Ignatz bellowed.

More cannon fire came spewing down upon them, a barrage from somewhere ahead and to the left. It was a brutal mixture this time that was far more accurate in finding targets. Explosive shells, cannon balls filled with black powder, began the volley and grapeshot ended it, canvas bags stuffed with clusters of small iron shot that mowed the nearest horses down as if taking a saw to their flesh. It was ruthlessly efficient in decimating the ranks of the Stirland riders.

Small pockets of fire pocked the front and rear lines. The air stank of burned horseflesh. The cries of the fallen beasts were pitiful. The stink in turn made the remaining horses skittish.

Clouds of smoke rafted up from the smouldering earth. Many of the riders that had escaped the onslaught found themselves disorientated by smoke and noise, their mounts turning frantically on themselves, bucking and shying blindly. Too many of the frightened beasts stumbled into the craters, falling badly and breaking their necks and legs.

Despite the brutal efficacy of the bombardment it was merely the opening salvo in what was a massacre.

Vorster struggled with his stallion, exercising a heavy hand on the beast to keep it from bolting. He could see precisely where the Talabeclander emplacements were situated. The main range of cannons was strung out in an arc across the top of the Färlic Hills, at the far end of the bowl, while flanking positions bore down on either side.

He spat and swore bitterly. Ignatz was every bit as big a fool as Jaeger. How could any commander not know that the Talabeclanders had a triangulated bead on anyone that entered the valley?

This head on assault was nothing short of madness. Vorster wheeled his horse around, looking down the ruined line. Another barrage would decimate their ranks, effectively rendering them impotent. Ignatz *had* to be able to see he had made a mistake, had to. He was just too pig-stubborn to order a retreat.

Vorster watched in horror as Ignatz lowered his sword arm, thrusting his blade forwards into the booming din ahead and gave one almighty cry, '*Charge!*' The cavalrymen spurred their horses into full gallop and into hell's chasm.

Within the blink of an eye the horse and rider alongside Vorster vanished from view as a cannonball ploughed into the mare's skull only to explode through its ribs, taking the rider's leg with it.

Vorster kept his hands on the reins, too afraid to wipe the kiss of warm scarlet from his face. He gritted his teeth and spurred his mount on, jumping it over the corpse of another fallen mare. Huge puffballs of smoke rose silently from the hills over to the right, followed seconds later by the roar of another barrage. Bone and horseflesh blossomed across the battlefield to the cacophony of shrill screaming.

Still the Stirlanders plunged forwards, closer to the ranks of the Talabeclanders and their guns, closer to their objectives, and right into the curtain fire from the Talabecland fusiliers.

The sudden furious pop, pop of muskets pierced the deep booming rumbles of cannon fire like dry twigs snapping on an open fire. One after the other, horses reared, and Stirlander cavalrymen were thrown back, their bodies riddled with bloody punctures.

Vorster quickly lost sight of Ignatz, and the other cavalry commanders in the thick blanket of smoke and dust that had descended upon the battlefield turning day into night. He orientated himself by the drum of thundering hooves until suddenly he was thrown from his horse.

Whether it had stumbled or had been hit he couldn't say. It was gone. Gunfire rifled the air, adding to the chaos of battle. He heard a brief whinny and then there was a moment of shocking silence. He tumbled through the dirt and staggered to his feet, drawing his sword. He stumbled forwards. His head reeled. Though the roar of battle was at hand, he could see none of it. Smoke rendered him utterly blind. Occasionally he heard the drumming hooves of a horseman galloping by, but he was gone again before he could call out, and just as quickly he was lost in the smoke again.

Then… then the tide of battle took another turn.

Vorster heard the clash of steel.

It was an unmistakable sound, and it meant only one thing: the Talabecland army was on the field!

Vorster raced blindly towards the din, his sword outstretched, thinking only to fight his way free of the slaughter. Twenty paces into the smoke he came face to face with a mighty Talabecland cavalryman bearing down on him, sabre raised.

Vorster stood his ground, braced for the blow to land. He struggled to regulate his breathing, slow it so that panic didn't overwhelm him. He waited, only to side step at the very last moment and ram the tip of his blade into the side of the charging animal. The gash was deep and bloody, cutting into the horse's stomach and spilling its guts. The horse bucked furiously, throwing its rider to the ground ten feet beyond Vorster.

The rider landed badly. His neck was obviously broken, but he was still alive and struggling to breathe. The fallen man's eyes bulged with fear as he watched his enemy approach, utterly helpless to do anything about it.

'Please…' the man begged, barely forming the word.

Vorster was merciful and quick.

He hoped, when it came to it, that some Talabeclander would do the same for him.

* * *

THE END, WHEN it came, was inevitable.

He fell beneath the swords of two men, beaten into the ground by the savagery of their blows.

He crawled in the dirt, but he would not beg.

His sword had fallen so far from his fingers. He did not want to die without it in his hand. He needed to reach it. He tried to move, but a fierce kick in the side of the ribs lifted him bodily from the mud and left him clutching at his gut in agony. He gasped but couldn't catch his breath. A second kick turned him over so that he lay face up, looking at the sneering face of his enemy.

Vorster, tried to breathe, but the heel of a well-placed boot came down to crush his windpipe.

He clawed at the leather, but was helpless against its force.

He gave up, waiting for the inevitable killing stroke, be it stamp or stab.

The cold tip of steel rested against his eye socket; the enemy was not ugly, not some monster. He could have been looking at himself. He felt a surge of sadness that it should come to this, here. The young Talabeclander officer leaned over him. 'Why?' his voice shook with raw emotion.

Vorster struggled for air, aware that there were others surrounding him, but he would not answer.

'You knew it was madness...'

Vorster felt the rage within. He could see his sword. The leather wrapped hilt was five feet away, no more, if he could just reach it...

The boot pressed down harder.

'For all your leader's folly, you showed great courage this day, soldier,' the young Talabeclander said, admiration in his tone. 'It would be a shame to kill you, so please do not give me the excuse. You will be our heroic guest. I cannot say whether it will be a long stay.'

The last thing Vorster Schlagener heard as he slipped into unconsciousness was, 'Dress his wounds. Then bind him and take him away.'

UNDER FLAGS OF truce the dead and wounded were brought back from the silent valley.

There was an air of disbelief about the high command. Anger at the stupidity of one man grew into grief as they built huge pyres for their dead.

Of the 365 men who had charged down the valley less than sixty returned. Ignatz, the man responsible for the debacle, was not amongst them. Corpses littered the battlefield.

Horses streaming with blood and unable to get to their feet bit at the short grass with froth-covered teeth.

The occasional sharp, melancholy cry of a horse dying beneath the farriers' knives filled the air.

CHAPTER SEVEN

The Lahmian Temple
Nuln, the Imperial City

THE WOMAN, NARCISA, fascinated Skellan.

She was an enigma.

She moved freely amongst the living while he was forced to hide in the gutters and the Unterbaunch beneath the Alt Stadt, eating off scraps while she played the social butterfly, moving from arm to arm of the rich and influential, laughing, charming and seductive. They loved her. Night after night he spied on her from the shadows, watching her nocturnal promenades with actors, merchants, aristocrats and men of undeniable power. She gravitated towards those who had power, or had some kind of influence over the power-mongers. No one seemed to notice her nature. Certainly there was none of the hysteria that would have accompanied Skellan revealing his presence to the cattle. They adored Narcisa. They flocked to her, feted her and pandered to her, all in the hope of getting closer to her flame that they might bask in her glory. Though of course if they succeeded in getting close enough, Skellan knew, they would get burned, but how many moths cared about that as they flocked to the flame?

She was clever, ruthlessly cunning and selective in her feeding pattern.

He quickly realised she was feeding off each and every one of the gentlemen callers he saw her with – a little here, a little there, a kiss turned overly playful, a cut tenderly administered. There were ways of drawing blood that they didn't even notice. Narcisa was tender, loving and amused by their jokes, and she made them all feel like fortunate fools. It amazed Skellan that none of them noticed just how 'too good to be true' the Lahmian was. Still, the cattle were not the brightest of creatures.

Occasionally he followed her back to her chambers and would sit while she put on a show for him, seducing the bright young things, and then taking what she wanted in return for what they wanted. He appreciated her performances, but resisted the urge to take a lead role in her little tragedy of passion.

Over nights of watching, Skellan came to realise that she was not alone, far from it. When he knew what to look for it became easier to spot them. During his stalking of Narcisa she encountered perhaps fifteen more of her kind – blood-sucking females seducing their way into positions of influence in the hierarchy of Nuln.

Walking still pained him. The witch hunter's bolt had left its mark, the head buried deep in his arse. He had pulled it out, but the damned thing was tipped with silver so it had burned him deep inside and refused to heal. So he walked with a limp, dragging his left leg slightly. It added to the illusion though. Any who spotted him would have assumed, naturally, that he was some sort of cripple left to beg, following the mayhem of the civil war.

Some nights he followed Narcisa, other nights he followed one of the other girls. They were all curiously similar, beautiful, more beautiful than the courtesans and hangers on that had flocked to Konrad, most certainly, and easily as beautiful as Vlad's own Isabella who, in Skellan's memories of her, was an exquisite beauty. He had never thought to see such beauty in the flesh again.

THE DARKNESS HELD, refusing to give way to dawn.

It was cold. Winter was close.

A horse drawn carriage rumbled past his hiding place. The animal's hooves sparked on the cobbles and streamers of steam coiled out of its flared nostrils. It stamped hard on the ground, whinnying.

Skellan backed away into deeper shadow, willing the beast to walk on.

The horse shied, kicking out, and then came down, breaking into a canter. The carriage driver pulled back on the reins and cried, 'Ho, girl!'

The horse didn't calm until it was well past Skellan's hiding place.

The clouds were thick, promising snow.

Skellan walked in the shadows, never far from the woman's side. She knew he was there. Still he refused to step out into the false glow of the streetlights. He felt uncomfortable, the beast stalking beauty. He had to remind himself that she was no damsel. The woman was every bit the predator he was. Moreso, perhaps, as she fed on countless men, keeping them alive as long as they furthered her ambitions. There was a callousness to it that was exciting to him.

He was moving into familiar territory.

It felt like an age since he had hunted these streets with Mannfred, but they had not changed so much. He remembered, with a sly smile, the various tastes of the Family Liebowtiz as they had succumbed. That night of the long knives had been one like no other. He had revelled in the culling. They had died in so many inventive ways, defenestrated, despoiled and degraded, that the ingenuity of the murders challenged him even now. It sent a thrill of pleasure through Skellan just thinking about it.

Indeed, the city still reeled from it.

The influence of the family had been severely weakened – to the point that a splinter of the family had emerged with a variant pronunciation of their name: Liebewitz. It was a subtle difference in tonal delivery, but it set them apart from the tragedy. Rumour had it that it was a half-brother of one of the dead that had surfaced from somewhere to claim the family fortunes and with no one to stop him, he had succeeded. There were all sorts of suppositions about him having been drummed out of the family when they were still alive, but Skellan wasn't interested. The original pronunciation of the name had all but died out, it seemed. But then, few liked to be reminded of the horrors Skellan and von Carstein had visited upon the city. It was natural that the survivors would try to distance themselves from that dark time. It had been then that he had learned the truth about the stranger he travelled with and about his hungers – that it was Mannfred, Vlad's first born. Soon after that, Mannfred had left him to travel into the Lands of the Dead in search of the dark wisdom of the great necromancer, Nagash.

She led him through the Sonder district into the Smalz quarter. Businesses became few and far between and the houses grew gradually more impressive with colonnades and almost skeletal stone structures. A great many of the houses were dominated by sharply pointed ogive arches, ribbed vaults, clustered columns, sharply pointed spires, flying buttresses and decorative detail. On one such mansion, Skellan saw grim-faced gargoyles and on another what appeared to be butterflies attacking a terrified man. It was all an exercise in indulgence, a way of showing off the owner's wealth. It was gratuitous and ugly to his eye.

Further removed from the press of people it became colder, too. He drew his collar up, covering half of his face. The cold was no real discomfort; it was more the illusion of fitting in. One of the cattle seeing him wrapped up against the elements would think nothing of it, just another poor sod out in the cold, making him instantly forgettable. The alternative, Skellan standing on the corner in his shirt oblivious to the cold, would stick in the mind of any who happened to see him.

She stopped at a set of imposing iron gates, easing them open and slipping through. A serpent had been woven around the black iron bars of either gate, fangs bared in threat. Skellan didn't follow, at least not directly.

He waited across the street from the iron gates, watching. The mansion was walled off. The wall was nine feet high and topped with creepers and flowering vines. The trick was making it look as though he belonged. An interloper stood out a mile if he acted like one... Skellan was not by nature a patient man, though. Waiting went against the grain. He looked up and down the street for a good spot from which to carry out his surveillance. The street was empty save for two carriages. Lime trees lined the far side of the road. The lime was a fascinating species of tree, said to grow on unmarked graves. The wind dragged through the leaves, creating an unnerving susurrus that sighed through the trees.

He was grateful that there were no horses or dogs for him to concern himself with.

He walked slowly across the cobbled street, approaching the gate. The wall, he saw, was actually topped with shards of broken glass that were hidden beneath the flowering vines. A few of the broken pieces poked through the green.

The snake appeared to be made out of copper, the elements having oxidised it a bilious shade of green, and they were deceptively well crafted, cast from a single mould and used as a sheath on the iron bar. He touched one of the copper snake's teeth. It was sharp enough to draw a bead of blood with the least bit of pressure.

Skellan focused his senses, picking out the sweet fragrance of a woman's perfume and the damp of bark surrendering to mould, with the faint overlay of a more astringent musk. It took him a moment to isolate it: catsfoot, or cudweed as they called it back home. It was an aroma he hadn't smelled in the longest time. Lizbet had sworn by it as a cure-all, good for loosening bowels and efficacious against even the most potent snake bites. He heard the caw of a crow, the rustle of the wind through the lime leaves, and the more distant murmur of water.

He felt the first snowflake of the night on his upturned cheek.

Skellan looked at the sky. A storm was coming.

He eased open the iron gate, pushing it back on protesting hinges, and slipped into the grounds of the mansion house. The grounds were well tended, the rose bushes dead-headed, the japonicas cut back, even the vines clinging to the façade of the manse were well maintained in a careful state of managed disrepair, giving the old house an edge of wildness that Skellan found appealing. Left of the serpentine drive lay a small lake, frozen over, and behind it an architectural folly that acted as a small boathouse. On the right were more gardens, a grove of beech trees and a huge stone mausoleum.

He skirted the high wall, keeping to the fringe of the well-cultivated garden until he reached the mausoleum. A line of gravestones stood like broken teeth across the front of the building giving it something of a grim smile. Each of the tombstones was engraved with the mark of the snake. It was obviously some sort of family crest, tied for who knows how long to the old house. The motto 'Es liegt im Blut' was carved into the lintel above the mausoleum's door. 'It runs in the blood.' Skellan couldn't help but smile at the obvious irony of the words.

He tried the door. It was sealed.

Instead of forcing his way in, he sat with his back to one of the gravestones, watching the comings and goings of the house and its nocturnal visitors. They came and went in pairs and alone, the women of the night. It seemed they all returned to the manse after feeding, to share whatever they had learned with whoever dwelled there – almost certainly their hidden mistress, just as Mannfred had assumed.

The manse evidently served as the focus for their infiltration of the echelons of Nuln's society.

Again he was disturbed that the Lahmian's could live in such obvious opulence and not attract the wrath of witch hunters and bigots claiming the holy bloody right of Sigmar to crush anything they didn't understand. The depth of their deception was staggering.

Flakes of snow were drifting down, whipping up over the top of the gravestone and away, melting before they reached the ground. Skellan wrapped his cloak around him and pulled the hood up over his head so that only the broken profile of his nose protruded. He itched at the leather patch across his eye. Judging by the moon's position it was well past the middle of the night.

Despite, or because of, the lateness of the hour, the manse was far from deserted. He watched as two young debutantes in high boots and long fur coats walked arm in arm out of the main house. They talked lightly, giggling as they walked around the rim of the lake. Together they slipped through the gate and back out into the city proper, destined, no doubt, for some aristocratic bed somewhere. The trailing edge of their laughter reached him as they passed by on the other side of the wall.

Still he waited.

More women came through the gate, more left.

The women frequently turned and seemed to stare right at him as though sensing his presence in the grounds, but none saw him.

Finally Narcisa emerged from the house.

Skellan detached himself from the shadows and moved up behind her, catching the Lahmian by the throat as he wrapped his other arm around her waist. He leaned in close, whispering in her ear: 'My master would meet your mistress, Lahmian.'

The woman didn't flinch. 'Then perhaps he would care to ask instead of sending his brute in to force an invitation?'

Skellan added pressure to her throat, knowing even as he did so that she had no need of breath. Frustration caused him to squeeze savagely enough to crush her windpipe. He felt her stiffen against him, resisting. Beneath the pretty curves her musculature was a match for iron. He struggled to hold her.

'Make it happen.'

'The Eternal does not see commoners, vampire,' Narcisa said, sneering.

'Oh I think she will make an exception for this commoner.'

'Do you think we don't know who you are? Who your uncommon master is? You really are a clueless brute, aren't you Jon Skellan?'

'How could you...?'

She twisted, so that her mouth was beside his ear, reversing their roles of captive and captor. Her eyes, he saw, were different: one glaucous blue, the other flecked with hazel. The imperfection only served to make her all the more appealing.

'We are observers. We watch; we listen. We do not bluster and preen, craving attention and approval for our wickedness. We simply observe. It is amazing what you can learn by paying attention to the world around you. Of course, you wouldn't know as you are too busy playing the thug for your master. Does he call you whelp?'

'I could end your life here, with my bare hands, woman. Do not push me into something you would not live long enough to regret,' Skellan rasped.

'See? Bluster. You need my help to see to it that your master, the new Count of Drakenhof, if I am not mistaken, and I am seldom mistaken, meets with my mistress. Do you think ending my life would please either of them? One might go so far as to suggest it would bring a world of hurt down upon your head, vampire. So, why don't you try again? Tell me why I should help you?'

'You have a good thing here, you and your kind, but don't make the mistake of believing it will last forever, Narcisa. It won't, I promise you that.'

'So you threaten me again in an attempt to earn my trust and win my support? You really are quite the animal, and I don't mean that as a compliment.'

She turned easily in his arms, as he arched back, releasing the beast within. His face twisted as he grabbed her by the hair and yanked her head back. He lunged forwards, sinking his teeth into her throat and tearing out a mouthful of her tainted flesh. He tasted her black blood, swallowed gluttonously and then pulled his head back. Skellan savoured the look of fear in her eyes. To be feared was an intensely erotic feeling. 'You taste... luxurious. Now,' he said, licking her blood from his lips. 'My master will meet your mistress. You will make it happen.'

She nodded, all the fight gone from her body.

They were not equals. For all that she might have wanted to pretend otherwise, playing the aristocrat, Skellan had shown that the beast was more than a match for beauty. It had taken a single moment of blistering savagery to impose his will on her. She had buckled, leaving him dominant.

BEYOND THE CITY gates peasants fired up by the witch hunter Moroi stormed the Strigany caravans.

The winter night could not have been bleaker. A thin patina of snow had fallen, but instead of adding an edge of romance to the city streets it only served to drape a ghostly veil of despair over a world locked in winter. A bitter wind chased through the narrow streets, sending corkscrews of snow twisting across the frozen cobbles.

They ran through those narrow frozen streets, shouting and screaming, torches blazing. They swarmed over the Strigany camp, pulling caravan doors open and shattering windows. As the mob mentality gripped them, righteousness turned to fury. A thick muscled townsman threw his burning brand through the door he'd just yanked open. He stood there waiting for the fire to catch, blocking the exit. As the travellers emerged from their caravan, coughing and choking on the smoke, the townsman thrust another burning brand into their faces, blinding them with fire. As they backed away he tossed a second brand into their home while around him others followed suit, throwing open caravan doors and shattering windows, setting light to the caravans. The screams only served to ignite their anger, the mob feeding off the fear. They plunged into the burning caravans and dragged the Strigany out by the hair, kicking and screaming. One weasel of a man thrust his firebrand into the face of an old grey haired crone. The air quickly smelled of burned meat and brimstone as her hair charred away from her scalp.

'Is it here, Moroi? Can you feel its presence?' Arminus Vamburg whispered, his breath conjuring wraiths of mist to hang like a veil between the living and the dead. The violence of the mob frightened the man, but it was a necessary evil. They couldn't hope to flush the beast out without it. The waning moon was a sickly silver eye barely floating above the rooftops. Vamburg ignored the icy chill worming its way into his heart, and wiped the sweat from his brow before it could freeze there. His lips were chapped from the wind's perpetual kiss.

Moroi nodded once.

A cruel wind drove the clouds through the sky, continually masking and unmasking the moon, so that the trees lining the street appeared to shamble like rows of gnarled corpses

'Bring out the beast!' Moroi cried.

Others took up the chant, banging on the sides of the caravans.

Snow began to fall thicker, a flurry blowing up into a storm. And from out of the centre of the storm came the beast.

It was not a giant and did not have two heads or blood-dripping fangs. It was a warrior with a huge double-headed warhammer in its meaty fists. It was not the wolf he had chased, but the sickness surging through his body told Moroi that the man walking towards him through the snow and fire was most assuredly a vampire.

The bravura leaked out of the living as they felt the power of the vampire, the dark aura of fear that the creature exuded. Some fell to their knees, while others scrambled back, trying to hide within the shadows, close to the walls. Only Moroi and Vamburg stood their ground, unflinching.

'Funny thing, death,' Jerek said, his voice bereft of inflection. 'You would think it would hurt more.' Then, almost wistfully, he asked 'Have you come to put me out of my misery? I should like that, but it isn't time. There are still things I must do.'

'Your life is forfeit, vampire,' Moroi said.

'I have no life, *mortal*,' Jerek answered. His bitter smile widened, his thin bloodless lips peeling slowly back from the white of his carnivorous teeth. 'Isn't that why you are here? Don't do this, please. Don't. Just walk away from here. Let this be one of those rare occasions when all these others live.'

'You cannot live if you are not alive.'

'I meant you.'

Moroi raised his handheld crossbow and aimed it at the beast's heart. He fired two bolts, less than a second apart, and he knew, even as he squeezed down on the trigger that his was aim true.

Jerek's hand lashed out, deflecting the first bolt so that it spun harmlessly wide, and snatching the second out of the air. He snapped it derisively.

Vamburg pulled a flask of blessed water out of his leather satchel, unstoppered it and hurled it into Jerek's face, babbling a line of prayer. The beast's skin hissed and steamed where the water hit, but it didn't slow his advance. He came at Vamburg first, surging forwards, the monster tearing out from beneath his skin as he launched himself into a blistering attack the man had no earthly hope of fending off.

It was brutal, savage, ugly, and tragic.

The man threw up his hands desperately trying to deflect Jerek's fury, but it was useless.

Jerek's fingers sheered through half of Vamburg's face, ripping his nose and half of his cheek away in a single bloody tear. The man's screams were hideous to hear. His blood soaked the settling snow. The speed of the attack was dizzying, the ferocity nauseating. Crouching over him, Jerek grabbed both sides of his head in his hands and snapped his neck clean in two with a savage twist. He dropped the man and reared back and howled. He did not feed. Indeed, for the shocking nature of the attack, more shocking still was that the beast retreated from the spilled blood.

There was a second when the entire street was locked in shocked paralysis and then Moroi hurled himself at the beast, only to be battered back almost inconsequentially. He sprawled in the thin layer of snow, scuffing it up as he scrambled, trying to get back to his feet.

Jerek rose, standing over the witch hunter.

The crowd of vigilantes stared, torches spitting sparks that danced high into the air. The sparks conjured wraiths of steam that spun away in tight spirals. None dared move. Their pitchforks and makeshift spears hung slackly in their hands, their wooden stakes clattered to the floor as fear – real genuine terror – wormed its way into their hearts.

'Do not make me kill you, man. I have no taste for blood. There is something I must do. Then I will seek you out and you can end my life. If you try to stop me, I will kill you. I promise you that. You have my word, as a wolf of Ulric.'

'Your *word*?' Moroi spat, nursing his bruised and bloody chin. 'You kill my friend and expect me to let you leave, on your *word*?'

'No, I expect you to come after me and die. I just don't want to be forced to kill you. I have enough blood on my hands. I have no desire to add yours.' He turned his back on the witch hunter, as though goading him to try.

'You are an affront to nature,' Moroi swore. 'And I will come after you beast. I will come after you and kill you. That I promise.' For a promise it sounded dreadfully hollow, even to the witch hunter's ears.

None of the would-be vampire slayers stopped him as Jerek walked away into the darkness.

SKELLAN STARED AT the curious bird.

It was neither crow nor raven but some kind of unnatural blend between the carrion eaters and something else entirely. It was a strige, a hideous cross between bat, bird and wasp with four small, pincer-like legs. It was rusty-red with a dangling proboscis. The name meant owl in the old tongue, a nocturnal bird. In more modern parlance it meant witch, which was decidedly more fitting, Skellan thought. He was uncomfortable around the strange bird, but Mannfred seemed to have taken a liking to communicating through it of late.

'Is it arranged?'

'The Lahmian has agreed to facilitate a meeting between you and one she calls the Eternal.'

'Good, good. You have done well, my friend. I am close. I should enter the city within the week.'

'I don't know... There is a peculiar tension to the place these last few days, like something is primed to explode. It makes me uncomfortable. The humans are restless. No doubt it is some part of their never-ending quest to tear their civilisation apart, but be that as it may, I think we should exercise caution. For one, I would avoid coming in overland like the plague. Better, I think, to enter via the tunnels. There is a concealed jetty that disembarks directly into a vast underground labyrinth beneath the city.'

'Indeed,' Mannfred agreed thoughtfully.

'It would also serve us to be cautious around these Lahmian women. I do not trust them. They spend their lives lying and trading information for power. I would not put it past the bitches to sell you out to the Imperials in return for turning a blind eye to their presence in the city. They have the fools eating out of their hands while they eat out of their necks!'

'Then pity the fools who get in my way.' There was no arrogance to the statement. It was delivered flat, matter-of-fact and all the more chilling for it.

'Still, the less they know of your movements the better.'

'Agreed. Something is disturbing you, is it not?' The bird-thing craned its neck curiously, peering at Skellan. Its scrutiny made him uncomfortable.

'There was some kind of riot this past night. A Strigany caravan was burned to the ground, the gypsies run out of town. I believe someone told them I was sheltering with the Strigany and that is why the caravan burned.'

'They know you are in the city?'

'No... well, not exactly. A damned witch hunter put a silver arrow in my arse. I know he is looking for me.'

'That was... unfortunate.' Mannfred's disappointment was palpable. 'What do you intend to do?'

'Oh, I intend to string him up – dead of course.'

'Good. See that it is done before my arrival.'

MOROI COULD NOT find it in himself to mourn his friend.

Arminus Vamburg's grave looked like a black wound in the earth, surrounded as it was by three inches of snow. Winter had taken a hold of Nuln. Vamburg's coffin was a simple wooden box bare of any ornamentation. It rested beside the hole, on ropes that would be used to lower it into the ground. Moroi couldn't take his gaze from the coffin. He couldn't accept that his friend – his only friend – lay inside, waiting to be interred, dead. The beast had done this, murdered Vamburg without compunction or guilt. It was a stone cold killer – and yet it had promised to return, to find him in order to die at his hand when its work was done.

There was a surreal quality to the events of the last night that turned his thoughts inside out.

The priest of the Garden of Morr, an old man dressed in a long black robe of mourning, read words meant to comfort him, 'Into thy hands,

Oh Morr, we commend thy loyal servant Arminus, our dear brother, may he serve at your side in death as he did in life, steadfast and true. We beseech thee to protect his soul from the devilries of those who would extinguish his light like a candle that has burned out, rather than renew it like the blazing fire that is faith.'

A gust of wind churned through the garden, drowning out the priest's frail voice.

Moroi helped the sexton lower the coffin into the grave. He bent low against the bitter wind. He told himself that the tears on his cheek were due to the stinging wind even though he knew they weren't. There was no comfort to be had in the ritual. He cast a handful of dirt over the coffin lid and left before the old priest had finished his supposedly soothing words.

He walked slowly back towards the temple. There were no temple guards, which he found curious, even for a small temple. It was uncommon in this uncertain time for the holy houses to be left undefended. To attack one's faith was an almost certain way to undermine a man's courage, and a fearful man died most easily. Moroi shrugged off his momentary unease and opened the door. As he stepped inside, the feeling of nausea was overwhelming.

He walked slowly through the narthex. There was an unnerving quality to the silence.

The old temple was half in shadow, the small windows not generous with the light. It was cold – as cold as it was outside. The chapel was austere. He bowed low to the marble statue of Morr as he passed by into the nave. The god turned a blind eye to his tears. Moroi rose and walked down the central aisle, listening. There was a sense of wrongness about the place. His eyes roved across the tiny chapel. With every step the pain in his skull increased, the blood swelling against the bone.

The air in the temple smelled of snow and something else, something more redolent and utterly out of place – decay.

Halfway between the altar and the door a man stepped out of the shadows. The man was tall and wiry, his thin-lipped face sharp and laced with scars. He moved with a pronounced limp. Moroi's heart skipped a beat as the man moved menacingly towards him. His features were bony, lending an angular quality to his face, and a black leather patch covered one eye. His presence was repulsive.

'No crossbow today, witch hunter?'

Moroi reached for where the crossbow ought to have been – only it wasn't there. It was back in his room. He hadn't wanted to attend the funeral of his friend armed. It had felt wrong, to honour death with the tools of killing so close at hand. So much for respect. Moroi cursed his stupidity as the beast came at him. He should have known the vampire would hunt him out at his weakest moment.

'You're not– '

'Not what?' the man interrupted.

'Not him... you're not the vampire... not the wolf.'

'Oh, believe me, witch hunter, I am *all* the vampire you will ever need.' A moment later the creature had him by the throat and leaned in close, the sickness of his foetid breath harsh on Moroi's face. The witch hunter struggled desperately to raise his arm, to push the beast away, but the vampire's grip was like iron. He held him close in a parody of a lover's embrace. Moroi kicked and writhed futilely in his grasp.

The beast shook his head, tutting slowly, and hurled Moroi back across the row of pews.

Moroi screamed in agony as he came down hard on the wooden backs of the pews, bones in his spine cracking.

'Oh don't die on me yet, little man. I have such pain to show you. For you I shall make death exquisite suffering. Morr will welcome you with open arms, overwhelmed by your agonies. They will be legendary even amongst the dead.' The vampire stepped up close, leaning down to stare at the witch hunter, folded over the back of one of the overturned pews. He tutted again.

The agony was blinding. Moroi couldn't move his hands; they hung lifelessly at his side. He tried to concentrate on moving his fingers but had no control over them. The pain was savage. It blossomed out from the centre of his spine. He couldn't support his head. His back was broken.

The beast hauled Moroi up by the throat, choking him as it lifted him bodily off the floor. 'I'm not letting you get away from me that easily.'

Morai couldn't speak. The force of the vampire's grip crushed his windpipe. Blackness swelled up, threatening to overwhelm him, but even as he tried to lose himself the beast denied him, hurling him again. The witch hunter's head cracked sickeningly as he hit the foot of the stone altar. His vision blurred, failing completely in his left eye. He felt the warm stickiness of blood matt in his hair and spread slowly down his neck.

The last thing he saw was the beast grinning as it toyed with his throat, seconds before ripping it open.

SKELLAN STUMBLED TOWARDS the great iron-banded temple doors, but collapsed more than ten feet shy of them.

Revulsion tore at his body.

He had kept it at bay by sheer force of will, refusing to show weakness before his quarry. Finding Moroi had been easy; human weakness was the answer. His companion was dead and the witch hunter would inevitably be there for the internment. Now, with the deed done, the power of the holy place took its toll on him.

He forced himself back to his feet, screaming at the agony the defiance took out on his body.

The sanctity of the place tortured his perverted nature. He was sure he couldn't have survived if not for the fact that the Sigmarites had held him hostage in the Grand Cathedral for so long, fostering in him a tolerance for the excruciating agony that came along with his violation of such a holy temple. It inured him to the repellent 'holy' places and that it was their doing was delicious irony that appealed to the darker side of Skellan's humour.

He was strong, stronger than he had a right to be, but then his sire had been potent – a rival to Vlad himself. It had been Posner who had risen up when first Vlad fell, not his whelps, Konrad, Fritz, Pieter or Hans. Even Mannfred had hidden himself away. Only Posner had had the strength to dare attempt to fill the vacuum that Vlad von Carstein's 'death' had left – or was it greed, lust and all of those other base human emotions that had driven his sire?

Strength was the one thing Skellan admired above all.

A lesser vampire would have lay curled up on the floor of the aisle waiting to be put down by some holy fool with a wooden stake. Not him.

He was strong enough to rise.

Behind him the corpse of the witch hunter hung from chains looped around the timbers of the vaulted ceiling. His corpse was torn open, the white bone of his ribs cracked back and parted like a whalebone corset, his anatomy laid open for all to see.

The witch hunter's heart lay on the altar, and beside it a small pool of blood gathered where it dripped down from the ragged wounds.

He only wished he could have remained long enough to see the aberrant horror on their faces when they discovered the corpse. It was self-indulgent, of course, to want to savour the full extent of his brutality.

He didn't have the time for such idle fancies. Preparations needed to be made. The witch hunter had unwittingly given him something more urgent to worry about. He wasn't the vampire, that's what the fool had said. Skellan had dismissed it in his hunger to dispense pain, but the words returned in the calm after the blood-thirst. If *he* wasn't the vampire that could only mean one thing: the witch hunter had been on the trail of another rough beast. Not, surely, Narcisa or one of her breed...

So who then? Who was here?

And more pressing, what kind of threat did they pose?

He limped out of the temple.

And he knew.

You're not the wolf... But he knew who was.

Oh yes, he knew. The Strigany caravan had burned because it was sheltering the wolf, and that wolf was Jerek. It had to be. That meant Jerek was here, hiding somewhere in this stinking warren of streets. But what was he doing here? Why Nuln? Why now? Did the old wolf know that he was here? Was he hunting Skellan with some stupidly noble idea about putting him out of his misery? He wouldn't put it past the insufferable buffoon.

Let him try, Skellan thought. Instinctively, his hand strayed to the eye patch, a bloody finger scratching beneath it at the ruined flesh. It was a permanent reminder of the score he had to settle with the old wolf.

It would have to wait, for now.

HE WAITED FOR Mannfred in the shadow of the mausoleum.

It was snowing again. The fat flakes swirled in the air, not thickly enough to hide the door of the manor house or the comings and goings of the dead girls, but enough to deaden the sounds of the world. It was winter; of that there could be no doubt, yet the women showed no signs of being affected by the cold. They walked and whispered and giggled, shawls drawn up to the pale blue blush of their throats. Skellan studied them. They were like birds, flocking, preening, primping and posing, craving the eye. The unnaturalness of their vanity still surprised him. Both dead, both monsters in the eyes of humanity, they lived in different worlds. It was as though death held no dominion for the Lahmians.

He had seen Narcisa twice already tonight. She refused to meet his eye, which pleased him. She knew her place now, recognising him as her superior. She moved coyly, giving him time to watch. He found himself remembering her scent and feel. He would have her, he decided, relishing the prospect. When the time came she would scream out his name. He smiled.

Narcisa had promised that the Eternal would give them an audience, as if she had a choice. He barked a short harsh laugh at the notion of a *woman* daring to laud it over him. *Oh sweet Narcisa you will beg and scream,* he decided, *and I will grow drunk on it.* He would have her on her knees pleading for mercy as he very slowly and very deliberately hurt her. He found himself imagining it, the images so real in his head that they could have been hallucinations.

He watched the peculiar dance of the snowflakes, the twist of light and shadow. He held out his hand, catching flakes. They didn't melt, so cold was his skin.

He turned, imagining he heard something behind him, a careless footfall crushing the fresh snow. He was alone in the ever-whitening graveyard, the flakes settling around him. He didn't feel the cold. His blood was far colder.

The solitary depression of a footstep in the otherwise virgin white didn't go unnoticed.

He wasn't alone.

He didn't move.

He listened, searching for the slightest sound out of place. The fine hairs on the nape of his neck prickled, as did those on his forearms.

Skellan had used Mannfred's strige, that vile undead creature that looked, in truth, like nothing more noisome than a cadaverous plucked chicken, to tell his master of the labyrinthine tunnels beneath the city, and the jetty hidden within the walls of the riverbank. He had suggested discretion. The Vampire Count had agreed it made sense to avoid the city proper. Only a fool revealed his hand so early in the game. He would enter the city from below, and move through it out of the sight of prying eyes, negotiating the old tunnels.

Skellan expected him to emerge from the mausoleum. The old tomb was almost certainly connected to the subterranean walkways.

He turned in a full circle, until he had *almost* succeeded in convincing himself he was alone.

He waited for the watcher to reveal himself. He studied the yellow of the lamps as they flickered in the windows of the manor house and the comings and goings of the elegant Lahmians. It was all he could do to remain hidden. Their carefree sashaying as they walked, arms linked, down the long gravel drive infuriated him. They knew he was there. They looked his way with a casual toss of the head. The shadows masked their true expressions, but he knew they were sneering. Over the next few hours he would turn their comfortable little world on its head and strip them of their smugness. Then he would sneer at them.

'They are exquisite corpses, are they not?'

The sound of Mannfred's voice startled him even though he had known all along that the Vampire Count was close by.

'I've tasted better,' Skellan said, even as he said it remembering the richness of Narcisa's tainted blood as it trickled down his throat. It was a lie, he hadn't.

'Somehow I doubt it,' Mannfred said, as though reading his mind.

Skellan turned to face his master, but found he was looking at shadows and the bare expanse of the white stone of the mausoleum wall. It took a moment to discern the vague blur around one of the carved columns where the air seemed agitated. He looked down and saw the lone footprint and looked back up studying the peculiar blur of the air intently. The more stubbornly he stared at the curiosity the more substantial the shape hidden within it became. Even knowing what was causing the peculiar displacement of the air it was difficult to focus on the blur for any sustained length of time, made more so by Skellan's monocular vision.

Finally, the Vampire Count drew back his hood and emerged from the shadows. His expression was sardonic. He knelt, dusting his hands in the grave dirt, a curious mark of respect for the interred and rose again. 'Shall we?' He set off without waiting for Skellan's response, flinty chips of gravel crunching under his boots.

Skellan hurried after him.

A fair-haired beauty turned, shying away from them as they approached. Mannfred sketched an easy bow. Skellan ignored the woman. He caught up with the Vampire Count as he knocked twice with the huge snake-headed knocker on the iron-banded door. The door opened before the cries of the metal had fully faded. For a moment Skellan thought it was Narcisa who stood in the doorway, but he quickly realised it wasn't her. The differences were subtle, cheekbones more aquiline, eyes ever so slightly more almond-shaped, lips fuller. She stepped aside to allow them to enter. She wore a silk ball gown of emerald green that clung perfectly to her body, accentuating every curve.

Skellan moved deliberately close to the Lahmian, causing her to back up another step.

The inside of the manor house was another world entirely. He wasn't sure what he had expected from the brief glimpses he had managed, but on the evidence of the foyer alone this wasn't it. Heavy velvet drapes the rich red of blood were cinched in place by golden snake heads. The serpentine emblem was repeated everywhere, in the gilding of the picture frames, in the weave of the carpet beneath their feet, in the metal casing of the crystal chandelier, coiled around the table lamps and the bole of the hat stand, and even carved into the door jambs. The foyer was dominated by a huge double-sided marble staircase. Its wrought black iron banisters were fashioned as rearing cobras. The jewelled eyes of dozens of snakes studied them, and amid the statues and carvings Skellan saw movement, the sinuous ripple of a living serpent. It came across the carpet, forked tongue flashing out. The woman knelt, holding out her arm for the serpent to coil itself around.

Stroking the reptile she bade them follow, and instead of climbing the stairs, led them through a narrow twisting corridor to a glass ceilinged arboretum filled with lush, green life. She ushered them towards a bench in the centre of the vast chamber. She raised her hand to an overhanging branch and whispered something, causing the snake to slither off her outstretched arm and curl itself around the branch. Skellan saw at least fifteen various species of snake draped on branches and more curled up at the bases of the exotic trees. He had no desire to wake any of them.

'The Eternal bids you wait a moment with her children while she readies herself for your visit.'

She turned to leave.

'Stay with us,' Mannfred said, touching her arm.

She glanced down at the hand resting on her arm and nodded, 'As you wish.'

'Good, good. Now, tell me a little about your mistress. A good guest should always know something about his host.'

The girl smiled faintly. 'It is not my place.'

'Don't be coy, girl, it doesn't suit you,' Skellan said, moving to stand a single step behind her and leaning in so that she would feel his breath on her skin.

'Very well,' the Lahmian said, stiffening visibly as Skellan laid his hand softly on the nape of her neck, fingers brushing her throat almost tenderly, almost.

A white mouse scurried across the stone floor. A viper fell from a branch directly above it and had swallowed the creature whole in the time it took to blink. Skellan watched the snake's body distort as it digested the mouse. Satisfied, the snake slithered away into the shade.

'The Eternal is the oldest of our kind in these parts, and as such is our queen. She is as wise as she is beautiful. As–'

'On second thoughts, silence is a virtue,' Mannfred said, somewhat dismissively cutting across her. He ought to have noticed the signs. The woman was under some kind of thrall. He had no interest in hearing whatever lip service she had been programmed to puppet. Anger flared in the woman's eyes but it never reached her lips. She curtseyed, turned on her long stiletto heel, and walked back into the main body of the house, her skirts swishing around her as she went.

The Eternal made them wait.

Skellan knew he was not patient, but Mannfred seemed prepared to wait all eternity for the woman to dignify them with her presence. He walked around the stone dais that marked the centre of the arboretum, touching the leaves, feeling the varying consistencies. He pushed back a branch to reveal a huge elaborately carved stone head. It was an impish thing with a bulbous nose and cherubic cheeks, and a row of razor-sharp fangs. It was a quite repulsive little monstrosity. Mannfred let the branch fall back across the stone facing, hiding it once more. He moved three more steps and knelt. Skellan saw him pluck up the only red flower, a beautiful orchid with a yellow stamen. He plucked the petals away from the stem one at a time, denuding it slowly. He scattered the petals at his feet and then walked over them.

Skellan sat down on the bench content to let Mannfred explore. There was little in the curious indoor garden that interested him. He leaned back, allowing his head to tilt back so that he could see the ceiling. It was glass and metal, domed with huge windows allowing the moonlight in yet keeping the cold of winter out. The heat from the arboretum kept the snow from settling on the glass. It was a breathtaking construction. Ultimately, Skellan didn't care what they did with their glass and steel and stone. It was all the same ephemera of life that slipped through time's fingers like grains of sand.

He closed his eyes, thoroughly bored.

He would find a way of making the arrogant bitch pay for the insult. He imagined, for a delicious moment, walking through the Eternal's house, claiming her followers one by one, stripping them just as painstakingly as Mannfred had the orchid, and just as lethally. Instead of those gossamer fine petals he'd peel away tendon and muscle from bone, transmogrifying them into blood red roses of flesh. He licked his lips. He could taste their fear. It was intoxicating.

A rattle-tailed serpent brushed up against his foot. He watched it. For a moment it seemed as though the cold-blooded reptile had no interest in him, but then it reared back, fangs bared to strike. Before the snake could sink its teeth into him Skellan snatched it up. The creature hissed and squawked as he forced its jaws further apart until the bones started to crack and the skin split as he tore the snake in two savagely. He threw the remains at another reptile hoping to start a feeding frenzy with the blood.

He looked down at his hands. They, half of his arms and the left side of his shirt were covered in blood. He lifted his fingers to his lips and tasted it. The reptile's blood had a peculiar tang to it. It was less iron-rich than its human counterpart, earthier.

The woman reappeared a moment later. She had changed. Instead of her silk dress she now wore a simpler shift of raw cotton. As with everything else in the manor it bore a serpent's crest. She looked, if anything, more doll-like and beautiful in the sackcloth, as if the richness of her dress had somehow detracted from her essential beauty. Free, now, she radiated poise and allure in equal measure. She inclined her neck, studying the blood on his hands. A smile flirted with her lips as she said, 'The mistress will see you now.'

Skellan stood, staring at her. All that time, and for what? A damned change of *clothing*? He struggled to remain calm, barely managing to bottle his anger. His lip curled into a snarl.

She pointedly ignored him.

'Do you think it was wise to bathe yourself in the blood of one of the woman's pets?' Mannfred asked.

'No, but it was satisfying.'

'It will certainly give our host pause for thought, I'll grant you that.'

They followed the woman out of the arboretum, but not the way they had come. She led them between dragging branches that scratched and snagged at their clothes and hair, behind the great stone head, to an opening concealed in the back of it. Fourteen steps led down. They descended slowly into darkness. At the bottom the woman struck a light and lit a taper. She pulled a reed-wrapped torch out of a black iron sconce and plunged into the darkness, leading them down, down, deeper and still down.

Their footsteps echoed in the cramped confines of the tunnels. The passageways were incredibly claustrophobic. The sheer weight of the earth pressed down on all sides threatening to transform the warren of tunnels into a barrow. Skellan touched the walls. They were cold, sheened with a fine coat of mucoid slime. His fingers came away slick and sticky. The temperature dropped steadily without falling below a pleasing chill.

Still they descended, the woman leading the way.

The quality of sound changed; the pressure of the earth above dampening it. Their footsteps became leaden. Water dripped tantalisingly somewhere away in the darkness beyond the edge of the torch's glare.

Skellan had a bad feeling about this latest turn of events. He didn't trust the woman, or any of her kind. He had observed them well enough to know that they were devious creatures capable of almost any treachery. He slowed, walking in the furthest part of his shadow. He watched her back, watched the arch of her spine, her musculature for some sense of tension, and beyond her watched the flicker and dance of the flame's caress as it turned the oppressively dark, dank passage into a place of light. The light, if anything, was less reassuring than the dancing shadows. He was at home in the shadows; they were his natural habitat. He was a hunter. He relied upon stealth. The light lied. It pretended to reveal all of its secrets, expose its dark places, but it never did, not fully.

The tunnel widened into a spectacularly gaudy antechamber painted in splashes of bright colour, greens and reds and foiled with gold. The room was dominated by two huge urns that stood either side of a door. Shadows clung stubbornly to the door, making the embossed relief figure of a jackal-headed man stand out in stark relief. The jackal man held a staff that appeared to be in the process of transforming into a snake. There was an iron ring in the creature's mouth. The Lahmian walked up to the door, grasped the ring and knocked three times, slowly, deliberately and loudly.

Beyond the door a woman's voice uttered a single word, 'Come.'

Their escort opened the door and stepped aside to allow them to enter the nave of a vast subterranean temple, although whatever gods it venerated, they were none that Jon Skellan was familiar with. The one they called the Eternal sat on a mighty snakeskin throne where in any other temple the altar would have stood.

She was not beautiful by any stretch of the imagination.

She was old and haggard, her skin so deeply lined that it was impossible to make out her eyes from the shadows they conjured. She wore a simple black shift and a tiara of gold and copper hammered into a perfect circle. The serpent's head consumed its tail. The blood-rich rubies of the tiara's eyes glittered in the torchlight.

'It has been a long time, Kalada,' Mannfred said, dropping smoothly to one knee. 'I would say you haven't changed but I would be lying. The years have ceased being kind to you.'

The Lahmian smiled. On her it was anything but a pleasant expression. 'Flattery will get you nowhere, von Carstein. What gives you the right to enter my home?'

'You know her?' Skellan asked, still trying to take in the immensity of the subterranean temple with its unfamiliar fetishes and statues to gods he didn't recognise: figures with reptilian heads, huge distended jaws and jagged teeth, figures with avian features, owls and contemptuous birds, and others with the feral lines of cats and dogs. They were all painted with archaic symbols Skellan did not understand. He wasn't particularly fond of feeling like a simpleton. It rankled, like so much of the pomp and circumstance of the whole charade.

'From another life, one that was not kind to her,' Mannfred turned his attention back to the woman on the throne. 'I had thought you dead, Kalada.'

'Death is no great mystery to us, is it, my dear? No, on the contrary, death is familiar, comfortable.'

'Indeed. Circumstance has made you wise, I see.'

'No, Mannfred. It was age that did that. Circumstance made me vengeful. Give me a reason, Mannfred, a single reason why I should not unleash a thousand agonies upon you and your manservant as retribution for violating my home, one reason.'

Skellan bristled, ready to fight if the witch was intent on forcing their hand. It would be on his terms, not hers. He tensed, cracking the bones in his neck as he turned first left, then right. He breathed deeply, drawing upon the beast within, summoning it. His face contorted, the scar tissue of his cheeks tearing and changing as he growled.

Mannfred laid a hand on him, stilling him. 'It is not time for brute force, my friend. There are other answers at our disposal.' He turned to the woman, Kalada, the Eternal as she had mockingly dubbed herself. He held out his hand to her. She saw it immediately, the plain band amid the more elaborate rings. Her eyes widened. She looked up at his face as though seeing him properly for the first time. She held out her hand to him. He took it and raised it to his lips. She in turn took his and duplicated the kiss. Something had happened between the pair, but Skellan was baffled as to what exactly it was that had transpired.

'What do you want of me and mine?' The Lahmian asked bluntly.

'I would call on the old bonds, Kalada. I would, for a short while at least, offer truce between my blood and yours.'

'Why do you think I, or my queen, would countenance such a thing?' Skellan could tell she was genuinely curious.

'To cause strife among the living.'

'Again, why do you think we would seek such a thing? We are well situated here. We have influence, power: true power. We don't have to skulk in the shadows and hope the masters of this other world don't come looking to slay us. They crave our company. They dote on us. We are a status symbol, something to be associated with not shied away from. We have the ears and hearts of the aristocracy, the artists and artisans. We are the true rulers of the world above us, or at least this part of it. So why oh why would we want to meddle with what so obviously suits our purpose? We are not the fools who would kill the goose that lays our golden eggs. To put it simplistically for you, we like this city – our city – just the way it is.'

'Think beyond a few streets woman. Imagine grand designs of power. Dare to dream what is possible.'

'You make the mistake of assuming we want or need more than what we have, von Carstein. It was ever thus. You and your kind seek to impose your greed for glory and lust for power onto the rest of us, turning us into something you can understand.'

'Not so.'

'Oh but it is, it is, painfully so.'

Something stirred in the darkness, deeper in the belly of the temple. Skellan spun around, fangs bared, ready to launch himself. He was jumping at shadows. There was nothing there.

And yet...

And yet he could smell something, something he couldn't see. Skellan's lips curled in a threatening snarl, a low growl percolating in his throat.

'Down boy,' the Eternal said, derisively. 'Rein your beast in, Mannfred. I'll have no blood spilt in my home.'

'A little late for that,' Skellan said, grinning spitefully. 'One of your little reptiles had an accident.'

'At ease, Skellan, we are guests here.'

'For now,' Skellan rumbled. He didn't trust the woman. Anyone who adopted a snake for a fetish was inherently conniving and mistrustful. She would reveal her hand eventually, and when she did he would bite it, tasting her old withered blood.

'We have a bond, Kalada, you and I, my people and yours. There are old ties between our bloodlines. Was Vashanesh not husband of Neferata? Did he not sup of the elixir at her side, sharing blood with your queen? Those ties, no matter how much we might profess otherwise in our anger and arrogance, cannot be broken. They are the ties that bind. They are the threads that make us who we are. It has always been so.'

'That was a long time ago,' the Eternal conceded grudgingly. 'It is irrelevant now.'

'Not so. As ruler of my people I am, to put it rather simply, heir to the great one himself, and as such would invoke those old bonds, Kalada. I would have you and your people at my side, equals in the new Kingdom of the Dead.'

'Why?'

'You said it yourself. You can go places we cannot. Where we are forced to hide from humanity, you seduce it. Together we would pose a threat far greater than we do alone. Imagine. We would be irresistible, mighty. Join us, Kalada. Undermine the cursed Empire from within while we muster the dead and attack from without.'

'You assume again that we dream of conquest. What you offer is hypothetical. Your sire and your mad brother both failed, why should we believe that you are capable of anything other than the same miserable failure? You talk of dominion but offer no proof of your might, no proof that you are capable of matching your words with actual power. What we have now is concrete. You ask us to risk what we have, throw in our lot with a bloodline of failures, on the promise that you are different? Somehow more than your sire? More than your mad brother?'

'What would you have me do to prove myself, Kalada?'

'Show me your might. Show me your armies. Show me what makes you more than your kindred, von Carstein. Show me you have what it takes to back up your pretty words with actions. Show me you are more than just another failure. Then, and only then, I will consider your plea. Now leave me. Seeing you once more has not been a pleasant experience. Some corpses are best left dead.'

CHAPTER EIGHT

A World of Victims and Executioners
Obelheim, Talabecland

ACKIM BRANDT WAS true to his word. They had been treated well by the Obelheimers, though well was a relative term. They were prisoners of an opposing army. They were not the honoured guests of some sultan in a far-flung corner of Araby. They weren't beaten. They were fed and although the gruel was far from nutritious, the lumps of potato and occasional chunk of rancid pork and strips of gristle kept them alive.

That was what it was all about, keeping them alive.

Ackim Brandt was no fool. Living they had at least some basic economic value to the victors. They could be used to barter for concessions and the return of their own people from the Stirlanders. Martin, in turn, would be feeding the Talabeclanders he held captive. Anything else would have been inhuman. Both Brandt and Kristallbach understood the basic folly of war: that there was no more stupid a notion than the one that claims a man has the right to kill another simply because he lives on the other side of a river and their rulers have a quarrel. The men have no quarrel with each other, and yet they are supposed to do the dying.

Vorster Schlagener huddled up against the stockade wall, rough logs digging uncomfortably into his back. The weather had turned, finally. It was bitterly cold. He couldn't remember the last time he had felt warm. They each had a blanket, but the wind cut through them, rendering them useless. The others moaned. They were soldiers, it was what they did. If they weren't complaining they were most likely dead. He barked out a short bitter laugh at that.

Meinard stood guard with two other men, Jasper and Brannon, although they hardly 'guarded' anymore. Tonight, as last night and the night before, the hours were being passed in a game of chance.

Meinard stank almost as badly as the men he tended.

It was no surprise.

When he wasn't playing gaoler he was tending the pigs, mulching the swill and mucking out the slop. Vorster could see the similarity in Meinard's dual responsibilities – they were all animals, after all.

The other two weren't much sweeter.

The guards were a lot friendlier towards him than he would have been in their place, but none of them were prepared to talk about the conflict. He had no news of home and no idea how the war was being played out. They could have been days away from rescue or hours from damnation and none of them knew either way. The world had stopped for them after Ignatz's bloody stupid charge.

Soldiers loved to talk, though, so they found other things to moan about. Days and weeks of captivity locked up in a rat infested, pigswill reeking pen gave them precious little else to do. During all that time Meinard had never come across as much of a liar. Vorster had slowly and carefully drawn him and his replacements, when they came to relieve him, into a conversation that went beyond the pillow virtues of women, the various flavours and tastes of beers brewed traditionally in oak vats in different regions and things of equally minor consequence. Still, even when they had formed something approaching friendship, there was no talk of the war or the bravura of comrades-in-arms marching out to face the world as he would have expected.

Brandt was a little more forthcoming about the things that really mattered. He visited Vorster after sundown on three consecutive nights, pulling him out of the stockade to question him about the Stirland command and what he knew of Martin von Kristallbach's plans. Brandt was no simpleton. He knew that Vorster was little more than a foot soldier, but he had taken a special interest in him. He had heard of the existence of tunnels within the mountains, some that might even stretch below the plains, though how far and how extensive they might be he had no clue. He was, he explained at great length one evening, acutely aware of the possibility of one or more of those tunnels being dwarfish in origin and going through the earth from the Worlds Edge Mountains, beneath cities like Eichenbrunn, Leicheberg, Langwald and perhaps beyond like some great subterranean road winding beneath the Empire leading who knew where. Halstedt? Julbach? Schollach? Kircham? Blutdorf? Ramsau? Further afield into Averland? Reikland?

It wasn't, Ackim Brandt assured Vorster, a major concern. The way in which he said it gave the lie to his words. It was a problem. It was precisely the sort of problem that would drive the soldier to distraction trying to puzzle through it. Brandt didn't like the fact that these supposed underground roads existed. They were unknown variables that impacted upon his carefully thought out strategies. Worrying about them drove Brandt to distraction. Did Martin know of these tunnels? Indeed, were there any tunnels at all or was it all just smoke and mirrors to distract the Talabeclanders?

It wasn't out of the realm of possibility that Martin was to blame for the disinformation, if it was disinformation. The man was nothing if not shrewd. He would have been well aware of the uncertainty such a rumour would spread in the enemy camps. No one wanted to fight an enemy he couldn't see. No one wanted to chase his own shadow across the battlefields. No one wanted to fight against an army of what might as well have been ghosts, able to disappear out of sight, beneath the ground, at will.

Vorster understood that these evenings together were intended to give him a unique insight into the mind of the enemy, but perhaps the most startling revelation of all had been how utterly normal Brandt's men, and Brandt himself for that matter, were. It was difficult to cast aside prejudices, but if he were to be truthful, Brandt was not so different from Vorster. They might have been cut from the same cloth.

Vorster was impressed with how Brandt looked out for the good of his men.

Vorster had been a soldier for a long time. He had served with good men, great men and fools. He had seen those good, great, and foolish men forced into making some tough decisions. They seldom flinched from those unsavoury choices and neither, he was sure, would Brandt if it meant the difference between one life or many.

In that way Vorster's captivity was an eye-opener.

Every day it became a little more difficult to think of them as the faceless enemy so full of evil, child killers and murderous swine, because every day he grew a little more familiar with their faces and their dreams, heard talk of their families and realised that in another time he would have been proud to call Meinard, Jasper and Brannon friends, and wouldn't have hesitated to serve in a battalion led by Brandt.

Does that make me a traitor, he wondered, and not for the first time? It didn't help matters knowing full well that he was their prisoner, alive still only because of Brandt's whim. The man had admired his courage in the face of stupidity. For that he had given him, and the others, their lives.

He couldn't decide if it was natural that he should feel some kind of bond being forged between him and his captors or if it was another layer of deceit in the enemy's game?

Their chosen games were knucklebones and five card blind, not that he had anything to lose. Jasper assured him they were happy to take his marker because, given the circumstances, it was the least they could do. Vorster lost a lot of money that he didn't have in the hope of loosening a tongue or two, but it was useless.

Jasper studied the five dog-eared cards in his hand and tossed a coin onto the makeshift table. 'I'll take one blind,' he said, laying the fifth card face down.

Brannon dealt Jasper a fresh card and turned to Meinard, 'In or out, big man?'

'In,' Meinard grinned, dropping his own coin onto the tabletop. 'I'll take two, one for each eye.' He discarded two of his cards.

Brannon turned to Vorster. 'How about you? You want to gamble your life away on the turn of a card?'

Vorster smiled. 'With sweet talk like that how could I resist? Give me two.' Vorster took the cards and arranged them in to the familiar pattern of the Blind Man's Curse, a good hand. Not the best, but probably better than anything anyone else at the table was holding.

'So ladies, let's be seeing you, shall we?' Brannon laid his own pattern on the table with a cock-eyed grin. Beggar's Bluff, not worth the paper the cards were painted on.

'Not your day, is it sunshine?' Jasper remarked, arranging his own pattern on the table, the Penitent Vagabond. A fair hand and on another day it might have walked away with the pot, but not today. Jasper licked his lips nervously as he watched Meinard place his own cards down, the Blood of the Gypsies. No wonder Meinard was smiling. The Blood of the Gypsies was a very good hand. There was only one problem; to make the pattern he needed the Gypsy Child card, which was part of the Blind Man's Curse pattern. Meinard, Vorster realised, was cheating. He wondered how the man was doing it, but then thought of the unusual dexterity that Meinard had with ropes and assumed it was down to some form of palming. The others were looking at him expectantly.

'Ah... I think we are about to witness a miracle my friends,' he said with a smile and laid his five cards down, one after the other, resting the Gypsy Child on the top of the pile and holding a finger over it.

'Why you no good son of a bitch,' Jasper muttered, but he wasn't looking at Vorster, his eyes were firmly fixed on Meinard.

Meinard grinned and shrugged.

Brannon reached across the small table and grabbed Meinard by the wrists, triggering whatever mechanism Meinard had secreted up his sleeve and sending the hidden cards scudding across the table.

'I want my money back.'

'Of course, of course,' Meinard said placatingly, still pinned by Brannon. 'It wasn't as if I was going to keep it.'

'Of course you weren't,' Jasper agreed amicably.

Vorster felt it first, the earth shivering beneath his feet. It was subtle but unmistakable. He stopped listening to the accusations and placed his hand flat against the dirt floor. The tremors were steady, rhythmical – marching feet. 'Shut up,' he hissed, dropping to his knees and pressing his ear to the ground. The others fell silent. Vorster listened. They were still a long way off, a league or more at least, but it was as though the very earth itself were protesting at their passing.

'Oh, Sweet Shallya, Mother of Mercy,' Meinard said, his face grown suddenly pale.

'How far?' Brannon asked curtly. He had already begun packing the cards and the makeshift table away.

'Not far enough,' Jasper answered for him.

They weren't the only ones who had heeded the signs. War was coming closer. Outside the tent the commotion mounted, and the horses whinnied and fought against their handlers as a palpable air of fear descended on the camp. The tent flaps were drawn aside and Brandt stepped through the gap. Instead of his usual implacable calm he wore a harried expression.

'Good news, boys,' Ackim Brandt said. 'Word's come from Martin. An exchange has been agreed. You're going home.'

Vorster studied the man's face, looking for the lie. He had come to know Ackim Brandt well during their months of captivity.

'Up,' he said. 'Come on,' he gestured for Vorster to stand. 'Come with me, there is something you need to see. You three, escort our reckless hero.' Brandt was breathing hard, Vorster realised. He was afraid. It was obvious. Martin had brought Stirland to their door. He had good reason to be afraid. Vorster got to his feet. Brandt turned and left. Jasper nodded for Vorster to do likewise.

Outside, the air had a real bite to it. He sucked it down in great mouthfuls, having not tasted fresh air for days. The camp was a hive of activity, soldiers moving purposefully about their business dousing campfires and ordering their possessions as though they expected the order to move out at any moment. Vorster looked up towards the many peaks of the Färlic Hills. Freedom was close enough for him to taste it.

'Thank you,' he said to Brandt.

'Don't thank me soldier. You proved yourself more than merely a worthy adversary. Indeed, after that irrational charge your damned idiot of a leader Ignatz decided upon, you handled yourself well enough for me to wish you were one of my men. I do not say that lightly. In another time I like to think we could have...' He didn't finish the thought. 'For all that though, the reality is that you were lucky. If it weren't for the fact that the day after that debacle Oskar Zenzi captured Jakob Schram you would all be dead by now.' He paused, as though expecting Vorster to interrupt, question him. Vorster remained silent. 'Schram is a runt of a man, for sure, but he is a well-connected runt of a man none the less, a distant relation of Ottilia herself, I believe. Your man has agreed to a trade, all of your lives for this one aristocratic buffoon. It speaks well of Kristallbach that he was determined to see you all returned. Indeed, it is the mark of the man that he values his men-at-arms as highly as another ruler values her family, no?'

Someone shoved him in the back and he stumbled forwards, following Brandt as he wove a path through the industrious soldiers until they came to a small rise on the outskirts of the encampment. They looked down across a much wider valley and a vast spreading plain below. Huge dust clouds churned up the horizon. The darkness was advancing, bringing on a premature night as the men of Stirland marched. Vorster's breath caught in his throat as the sheer magnitude of the force registered. It must have been four thousand men... more.

'They wrote in the old days that it was sweet and fitting to die for one's country,' Ackim Brandt said, looking at the men he would have to fight all too soon. 'They understood nothing, did they? There is nothing sweet or fitting in your dying. In war, good men die like dogs for no good reason. Come, let's get you and your men home shall we?'

THE EXCHANGE TOOK place less than a quarter of a mile from Ignatz's Folly. That was how the survivors had come to think of the arrowhead tip of Ramius Point ridge.

They were going home, or rather returning to the front line with Stirland to fight anew so that more of them could die on the right side of the river.

None of them had dared dream of any sort of homecoming during their days of captivity. To dream of home was just another torment. It weakened the soul. It ate away at their strength more completely than hunger or fear ever could. They had no need of fresh agonies. But now, together, walking towards the ridgeline of Ramius Point they could begin to hope. They were going home.

Vorster led the survivors. They held their heads up high, walking towards Martin's army. They had not broken. They had not died. They were survivors. During their months within Brandt's camp the ghosts of battle had taunted them. Cannon fire, the cries of the horses, the screams of the men and ringing steel had been keeping them from sleeping and driving them beyond the point of exhaustion.

Now they were free. Well, almost. They were out of the godforsaken stockade and were going home, sixty of them, bound hand and foot, shuffling along in a winding column. It was a long walk, but Vorster welcomed the clear sky over his head and the wind in his hair. He swore he would never complain about being stuck outside in the middle of nowhere again, knowing even as he made the vow that he would break it. He was a soldier. Complaining about the elements was his lot in life. The day he stopped complaining about the blasted snow or the blessed rain was the day he died. He looked at the rest of his men and smiled. He thought of them as his men now. They had made it.

Ackim Brant raised a hand, holding the line.

Across the field, Martin von Kristallbach walked forwards breaking the line of men, a trio of war hounds loping by his side. The man moved with the surety of a warrior not a woodsman. So changed was Martin by the conflict that Vorster would not have recognised him. He knew the look on his face. The man was haunted by daemons.

'But then who isn't?' Vorster asked himself.

'Soldier?' Brandt queried.

'Just thinking aloud.'

Together they walked across the snow-covered field and met the man halfway. Vorster studied his liege as he approached. His hair and beard had grown almost wild. They lent him a terrifying aspect. He moved with the authority of someone used to being respected. With three war hounds running at his side, Vorster wasn't surprised. The sight of the animals loping easily at his heels was enough to strike terror into the heart of even the stoutest soul. He was a born leader.

'Are you the Ottilia's man?' Martin asked, looking Brandt up and down.

'Aye, I am. You?' Brandt held out his hand for the man to take.

'Martin von Kristallbach.'

Brandt started visibly at the mention of the name but didn't withdraw his hand. Kristallbach smiled slowly as they shook. Kristallbach wasn't a man to let his lackeys do the unpleasantries while he hid in the command tent.

'So you know me?' Martin asked. 'Well, my new found friend, shall we be about our business? We have Schram here, and I see a few familiar faces. I thank you for looking after my people.'

One man in return for sixty marked this Schram as important, Vorster realised. But then Dietrich Jaeger was important to someone.

'I would that the situation was different,' Brandt said, surprising Vorster with his candour.

'No one ever claimed there was a good war, soldier, nor that there was a bad peace.'

'Indeed,' Ackim Brandt agreed. 'We shall grant you twenty-four hours with which to make your passage out of our lands, after that, we must begin the dance all over again.'

'Twenty-four hours is generous,' Martin said. He reached down absent-mindedly scratching one of the dogs hunkering at his feet. 'Though I suspect not enough for these men, no matter how fair your treatment of them has been. I cannot put them through the march.'

Brandt craned his neck to look at the ragtag bunch of men he had escorted to the exchange. Vorster followed suit. Martin was right; they were in no shape for an extended march. He understood why Martin had brought the full force of his army down onto this foreign field. He was prepared to fight for the sixty-something men.

Brandt mulled the dilemma over for a moment and then nodded, satisfied. 'Seventy-two hours, then we come after you. That should give you long enough to cross the river.' Vorster understood the reference; Brandt was giving them a chance to go home. He had no quarrel with these men, any of them. He was merely a man living on this side of the river doing his ruler's bidding, and for a few hours at least, there would be no conflict between them.

Martin held out his hand. 'You're a good man, Ackim Brandt. If the Ottilia ever tires of you I want you to know there is a place for you in Stirland.'

Brandt took Martin's hand and shook it, once, firmly. 'At the business end of someone's sword, no doubt,' Brandt chuckled. He gestured to one of the guards who had accompanied him to loosen the prisoners chains, and it was over, as simply as that. The prisoners walked across the snow-covered field. They were greeted with huge grins, and hugs and slaps from comrades they thought they would never see again. The mood was buoyant. It was a good moment. For that little while at least they could forget about the fact that tomorrow or the next day or the next they would be fighting again and the day after that some of them would be lying face down in the mud, food for crows. There were precious few good days in war.

One man came back the other way. The difference in his demeanour was remarkable. He looked like a whelp that had been whipped one too many times. He was broken. His hair ran wild and his beard was scraggy and untamed. He shuffled, Vorster realised. He didn't walk. His head was down, the fire in his eyes out. Jakob Schram hadn't enjoyed his captivity. Brandt's men seemed none too happy to see the young aristocrat returned to their ranks either. Schram was obviously their Dietrich Jaeger.

Speaking of Jaeger, Vorster saw the arrogant son of a bitch loitering behind Martin's back, close enough to bask in the Elector Count's aura and pretend familiarity. Vorster hawked and spat. The man made his skin crawl.

He waited until the last man had crossed over to the other side before he gripped forearms with the man who was his enemy, the man who had somehow become – if not his friend – someone he admired, liked even.

'Go with Sigmar, my friend,' Brandt said.

Vorster nodded. He inclined his head to Meinard and the others in silent farewell, and turned back to Ackim Brandt.

'You know if you ever do decide to take him up on that offer I am expecting you to put in a request for Vorster Schlagener to be seconded to your regiment. I'd walk to the ends of the earth for a leader like you, my friend.'

Brandt smiled. It was the most natural of gestures on his open face. 'If I ever do find myself on the other side of the river I can't think of a soldier I would rather have at my side. Now go before I change my mind and keep you here. I have a feeling we're going to need a few more men like you if we want to whip that man of yours.'

Vorster chuckled. 'Ah neighbour, if only that were so.'

'Isn't that always the way of things?' Ackim Brandt said, his gaze drifting towards Jakob Schram's back.

VORSTER TRIED TO bite his tongue, he really did, but face to face with that dimwit Jaeger there was nothing he could do. His anger had been simmering from the moment he'd seen Jaeger skulking behind Martin's shoulder. Half a minute in the man's company and it got the better of him. One look at Jaeger's smug expression was enough. The fop had the gall to expect thanks for saving them. His skull was so thick that the cost of his own actions hadn't penetrated the bone. He wilfully refused to understand that his arrogant stupidity had condemned hundreds of good men to needless deaths. Instead he chose to stand before the survivors and play the role of benefactor, the caring father with arms wide open to welcome the prodigal sons home.

Vorster wanted to smack him in the face and wipe that damned stupid grin off his fat lips.

The words just spilled out of his mouth.

'You!' Vorster bellowed, grabbing a horrified Dietrich Jaeger by the lapels and hauling him up so the fool's spluttering face was only inches from his own. 'You sanctimonious son of a bitch! How *dare* you stand there like some bloody hero lording it over your minions! Do you have *any* idea what you did? Do you?' Spittle frothed at Vorster's mouth. He threw the officer backwards. Jaeger staggered and stumbled trying to keep his feet. Vorster slammed an open palm into his chest and sent him sprawling to the dirt. He stood over the man. 'Did you stay long enough to watch your own men die? Did you? No, of course you didn't. You went back to your bloody pavilion for a nice goblet of mulled bloody wine, didn't you? Sigmar's balls, you disgust me, Jaeger. You're less than human. You're a fool and that wouldn't be so bad if you weren't so damned smug about your own stupidity. That man there,' he turned to thrust an accusing finger at Ackim

Brandt's retreating back, 'is a hundred times the man you are. He cares more about his prisoners than you do about your own men!'

'How... how... you... How *dare* you?' Jaeger gabbled incoherently, enraged.

'I dare because I watched friends split open by axes. I dare because I lay amid their corpses as the birds plucked at their eyes! I dare because *you* were too bloody stupid to know your arse from your elbow and sent me to die! You sent us running across their guns. It was suicide and you were too goddamned dense to realise it!'

'I'll have your head!' Jaeger thundered, pushing himself up onto his elbows, his face purple as though he were in the grip of an apoplectic fit. 'How dare you, you ungrateful whoreson? I'll have satisfaction for your insults.'

'Are you truly *that* stupid?' Vorster shook his head. 'Of course you are. Very well.' Vorster reached instinctively for the sword that on any other day would have been at his hip.

'Oh no, you oaf,' Jaeger said, on his knees. 'You'll do this right. You'll face me man to man. I will have satisfaction or an apology.'

He teased off his dirt-smeared glove and threw it in Vorster Schlagener's face.

Vorster stared at it in disbelief. The glove lay in the mud. He stepped on it, grinding it under his foot. 'You outrank me, *sir*. You are petty aristocracy and I am a non-commissioned officer. There's no good reason for a duel.'

'There's every damned good reason you egotistical pup. You need a lesson in manners and I am just the man to teach you.'

'In which case I shall very much enjoy killing you.'

Vorster half-expected someone to get between them and call an end to the nonsense, but no one interceded. Vultures gathered around to watch though. The spectacle was compelling.

Oskar Zenzi held out a hand to Jaeger, helping him to rise. 'I will stand as your second, Dietrich. Who will stand as this blowhard's man?' Zenzi turned around. 'Anyone?'

'I will.'

The crowds parted to reveal Ackim Brandt standing in the middle of them. The commotion had obviously drawn his curiosity. Vorster started visibly. He had thought the enemy soldier had returned to the safety of his own ranks, as any wise man would have. To see him, coming through the press of people to support him was a sign of friendship beyond anything he could have imagined. It showed, more than anything, that they were all men divided by an enemy of their own making where not so long ago they had stood side-by-side against a common threat. Still, in this new political climate it was unusual to say the least.

He wasn't alone. Meinard and the other guards had remained with him, or returned.

The sight of Brandt reduced Jaeger to apoplectic rage. 'How dare he? How dare this scum walk amongst us so brazenly? Will you stand for it, Zenzi?'

'Oh, yes,' Zenzi mumbled, obviously flustered by this peculiar turn of events. An honour duel between unequals, the lesser man's second none other than an enemy commander – it was unheard of in polite society.

They weren't in polite society, they were on a battlefield. Manners and civility were for the dead, he decided, extending an unusual courtesy to the man they had come to parlay with. It was a rare moment of peace in what had been a long hard campaign.

'We are all men of honour,' Zenzi decreed. 'It is our opinion that honour is best satisfied between equals. As men of the Empire we are all equals.'

'Though some are less equal than others,' Jaeger blustered. No one was listening to him.

'Are you prepared to apologise to this man, friend Vorster?' Brandt asked, ignoring the raging Jaeger.

'No. I am quite prepared to kill him though,' Vorster said, without a hint of mirth in his voice.

'Then it seems our course is set. As the challenger your man has the right to choose weapons. Let us not draw this out any more than we need to. I suggest these.' Brandt drew a twin pair of beautifully hand tooled pistols.

Seeing them, Jaeger's eyes lit up. 'Oh yes, quite fitting. They will do just splendidly.'

He held out a hand eagerly.

'Make your choice.'

'This one, no, no, this one. Yes.' Jaeger took the second of the two even though there was no visible difference between them. Brandt smiled and handed the first pistol to Vorster.

'A single cap. Kill or be killed. If you fall, your charge will be seen as unfit and your opponent exonerated of all wrong doing. This we swear before an audience of equals.' Both men nodded. 'Very well.' He removed a small blackpowder pouch and emptied just enough propellant for a single shot from each weapon, and handed both men a lead ball. 'You will follow my mark. Stand back to back.'

They did. Vorster felt strangely calm. He pressed the powder and shot into the pistol, and kept the barrel held upright, resting beneath his chin.

'I will count out ten paces. On ten you will each turn and loose a single shot. That shot shall signify the validity of this fight and settle all needs for honour. Is that understood?'

'It is,' Dietrich Jaeger said solemnly.

'Understood,' Vorster said.

'One last chance, gentleman, are you quite sure you want to go through with this?' Brandt asked.

'Of course I am,' Jaeger said. 'I am completely in the right. I have nothing to fear from this ruffian.'

'Very well, and you, Vorster? Do you wish to withdraw from this contest? There would be no shame in saving a life.' The way Brandt said it left the crowd in no doubt as to what he believed the outcome would be.

'This isn't for me. This is for every one of the men that *Captain* Jaeger condemned to death with his orders. This is for my friends and my brothers. I will not sully their memory. In one shot I shall avenge them all.'

'There is no satisfaction in vengeance,' Brandt said almost too quietly to be heard.

'Perhaps not,' Vorster conceded, 'but there is retribution.'

'Oskar Zenzi, do you wish to officiate? These are your men, after all.'

'Ah, no, I think perhaps given the irregularity of it all it is best that I defer to you.'

'Very well, then on my word! Gentlemen, begin! One!' He counted out the steps. 'Two!' Eight seconds and he could be dead. The thought, rather surprisingly, didn't disturb Vorster. Indeed he was curiously detached. His hands were steady. He took another step. The world came alive around him even as it slowed to a treacly crawl. Scents heightened, suddenly overpowering: grass and mud and sweat, piss and fear were all there in his nose, alive. The colours of the grass, the sky and the clouds intensified. The grass became greener, more verdant, the sky cerulean and the clouds purer. He was alive, experiencing these things for the first time despite the fact that he had lived with them all of his life. The sudden fear of their loss ought by rights to have undermined him. It didn't. It invigorated him. This was his world, the living world, the world his men had been denied because of Jaeger. 'Three! Four! Five!' Brandt cried out, marking time. Vorster walked resolutely on, keeping perfect time with Brandt's count.

'Six!'

Vorster breathed deeply and held it.

He saw the implacable face of Martin, a silent spectator on the fringe of the crowd. Vorster chose to believe he saw something else in the Elector Count's cold eye – a belief that justice was being served.

'Seven!'

He let the breath leak slowly out between his lips.

'Eight!'

He closed his eyes, focusing on the rhythm of his heart and the slight breeze on his face. He could picture the entire scene, down to the faces in the crowd: the men of Talabecland, Ackim Brandt facing the Stirlanders, the flustered supporters of Jaeger and unseen by all but a few, the unflappable count.

'Nine!'

The *dub-dub-dub* against his chest accelerated rapidly. His breathing grew erratic. Still his hand was steady, the tip of the pistol's barrel unmoving against the underside of his chin.

'Ten!'

Still with his eyes closed, he exhaled, inhaled, exhaled.

'Turn!'

He opened his eyes, spun on his heel and levelled the pistol at Dietrich Jaeger's face, but he didn't squeeze the trigger.

Jaeger was marginally slower in the turn, but he brought the gun up quicker, snatching the shot.

Vorster felt a sudden burning in his left shoulder and saw the horror sweep across his opponent's face. He'd hit, but in rushing the shot he had failed to make it count. Vorster had all the time in the world to take his aim and fire at the helpless Jaeger. They all knew it. It had ceased to be a duel and had become an execution.

All colour fled from Jaeger's face. He threw up his hands and whimpered: 'Please.'

Vorster waited, allowing the adrenaline to seep from his system, for his heart to slow to a regular beat, and for the breeze to still.

Jaeger staggered back a step. 'No, man! Stand!' Brandt barked.

Vorster drew slow and careful aim. One shot. He didn't need more.

He fired.

The lead shot took Dietrich Jaeger through the right wrist, shattering the bone into splinters. The man screamed and fell to his knees, clutching his ruined hand. He looked up at Vorster. He knew. It was in his eyes. 'You could have killed me,' he rasped between clenched teeth, biting back on the pain. 'You didn't. Why?'

Vorster walked towards the fallen man. 'I didn't need to,' he said simply. 'You're humiliated in front of these men. You panicked when it came to the moment of truth, just as you always panic. You couldn't run away despite every nerve and fibre of your being screaming out for you to flee, and you would have if Brandt hadn't chastised you. You would have run for the hills, no better than a common deserter. You are finished Jaeger. Everyone here has witnessed your fall. You'll never hold a sword again. That is good enough for me. Hell, most likely the field surgeon will have to amputate. I did that, but I will not have your death on my conscience.'

Brandt came to stand beside him. He took the gun from him.

'Compassion isn't weakness. Believe me it will cure more sins than condemnation, my friend.'

'There is wisdom in that,' Martin von Kristallbach said. Neither of them had heard the young Elector Count approach. 'So, tell me soldier, have you decided to take me up on my offer? It would seem I have a vacancy for an experienced officer.' Martin looked down at Jaeger, his distaste all too apparent on his plain, open features. Before the shamed officer could object he told him, 'You brought this on yourself Dietrich. Own your mistakes. Be a man. Now get up, there's no need to add to your humiliation.'

Dietrich Jaeger struggled to his feet. He was bleeding quite badly, but Vorster's shot hadn't ruptured the main artery. He would live. Zenzi supported him.

'Go see the chirurgeon. A soldier who can't hold a sword is no good to me,' Martin said. He turned to Vorster. 'Now, tell me, soldier, what am I to do with you? Wilful disobedience, calling out a superior officer, endangerment of life.' He looked squarely at Ackim Brandt as he said, 'Consorting with the enemy. Your list of crimes is a lengthy one.'

'I will suffer whatever punishment you deem fit, my lord,' Vorster said solemnly.

'Indeed you will,' Martin agreed, 'Sergeant Schlagener.'

It took a moment for Martin's words to register. He thought for a second that he had misheard. 'You're not discharging me?'

'Why on earth would I do that? I am surrounded by fools. A rough diamond is far preferable to a lump of coal, sergeant,' he turned back to Brandt. 'Now, about that offer–'

Before he could finish a murmur arose from the surrounding men. They turned to see a plume of snow-dust rising from one side of Ramius Point, and out of the mist came a rider, pushing his mount to the point of collapse. Ribbons of steam corkscrewed from the exhausted beast's nose. The rider kicked hard, spurring the animal on. Unease spread quickly through the ranks. Whatever word the messenger carried it most certainly wasn't good news.

'They're coming! The vampires are coming!' the man yelled over the wind.

For the second time in as many minutes Vorster Schlagener didn't trust his ears. Only this time, he prayed he had heard wrong. It was impossible, the threat was ended. There were no vampires. It had ended at Grim Moor. The dead did not rise, not now. They stayed dead. He wanted to ask if the man was sure. Then he saw the pure horror wrought across his pale face and knew beyond a shadow of a doubt that they had all been idiots, tearing each other apart, while in the shadows the vampires had been watching, enjoying the savagery that only mankind was capable of.

Vorster knew fear.

CHAPTER NINE

A Band of Brothers
The Dwarf Stronghold of Karak Raziac
Beneath the Worlds Edge Mountains

KALLAD STORMWARDEN COULDN'T rest.

The dwarf dearly wanted to just close his eyes and have the world go away into dreams, but there was no hiding, even here, deep under the mountains.

He had hoped after Grim Moor that he would be able to find some kind of peace. He had faced his father's killer and watched the daemon struck down by Helmar and his Runefang, but there was no peace.

Peace, such a fleeting thing, even for one as long-lived as Kallad. When he closed his eyes he heard the raven's caw: *Mannfred!* And recalled the vampire, Skellan's words: *The greatest of all is coming. You do not want to be here when he returns.* It was impossible to shake the memory, to move on.

He had been content to pick up the hammer for more useful purposes, for a while. He had worked in the smithy with Keggit and his brother Rerle, but Kallad had had no great skill for it. Despite his brother's patient teaching, everything he turned his hand to ended up going back into the fire to be melted down again. He quickly tired of failure. Gegka Darkcutter offered him a place in his crew, mining the deeps of the Underway. Kallad had no wish to go deeper; memories of the subterranean prisons of Drakenhof plagued him still. For a while he ran with Iori Slatebreaker's hunters, bringing down mountain game to feed the families of the Karak, but he tired of that, too.

Even in Karak Raziac, surrounded by his own kind, the dreams tormented him, making sleep impossible. He prowled the stone halls of the stronghold or went out beneath the sky and haunted the mountainside. He was a ghost, a shadow. He slowly came to understand the truth. He had died out there on that battlefield, not a physical death, but a death all the same. If his nocturnal perambulations disturbed the others they were loathe to say so, at least to his face. They knew his pain. Few he encountered spoke with him. He was, they whispered behind his back, cursed. He was the son of Kellus, the last child of Karak Sadra. He had fought the vampires, stood beside Grufbad at Grim Moor, and for that they welcomed him among them, but he was not one of them, and he never would be. Instead of friendship they offered pity.

He was disaffected.

He had had his reckoning, but rather than completing him revenge left him hollow.

He sat alone on the hillside, waiting for the spectre of death to come and claim him. He shouted a challenge to the mountain, his axe Ruinthorn above his head, shaking it at the thunderheads and the sky. He looked for ghosts coming over the peaks. He knew what it was: survivor's guilt, they called it. He lived where his family, his entire people, had died. He was the last of them. He carried all the guilt that went with outliving his clan, the guilt that went along with failing them.

'At least they died free,' Kallad whispered, his breath conjuring wraiths of mist to hang like a veil between the living and the dead. The failing sun was a sickly yellow eye on the horizon. The snow was cold beneath him, but he wrapped himself in furs. It was true, though it was little consolation. His people had died free. They had marched to Grunberg and they had laid their lives down in a fight that wasn't theirs. They had done it for the manlings. They hadn't run away, hadn't hidden in the mountains waiting for the evil to pass over them. They had stood up, and because of that they were heroes, each and every dwarf of Karak Sadra.

He was proud and sad.

He had to believe it had been worth it.

Mannfred is coming!

That one line undermined their sacrifice.

The ground beneath him was colder than death. His sweat had become a brittle frost that clung to his face like a second skin. A fine dusting of snow had settled on his jerkin and rough trousers. Kallad ignored the icy chill worming its way into his heart.

Behind and before him, the many ridges of the Worlds Edge Mountains and their snow-capped peaks reared, reaching into the sky. Beneath him lay Blutfurt, Nachtdorf and the forest between the two, her white-laced leaves rustling. The north wind whispered fragments of the wood's darkest secrets, hints of the hearts it had stilled and the dreams it had buried in its rich soil. Beyond that were the rolling hills that the manlings called the Unhiemlich Hügelkette, or Eerie Downs. Their name was apt. The nearness of the rolling hills was oppressive.

He shook off the uncomfortable sensation of eyes watching him and resumed his laborious trudge down the mountainside, the wind crying traitor in his ear. He ignored its mocking voice, knowing that the whispers would be endless and unforgiving. It was the burden of being a survivor. The ghosts he had left behind whispered and taunted him with the voice of his own guilt, ghosts that could never forgive him for being alive while they rotted in some unmarked grave.

Kallad pushed on until he came to the edge of a frozen tarn, his thoughts introspective, jagged memories weighted down with the sorrows of a dwarf who had turned his back on his friends when they had needed him most.

It didn't matter if it wasn't true. It didn't matter if he had carried the fight to von Carstein's aberrant army. It didn't matter that he had been with them at the end to slay the beast. His guilt didn't care for any of that.

'What good would it have done for me to die with 'em?' he yelled at the wind, finally sick of its taunting. His voice was thick, raw, strained.

It's not about dying, the wind whispered, *it's about living. You've stopped living, Kallad Stormwarden.* He might have stood there, frozen, for an hour or a day, listening to his guilt echo off the rocks; a dwarf on a mountain being judged and found unworthy by the ghosts inside him. *Worse, you've stopped watching for the oncoming storm... and now it comes. Can't you feel it? Can't you feel it in the air? The presence of evil is building.*

'I could lie down now.' He barely breathed the words, taking their silence as judgement. 'I could close my eyes and never wake up. The cold would take me before dawn.'

To join them in death would have stopped the shades from being alone, but it was not them who were alone, it was Kallad. The wind knew that. It had stopped listening to the survivor's lies. It knew he could no more lie down and die than the sun could cease to shine or the seasons stop turning. It was a survivor's nature to survive, to go on living no matter the costs to those around him. A survivor would find a way.

He wiped the sweat from his brow before it could freeze there. His lips were chapped from the wind's perpetual kiss. Kallad hadn't realised just how thirsty he was until he knelt and brushed away the thin coating of snow from the surface of the frozen lake. Quickly, he used the wooden handle of his axe to chip a series of cracks in the ice, breaking a small slab free. He teased his gloves off and rubbed some life back into his hands before he pushed the ice under so he could scoop a handful of water to his lips. It tasted heavily of minerals and dirt, but it could have been wine to the lips of a drunkard. He drank deeply, wiping at his beard where the water ran down his chin, and scooped up another mouthful.

When he lowered his cupped hands from his face, Kallad faced a miracle reflected in the still water. Not one face but three looked back at him: his own drawn, exhausted reflection and two faces he knew better than his own, faces haunted by the death he had left them to back at Grim Moor. Skellan's ruined features showed a spider web of cuts and purple bruises that stood in stark contrast to the other man's: Jerek von Carstein.

Mannfred is coming!

No matter what he had told himself the beasts were far from slain. The storm had abated. It hadn't blown itself out. There was fighting, and dying, to be done. The vampires were out there, alive, as alive as those things could ever be. They were eternal. Their blades were like snakes of lightning on the battlefield, weaving a deadly magic as they danced. Kallad's fingers moved towards the illusion painted so thinly on the water. He wanted to reach out to banish the illusion, to drive the dead away.

Kallad plunged his fist into the icy water.

He swirled the water with his fist, dragging it around the small hole in the ice to drive the faces of the dead men away.

'It's the cold,' he told himself even as his nostrils flared at the scent of death carried by the wind. 'It's the cold making me jump at ghosts.'

He felt unbearably old, despite the fact that he was a child beside others of his kind. Kallad had long since ceased counting years and instead racked up experiences. He had lived through more than almost every dwarf in Karak Raziac. There were a few of their number who had lived even half as much life, heroes like Grufbad, Goriki Earthrunner or even old Runik Greybeard, who was rapidly becoming Runik Whitebeard, though none dared tell the old curmudgeon. Kallad had seen more than anyone should have to.

He remembered his father giving him his full name, Stormwarden. It could have been yesterday. He had pledged to guard against the oncoming storm. Looking at the snow churning across the bleak mountainside, he couldn't decide if he had failed in that as well.

Mannfred is coming!

He made a decision. He would seek out King Razzak and explain that he couldn't simply wash his hands of it, not while he knew the vampire nation was growing once more. They were licking their wounds, they weren't banished. That was why peace eluded him.

He trudged back towards the stronghold.

It felt good to have made a decision.

For once his ghosts were silent.

His decision pleased them.

KING RAZZAK'S GREAT hall was a monument to dwarf architecture and engineering. Eight giant foe-pillars supported the vaulted ceiling. They were three hundred feet high, carved with giant frescos of battle depicting great triumphs of the clan: scenes of death ranged back beyond the War of the Beard, orcs blinded by crossbow bolts, trolls slain by axe and warhammer, the skulls of ratmen and goblins cleaved in two. Each foe-pillar held a thousand deaths.

Kallad looked up at the ceiling; it was impossible not to. The builders had designed the central hall as a spectacle to be entered from above and descended into, allowing their craft to be best displayed. The second and third tiers of the ceiling were threaded with gold and silver wires that caught and reflected the light from the torches blazing all the way down the winding staircase to the mosaic-tiled floor of the grand hall. A huge bas-relief of Grimnir dominated the centrepiece of the ceiling, the dwarf god clutching his fabled twin axes, one either side of the aisle carved through the heart of the mountain. More carvings showed the defeat of the dwarf's foes.

Hammers rang out, bellows hissed and huffed, the engineers hard at work developing, Kallad seemed to remember, a huge mechanical water pumping system to aid the excavations of the Underway. Kallad walked slowly down the twisting stair, drinking in the grandeur of Karak Raziac. This was the artistry of his people at its finest. His fingers trailed along the outer wall. He imagined the memories locked within those old stones.

His footsteps echoed as he walked the length of the wide aisle. Midway down the aisle a huge iron fist, twice his height and more than four times his girth, dominated the floor. It was a symbol of the Karak's might. Kallad walked around it.

Razzak's throne was on the other side of the fist, on a raised dais of black stone. Like the dwarf lord himself it was a squat robust piece of furniture carved from the very rock of the mountain and set down in the middle of the great hall, as immovable as Razzak was when he put his mind to it.

The dwarf king was not on his throne. Razzak was a hands-on ruler. He didn't have his dwarfs do anything he wasn't prepared and capable of doing himself.

Kallad found him with the engineers, sleeves rolled up, getting his hands dirty, lifting and carrying immense cogs and wheel-gears for a huge water pump. They were in a vast chamber with a foundry at one end, steaming water vats and other curious devices churning out an infernal amount of heat. Hammers clanged and dwarfs grunted, and then the rhythm of the work broke down and one red-headed engineer cursed, sucking at his thumb where he'd hammered it solidly with the head of his tool. That shift in timing turned the regular clang-beat-clang into a discordant cacophony of hammering, cursing and beating that had Kallad covering his ears.

Thokën Kragbeard, one of Razzak's wreckers – engineers who specialised in demolition and destruction – looked up and saw Kallad standing in the doorway. He took his goggles off and wiped the sweat from his brow, smearing a great link of soot across his forehead. Thokën put his fingers to his lips and whistled sharply. The hammering stopped almost immediately.

Razzak looked up from the sharp-toothed cog he had been rolling across the floor as Kallad walked towards him. One look at the dwarf's face told the king all he needed to know. He passed the huge cog-wheel to another one of the crew and dusted his hands off on his bare chest.

'Can we talk, sire?'

'Aye, we can. It's one of the marvels of Grimnir. That an' opposable thumbs. You got something you need to get off yer chest?'

Kallad looked around the room. These people had done their best to make him feel a part of their clan, but he didn't. In that, he had failed them more than they had ever failed him. 'Yes.'

'Walk with me, lad.'

Razzak untied his apron, rolled it into a ball and left it on one of the many work benches. 'She's gonna be a beauty when she's up and running. You should hear the motor purr. Grakchi is a genius with this stuff. She ought to be able to pump three or four hundred buckets an hour. We'll have the deeps cleared in no time.'

No time to a dwarf of course, was relative, a year being a blink of an eye.

Kallad nodded his appreciation.

'So you are leaving us?' Razzak asked, turning his back on the machine.

'Aye, I think I am.'

Razzak studied him thoughtfully. Finally he asked, 'Do you intend to tackle your monsters alone?'

The question threw Kallad. He didn't know what he had expected Razzak to say, a plea to stay, perhaps, but not this. He had become so accustomed to being alone while hunting his father's killer that the notion of doing it any other way had never occurred to him.

'You are not the only one alone now, Kallad. Look around this room. Five here lost their life-mates to the Vampire Counts. Three more have no family outside the clan itself. War is hard on everyone, but you need to remember that no matter what you feel, you are not alone. You are one of us.'

'I don't understand.'

'No, perhaps you don't. It must be hard, having to carry the guilt of outliving your clan inside you. Look around, just in this room. Tell me what you see.'

Kallad did as he was asked. He turned slowly, taking in all of the hustle and flow. 'You're building a water pump,' he said finally, not sure what exactly he was supposed to be seeing.

Razzak smiled. 'So you *do* see it even if you don't understand exactly what it is you are seeing.'

'If you say so.'

'Let me explain,' Razzak put an arm around the younger dwarf and led him away. They talked as they walked through the vast network of tunnels and underways. 'We are clan. It is more than just a concept, it is our identity. It defines us, and because of it we are never alone. Those who can do something do what they can, those who can't find other ways to help, but every son and daughter of the clan is vital to the clan as a whole. Alone, no one, not even Grakchi, could assemble this monstrosity. He can imagine it, but he's no smith. He couldn't fashion the pieces needed for the complex mechanisms. Even then few of the foundry workers have the skill to fashion the intricate pieces, so these are hand-tooled separately. Do you see now? Ask yourself who is more valuable? If neither one can function without the other they are both essential. The clan is the same. You, my friend, are essential. Whatever you may think, you are a part of us.'

Kallad nodded, grudgingly. 'Aye, but what's that got to do with the price of fish?'

'Talk to Belamir, Cahgur and a few of the others. I don't believe you have to do this alone. I think this is still something for the clan. Perhaps they would accompany you. After all, the world has changed for them almost as much as it has for you. Like you, they are refugees of the war. I think they would appreciate the chance to strike back. Otherwise, the vampires have taken all of your lives as effectively as if they had sunk their fangs into your necks.'

'RAZZAK TOLD ME you'd got some brainless plan about takin' the fight to them pointy-toothed whoresons in Sylvania?' a bespectacled Cahgur laughed as Kallad outlined his plan to march into the darkest corners of Sylvania and root the undead out of their hiding places, not stopping until he had ended their threat once and for all. 'All I got to say is you and whose army?'

Kallad grinned, the grin of a madman. He didn't care. 'You in?'

'I'd have to be a raving lunatic,' Cahgur said, shaking his head in wonderment.

'So are you in, laddie?'

Cahgur chuckled. 'I must need my head read for sayin' this, but aye, I'm in. Why the kruti not, eh?'

The response was much the same from the others he approached. They looked at Kallad as though he were some 'zaki' dwarf wandering the mountains, but then the fire lit in their eyes and they held out their meaty hands, joining his band of brothers.

They were seven when they set out from Karak Raziac: Molagon Durmirason, Skalfkrag Gakragellasson, Othtin Othdilason, Belamir Kadminasson, Cahgur Ullagundinasson, Valarik Darikson and Kallad Stormwarden. They made an unlikely brotherhood, but they all had something in common: they no longer fitted among their own people. The wars had affected them too personally, too deeply. They left without ceremony, just like any other mountain patrol going in search of greenskins, only their quarry was far more dangerous than an orc or goblin.

The mood was sombre.

Kallad walked, looking up at the sky, at the skeletal branches of the trees and the freshly fallen snow. Each place offered its own unique hint as to the enemy's movements if you knew what to look for. He sought black crows and the paw prints of wolves in particular.

They walked along in silence for the better part of the day, each lost in his thoughts. They made camp in the shadow of the mountainside that first night.

'You're all gonna think I am mad,' Kallad said, around the campfire.

'Most likely, aye,' Belamir agreed, warming his hands briskly over the fire pit. 'But tell us anyway. It ain't like we're strangers to a bit of madness.'

Kallad scratched at his beard. 'Right, well, I ain't told you how I know the beasts ain't dead, now have I?'

'Ooh sounds like a story, good, good,' Molagon said, biting off a hunk of stone bread and chewing loudly. Cahgur swallowed a chug of robust ale, preferring it to the dry bread. He was more than happy surviving on nothing but ale for a few days. Belamir clanked tankards with Cahgur.

'Well, depends on your disposition, I'd say, an' whether you are willing to believe in some weird stuff. See, I was there at the end, with Grufbad and Helmar when the lad stuck the sword in, finishing off the blood count. But it weren't just us. In the middle of this hellish battle we had some help. Unlikely help, you might say. There were two other vampires there that helped bring down their leader. One calling himself Jerek von Carstein,' Kallad began, telling them the story. It was the first time he had spoken of his pact with the undead.

'He came to me in the dark, claiming to be a friend. I didn't believe him. All he had to say was, "Then let's hope that by the end of the night I am."

'I heard him out, even though I didn't trust him. My thought was to strike him down. He knew it, I knew it. Why should I trust him? His explanation? "Because of who I was," he said. "Not who I am. Because as the White Wolf of Middenheim I gave my life trying to protect the same thing you are trying to protect, and because, for some reason, a spark of whatever it was that made me still burns inside here,"' said Kallad. Jerek's words were poignant. Kallad could not resist the opportunity to turn into a storyteller, mimicking the vampire's grave voice as he leaned into the fire. "I was a ghost, trapped between the land of the living and the nations of rot and decay, and nothing in either world."

'It was a grand speech boys, I'll grant the beast that. His words stirred something in me. I mean, I believed him. I could just tell he was telling the truth and the strength it must have taken to hold back the beast inside him, well, I wasn't dense enough to think I could fight my way into the heart of their army and take down the blood count by myself. So we made a deal. He told me how the first war with the Vampire Counts was won by guile, not force. He explained that von Carstein had a talisman of incredible power that enabled his dead form to regenerate, and that the talisman was stolen during the Siege of Altdorf. See, it was that theft that allowed the Sigmarite priest to slay him once and forever.'

Kallad leaned in over the fire pit, warming himself on the blaze. Licks of flame danced erratically, throwing shadows across his face. An owl hooted somewhere in the distance. It was a melancholy sound, answered a moment later by a lupine lament. There was no way of knowing if the beast was a true wolf or a were-creature. The howl sent a shiver of ice into his heart.

'We know the story,' Othtin said, impatient to get to whatever nugget of mystery Kallad had alluded to. 'The Vampire Count's ring; the thief stole it and gave it to the priests.'

Kallad looked at him across the fire. 'You think you know the story. There's a world of difference. Jerek shared a secret about the damnable count's ring. This secret has robbed me of peace.'

'Go on,' Belamir urged, leaning forwards, sold on the tale.

Kallad waited, looking slowly around the circle of faces. 'The ring wasn't in the vampire's grave.'

'So?'

'Think about it, you don't need me to explain it all.'

None of them dared say a word.

'If that ring resurfaces, any beast wearing it, well he'd be like that scourge, Vlad, and damned hard t'kill. Jerek was looking for the ring.'

'He wanted its power?' Othtin asked, appalled at the thought of another dread beast rising to challenge the stability of the Old World.

'No, he said he wanted to make sure the damned thing was destroyed.'

He let that sink in.

'That was the pact we made. I told him what I knew, which was precious little. I tracked the thief down in Altdorf, where he'd been taken in by the Sigmarites. He lost his hands, and the ring, to one of the vampire's kind. Jerek knew what I was, the last of my clan. He'd been there, seen my father fall. He understood the anger inside me, the need for vengeance, because, like me he said he bore a grudge against the monsters that had made him into what he was, a monster in their image.' Kallad lowered his voice, lending his words an ominous quality. 'We were not so different, the beast and me. He told me, "I will not lie down and let them swallow my world whole. I will not stand by and watch it plunged into eternal night. I will not watch it become a place of blood and sorrow. That ring cannot be allowed to adorn the finger of a vampire. It cannot. The world cannot withstand another dread lord of my sire's ilk." And his words sent a chill to my core, brothers, because in them I heard the truth. He had me over a barrel. He had saved my life, see, from the other vampire, the one he called Skellan. I didn't like it, but he was at pains to point out that I didn't need to. All I had to do was accept that he was less than human, more than vampire, something else entirely and nothing completely. He claimed no loyalty to the dead and only wanted to do what he had always done, protect the living.'

'Are you tryin' to tell me that the damned beastie didn't want the ring for himself?' Cahgur asked in disbelief. 'Do I look like I am still sucking at my ma's teat?'

'Trust me,' Kallad said. 'He didn't claim the life debt I owed him, though he knew full well he could. He was aware what it means to save a dwarf from certain death. He didn't care. He wanted my help given willingly or not at all. What he was asking for was nothing more than help preventing a dark and hungry god from arising. We sealed the pact, and he upheld his end, he helped me get close to the necromancers and kill the mad vampire. We never would have done it without him.'

There was a long moment of silence before Belamir asked, 'What did you promise him?'

Kallad looked at his new comrade across the fire's heart.

'I told him I'd aid his search for the damned ring.'

'And this is what you want us to do? To scour the earth for some magical ring? Why didn't you say this when we set out? This ain't exactly hunting the beasts in their stinking lair!'

'Would you have come, Othtin?' Kallad Stormwarden asked, bluntly.

The dwarf shrugged. 'Maybe, maybe not.'

'This is not all the story is it?' Valarik Darikson asked, thoughtfully. 'It don't feel... What's missing, Kallad? You're dancing around something. Just come out with it. What aren't you saying?'

Kallad picked up a stick and prodded at the embers. Sparks fizzled and hissed and ash fell lazily back down to the ground. They deserved to know.

'At the end, on the field surrounded by the dead, Morr's birds carried a message for us, the living,' Kallad said. The stick snapped as he thrust one end into the dirt.

'What was it?'

'Mannfred is coming!'

Kallad threw the other end of the stick into the fire. The flame roared as the embers scattered, scaring the hell out of his new companions. He grinned.

'You whoreson!' Othtin grumbled, clutching at his chest. 'You scared seven shades of crap out of me!'

'I need a bloody beer after that!' Cahgur said.

'Aye, but what does that mean?' Belamir asked, knowing that any chance of understanding the message lay in getting to the root of Kallad's reluctance to explain it.

'Mannfred's the worst of them, that's what Skellan said.' Kallad shivered at the memory. He made a show of rubbing his arms briskly as though to massage the heat back into them. 'He all but killed me when I faced him... and...' And this was the wisp of memory that plagued him. It was like some perverse engineering puzzle all coming together layer by layer. 'I killed him. I mean I split him in two with Ruinthorn here, but that bastard didn't die.'

Skalfkrag Gakragellasson, who hadn't said a word during the telling of the tale, understood first. It came out of his mouth like a death sentence, 'He has the ring.'

'He has the ring,' Kallad echoed.

'So we *are* hunting a creature then,' Othtin said. 'I like that better than looking for some stupid trinket.'

A few of the others nodded as the true underlying nature of their quest became clear.

Kallad nodded. 'Aye, we are.'

'But it's like a vein in a mountain, you can dig and dig and dig and never strike it. How'd you propose we find this Mannfred?' Cahgur asked.

'I have been in his home,' Kallad said. 'I have been imprisoned in the dungeons and the dark beneath his castle. They call it Drakenhof. It lies in the barren wilderness of Sylvania, out of reach of the Empire. It is a vile place, but I know a few of its secrets. I know a way back into the castle through the old underways from the Worlds Edge. Now, I'm gonna ask you fellas again. Who's with me? Anyone wants to return to the stronghold, there won't be no grudge here. This is above and beyond what I can ask of you. Chances are we won't come out of that place alive.'

'My kind of odds,' Othtin said. 'I'm in.'

'Aye,' Belamir chuckled, 'why'd I want to be going home just when things are about to get interesting? You're a strange lad, Kallad Stormwarden.'

'We're brothers now and our bond is stronger than steel,' Molagon Durmirason said. 'We've seen some of the worst the world has to show us. Alone, we are outsiders, but together, together we are clan.'

He held his hand out across the fire.

'It's gromril at least.' Belamir reached out and placed his on top.

Othtin did likewise. One by one the others reached across the guttering fire as it failed, adding their hands to the pile, sealing the brotherhood.

They would return to the belly of the mountains, to the cells where Kallad had been held prisoner, to the soul cages where he had been forced to fight for his life for the entertainment of the blood count, back to the one place he had vowed he would never revisit: Drakenhof.

He pulled his hands away from the others.

He felt whole for the first time in as long as he could remember.

He would have been lying to himself if he tried to pretend it was the company of strangers that contented him.

He was finally fulfilling his promise to Jerek. He had decided to live the rest of his life and make it count. He was going after the beast. He would most likely die in the coming fight but that, didn't matter. He had stopped running away. He had made a decision to stand and fight in the face of the oncoming storm. He picked up Ruinthorn and pushed himself to his feet. The old axe felt comfortingly familiar in his hands.

'Well, lads, what are we waiting for?'

CHAPTER TEN

The Mirror of his Dreams
Nuln, the Imperial City

JEREK VON CARSTEIN huddled in the shadowed doorway of a disused oast house. He could smell the last few kernels of hops and the mulch of rotten straw. The air reeked of disease. He hadn't fed on *real blood* in so long. He couldn't remember when he had last tasted it. No, he could. He didn't want to, but he could. Rats and cats, and dogs and birds were pale substitutes that barely sated the rising hunger in him.

His mind was useless. Words, random, disconnected words, floated through it. He grunted and moaned, drew his legs up to his chin and pressed back deeper into the doorway, wanting to disappear.

Passers-by flipped occasional coins at his feet, mistaking him for a vagabond unable to conquer his daemons. He left them. He remembered fragments of memory: the caravan, the old woman, the witch hunters, the bloodthirsty crowd, the dead man at his feet and his blood on Jerek's tongue. Oh yes, that he remembered. That taste he couldn't forget.

The guilt was killing him.

He had tried so hard not to kill. He had tortured himself with the hunger, grubbing around eating vermin, anything other than touch humans. He had wrestled his instincts, his needs, the drives that made him what he was and he had failed. They had corralled him into a corner of fire and hate, and he had lashed out, frightened. In that one moment of brutality it had all come undone.

He tortured himself with the face of the dead man.

Jerek closed his eyes.

He hadn't fed in so long.

He had tasted the blood on his teeth and tongue and lips as he had killed the man, but he hadn't fed. He hadn't suckled at the wounds gulping down that heady elixir.

But he had *wanted* to, and that shocked him. After everything he had done to bury his nature, the first whiff of blood and he had wanted to undo it all and feast on the damned human.

He hated himself for what he had become.

They had found the witch hunter strung up from the ceiling of the temple of Morr. He had been mutilated, laid open like a lesson in the secret of anatomy. The murder was the talk of the city. The watch had scoured the streets, dragging hundreds of vagrants and undesirables into custody. Jerek had been forced to flee below ground until even that sanctuary had become unsafe. They had descended with dogs, savage animals that they unleashed in the tunnels trying to cleanse them. Jerek had fled to the rooftops before being forced to move on by the agonies of the sun. So he had become one of the hundreds of beggars, faceless and unmemorable. It hadn't always been easy to hide. A wandering Shallyan had come to give benediction to the poor when she collapsed, suffering from a fit of hideous convulsions. She had fallen two buildings away from where the vampire hid. He had run before anyone could capture him.

That was his life now – he ran.

Jerek hunched up against the doorframe. His hands trembled, as if he was some addict coming down from a Crimson Shade high.

He shook with an undercurrent of violent seizures that wracked his corpse. He wanted nothing more than to cease to be, but he couldn't die, not while the fractured visions still mocked him.

And they did, day and night, night and day.

They refused to leave him be.

He killed rodents and birds when they dared come too close, and drank. They offered little more than a dribble of blood, but it staved off the fiercest of the madness, though day by day it was growing evermore difficult to resist the pull of delirium. He forgot who he was at times. His only anchor on sanity was an image: a white wolf. As long as he could recall the wolf he knew *what* he was. At the worst of times that was enough.

He opened his eyes at the sound of a carriage rolling by. There weren't many carriages in this part of the city. Those who could afford them had little business in the squalor of the Alt Stadt, little *respectable* business.

The beautiful, open-topped carriage, was pulled by a black mare. A woman of uncommon grace disembarked. The dress she wore would have paid for the entire street with its sequins and pearls alone. He was drawn to her face. It was haunting though not attractive in any traditional sense. She moved past the window of a thruppeny bazaar with all sorts of junk and curiosities on display through the glass. The place was a veritable cornucopia of enticements and behind it, Jerek knew there was a low-rent knocking shop aimed at satisfying all the other curiosities a body might have. There was something about the woman, not merely that she was out of place in the Alt Stadt's hovels, something more than that. It took a moment for him to see what it was.

Though she faced the sun, he saw that she cast no shadow.

He looked at the glass window as the shopkeeper dimmed the oil lamp. Her reflection wasn't caught by the window, but seeing and understanding were two completely different things. It took Jerek the longest time to realise *what* he was seeing, or what he wasn't.

She cast no reflection and no shadow.

He stared at the woman, praying fervently that she would not turn and see him. He struggled to his feet, needing the wall for support. His head swam dizzily. The woman was half way down the street before he managed a first unsteady step. Jerek lurched forwards. A rat scuttled over his foot. He twisted and saw that two more of the fat-bellied rodents had come out of the cracks and were sniffing around him in search of food. Without thinking he leaned down, almost falling, and scooped one of them up and crammed its wriggling body into his mouth. The rodent died in a shrill squeal. Its blood dribbled hot and thin across his tongue. Jerek swallowed, wishing even as he did that it was human. He fell to his knees and snatched up the second and third rats, draining them greedily.

When he looked up, momentarily lucid, the woman had gone.

He stumbled forwards, lurching down the street, looking left and right for any trace of her, but she had disappeared.

It didn't matter.

He knew that he had seen a female vampire walking through the slums of the old city, and that was just the beginning of the peculiarities he began to notice.

A few days later he saw a black bird perched on a blacksmith's sign. The bird took flight in a burst of feathers leaving the weather-beaten sign creaking in the wind. He turned away, thinking nothing of it until he saw a second black bird perched on a roadside marker, watching him, and a third on a fence post. Their scrutiny was unnaturally attentive. He ran at the birds, scattering them.

They didn't fly far, one coming to rest on the guttering of a nearby hovel, the two others landing on the top of a low broken wall. Jerek turned wildly and the nearest bird squawked, but it didn't fly away.

He walked towards it slowly, reaching out. The raven cawed harshly and sank its beak into the soft skin of his hand. Jerek wrenched his hand away and swore as the raven took flight. It circled his head three times before flying away over the rooftops. He turned on the two birds perched on the wall. They studied him with their yellow beady eyes, and as he reached towards it the nearest bird cawed, sounding for all the world as though it said, *Jerek?* He flinched, startling the birds.

They were gone a moment later – disappearing in a flurry of black wings.

He stood alone in the middle of the street, turning left and right.

The bird had known him. It had recognised him.

Was it part of the madness? Had he imagined it? Was he like Konrad now? Hearing voices and threats in all these unlikely places?

Three nights later he saw Jon Skellan.

He knew it was Skellan even though he never saw his face. Jerek followed him a while, long enough to see him slip into the grounds of a huge manor house on the outskirts of the city, in one of the more affluent districts. Jerek stayed back, following at a distance. His only thought was that if Skellan was there then his master couldn't be far away.

He saw women come and leave the house that Skellan had entered, hauntingly beautiful courtesans. Each one put him in mind of the woman he had seen leaving the carriage, the woman with no shadow or reflection. They were vampiric in nature. He sensed the blood curse on them. How pretty they were and yet how lethal. He mourned for the women they had once been before they had become these loveliest of the dead.

He slept in the old mausoleum within the grounds of the manor house. It was the first good day's sleep he had had in months and he was forced to take it amongst the dead. Come dusk he left the house of corpses in search of a man who could help him, not that he expected help. He skirted the better neighbourhoods, moving by rooftop until he found a staircase leading down into the Unterbaunch. He ran along the dark passages, more vital than he had felt in months. He ran up to the first man he saw and pressed him against the wall. 'Do you know where I can find a hedge wizard?' Terrified, the man shook his head. Jerek dropped him and ran on, going from person to person asking them the same desperate question. Time and again he was greeted by fear and ignorance until he slammed a young woman up against the lichen-smeared wall of the tunnel and instead of collapsing in fear she nodded hurriedly, eager to please.

'Where?' Jerek rasped, not letting her go.

'I know some stuff, little tricks mainly,' she said.

He grinned, and as his smile widened so too did her eyes as she saw his fangs and understood what he was.

'Please, no, mister. Don't kill me. I–'

'Can you change this?' He put his hand in front of his face to show her what he meant. 'Can you make me look different? I need to look like someone else.'

'I don't know,' the girl said, 'never tried to do stuff to someone else.'

'Anyone else, please.'

'And you won't kill me after, like? So I can't say what you look like to no one?'

'No,' he promised.

'Why should I believe you? I mean you are... you are... you know.'

'I know,' Jerek said. 'Please, do what you can. I need to be different. I need to get close to a man so that I can kill him.'

'Oh, no, I can't do that I mean, no. I–'

'He's not a *living* man. He's a monster. I promise you.'

Then his knees buckled. He could smell the heat of her pulse so close to his lips. He could hear the echo of the great song of her life that pumped in her veins. He could just lean in and taste her, take just a little of that vitality for his own. All he had to do was bite... He shook his head, struggling to quell the blood lust. 'It is the creature that killed the witch hunter in the temple of Morr.'

He knew it was true. He knew that Skellan was the vampire the witch hunters had been tracking when they had raided the Strigany caravans. It made a sick sort of sense. Skellan had been dogging his trail every step of the way.

'You aren't lying to me are you? I mean...' she left her second question unasked.

Jerek trembled as he let go of her. 'He is one of the beasts that served the mad count, and his sire before him. He is the worst sort of monster, this I swear. He is a killer to the core and his presence in your city augurs ill.'

'And you can kill him?' the girl asked.

'I don't know,' Jerek admitted. 'I am not the man I was.'

'But you are a vampire.'

'I am, but I was a Knight of Ulric before I was damned to this unlife. I would rather be the man I was.'

She looked at him and instead of fear he saw pity in her eyes. He hadn't expected that. She reached out and touched his cheek. 'I will try,' she promised.

It was all he could ask.

* * *

SHE LAID HER hands on his face.

There was an uncommon cold to the touch, but it quickly flowered into heat. Jerek felt it below the skin, rising to the surface. She whispered words of power as her hands moved, reshaping his face. Only he didn't feel different; his eyes, his nose, his cheeks, he felt like himself. Still she moved her hands, feeling out the contours of muscle and bone, re-imagining them in her mind, reconstructing them in the glamour she wove around his face.

She held a fragment of mirrored glass up for him to see when she was done. He had been about to knock it from her hand, determined not to see the emptiness, but he was there, trapped in the reflection. Only it wasn't him, it was some other, unlike him in almost every way. Fine narrow boned features, light blonde hair and eyes of pale midsummer blue looked back at him. The face she had given him was handsome, too handsome he feared for a moment. It would draw attention to him. People would remember seeing him, and then he realised it didn't matter because once the glamour fell he would be himself again. For a little while at least he could pretend to be human. 'Thank you,' he said, feeling out his new face.

'I don't know how long the glamour will last,' the girl admitted. 'I've never done it on someone else. A day? A month? An hour? I have no idea, but I hope it is long enough for you to do whatever you have to.' she handed him a small clay disk. 'If you need to be rid of it for any reason, break this. They're tied together. With the disk broken the illusion won't be able to sustain itself. I don't know how it works, only that it does. My father taught it to me. He liked his tricks.'

Jerek smiled, trying out his new face. 'I don't know how to thank you.'

'Don't kill me,' the girl said.

He touched her face, his fingers lingering on her rich red lips. She shivered beneath his touch. He felt her pulse, felt the lure of the blood, and rested his fingers to his own lips.

'You have my word,' Jerek said.

JEREK LEFT THE Unterbaunch a new man.

The sun was low in the sky. He felt it sting his skin. He covered himself as best he could for fear that any exposed skin might suddenly ignite. He was weakened, but he didn't know how weak he was. He clung to the shadows, scant as they were.

He knew where he had to go. The manor house.

It was the only link to Skellan that he had, and that made it his only link to Skellan's master, Mannfred.

He had no thought other than to confront the Vampire Count and, if he could, to slay him. If he failed, well he would be dead, truly dead, and then he would know peace. Given the choices and the torments of his unlife Jerek knew he couldn't lose, no matter the outcome.

He walked the snow-covered streets, watching the early evening bustle as businesses closed for the night. It was too early for the city's other life to begin in earnest, though here and there as he crossed the entertainment district he saw the red glass oil lamps light up in the windows, welcoming business. Row upon row of ladies of every imaginable shape and size sat on their window ledges whistling and calling down to the wide-eyed young men on the street below. The street had its share of tenements with leaking gutters and grimy stoops as well as almost palatial buildings with mosaics and marbled pillars. 'Eclectic' best summed up the contrary building styles in this modest district, but perhaps that shouldn't have been such a surprise, considering the variety of tastes the street hoped to cater to.

The first thick flakes of snow were in the air as Jerek hurried towards the manor house.

'Up here, handsome, you can shelter from the snow,' one of the street's ruddy-faced matrons called from her window in a brownstone tenement. The years hadn't been kind to her.

For a moment Jerek didn't realise she was talking to him. 'Ah, not tonight, gorgeous,' Jerek said with a smile and a hand on his heart. 'Tonight there is only one lady for me.'

'Ah, then she's a lucky girl.'

'Let's hope she sees things the same way, eh?'

A pair of young men staggered arm in arm out of a door across the street, nearly tripping as they navigated the short flight of stairs down to the icy cobbles. At the doorway an equally young girl with the feathered hair of a raven blew the boys a kiss.

'You could have left one for me,' the old matron called to the girl from her window.

'Next time you can come over and join us, Esme,' the girl called back. 'Between us, we'll kill 'em.'

'Aye, that we will, lassie, but at least they'll drop happy.'

The banter continued as Jerek ducked around the corner into a side street. His thoughts ran wild. He could smell them all, the ripe flesh leaning out of the windows, the blood pumping through their breasts as they forced themselves into their corsets and cinnamon and strawberry coloured dresses. It would be easy to walk into one of the bordellos and take a girl. Her death wouldn't be noticed until morning and he would be long gone by then. Feeding would give him strength. He would need strength if he hoped to face Skellan and his master. That was how his mind worked when the hunger was upon him, it reasoned with him, showed him how he was weak and told him what he needed to be strong. It wheedled and pleaded, and finally cursed and kicked, and demanded to be fed.

It was growing more and more difficult to resist it.

He hurried away from the temptations of the street.

He found a stray dog four avenues down. The mutt was on its last legs. Jerek got down on his knees and whistled low and slow, calling the dog over. It came willingly enough until it was a little less than ten feet away and then its fur raised in a ridge along its back. Before the dog could bolt Jerek lunged forwards and grabbed it by the scruff of its scraggy neck. He dragged it close and even as it snapped and snarled, feral, he broke its neck and fed. The blood was sour. It barely touched the need inside him, but it was blood.

It would sustain him, keeping the fractured memories and the madness at bay a little while longer.

He left the dog's carcass at the side of the road, the snow stained red around it, and walked back to the black iron gates of the manor house.

He waited a while, watching from hiding. As on his last visit the courtesans came and went, always in pairs, giggling and preening as they walked out of the gates only to return hours later, their cheeks ruddy from their nocturnal jaunts. They had fed, he knew. He could smell the blood and the sex on them.

Jerek waited until the street was clear and eased open the gate. He slipped inside, moving quickly. He darted into the cover of the trees, using the shadows to edge closer and closer to the house. Oil lights burned in the lower windows. He watched as two courtesans closed the gate behind them and walked arm in arm up the drive to the door. He followed them, breaking into a run over the last few yards. By the time they realised danger was close it was too late. He caught up with them on the porch.

'Good evening, ladies,' he said, leaning in close, an arm on each of their shoulders.

The women turned, pleasant smiles gone. They were neither frightened nor surprised. 'You stink, but then your kind always does,' her voice was coldly mellifluous. 'What does your master want with the mistress now?'

'Ahh, what doesn't he want? You know how he is, after all,' Jerek said, imaging it was something Skellan might have said in similar circumstances. They obviously thought he was working with Mannfred, just another lackey, so he thought better of correcting their mistake and decided to play the part. Being taken for an ally would make things easier. 'Better take me to her, wouldn't want to keep the lady waiting would we?'

* * *

THEY LED HIM through a hall dedicated to a vast array of serpents, and without preamble down into a vast subterranean labyrinth with countless tunnels feeding into one another. Somewhere, almost certainly, they linked into the warren beneath the Alt Stadt.

Jerek followed the women.

He followed them through a series of turns and twists and narrowing corridors into wider tunnels until they reached an antechamber, and beyond it a door that led into the nave of a vast subterranean temple. The mistress reclined lazily on a grotesque snakeskin throne.

She was ugly, though not merely physically. Her essence was ugly. Jerek walked into the grand chamber and felt it, a physical thing that had sickness clogging in his craw. He looked at the woman even as she looked at him. She was old, gaunt, her skin slack as though, like the reptiles she venerated, she was in the process of shedding it. She wore a simple black gown and a tiara of gold and copper hammered into a perfect circle. The serpent's head, he saw, consumed its tail. The blood-rich rubies of the tiara's eyes glittered in the torchlight.

'What does Mannfred want with me now?' the woman asked, cutting to the quick. 'He has our aid; does he seek to bleed us dry?'

Jerek stood his ground, offering no hint of diffidence. He couldn't imagine an arrogant whoreson like Skellan bowing and scraping before the old woman. 'He sent me to the city above to deal with a problem, and then bade me visit the mistress to find his whereabouts. It is done, so I have come as I was told.'

'Who does the vain Morr-loathed maggot think he is to use *me* as his messenger?' The woman leaned forwards in her throne, hatred blazing in the black pits that ought to have been eyes. 'I am Kalada, I am the Eternal, beloved of Neferata. I am the true dark heart of this city. I am the black angel they pray to when the lights are out and the old superstitions grip them. I am the unseen threat lurking in the corner of the eye. I am *not* some worm he can order around as the whim strikes him.' Venom dripped from her words.

Jerek stood his ground, affecting a Skellanish swagger. 'Not my problem, lady,' he said, hoping he sounded as egotistical and cocksure as Skellan would have in his place. 'I don't want to bring *his* wrath down on my head. So do us both a favour, tell me where he is and I'll get out of your hair, and you can carry on playing the dark mistress to your heart's content.'

She looked at him as though he were dirt beneath her fingernail, something to be rooted out and disposed of.

'Like the maggot he is, he's down below, crawling through the slime and putrescence of the old dwarf underways that the rat people have infested. He creeps and creeps, and squirms and creeps, inch by inch and out of sight, leading his damned army through into the heart of the Empire without ever being seen. One of my handmaidens will see you to the door, but from there you are on your own. If you try hard enough I am sure you will be able to smell his stench somewhere down there amid the filth.'

CHAPTER ELEVEN

Like a Wolf to the Slaughter
The Old Skaven Underways
Beneath the World

THE DEAD WALKED unseen.

They moved with grim determination, unhindered by hunger and other earthly concerns. They came on, a relentless tide beneath the earth, hundreds of them, thousands as they were drawn down through the dirt to be born again into the agony of unlife. Mile by mile more and more white bone and diseased flesh clawed their way into the tunnels, joining the subterranean dance macabre.

The underways were so vast and complex that it was impossible to map or indeed plot a path through them. Some were wide, others unbearably cramped and claustrophobic. In places methane-burning cressets lined the winding tunnels, hinting at some subterranean life, the glass spheres casting ghastly flickering light over everything. Other stretches of tunnel were a dark nightmare of squalor and filth as they rose nearer to the surface, moisture running down the walls and effluvia and human waste washing down from the city. The filth was knee-deep in places. The stench was overwhelming. The darkness was prowled endlessly by shadow-shapes that skittered and chittered before disappearing before the ceaseless advance of the dead.

Mist crept along the floor in places, coiling around the shuffling feet of the dead and the damned. The mist was clammy as it writhed sluggishly around them.

Mannfred von Carstein drove them on mercilessly, bending the shuffling corpses and shambling skeletons to his will. His hand closed around a talisman he had unearthed in the rubble of the old tombs at Khemri, in the baking deserts of the Lands of the Dead. It was a peculiar device of little worth; though he had found it deceptively powerful when it came to influencing the more mindless undead. It was an ugly trinket to the eye, a small oval shaped pendant carved from obsidian with a central eye surrounded by odd pictograms of what looked like animal-headed people. The jewel itself was gripped in a silver hand setting with pointed talons. He felt the Eye, hot against his skin, amplifying his will so that none raised by the necromantic arts or held together by the dark wind of Shyish, could resist him.

Here and there the dead were assailed by gouting spouts of flame from fissures in the earth, always accompanied by a deep rumbling tremble from down below. Noxious fumes hung in the air of the webway of tertiary tunnels.

Occasionally the rhythmic cadences of dull drums and hammering reached up from below.

Cracks and chasms in the labyrinth vented greyish plumes of steam, and the stink of sulphur along with the stench of matted fur and excrement was carried by the subterranean winds.

Patches of yellow oil corroded into raw iron ore set into the tunnel walls. It was slick to the touch and reeked like lamp oil. Occasional strings of long, thin, spiny, brown hair caught on jags of rock. The air smelled of festering wounds.

There were prints too, in the dust, like the treads of large hunting dogs, only narrower, with elongated claws that left scratches in the clay ground.

The deeper they went the more walls they passed that had been daubed with the mark of the Horned Rat.

By then they had gone too deep, but there was no turning back.

THE RATMEN CAME shrieking, chattering and squawking out of the darkness, ringing their plague bells and wielding swords and daggers of bone. If they were words, they were none the dread count could decipher. The sounds were a cacophony of rapid trills, short, clipped and they often sounded as though they were repeated several times. Beneath the chatter lay a low grating noise.

Vermin swarmed over and around them, scores of bloated rats and ferocious bug-eyed rodents. Their thick worm-like tails quivered excitedly as they sank their teeth into the front ranks of the dead and tore at the rancid meat. There were no screams from the dead and no cessation in their relentless march. They dragged the rats forwards even as the rodents devoured the flesh from the calcified bones of their undead enemy.

The ratmen held their ground, banging spears and swords against the clay floor and rock walls, raising a cacophony of sound that was deafening. It folded in and in, and in again on itself, intensifying and amplifying the din until it became a single wall of noise.

In the flickering light of the glass spheres the many and hideous wounds of the ratmen were visible. Their feral snouts were torn and gnarled, gangrenous, teeth broken, lips torn back, eyes missing, ears ripped off. Others showed signs of mutation, their claws twisted and warped so that they became weapons grafted into their virulent flesh, their musculature bloated and twisted so that their reach doubled, their legs double-jointed around the knees, enhancing their natural pounce.

The tunnels were cramped, claustrophobic, with the dead lurching and stumbling forwards into one another. Strips of flesh clung to bones, draping them like rags. There was no room for more than three or four of the small ratmen to come at the shuffling dead at a time. Even so there were hundreds of them spilling out of every crack and crevice, clothed in rags and scraps of armour marked with the triangle of the Horned Rat. Sheer force of numbers held the dead in a nexus of tunnels where fifteen passageways crossed one another. The dead air reeked of sulphur and brimstone. They came from all sides, dropping down from above and climbing out of fissures below, a swarm of vermin.

Noxious fumes filled the tunnels, choking cloying fumes that sapped the air from around the dead. It was a pity for the rats that the dead had no need of anything as prosaic as air. The battle was joined with a clash of bone and fur on rusty blades. A sleek black-furred rat-man swung the ball joint of a human leg embedded with a razor of saw-toothed bone into shambling zombie. The bone stuck in rancid flesh. Shrieking, the skaven warrior tore his makeshift weapon free of his dead foe and slammed it again and again into the dead man's rotten face. The bone razor made an ungodly mess, slicing through nose and cheek, opening an impossibly wide smile of flapping skin. Then the dead fell on the rat man and the shrieking turned to terrified screams as the zombie's chipped and broken finger bones clawed into its eyes and pulled at its skull, until it had opened the ratman's head and was feasting on the mulch of brain beneath.

Green ribbons of crackling light arced through the fumes, tearing the flesh from the bones of the front line of undead. The corpses staggered and twisted in the hideous parody of a dance, flesh flensed from bone. There were no cries. Agony was silent. Rats swarmed over the fallen meat, their teeth grinding and tearing at the rancid flesh as they chewed and swallowed, feasting ravenously.

Gnats and flies swarmed in behind the smoke, biting and stinging, a multitude of insects buzzing around the faces of the dead, into ears and mouths as they flapped, up noses, in eyes with such cohesion to their pestilential assault that they formed a solid veil of insects.

Mannfred moved effortlessly through the ranks of the dead, muttering an arcane curse beneath his breath. The flies swarmed around his face. The dead fell away from him as he walked slowly and deliberately to the front of their number. A foul stench of death arose, thickening into a cloud that gathered around his clenched fist. The flies fell, the sheer incessant buzz of their wings suddenly silenced. With a horde of ratmen clamouring to reach him, fighting over one another, Mannfred raised his fist to his lips and opened his fingers. He blew once, sharply, sending a thick plume of smoke out over the fat-bellied ratmen. The stench of death clung to the living, fed on their fur, as dissolution set in wherever the smoke touched, the smell growing ever more sickening as the fur, hide and flesh rotted from their bones. They fell at his feet.

It was a cruel death, but the cloud dissipated before it could claim more than a third of the rodents. Their cries were wretched as they writhed on the ground. The vampire relished them. Beneath, behind and between the screams of the dying, Mannfred heard the drums.

Only they weren't drums.

The ground trembled beneath his feet. It was a small movement at first, a rumble, but it quickly grew in intensity until the dirt and clay of the ground buckled beneath him. He reached out as a section of the ceiling came crashing down, crushing a handful of rats beneath the rockfall.

All around the dead, the walls of the tunnel collapsed and the ceiling caved in. As the rock and dirt spilled into the passages the blighted skaven poured in after it, riding the wave of debris, talons bared, glittering with virulent poison. They fell upon the dead like a plague.

A hunchbacked ratman scuttled forwards, a crystal sphere in its grubby paw. Chittering and shrieking it lobbed the glass ball up at the ceiling above Mannfred's head, shattering it. A deleterious yellow-green choking gas billowed out. Mannfred breathed deeply of the poison wind, feeling its blistering bite at the back of his throat. Mannfred blew the vile gas from his lungs and levelled an accusing finger at the creature that had hurled the glass sphere. The gas ignited, an arc of flame billowing from his lips all the way to the ratman's furred face. The skaven writhed around on the floor as the fire ate into him.

Mannfred turned his back on the dying rodent.

A beast came to the fore with a glittering blade that pulsed a sickly green in the ghastly light, throwing its taint across the ranks of the dead. The skaven was a giant, more a rat fiend than a ratman. It swatted aside a corpse, smashing its skull against a huge boulder. The sword danced in the creature's hands, weaving a pattern of death in the air as it advanced on Mannfred. It was obviously a champion of its kind. It moved with the arrogant swagger of strength.

Mannfred touched the talisman, focusing on the image of his damned legion parting to allow this monstrosity through to face him. Before him, the shuffling dead mirrored the image in his mind, a path opening up through the heart of them.

Mannfred drew his blade and moved to meet it, ignoring the melee around him. Venom dripped from the ratman's fangs. Mannfred bared his own fangs, his lips curling back into a feral smile, every bit as predatory as the skaven's snarl.

He blocked the creature's first swing wordlessly. The blow sent shivers down his arm and a sunburst of pain up through his fingers as though the blade somehow contained lightning harnessed from the sky. His rage bellowed from his mouth as he threw his head back and screamed, launching a blistering series of cuts that the beast barely knocked aside as it stumbled backwards into the bodies of its fallen comrades.

Mannfred lunged forwards, refusing to allow a moment's respite.

He cut low, bringing his blade up in a vicious arc, the tip of the sword piercing the underside of the warped ratman's jaw, and up through its mouth and into its brain.

The giant ratman didn't fall.

It staggered back, massive convulsions wracking its body, and reared back on its hind legs, tearing the blade free of its skull. Ichor dripped down the front of its battered battle armour. Whatever maddening battle drugs fuelled its system, the creature refused to fall.

It lashed out with its loathsome blade, cutting deep into the Vampire Count's shoulder.

It was no ordinary sword.

Agony sang in his tainted blood.

Fire burned beneath his skin.

The blade was laced with some kind of corrosive mixture. On a living thing its kiss would no doubt prove fatal. As it was, Mannfred felt the sickness of the warped blade's bite, and the sting as its infection spread throughout his body. His back arched as his cadaver contorted, railing against the pain of the cut in his shoulder.

Even as he straightened, he felt his flesh knitting, the answering fire spreading up his arm from his fingertips.

His grin was ferocious.

Mannfred moved in close enough to breathe in the stink of the skaven's corrupt flesh. He hammered his fist into the ratman's snout, following the blow with a balletic sword-arm cross, his blade cutting deep into the bone of his opponent's neck.

He stepped back, admiring the efficacy of the blow.

The ratman remained on its feet for a moment, its head lolling on its neck, attached by a single tendon and a patch of fur. Then it fell.

He cut the beast's head from its shoulders and hurled it at the ravening horde of rats and mutant creatures from the deeps of the Old World.

Then, standing over the corpse, he bade it rise, not the valiant enemy it had been, but a headless warrior of darkness and spite. Around him more and more of the fallen ratmen rose, joining the ranks of his abominable army, turning on the rats in the tunnels with stunning savagery. The headless rat was lethal, its vile blade cleaving flesh from bone, the touch of its weeping shaft corroding fatally through fur and scraps of battle armour to still the rabid vermin hearts of those rash enough to get in its way.

Mannfred stood in their midst, silently watching.

Every ratman that fell rose again, joining silently with the ranks of the undead.

It was time, he knew, to lead his army to the surface.

Like the grand puppet-master he was, Mannfred drew the newly dead rats and skaven to the fore of his army. These creatures would come up from the underground to strike fear into the hearts of the living.

Winter would bring a war unlike any that humanity had ever witnessed.

JEREK WALKED IN darkness.

He heard cries and other, stranger, sounds echoing up from the deeps. He ignored them. He wasn't here for whatever daemons lived this far down in the underways. He was hunting other game. Skellan had disappeared down this hole and he would find him.

The handmaiden, Narcisa, led Jerek deep into the tunnels beneath the subterranean temple. She didn't talk. In the occasional flickers of light from the oil lamp she carried, Jerek saw utter distaste in her expression. He didn't try to talk to her. He watched her as she walked. Everything about her bearing betrayed her profession. She was arrogant with her flesh, enjoying the attention of his eyes. She was barefoot, but not once did she so much as flinch as she walked over rock dust and chips of stone.

Eventually, she stopped at the mouth of what appeared to be a vast cavern.

'You aren't like him, are you?' she asked suddenly. 'You're different. He talks and swaggers, and needs to be the big man, but you are different. You're quiet. That, back there, with the Eternal, was an act, wasn't it?' It was barely a question; she knew full well she was right.

Jerek nodded without saying anything.

'He is down here,' she said, walking ahead slightly and pointing. The way she said *he* betrayed a surprising level of hatred. 'There is a shaft that plunges several hundreds of feet into the darkness, try not to fall down it.'

'I'll do my best,' Jerek said. 'You've met him haven't you?'

She turned to face him, nostrils flaring. She wasn't pretty when angered. 'Oh, I met him,' she said. She pulled at a red silk kerchief she wore tied around her throat, baring two hard pink scars of puncture wounds. 'He gave me these.'

'He fed on you?' Jerek asked, horrified by the thought of tasting undead blood. Surely it was poison...

'He fed on me,' she admitted, as though confessing the violation burnt her tongue.

'It's not... it's not *right*,' said Jerek, still struggling to come to terms with the idea of a vampire feeding on a kindred creature. 'Why would he?'

'Potency, fool. Are all of von Carstein's gets so simple? To drink the blood of a vampire is to absorb some of its essence, its strength.'

'But it is an abomination,' Jerek said, aghast at the very notion of it. It was parasitic.

'Oh you truly are simple, aren't you?' the Lahmian handmaiden said, shaking her head in disbelief. 'It is about the quest for domination. He seeks to imprint his power on me, cause me to cow to his will, to see him as my master.' She laughed bitterly at the prospect.

Jerek struggled with the image. 'Did you bow to him?'

'Never,' Narcisa said vehemently.

'Good. Skellan doesn't deserve benediction. He is a monstrosity.'

'And yet he is your kin?'

Jerek shook his head. 'He is no kin of mine, woman. I intend to end his miserable existence here and now.'

'Yet you serve the same master, curiouser and curiouser. This is something else you did not mention to the Eternal. I wonder, does that mean you are lying to me, or did you lie to her?'

'I have told no lies.'

'Oh I think you have,' Narcisa said. 'I can read men. You lied like all men, to get what you want, only this time it wasn't soft legs around your head. You truly do intend to kill him, don't you?'

'I do. His head is yours, if you would have it, to appease his violation.'

She laughed again, this time genuinely amused by his offer. 'Oh, men have violated me in worse ways than his brutish assault. I live through their abuses day and night for my mistress. Do you think I lie with them for my own pleasure? A suitor would offer me his heart if he sought to impress me. Or are these pretty words nothing more than a tisane so that I will offer my throat to you as well?'

'I am not tempted by your blood, woman,' said Jerek.

'Again, you lie. I can feel your hunger. You would take me in your arms and deliver the sweetest, tenderest bite, and then you would feed. You are starving. Do you think I cannot tell? You stink of vermin; the blood of rats and mice is on your breath. You are weak and yet you would go up against a monster. That makes you either a hero or a fool.'

'Isn't foolishness the trademark of a hero?'

She ignored him. 'I take you, at first glance, for a fool. You hunger for a taste of me and my blood would give you the strength you need to match the beast you hunt, yet if I offered my wrist you wouldn't bite, would you? That is why you stink of animal blood. You wouldn't give yourself an advantage because you hate what you are. You loathe yourself to the point that even if I offered myself willingly out of hatred for your enemy you would not drink.'

'You have the right of it,' said Jerek. He met her gaze with defiance. 'I will not drink of you, woman. I come here to end things, not begin them anew. Blood solves nothing.'

'You are a peculiar creature.'

'I am a wolf,' Jerek said, summoning the image of Ulric's blessed white wolf in his mind. For a moment he felt whole, strong. The feeling faded as the image dissolved.

'And I am a lamb,' the Lahmian said, with no hint of irony in her voice as she held out her wrist for him. 'Feed on me. It is your nature, surrender to it. You must if you hope to defeat him. Alone you are not strong enough.'

Jerek found himself thinking about it, imagining lifting her wrist to his mouth. A heady rush of sensations washed over him. Even the awareness of the possibility was euphoric. He couldn't begin to think what the effect of the actual blood would be.

Jerek pushed her hand away.

'No.' He shook his head, backing away from her.

Narcisa sighed. 'Then you truly are a fool.'

'I'm not a fool,' Jerek said, 'but more importantly, I am not a parasite.' Jerek clenched his fists in frustration. 'You don't understand. I am damned already. I will not make matters worse.'

She laughed in his face. 'You cannot make matters worse. You can only die. Your only option is oblivion. Is that what you want? It is isn't it? That's what you want.'

'Not yet,' Jerek said. 'When this is over, perhaps, but there are things that must be done before I can rest.'

'You mean killing. There's killing to be done before you can rest.'

'Yes.'

'Then you better hope he doesn't kill you before you kill him.' Narcisa re-tied the silk scarf around her throat. 'On the far side of the shaft lie three tunnels,' she said matter-of-factly, as though their conversation had never veered into the realm of murder. 'One leads to the lair of the rats. One, eventually will take you to a dawi stronghold in the Worlds Edge Mountains if you walk to its end, and the other branches out into countless tributaries. You could walk them for a thousand years and not find your way back to the surface.'

'How will I know which to take?'

'You won't.'

She left him there, alone, in the dark.

TIME LOST ALL meaning.

The dark was his lord and master.

He searched.

He walked.

He listened.

Every so often he made a mark on the floor with a fragment of stone he had found. It worked like chalk. He drew a crude sign of Ulric, hoping his god would lead him back home when he was done.

It could have been a day, a week or a year. He heard strange things, chitterings and skitterings, but stayed away from their source, respectful of whatever daemons lurked in the underways. Mostly the passages were silent but for the occasional drip of damp water from above and the scuff of his own feet. More than once he jumped at his own shadow, mistaking the shambling shape for something more fearful. He felt the touch of hunger returning, the seductive lure of those fragmented truths that heralded the onset of the depravation-madness. He tried to push them aside, focusing on the white wolf. It was a majestic creature.

Finally, he heard whistling.

It was faint at first, almost lost beneath the rush and swell of some louder sound.

It took him a moment to realise that he was hearing the crash of water. It was deafening in the confines of the underways. Rivers, he knew, ran underground as well as over land in places. The boom and crash was the cry of a subterranean waterfall. That he heard the whistling at all had to be the result of some freakish acoustics. Jerek said a silent thank you to the quirk of geology.

Jerek stopped. He closed his eyes, focusing purely on the sound. It barely carried to him, but he recognised the whistler's tune. He had heard it before: *The Lay of Fair Isabella*. The last time he had heard it was during the long siege of Altdorf all those years ago. Jon Skellan had been whistling it as he walked amongst the bones of the dead, picking a path back towards the Vampire Count's pavilions. It had stuck with Jerek because it said so much about Skellan's casual disdain for life. It was then he had known – known for sure and certain – that some small relic of his old self had survived the siring. So, in a peculiar way, he owed Skellan for proving he wasn't the monster he had thought he was.

Hearing the same song now went beyond mere coincidence. Jerek had long since stopped believing in random happenstance.

The whistling moved nearer, reverberating around the old tunnels. Jerek crept towards the edge of the burrow as it opened up into a vast cavern.

There was beauty in the Old World, or under it. The cavern was living proof of it. A river ran through it, falling away into blackness as it plunged over the lip of a huge chasm. The way the sounds echoed and folded back on themselves suggested it was a substantial drop. Spray rose back up from the depths creating a fine white mist that hung over the entire cavern.

Skellan sat on a rock, kicking his feet and whistling. He picked at his fingernails with a long thin sliver of wood. Jerek watched him for a moment, hatred bubbling inside him. He quelled it. Hatred would not serve him. Skellan was a stone cold killer. Hatred, rage, they were emotions, and emotions were weakness. That was Skellan's mantra. In this instance the old wolf knew he was right.

Skellan's lantern picked out the crystalline structure of one of the walls. Quartz and other facetted minerals caught, reflected and refracted the glare, conjuring ghostly rainbows across the mist.

Jerek walked slowly out into the centre of the cave.

He hadn't imagined a glory-hound like Skellan being capable of biding his time in some stinking tunnel when he could have been out in Altdorf revelling in the slaughter being wrought by his master. So what brought him down here and left him sitting idly twiddling his thumbs? The only thing Jerek could imagine was power. The vampire obviously believed there was something to be gained by hiding out down here while Mannfred fought. Did he hope to steal in and take advantage of the weakened count? Or was there something else down here in the darkness, some other fiend he sought to enlist? A fresh treachery to unleash? Nothing Jon Skellan ever did was simple or obvious.

The crash of water masked his footsteps until he was almost halfway.

'You don't appear to be a rat,' said Skellan, looking up at his approach, apparently unbothered and equally unsurprised by Jerek's sudden appearance. 'But then you don't look like much of anything.'

He tossed the wooden pick away thoughtlessly, and swung his legs down and slid off the rock.

'Well, you've seen better days.'

Skellan grinned. 'So what are you? Apart from lost?'

'I'm not lost, Skellan,' said Jerek. His voice betrayed him, he realised. For all the magic masking his face, his voice was still his voice.

Skellan raised an eyebrow in mock puzzlement. There was no indication that he recognised Jerek's voice, but then why would he? It had been a long time since their last encounter, Jerek reminded himself. 'Well, well, you seem to have me at a disadvantage, fellow. Obviously you're not a woman, so I haven't left your bed before dawn and broken your heart. No, to be fair, you could conceivably be a woman, but if you *are*, you aren't a particularly attractive one and I can't imagine I would have crawled into your bed in the first place, so that pretty much discounts an illicit tryst. Yet you obviously know me and I haven't the slightest idea who you are. I have to admit I am curious.'

'You know me, Skellan,' said Jerek. He walked slowly into the centre of the room. Skellan's small bull's-eye lantern was trained on him. Jerek didn't shield his eyes despite the discomfort.

'No, I don't think I do.'

Jerek knew he was babbling. It was too late for regrets, but he couldn't help but wish he had taken Narcisa up on her offer of blood. 'Oh, come on, Jon. We go back a long way, you and I. I'm hurt you don't remember me. I had hoped after our last encounter that I would be the face that haunted your dreams... Oh, that's it of course. You don't recognise this face do you? How about the voice?' Skellan said nothing. 'No? You disappoint me, Jon. You don't recognise a fellow Hamaya? Did Konrad mean so little to you? What am I saying? Of course he did. But Vlad? Surely you remember us standing side-by-side with my sire, facing the great walls of Altdorf together in those last days before his fall?'

Jerek slipped his other hand into his pocket and cracked the small clay talisman the girl had given him. He didn't feel anything, but he knew from Skellan's face that the glamour had slipped as soon as the token had broken. He savoured the momentary glimmer of fear in Skellan's one good eye.

'See, you do remember me. I knew you couldn't have forgotten me after all we've been through together, Jon.'

'What do you want, wolf?'

'What do you think? To finish what I started at Grim Moor. I tire of this perpetual dance of death and would have it over once and for all.'

'You've come to kill me? You don't have it in you, old man. You think you are a colossus, but I've got news for you, you're not the mountain you think you are. You're a mountain goat. There's a difference.'

'You talk too much, Skellan. You always have. I'm not here for you, you're the whipping boy. I'm here for your master.'

Skellan slapped his forehead in mock despair, and then burst out laughing. 'You're priceless Jerek, do you know that? Truly, I don't know how I will live without you in my life, but I suppose I will have to if you are hell-bent on hunting Mannfred. This is just too delicious for words.' Skellan moved forwards, arms open wide, as though to wrap him up in a huge bear hug. He stopped five paces from Jerek, a look of pure perplexity spreading across his ruined face. 'Oh my word, you actually think you can kill Vlad's heir, don't you? Wonderful – and yet so utterly tragic. Have you looked at yourself lately, wolf? You can have all the glamours in the world cast on your mangy carcass, but they won't disguise the fact that underneath them all you are a wreck,' said Skellan. He appeared to think for a moment. 'I don't like you, Jerek. You know that. Even so, I have no reason to lie to you. You won't last two minutes if you go up against him. He isn't like Konrad, and even that madman whipped your arse for you if I remember rightly. Trust me, wolf. I've seen him fight. He is everything Vlad was and more.'

'I'll take my chances if it is all the same to you, Jon. You are obviously down here waiting for him. Just tell me where he is.'

'Ahh, but see, I can't do that, old man. As much as I'd like to see your ashes scattered to the four winds, I can't let you take that fight just in case by some miracle you do go and kill him. It would all become so terribly messy if you did. You see, as unlikely as that is, Mannfred's demise would cause rather a problem for me. We've got plans. You don't think I enjoy loitering in this pit do you? Let me just disabuse you of that notion if you do. I don't, but there's a reason for it. I'm waiting for Mannfred, you see. The war has begun and the living are completely oblivious. He's the greatest of all of us, wolf: the grand schemer. Do you think Konrad's insanity was mere chance? Do you think Vlad's fall was a divine gift of Sigmar? It was all him. He has been playing the longest game of all. Even now he brings the greatest force the Old World has ever witnessed to bear, and the humans are clueless, because they cannot see it with their own two eyes. He will be culling them before they even realise he has come up from underground. To allow you through, to help you kill him, hurts me, not in any sentimental way; it's all about self interest. It would undermine my power.'

'Then it would seem we are at an impasse. I am here to kill him, you can't have me succeed.'

'There's no impasse, wolf. I'll just have to kill you myself. I hope you have coin enough to pay the ferryman. Oh wait, you don't have a soul to take that particular journey, do you? Shame; you'll just have to content yourself with oblivion.'

'And you think that should frighten me? What have I got to fear from oblivion? I am made from the dust of the earth and to the dust I shall return. Death, a second death, holds no fear for me.'

'I almost believe you old man, but then I look at you and see how desperately you've clung to this half-life of yours and that tells me different. You're scared. You've grown fond of this stinking place haven't you?'

Jerek reached slowly for the warhammer at his belt, but it wasn't there. He couldn't remember the last time he had held it. His heart sank.

Skellan laughed, seeing him come up empty handed. 'Well you are in a pickle aren't you, old wolf? I *almost* pity you. As it is I'll just have to kill you all the more quickly.'

'This is the beginning of the end, Skellan,' said Jerek as he unleashed the beast within. His hands stretched, fingers elongating, nails hooking into talons. His face shifted too, altering as completely as when it had been under the spell of the urchin girl's glamour. His brow broadened, the ridge of his eye sockets arching, becoming more atavistic as he connected with the beast.

Grinning, Skellan cracked his knuckles and squared up to the wolf. He moved quickly, spinning on his heel and lunging backwards for his sword, which he had left leaning against the rock.

Jerek reacted instantaneously, springing forwards and slamming into Skellan's back.

They came down hard, sprawling across the rocky ground.

Jerek grabbed a tangle of Skellan's hair and slammed his face hard into the ground. The sickening sound of bone splintering was lost beneath the roar of the waterfall and Skellan's matching howl as he unleashed the beast within.

Jerek tried to hammer Skellan's face back down, but Skellan contorted around beneath him, prying his fingers up into Jerek's face and mouth, pushing his head back as he sought the leverage he needed to dislodge the wolf from his back.

Jerek crunched down into Skellan's fingers, taking a huge bite out of the bone. Skellan shrieked, partly in agony, partly in anger, and wrenched his arm back, throwing Jerek bodily. Jerek sprawled sideways, rolled over and came to his feet panting hard.

Skellan dropped into a fighting crouch.

They circled one another warily.

Skellan's grin was feral.

'Are you frightened, wolf? Yes, yes you are. I can smell it right there with the stink of rats and dead birds on your breath. Why would you be frightened if you hadn't fallen in love with this life, eh?'

'I have no love of this life, believe me.'

'*This* life,' Skellan mocked, 'but what of your life before? That's it, isn't it? You still yearn for what you were! That's possibly the most tragic thing I have ever heard! I *love* it!' Skellan's arm snaked out and he slapped Jerek open-palm across the face. Jerek rocked back on his heels, rolling with the blow. His head came back around slowly.

'Don't tell me you don't see ghosts, Skellan,' said Jerek, answering Skellan's slap with a double-handed clap to either side of the vampire's throat, a blow that would have shattered a mortal man's neck. Skellan barely registered the strike, backhanding Jerek contemptuously. 'I know what happened to your wife,' Jerek said. 'Don't tell me she doesn't come to you at night, in your dreams. If one of us had cause to long for his old life it is you, not me.'

Skellan hawked up a wad of loose phlegm and spat in the wolf's face. 'She doesn't come to me. She is at peace, something neither of us shall ever know.

The bellow of the waterfall was an indelicate thunder booming throughout the cavern. Jerek straight-armed Skellan in the forehead, snapping his head back. He followed the blow up with a savage left hook, driving his fist into Skellan's throat. Skellan answered with a clubbing right and four successive rabbit punches to Jerek's kidneys, lifting him bodily into the air. As he came down Skellan hammered a right cross into his face, shattering his nose in a bloody spray.

Jerek shook his head. His vision swam alarmingly, the world tilting around him as Skellan followed up the initial onslaught, stepping inside his wild swing and hammering home an elbow to the side of his head that had Jerek sprawling at his feet.

He stood over the wolf, a look of utter disdain on his ruined face. 'You really thought you could do this?'

Jerek swept his leg around, cutting Skellan's feet out from under him. Skellan came down hard.

Jerek pounced on him, tearing at his face and throat with his teeth. Skellan tried to throw him, but couldn't break Jerek's hold. He slammed his head forwards, his forehead connecting viciously with Jerek's already broken nose. Jerek clutched at Skellan's face, thrusting his fingers into all of the soft places they could find. He felt the heat of Skellan's tainted blood swell up around them. Skellan screamed and threw his weight to the side. They rolled, Skellan's greater strength giving him the upper hand momentarily. He straddled Jerek, pummelling his fists over and over into the vampire's face. Jerek took the beating. He delivered a single savage roundhouse of a punch, his fist cannoning into the underside of Skellan's jaw. Skellan spat blood as he sank back, shaking his head, even as Jerek pushed him away.

Jerek forced himself back to his feet. He stumbled back a step.

Skellan stared at him, his one good eye bloody, the eye patch torn away from his ruined eye to reveal the ragged wound Jerek had inflicted upon him back at Grim Moor. He pushed himself up onto his knees, coiled, ready to spring forwards. Skellan smiled bleakly. It was an ugly expression on his ravaged face.

Jerek backed up another step, bracing himself for the charge.

He felt the spray of the waterfall on his back and realised he'd somehow managed to be manoeuvred around until the chasm was at his back. He didn't dare risk even a brief glance over his shoulder to see just how close he was to the fall. He had to rely on his other senses. He concentrated on the echoing crash of the water. It was louder, resonating within his bones. That, combined with the kiss of the white mist on his neck was all the evidence he needed to know he was too close to the edge.

Before he could take another step in any direction, Skellan launched a blistering attack, coming out of his crouch like some dervish possessed, spitting blood and hissing. He hit Jerek full in the chest. For a moment they hung there before Skellan's momentum carried them both back over the chasm's edge.

They fell backwards through the fragmentary rainbows.

The drop was vertiginous. Water sprayed over them as they tumbled and twisted, falling through the air. Skellan tore at Jerek, trying to break free of his hold long enough to mutate into avian form. Jerek refused to let him go. Skellan shrieked, driving his head forwards to butt Jerek full in the face. The rush of air ripped and pulled at them as they tumbled head over feet, still locked in their immortal struggle, into the cannonade of water. The sheer elemental might of the waterfall ripped them apart, throwing Jerek back against the jagged rock wall, buffeting and bludgeoning him against the jagged stone before hurling him clear.

He lost sight of Skellan in the torrent of water.

Then he hit the ground with bone-shattering force.

He lay, broken, at the bottom of the fall, barely able to lift his head. Skellan was nowhere to be seen. The subterranean waterfall rose hundreds of feet above him. The agony escaped his lips. He tried to move, but couldn't.

'Well – that hurt,' said Skellan, his voice was barely audible above the water.

Jerek tried to crane his neck to get a better view of his surroundings. He lay on a narrow ledge of rock that ringed a still deeper chasm. A lambent glow of orange came from below, molten in its intensity. A slender stone span bridged the chasm. Beyond the bridge lay another ledge of stone and beyond that a great pool that was fed by the constant spume of water. Splashes lapped over the lip of the pool, spilling across the narrow ledge and over the crevice. White steam rose in great clouds where the water hit the fiery pit below.

He couldn't see Skellan for the steam.

Then he saw his own leg. It was a bloody mess, broken in two places below the knee so that it stuck out at an impossible angle from his body. White bone pierced his trousers.

He tried to rise and fell back in a sunburst of agony.

'I'm coming to get you, wolf,' Skellan taunted.

Jerek closed his eyes against the pain. He knew what he had to do. There was no choice. He couldn't allow himself to think about it. If he did he wouldn't be able to go through with it. He tore a strip from his ruined trousers, wadding it into a ball and bit down on it. Even that little movement was torture. He couldn't bear to look as he began to feel out the broken bone. He gripped the ruined leg hard and pulled down, forcing the bone back into place. The splintered edges of bone grated against each other. For a moment he thought he was going to black out from the pain. As it was the rag fell from his mouth and his screams drowned out the crash of the water.

'You're dead, old man. Dead, dead, dead,' the words echoed around the cavern, folding in on themselves insensibly, diminishing into a babble of water. For all his taunts, there was no sign of Skellan. Jerek could only assume he was hurt.

Tears streaming down his cheeks, Jerek forced himself to sit up.

He swayed dangerously and almost fell back. Jerek forced himself to remain upright even when it felt as though the world fell away from under him. Biting back on the pain, he struggled to look around the cavern. He could see Skellan, lying on his back on the far side of the narrow stone bridge. He had fallen badly, but there was no way for Jerek to know precisely how badly. He had to move, he knew. He had to finish Skellan before Skellan finished him.

'It ends here, Skellan,' promised Jerek, taking hold of his ankle. There was nothing to brace himself on and the rag had fallen out of reach. 'One, two, *three!*' He gasped and yanked down hard on his disjointed ankle on three, the word tearing from his mouth in a shriek. The pain was excruciating as he forced the shattered bones together, pressing them until they ground into place.

'You scream like a little girl, wolf,' Skellan mocked. He hadn't moved in all the time they had lain there.

'I'm coming to eat your heart, Skellan,' Jerek called across the chasm. 'Run if you can. Oh, look, you can't.'

Jerek gripped the rock wall beside him and clawed his way up it through the pain barrier until he stood on his broken leg. He gritted his teeth against the pain and began to walk slowly, dragging his lame leg behind him.

Twice he stumbled and almost fell as he crossed the bridge over the lava pit. The heat coming up from the fissure was overpowering despite the fact that the pool of molten stone was hundreds of feet below.

Skellan hadn't moved.

The reason, Jerek saw, was that a huge stalagmite had pierced his lower stomach and abdomen and jutted up out of the wound like an accusing spear, effectively pinning Skellan to the ground.

Jerek stood over the fallen vampire.

'It's over, Skellan. You are dead.'

Skellan shook his head, and reached up stubbornly clasping the stone spear as though intending to haul himself off it. 'Not yet, wolf, not yet.' But his voice was already fading, taking on a distant quality.

Jerek shook his head.

'Can you see the darkness? Is there anything there for us?'

'No,' Skellan said. 'There is nothing.' But a smile began to spread slowly across his face.

'What do you see, Skellan? Tell me.'

'I see you, wolf. I see you dead at my feet,' and, screaming in sheer bloody agony Skellan heaved himself upwards, his guts unravelling out of the huge ragged wound in his back like a huge skein of yarn. He fell back, pushing the stalagmite deeper, opening himself up. 'You can't kill me,' said Skellan, but it was obvious to both of them that he didn't believe it.

'I don't need to,' said Jerek. 'You aren't important. It was never about you.'

He knelt beside Skellan.

'May you find some kind of peace.'

'Go lick yourself, wolf.'

Jerek placed his hands on either side of Skellan's head, holding it firm as he leaned in close. He could hear it above the cry and crash of the water, the siren song of the blood. Narcisa's words came back to him: *to drink the blood of a vampire is to absorb some of its essence, its strength.* Lust, hunger, need, the base primal instinct to feed drove him and this time he surrendered to it, surrendered in hate and need, and desperation. Jerek leaned in, sinking his teeth into the vampire's throat, and drank deeply even as Skellan struggled weakly to fight him off. Skellan's corpse kicked and bucked and thrashed until the death shudder took him and he lay still. It was unlike any blood he had ever tasted: thicker, richer and more potent. It sang in his throat even as he sucked it down greedily. This was his blood, the blood of the vampire. This was a distillate of life eternal. This was power.

This was his curse.

This was his damnation.

He was a creature of the blood, a monster.

It was in him, this sickness, this power, and he enjoyed it.

He had proved himself a beast. Vlad von Carstein had been right when he had chosen him all those years ago. He did make a good vampire.

Jerek rose, wiping the last trace of tainted blood off his lips.

Skellan wasn't dead, not yet, but drained there was no life in his corpse. It would return though, given time. Jerek couldn't allow that to happen. An evil of Skellan's enormity could not be allowed to rise again. The world had hurt enough.

Jerek reached down and hauled him up off the stalagmite. He carried him, limping and shuffling to the centre of the narrow bridge. He felt strong, stronger than he had felt in years, despite his wounds and the fire burning up his leg. Skellan's vitality flowed in his veins.

He held Skellan's corpse out over the chasm. It felt light in his arms.

'May you finally be reunited with your woman, Jon Skellan,' Jerek said solemnly as he let go. He watched Skellan's corpse tumble head over feet until it disappeared beneath the smooth sea of orange and red flames hundreds of feet below, swallowed, cremated by the molten rock.

There would be no resurrection for Jon Skellan, of that Jerek was sure.

'From dust to dust returned,' he said, ending the prayer of interment.

Skellan had, at the very last, been smiling. Perhaps he truly had seen her ghost come to carry him home and that was the reason for the smile. Perhaps his last breath had been taken saying her name.

Jerek wanted to believe that it was so, wanted to believe that there could be some form of redemption for his own monstrous soul. He needed to believe it, but he knew it was a lie.

Skellan hadn't been smiling.

Death's rictus had been locked on his cold hard lips, and now there was nothing.

Both flesh and spirit had been destroyed.

Skellan was gone.

Jerek made the sign of Ulric as he watched the lava bubble and pop.

It was as though Jon Skellan had never been.

Jerek walked back across the narrow bridge. Somehow he needed to escape this chasm, but first he needed to rest.

He had lied to Skellan. This wasn't the end. It was the beginning. He had finally sacrificed himself. Becoming a monster was the only way he stood a chance against the greater monsters he hunted.

Drained, he slumped down against the wall, listening to the delicate sound of thunder rumbling deep within the earth until he succumbed to a fitful regenerative sleep.

There was no rest, though.

His dreams were haunted by a white wolf, the elusive animal leading his dream-self a merry chase through the subterranean world of his nightmare.

He came awake gasping, 'I am the wolf,' and he knew it was true. He had at last become the predator that Vlad had always known he was.

CHAPTER TWELVE

Small Magics
Ulthuan, Fabled Land of the High Elves

HIGH IN THE mountains of Saphery, overlooking the Sea of Dreams, the eight winds were stirring.

In the shadow of the White Tower, Finreir tried to clear his mind of all conscious thought and distraction, but a single image refused to leave his mind's eye.

Boots, running, knee deep in the snow; thick heavily worked steel greaves; the chinking of armour; a run succumbing to abject panic; a darkness the likes of which he had never known in pursuit.

Finreir's nostrils filled with the scent of animal hide and the sickly bitter taint of evil. It clung to the winds. He sensed a great gnashing of teeth, a great goring of blood and felt as though he were the black crow high up above, watching it all. Trees, like black fingers thrusting up out of the ground, rushed passed his vision as the booted figure continued his desperate flight. The head of a glinting steel axe was brought to chest height as the exhausted runner could flee no more.

He turned on his pursuers, to face his own damnation.

He was a small man, tiny against the harrying pack.

Not a small man… a child of Grimnir, a dwarf, his face bloodied and bruised.

Evil was coming for him.

His only protection were the eight winds, none of which he could touch, and the axe in his hands. The eyes of his hunters were bloodshot, virulent, filled with hate and lust and hunger, and a single name rang out from within their minds: Mannfred.

Finreir came out of the trance with a start, his hands trembling and sweat beading on the back of his neck. His breath came thick and fast as though he'd been running, and in that moment of revelation he could not tell whether it had been a true vision or a snatch of someone else's nightmare.

He staggered to one of the doors of the White Tower and leant his hand against the cold stone, embracing its calming serenity. The old tower was implacable. His chest heaved. He had never known evil quite like the insidious dream-presence.

He sensed a disturbance in the balance of nature. This was more than a mere malevolent presence. This was a force intent on consuming everything in its path like a sickness.

In that moment he saw a twin-tailed hawk swoop down and snatch a mouse from the fields, and wondered if the dwarf he had seen was still alive or if indeed he had even been born yet. Such was the nature of a vision quest. Its truths could be illusive or they could provide moments of clarity greater than any spy glass.

There was only one creature that could tell him if what he had seen was history or deeds yet to come, and that was the creature through whose eyes he had seen the hunt unfold.

IT TOOK THE mage, Finreir, a long time to feel comfortable confined once more in his robes. Nature's magics felt more intimate and liberating when stripped down for the ritual. That was why he had removed himself from the White Tower. Most of his kin looked unfavourably upon his quirks since, as a high elf, modesty was expected of him and, as a sorcerer, discipline. In truth he lacked neither, he simply saw things differently and that is what set him apart.

Finreir believed deeply and passionately that although the Ulthuan civilisation was an ancient and wise one, those who dwelt upon the island did not know everything, and that lack of knowledge fed his unceasing curiosity. By night's end he had begged the indulgence of the council. As the youngest adept to have been bestowed the gift of High Magic he held considerable sway, despite the fact that he was still a child amongst his own kind.

But there were certain elves who simply did not accept him.

'You are still young, master Finreir, prone to impetuosity. It is understandable for one who has achieved much in such a short time, but the affairs of men are of no concern to the Asur. We don't deny what you have seen, but with maturity comes wisdom. In time you will see that it is not for us to decide the fate of the Old World. They have little knowledge of our kind and we would have it remain that way for a while longer.'

Finreir had taken their chastisement with good grace, but the affairs had sought him out – on the eight winds, no less – and only an ignorant elf would turn his back on that.

Within the hour he had convinced three elf warriors to accompany him.

Something was infecting the entire Old World, something that had been brewing remorselessly over time.

An ancient sickness bubbled up from below, incipient enough for its influence to taint the very winds themselves. He had tasted it on Shyish. It caused Chamon to burn. It infused Ulgu with its noxious stain. It made Gyrun reek with its corruption. Already it had touched Aqshy, Ghur and Hysh. None were immune.

That was the power of the evil he hunted, but that did not seem to concern the council.

Finreir felt deeply that such a threat could not be allowed to go unchallenged.

The truth of his vision must be sought before a clash of civilisations wrought chaos across all the lands. Life was precious, even a dwarf's.

He issued various orders of preparation before returning to the heights of the White Tower.

Finreir swept up the winding stairs, rising higher and ever higher until he was one with the sky, miles above the surface of the earth. He stood in the immense domed ceiling of the tower, the vaulted windows glassless, exposing the inner chamber to the confluence of all the winds. He stood in the centre, the winds surging around him, whipping around in a vortex, howling in an unrelenting gale. Up here where the winds could move unfettered he held his hands aloft, touching them and letting them touch him. He became one with the ultimate power of the winds.

All of his senses had been subsumed by the winds. The winds were his senses now, his sight, his sound, his touch and taste. The reek of corruption swelled within him like a cancer. Out there, flying upon the winds, he found empty husks stripped of life and soul to serve as sentinels. Once they had been birds. Now they were mindless automata, soulless. They were limbs of the dark force, extensions of that malevolent mind. Their unnatural presence chilled him to the core.

This could not have appeared overnight.

Why, he thought, had no other elf seen this before?

Had the arrogance of his kin reached such dizzying heights that a threat such as this would pass unchallenged?

Finreir reached out with his newfound senses, seeking his quarry. He touched the hills of Lustria, scoured the coast of Araby, swept across the Sea of Claws and down the rivers of Middenland. He brushed the Mound of Krell, and rode the Grey Mountains. He skirted the forests of Loren and then the scent, light on the wind drew him towards Black Water and beyond to the dark spires of Drakenhof.

The stench of death was ever present. The carrion seekers circled in the air. There, laid out before him, was a trail of withered black trees that slowly gave way to a forest of bones impaled brutally upon stakes and left out to be bleached by the sun. There, pecking at the eye socket of one hapless soul, was the crow that had taken him on his vision quest, and on its breath a single word: Mannfred.

He looked the crow in the eye.

The crow blinked and inclined its head, aware that it was being watched from a distance. In the White Tower high above the world Finreir whispered, 'Take me to him.'

The bird took flight.

Soaring high about the gothic sprawl of the castle below, its black wings danced across the eddies sending him soaring across the plains of the Moot. Following the River Aver and high above the black forests of Nuln, the crow swooped in on Altdorf and circled a city whose walls were empty and whose people had no protection from the advancing legions of darkness outside them. Finreir gasped, aghast at the display of such dark might, but the crow seemed disinterested in such esoterica. Whether a soldier was living or dead in this nightmare landscape made little difference. It would feed soon enough.

The crow extended its talons as it saw its quarry and swooped down to the head of the advancing lines, its gaze fixated on one man, Mannfred.

The bird came down, resting upon the vampire's shoulder. Mannfred flicked it away with an irritated swipe, but the crow refused to leave. Finreir could taste the influence of an even more illusive and malign force influencing even this wretched creature.

Finreir demanded one last thing of the bird, 'Who puppets this monster?'

The crow buried its beak into the side of Mannfred's face, drawing blood and unleashing a tidal surge of hate that lashed back across the winds of magic all the way to the heights of the White Tower.

Finreir was pulled off his feet and hurled up into the vast vaulted dome of the chamber, slamming his willowy frame into the finely carved stone. He fell back to the floor, broken.

He knew only one thing as he slipped from consciousness – the vampire's protector was the dark, slumbering evil of Nagash.

CHAPTER THIRTEEN

Promises Broken
The Underways Beneath Nuln

JEREK SAT, SLUMPED against the jagged rock-face.

The waterfall dwarfed him, the cascade of white water pouring down the falls from hundreds of feet above.

There was no way up that he could see, except for what looked like an impossible climb up the near sheer rock face.

Jerek closed his eyes. He had no wish to taunt himself with this fresh failure. He had come so close. He had... an idea.

He concentrated on the image of a bat in his mind, trying to become it just as he so often became the wolf, but he felt no answering surge, no transformation. He pictured a bird, a huge black winged thing, but still his body refused to surrender its form. He willed himself into its shape, trying to fall into the wings, but it was useless.

He fell back against the wall, grunting in frustration. He slammed his clenched fists into his thighs, angry at his own impotence.

It ought to have been the same, simply a case of transforming. He could feel the wolf beneath his skin, so eager to be released, but the other forms refused to take shape.

He dug his nails into the dirt and rock beside him, trying to swallow back his frustration.

He was healing rapidly, the process accelerating beyond anything he had experienced since his siring. It was Skellan's blood. It invigorated his reparative system. Narcisa had been right when she had claimed that feeding on one's own somehow leeched their essence, but Jerek knew it wasn't going to be enough. It could be days before his leg was strong enough to take his weight.

He tested his broken leg. It had been hours at most since he had come crashing down the subterranean waterfall. It didn't matter that the bones had already begun to knit, there was no strength in them. His lungs were full of water from the steam he had inhaled. He had no need of air, but the water set a fire inside him that dragged on his strength. He looked up at the daunting climb. There was no other way out of the chasm. Somehow he had to scale the wall. He wasn't built for climbing, lacking the lithe grace of Skellan. He was heavy set, powerfully muscled, broad shouldered and bullish. His weight and size were detrimental, but it didn't matter in the grand scheme of things. He would haul himself up by bloody fingernails if that was what it took. He would not fail now, not when he was this close.

The heat of the lava drew sweat out of him and with it his resolve. He looked back up at the climb and knew there was no way he was going to make it.

He had an unnatural thirst on him, although it was more about blood than water.

Now that he had succumbed, he knew that the thirst was going to worsen until he slaked it again and again, and again. He had to escape. He had to make the climb, find Mannfred and end his threat so that he could finally find some rest.

That was all he wanted, to rest. He had lived too long and seen too much. When he closed his eyes, ghosts of the conquered drifted across his mind, butchered corpses dressed up like mannequins to puppet out his memories.

'I am the wolf,' he said aloud. His words echoed up and down the chasm before being snatched away and drowned beneath the crush of water.

He pressed his back against the wall, using it to take his weight as he struggled to stand.

Despite the incredible healing properties of his tainted blood, the bones of his shattered leg were weaker than he had thought. Even a little weight would undo the healing process, the pressure driving the freshly knitted bones apart. He leaned heavily on his good leg, clutching the wall and working himself around so that he could begin the arduous climb.

The rock was slick with damp backsplash from the waterfall.

He felt out a handhold and pulled himself up, taking all of his weight on three fingers of his left hand and holding himself there, a few feet above the ground, while he felt out a second handhold. Jerek shifted his weight, easing himself another few inches up the climb.

Two more and he found a toehold to take his weight while he leaned back, trying to visualise a path up the cracks and crevices to the top.

It was far from easy. There was no natural route that he could see, only several difficult traverses that would involve perilous moments hanging on by fingertips and with hope. He had no choice but to risk it, knowing that the stalagmites were far enough away so that falling shouldn't prove fatal, but there was the threat of the second crevice and the lava pit should he fall too far.

He forced failure from his mind and dragged himself up another two feet, grunting as his toe slipped off a narrow ledge. He clung to the rock, scraping his foot back and forth until it snagged on the tiny ledge and held firm. He looked down, but even as he did he knew he shouldn't have.

Already, it was a long way down.

It took twenty agonising minutes for Jerek to manipulate his body around so that he had moved out of the spray. Twice his fingers slipped, but he didn't fall. His fingernails had cracked and one had torn free, leaving a bloody mess. His shoulders and arms burned with the exertion. The muscles trembled violently as he struggled to support his weight. He didn't dare risk taking any of the strain on his wounded leg. Grunting, he leaned out to look for the next few handholds.

His hands were too big; they made gripping his fingers on the narrow ledges almost impossible at times. He felt himself weakening with every new reach and stretch. Still, a little over an hour later he reached up, his fingers snagging the lip of the chasm, and with one last almighty heave, he dragged himself back up to the top. He lay on his back, panting and looking at the rainbows and fragments of colour from the crystalline walls. His fingers were raw and bloody. His entire body ached.

Jerek tried to stand, but his leg gave out beneath him.

He lay there, fading in and out of consciousness.

The pain was excruciating.

He dragged himself across the ground, clawing his way to the boulder that Skellan had been sitting on, and lay propped up against it. He felt out the knitting bones, testing them without pushing them to the point where the marrow ripped. They were stronger again, but it would still be a day or more until the leg would be able to take his weight.

There was nothing he could do but rest and let the *unnatural* take its course.

He lay in the dark, listening, trying to discern whispers and sounds, convinced that somewhere out there Mannfred and his dead were scheming. If he could just listen hard enough, perhaps he could make out words in the echoes of the peculiar subterranean sounds.

* * *

When at last he was strong enough to walk, Jerek took Skellan's sword and used it as a makeshift crutch. He tore another strip from his ruined trousers and wadded it around the blade's point, tying it off so that the drag-and-carry of the crutch wouldn't damage the weapon beyond repair. He would have need of it soon enough.

It was a long walk back to the surface.

He had come to hate the dark and the claustrophobic confines of the tunnels. The subterranean underway was grim and oppressive, the weight of the earth constantly pressing down on him. It was too akin to being buried alive, and that was an experience Jerek was none too eager to relive. He still suffered traumatic flashbacks to that moment in Morr's garden in Middenheim when his eyes had first opened on the darkness of the tomb and he realised he had been cursed to this unlife. Being born again was not something any man should be forced to experience. Jerek shuddered at the memory and walked on.

It was impossible to tell if he was walking in circles, doubling back on himself and treading the same tunnels over again.

He began noticing signs scratched into the walls, the mark of the Horned Rat. Not wishing to stumble upon a lair of the loathsome ratmen, Jerek turned back, looking for other pathways that led slowly upwards. That was how he found his way out, looking always for the slight incline to confirm that he was moving in the right direction. Every so often he would come across one of the marks he had chalked on his descent. Whenever he saw the sign of Ulric he felt a surge of hope. He would make it. His god hadn't forsaken him.

As he wandered the dark underways he puzzled away the labyrinthine deceits. The Lahmians had joined forces with von Carstein, of that there could be no doubt. The concubines and courtesans were paving the way for his armies, lulling the influential and powerful humans, bedding them and robbing them of their secrets, which in turn they delivered to Mannfred as their part of the pact. No doubt the whores whispered in their beau's ears subtle misdirections of where the Vampire Count would strike should he ever have the strength to pose a threat to the living, planting arrogance where there ought to have been fear. It was cunning, but then everything about the new count was sly.

What Mannfred offered in return, Jerek dreaded to think?

He was forced to rest more often than he would have liked, but rest served to make him stronger. After a few days he had healed beyond the need for a crutch and fastened the sword to his belt. He was building strength in his leg.

Eventually the sporadic marks of the wolf led him back to the familiar tunnels of the Alt Stadt and in turn back to the Eternal.

There was no warmth on the old woman's face as Jerek barged unannounced into her chamber.

'How dare you defile this place?' Kalada rasped, her voice rich and sibilant.

Jerek threw Skellan's sword down onto the floor at her feet.

'You chose the wrong side in this war, whore,' said Jerek.

Outrage turned to fear as she saw the blood on him and understood the significance of the sword.

'What do you want?'

'Nothing that you can give me.'

'What do you mean to do?'

'Everything, but first I mean to finish you.'

'You don't have the strength.'

'Is that an assumption you are willing to risk your life on? You might want to think about picking up that sword. I'll give you a moment to think about it. I'd hate for you to die without at least a struggle.'

Before she could move Jerek swept across the five steps between them and took her in his arms. The physical violation of her skin pressed tight against his was clammy and repugnant. He tightened his grip, feeling her brittle bones crack. She struggled, but his grip was iron. His expression never wavered as he leaned in closer and whispered, 'Say goodbye to all of this, witch,' his lips close up against her ear.

She whimpered as he yanked her head back. She was ancient. Her bones might have calcified and become delicate, but there was power in her blood. Hatred blazed in her eyes. There was a frightening power within her. Kalada's lips parted, jaw distending hideously as she lashed out at him, her nails clawing at his face, as Jerek sank his teeth into her throat.

It was the sheer audacity of his attack that was her undoing. She was so old, so used to deference, to temerity from her servants that she never imagined, not even for a beat of her dead heart, that a ragged peon of von Carstein's could prove her undoing.

Shock registered in her eyes, but by then it was too late for her to do anything but die.

For the second time since coming below ground Jerek drank the blood of his kin. The first mouthful was intoxicating. She bucked in his arms, her nails breaking against his cheekbone as they gouged bloody black runnels across his face. Still he drank another greedy mouthful. Unlike Skellan's blood, Kalada's was a heady elixir. The potency of the tainted blood surged through him, revitalising Jerek. He swallowed mouthful after gluttonous mouthful until the Eternal stopped screaming and collapsed slackly in his arms. He pressed his hand flat against her breast, pressing down with his cracked and bloody fingernails until they pierced the skin. The woman convulsed once, viciously, as his questing fingers forced aside the tough cartilage and pulled apart the bone cage of her ribs, exposing her withered heart to the stale air. It smelled rank, of corruption and complicity.

Jerek tore it from her chest and took a bite out of it as he let Kalada's corpse slump to the floor. It was tough, like old leather as he worked it with his teeth, and tasted of bile but that didn't stop him from taking another bite, chewing it slowly and swallowing it down. Piece by piece he ate her heart out, and then walked around the subterranean temple, overturning the oil lamps and igniting the tapestries and curtains until there was a fierce blaze taking shape. He stood awhile and watched to be sure that the place would burn, expunging the Lahmian witch and her cult from the face of the Old World. Each crackle and hiss of flame and snap and cackle of wood cracking and splintering as the dissolution set in and the temple drowned in flame.

Jerek reclaimed the sword and strode out of the temple, content that through his actions it would look for all the world as though Mannfred had betrayed the Lahmians, breaking their foul pact.

CHAPTER FOURTEEN

A Matter of Little Faith
Across the Battlefields of the Empire

VORSTER SCHLAGENER LIVED. That was his greatest achievement as a soldier in Martin von Kristallbach's army. No matter how desperate the fight for survival became, Vorster Schlagener lived. It was a useful skill for a soldier and it had been noted among his superiors and the men beneath him.

Better a lucky officer than a tactical genius, he heard one man say, in defence of the mess they found themselves in. And it was true. As a soldier, Vorster would have always chosen to fight beside a lucky man in the hope that some of that luck might rub off.

Where others fell, Vorster somehow remained standing.

It went beyond useful. He became a talisman for the men around him.

He smiled at their talk of luck and the jibes about fate playing a hand. The truth was that none of them wanted to jinx whatever hoodoo kept the young soldier alive. Instead they sought to reap the benefits of his bravery.

As others fell, good and bad men both cut down before their time, Vorster found himself rising through the ranks until Martin himself named him Kreigswarden.

He tried to be a decent man and a fair leader, but it was difficult. Over the months he had developed a deeper appreciation for Ackim Brandt.

It had been more than a year since that first desperate cry of, 'The vampires are coming!' And they had been fighting on three fronts in a bitter and bleak winter war. Snow swarmed in the air, whipping up a storm. The chill penetrated his furs, gnawing into his bones. The wind driving the flurry was biting cold, its teeth cleaving into his flesh, stinging all sense of feeling out of his hands. He rubbed them briskly together.

The winter had been the harshest in living memory. Cattle had died of lung blight, calves and foals were stillborn as the damned cold refused to relinquish its hold. The granaries and food silos were long since depleted. People were starving. Starvation led to discontent. With the uneasy peace it wouldn't have been a stretch to imagine neighbours turning on one another if the rumour of a decent meal became too much for them to resist. Regional affiliations ceased to matter. It became a question of survival. Remote settlements were cut off by blizzards. Every homestead suffered losses. The weak and infirm died from the extremes of the elements if starvation didn't take them first. It was all about filling empty stomachs.

Vorster was hungry. He couldn't remember the last time his belly had been full.

It was dark and he couldn't sleep so he had come outside to watch the silent enemy on the hills around them. The hillsides were lined with the army they said could never return.

It was difficult for Vorster to mask his bitterness.

He drew his sheepskin cloak up around his throat.

He turned his back on the dead and trudged back through the knee-deep snows to the pavilion that Ackim Brandt was using as his command tent. He pushed open the canvas flap and ducked into the tent, the storm blowing in behind him. Vorster stamped the snow off his boots and rubbed his arms vigorously, trying to massage his circulation back into some semblance of life. He wasn't the only insomniac. Brandt looked up from the maps spread out across the table. He raised a curious eyebrow.

'No change,' Vorster said. 'They're waiting for something, but I'm damned if I can work out what it is. It's obviously not the night, it's darker than a Shallyan priestess's puckered behind out there, and it's not the snow. Not even the damned phases of the twin moons seem to be making a blind bit of difference. I don't get it.'

'Hmmm,' Brandt mused, moving around the table. He steepled his fingers thoughtfully. The map spread out before him depicted the entire battlefield. It still fascinated Vorster to see a war played out so clinically with coloured flags for forces, hostile and friendly regiments, mounted knights and pistoliers. He had spent years down there on the killing ground unable to see the elaborate dance that was any given battle in all of its complexity. To him it was all about the fog of war, the fighting narrowed in around him in a clash of steel and spray of sweat and spill of blood, with him never really seeing anything more than a few feet beyond the tip of his sword. Brandt's world was different. Brandt saw it all dispassionately, like a hawk from above. It was like a ballet as opposed to a jig or a reel, every dancer moving in time to create something grander, something so much more than the sum of its parts.

That was what marked Brandt as special.

Interestingly, over the course of the year they had spent fighting together, Vorster had come to think of Brandt as a friend, but that didn't prevent him from being awed by the man's stratagems. He had never imagined they might end up on the same side, but petty feuds had been buried with the resurgent threat of the undead.

The Talabeclanders joined forces with Stirland's greater strength to fight back the skeletal armies of von Carstein as they came swarming up from the underground.

Even together they were constantly being pushed back. Something eventually had to give, and they all knew what it was. The alliance was a fragile one, both sides knew that, but if they hoped to live out the storm of the Winter War they knew that they had to stop tearing at each other's throats and fight side by side – fight as one.

They could and would turn on each other again if they survived. As he had promised, Ackim Brandt requested Vorster be seconded to his force. Martin had been more than happy to grant the request. It was a tie that bound their pact. Vorster knew that the elector count was using him as a diplomatic manacle around Brandt's ankles. It was a strange position to be in. He liked, even admired Brandt, but his loyalty lay with Martin. The pair of them had fought side by side during the opening months of the campaign, each gaining the trust of the other and creating a bond quite different to the one that captivity had formed between Brandt and Vorster.

Brandt crumpled a paper knight in his fist and threw it on the floor, unable to mask his frustration.

There were heroes out there freezing to death and the galling thing was that the cold didn't touch their enemy. It was not an equal battle. Vorster knew that they needed to find a way to neutralise the elements, but for the life of him he couldn't see a way around the simple truth that the cold was their biggest enemy. They had fought the dead for so long, they were almost common place. The sight of reanimated bones didn't immediately strike fear into the hearts of the men. It galvanised them. They knew that the dead could die again and again and again. They knew that the vampires could fall and the zombies could be returned to the dust of the earth. They knew that they could live. It was what they did, they were soldiers. They lived.

'Can't you feel it?'

Vorster nodded. He could. He had no idea what it was, but he could feel *something*. It was like a clawed finger hooking down into his gut and agitating the digestive acids. 'Do you think it's him?'

'Von Carstein? Taal's teeth, I hope not,' admitted Brandt. The man was a champion, a conqueror, but he wasn't a fool. The Vampire Count would be more than a match for their already exhausted forces. The dead had kept them on the run for four weeks already, harrying them and picking away at the men one night after another. He looked down at the map. Even he could see they were being shepherded into a dead end.

If they couldn't choose their own place for a last stand – the thought was interrupted by a peculiarly uncomfortable sensation, what his mother had called a goose walking over her grave. Vorster turned, his hand instinctively going towards the sword on his hip. There was no one behind him. He couldn't shake the feeling of being watched.

'I felt it,' he said. 'We aren't alone.'

Brandt nodded. 'It's been out there a while.'

'What is it?'

'If I were being forced to bet my life on it, I'd have to say a vampire. Its presence is repugnant.'

'An assassin?'

'I doubt it,' said Brandt. 'Murderous stealth isn't exactly our enemy's style.'

'Look at us, jumping at ghosts.'

'Not ghosts,' Brandt said, pointing at the shadow-thief creeping around the side of the pavilion wall. The guttering oil lamps picked his silhouette out against the canvas. Brandt held a finger to his lips. Vorster watched the intruder move towards the tent flaps. He drew steel, ready to fight for his life. His palms were slick with sweat, his heart palpitating. He stepped aside, blade-tip levelled at the black gash that was the tent flap.

The intruder never came through it.

They waited.

The creeping edge of fear made turning his back on the entrance impossible. Vorster couldn't think straight. He strained to listen, but there was nothing out there to be heard beyond the faint susurrus of the snow falling. He moved towards the tent flap, ready to throw it open. Brandt held up his hand, stopping him. 'We do not rush out into the unknown, my friend. Haste is a death sentence.'

'What do you suggest?'

Brandt moved away from the corona of light, withdrawing a dagger from his boot and slashing through the tent's wall where the shadow was deepest. He slipped out into the night on the other side.

Vorster followed.

They circled the pavilion until they found the interloper's prints in the fresh fall of snow. The track's betrayed his passage. He had moved off beyond the tents. They followed, expecting the tracks to lead to the owner of the shadow. They didn't. They led them into the first stand of trees and then deeper before they petered out into nothing, leaving Brandt scratching his chin, perplexed.

Vorster turned in a slow circle, but with the leaves and branches intermeshing to blot out the moon it was nigh on impossible to see anything beyond shadow and more shadow.

He heard something, a crackling of branches. The sound echoed from tree to tree. He looked up instinctively and saw something black scamper from branch to branch scared out of its hole.

Then the creature swooped down on them from above, black fur cloak billowing out behind it as it came.

Vorster lashed out with his sword blindly, catching the black shape high across the shoulder. Before he could follow up with a reverse cut and thrust, the creature had him on his back in the snow, the wind knocked out of him.

'Listen to me,' the creature rasped and then it was spinning away to the side as Brandt's blade lashed out, slicing deep into the fusty wool of the beast's tunic.

Brandt edged forwards in a tight fighting crouch, black blood on the edge of his sword. Vorster scrambled to his feet. His sword had fallen ten feet away and there was no way he could get to it. Fear gripped Vorster, a cold fist clenching around his heart. He looked around frantically for a weapon, anything he could use to defend himself with. The beast's blood stained the snow between them.

No one moved.

'Listen to me,' the vampire repeated.

'Shut your vile stinking mouth, beast,' Vorster snarled.

'I could have killed you if I wanted to.'

Vorster stared at the creature. It was wild, feral. Its very nearness gnawed away at his gut. Brandt edged closer.

'You want to speak, beast, then speak,' Brandt said. There was blood on his shirt from a cut high on his left arm.

Looking from one to the other it was impossible to tell which was the monster. Brandt's face twisted into a bestial snarl whereas the vampire's face remained devoid of any emotion.

'I have a message. I need it delivered to Altdorf.'

'And why should we believe you, beast? You come skulking in the night like some cut-throat assassin. What is to say this isn't a lie to disarm us? What is to say that there is any message for the capitol? Your kin are renowned as princes of deceit.'

'I am not one of them,' the vampire said. There was something in his eyes that terrified Vorster. It took him a moment to realise what it was: compassion. Of all the traits of the living it was the last thing he had expected to encounter in the dead.

'Then what are you?'

'My name was Jerek Kruger. I fought as Knight Marshall of the Knights of the White Wolf. I was the wolf itself. I slew the first Vampire Count. This... this incarnation... is my punishment. The beast robbed me of my humanity. Now I am nothing. I would end things. There has been too much death.'

'Yet you come to us in the night? You creep among us. You do not enter my tent and seek to parlay. Instead you fall on us from the trees.' Brandt pressed a hand to the shallow cut in his arm. 'You draw blood.'

'But,' the vampire countered, 'I do not feed.'

'Why should we believe you?' Vorster asked, finding his voice. The fear inside refused to subside.

'Because I am your only hope, young man and because you do not want to suffer my fate. Because on the morrow the dead will come swarming down from those hills and you cannot hope to resist them, because without me you will die.'

'You paint a grim picture, dead man.'

'I tell the truth. I do not waste words painting pretty pictures or whisper sweet sounding deceits. There is no point.'

'What do you want from us?' Vorster cut to the chase. He cast a calculating glance in the direction of his sword; there was no way he could possibly reach it before the beast fell on him. Would Ackim Brandt be fast enough to get between them and save his life if he made a rush for the blade?

'Don't think about it, soldier,' the vampire said as though reading his mind.

Vorster took an involuntary step backwards, his boot scuffing up snow. Wraiths of foggy breath corkscrewed from his nose and up through the air in front of his face as though he were a bull gathering himself to gore his enemy. He saw Brandt watching him, saw Brandt's left hand flex into a fist. It was a subconscious reflex. It was Brandt's tell. Vorster had fought alongside the man for long enough to learn the idiosyncrasies of Brandt's fighting style. Every soldier had certain tells that betrayed them in combat: a twitch, a flick of the eye, something that telegraphed their intentions a split second before the actual attack. Such a weakness could be lethal against a foe familiar with it, although it was seldom that one man would face another in anything like ritual combat. War was dirty and fast, the brutality of it more than outweighing the finesse of reading an opponent's body language. That clenching of his left hand was an unconscious thing, a tic, but

Vorster had seen it often enough to know that Brandt was bracing himself for violence.

'I am not a great lover of magic, but I have seen enough to pay heed. A creature came to me inside my head, painting a memory for me and bade me deliver it to you. His message could turn the tide of the war in favour of the living, forever. Can you take the risk of ignoring it?'

'You had a dream? You expect us to spare you because of some damned dream?' Vorster asked harshly.

Jerek shook his head. 'It was no dream. The creature's name was Finreir, his words carried on the winds. He had power, true power. He was unlike any living creature I have ever encountered. He showed me things, secrets.'

'What are these great secrets then?'

The vampire shook his head. 'They are not for you to know.'

'Then deliver the message yourself.'

'Are you naïve enough to believe that is a possibility, soldier? No, I thought not. We both know I cannot walk amongst the living, not now, not with the dead coming up from the underways and the vampires abroad. I would be hunted down, staked, mouth stuffed with white roses and my corpse buried face down in the dirt. I can see it as clearly as I could if I had been gifted with foresight. You must send runners where I cannot go. I'll write the message down. It has to be this way.'

The urgency of the vampire's words disturbed him.

'I am not comfortable with this,' Vorster told Brandt. 'I feel as though we are being played for fools.'

'Deliver the message and you will be undoing the Vampire Count's threat.'

'It cannot be that simple,' said Brandt doubtfully.

'It was the first time,' said Jerek. 'There was no gift from Sigmar. It was a message, yes, but there was no divine source. The message that proved the key to the fall of Vlad came from his own get. He was betrayed.'

'Now you intend to emulate the betrayer,' Brandt said, ironically. 'What is your price, daemon?'

'Peace,' said Jerek.

'Are we to believe that a bloodsucking fiend could suddenly turn pacifist?'

'I don't care what you believe, soldier. The truth is all that matters to me now.'

'Come with us to Martin,' Brandt said. 'Make your case. The import of your message will decide whether you live or die.'

'No,' Jerek said, shaking his head. 'I will not beg Stirland. As grateful as I am sure he would be for my betrayal of his enemy, I am not fool enough to believe that his benevolence would extend to me walking away from his Runefang with my head still attached. I was the Wolf of Middenheim, but to van Kristallbach I am von Carstein's get, nothing more nothing less. No, if I had wanted the elector count I would have drawn him out here. I chose you. I have watched you. You are soldiers, much as I once was. Those are your men out there freezing to death. You care about them. You don't want them to die needlessly so you will send runners to the cathedral in Altdorf. You will see that my words are heard by those who need to hear them.'

'What would you have us say?'

The fate of the living hung on the seven words Jerek told them.

MANNFRED VON CARSTEIN's legion of the damned marched on through the driving blizzard, oblivious to the battering of the elements.

The snow swirled in their wake like white devils and crunched under the bones of their skeletal feet.

The dead came on endlessly.

They had no need of comfort.

They keened and cried and wailed, their lament tormenting the landscape. Not once did they stumble or fall.

They were a relentless tide.

Thousands upon thousands of rotting corpses and bare bones, clad in scraps of armour, leather straps rotted through, and breastplates and cuirasses hanging lopsidedly off the cadavers, marched on.

The ghosts were the worst. They were both pitiful and terrifying. The restless shades seemed ignorant of their own deaths and fought blindly, against and among themselves, over and over. Their non-corporeal forms re-enacted the battles that had seen them fall, only for the ghosts to rise over and over for 'One last push!' and 'One more charge!' before they fell to the cries of, 'They come, they come!'

Ethereal screams haunted the fields as the shades threw themselves once more into the fray.

The clash of ghostly swords and the cries of the fallen were ever present.

Adolphus Krieger stood in the middle of it, basking in the memories of slaughter. Feeling the sorrow and fear radiate from the ghosts deep into his bones was akin to the joy he felt during torture and the rapture that the act of killing delivered. He fed on it every bit as greedily as he fed on blood. He was a cruel creature. Mannfred had turned to him when Skellan had failed to return. They were similar monsters. Their natures were the same. They were a match in their appetites for cruelty, as bloody as cleaving a co-joined twin at the spine. They were butchers. Krieger turned and turned again, brushing his fingers through the ghostly warriors, shivering with delight at the static lightning-charge that coursed through his body at the contact. He drank down their misery like the finest of wines, the headiest of liquors. The screaming and wailing and gnashing of teeth rose into a symphonic roar swelling over the field.

Soon the dying would be real enough.

Soon the screams would be true.

Soon the ghosts would be joined by more, newer, fresher shades.

Soon the living would join the dead.

For now they fled, in utter terror. The priests in the temples had sworn, had promised, that these armies could never return, but they had been proved liars and fools.

The skeletal fingers of the long and recently dead clawed up through the earth around Krieger, as the rank and file of von Carstein's armies shambled out from the underways.

They emerged within a day's march of Altdorf itself, behind the lines of the defenders.

The Winter War would be remembered for its legendary suffering. With the men out chasing shadows, the women and children were left alone within the city walls to bleed and die, and to satisfy Adolphus Krieger's need for pain.

He strode ahead of the main body of the army.

The vampire was the vanguard, the hammer to the forge's fire.

The ripple of fear would chase away from them, all the way into the heart of the city. There was no time to flee. No time to panic.

In the distance the grand spires of Altdorf reflected the moonlight back up to the heavens, and the dead marched on.

CONFESSION WASN'T GOOD for the soul, and when committed to paper in the form of history those weighty tomes were nothing more than links in hefty chains. They weighed down upon the reader, testing his faith to the core.

Kurt III, Grand Theogonist of Sigmar, holiest of holies ran his crooked fingers across the spidery scrawl of his predecessor's submission, and he was afraid, deeply afraid. Outside the walls of Altdorf the dead gathered, but Kurt was besieged both from without and from within.

How could such a devout Sigmarite commit such filth to vellum and in so doing cast such untruth in stone? How could such a great man fall so far? The irony was not lost on the priest, given that Wilhelm had plunged from the battlements of Altdorf locked in the Vampire Count's deadly embrace. Death was not averse to irony.

Kurt refused to believe the story unfolding within the diary.

He hurled the book across the floor, the pages spreading like wings as they hit the black iron dogs of the open fire. One of the pages blackened and burned. For a moment he thought about leaving the book there and letting Wilhelm's confession be consumed by the hungry flames, but only for a moment. He couldn't do it. He couldn't be responsible for the death of history. The words, that spidery scrawl, were all that remained of Wilhelm's fatal encounter with the first Vampire Count. Somewhere in there, surely, was the key that would set them free. Vlad had fallen, so too would his vile progeny.

'No, no, no, no.'

He slapped out the first wisps of black smoke as they smouldered through the ancient leather.

He couldn't let the book burn.

And yet he couldn't move beyond the confession, the lie, that Sigmar's hand had been nowhere near the dank crypts while a sick old man prayed for a miracle.

'You want me to believe that it wasn't Sigmar who came down?' He made the sign of the hammer across his chest reflexively. 'You want to believe it wasn't Sigmar who granted you the strength to battle, despite the sickness eating away at your flesh? You want me to believe that it was a vampire that delivered to us salvation? God help me!' Spittle frothed at his quivering lips as he threw his arms up in anger and despair. He spun around, lashing out at the oil lamp on the table, sending it crashing across the floor. Blue flame spread virulently across the flagstones. He watched the flames dance, allowing them to burn themselves out.

He tore out a single sheaf of vellum from the binding of the unholy book, crumpled it and threw it into the fireplace. For a moment it looked as though the page would resist the teeth of the fire, immune to its heat, but then it blackened and shrivelled, and finally burst into all-consuming flame, taking its lies with it. He tore another handful of pages from the book and raised his arm as though to hurl them into the fire, but he let them slip through his fingers and fall at his feet.

Exhausted, he sank back into his chair, staring at the ancient diary.

'What am I supposed to do? What do you want from me? What am I to do when the progeny of unfettered evil bears down upon us and there's no thief to steal us a victory? Am I to fall upon my knees and beg for mercy from a creature that knows no such thing? Am I to fall upon my knees and pray to a god who abandoned us before? Am I to hurl myself from the spire and fall upon the pikes of their advance? I don't know what I am supposed to do.' That was the truth. He leaned forwards, drawing closer to the book. 'What is the point in prayer when I am praying to a lie?'

Fat tears of frustration broke and rolled down his cheeks, falling onto the scattered pages of the old priest's confession.

A knock at the door dragged him from his melancholy.

'Come,' he said, looking up.

The heavy door swung open and a young messenger entered, wearing the colours of Stirland. The grime of the road was beaten deep into his features.

'What is it, boy?'

The messenger reached into his satchel and withdrew a missive bearing the red wax seal of von Kristallbach. He handed it to the old man, eager to show that he had not broken the seal. Kurt took a knife from the table, still wet from where it had been slicing the flesh of an apricot. He slipped the blade beneath the seal and cut it loose. He teased the single sheet of parchment out of the envelope and brought it over to the light.

He read the single line with weary eyes and felt the hand of Sigmar rest upon his shoulder.

'What is it, sir?' the messenger asked, even though it wasn't his place.

A glimmer of a smile touched the Grand Theogonist's thin lips. 'It is salvation, my boy, salvation.'

He read the single line of text again: *What can be bound can be unbound.*

THE GRAND THEOGONIST swept purposefully through the dark halls of the cathedral and across the courtyard, acolytes swarming around him, one handing him his cloak, another trying to impress upon him that perhaps there were other options.

'Perhaps the priests of Taal have another copy of the book, your grace?'

Kurt held out his arms for the acolyte to dress him even as he argued.

'There are no other copies of the nine books of Nagash.'

'Are you sure, your grace?'

'Positive. The only known copies were destroyed here, on this very soil two centuries ago. Where are my horses?'

'They're in the courtyard, your grace.'

Kurt spun on his heel and marched out into the snow-filled air, saying, 'I ride for the libraries of Arenburg. There, perhaps, we might find something. The scribes are far more knowledgeable than I.'

'You do yourself a disservice, your grace. Your knowledge and our resources here are unrivalled.'

He reached the horse.

'Were not books taken to the scholars at Middenheim or the scholars of Nuln? Not that it matters. You'd never make it through. Listen to them, your grace. They're here.'

Ignoring the acolyte's warning Kurt said, 'No, no, no, young Kristoff. The books were burned in pyres. The priests gathered them, drenched them in oil and sacrificed them to the fires.'

He swung himself up onto the horse.

In the distance they heard the screams of retreat as people fled from the undead scourge. Thousands of rusty swords clanged and hammered, and beat against shields conjuring thunder that boomed and rolled across the great city. The dead were encircling the city walls like a noose around her delicate neck.

'Here... under our very feet, are the ashes of those books.' Kurt glanced up in the direction of his room, the dance of flame on the burning confession still playing out across his mind's eye. Something lurked in the shadows, tantalisingly close. 'The pyres were here,' he repeated emphatically, 'here.' The letters on the illuminated page had been in different inks. When one had touched the flame, he recalled the way that they had flared on ignition. For one brief moment he had been presented with the answer. Only now did he see it. 'What's beneath our feet, Kristoff?'

'The ashes?' the young acolyte asked, a little bewildered.

'No, Kristoff, the catacombs.' That was it. That was what he had seen in the burning paper, only he hadn't recognised it for what it was; he'd been too busy feeling angry with his god. There were no answers at Arenburg. They were here, buried deep. Like all true secrets, the words of the *Liber Mortis* had been lost for so long that they had become legend, and legends were stories, and stories were make believe... only, they weren't, of course. For every lie there was a grain of truth.

He didn't wait for the acolytes to follow. He dismounted and swept across the courtyard oblivious to the snow, through the majestic double doors into the cathedral, and down into the catacombs. His footsteps rang out hollowly, echoing up and down the dark passages. He snatched up a flaming torch and plunged deeper into the secret places of the house of worship. Light danced off the carvings lining the rows of ornate priestly sarcophagi. He walked slowly down the line, shadows dancing all around him. The musty smell of cold damp stone filled his nostrils. He heard scuttling – rats hugging the walls.

He cast about left and right, looking for something to call to him. He wasn't certain what he was looking for, but he had renewed faith – it would present itself to him. Here was the history of the priesthood laid bare, his forebears in stately repose, guardian swordsmen hefting their blades aloft in exultation to Sigmar.

All, that was, except one, in a dark recess further down the hall.

The stone swordsman's blade stabbed down into the lid of the sarcophagus of a child's tomb at its feet, as though guarding against some infernal evil.

The other sarcophagi bore the names of those interred, but this one bore two simple couplets, engraved into the façade of the tomb. He held the torch closer so that he could better read them. *Child of Death, Free of Death.*

He knew the inscription well. He had always thought it such a sad one, but now, reading those words again, he began to unravel the secret hidden in plain sight. *Child of Death, Free of Death.*

In the old scholar's tongue the couplets meant the same thing: *Liber Mortis.*

The same word for child and free had a third meaning.

Liber also meant book.

Liber Mortis: the book of the dead.

A chill shivered down the ladder of his spine.

How many times had he, and others, passed the tomb without a second thought? They had chosen to hide one of the most repellent artefacts of the undead nation beneath the holiest of holies. All that it needed was someone with the eyes to see beyond the simplicity of the message. He made the sign of the hammer again, uttering a soft prayer to his lord.

He was not alone.

Anxious footsteps echoed down the stairs towards him.

'Your grace? Are you all right?'

Kurt gripped the lid of the sarcophagus and leaned his back into it, heaving with all of his might. 'Come!' He called. 'Come help me!'

The acolytes rushed to his aid, throwing their combined strength into the task, gradually prising the stone plinth from its resting place and smashing it to the ground. Holding their torches aloft, they gathered around the open tomb as the grand theogonist rummaged around inside.

There was no body.

He lifted out the unholy manuscript and held it at arms length, already feeling its insidious evil worming its way into his heart.

'Come! Sometimes it takes evil to fight evil. Let the wretched carry out burdens and squabble amongst themselves. Sigmar is with us!'

'Sigmar is with us!' they repeated.

MANNFRED STOOD BENEATH the imposing walls of Altdorf and surveyed all that he had wrought. He was the wrack and ruin of mankind.

He had not expected the seeds of the fear he had sown to be so fruitful.

The living had fled.

Chill winds swept along the empty battlements, rattling the unlit braziers at each abandoned sentry post. Where normally the flames would be lit to mark the beginning of man's domain the braziers remained unlit, testament that death had encroached beyond the humanity's defences. The once flaming braziers that stood watch over the city illuminating its night had fallen into darkness. Their fires had burned out with no one there to tend them, the embers long since dead and their rattling bronze wailed in the night, beaten by the winds without mercy.

Mannfred roared with laughter, turning around to his troops, raising his fist. 'Now they cower! Finally they heed the lessons taught by our kith and kin! Altdorf is ours!'

Adolphus Krieger stepped up beside him, a finger to his lips as he hushed the whole army, even his leader. A slow, cold smile spread across his lips as the lone cry of a baby echoed from the narrow streets behind the high walls and out across the horde. Delicious victims waited for him.

From out of the darkness a lone black bird descended. It swept low, settling on Mannfred's broad shoulder. The Vampire Count swatted it away, but the bird would not be cowed. It bit a chunk out of the side of his face, drawing blood, and in that moment, a name rose in Mannfred's mind, as though he had been touched by another remote force, one other than the slumbering malevolence he had unearthed deep in the Lands of the Dead.

'Finreir,' he said, tasting the name. A face flowered within his mind's eye.

'What are you talking about?'

Mannfred reacted quicker this time, snatching the crow from his shoulder. He snapped its neck and threw it to the ground.

'Nothing,' he replied.

'What are we waiting for?' Krieger muttered.

'We are not waiting, we are savouring the moment,' said Mannfred. 'Where my sire failed, I have risen to best them all. It is I, Mannfred, who stands before the terrified city. It is I, Mannfred, who will drink on the blood of Altdorf's finest. It is I, Mannfred, who will claim this greatest of prizes. This is my destiny!' His words carried out over the dead, his voice spiralling in its intensity whipping the hordes into a frenzy of bloodlust. It was no *natural* lust. The sheer power of Mannfred's words imbued the ranks of the dead with his own hunger. The ghouls panted and salivated, goaded on beyond reason by the mere promise of meat. 'Now, we break open this rotten carcass. It is time for us to feed!' He launched his sword at the city gates to manic cheers from the animate cadavers.

They surged forwards throwing themselves at the gate, trampling one another underfoot in their lust to be the first to breech the wall.

Mannfred stood in the centre of it.

This was his moment of triumph, the breaking of humanity.

Then, high on the walls, he saw a lone figure wrapped in holy vestments, battling against the elements. It was almost comic. One man, no matter how holy, couldn't hope to stand against the might of the vampire nation. Mannfred smiled, waiting for the fool to be torn limb from limb by his wretched horde.

Unperturbed the figure strode to the very centre of the battlements, showing no fear.

He reached into his vestments and produced, not a shield nor a sword but a book.

'What's this fool doing?' Adolphus Krieger asked. Then his face split into a manic grin. 'He's going to sing for us!' The notion delighted the vampire.

The voice that came down from the battlements was not miraculous or musical. The intonation was flat, emotionless, but somehow the words carried.

Mannfred recoiled in horror, recognising the arcane tongue immediately.

'It cannot be,' he said in disbelief.

Suddenly the ground quaked beneath his feet. The high walls trembled and the rumble of the storm took substance. The rhythmic beating of the undead's shields faltered before the might of holy wrath. Without warning, lightning cleaved the sky, forks spearing down before the battlements. The blistering maelstrom swarmed around the priest. One by one, the braziers at the guard's posts exploded into flame, the detonations shooting pillars of fire up into the heavens.

In desperation, Mannfred screamed at his armies, '*Bring me his head!*'

Krieger leapt to the attack, running for the priest. On his sixth step his body shimmered into vapour and from the smoke a huge black bat took flight, its wings skimming over the upturned heads of the skeletal army, and ploughed through the blizzard remorselessly.

Another line tore from the priest's mouth as the Great Spell of Unbinding took shape, its echo so powerful that Krieger's ears began to bleed. The bat slammed into the wall and tumbled to the ground, its wings ripped by bone and rusted armour as the mindless dead fell upon it.

This was not the moment of glory Mannfred had believed was his by right.

Krieger's body took shape at the foot of the mighty walls, battered and bruised, and bloodied beyond all recognition. The vampire roared his anger and frustration, but undeterred continued to scale the backs of the skeletal army as they ramped up against the stone walls.

The Grand Theogonist turned the page to read the final line of the incantation. His trembling lips tripped over the final words, sheer exhaustion consuming his fragile body. He had done all that he could do, more. His knees buckled and the book tumbled from his fingers and fell, pages torn apart by the gale. The skeletal army arrived atop the battlements and reached out to grasp him.

Kurt closed his eyes and offered himself up to the mercy of Sigmar. It was out of his hands now.

As Krieger climbed higher, scrambling against the bones of his makeshift ladder, his foot suddenly gave way, ploughing into the disintegrating chest cavity of a dead foot soldier. He struggled to pull his foot free and regain some kind of balance, but wherever he lashed out he found nothing but crumbling bone. The dissolution set in. One by one the soldiers of the undead army fragmented, collapsing in on themselves as whatever magic bound them to this hellish form degenerated.

All around Mannfred skulls rolled off shoulders and swords and sword arms clattered to the ground in tainted heaps. The chiming of desiccated muscles and stringy sinew snapping rang out across the battlefield as mass atrophy took hold.

Mannfred stood, despairing at the absolute collapse of his forces.

Piles of bones gathered at his feet, rapidly disappearing beneath flurries of fresh snow. The glowing torches of Altdorf looked down upon him in mocking disdain. The living had found themselves an unlikely hero, not a man of the sword, but a man of the cloth. Because of one man's faith, the dead were forced to flee.

CHAPTER FIFTEEN

A Small Matter of Revenge
Drakenhof Castle, Sylvania

KALLAD STORMWARDEN BROKE his vow.

He hoped Grimnir would forgive him.

He led his dwarf brethren through the dark crags and into the belly of the Worlds Edge. The reality of being back in the tunnels was considerably less troubling than the fear he had allowed to fester. Cahgur suggested that they held off from lighting the torches until they were deep beneath the mountain so as not to risk smoke or light signalling their arrival to the unsuspecting world above. Kallad agreed, although the ground seemed slick and treacherous underfoot. The ragged sounds of his own breath filled his ears, but something seemed different.

The return of the echo was muted.

They pushed on, deeper into the darkness.

They became increasingly aware that some quality within the tunnels had changed. The air thickened with moisture. It wasn't damp. It was hot.

Belamir huddled in close with Kallad and Valarik.

'I can't stand this dark,' Belamir cursed. 'I'm gonna end up on my arse!'

'Strike a flint, fer Grimnir's sake and let's get some light in here.'

The rasp of the flint being sparked was followed by the sudden bluish flare and the drawing of flame. Valarik ignited the tinder and in turn a torch. The dwarfs squinted against the brightness, waiting for their eyes to adjust. Only then were they able to fully comprehend the horror unfolding before them.

'I have no liking for this,' Molagon said. 'Not one little bit. It's unnatural.'

'Well this is what we came for, what did you expect?' Kallad asked. 'The glittering halls of Grimnir and the magnificent forge of Grungni?'

The others laughed, but it was nervous laughter. Only now were they beginning to form an appreciation for what he had been through. His bravery was no bluster.

The walls were slick with blood, hot fresh blood turned black by the dark stone. It reeked of the forges of the metalworkers. Kallad knelt and pressed his fingers into the blood, raising it to his nose. It stank with a tang of iron. Dwarf blood, he knew from the higher iron content, and it was fresh, which meant that he had been wrong.

He hadn't rescued everyone. Some had still died down here. Some were still dying. He unclasped Ruinthorn and plunged headlong into the darkness.

THE SOUL CAGES were empty when they arrived.

They creaked and groaned on black iron chains, suspended over fire pits for cleansing, to burn the blood and faeces off. The sight of them brought back bitter memories of his time in the arena.

Othtin set off across the floor, ducking beneath one of the swinging cages.

'Not that way,' Kallad said. 'Trust me there are no glittering halls that way.'

Othtin stood stock still and turned slowly to face Kallad. He raised an eyebrow. 'How about Grungni?'

Despite himself, it made Kallad smile.

'Not unless he's fighting in the arena.'

'So which way then?'

There were five doors leading off the cleansing room, one on each point of the pentagram. Two led down towards more prison cells, one fed off towards the galleries surrounding the arena, one to the arena itself. Only one led up to the galleries above. Kallad pointed. 'That one.'

'Where does it go?'

'Up.'

'I don't like all this quiet,' Skalfkrag grumbled.

'I can't say I'd prefer a welcoming party,' Kallad said.

'Unless they brought ale,' Belamir chimed in.

'Then why are we standing around here yapping, I'm parched.' Valarik smacked his lips, clapped his hands and led the way.

They moved single file up the tight corridor. Grooves had been worn in the middle of the steps from the shuffling feet of countless condemned men. They crept on. The place was eerily empty. They had come prepared for grisly work and had thus far met nothing. Considering the enemies that could have been waiting, Kallad claimed it as one little victory.

They were not here to fight a war.

They were here to kill quietly and leave.

THE STRAINS OF a haunting melody began to filter through from the throne room.

The smell of perfume and wine filled the air.

Kallad stood on the threshold watching a beautiful, naked harpist playing her fingers down to blood. The filaments of the instrument were so fine that they cut into her ivory skin like wire, and still she played on through the pain, feeding it to the threnody to make it all the more elegiac.

His clan brethren fanned out behind him, drawing their hammers and blades silently.

The lord of this wretched domain reclined languidly in a chair with his back to them, his effeminate hand clutching a lace handkerchief. A crystalline goblet, half-full of rich ruby blood, coagulated on the table beside him.

'Come to me, woman,' the vampire commanded. Her fingers trailed across the final notes, enthralled. She rose and moved with grace to kneel before him. The vampire took her ruined fingers in his hand and raised them to his lips to drink. Her eyes fluttered closed, her breast heaved and her breath hitched in her throat as the beast drained her.

It served as the perfect distraction.

The dwarfs crept silently across the marble floor, using the shadow of the obsidian throne as cover until they could be certain that there was no one watching who could alert Mannfred from the galleries above. The lord of all darkness was unprotected. All Kallad could think was that this had to be a trap. It was too easy, but, for all that, he wasn't going to pass up the opportunity. Cutting off the snake's head might not kill it, but it was satisfying to watch it flail around in pain.

'Mannfred,' Kallad said, 'I'd like to reintroduce you to Ruinthorn. I believe you've met.'

Without waiting for the Vampire Count to turn around, Kallad slammed his trusty axe into the back of the vampire's head, splitting the beast's skull in two. There was a moment of utter disbelief. The beast was dead.

'Right,' said Cahgur. 'Let's see about that ale then, shall we.'

'Stay your thirst, Cahgur,' Valarik said. 'There's something very wrong here.'

'Yes, it's a bleedin' castle full of vampires,' Skalfkrag said, stating the obvious.

'Really? Then where are they?'

'Let's get this wee lassie out of here. There've been enough victims already.' Othtin reached out to take the harpist's hand and led her to freedom, but as their fingers touched, the girl recoiled and turned on them, her face contorting like some wild banshee as she opened her mouth and screamed.

'Shut up, lassie,' Othtin said, bewildered. 'What do you think you're doing?'

Kallad Stormwarden could see in her black eyes that she wasn't screaming out of fear. She was screaming for help.

'Oh, bugger.'

He didn't even think about it. He buried Ruinthorn in her throat silencing her screams.

The others stared at him in horror.

'She was one of them,' he said. It was all he offered by way of explanation.

'So what about this ring then? Isn't it meant to bring him back from the dead? Maybe we should take it off his hand before it can do the business.'

'Aye,' Valarik agreed.

Kallad stepped over the bodies. Ruinthorn had obliterated Mannfred's features, cleaving through his face, rendering him unrecognisable. The signet ring on his finger was all the proof he needed that he'd killed the right monster. He saw the feral bat shaped around the ring and knew it as von Carstein's mark. He took the beast's ring, finger and all.

He hefted his axe up onto his shoulder.

'Let's go,' he said, but their retreat was already being countered.

Two vampires leapt through the stained glass windows above the gallery. A third loomed in the doorway. The girl's cry had been answered.

THE BREATH OF talons brushed across Kallad's throat.

The dwarf was fast.

He smashed the vampire's claws away with the butt of Ruinthorn and reversed the blow, bringing the axe-head up to thunder the flat of it into the beast's face.

The other dwarfs instinctively scattered so as to make the vampires work for their targets.

Warriors never willingly bunched up.

Kallad hammered the blade into his opponent's grinning face, opening its leering smile all the wider. The dwarf launched into a whirlwind spin, Ruinthorn arcing out in a lethal silver flash. Just as the next vampire launched forwards, the axe sheered through both of his fangs and tore out of the side of his face. The beast went down in a spray of tainted blood.

Valarik was not so lucky.

He charged at the fiend barring the threshold, axe raised above his head, but the vampire was faster. It leapt over the dwarf's wild swing, taking the flesh of Valarik's throat with him. The dwarf was dead before he hit the floor.

Cahgur and Skalfkrag fought side by side, beating the unlife out of a fallen vampire. Their hammers mashed the creature to a bloody pulp.

'To me!' Kallad yelled, unhooking a peculiar looking mechanical crossbow from his belt. He took aim and squeezed down on the trigger, releasing the grapple. It sailed up over the gallery's balustrade and clattered into place. He tugged down on it hard to make sure it was secure. He wrapped his arm around the rope and hit the spring-loaded winch propelling him out of the clutches of the vile beasts.

Kallad grabbed on to the top of the stone balustrade and hauled himself up onto the gallery. Gasping for breath and acutely aware that his brethren were locked in a desperate battle below, he jammed the crossbow-winch into the balustrade, hammering it tight with the butt of Ruinthorn. Moving quickly he disconnected the metal grapple and tossed one end of the rope down. Kallad speared the hook into the winch mechanism turning it into a handle.

Belamir grabbed the trailing rope and began to climb. Kallad spun the winch frantically, pumping his arms. Moments later Belamir was hauling himself up over the top and throwing the rope back down. He unshouldered his own rope and sent that over the top as well, allowing Othtin and Cahgur to climb together.

'Hurry!' Molagon bellowed. More vampires were arriving, closing in all the time. Skalfkrag was being forced back into a corner, three vampires slashing and clawing at his face even as his warhammer caved in temples and gouged out eyes. He fought like the mad dwarf that he was.

The ropes were thrown down again, slick with sweat and grease from going through the winch. No one was holding the end of the second rope. It fell in a serpentine coil, leaving the single rope dangling.

Molagon grabbed for the rope and missed. A vampire hurled itself into his back, punching him off his feet. As the beast's fangs came down to tear open the back of his throat, Skalfkrag landed on its back, driving the wicked point of his hammer into the top of its skull and opening the back of the creature's head up.

Molagon crawled out from beneath the dead vampire.

Together they grabbed the rope, but their weight was too much for the winch and Kallad's tiring arm.

Cahgur and Belamir reached through the balustrade, struggling to grasp the rope and pull their friends to safety. Hand over fist, they dragged them higher. With the two dwarfs hanging in the no man's land between the gallery and floor, the load on the rope suddenly grew lighter. Skalfkrag's screams rang out through the great hall. Talons had sheered through the muscle and bone at the base of his neck, rendering him crippled. He fell and lay there, helpless, looking up, unable to defend himself as the beasts gathered around.

Kallad couldn't watch as the vampires fell upon his friend.

'Look away,' Belamir said, revulsion clogging in his throat. 'Give him his dignity.'

Cahgur helped Molagon up onto the gallery.

Down below one of the beasts looked up, and grinned, relishing the hunt. The air around him shimmered as his body slowly shifted into the form of a great black bird.

The bird flew at Kallad's face.

Swinging Ruinthorn, Kallad split it in two. Both bloody parts fell at his feet. He was running before they hit the floor.

Broken glass and jagged lead crunched beneath his boots as he launched himself through the shattered remains of the great stained glass window. The others came behind him. The icy wind almost snatched Kallad off his feet. He slipped and skidded on the slick roof tiles, casting around, looking for a way down.

The blizzard had mercifully blown itself out for a while.

He saw huge claw marks gouged through the ice and into the very masonry of the castle, the feet of their maker almost certainly larger than the dwarfs were. Kallad had no desire to meet the beast responsible for them. He pulled a set of spikes from his pack and stamped them onto his boots hurriedly before running. He traversed the roof, peering over the edge, searching for a way down. The path across the top of Drakenhof led towards a far tower, its roof in two parts, a spired top and a mid-section collar that, Grimnir be with them, they could jump down onto.

Four vampires appeared on the crest of the roof behind them. They had unleashed the beast within, their faces contorted into vile animalistic masks. They moved with ungodly grace across the slick tiles, always in balance as they scuttled forwards.

The dwarfs knew where to pick their battles, and an icy rooftop was no place to fight a vampire.

Kallad leapt from rooftop to rooftop, across the uneven gothic gables, slipping and sliding on the treacherous ice every step of the way. Only the spikes on his boots prevented him from careening off the gables. He pulled up short, confronted by a sea of corpses impaled on spikes, some so fresh that their blood was still oozing down through the runnels in the earth and into the belly of the old world. He knew, sickly, where the blood in the tunnels had originated. It was another crime that the Vampire Count had on his undead soul. Anger swelled inside Kallad. The scourge of the vampires was relentless.

'We did what we came to do,' Kallad said. 'We can't take them all. We have the ring. There will be ample time for retribution.' He threw himself across the gap to the collar, barely making the jump. The wind howled around him, bullying him off the parapet.

He fell to the earth like a stone.

The others came down behind him, the rooftop vampires breathing down their necks.

They stared for a moment, confronted by the forest of the impaled, and then they ran.

CHAPTER SIXTEEN

Duel

Marienburg, the Imperial City

FINREIR BROKE BREAD with the humans.

'The Vampire Count lives despite the would-be assassination, I see.'

The men of Marienburg were still uncomfortable in the elf's presence. They looked upon him with something akin to awe and suspicion, as though, Finreir thought, a god walked among them. What he did here at Marienburg would shape how humans and elves interacted for centuries to come. In some ways they were like children, blood-thirsty children, admittedly, but children none the less. Finreir was here to turn the tide against evil, although he was not entirely convinced of human kindness and was in half a mind to recommend on his return to Ulthuan that these creatures be watched from afar with keen eye. That is if they did not strip him of his status due to youthful impetuosity first. No doubt his expedition would trigger repercussions. Three elves breaching the seclusion of their people, indeed betraying their existence to these short-lived humans, could not go unpunished, but there was cause, good cause.

At the very least the humans deserved to survive this onslaught.

On an intellectual level, he suspected that given time the humans would learn to accept him, but they did not have time. As it was they deferred to him, which suited his purpose for now. It was a deference brought about by fear and suspicion, but again that suited him. It struck him yet again as remarkable that human and elven life spans were so different. At 60 years old in the human world he was not a child, but a wise elder and he was treated with respect accordingly. The feeling was good. He was not about to correct them.

'I do not understand,' said Johan Kleine, captain of the city guards. 'You've only been here a week and you know more than we do about the wolf at our door.'

'One needs only to listen to the winds to know the truth,' the elf said, not bothering to explain further. 'Mannfred has spent much of mid-winter licking his wounds and replenishing his forces. You humans are so eager to die and join his ranks. He grows in confidence daily. Three skirmishes in as many weeks, and three times your forces have been driven back. It has been a month since your last victory. The tide of war is against you, but eventually tides always roll in. Such is the ebb and flow of war. He will be here before sundown so the only question that remains is will Martin von Kristallbach reach us in time or should we make peace with our creators?'

'We can't afford to be optimists. We have to prepare for the inevitable.'

'Death is always inevitable, soldier,' said Finreir philosophically. 'It is merely a matter of when we choose to depart this mortal coil.'

They were in a huge tower room armoury, the forges below belching out steam and smoke. There was the sizzling of water as weapons were plunged into cold baths to temper them. Around the room other soldiers were gearing up. The place reeked of linseed oil, beeswax, leather, horse-hair and sweat, lots and lots of sweat.

The room was awash with the din of preparation: the clank of metal, the rasp of whetstones on steel sharpening swords, the sound of knives splitting quills and trimming the willow, the gentle whistle of fletchers biting down on the feathers as they bound them with sinew to arrows.

Johan Kleine cinched the strap of his metal vambrace into place on his lower arm. A page knelt at his feet, helping him fasten his greaves securely. He adjusted his scale hauberk so that it sat comfortably on his shoulders. Another page fastened his fauld to his abdomen once his cuirass had been secured.

The heat from the forgers beating out arrowheads and casting cannonballs, and from the hot lead of musket balls was fierce. The deafening hammer blows of armourers hammering out dents from the breastplates and other oddments of armour beat out the rhythm of the drums of war. The men wiped the sweat from their brows with hands thick as ham hocks and black with soot. Once an hour, more pages rushed into the chamber to slake their thirst for ale. It was an endless carnival of motion.

In the middle of it all, implacable, stood the mage Finreir, surveying the machine of war as it gathered momentum.

The heavy oak doors of the massive chamber opened. Three elf warriors strode imperiously into the room to confront the mage.

'Does Mannfred approach?' Finreir asked his kinsman.

'He does, and he will rip through these humans without breaking sweat. Look at them with their toys of war, Finreir.'

'They do what they must to bolster their failing spirits.'

'Then why won't you let us fight alongside them?'

'We did not come to watch carnage. It gives us no pleasure,' Málalanyn added.

'A wise commander studies his enemy before he weighs in. Impetuosity wins nothing.'

'Do not presume to lecture me on the tactics of war, mage. Battles are won by overwhelming force. If it has already come to blows the study of the enemy is meaningless. It is time to put an end to this haemorrhaging,' Aelélasrion said.

'These humans are brave,' Rinanlir, the last of the three moved out of the shadow of his brothers, 'but they are not endless in number.'

Finreir turned his back to his kin and stepped to one of the arrow slits, contemplating what awaited them over the horizon. He had touched Mannfred's evil and recognised the steering hand of Nagash. He realised that he would not be able to discern the slumbering evil's scheme unless he removed his proxy. It was time to remove Mannfred von Carstein from the game.

'Prepare your horses,' he said, simply because there was hope.

At dawn he had reached out across the winds, scrying the lie of the land. Events unfolding across the generations of the Old World were greater than he had anticipated. The humans had already fought this battle and won countless times, but they had made catastrophic mistakes, mistakes that could not bear repetition. The forces of Stirland under the banner of Martin von Kristallbach combined with the might of Altdorf and regiments from Talabecland were marshalling. They did not know, Finreir. How could they? But through the eight winds the mage knew them. The minds of the humans were akin to open books hungry to be read.

Beyond the trees he saw roiling dark clouds rolling in and felt the touch of darkness. This was no natural night rolling towards them. Dusk was not for another three hours. Mannfred was growing in confidence. Already he was arrogant enough to turn day into night in his hunger to bring the battle forward.

With Martin's forces gathering behind the dead it fell to Marienburg to be the rock against which Mannfred and his damned legions could be smashed. The strategy was clear: to hold out for as long as was humanly possible.

Finreir turned back to face Aelélasrion. The elf's words made what he was about to do all the easier. 'The humans are coming. Ride for Martin von Kristallbach, tell him that his hour has come. We will hold Mannfred at Marienburg. We invite the leader of men to come, to smash the Vampire Count upon our rock.'

'How dare you banish me on some menial errand? I am not your lackey! I am here to fight!'

'Then if you want something to fight you had best hurry, Aelélasrion.'

Finreir knew Aelélasrion's anger would only serve to quicken his passage to Martin. The warrior would be hungry to return in time for the meat of the battle. 'Remember, they have never met our kind before. Try not to frighten him. He is rather useful.'

'I am a swordmaster. I am no messenger boy, Finreir. Get someone else to run your errands.'

'I was not opening the matter up for debate, Aelélasrion. You have your orders. I suggest you ride, now.'

Aelélasrion stiffened as though to voice more complaint. Instead a moment later he said, 'He doesn't know us. What if he doesn't believe me?'

'We can only trust that he will; our lives depend upon it.'

Aelélasrion bowed deeply and swept out of the room.

A deep basso-profundo horn rumbled, shaking the very foundation of the armoury tower.

The enemy had been sighted.

THE MASSIVE TEETH of the portcullis hung over the maw of the city wall, hungry to bite down as the defenders marched out to face their foe.

Archers lined the battlements, their barbuts gleaming in the last glimmers of daylight. A single archer, crouched, nocking an arrow as he aimed his recurve bow high. The man had been chosen from the ranks of the city, a champion archer from the last tourney. Breathing shallowly, he drew back his arm until the catgut had dug so deep into his fingers that he had lost all feeling. The arrow felt unwieldy. He had never fired its like before. Its balance was unnatural, but he followed Finreir's instructions to the letter. He made a silent count of ten before he loosed the sorcerer's arrow high into the black sky.

As the arrow left the bow, the archer recoiled as it unexpectedly burst into flame. Its red glare streaked over the heads of the dead before exploding in a shower of shimming fireballs that hung in the air, revealing the extent of the enemy they faced.

The front line swelled with the slack-skinned putrescent flesh eaters scuttling forward. Behind them came the Black Hand, skeletal knights in rusted armour, under the command of Adolphus Krieger. Unmatched terror emanated from their corpses, fear rolling across the battlefield. Mannfred's own grave guard, wights wielding deadly wight blades and clad in gleaming black plate, brought up the rear.

On either flank were the Black Knights, the right led by Gothard, the Undying Wight Lord, and the left by a faceless vampire, a white rose emblazoned on his chest. The knights reined in their skeletal steeds, chomping at the bit, hungry to taste man flesh.

Finreir and the two elf warriors, Rinanlir and Málalanyn, emerged from the great mouth of the city, the rank and file of humanity swelling out behind them to face the undead.

The human forces, led by the army general and an experienced and battle-scarred veteran, Syrus Grymm, flanked Finreir to the left and to the right in ranks ten deep and one hundred wide, spreading out across the killing ground of the battlefield. Down the entire length of the city walls before them a harsh snow-filled landscape rolled out for yard after yard, until the first line of undead foot soldiers stood mockingly just out of arrow range.

The undead army roared as one at the living, their mere existence taunting them, beckoning them closer, but the humans would not move.

Mannfred gave the signal to the left flank.

Gothard responded by spurring his nightmare steed into a charge, leading a single probing wave of Black Knights down the length of the men's front line. They immediately drew fire from the frightened archers up on the battlements, but curiously the infantry did not flinch or recoil. Instead as the riders of the dead raced back and forth, their presence goading the living, the entire rear line of Marienburg's innocuous looking foot soldiers sprang into action. Grabbing up sharpened pikes that had been concealed in the snow, they raced to the front line and ten deep thrust their pikes into the ground, erecting a barrier that no riders, undead or otherwise, could ever hope to penetrate.

It was little more than a trace memory, a ghost of who he had been, but he felt it: satisfaction. He had forced the living into showing their hand. Gothard led his riders back to their place on the left flank to await further orders.

Mannfred saw instantly that he must send in his foot soldiers.

He ordered the flesh eaters – and only the flesh eaters – to advance.

The cadaverous ghouls salivated and slavered, shrieking with delight as they surged across the no man's land between the forces, banging gnawed bones and clubs to raise a cacophony of sound. They broke into a run, brandishing their chipped and rusty swords above their heads.

Finreir nodded once to Grymm and once to the sergeant of the archers on the battlements who raised his arm in acknowledgement. The man's arm came down with a cry of, 'Loose!' A rain of steel poured from the heavens.

Arrow upon arrow thudded into putrid chests and pus-filled arms, cutting down wave after wave of the damned flesh eaters.

A cold smile spread across the Vampire Count's grim face. The living had taken the bait. He called forth his necromancers, bidding them have the newly dead rise. The fear in the faces of the living was a wondrous sight to behold

The dead flesh eaters rose from the dirt right on top of the terrified pikemen.

Finreir had anticipated this manoeuvre too.

A second row of archers sprang up from behind the first along the high walls of the battlements, crossbowmen bearing flaming bolts soaked in naphtha. They took aim and fired upon the undead.

Adolphus Krieger chuckled bleakly at the obvious mistake. The living were commanded by idiots. 'They fire on us, they fire on their own pikemen,' he said, pointing out the irony that already the pikes were burning as the flesh eaters surged relentlessly forwards, throwing themselves onto the defences. Soon they would be reduced to ash and that would allow the riders back through. 'We must press the advantage!'

Mannfred gave the order for Krieger to advance with the Black Hand, marching on the centre. At the same time, he released the dire wolves to undertake continuous hit-and-fade assaults on the flanks of the living forces, augmenting the knights' more powerful cavalry charges with constant harassment attacks and drawing the archers' fire away from Krieger's foot soldiers.

Across the battlefield Finreir felt deep satisfaction that the arrogant dead had fallen for his double bluff. His only remaining fear was that Grymm and the living could not hold their line or their nerve long enough for the reinforcements led by Martin of Stirland to arrive and smash through the exposed ranks of the damned.

Mannfred threw up his hands, the lethal incantation screaming off his tongue. Ribbons of dark energy coursed from his cruel fingers, rippling out across the battlefield and ensnaring his front line. The flesh of the risen zombies became thin and desiccated as Mannfred's magic took hold. Compelled to thrust out their arms, they grasped for the nearest living being. Flesh decayed beneath the zombies' touch, fell conduits for the vampire lord's power. Their victims didn't even have time to scream.

Finreir reacted swiftly, raising his ivory staff and planting it firmly in the ground between his feet, but it was too late for many. The ground shook so violently that forces on both sides lost their footing and fell. In response, the snow and dust raised up from the ground beneath the living hung in the air for a moment, before blasting across the battlefield into the faces of the flesh eaters, like a maelstrom. The ice and the snow scoured the ranks of the dead, ripping the very flesh from their bones, pitting their bodies and obliterating them before the eyes of the humans.

There was nothing left for the necromancers to raise.

Mannfred raged in the cold heart of the undead army's ranks, his eyes blazing.

Finreir turned to his kin. 'Remove the necromancers from the field, brothers.'

Rinanlir and Málalanyn set off at a mad dash, using the chaos of battle as cover. None could touch them. Their swords whickered out occasionally, cleaving a path out of the flank, seeking the opportunity to cut back inside and catch Mannfred's sorcerers unawares. It was a simple but effective manoeuvre, surgical in its precision, elegant in its execution. The two elf swordmasters made light work of all in their path, but they did not underestimate the long-reaching powers of the magicians. Speed was of the essence. Within feet of the necromancers they felt their blood beginning to boil and their energy draining as the flesh began to melt around their bones.

Málalanyn brought one of Mannfred's grave guards to his knees and, leaping from the undead warrior's back, launched into the air, scything around in a deadly arc. His sword cleaved through the skulls of a surprised coven of necromancers. He landed in the midst of the dead, sword planted in the ground. He looked back at Rinanlir and said, 'Your turn.'

But there was no one left to kill.

'You take all the life out of fun, my friend,' said Rinanlir shaking his head. 'Perhaps we should take the initiative to kill a few more of these… things.'

Mannfred's elite grave guard, seven feet tall, were already closing in on the company of two elves.

'This could be interesting,' Rinanlir said, raising his sword in readiness.

Before a single blow could be landed, Finreir's presence touched their minds, ordering them back to the line.

As they turned to withdraw, they saw that Mannfred was already unleashing his next gambit, the bones of the long-dead clawing up from the earth in a vile parody of birth. But Mannfred's rage was not sated. Out at the extreme flanks of the living's lines, a foul stench began to form, filling the senses. The noxious fumes came not from without, but from within the very flesh of the soldiers, the rank corruption causing their flesh to rot and fall from their bones. The soldiers screamed in absolute terror and utter agony.

Gothard seized his chance, and the once proud warrior of the Knights of the Divine Sword led his riders in a wild charge at the human's flanks, racing them down the rear of the human forces. His damnation tore through him, flickering half-memories of a time before Mannfred had raised him from the dead, a conscript to his damned army. Emotions were alien now. There was no sense of self, no recognition of the banner of the Divine Sword, no stirring within him. He hungered for nothing more than the death of self. He lived on merely to fight, to serve, to destroy all that he had once held dear. He was destruction, wrath personified.

Finreir closed the noose on the perfect play, signalling Syrus Grymm to lead the remaining forces out, holding the flanks to face inwards and slam shut the steel trap, cutting off Mannfred's riders from the rest of his hellish legions. Held as they were at the foot of the city walls, the ranks of crossbow men and archers above loosed everything they had.

A swarming sound filled the air, a swirling black vortex of flesh eating insects streamed across the killing ground from Mannfred's fingertips, chewing a path through the living. The insects swarmed into mouths and eyes, and up the noses to clog the throats and choke the life out of the soldiers in their pestilential path.

Finreir cried, 'Stay out of the light!' as static blue charges lanced from him into the soldiers next to him and on from them, cascading into the next and the next, and the next until every living soul was alive with raw power. The static light drove back the unnatural darkness, cracking open the sky. The light was so bright that the flesh eating insects combusted, flaming like a shower of hot coals falling into the snow with a hiss.

In the distance, the sound Finreir and the living had been longing for, Martin's horn, heralded the arrival of reinforcements. Banners flapped in the wind, regiments of Stirlanders marching side by side with an army carrying the banner of Altdorf. Thousands of soldiers were moving with rhythmic precision across the fields. They banged swords on shields, hammering out their defiance as they advanced. The clamour had little effect on the dead, immune as they were to such primal instincts as fear, but it served to rouse the living, renewing strength in exhausted limbs, giving them fresh hope that they might yet live despite the uncompromising evil they battled.

Finreir smiled. Such was the power of hope. A single spark could banish an all-engulfing darkness.

Mannfred cocked his ear. How had he not seen this? His blindness incensed him. Finreir had drawn his Black Knights, and his rear was completely unprotected. Mannfred had expected to make an assault upon a city. He had not expected that the assault would be upon him. Finreir had played him masterfully, but the game was not over yet.

Krieger, almost at the front line of the living, came to the same realisation. He unleashed his will, invigorating the Black Hand with the sheer malevolent force of his presence, spurring them into a wild frenzy. They charged, concentrating his forces on a single point. The only task was to punch a hole through the living to rescue what was left of the Black Knights.

Mannfred did not wait to see if Krieger's Black Hand were successful. He wailed at the night, calling forth the banshees of nightfall. The wailing spectres would hold back the living long enough for them to flee.

This battle was over, but the Winter War was not.

CHAPTER SEVENTEEN

Carpe Noctem
Hel Fenn,
The Blighted Forests of Sylvania

AND SO THE living drove the dead relentlessly out of the Empire and back into the foul forests of Sylvania.

It was not one battle, not one decisive victory that did it. Scores of skirmishes and confrontations with a spiralling death toll matched the determination of the living not to fail. Swords clashed across hundreds of miles, the dead of countless provinces, hamlets, towns and villages gathering to rot in ditches so very far from home. The living swelled the ranks of the dead. Faith was stretched thin and hope was all but crushed, but that last stubborn flicker refused to die and from it blossomed an unflinching optimism. The living fought for their friends, their families and their land, the dead fought only for their master. It wasn't fear or hunger that drove them on, they were far removed from such base emotion, it was a weakness that death had cured them of.

Carrion crows hovered over the battlefields, picking at the remains of two hundred thousand souls. It was death on an unprecedented scale. That was the cost of the endless Winter War. For the living it seemed as though spring would never come, indeed, for more than a year it didn't. Though the snows came and went with the melt, death held the landscape in its icy grip. Morr's appetite for souls was so fierce that it could never be slaked.

There were too many skirmishes to remember, too many bodies to count, too much grieving to be done. It was an endless stalemate, no one's objectives truly met.

Battlefields were scoured and the fallen gathered into huge pyres. The cremation fires robbed von Carstein of more foot sloggers.

Even so, too many were born again into the ranks of the undead.

The clash of steel and the rasp of whetstones became the anthems of humanity.

The balance was precarious. The ebb and flow of slaughter never ceased. Martin, Count of Stirland and Kurt III, Grand Theogonist of Sigmar, marshalled the combined forces of humanity. Despite huge losses, they decimated the ranks of the undead more than once.

The strength of steel and the unbending determination of faith combined to forge two beacons of courage. They led by example. Martin von Kristallbach's horn rang out over the battlefields. He was not some fair-weather leader who sought the protection of the command pavilion. He fought with the rank and file, inspiring those around him with his bravery. Though others damned him for his reckless stupidity, none were prepared to carry the fight to the undead. Martin von Kristallbach was the unwavering beacon of humanity that inspired the living and drew the undead like flies.

Martin's grasp of strategy was instinctive and often daring.

Kurt witnessed a greater evil playing out on the battlefield and prayed to Sigmar for guidance. The Man-God granted him strength of purpose to do what must be done, the answer revealed when what appeared to be a ghoulish foe that had fallen at his feet begged him for release. The ghoul turned out to be no ghoul at all, but a revivified cadaver whose original spirit, imprisoned in its vile flesh, had been unable to cross over into the afterlife. Kurt recognised him. He had been cut down on the battlefield only hours before and somehow, through sheer force of character, had managed to regain a shred of control over his lips so that he could beg to be released from his own personal hell. If this had happened to just one man, how many thousands of others were, like him, denied salvation?

Honour was satisfied even if death wasn't.

For every victory the living claimed, the dead matched them.

The living learned their lessons well.

Martin refused to allow Mannfred the luxury of time.

The living harried his forces across the world.

Respite was rare and broken.

Under Martin's guiding hand, the men shaped themselves into a mighty foe-hammer. They beat down remorselessly on the flesh eaters and the Black Hand.

Differences cast aside, the men of the Empire refused to be humbled. In that, they reaped what they sowed. Their courage brought them small victories. Each small triumph spurred them on as the nature of the war shifted. There were cowards, of course, but there were heroes too, ordinary men like Vorster Schlagener, whose bravura, courage and skill on the battlefield earned them reputations among the men.

Fewer and fewer skirmishes took place on the wide open fields of battle as the conflict became a guerrilla war, the living being forced to scour the woods for the vampire's foul army.

The dead were not content to be victims.

Mannfred deployed all of his cunning to make the hunt lethal, fashioning traps, pits and spikes, nets and more wily artifices to ensure that the living trod softly, forever fearful of their hidden enemy.

Still, the deadlock could not last.

VORSTER EMERGED FROM the trees, blood caked around a wound on the side of his head.

An open plain sloped up gradually to a sharp ridge. Beyond it stood yet more trees.

He felt nauseous. He had taken a blow to the head that morning. A cudgel had lifted him off his horse and left him unconscious in the mulch of fallen leaves. Twice since coming around he had found the world spinning beneath him, his vision blurring. He wasn't about to complain. He was alive. Fifty men had fallen. It was a sobering thought.

Vorster Schlagener and Ackim Brandt rode side by side up the ridge, along with one hundred men who were part of Stirland's ranger advance, scouting out the lie of the land.

Hel Fenn spread out before them. Fog had settled in. Wisps of white drifted through the twisted trees, moving sluggishly on the breeze that came from the stinking swamp. The cloying reek of the place was foul.

The ball of the sun hung low in the sky, the light fading fast.

Vorster's first thought was that his mind had been damaged by the blow to the head. It looked for all the world as though the blackened limbs of the trees were moving!

He steadied himself in the saddle, closed his eyes and opened them again, the wave of sickness passing.

It was no fever-dream.

The bones of the forest were on the march, the dead streaming out of the withered trees in droves.

Vorster's horse shied as it caught the stench of rotting flesh.

A thrill of fear chased up the length of his spine.

More poured out from the forest, endless columns of walking dead.

They were not alone.

Wolves loped along at their side and the sky grew black as a flock of fell bats converged in swirling clouds.

The dead spread out before them, thousands upon thousands, an endless danse macabre.

His breath caught in his throat. Vorster had faced the undead more times than most, and still the sight of them exerted a grip of fear around his heart that no other enemy could. He felt the first constricting touch of horror and struggled to banish it. Fear was a soldier's worst enemy and constant companion.

They came out of the forest, spilling endlessly across the plain.

'Do you think it's too late to burn the forest to the ground?' Ackim Brandt asked, irony bitter in his voice.

'How can they have grown so?' Vorster breathed in disbelief.

'The world is full of the dead, my friend. It is the living we have a shortage of.'

'Now *that* is a sobering thought.'

The darkness thickened. The shriek and chitter of the bats was the only sound across the whole battleground.

The truth was sickening. While playing hide and seek in the damned forests, the Vampire Count had drawn them into the jaws of a trap. He had lulled them into believing that in harrying his forces, chipping away at their number battle by battle, they were somehow winning the long war of attrition.

The proof of that lie was laying itself out before them in the form of a vast host of skeletons, ghouls, zombies, wights and, alongside them, the vampire's peasant levies.

'What man would willingly march to war under the banners of the undead?' Vorster asked. He still found it difficult to come to terms with the fact that any of the living could willingly choose to throw their lot in with the vile dead.

'They fight for their cruel masters because they fear them, my friend. It is as simple and as sad as that. Fear can drive a man to do many things.'

Vorster shivered.

'As hard as it is for us to comprehend, they see von Carstein as their legitimate lord. It infects them with a twisted sense of loyalty. To them *we* are the invaders and they are merely protecting their homeland.'

'Then I pity them,' said Vorster, earnestly.

'Pity is better than hatred. That way lies madness. The best we can hope to achieve is to bring death to a few of them. Doubtless it is a release from a much worse fate.'

Two hundred thousand strong, at least, and still the undead spilled from the cover of the trees.

'So this is to be our doom,' Vorster said to the man beside him.

'It would seem so,' Brandt agreed as it became sickeningly obvious that for every human there were twenty or more creatures dragged back from beyond the grave, hungry to kill them.

'Why do we even bother with the charade? How can we do anything other than die here?'

'Look at our choice of masters. Should we die in battle, we'll still be enlisted into this war, my friend.'

They watched with mounting horror as still more and more of the corpses shuffled out of the forest, forming into hellish regiments in complete silence. No order was shouted, no trumpet bayed.

Then they saw him, a distant smear in the dusk's light. The Vampire Count's silhouette was unmistakable.

He threw his arms aloft, the sky answering with a devastating crack as lightning trembled and flashed around him. The harsh bluish-white light revealed the full extent of his forces. The vast fen was a sea of dead. They surged forwards as still more corpses swelled in behind them, a relentless tide rolling towards the living.

Brandt called a young rider forward.

'You see what we face, soldier?'

The fresh-faced rider nodded sickly, making the sign of the hammer across his chest.

'Good. Carry it with you. Martin is half a day away. Drive your horse into the ground. Ride the poor animal until she drops. There is nothing to be gained from sparing her. You *must* get word to Martin. Tell him the vampire has found new strength and has been waiting for us. Should he find us amongst the enemy, beg him to be merciful and slay us quickly. Now ride like the wind, soldier.'

THE SUNLIGHT STREAMING in through the stained glass window refracted into the eight colours of the winds.

Finreir stood over the battle plans, playing at general, pleased with himself and his first victory, and eager to march deeper into the lands of the Vampire Count to press home the advantage he'd secured.

He looked up.

One by one the colours wove themselves into the tapestry of a man, no, not a man, an elf.

The spectral projection of his tutor, Areiraenni, took shape and stepped out of the glass window to stand before him. The old sorcerer was not amused.

'I see you play at soldiers.'

'I am making a difference, master. The humans need us.'

'The humans need many things, Finreir. We are not one of them. You were forbidden from coming here. You are to return to Ulthuan immediately.'

'But I have so much to do.'

'It is not a request. The council has issued an edict. You will carry it out. If you cannot find within you the discipline that is required I will recommend that you begin your studies all over again, and I shall remove myself from the council for I shall have failed in my role as your teacher'

'If I can just show you what I have found here, master, the threat the humans face,' he walked over to the map. 'So many battles, but they all rise from the same darkness. The sleeping one's influence is undeniable. If he is allowed to wake–'

'Finreir, are you so naïve as to think you are the only one that has seen what is happening here? The council sees wisdom in not interfering. This is the fight of humans. It will define their place in the world. If they fail, well, they have no place living. You must allow nature to take its course. There is a reason for everything. You will come voluntarily, or we will forcibly remove you.' With that, the shadow-shapes of two guardian elves began to form on either side of the sorcerer's projection.

'Tell me something, Finreir, does Málalanyn live?'

'He does master. Your son acquitted himself well in the battle. He will become a fine warrior one day.' He saw upon the old elf's face the relief that only a worried parent could know.

'My apologies if I have offended the council, master. It was not my intention.'

'You will apologise to them in person within the month. I suggest you also beg for their forgiveness. I also suggest that you take the shortest route possible, Finreir. Your proclivities for exploration will not be tolerated further until you come of age. Is that understood?'

Finreir understood perfectly well, but he would continue to watch over the humans from afar. There was nothing the council could do to stop that.

KALLAD STORMWARDEN STUMBLED out of the forest.

Cahgur and the other survivors staggered out behind him, exhausted.

They lay in the snow, peering up at the sky, wondering how, why, they still lived.

Cahgur sniffed the air curiously. 'Do you smell ale?'

'We're running for our lives and *that's* all you can think about?' Othtin asked in disbelief.

'Well it's not *all* I can think of, but it is a goodly portion of it,' Cahgur said, sitting up. 'Seriously, can you smell it?'

He looked around, trying to see where the tantalising smell was coming from.

A small ramshackle cottage sat to the side of deeply rutted tracks. They were on a trade route of some kind, although it was unlike any trade route the dwarfs had been on before. This was a road no traveller dared veer from. The cartwheel ruts were deep and rigidly adhered to. The long, skeletal fingers of the withered trees dragged low enough to snare any passing coaches.

'Is that a house?' Cahgur pointed at the dilapidated building.

'Surely not, who'd be mad enough to live out here?'

There were more horses tethered outside than they would otherwise have expected from a hovel.

'It looks like an inn to me,' Othtin said.

Kallad pulled himself up to his feet using one of the dragging branches. He sighed wearily. 'Well, whatever it is, it's got four walls and a door. That ought to be enough to keep a vampire out for the night. At the very least if they are still chasing us by dawn anyone in that building just joined our wee gang.'

He set off in the direction of the building.

'What if they're already in the other fella's gang?' Belamir wondered. 'Oh, did I say that out loud?' He grinned at the others. 'All this running works up a thirst.'

'Skalfkrag and Valarik would have loved this place.'

'Aye, that they would, laddie, that they would,' said Kallad.

THE DOOR TO the taproom swung open on the creek of rusted hinges.

Kallad felt as if he had stepped back in time.

He walked through the rotten sawdust up to the bar where an emaciated barkeep towelled out a pewter flagon. Kallad reached into his pouch and pulled out the dead vampire's ring, finger and all, and slammed it down on the ale-stained bar. 'I'm here to see about a bloodsucker.'

'He's been expecting you. He sleeps in the basement.'

Kallad nodded.

His kinsmen were shocked. 'You knew we were coming here?' Cahgur asked, shaking his head.

'Nothing on our journey is without reason,' Kallad said.

'So what's down there?'

'Nothing you want to see. I'm here to settle my debt.' He slapped a handful of coins on the bar. 'The drinks are on me. Try not to fall down. We might need to leave in a hurry.'

'I don't like the sound of that,' said Molagon.

'But I do like the smell of that ale,' Cahgur said, grinning, willing to forgive anything for a dram of the wet stuff. 'So, barman, busy yourself, I've worked up a fearful thirst.'

Kallad left them drinking and disappeared into the dank cellar beneath the inn.

The first thing he noticed was the smell, the musk redolent of the grave.

Kallad said into the darkness, 'There are easier places we could have met.'

'Ahh, maybe so, but none more scenic.'

'You're a strange one, even for a dead man. If you weren't dead already I'd have half a mind to kill you where you stand.'

'There's time for pleasantries later. Do you have the ring?' Jerek von Carstein asked, emerging from the sanctuary of the shadows.

Kallad gladly gave him the finger.

Jerek unwrapped the small muslin bundle hastily, his hands shaking with anticipation as he removed its contents. He stared at it for a moment. The dwarf could not fathom whether his disbelief was born of pleasure or disgust until the ring finger went flying across the room, clattering off an unseen wall. 'It is a very pretty ring, dwarf, but it is not the ring I asked for.'

'You wanted Mannfred dead,' said Kallad. 'I made sure of it. I walked into the very heart of his damned castle and cut off his head while he sat on his stinking throne. That is his finger. That is his ring.'

'That was not his ring. You did not kill Mannfred. You killed Mannfred's man.'

'What are you saying?'

'The Vampire Count is still at large, as is the damnable ring. You merely ensured he has one less decoy in the world, one less thrall willing to die for him.'

'You mean to say it was all for nothing?'

'Not nothing,' said Jerek and then a moment later, 'Yes, nothing.'

'I lost two dwarfs for that bloody ring!'

'Careless.'

'I consider this debt settled,' Kallad said.

Jerek moved in swiftly. 'Know this, dwarf. I do not consider it settled. We had an agreement. If you do not deliver the right ring, I consider your life forfeit, and I *will* exact payment.'

There was nothing he could say to that. He trudged wearily back up the stairs to the taproom and determined to console himself with ale.

BUT KALLAD HAD no taste for it.

He sat apart from his compatriots, nursing a tankard.

Then a hooded man he had never seen enter the bar spoke, 'You look lost, dwarf.'

'What's it to you, stranger, whether I am lost or found?' he demanded with suspicion. He couldn't see the stranger's face; the hood was drawn down so completely as to obscure it.

'I cannot linger, dwarf, but know that I have come to deliver a message.'

'Who the bloody hell are you?'

'Names are not important.' the stranger pulled back the hood to reveal aquiline features. Something about him seemed unreal, insubstantial. 'I was with you when you fled Drakenhof. I was with you when you stumbled through the forest of bones.'

'Well I didn't see you. You could have lent us a hand!' Kallad grumbled sourly.

'There is little a carrion bird can do but watch. You acquitted yourself well.'

'What, by Valaya's buttocks, are you talkin' about, fella?'

There was something not quite right about the stranger; he did not look human. He knew instinctively he was no vampire, but equally, he knew he was no man either. No, the more Kallad stared, the more he realised exactly what the stranger was: an elf.

'I don't have much time, dwarf. I am not going to waste it explaining insignificant details to you. I am here to deliver a message. Know this, Kallad, son of Kellus, last dwarf of Karak Sadra: All of the Old World is in jeopardy. The life of every living creature hangs in the balance. The war with the undead wages still. It cannot be fought by man alone. The dwarf nation will determine whether the Old World as we know it stands or falls. That is your destiny, Kallad. That is the storm you were born to ward, Stormwarden, son of Kellus.'

'How do you know who I am, and who are you to tell me what my destiny is? Answer me, elf! And give me one good reason why I should believe a word out of yer treacherous mouth! Now!'

'The forces converge. You must away to Hel Fenn.'

Kallad launched forwards, clutching at the stranger's cloak. It turned to rags in his hands and crumpled to the floor.

There was no sign of the stranger.

Across the room, Belamir and Cahgur roared with laugher. 'Kallad's drunk off his arse. He's arguing with the curtains!'

MARTIN OF STIRLAND held the higher ground.

His left flank was sheltered by forests and farmland, and to his right stood the ruins of an old stone fort. Ahead lay a raised track running parallel to the bottom of the hill. His position was strong, but it wasn't perfect.

Martin von Kristallbach arrayed his artillery pieces across the crest of Thunder Ridge. Both cannon and mortar had good vantage over the approaching enemy. He did not want to risk a repeat of what Gothard's Black Knights had attempted at Marienburg. He gave particular attention to supporting his flanks, which he did by installing brigades of his elite Ostland Black Guard under the aegis of Vorster Schlagener in hiding among the masonry of the ruined buildings. The vast bulk of his army, the infantry under the command of Ackim Brandt, the cavalry answering to Dietrich Jaeger, he kept hidden behind Thunder Ridge, while he stationed huntsmen and free companies out in plain sight, as his bait.

For all his strengths, Martin had a weakness too, and one of the most human, forgiveness. Jaeger had been disgraced, humiliated by Vorster, and had turned into a laughing stock amid the rank and file, but Martin had found it in him to give the man a chance at redemption. No man, the count said, deserved less. He had served in several of the smaller skirmishes, acquitting himself well. It was as though in shame he had decided to become a hero, placing little value on his own skin. So Jaeger had the cavalry with Martin's blessing.

The landscape, and a huge slice of luck, would decide this battle. Martin had every intention of drawing Mannfred in, blindsiding him with the grandest of ambushes.

In the calm before the battle, a priest of Morr walked within the ruins before the bowed heads of the Black Guard, bestowing upon them the blessings of the god of death and dreams. Four thousand of the fearsome black armoured warriors hid within the old fort, another thousand at the farm. Each warrior carried with him a pouch containing two silver pieces. The coins were an offering to pay their way into the afterlife should they fall on the field of battle.

Although he was not one of them, and did not wear the lacquered black plate and hauberk of a true Black Guard, Vorster took the blessing gratefully. He, like every man in the regiment, had worked his way up through the ranks, earning his place in the battle with deeds and courage not birthright and patronage. He was proud to stand beside them and would be equally proud to fall with them. Beside him Vladimir Ludennacht, champion of the Elector Count of Ostland, bowed his forehead until it touched the hawk's head embossed upon the gleaming hilt of his zwei-hander great sword. The weapon was truly a thing of beauty eager to cleave undead flesh and bone.

It would not have to wait long.

THERE WAS NO signal that Vorster could see.

When Mannfred's army came it did not pause to bluster, to wail, to gnash or to goad. It simply continued its eerily silent advance until the skeletal riders and a vast regiment of bone-white infantry under prior orders from the Vampire Count altered course and made directly for the old fort on the right flank of Thunder Ridge.

With that one simple manoeuvre the battle of Hel Fenn had begun.

'Hold,' Vorster whispered. 'Hold.' He held up a hand to stay the men under his command, and from his vantage point, continued to watch the creeping advance of the undead draw ever closer to their hiding place. The bones were here for one purpose and one purpose alone. They were not here to frighten or to send a message of fear to the humans. There was no need of fear now. No, they were here to kill them.

The skeletal riders surged forwards, cantering across the no man's land. They met no resistance. The lie of the ruins was inviting, but entering would have forced them into a narrow formation, compressing their flanks. Their commanders were reluctant to sacrifice their mobility before the skeletal foot soldiers were in place.

Ludennacht was itching to attack. 'Why don't they come?' he whispered, barely breathing the words.

'They are looking for the advantage. We must not surrender it to them,' said Vorster calmly. 'Hold.'

The dead crept forwards inch by inch without pause or thought as they clogged into the funnel betwixt and between the rubble.

Vorster had the spot all marked out: three paces, two, one.

Now!'

All four thousand of the Ostland Black Guard came out of hiding, swinging. The dead had no comprehension of what hit them. Slow to react, the first lines were reduced to nothing more than shattered bone and weeping marrow within minutes as the Black Guard's great swords cut a swathe through their ranks. Not once did the undead cry out as they fell beneath the barrage of blades. For a moment Vorster dared to believe that it might be over quickly. It wasn't. He ducked a wildly swinging blade. The edge caught him high on the shoulder. A little higher and it would have opened his neck. As it was the blow glanced off his armour harmlessly. The man beside him fell, only to be replaced by another. A corpse stumbled at Vorster's feet. Before he could banish it to whence it came, the creature lashed out, scratching Vorster across the face with foetid fingernails. A ribbon of blood ran down the warrior's cheek. He did not wipe it away – another corpse swung for him before he could. Vorster matched blades with the undead as they continued to surge forwards in wave after wave of rusted metal and makeshift weapons. The ruins stank from the rotting marrow of their broken bones. With each blow that cracked open a bone, the stench intensified. The Black Guard's repel was fluid. As the undead army probed for weaknesses the Black Guard shored up their line, never once allowing them through. This would have remained a precarious defence, but Martin had had the foresight to prepare a masterful counter-strike.

Pistoliers and musketeers rained down a ceaseless hail of lead from the upper levels of the ruins. The cacophony was deafening.

Runners raced frantically to fetch shot and blackpowder to keep the volleys going.

A rusted blade nicked Vorster's shoulder. He battered it away, barely ducking beneath a wild swing meant to separate his head from his body. Crouching low he drove his sword into the wretched creature's gut, opening it wide. The creature fell at his feet.

More gunshots cracked, raining down death from above, and it was not long before a cloud of billowing smoke from the sheer volume of shots enveloped the fort.

For the first hour the right flank held.

For the second hour the right flank held, barely.

Nameless men fell around Vorster, good men who had lives and all the accoutrements that went with them. Those same good men began to ris drawn back to hellish unlife by the Vampire Count before they were bludgeoned to broken bone and mashed flesh by their friends.

And still the dead kept coming.

FROM HIS HORSE, Martin von Kristallbach watched the battle unfold and prepared himself for Mannfred's next move, sickeningly sure of what it would be.

Martin had read it right. True to form, the Vampire Count readied his forces for an attack on the left flank. Behind the walls of the farmhouse, the remaining one thousand Black Guard lay in wait alongside heavy cannons and a regiment of ordinary footsloggers, but the foot soldiers were not battle-hardened like the elite guard. Martin had bet everything on Mannfred attacking the right flank first. As a result the left was inherently weaker. He feared it would be the first to fall, and with good reason.

He watched and he waited, and he feared.

'Sir! Sir!' a runner cried, stumbling across the snow-packed sod.

'Runner, report,' Martin said, not taking his eyes from the field of battle for a second.

'Look to left flank, sir!'

'What about it?'

'There are dwarfs arriving, hundreds of them. Their leader pledges his allegiance to the flag and vows to fight until every shambling rotten undead piece of filth is dead again. Those are his words, sir, not mine.'

Martin sat forwards in his saddle, unable to believe his luck. He spied the tree line and within it, the first stirrings of movement. 'By Sigmar! We *will* win this day! Send word to their commander, what's his name?'

'They come under the banners of Karak-Kadrin, Zhufbar, and Karak Raziac, sir. Their leader calls himself Stormwarden.'

'Then send word to this Stormwarden that the Empire thanks him for his bravery and will not forget this day. Tell him to marshal his might and remain hidden within the tree line. Let the vampire think we are weak, and when he tries to press his advantage, crush him.'

'Very good, sir.'

The runner sprinted for the trees.

For the first time since the fighting began, Martin allowed himself the ghost of smile.

MANNFRED'S ARMY ADVANCED with speed on the left flank, hoping to catch the living off guard.

Chariots at the fore, manned by skeletal archers, flanked by dire wolves and trailed by peasants, they saw the gap in Martin's defences and rushed to exploit it with a would-be hammer blow.

The Black Guard rose heroically, presenting themselves as a target.

The undead charged them at a frightening clip. The sickle-shaped scythes set into their wheels sliced through the air, and as they met the living, sawed through their knees.

It was an undead victory that would not last long.

Kallad Stormwarden whirled Ruinthorn above his head, leading from the front as the dwarfs came streaming out of the trees, accompanied by the rapid-fire volleys of their quarrellers. His blade rasped through the ranks of the enemy, opening up a bloody path. Kallad plunged into it, bellowing his rage as he swept Ruinthorn around in savage arcs. The axe was lethal close up. The dwarfs charged in behind him, hammering into the backs of the dead, cutting them down. Axes shattered skulls and ribs, and cleaved through pelvises and every other foetid bone in their stinking bodies.

The dead fell silently.

Kallad drove his axe into the ribcage of a cadaverous brute, splintering it in two. The stench was sickening. Ruinthorn cracked the skeleton open as if it were the brittle shell of a nut. A scythe cut the air beside his head, slicing into his helm. The blow rattled his brains. Reeling, Kallad answered it by disembowelling the offender. The battle raged around him. He was a rock. He would not fall.

He was the last son of Karak Sadra. He was not fighting for himself, for the living. This was for the dead. His dead. The living rallied around his glittering axe. Blood flowed.

Again, the flanks held, despite all the odds.

It was painfully obvious to Martin that should one fall it would be a disaster.

Mannfred was forced into engaging the centre.

The undead army moving across the plain was vast. Blocks of skeletons marched in perfect unison, thousands strong, shattering the silence by crashing their spears against their shields. Zombies shuffled, gnashing their teeth, and scores of dire wolves slavered behind them. The air above the host was black with bats, blotting out the sun. It was mid-morning, but it was as though dusk had come early.

'Good,' Dietrich Jaeger said to the waiting cavalry around him, 'We shall have our battle in the shade.'

The stump where his hand had been itched. He scratched at it. It always itched when he grew excited. He was reminded of his shame.

'It will not happen again,' Jaeger pledged. 'Today is ours for the taking boys!'

The air thrummed with the beat of wings and the ground shook under marching feet.

Martin von Kristallbach wheeled his mount around to see the full extent of the slaughter. They were so many, the dead. Legion. The living could not hope to stand against their might.

'If we are to die here, then we die,' he said to the dispatch rider beside him. The man looked terrified by the prospect. Martin could not blame him. 'But let's see if we can't drive them all the way back to hell, eh?'

He sent orders to the artillery on Thunder Ridge – hold the line at all costs. The men cheered as the great cannons and mortars boomed and kicked into action, blasting shot at the approaching dead. Clods of mud were thrown into the air as the cannon balls hit the ground and on the bounce battered the skeletal ranks. Gaping holes appeared in their masses, bones shattered, bodies breached.

Martin kept the reserve firmly hidden behind the ridge and sent only the front ranks forward to weaken the enemy advance. This thin line was dubbed the forlorn hope by the men who waited behind it.

JEREK SHELTERED IN the trees.

He wore the face and body of a huge dire wolf.

It was fitting that the final moments of the White Wolf of Middenheim should see him transformed thus.

From his vantage point he could see both sides of Thunder Ridge clearly.

He watched as Mannfred's forces engaged a weak looking centre. The spearmen of the Empire stood in ranks only four deep. Though they fought valiantly, they had nowhere to go but to slowly retreat up the hill, back towards the artillery.

Jerek could not help but smile as, invigorated by this turn of events, Mannfred ordered the bulk of his army to surge forwards with renewed vitality, victory in sight. But Jerek could see what the vampire could not, that Martin's forlorn hope was nothing but a clever feint to draw the Vampire Count in.

As each defender fell in the weak looking line, another would race up from the hidden reserves behind the ridge to replace him, so in effect the wall was eternal and could never be broken while appearing to Mannfred to be forever on the verge of collapse.

It was ingenious.

With so much of his army committed, it opened up a gap at Mannfred's end of the battlefield, giving the Elector Count of Stirland the chance to decapitate the Vampire Count once and for all.

'RIDE!' MARTIN GAVE the order to Dietrich Jaeger.

The shamed soldier spurred his mount forwards, answering the order.

Vorster watched as Stirland's cavalry spread out across the plain, their trot increasing to a canter as they advanced around the ridge. They gave the horses their heads, galloping. Their wave of steel and courage smashed into the undead and broke them utterly.

Jaeger brandished his sword in his left hand, a relic of his duel with Vorster. The soldier felt no guilt at the fop's ruined hand. He could easily have been left dead on the duelling field instead of maimed. At least fate had given him the chance of redemption, claiming another small victory.

And there it should have ended.

The cavalry charge had achieved more than the allies could have hoped, but they should have turned back to the Empire lines, regrouped and made ready towards another foray.

Vorster watched in disbelief as Dietrich Jaeger succumbed to vanity.

Instead of breaking away and fading in search of a more accessible target, Jaeger continued the charge towards Gothard, looking to bring his head home to Martin as a trophy.

The fop chased the Black Knights until he was deep beyond the undead lines. He fought like a daemon possessed. The cavalry rallied around him, cutting and killing, opening corpses and flesh eaters alike. But it wasn't enough.

Disbelief turned to horror as Mannfred commanded his elite grave guard to form up into spear blocks and cut off the cavalry's escape.

Jaeger, who had been so focused on bringing down Gothard, failed to notice the gravity of his error. Vorster had no such blessing. He stood slack jawed as Mannfred's counter ensnared Jaeger and all of his men. Their horses were exhausted. With nowhere to run as Mannfred's noose tightened, no amount of hack and slash from the riders could prevent a thousand undead spearmen from goring the horses to death. With the riders either crushed beneath the weight of their dying animals or left to fend on foot, Mannfred's necromancers were quick to raise the horses from the mud and snow to trample their former masters to death.

Dire wolves prowled closer in packs, hungry for the flesh of horse and man.

Vorster watched with barely suppressed fury as the blowhard Jaeger tried to rally his troops. Around the battlefield the cannons fell silent, the gunners frightened of hitting their own men.

The distraction cost him dearly. A callow-faced flesh eater grabbed hold of his legs and pitched him into the sludge of snow and mud. Two more were on top of him in a heartbeat, trying to claw through his armour to his heart. He struggled to fight them off but they were relentless, in his face, biting, tearing their fingers bloody trying to open him up. And then the skull of one opened, crying blood down on him where the back of it had been cleaved in two. The second fell across him, a huge gaping wound in its back where a steel blade glittered red, slick with ichor. Vorster rammed his own blade up into the throat of the last one and rolled clear.

He didn't see who had saved him. All around him swords flashed wildly as men fought for their lives.

And then, for a moment, respite in the frenzy.

'So much for redemption,' he breathed in the lull, his words carrying.

In the midst of it, Dietrich Jaeger cut and ran for his life.

For a moment he was master of his fate, and because of it, Dietrich Jaeger died a hero. For all that, Vorster could see the terror in his eyes as he ran at the dead, hacking a path through a shambling horde of zombies.

He fell to an arrow in the back.

Jaeger's folly had cost Martin his cavalry.

MANNFRED VON CARSTEIN watched in delight as barely one hundred knights managed to scramble from the encirclement and make it back to the Imperial lines.

He felt buoyed by this success.

He ordered his reserve to finally be brought into play. They joined the grave guard bringing up the rear. The entire strength of the undead rolled forwards, giving no quarter to the living.

He could taste victory.

It quickly curdled in his mouth.

An ink-black bat swooped low, out of the maelstrom above, skimming across the bleached-bone skulls of the skeletal horde, its leathery wings beating urgently. In one swift tumbling movement the bat's shape shifted, and a grim-faced vampire scout stood before him. He delivered a dire warning about the shape of the battlefield.

'My liege,' the vampire bowed low. 'Reinforcements march for Stirland beneath the banner of the Knights of the Divine Sword. The Grand Theogonist himself leads them.'

'Does he have the damnable book?'

'I cannot tell.'

'How long until he joins the fray?'

'An hour, maybe two, but no more than that.'

Mannfred was again swayed by the sight of the forlorn hope across the ridge. He clenched his fist in bitter frustration. 'Surely one decisive blow will break them.' It occurred to Mannfred that the reason the flanks had resisted him thus far was down to Stirland's folly. The man had obviously committed the bulk of his troops to them. Mannfred had been fighting the battle under the misconception that Stirland was stronger than he was and had withheld a reserve force out of sight somewhere. The arrival of the priest told him otherwise. The Knights of the Divine Sword were the reserve and they had not even reached the battlefield. Time was of the essence. The living were stretched thin, to the point of breaking. He could not afford for the wretched priest to take up his position and bolster them once again. 'Would someone rid me of this damnable holy man?' No one answered him.

Mannfred decided that swift action was required.

There could be no waiting.

He ordered his forces to quicken their advance, throwing all their weight at the centre.

The forlorn hope must fall.

It was an error of judgement that would prove fatal.

THE GRAND THEOGONIST, Kurt III, received his orders from Martin and understood what was required of the Divine Sword.

They formed an armoured column, like one half of the pincer of a mighty demi-kraken. Thousands of knights resplendent in full battle armour rode onto the field of death. They held aloft flaming torches. The reddish hue of fire danced across the contours of their burnished plate armour. They were an awesome sight to behold, riding out of the storm. The snow seemed to melt away from them.

Spurring their warhorses into a wild charge, they punched a hole clean through the ranks of the dead. Trailing their sword arms low, the knights wielded their flaming brands like great swords and thrust at the horde of undead, igniting the rags they were clothed in. The fire spread like a plague. The sweet stench of cooking flesh wafted across the battlefield.

They did not scream.

Ablaze, they marched ever onwards, driven by Mannfred's unbending will.

It was not long before their charred bones became so brittle that their legs snapped like twigs as they marched and then crumbled into a fine coating of black soot, dusting the snow.

The horns of the Divine Knights blared out, sending a message of hope to the defenders. The dwarfs, seeing the dead burn and the knights riding through the fire, fought with renewed purpose.

The clash of steel on bone was sickening.

The flames roaring around him, Kurt III, Grand Theogonist of Sigmar, signalled to the entire left flank that now was the time to break from defence and drive forwards down the ridge, corralling the enemy into the centre ground.

Across the battlefield, on the right flank, Vorster, exhausted, bloodied and sweating, his battered armour hanging heavy on his bruised and equally battered body, matched the signal, three sharp blasts on his trumpet, signalling Ackim Brandt to lead the reserve and charge at the right flank.

Just as the Knights of the Divine Sword had punched through on the left, so Brandt's reserves smashed through on the right.

Their legs pumped, knee deep in thick snow, their feet slipping and sliding through the treacherous icy bog. It mattered little that the men were fresh into the battle.

The only thing that mattered was that they carried out this single manoeuvre at speed.

They began driving the enemy into the centre ground.

By now Mannfred's shock at seeing not one regiment but two ente the fray must surely have worn off. He would be able to see clear that Martin's ultimate strategy was to envelop his undead horde in two mighty pincers and crush them.

Identifying a plan and neutralising one were two different beasts.

Orders and counter orders rippled down the enemy lines.

They only served to wreak confusion as the legions of foot sloggers, flesh eaters, dire wolves and ghouls quickly discovered that they had nowhere to advance to, nor retreat from. They were bogged down and defenceless.

Kurt unleashed the Divine Sword.

The knights raced to encircle the battlefield, driving the stragglers from Mannfred's army deep into the fray at the centre. They joined up with the right flank.

Mannfred's entire army was trapped within the noose.

All that remained was for Martin von Kristallbach to tighten it.

High above Hel Fenn he ordered the gunners, the cannoneers, the musketeers and the pistoliers to begin a relentless and unceasing bombardment of the heart of Mannfred's ensnared forces.

All around the Imperial circle, pike- and spearmen rushed forwards, slogging through the mire, to form the teeth upon which the undead would be devoured.

MANNFRED, TRAPPED IN the centre, panicked. It was not an emotion he was familiar with. The alien sense of fear had him reeling. He spun his nightmare steed around in circles, yanking at the reins. Flame billowed from the beast's nostrils. The scent of blood filled the air.

Everywhere he looked, the living pressed in.

A low-lying undercurrent of chanting took shape. It possessed a steady melodious rhythm that seemed to enthral the outermost lines of the dead, holding them at bay as surely as any sword or axe. The devout priests of Taal were joining the circle. It was their song that penetrated into the cavities of the corpses searching for their souls. Ordinarily an undead warrior was a hollow husk devoid of any holy light, but as the grand theogonist had discovered, when some of the humans fell their bodies were being raised so quickly to fight in the undead legions that their souls had not yet crossed over and were trapped, often powerless inside the meat of their former selves.

Now, one by one, a shining blue corona of holy light blossomed around random carcasses.

SEEING THE SPECTRAL lights flowering across the battlefield, the Grand Theogonist saw the extent of his task and began his invocation. The flurry of thick winter snow sparkled like fireflies around the glowing corpses. It was a glorious sight, proof of the divine.

He threw his arms up to the heavens beseeching Sigmar's intervention with Morr, god of death and dreams, on behalf of these wretched souls. They deserved to die warriors' deaths. They could not do so as prisoners. He prayed for Sigmar's help to break the bonds of Mannfred's will and giving each man back his destiny, and more importantly, his death.

The final words of the invocation spilled from his tongue and a miraculous sight took hold. Throughout the ranks of the dead, soldier turned on soldier, the illumed against the shadowed.

It reduced some of the soldiers to fighting with tears streaming down their cheeks as men they had fought side by side with during the long bloody days of the campaign were allowed to fight and finally die with dignity.

As each shadow fell, Mannfred's army simply diminished, but with each illumed that fell the mesmeric blue corona that had come to define them found release, coruscating down into the snow and billowing out in one final pulsating glory that illuminated the ground at their feet, to the earth returned.

MARTIN VON KRISTALLBACH saw the final chapter of the battle with perfect clarity.

As the last of the illumed faded, their essences rippling out through the cracked ice and muddy snow, he saw the opportunity to finish off Mannfred's remaining forces. He led the charge to tighten the noose he had so masterfully looped around the Vampire Count's neck.

With Vorster and Brant stepping up, aiming to meet him in the centre, the hack and slash of cruel battle was undeniably in their favour.

The other regiments picked their targets and seized the night.

THE KNIGHTS OF the Divine Sword wheeled their mounts in their hunt for the wight lord known as The Undying.

The knights still knew their enemy as Gothard for he had been one of them.

They saw his slaying as their sacred duty, not because they hated him for the monster he was, but because they loved him for the man he had once been.

As one, they made for the once proud champion of their order and raised their great swords in his honour before raining them down upon his corrupt flesh and finally laying him to rest.

His death was savage. Even after he had fallen they cut him limb from limb, hacking his corpse into ruined pieces.

KALLAD STORMWARDEN SPIED Mannfred, Adolphus Krieger at his side.

'Come on, lads. This is what we're here for.'

Belamir cracked four skulls in a wide sweeping arc.

Othtin mirrored the blow, caving in the chest cavity of a zombie.

Gasping for breath, Kallad rammed his head into an undead beast's maw and fell upon it, Ruinthorn splitting the beast from throat to gut.

Cahgur lunged forwards, thrusting the head of his warhammer up under the chin of the zombie before him. The blow came out of the back of its skull, sending a spray of rotten brain showering over the shambling undead that remained behind.

Molagon cut the legs out from under a stumbling skeleton. The bone splintered, and even though the thing fell it still clawed on through the snow grasping for the dwarf's boots. Molagon stamped on its head, grinding the bone to dust beneath his hobnailed boot.

Seeing the skeletal horde humbled and no longer the terrifying force they had once been, the dwarfs regarded them as little more than an inconvenience on the path to their ultimate goal.

Hacking and cleaving at bone, they lopped heads and severed limbs, driving towards the two vampires.

WITH HIS ARMY collapsing around him Mannfred saw a path opening up.

The crush of the dead had thinned.

The battle was all but lost.

He did not have to lose the war.

Now was the time to make good his escape.

Adolphus Krieger saw it too. With chaos reigning around them it was pointless to stand and fight. He pointed the way with his black blade.

They plunged forwards, leaping their nightmarish mounts over the bodies of the fallen in their haste to make it through the opening before it slammed shut and the opportunity to escape was snatched away.

Hammer blows rained down on the legs of both steeds, from nowhere, crippling the animals. The two vampires came crashing down headlong into the snow to the agonised screams of their mounts. Krieger's nightmare reared up, flames snorting from its muzzle as the animal's legs buckled and then fell directly on top of him.

Pinned under a tonne of panicked animal, even the vampire's formidable strength could not save him.

Two dwarfs stood over him.

Together they raised their hammers and piled them into his skull again and again and again until it caved in on itself, spilling the beast's brain across the battlefield.

Kallad Stormwarden blocked Mannfred's path.

'I killed you too fast the first time. I shall not make the same mistake a second time,' said Mannfred coldly.

'Are you the beast or just another one of his proxies?'

'What do you think?'

'I'm not a fan of thinking, it interferes with the killing.' Kallad looked down at the beast's right hand. He wore but a single ring, a plain signet. It looked utterly unremarkable beside the vampire's gaudy ceremonial finery. The plates of armour were decadent and impractical, offering no protection from the enemy's weapons. He needed no such protection. He had other means of defence. The plates were designed to allow the dexterity needed for spellcraft. 'Just so you know, whether yer him or no, I'm gonna batter yer anyway.'

Mannfred opened his mouth to respond, but stopped short, sensing movement to his right. He whirled around with hideous grace to see another dwarf charging straight at him. Kallad raged, but his moment had been shattered.

'*What do you think you're doing*!'

Molagon responded, 'Not standing around scratching me backside talking to the whoreson, that's for sure.'

It was the last thing he would ever say.

In a blur of motion, Mannfred lunged at the attacking dwarf, his entire form shifting into a slick coat of grey fur and the snout of a huge dire wolf. The beast buried feral claws into Molagon's belly, opening him up with a savage slash.

With a mouthful of snarling teeth, Mannfred bit out his throat.

Kallad screamed his pain. He could not save his friend, but he could kill the beast.

Belamir and Cahgur abandoned Krieger's corpse and ran to engage the dark lord.

Kallad split the wolf's spine with Ruinthorn, chopping the mighty axe deep into the Vampire Count's arched back. The beast howled its pain and bolted for freedom, Kallad struggling to restrain it, but Ruinthorn's purchase became slick with blood and quickly tore free of the wolf's flesh as the creature writhed beneath it.

The wolf disappeared amid the legs of the dead, racing for the cover of the woods.

The dwarfs set off after it, struggling through the blood and the mud, and the churned snow.

Suddenly a terrifying howl rang out across Hel Fenn. As Kallad emerged into open ground beyond the line of the Taal priests he saw a second huge wolf come barrelling down towards them from out of the trees.

Not them, he realised... towards the beast that was Mannfred!

THE TWO WOLVES clashed in mid-air in a fury of fur and teeth, and claws.

Neither beast could get the upper hand.

They tumbled in the snow, kicking and biting, snapping at each other furiously until suddenly one emerged atop the other, pinning him dow by the chest and biting down on a hammering paw, chewing it clean off. The victor having claimed his prize had no interest in whether his prey lived or died. The vanquished wolf yelped pitifully, staggered to its three remaining paws and limped away towards Shadow Lake, leaving nothing but a trail of blood in the snow.

But who had injured whom?

Kallad could not tell.

THE PAIN WAS excruciating.

Mannfred could barely see as he stumbled forwards. He felt his grip on his lupine form slacken. He could not maintain it. He felt the fur go first, melting away from his arms. His sense of smell diminished, lost to the overwhelming reek of blood. He collapsed to the snow and crawled forwards on his one good hand and knees.

He looked around to see how far he had made it from the battlefield, but no more than a few hundred feet away he saw the damnable dwarf raising his fingers to his lips and unleashing an ear-splitting whistle that drew every living eye in his direction.

He watched as Kallad levelled Ruinthorn, pointing the axe at him, yelling, 'The beast is injured!'

Within moments Martin and his cavalry were closing in.

Mannfred groaned and stumbled to his feet. The snow was thick and deep, obscuring the treacherous nature of the terrain beneath. He ran, fell, ran and fell again.

The second wolf padded along beside him, tantalisingly out of reach, taunting him, making sure that whenever he ducked out of sight of the Empire forces he drew them back to the vampire's trail.

'Who *are* you?' Mannfred yelled at the beast.

It didn't answer. Its silence mocked him.

Shadow Lake lay hidden within the depths of the forest.

It was towards here that Mannfred ran, with its underwater caves and grottos hidden within the reeds. If he could only reach it, it would be the perfect hiding place for respite and recovery.

If he could only reach it.

MARTIN, VORSTER AND Ackim Brandt spurred their mounts forwards, answering the shrill whistle.

The horses lengthened their strides, eating up the snow-covered ground as they made for the dwarf axeman.

Mid-gallop, Vorster Schlagener reached down and scooped Kallad Stormwarden up, helping the dwarf commander into the saddle behind him. Kallad clung on for dear life, but was thankful for the human's intervention.

'I'll not be missing out on this,' the dwarf rumbled.

Together they bore down on the last of the Vampire Counts.

Darting between the thinning trees, they were forced to slow when they hit the marshes, but it was of no consequence. It was obvious to all that Mannfred had nowhere else to run.

They dismounted and drew their steel, closing in for the kill.

DESPITE THE WEIGHT of the Runefang in his hands and the thrill of victory in his heart, Martin von Kristallbach was not fool enough to have banished his fears completely. He approached the vampire with caution, knowing full well that an injured animal was always at its most dangerous when cornered.

'I will burn your corpse, vampire, and make sure your kind can never return.'

'So *this* is how it ends?' Mannfred held up the bloody stump where his right hand had been. 'I seem to have lost my... protection.' He threw back his head and laughed bitterly. 'Take me then. End it. Or are you afraid? I may be weakened, human, but I could tear your heart from your chest and feast before you knew it was gone. So, are you man enough?'

There was no more need for words.

Vorster and Brandt stepped aside to allow Martin, Elector Count of Stirland, victor of Hel Fenn, through. He swung his Runefang with such decisive might that Mannfred von Carstein was hurled back into the black lake, truly dead before the brackish waters closed over his corpse.

Skull cleaved in two, the last of the Vampire Counts was no more.

TOGETHER, VORSTER AND Ackim Brandt walked back to the battlefield, leading their horses by the reins. The moment Mannfred had died, the remnants of his army had crumbled to dust.

Handfuls of peasant levies crawled around in the snow, weeping. How these pitiful wretches could fight for the dead, could mourn the undead, baffled them. They lacked the courage or good grace to fall upon their own blades and hasten their journey to join their vile masters.

Thick palls of smoke clung to the fen where the living had gathered their dead into huge pyres and begun the grim work of cremation. The casualties were horrific.

Vorster and Brandt stood, awed by the slaughter, wondering how they had survived.

THE DEATH TOLL was severe.

They walked among the casualties, unable and unwilling to appreciate the true extent of the horrors they had lived through. Bloo soaked into the battlefield; the blood of good men. Vorster could n begin to count their losses. Thousands upon thousands lay dead in the field.

The Knights of the Divine Sword knelt in a circle, heads bowed in prayer, willing the souls of the fallen on their way. More than three thousand of their brothers would never lift a sword again. Their prayer became a song of farewell as they lifted up their heads, their hearts and voices breaking as they serenaded the dead.

The survivors of the Ostland Black Guard began gathering the bodies of their kin for the huge funeral pyres. There would be no night, only endless day as the red flame turned the black sky day bright. They moved the dead with tenderness and compassion, each one treated like the hero he was. More than two hundred Black Guard joined the flames.

The Priests of Taal moved through the carnage, bestowing blessings and prayer on the few who clung stubbornly to life, and offering guidance to the souls of the departed so that they might find Morr and know peace despite the brutality of their slaughter. They made no distinction between rank or duty, between the shredded hide of a woeful flagellant, religious zealot or crossbow wielder, musketeer and gunner, pike man and foot soldier.

They all deserved peace.

KALLAD STOOD BY the lakeside in quiet reflection.

The humans were gone now.

Martin had thanked him and offered his sorrow at the losses his people had suffered, and promised that dwarfs and men should stand together. They were stirring words, words that ought to have resonated within him. Kallad made the right responses and when they parted company it was as new friends.

But as Kallad remained, looking at the frigid waters of the icy lake where Mannfred had fallen, a single thought weighed heavy on his mind.

'Someone stole his bloody ring.'

He had a reasonable idea that he knew who.

The wolf.

It wasn't over, not yet.

For all the dying, the deed wasn't done.

Cahgur and Belamir joined him by the water's edge.

'I could do with an ale, I don't know about you?'

EPILOGUE

Buried Undead
Somewhere in the Old World

KALLAD LAID ANOTHER course of mortar and set a brick down on top of it.

From his side of the growing wall Jerek said, 'I heard a story once, an old lady told it to me.'

'Aye?'

'It was a sad tale. I didn't understand it at the time, but I do now. It was about a boy and a girl. The boy fell on the field of battle to a bitter blow, his body cleaved in two, disgracing the family with his failure. "None shall grace him with sepulchre or lament, but leave him unburied, a corpse for birds and dogs to eat, a ghastly sight of shame," proclaimed his father. The girl, his sister, gathered all of her courage and defied their father the king, standing proud. "I owe a longer allegiance to the dead than to the living. In that world I shall abide for ever," she whispered, sprinkling grave dirt over her brother's broken corpse. Livid, her father walled her up in his castle for he was a vengeful soul who did not like being shamed in any way.

'The woman who told me this story said it was my curse. I did not understand it at the time, but I do now. I know what it is to be trapped between both worlds – the dead and the living.'

'So you have taken her words to heart and made them your doom?' The dwarf knocked the errant brick into place, smoothing off the rough edges.

They were in an old ruin in wastelands far from Imperial civilisation.

'I have no alternative, dwarf, I cannot allow this thing to stay in the world unprotected. I cannot risk another uprising. I could not live with the death of the world on my shoulders.'

Jerek spoke the truth. There were no other options. If Kallad slew the vampire the problem of the ring would not go away. Dwarfs did not live forever and the memories of what had happened with the Vampire Counts would inevitably slip away, pass into history, into legend and finally, myth, losing the cold hard immediacy and reality of what the ring represented. There would always be another Skellan, another Mannfred, another Konrad. There would never be another Jerek. The man's humanity was awesome. How it had held off the sickness of the blood curse, he had no idea.

'The ring doesn't just need a guardian,' said Jerek. 'It falls to me as the last surviving heir of Vlad to see that its evil is negated once and for all. I know with certainty what it represents, because I was there. I know what it can do. I will not die and leave it unguarded.'

Kallad set another stone in place. The wall was almost complete.

'Without feeding you will go mad.'

'Forget about me. Of the two of us, only one of us has an actual life to live.'

Kallad laid another brick, and another. The wall crept slowly higher.

'Farewell, Jerek. For all that you're a bloodsucking fiend you are not a bad man.'

The vampire laughed as Kallad laid the last stone in place, sealing him in his immortal tomb.

The vampire stared at the wall, alone, and waited for a death that would never come.

ABOUT THE AUTHOR

British author Steven Savile is an expert in cult fiction, having written a wide variety of sf (including Star Wars, Dr Who and Jurassic Park), fantasy and horror stories, as well as a slew of editorial work on anthologies in the UK and USA. He won the L. Ron Hubbard Writers of the Future award in 2002, was runner-up in the British Fantasy Award in 2000 and has been nominated three times for the Bram Stoker award. He currently lives in Stockholm, Sweden.